The human imagination is a marvelous tool. It enables us to enjoy fantastic imaginary adventures that aren't available in real life.

Dan Pekarek

The
Ultimate
Adventure

Daniel L. Pekarek

PEANUT BUTTER PUBLISHING

Seattle · Vancouver · Los Angeles · Milwaukee · Denver · Portland

ISBN: 0-89716-900-X
Library of Congress Card Number: 99-067088

First Printing September 1999
Second Printing June 2001
Printed in the United States

Published by Peanut Butter Publishing
Seattle, Washington

Peanut Butter Publishing

2207 Fairview Ave. E. Houseboat #4   Seattle Washington 98102   (206) 860-4900

ACKNOWLEDGMENTS

I owe a special debt of gratitude to my parents, Lawrence and Lavina Pekarek. Many years ago, they insisted that I get an excellent education. When I was in grade school and high school, they constantly encouraged me to study and earn good grades. Also, I appreciate the hard work they did to help finance my college education. The knowledge I gained was essential to writing this story.

A special note of thanks goes to my wife, Joan, for all of her support, encouragement, and helpful suggestions. One of her best suggestions was that I read *Revising Fiction* by David Madden. The information presented by David Madden was thought provoking and helpful.

Many thanks to Bob Burke and Pat DeBurgh. They gave me several books on creative writing and grammar, which contained answers to most of the technique problems that I encountered. *A Writer's Reference* by Diana Hacker was especially useful as was *Professional Fiction Writing* by Jean Z. Owen.

A special note of gratitude goes to Peter Fisher, M.D., for proofreading *The Ultimate Adventure* and reviewing the medical aspects of the story. Also, I greatly appreciate the proofreading and ideas provided by Al Bjorgen and Jim Gaut.

The following friends and family members also deserve a heartfelt thank you for their interest, support, and thoughtful ideas: Chuck Groat, Sheila Cavan, and Charles Feske, D.D.S.; my sons, David and Mark, and my daughter, Caryn; my brothers, Alfred, Roger, and Eugene, and my sisters, Nancy and Bonnie. I especially appreciate the patience and persistence of Robert Crenshaw for helping me get acquainted with my first computer and its related equipment.

Acknowledgment of Professional Services
I am greatly pleased with the professional services provided by the following individuals:
Elliott Wolf for managing the publishing process
Elizabeth Lake for copy editing
Dave Marty for cover design
David Pekarek for creating the cover images

Preface

How does an author write a story? Where does the idea for the story come from? The basic idea for this book came to me more than forty years ago when I was a teenager living with my parents, brothers, and sisters on our dairy farm in central Minnesota. In some ways, life on the farm was difficult. There was no shortage of hard work. However, some jobs were easy, even fun. Cultivating corn was one job that I enjoyed. Sitting on a tractor on a warm summer day was pleasant, but as the days wore on, it always became quite monotonous. Dealing with the monotony caused me to develop a very active imagination. I constantly went on imaginary journeys into fantasy-land. An imaginary adventure that kept reoccurring is now the story-line for this book.

It took me nearly ten years to write this story. This might seem like a long time, but I never hurried the writing process; rather, I patiently worked with my characters until the scenes they were involved in came alive.

From the beginning, my primary objective was to write a story that would be fun to read. To that end, I have given this story a positive, upbeat mood by creating characters who enjoy life and believe that their lives are what they choose to make them. It is my hope that you will enjoy getting emotionally involved in their lives and find this to be a thrilling imaginary adventure.

THE ULTIMATE ADVENTURE is a story that I believe will happen because it is part of human destiny. Someday, humans will journey to the stars, and Earth-like planets will be discovered. Some of them might be inhabited by beings far more advanced than we are, but some of them might be the way Earth was during the dinosaur age. In THE ULTIMATE ADVENTURE and its sequel, both possibilities are encountered.

About the Author

Daniel L. Pekarek was born in a farm house in central Minnesota on July 24, 1940, grew up on the dairy farm owned by his parents, Lawrence and Lavina, received a Bachelor's Degree in Aerospace Engineering from the University of Minnesota in 1963, worked as a wind tunnel test engineer for seven years, worked in professional sales for a small contractor for 22 years, is currently a poker dealer at Diamond Lil's in Renton, Washington, is a member of The Planetary Society, enjoys reading The Planetary Report, Astronomy, Discover, Reader's Digest, and Aviation Week and Space Technology, enjoys reading realistic science fiction, started writing THE ULTIMATE ADVENTURE in 1989, plans to complete the sequel by July, 2001.

ONE

The Long Journey Begins

On July 15, 2092, Captain Jerry Jerontis was working in his office onboard the starship, Challenger, currently orbiting Earth at an altitude of 280 miles. He was gazing at one of his computer monitors reviewing a list of tasks that remained to be done before departing Earth on a voyage to the Alpha Centauri System. While he studied the list, the possibility that his starship might be sabotaged kept entering his mind. Captain Jerontis took the sabotage threat seriously, but he hoped that it was nothing more than the ranting of an extremist group that had vowed to stop his mission to Alcent, an earth-like planet orbiting Alpha Centauri A.

At age 42, Jerry had been preparing for this mission for more than twenty years. He had signed an employment contract with NASA even before graduating from the University of Minnesota with a Master's Degree in Aerospace Engineering. Having been involved in the design, construction, and testing of the Challenger from day one, Jerry knew every inch of the giant starship and felt that it was his creation, his starship. Even though he would never return to Earth, Jerry was eager to get the mission underway. This would be the first manned interstellar voyage ever attempted by the human species, and Jerry was determined to make it a success.

The long journey to the Alpha Centauri system would be dangerous because of the speed and distance involved. The Challenger would reach a speed equal to about three-fourths the speed of light, and humans had never before attempted travel at such a fantastic speed. But even at this tremendous velocity, the journey would still take six-and-one-half years, more than enough time for tragic accidents to happen.

If the people on the Challenger survived the long, high-speed journey, then they would face the hazards of living on a savage alien planet. Finding a way to safely live on a planet inhabited by huge dinosaurs, some of which would be deadly carnivores, would be problem enough; but perhaps, an even greater danger would be posed by organisms too small to be seen. The human immune system would have to contend with alien germs that it had never experienced. Could it defeat them, or would serious illness and numerous deaths occur? Would disease doom the colonization attempt, or would medical technology be up to the task of defeating any alien germs that the human immune system was unable to defeat?

Along with the suspected hazards, Jerry fully expected to encounter unforeseen dangers that would challenge his ingenuity. He had given his imagination complete freedom to envision dangerous situations, but he realized that predicting every unknown hazard was impossible. Even so, Jerry was confident that he and his crew would effectively deal with anything that they encountered.

However, before the mission could begin, one major task remained: the Challenger had to be joined to its propulsion stages. In less than an hour, the space tug, Goliath, would dock with the Challenger. Fueled with antimatter, Goliath's basic mission was to move large payloads between low Earth orbit and various lunar bases. Shortly, it would begin the transfer of another large payload, the Challenger, from low Earth orbit to its fueling station in orbit at an altitude of 125,000 miles. The huge quantity of antimatter fuel required for the interstellar mission was accumulated and stored in this high altitude orbit because of the enormous amount of destructive energy that would be released if an accidental explosion occurred.

While awaiting the arrival of the Goliath, Jerry reflected on some major events in human history. Jerry noted that people had dreamed of flying for centuries before it finally became a reality at Kitty Hawk, NC in 1903. Then, in just 66 years, man had set foot on the Moon. In 2020, the first manned lunar base became operational, followed by a similar base on Mars in 2036. In 2046, Earth's first unmanned interstellar probe, Star Voyager, was sent on a long journey to the Alpha Centauri System. Twenty-six years later, in 2072, it discovered a life-filled, earth-like planet orbiting Alpha Centauri A. Now, in 2092, people were about to follow the path pioneered by Star Voyager.

Jerry considered his mission to Alcent, the third planet of Alpha Centauri A, a truly epic event in the evolution of the human species. For the very first time, people would journey to another planet with a breathable oxygen-nitrogen atmosphere and a temperate climate, a planet where a new civilization could grow and prosper without support from Earth. Now, after twenty years of preparation, the most epic voyage in human history was about to begin. However, as had frequently happened in technological development, there have been individuals and groups who have tried to stop the process, and this time was no exception.

Over the years, two fanatical extremist groups had led an ongoing publicity campaign to stop Challenger's mission to establish a human colony on Alcent. Environment First, an extremist animal-rights group, promoted the idea that the arrival of human beings on Alcent would pollute the pristine environment and be dangerous and destructive to the life forms already living there. A fanatical religious cult declared that all of Earth's problems were the result of the human species being infected with the devil. It maintained that if the Challenger were allowed to carry people to Alcent, then it would also be infected with the ravages of the devil. Both of these groups had attempted to generate overwhelming political opposition to the Alcent mission with street demonstrations, civil disobedience, and the dissemination of propaganda. However, they failed to stop the mission in the political arena and had recently resorted to terrorist acts against NASA facilities. So far, they had killed thirteen people and seriously injured thirty-seven. They declared that they would not fail and stated that they had already implemented a plan to stop the mission.

Captain Jerontis took their declaration seriously and considered some obvious possibilities. Planting a bomb on a spaceship orbiting 280 miles above Earth would be a difficult task for even the best smugglers to accomplish. If this was their plan, the bomb would most likely already be onboard, since their only option to transport the bomb to the ship would have been to disguise it and conceal it among the ship's supplies, which had already been delivered. However, Jerry thought this unlikely, since everything on the ship had passed through meticulous security checks, including intensive examination by sophisticated bomb detection equipment.

Sabotage by one of the construction workers was possible, but would almost certainly have been detected, since all work was carefully inspected and tested by three independent crews, who took great personal pride in discovering imperfection. The goal of this procedure was to make the huge starship free of malfunction during its long voyage to Alcent. Also, all individuals working on the Challenger had survived thorough security investigations.

With enough money, anti-satellite missiles could be bought from black market arms dealers. Several models had enough range to attack the starship in its current orbit. However, Jerry doubted that either of the radical groups had the money or expertise to carry out such an attack. But as a precaution, the USAF had stationed several missile interceptors around the starship.

Perhaps, the threat was nothing more than a psychological ploy, an attempt to save face. Rather than admit that they had failed to stop the mission, extremist leaders could use such a threat as a way to keep their followers fired up, gain additional publicity, and give a starship commander one more thing to worry about.

Totally engrossed in thought, Captain Jerontis was startled when the ship's communication system suddenly snapped to life with a boisterous greeting, "Ahoy there, Captain J.J.! This is your old college football buddy, Moose, ready to give you a lift to your fuel stop. We expect to dock with the Challenger in ten minutes. Then, we'll light our tail pipes, annihilate some matter, and begin orbital transfer."

While turning to face the rearview screen, so that he could monitor the approach of Goliath, Jerry responded, "Sounds like the same old comic I've known all these years, and I might add, one who seems to be in an exceptionally high-spirited frame of mind."

"Just a natural part of my vibrant personality which you serious types might have a difficult time relating to. However, I am going on a much needed vacation. After all, I have been shuttling payloads to and

10

from the moon for the last six weeks. Just as soon as I've delivered you to your fuel stop, I'll have four weeks on Earth, which I intend to spend on a warm sandy beach in the South Pacific that is famous for its elegant bikini-clad scenery."

Captain Jerontis felt a need to respond to the jibe at his serious personality, but decided to wait for a suitable opportunity and just said, "Sounds like you haven't changed much over the years. Here we are, practically on the eve of mankind's greatest adventure ever, and where is your mind? Somewhere off in a distant erotic fantasy land."

"That's the kind of comment I would expect from the predictable, no-nonsense Captain J.J. that I've known practically forever. But, it's probably not your fault. Who knows, if you hadn't been so dedicated to this Alcent Project all of your adult life, you also might've developed a keen sense of appreciation for some of the more playful aspects of life."

"Getting my starship ready for our long journey has definitely dominated my life, and I really haven't had much time for anything else."

"Before I drop down to Earth for a well-deserved vacation, maybe we could have lunch, and you could give me a tour of your ship?"

"Are you sure you can spare the time? I wouldn't want something as trivial as a tour of Earth's first manned starship and lunch with its captain to delay your pleasure trip to some exotic beach in the South Pacific."

"In the interest of helping you get into the proper frame of mind for your long voyage, I am willing to make the sacrifice."

Captain Jerontis thought Moose's mild psychological jabs at him were probably his way of handling the emotions involved in saying a permanent goodbye to a life-long friend. Even so, Jerry felt Moose would be disappointed if he didn't make an appropriate response before their final parting. Jerry thought back to their college football days when he was starting quarterback and team captain. He remembered his teammates who gave him the title, *Captain J.J.*

Moose, whose real name was John Moosebeck, was the starting fullback. Standing six feet two inches tall, weighing 260 pounds, and having very little body fat, he was an immensely powerful man. He was very quick on his feet, and he had had the habit of running through defenses like a charging bull moose during mating season. His highly vocal fans, without even bothering to consult him, decided to simplify his name. But even without his physical dominance on the field, his boisterous aggressive personality, which tended to overwhelm those around him, could easily have earned him the title, *Moose*.

With the Challenger now only minutes away from leaving its 280-mile orbit to begin its ascent to a new orbit at an altitude of 125,000 miles, nearly all of its twenty-four crew members were at view ports for one last good look at Earth. People had left Earth before, but had always had the option to return. This time, there would be no return. All that had been home would soon be forever left behind.

The Challenger's crew members had all demonstrated the ability to deal with the emotional stress of permanently leaving Earth. However, many otherwise well qualified candidates for the mission had been eliminated by psychological tests which detected a high probability of a chronic long-term depressive reaction to the emotional stress involved in permanently leaving mankind's birthplace.

Over the years, Captain Jerontis had occasionally thought about the emotional impact of leaving Earth. But it didn't have a very strong effect on his emotions because leaving Earth was always in the distant future. Now, leaving Earth was only a few days away. Jerry allowed his mind to drift into some of the fond memories he had accumulated over the years. He thought about a hiking trip that he had made to a remote wilderness lake in northern Canada. Then, he wondered what it would be like to hike along the shore of a lake on Alcent where all lakes would be in wilderness areas.

Jerry's mind was suddenly jarred back to reality when his communicator came to life with a message from Moose: "Captain J.J.! Our instruments indicate the completion of docking. Please confirm."

"Affirmative."

"Our best transfer orbit requires that we have ignition in about seventeen minutes."

"Okay. Let's begin a fifteen-minute countdown in two minutes. That will give everyone plenty of time to prepare for acceleration and to let us know of any reason to delay it."

Countdown began on schedule and all crew members prepared for several minutes of 1g acceleration that would put them in a high energy transfer orbit. After having been weightless for several weeks, even acceleration that was only equivalent to Earth's gravity would feel exceedingly heavy.

The option to use a high energy transfer orbit was one of the benefits available from antimatter propulsion. In the interest of saving time, Goliath's propulsion system would accelerate it and the Challenger to a much higher velocity than was necessary to accomplish orbital transfer. Before arrival at the fueling station, Goliath would again fire its engines to cancel out the excess velocity and complete the rendezvous and docking. Total elapsed time would be just a few hours. In the early days of the space age, such an orbital transfer and docking would have required a few days because of the minimal amount of energy available from the best chemical fuels in use then.

An hour and a half after Goliath's engines had been shut down, with nearly half the distance to fuel stop already covered, Captain Jerontis was taking a restful break in his quarters when Mike Johnson, the chief engineer, appeared at the entrance and said, "Captain, I need to talk to you."

"Come in Mike. What can I do for you?"

Mike looked into Jerry's eyes and calmly said, "I've decided to leave the mission. I want to stay on Earth."

Mike's announcement hit Captain Jerontis like a bombshell, and for a few moments, he stared at Mike in dumbfounded disbelief. Then, he said, "I am surprised to the point of being shocked. What has led you to this decision?"

Mike was silent for a few moments as if to collect his thoughts; then, he said, "For the last hour, I've been watching Earth steadily recede in the distance. In a few weeks, we'll be out of the solar system, and Earth will be so far away that we won't even be able to see it without a telescope. Thinking about that really bothers me. I have a lot of friends and close family ties on Earth that I really do not want to permanently leave."

"All of us are leaving behind people that we love and memorable places that we like to visit. This isn't easy for any of us, but the mission we're going on is the first manned interstellar voyage ever attempted by humans. The planet we're going to appears to be at the peak of a dinosaur age. We are going to study the life forms on this planet and build a new civilization there. We are about to embark on the greatest adventure ever attempted by the human race. Are you sure that you don't want to be a part of this?"

"I have devoted a major part of my life to this mission, but watching Earth steadily recede in the distance has given me an overpowering gut feeling of emptiness and sense of loss, and we haven't even left yet."

"All of us will feel some sense of loss. I think that's normal; after all, we are leaving much behind. We are leaving the birthplace of the human race, but we are going to lay the foundation for a new society. In essence, we are going to give birth to a new civilization. Thinking about that might help you deal with your sense of loss."

"I have thought about all of those things, but that overpowering gut feeling of not wanting to leave behind everything that I've had here on Earth just keeps coming back."

"Have you discussed your feelings with Doctor Nemard?"

"No, but I don't think I need to. They're too strong to be just a passing whim. I think it would be best if you would replace me, so that I can stay on Earth."

"Very well, but I will hold your request for a few hours in case you change your mind. You've been an excellent chief engineer, and I would very much like to keep you on the mission, but I will respect your decision."

"Thank you," stated Mike as he released his seat belt, gently pushed off, and floated out of Captain J.J.'s quarters. Then, Mike went to the observation deck for another look at the rapidly receding Earth.

Looking down on the Pacific Ocean, Mike observed a beautiful bluish-green world partly covered with soft white cloud patterns, which looked like tufts of cotton. The planet had a calm peaceful, almost fragile, appearance. Best of all, it was home. The thought of leaving it revived and enhanced Mike's earlier feelings of emptiness and forlorn sense of loss. But perhaps the real reason for Mike's intense feelings was the one that he did not discuss with Captain Jerontis, the one that he had to keep to himself for the time being. If his plan worked, the captain would find out about it soon enough.

Mike drifted across the observation deck to look in the opposite direction. He quickly located Alpha Centauri A and Alpha Centauri B shining brilliantly in the deep blackness of space. After looking at them for a few moments, Mike tried to turn away, but he could not, for the twin stars had captivated his attention in an almost seductive way. As he continued to gaze at them, they seemed to take on the aura of a pair of beckoning beacons that were somehow trying to entice him into staying on the Challenger for the long voyage to a new home on Alcent. Mike thought about the life-filled planet and some of the images returned by Star Voyager's video equipment. Some of these images were deeply mysterious and vividly implanted in Mike's memory. Mike was able to clearly visualize them. As he did this, a deep-seated desire rose from the depths of his mind, a desire to go to Alcent, a desire for the exciting adventure of exploring the mysteries of this planet. Mike was torn between this intense desire and the need to stay on Earth. Mike asked himself, "Is it really necessary to leave the mission and stay on Earth?" Mike pondered the question and decided to carefully reconsider his options.

Meanwhile, back in the captain's quarters, Captain Jerontis was thinking about Mike's surprise request. Even though regulations permitted anyone on the mission to drop out at any time by simply asking, Captain Jerontis was puzzled by Mike's sudden move. Everyone on the ship had passed rigorous medical, physical, and psychological tests along with excelling in the project's arduous training program. After surviving all of this, it simply did not make any sense to voluntarily drop out a few days before departure. Captain Jerontis decided to discuss the situation with Doctor Connie Nemard, who was a very competent psychologist along with being the ship's medical doctor and a skilled surgeon.

Jerry went to Connie's office and told her about Mike's replacement request and his stated reasons for it. Then, he said, "I want you to look at the results of all of his psychological tests and see if there's anything there that might explain his actions. I'll need your report in less than two hours."

"I'll do that right away. Come back in an hour, and I'll be prepared to discuss it with you."

Jerry said, "Thank you." Then, as he turned to leave, he felt Connie's eyes seem to fix on him a little longer than appropriate for an office call. It sure looked like a lingering glance, thought Jerry. The possibility caused Jerry's face to light up with just the trace of a satisfied smile as he thought, she is a beautiful woman. Her golden blond hair and those deep blue eyes are riveting. She might even have a stunning figure, but these loose fitting NASA uniforms make that hard to determine. I guess I'd better stop thinking about her. This just isn't the right time.

Captain Jerontis returned to the quietness of his quarters to think. He was a firm believer in PQT, personal quiet time, and he liked to use it to anticipate and solve problems. With the responsibility of getting the big starship ready for its long voyage, he usually didn't have to do much anticipating to find an ample supply of potential problems to be concerned about. Jerry wondered what difficulties might result from bringing in a new chief engineer so close to departure. While considering the possibilities, he was interrupted by Moose who floated into his quarters through the open hatch and said, "Ready for lunch? I'm starving."

Moose and Jerry went to the ship's cafeteria and ordered a deluxe combination pizza. When it was ready, they went back to Jerry's quarters to enjoy their meal.

After they started eating, Moose looked at Jerry and said, "You are unusually quiet. What are you worried about now?"

Jerry met Moose's dark brown-eyed gaze and asked, "Didn't you have a successful, complete physical before your current tour of duty?"

"Yeah, I did, but why are you worried about my health when you have a starship to worry about? Do I look ill to you?"

"No, on the contrary, you look perfectly healthy. But did your physical find anything even minutely abnormal?"

"Not a single thing, but why are you so concerned about my health?"

"I will get to that in a minute, but first correct me if I'm wrong. You've been Captain on the Goliath for about a year now, and before that, you were its chief engineer for five years. And if my memory serves me right, you are an expert in antimatter propulsion systems."

"Yes, but what's all this leading up to? Are you writing a book about me or a resume for a job that I haven't yet applied for?"

"One more question, do you think that your ego could handle a demotion from ship's captain to chief engineer?"

Moose's dark complexion lit up with an expression of surprised disbelief, and he blurted out, "What kind of question is that? What do you know about my career that I don't know?"

"Mike Johnson has requested that he be taken off this mission, and I am planning to put you on the mission in his place instead of following procedure and using the backup chief engineer."

"Hole-e-e-e Shit! You are going to stir up a real hornet's nest among the professional bureaucrats at NASA Command if you make a major change in your staff on your own!"

"But that's the beauty of my plan. I won't be acting on my own. You will be my fellow conspirator. Together, we'll devise a plan to get you on this mission ... if you want it."

"An hour ago, I was relaxing on the Goliath daydreaming about the wonderful vacation I've been planning, which begins in just a few days. Then, I do nothing more than stop by for lunch, and what happens? You want me to cancel the scenario that I'd envisioned for the rest of my life and go jaunting off to another star with you on just a moment's notice."

"It is all rather sudden, isn't it?"

"Somehow, I get the feeling that you're enjoying putting me on the spot like this. I suppose you want an answer right away."

"Oh no! You can think it over for an hour or two, and then you can let me know. But right now, you should get back to the Goliath. We need to put the brakes on rather shortly, or we'll go cruising right on past our fuel stop."

"What do you mean! Our fuel stop! I haven't accepted your proposal yet."

"No, but I suspect you will. After all, you wouldn't want to admit that this old, serious, worrisome personality type might be a bit too daring and adventuresome for you to keep up with, would you?"

Visibly shaken and deeply lost in thought, Moose floated out of Captain J.J.'s quarters and returned to the Goliath. Shortly thereafter, he started the fifteen-minute ignition countdown sequence.

Meanwhile, Captain Jerontis buzzed the medical lab and when Doctor Nemard responded, he asked, "Have you reached any conclusions about the individual we discussed earlier?"

"Yes, I have."

"Good, I'll be right there."

When Jerry arrived in the medical lab, Connie gave him her report: "The results of all the psychological tests Mike has taken over the years show him to be an exceptionally stable individual. He is fully able to cope with the emotional stress of permanently leaving Earth and living in close confinement with other people during a long interstellar voyage. I believe that his replacement request is the result of coolheaded analytical thinking, not fluctuating emotions. A well thought out decision is not likely to be changed unless the reasons for the decision change. In my opinion, he hasn't given you the complete story behind his request. I think that you should honor his request and not make any attempt to change his mind. However, if he changes his mind, I see no medical or psychological reason to deny him that option."

Captain Jerontis thought about the things that Doctor Nemard said. Then, he commented, "I am not surprised by your findings or by your opinion, which makes his replacement request all the more puzzling. I wonder what he's up to."

"I don't know, but there is one possibility that you need to consider. As you know, there are a couple extremist groups on Earth who have stated that they've already implemented a plan to stop our mission. One way to do that would be to have someone on the Challenger sabotage it and then jump ship right before we leave. Who on the Challenger would be better qualified to accomplish this than the chief engineer?"

"I've known Mike for several years, and he has always been very ethical and trustworthy. There is no way that I could suspect him of doing anything to jeopardize this mission or the lives of the people on it."

"I agree with you, but under the circumstances, I felt that I had to mention the possibility."

"I appreciate that, and I agree with your reasoning. So, what I want you to do is this: during the last twenty minutes before our departure, I want you to roam the ship and make sure that everyone is onboard and at their assigned locations."

Just then, the three-minute pre-ignition warning klaxon blared out its urgent sounding notes forcing Captain Jerontis to head for the command console. He needed to be on station even though the Challenger was still under the direct control of the Goliath. The crucial sequence of maneuvers to carry out rendezvous

14

and docking was programmed into the Goliath's flight control computer, but to guard against malfunction, Captain Jerontis and his flight crew needed to monitor the sequence of events leading up to docking.

Fuel stop was not a fueling station in the sense that fuel would be transferred from storage containers to the Challenger; rather, it was an orbital base where the Challenger would be joined with two fully fueled propulsion stages. Docking maneuvers had to be executed with perfection, for even the slightest deviation from the required flight path and speed could lead to a collision with disastrous results.

As the countdown ticked down to zero, Goliath's antimatter engines ignited precisely on schedule. The burn continued for several uneventful minutes successfully completing the braking maneuver. Looking at the rearview monitor, Captain Jerontis saw the huge propulsion section, currently about a mile away, very slowly grow larger in appearance as the two modules of the giant starship drifted toward each other at a closing velocity of just a few feet per second. As the distance slowly decreased, Goliath's flight control computer processed information from extremely accurate laser range finders and other specialized docking sensors. Through precise use of control thrusters, the computer would bring the docking structures of the two modules into perfect alignment and reduce final closing speed to less than an inch per second.

As the two large structures approached each other ever so slowly, time seemed to tick away even more slowly. A full two-and-one-half hours passed by before the habitation and propulsion modules were physically joined in a slow delicate procedure. Now, the Challenger was for the first time a complete starship. However, it would not be allowed to maneuver on its own until its flight control systems were checked out, and the Goliath would remain attached to it until this checkout was complete.

While thinking about the extensive checkout that needed to be done, Jerry received a call from NASA Control.

"Captain Jerontis here," replied Jerry while on the way to his office.

"Captain, the press conference we discussed earlier has been pushed through the proper channels by the Public Relations Department and has been approved. A crew of three from SNS, a free lance science reporter, a syndicated aerospace reporter, and a newspaper reporter are scheduled for liftoff on a personnel shuttle in about three hours. They will arrive on the Challenger at about this time tomorrow. We want you to arrange a tour of the ship and work out a schedule with the SNS people for a live press conference."

"Have these people been investigated by security for possible association with the fanatics that have tried to stop our mission?"

"They and their equipment have been cleared. Pertinent information will be transmitted into the security program in your computer."

"You do realize that entertaining the media for a day might delay our departure."

"Unavoidable. NASA Brass wants as much positive publicity as possible to help drum up political support for other NASA projects. So even though one of the reporters has a reputation for being antagonistic and obnoxious, we want you to avoid making belligerent comments. Try to be a good host."

"That will be difficult if you are talking about the reporter I'm thinking about."

"There can be little doubt that we have the same individual in mind. Naturally, we objected to his presence on the news team, but SNS wouldn't back down and threatened to make an issue out of it. So we've delved into his professional life of recent years to try to anticipate the kinds of questions he will ask. We've generated some appropriate responses. This information will be transmitted to you shortly."

"We'll take a look at it and be ready for him. Thanks for your assistance."

Reflecting on the next day's press conference, Jerry decided that he would like to bait and then embarrass his least favorite reporter during a live broadcast to a worldwide audience. Since the reporter had always been an outspoken NASA critic, the trick would be to embarrass him in a way that would discredit him. Discrediting a loudmouth antagonist might help NASA politically. Perhaps, Doctor Nemard would be the right person for this job, thought Jerry. After all, as a skilled psychologist, she was certainly capable of playing with someone's mind.

Turning his thoughts to other matters, Jerry needed final decisions from Mike and Moose. If a new chief engineer had to be brought up from Earth, he would have to be on the personnel shuttle scheduled to takeoff in less than three hours. Jerry picked up his communicator, entered Mike's number, and received an almost immediate response.

"Hello, Mike here."

"Mike, this is Jerry. Now that you've had a few hours to reconsider, have you decided to stick with your recent request or withdraw it?"

"I've thought it over and have decided to stick with it."

"Very well. When the new chief engineer arrives, I expect you to give him a full briefing and work with him until our departure."

"Will do."

Having received Mike's final decision, Jerry punched Moose's number into his communicator and waited for a response, but he didn't get the expected one. Instead, Moose appeared at the entrance to his office, held up his communicator, and said, "Can I come in, or do you prefer to talk through these things?"

"Don't be silly, come in, and sit down."

Moose floated in and strapped himself into a seat. "I've given much thought to your offer, and I've decided to go with you as your chief engineer, if the offer is still open. I only worry that I am not familiar with the details of this ship, since I've never worked on it."

"But you are a brilliant engineer with twenty years of experience in spacecraft, and this ship's library has detailed specifications of every part of the ship down to the smallest screw and microchip. The computer will give you a three-dimensional image of any part or assembly by simply asking for it. I have no doubt that if anything on the ship were to malfunction, you could diagnose the problem, find the cause, and repair it."

"Thanks for the vote of confidence. Obviously, I agree with you, or I wouldn't be here. But is the offer still open?"

"I spoke with Mike just before you arrived, and he confirmed his replacement request. So now, we have to devise a way to get you on this mission and him off of it without arousing anyone's suspicions. Also, since we're departing in three days, we need to bring you up to speed in a hurry. Mike is currently working with a crew down at the docking interface. Since they're only completing the details of docking, I don't think much would be gained by sending you down there. So I'm going to take you to the engineering library and introduce you to the computer. By the time we leave Earth, I expect that you will have a basic familiarity with the systems that are mission critical."

"I will give it my best, and I will start with propulsion."

PRESS CONFERENCE

One day later, the visiting members of the media completed a partial tour of the Challenger under the guidance of Dianne Dawson, Life Support Officer. They were relaxing in the cafeteria enjoying snacks and beverages awaiting the arrival of Captain Jerontis and Doctor Nemard.

When Jerry and Connie arrived, Dianne introduced them to the press. Then, she introduced the press: "This is Michelle, a highly respected free lance science reporter. This is Sam from Satellite News Service. This is Caryn, a syndicated aerospace reporter. And this is Patrick with Associated Press."

After exchanging the customary greetings, Captain Jerontis said, "I am pleased to meet each of you. Welcome to our ship! You've had a guided tour through some areas and have had the opportunity to meet and visit with some of our crew members. Now, Dianne, Connie, and I will answer your questions about our mission. Michelle, you can be first."

"Captain, what is there about this mission that has motivated you to devote your life to it?"

"That's a big question that's going to take time to answer," replied Captain Jerontis with a broad smile.

"That's true, but this is the most monumental mission ever attempted by humans, and you are the captain. I would like to know why you are so devoted to it."

After a few moments of thought, Captain Jerontis said, "I am devoted to this mission because I believe that interstellar expansion is the destiny of the human species. Throughout time, all species have sought to expand their habitat as a natural part of the evolutionary process. We are no different. With the evolution and growth of our sea of knowledge, we've learned how to travel to other stars. We live on a planet that is becoming very crowded. We need more space, and the Universe is huge beyond comprehension. The Milky Way Galaxy alone contains billions of stars and millions of these are similar to our Sun. If only one percent of these sun-like stars have earth-like planets, it will be a very long time before the human species runs out of planets on which to establish new civilizations. Our mission to Alpha Centauri A is the first step in the interstellar expansion of the human race. It is a natural part of the evolution of the human species."

"That sounds like a paragraph taken out of a book entitled *Mankind's Place In The Universe*," commented Michelle, "but I can see that you believe very strongly in the things that you just said."

"I get the feeling that I didn't give you the answer that you were expecting."

"It's good to dedicate your life to what you believe in, but what is it about this mission that excites you personally? What is it that gives you a burning desire to want to go to Alcent?"

"The kind of life that we think exists there excites my spirit of adventure. Since I was a teenager, it's been a fantasy of mine to journey seventy million years back in time and visit Earth during the dinosaur age. Going back in time, living among those creatures, and studying them firsthand would be very dangerous; but for me, it would be the ultimate adventure. Well, I can't go back in time, but Star Voyager data indicates that life on Alcent may be similar to what existed on Earth during the dinosaur age. This mission gives me the opportunity to live on and explore a planet that may be in an advanced dinosaur age. Perhaps, some of these creatures have even evolved into fairly intelligent beings."

"Why do you say that?" asked Michelle.

"The Solar System is believed to be about 4.6 billion years old; whereas, Alpha Centauri A and its planets are believed to be 5 to 6 billion years old. If the evolution of life started as early in Alcent's history as it did on Earth, then the creatures now living on Alcent may have had an extra billion years to evolve compared to life on Earth. Earth's dinosaurs only ruled the planet for about 150 million years. If Alcent is in a dinosaur age, it is possible that it started a billion years ago. Intelligence could certainly evolve in that amount of time. But intelligent or not, it will be one super adventure to live among those creatures and study them."

"I can see that you are thrilled by the possibilities, but do you have the training to study dinosaurs?"

"I don't, but Dianne does. She has a PhD. in Biology and in Genetic Engineering. She will be in charge of all plant and animal research on Alcent."

Next, Captain Jerontis turned to Caryn who asked, "Could you give us a brief summary of your flight plan including the speed, time, and distance involved?"

"As you know, our destination is the Alpha Centauri system, our nearest interstellar neighbors. Specifically, we are going to Alcent, the third planet of Alpha Centauri A. It is 4.35 light-years away. That is 25 trillion 516 billion miles. Before the development of antimatter propulsion, it was impossible to make this kind of journey in a human lifetime. But with antimatter propulsion, the Challenger will accelerate at a steady 1g for about nine months to bring us up to a speed of about .77c, which is 77% of light speed. This means that we will be traveling at a speed of about 143,220 miles per second. This will be our cruising speed for about 4 years and 11 months. Then, we'll have approximately nine months of 1g deceleration. After a travel time of nearly 6 years and five months, we'll go into orbit around Alcent and begin studying it."

Caryn argued, "Even with an antimatter propulsion system, I don't understand how you can carry enough fuel to accelerate to such a tremendous speed and then have enough fuel left to slow down for your arrival at Alcent."

"I know this seems impossible, but you must keep in mind that the energy available from antimatter fuel is about 140 times greater than what is available from nuclear fusion and about 100 million times greater than what is available from chemical rocket fuels. To put this in perspective, if antimatter propulsion had been available in the late twentieth century, thirty-five milligrams of fuel (about the weight of a sugar cube) would have been sufficient to launch the space shuttle."

Caryn seemed satisfied, so Jerry turned to Patrick who asked, "Captain, with 24 people on this ship, how can you possibly carry enough food, water, and oxygen to last more than six years?"

Captain Jerontis said to Dianne, "This question falls into your area of responsibility."

Dianne turned her attention to the media. "We have a sophisticated life support system that recycles all waste materials to produce pure water and oxygen. Also, we are able to grow food from recycled waste."

"Can you tell us briefly how it works?" asked Patrick.

"Briefly? That will be difficult, but the key to the success of our life support system is genetic engineering. Through it, highly specialized microorganisms have been developed to attack and break down the various kinds of waste materials generated on this ship. Specialized genetically engineered plants also play a key role in the process. They are used to grow the materials that our food synthesizers need to make food. The plants also produce part of our oxygen. Is that brief enough for you?"

"I get the picture, and if you started giving me technical details, I might not understand them anyway."

"I might add one more thing; and that is, we do have substantial reserves of oxygen, water, and food for emergency use."

"I have one more question," asserted Patrick. "How well do your food synthesizers work?"

"With the various kinds of plant materials that we feed into them, they are capable of making anything that you can find on any menu on Earth."

"But how well do they work?" persisted Patrick.

"Since arriving on this ship, you've had two meals and a coffee break. How well do you think our food synthesizers work?"

"Amazingly well!" exclaimed Patrick who just now realized that he had eaten foods made by the synthesizers.

Captain Jerontis turned his attention to Sam and said, "It is your turn."

"Captain, since this project's inception twenty years ago, hundreds of billions of dollars have been spent on it. Don't you think it would have been better to have spent this vast sum feeding the hungry and housing the poor?"

"Sam, that question has been debated by the politicians in Washington, D.C. during each year's budget battle since day one. I really don't think there is anything that I can say that hasn't already been said many times."

"Captain, you are evading the question. I want to know what your position is on this vitally important issue."

"My position is that this is a dead issue. The money has already been spent. Earth's role in the project is nearly complete. We are almost ready to leave. Why do you persist in pursuing a dead horse?"

"Because it is important for the future. Other huge expensive boondoggles will come up that need to be stopped, so that the money can be spent on social programs. How do you feel about all the money that has been wasted on this project that could have been spent on social programs?"

"Well Sam, as you know, I am totally devoted to this mission. I firmly believe in it, and during the past twenty years, I have dedicated my life to its success. This hasn't left me with very much time to worry about social programs."

"But Captain, you must have some concern for the plight of the hungry and the homeless and the fact that the money soaked up by this project could have been used to help them."

"Of course I am concerned about their predicament. But you must realize that the money invested in this project isn't going to disappear into interstellar space when we leave the solar system. We are not taking it with us. It was all spent on Earth and provided meaningful jobs and careers for tens of thousands of people for two decades. Much of the money was spent developing technology for this mission that can also be used to improve life on Earth. With just a little imagination, even you should be able to figure out that the microorganisms genetically engineered for waste recycling on this ship could be used by the cities of the world to totally recycle their sewage, thereby eliminating a major source of environmental pollution. This technology would also allow cities to recycle their waste water, a very important capability to have in arid and semi-arid parts of the world where water is in short supply. The special genetically engineered plants that we use to produce our food mature rapidly and can produce an abundance of high quality food from a limited space. If grown on Earth on a large scale, an abundant food supply would by available. Hunger could be eliminated as a social problem. All you have to do is overcome the hysterical objections raised by radical environmentalists who claim that since these plants were genetically engineered, they aren't natural and therefore should not be released into Earth's ecosystem."

Jerry quickly turned to Michelle who said, "Speaking of radical environmentalists, they have vowed to sabotage your mission. Do you think your security procedures are stringent enough to prevent whatever it is that they've planned?"

"Since they have resorted to terrorist acts that have killed or injured several NASA employees, we must take them very seriously. Consequently, our security department has recruited the best professionals in the country. They are organized into two teams with one team responsible for establishing security procedures while the other team attempts to breach the system. By trying to outwit each other in daily computer games, they have given us a security system that we believe is nearly impossible to penetrate. Also, we are using the best security equipment that advanced technology has to offer. Some of it is so new that it hasn't even been marketed yet. Sam, you have a question?"

"I want to discuss the population of your ship. You have a crew of twenty-four with twelve crew members under the age of twenty and twelve crew members ranging in age from twenty-eight to forty-two. Why the age difference between the two groups? And what kind of selection process was used?"

Captain Jerontis turned to Doctor Nemard and asked, "Would you like to respond to these questions?"

Connie nodded, "To understand why the people on our ship fall into two different age groups, you need to consider the goals and responsibilities of our mission. Those of us in the older group are all experienced, highly trained professionals in our respective fields. We are responsible for the operation of this ship and arriving at our destination safely and in good health. Also, during our long journey, we will be responsible for the advanced training of the younger generation.

When we arrive on Alcent, our primary goal will be to establish a new civilization. That means having children and successfully raising them to become competent adults. After a six-year journey through interstellar space, those of us in the older group won't have that many child bearing years left to us. However, those in the younger group will be able to have and raise as many children as they want and thereby give our new civilization a solid beginning and a promising future.

As to the selection criteria, all applicants for a position on this mission had to take a series of intelligence tests that sought to determine one's ability to learn new material quickly. One's ability to rapidly analyze and solve unexpected difficult problems was also evaluated. To even be considered for a position on this mission, an applicant had to score higher than ninety-five percent of those tested.

Also, each person had to pass medical, physical, and psychological tests. Genetics played an important part in this evaluation; in that, a successful applicant had to show a family history free of hereditary diseases that would cause physical or mental disabilities. Also, since we will be starting a new civilization, the success of which depends on reproduction, only applicants with normal sexual desires were considered for this mission.

Individuals who passed all of these tests faced still more hurdles. Training exercises based on Star Voyager data were developed to help mission candidates learn the survival skills needed to stay alive in the dangerous environment we expect to find on Alcent. Physical endurance, cunning ingenuity, good judgment based on common sense, and the ability to successfully deal with unexpected situations were all essential to successful completion of this training. Sam, you have a follow up question?"

"Yes, I do. What exactly do you mean by the phrase *normal sexual desires*?"

"I am referring to individuals who want to love and be loved by a member of the opposite sex."

Sam retorted, "But what about people who prefer to live in an alternative life style? Weren't their civil rights violated by being excluded from consideration for this mission? Isn't this tantamount to discrimination on the basis of sexual preference?"

"Yes, it was, but I believe that I explained quite clearly why this discrimination was necessary."

"But your earlier statement implied that people living in an alternative life style have abnormal sexual desires."

"I suppose you could interpret my comment that way, but I am wondering why you are pursuing this line of questioning instead of asking us how we feel about our mission, how we plan to survive and prosper on Alcent, or what we will do during our long voyage."

"I have just uncovered a flagrant violation of the Civil Rights Act. Also, I've called attention to a socially insensitive comment of yours that is inconsistent with politically correct thinking and that is bound to be offensive to a large group of people in our society, many of whom paid tax dollars to support your mission."

"And that is what you think your viewers from around the world are interested in finding out about the greatest adventure ever attempted by mankind. Perhaps after you get back to Earth, one of your viewers could send you a book on human anatomy. After a brief study of male and female body parts, it should become readily apparent to you what would constitute normal sexual activity. Then, with some additional study, you could figure out how human reproduction works and how it is dependent on normal sexual activity. Then, you might be able to understand why discrimination on the basis of sexual preference was necessary for the success of this mission.

As far as politically correct thinking is concerned, I am still a citizen of the United States, and I have political freedom as guaranteed by the Constitution. Not you, or anyone else, is going to tell me what kind of thinking is politically correct. My freedom allows me to decide that for myself. Early in the twentieth century, there was an individual who told millions what politically correct thinking consisted of, and he used lots of guns to enforce his point of view. In case you're not a student of history, his name was Adolf Hitler."

Wanting to end the confrontation with Sam, Doctor Nemard quickly turned to Michelle and said, "Michelle, you have a question?"

"Yes, doctor. The Challenger is a big ship, but you will be confined to it for more than six years. What are you going to do during all that time? And how are you going to avoid getting cabin fever?"

"Some people would have a difficult time dealing with close confinement for that long a time. One of the purposes of psychological testing was to find and eliminate them from mission eligibility." Connie briefly turned to Sam and said, "I guess you could even consider that a form of discrimination."

Before Sam could comment, Connie turned back to Michelle, "As to your first question, I will monitor the health and well-being of each person on this ship and treat any medical or psychological problems that develop. Captain Jerontis and the rest of the crew will monitor the performance of the Challenger's various systems, do preventive maintenance, and repair anything that malfunctions. One of the most important responsibilities of the older generation will be to assist the young people with their continued training. For example, by the time we reach Alcent, I will have trained two of them to take over my responsibilities if there is an untimely end to my life."

"But you can't work all the time," protested Michelle. "What about leisure activities?"

"All the quality movies created on Earth in recent years are stored in our computer library, so that an individual can call one up for viewing in his quarters. Music, books, and games are also stored in the computer library. Also, during your tour of the ship, you were shown our gymnasium. In addition to the exercise equipment located there, it is large enough to play competitive games in. For those who are musically inclined, we do have some musical instruments onboard. Occasionally, we will have dance parties with either live music or with music stored in the computer. Also, we have each other for companionship and close personal relationships.

We have a machine shop. It is located on the deck below the gym. It contains all the sophisticated equipment we'll need to manufacture parts or repair existing parts that might malfunction on this ship. This shop is also available to those who like to design and make things as a hobby. For example, new items of clothing can be designed and made with the equipment in the shop. Our responsibilities will keep us quite busy, but we will find adequate time for leisure activities."

"You almost make it sound like a certain amount of time spent on leisure activities will be a part of the doctor's orders," commented Michelle.

"I think personal well-being is dependent on spending time on leisure activities, especially for people held in close confinement for a long time. But even though our crew members are energetic self-motivated individuals, they do love their free time, and I don't think I'll have to order any of them to spend more time on leisure activities."

After glancing at his watch, Captain Jerontis said, "We have time for one more question from each of you; then, we'll have to bring this interview to a close. Caryn?"

"Captain, why was the name *Challenger* selected for your starship?"

"That name was selected in honor of the seven astronauts who were killed in the explosion of the space shuttle, Challenger, on January 28, 1986. Patrick?"

"In view of all the hazards that you will face, how high do you rate your chance of success?"

"We will succeed! Michelle?"

"Captain, it seems to me that your survival for the next six years is dependent on this ship's waste recycling system. If it fails to function as expected, you could run out of oxygen to breathe, food to eat, or both. How large a safety margin has been built into the system? You have twenty-four people on this ship. How many people could you put on this ship before the system becomes overloaded? And what about the microorganisms on which the operation of the system depends, how do you know they will stay healthy for more than six years of interstellar space flight?"

Captain Jerontis smiled broadly at Michelle and commented, "That sounds like more than one question to me."

Michelle smiled back and responded, "But they're all closely related questions concerning one of your ship's essential systems."

Captain Jerontis nodded in agreement.

"Our life support system has a safety margin of 35 to 40%," Dianne answered. "So we would have to add eight, nine, or ten people to our crew before we would be in danger of overloading the system and placing our survival in jeopardy. As to your other question, several predecessor versions of this life support system have been in use on our space stations and lunar and Mars bases for several decades. They have proven to be very reliable. However, during our long voyage, I will be using my genetic engineering skills and this ship's research lab to improve the microorganisms and plants on which our survival depends. Sam?"

"Environmentalists have charged that your presence on Alcent will pollute the pristine environment there and that microbes carried to Alcent by you will pose a serious threat to the life forms already living there. How do you plan to protect the life on Alcent from this life threatening danger?"

Dianne replied, "When we arrive at Alcent, we will orbit the planet at a low altitude, probably around 200 miles. After studying the planet from this orbit for several weeks, we will launch sterilized, unmanned landing craft to locations of interest. These landing craft will be complex remotely controlled research labs. With them, we will do chemical analysis of air, water, soil, and plant life samples. We will discover and study a multitude of microorganisms. We will compare them to those that exist on Earth. Using computer models, we will determine how much of a challenge Alcent's microbes will be to the human immune system.

Also, our robot labs will be equipped with small remotely controlled flying vehicles that we will land on the backs of dinosaurs to collect small blood and tissue samples for analysis in the labs. In addition, the fliers will be used to collect urine and fecal samples for analysis. We will be looking at healthy animals, injured animals, and animals that appear to be sick. We will attempt to discover what kind of immune systems these animals have and if they are capable of dealing with microbes from Earth.

The big question that we will be trying to answer is whether life on Alcent is compatible or incompatible with life from Earth. We will want to know what the risks are before any of us go down to the planet's surface."

Sam appeared ready to argue with Dianne, but before he could say anything, Captain Jerontis said, "This concludes our press conference. All of you except Michelle will be leaving our ship in three hours to spend the night on the personnel shuttle. During the balance of the day, Dianne and Connie will show you areas of the ship that you haven't yet seen or areas that you want to see again. They will also introduce you to available personnel for interviews. When you return in the morning, they will again be your guides. Michelle, your request to stay onboard until we depart has been granted. You will stay with the group until they leave the ship. After that, Connie will be your escort and share her quarters with you."

Except for Sam, members of the media thanked Captain Jerontis for his time; then, he left the group and returned to the flight deck to check the progress of events leading to departure.

Michelle turned to Dianne and said, "One area you haven't shown us is the hangar deck. I would like to see the shuttles that you will use to travel to and from the surface when the Challenger is orbiting Alcent."

"Good idea," Dianne responded.

On the way to the hangar deck, Michelle asked Connie, "You are about to depart on a long perilous mission filled with uncertainty. However, when Patrick asked Captain Jerontis to rate your chance of achieving success, he declared, 'we will succeed!' Is this wishful thinking on his part, or is he really that sure of success?"

"He actually is 100% confident that we will be successful."

"But you are attempting to do something that has never been done before. How can he be so confident?"

"There is something that you must understand about Captain Jerontis, and that is that he approaches life with a *very* strong positive attitude. When he decides to do something, he just simply refuses to accept failure. He has more stick-to-it-tive-ness than anyone I've ever met. He just hangs in there and does whatever it takes to achieve his goals."

"But this is a huge complex starship that must function for the next seven years. Any number of things could go wrong."

"That's true, but Captain Jerontis has participated in the design, construction, and testing of this starship from the very beginning. He probably knows more about it than anyone. If he is confident in this starship, so am I."

Michelle thought about the firmness of Connie's comments. Then, she said, "I've talked to several crew members since my arrival, and all of them seem to be as confident in Captain Jerontis as you are. He seems to have the unquestioned loyalty of the crew. How has he won their loyalty?"

"Everyone knows that he is an expert on the intricate details of this ship and how everything works."

Michelle argued, "There has to be more to it than that. I know many intelligent people, and some of them just don't inspire loyalty in anyone."

"You just mentioned the key word."

"Which word was that?"

"*Inspire*. Captain Jerontis inspires confidence in the people around him."

"How does he do that?" Before Connie could respond, Michelle said, "Let me make this personal. How does he inspire you to be confident in his leadership?"

With no forethought whatsoever, Connie immediately responded, "I greatly appreciate his leadership style. He is a strong leader, but he is gentle. He never criticizes anyone; he encourages them. Also, I respect his knowledge, and I like the strong confident cheerful attitude that he always displays. Then, there is the seemly limitless energy that he always comes up with when he has a deadline to meet. Perhaps, his energy comes from his attitude, determination, and physical strength. He does have a strong athletic build, being six feet three inches tall and 230 pounds. He is muscular and has very little body fat. I think his energetic, youthful appearance seems to inspire people into thinking that he can do whatever is required."

Michelle noticed that Connie's face seemed to light up while she was talking about Captain Jerontis. Being a professional reporter, she decided to investigate this, so she said, "That was a rather long-winded answer to my question. You seem to know a quite a bit about your captain."

Not expecting these comments and not prepared to respond to their implication, Connie thought about them for a few moments. Then, rather than respond to what was implied, Connie said, "I am the mission psychiatrist and medical doctor. I make it my business to know and understand everyone on this ship, especially the captain."

Michelle sensed that there might be another reason for Connie's extensive knowledge about the captain, but she decided not to pursue it because she felt that she wasn't going to get any additional information. Michelle looked into Connie's eyes and smiled in a way that let her know that she understood.

A few moments later, the group arrived on the hangar deck, and Michelle said to Dianne, "Those shuttles look like sleek high-speed aircraft. Can you tell me a little bit about them?"

While pointing at them, Dianne said, "The big one is a cargo carrier and the small one is a personnel shuttle. Both shuttles have NTR propulsion systems that will allow us to travel between the surface of Alcent and the Challenger as many times as we need to without being concerned about running out of fuel."

"What is an NTR propulsion system?" asked Patrick.

"NTR means nuclear thermal rocket," replied Dianne.

Patrick appeared puzzled. "How does an NTR operate?" he asked Dianne.

"Its operation is quite simple. A working fluid such as liquefied air or ordinary water is pumped through the nuclear reactor's heat exchanger where it is heated to a temperature of several thousand degrees. This converts the liquid into an extremely high pressure gas that expands out the rocket nozzle creating enough thrust to accelerate the shuttle to orbital speed and lift it to orbital altitude."

"Why were NTRs selected to propel the shuttles rather than antimatter power plants?"

"Antimatter fuel is extremely expensive to produce and NTRs provide more than enough energy for travel between the surface of Alcent and the low altitude orbit the Challenger will be in. Also, NTRs are safe, rugged, reliable power plants that are easy to operate. The technology involved is mature."

While members of the press asked Dianne additional questions about the shuttles, Captain Jerontis was on the flight deck talking to Mike. Captain Jerontis asked, "How is our final checkout proceeding?"

"Very smoothly. The fact that we're not finding any problems shows just how well-designed this ship really is."

"Not only that, but everything has been tested and retested so many times that all problems should have been found and corrected long ago."

"We should be ready to test fire our engines in about three-and-a-half hours, but right now, we've reached a forty-five-minute break in the checkout schedule."

"Good, why don't you accompany me to the engineering library. There's someone there I would like you to meet."

A couple minutes later, in the engineering library, Captain Jerontis said, "Mike, meet your replacement, John Moosebeck. He has been glued to the computer since accepting the position and is rapidly becoming an expert on the intricate details of this ship. Right, Moose?"

Moose answered Jerry's question by nodding his head and looking at him with the tired eyes and facial expression of one who has been involved in hours of intensive study. Moose shook Mike's hand and said, "Pleased to meet you."

"So I finally get to meet the boisterous, flamboyant Moose I've heard so much about," Mike said. "How did you manage to motivate the bureaucrats at NASA Command to allow you to replace me with your life-long friend?" he asked Captain Jerontis.

Seeing the gleam in Captain J.J.'s eyes and the mischievous grin on his face, Mike said, "Never mind. Forget that I asked that question; I really don't want to know."

Turning his attention back to Moose, Mike said, "Attempting to learn the intricate details of this ship in just a few days is a rather tall order. Is there anything I can do to help?"

"So far, I've limited my study to the most crucial systems. I've been looking at propulsion, flight control, and life support; and they aren't much different than on the Goliath, just a bit more advanced. Maybe, sometime tomorrow, you could brief me on any peculiarities that you think I should know about."

"Tomorrow's checkout schedule has a two-hour break at lunch time, and that would be the best time for me."

Mike looked at Captain Jerontis, "I am curious to know what clandestine plan you've devised for getting me off this ship and back to Earth without arousing anyone's suspicions."

"I was going to send you back on the Goliath, but that would've only gotten you down to our main orbital base, and you would've had to wait there for a ride down to Earth. But we've had a stroke of good luck. The captain of the personnel shuttle that brought the news media up is a friend of mine. Tomorrow, I will give him a tour of the Challenger, and explain to him that there has been a personnel change and that he is to give you a ride down to Earth. There's no reason for him to be suspicious, and even if he were, I doubt that he would question NASA Command about it. The only risk is that he might inadvertently mention it during some other discussion with them, so I think I will invite him to stay onboard until we're ready to depart. And I will delay telling him about the personnel change for as long as possible.

On another subject, a really sharp-looking female reporter named Michelle has requested an interview with our chief engineer. Maybe, you could talk with her this evening after we've finished discussing the results of our engine test firing."

Mike grinned and said, "Well, I don't know if I want to be talking to any good-looking women when I'm trying to get this ship ready for departure. That might be too big a distraction. Just how beautiful is she anyway?"

Jerry collected his thoughts for a few moments. He smiled, recalling Michelle's features, "She has an attractive figure, a beautiful face, sandy-brown hair, and a light tan. I'd guess that she's about five-seven, maybe five-eight, and probably weighs around 130 pounds."

Noticing Jerry appeared to be breathing a little faster, Mike said, "It seems that she had quite an effect on you. From your description, it sounds like you took a pretty good look at her."

"She definitely got my attention."

"Well, if she's as outstanding as you say she is, I guess I could find a little time to talk to her."

Acting as though he would be doing Mike a big favor, Jerry said, "If it's going to put too much of a strain on your schedule, I'll tell her that you're busy and handle the interview myself. Depending on how it goes, I might even figure out a way to make her a part of the crew."

"That's okay," Mike quickly replied, "I'll talk to her. After all, she did ask for the chief engineer, and I haven't yet been replaced."

Moose grinned at Mike, "I heard she has a knack for asking tough questions. I hope she doesn't hit you with something that you're not prepared for. Maybe, I should take the interview."

"Thanks for the offer, but I'm sure I can handle it."

Four hours later, all primary propulsion rockets had been throttled up to sixty-five percent of full power for fifteen seconds and then, throttled back down and shut off. Mike, Moose, and Jerry were busily poring over the computer analysis of the performance data. The first one to say anything was Mike, "I see no anomalies here. In fact, I don't see how this test run could have been any better. Other than increasing our speed and raising the apogee of our orbit, not much else happened."

Jerry and Moose nodded in agreement, and Mike said, "Since this concludes today's checkout, I think it's time for me to look up a reporter named Michelle."

Before Mike could depart, Captain Jerontis stopped him and urged, "Remember, as far as the press is concerned, and anyone else for that matter, you are the chief engineer for this mission."

Mike nodded and left.

Moose declared, "I haven't eaten in hours, and I feel like devouring a large combination pizza with extra pepperoni and cheese."

"Do you ever eat anything besides pizza?" asked Jerry while on their way to the cafeteria.

"Of course I do, but pizza just happens to be my favorite food."

"I would never have guessed that."

A little later, when Moose and Jerry were well into their meal, Moose said, "You sure have excellent food on this ship."

"Yes, we do. We fortunately have a chef who is blessed with an intuitive ability in the kitchen. What amazes me is that he does this with basic ingredients and flavorings produced by our food synthesizers."

"You're lucky that someone with so much talent survived the strenuous training and testing program required of people for this mission."

"Actually, he didn't. He is the only person on this mission who didn't do all that well in survival training. However, because of his culinary abilities, NASA allowed him on the mission anyway, since they consider excellent dining essential to crew morale on a voyage of this length."

"I agree—good food is a bright spot in anyone's day. But now that I'm here, he isn't the only creative cook."

"What do you mean?"

"Have you already forgotten all the good meals that you've eaten at my house?"

Jerry thought about Moose's question for a few moments; then said, "I'll have to admit that you do know your way around a kitchen. But right now, I am more in need of a chief engineer than another chef."

"Once we get underway, the engineering workload might not be all that demanding. If that's the case, I wouldn't mind helping out in the kitchen. Your chef can't work around the clock, and he might like some time off now and then."

"True, let's keep that in mind."

"On another subject, are you worried about anything in tomorrow's schedule?"

"Not really. We actually have a fairly light schedule. Our checkout procedures resume at 8:30 AM with a two-hour break at 11:30. If no problems are encountered, checkout will be completed at 4:30 PM. The most crucial event is the full power engine test at 3:30, but I don't anticipate any problems. Our engines are just enhanced versions of the power plants you have on the Goliath, and they've been extensively operated at full power for nine years now. At 1:30 PM the next day, there will be a presidential farewell address, followed by our departure at 2:00 PM. Now that you're part of the mission, are you worried about anything?"

Moose leaned back, briefly pondered the question and said, "Twenty years ago, you and I won back-to-back national championships by working together with the rest of the football team dedicated to a winning effort. As I see it, our current situation is quite similar. If you can provide the same inspirational leadership now as you did twenty years ago, we should all end up dying of old age on Alcent."

"Now that my all-time favorite fullback is on the team, my job will certainly be easier. When Mike hit me with a replacement request, it sort of threw me for a loop. The engineer that NASA would have sent up to replace him is a very capable individual, but for some reason, I am not comfortable with him. I would've had a difficult time working with him. I don't think that he and I would ever have been a smoothly functioning team, and in a time-critical crisis, smooth team work is essential."

"Twenty years ago, playing football, we instinctively worked together. I remember it seemed like we were almost able to sense what each other was thinking."

"In a fast-paced crisis, that is important," Jerry answered with conviction.

After a few moments of thought, he continued, "Twenty years is a long time, but talking about our football triumphs brings back fond memories that seem so clear, almost like they happened only yesterday. Have you ever considered that both of us could be comfortably retired by now if we'd gone into professional football instead of into space? Think about it, we could be having a relatively risk-free life on Earth; instead, we are about to embark on a mission we may not survive."

"We all have choices to make. I believe an individual's state of well-being at any point in his life is the direct result of all the choices that individual has made up to that point in his life. Rather than play professional football, I chose to go into space because I enjoy the adventure of it. Facing and conquering the unexpected hazards one sometimes finds in an adventure into the unknown gives me an emotional high like none other. Knowing me as well as you do, you had to know what my decision would be when you gave me the opportunity to go to Alcent with you. Hauling cargo to and from the Moon has been getting a bit routine. I am starting to feel like a truck driver who has to drive the same route every day."

"I was pretty sure you would accept. After all, my offer to you was just one more unexpected challenge for you to conquer."

"It was definitely unexpected. You dropped it on me right out of nowhere, and it's definitely a big challenge. Moose checked the clock, "I think it's time for me to go back to the engineering library. There are a couple more systems I want to look at before I turn in for the night."

"I am going to my quarters to put in a call to my parents. I won't be able to see them in person before we leave, but the video phone in my quarters has a screen covering one entire wall. A phone call to my parents is almost like being at home with them. I'm also going to give my brother and sister a call."

"Say hello to them for me," requested Moose as he headed for the engineering library.

"Will do. See you in the morning."

Mike and Michelle entered the cafeteria just as Moose and Jerry were leaving. Mike introduced Michelle and Moose. After a brief exchange of greetings, Mike and Michelle picked up menus and considered what to order. Michelle said, "Can we order food to go and eat on the observation deck? Viewing the

Universe from above Earth's atmosphere is rather spectacular. Since this is my first trip into space, I would like to take advantage of the opportunity to enjoy it. It might even be romantic."

Mike assessed Michelle from head to foot. He smiled at her affectionately, "I have no objection to eating in such a setting with a beautiful woman."

"Thank you. You have a nice way with words when you get specific."

A short time later on the observation deck, Mike explained to Michelle, "Here in space away from the familiar reference points that you have on Earth, it's easy to become disoriented, especially in the zero gravity situation that we're now in. To start with, our current orbital position places us directly between the Earth and the Moon with the Sun at our backs. We can't see the Sun because the shields are in place to protect us from intense solar radiation and to keep the observation deck in darkness. To our left is Earth with the face that we see half in daylight and half in darkness. The longitudinal axis of Challenger is currently in upright alignment with Earth's axis of rotation, so that when you look at Earth, the north pole is at the top. To our right is the Moon, also showing a face that is half in daylight and half in darkness. That brilliant yellow star over there is Alpha Centauri A, and that bright orange star next to it is Alpha Centauri B."

Michelle silently stared into the heavens. As her eyes wandered from one point of interest to another, she was enchanted by the stunning beauty of the multitude of stars shining in brilliant contrast to the stark blackness of space.

Mike, meanwhile, stared silently at Michelle. His eyes wandered from one point of interest to another. She was enchanting.

After a couple minutes, Michelle's eyes wandered back to home planet. "Earth looks so tiny from up here. It really doesn't appear much larger than the Moon."

"We are considerably closer to the Moon than to Earth. In round numbers, we are a little more than 125,000 miles from Earth and somewhat less than 105,000 miles from the Moon."

"When I see Earth suspended against the background of infinite space from this great distance, it seems so small and fragile. It is hard to believe that it is teeming with life forms locked in competition for finite living space."

"I get the feeling that you've gained an entirely new perspective in regard to our place in the Universe," noted Mike.

"Viewing Earth and the Cosmos from this vantage point makes me feel like I am a rather small and insignificant part of it."

"That's a fairly normal reaction. I've experienced those feelings more than once. But, however inconsequential you may be feeling at the moment, you've become the important part of my universe."

Mike's words caused Michelle to glow with happiness. After a few moments, she said, "As a science reporter, I've written a number of articles on subjects in astronomy, and I've always known that even on a very clear dark night, observing the heavens through Earth's atmosphere greatly limits what you can see. But until now, I didn't realize how much beauty is obscured by the atmosphere. For the first time in my life, I am able to sense and appreciate the vastness of outer space and truly enjoy its magnificent beauty. The stars are so numerous, it seems like I can see millions of them, and they're so brilliant, sharp, and colorful that I feel like I am peering into an immense galactic treasure chest filled with colorful sparkling jewelry. And to top it all off, Star Voyager data gives us good reason to believe that there might be an abundance of life out there, making the galactic treasure chest even more precious."

Michelle stopped talking when she felt Mike's arms encircle her from behind in an embrace. She turned within his arms, so she could face him. In the soft romantic glow of light from the heavens, Mike noted that Michelle's natural beauty took on an almost angelic appearance. He responded by giving her a long tender kiss. He felt an involuntary tremble in Michelle as she responded. With a supreme effort, Mike managed to gain control over his rapidly growing desire and he said, "Before we get too carried away with this, I think you should tell me your decision in regard to what we've been planning."

"The way I feel right now, I really don't have any choice but to do what you're asking me to do."

Mike kissed her again and softly whispered, "That's what I was hoping you would say. Now, I need to explain to you what we must do to achieve our objective. Let's go to my quarters, where there won't be any risk of being overheard."

PRESIDENTIAL FAREWELL ADDRESS

Forty hours later, the Challenger and her human occupants were ready to go. All checkout procedures had been successfully completed. The Goliath and personnel shuttle had undocked and moved away to a safe distance. The SNS crew onboard the personnel shuttle was ready to provide TV coverage of the Challenger's departure. The Challenger's personnel had said final good-byes to friends and relatives in preparation for permanent departure from Earth, which was less than a half-hour away. All were facing TV screens awaiting the presidential farewell address, which was expected momentarily.

The presidential press secretary appeared on TV, "Ladies and gentlemen, the President of the United States."

The press secretary's image was replaced by that of the president, who said, "Today is truly an epochal occasion as we are about to witness the birth of a new era in human history, the beginning of interstellar expansion. People have dreamed about interstellar travel for centuries. The Challenger mission to the Alpha Centauri system is a fine example of a dream becoming reality. This mission illustrates that what can be conceived by the imaginative human mind can be achieved by free men and women working together when not held in check by lack of resources or by a stifling political system. Captain Jerontis, we are proud to send you and your personnel, the finest men and women that America has to offer, on this historical mission. Establishing a new civilization is a big responsibility. I urge all of you to study human history, learn from our mistakes, and not repeat them on Alcent. I urge you to learn from our greatest successes and carry these into your new civilization. Make it a great one that we can all be proud of. Our prayers are with you. Captain Jerontis, before you depart, if you were to leave an inspirational thought with our nation's youth on how to be successful, what would it be?"

"Mr. President, before I do that, I would like to express my sincere thanks and appreciation to all Americans whose hard work, dedication, and sacrifice made this mission possible. I especially want to thank the American taxpayers for funding for it.

To our youth, I will simply say that your freedom makes you responsible for your future well-being. Each day, when you get out of bed in the morning, simply say to yourself, *My future depends on the choices that I make today*, and then, think about it.

This simple concept was responsible for turning around the life of a close friend of mine. During his first eight years in school, he was disruptive and rebellious. He studied very little. He was well on his way to becoming an illiterate street thug. When he entered the ninth grade, his science teacher had a fairly large sign on his desk that faced the class. The sign said, *MY FUTURE DEPENDS ON THE CHOICES THAT I MAKE TODAY*. At first, this simple message didn't mean much to my friend, but as the school year progressed, it started to have a profound effect on his daily activities. Instead of hanging out with the local street gang, he started doing his homework. After a while, he chose to go a step further and spend some time in the school library researching subjects of interest to him. Anyway, he went on to attend a university, where he earned an advanced engineering degree and became a sports hero."

"I like that message," stated the President. "If your new society is based on that simple concept, it should get off to a very good start. In fact, I like that message so much that I think it should be prominently displayed in all of our classrooms and offices. Too many of us forget that freedom of choice is a potent double-edged sword loaded with personal responsibility. Making the right choices in daily life will lead to a much better future than making the wrong choices. May you and your personnel always make the right choices."

"Thank you, Mr. President."

Captain Jerontis turned to his flight crew and gave the order to start the fifteen-minute countdown. A few minutes later, Connie appeared and handed him a note that said, "All personnel are present and at their stations."

Jerry made eye contact with Connie, "Thank you!"

Shortly thereafter, the warning klaxon blared out its urgent sounding notes indicating that ignition was only three minutes away.

A flood of excitement filled Jerry's mind and body with the full realization that twenty years of hard work was rapidly coming down to a climactic moment. With a fresh flow of adrenaline, Jerry's pulse increased, and his mind raced through a series of thoughts: I am leaving Earth, and I will never return. Will I ever regret this? Will our voyage be a safe one? Has the Challenger been sabotaged in a way that has escaped our detection? What challenges will we encounter on Alcent? Will I always make the right choices? I will certainly try. Am I going to miss Earth? Will I miss my family and friends? Of course I will, but I can deal with that."

As the countdown entered the final minute, Jerry hoped that once they had ignition and were underway, his adrenaline flow would get back to normal. Meanwhile, his excited mind continued to race through thoughts of the past and aspirations for the future. Then, the final seconds ticked by: 9 - 8 - 7 - 6 - 5 - 4 - 3 - 2 - 1 - IGNITION!

TWO

Sabotage

TIME: 24 Hours A.L.E. (after leaving Earth)

While relaxing in his quarters, Captain Jerontis made the following entry into his log: "It is now one day after ignition, and the Challenger's antimatter engines have performed flawlessly. By providing a continuous acceleration of 1g, the engines have added 527 miles per second to our starting velocity. We are now more than twenty million miles from Earth, and the distant planet looks only like an exceptionally bright star."

After completing his log entry, the Captain turned to planning his activities and those of his crew. But his thoughts were interrupted by a call from NASA Command: "Captain Jerontis! We have a serious problem here. When the Goliath arrived at our main orbital base without its captain, we naturally conducted an inquiry to find out why. The Goliath's pilot explained to us that there had been a last minute personnel change on the Challenger with Captain John Moosebeck assigned to it as Chief Engineer replacing Mike Johnson. We have two problems with this. First of all, since this didn't go through proper channels, we want to know the reason for the change and who authorized it."

"The reason for the change is quite simple. Mike said that he did not want to leave Earth and requested that he be replaced. John Moosebeck is eminently qualified for the position and was immediately available, so I authorized the change."

"But you did not follow regulations. As you know, NASA has very stringent rules to follow in regard to who is on this mission. You should be disciplined for ignoring the rules."

"I understand the rules. But now that we've left Earth, the success of this mission is my responsibility. John Moosebeck is a very competent engineer with a distinguished service record. He and I work well together, and I am confident that he will do an excellent job.

Also, I had Doctor Nemard check his medical and genetic background, and she was unable to find any problems of consequence. I believe that I have acted in a responsible way. But if you think disciplinary procedures against me are in order, I would suggest that you punish me by canceling my paychecks for the next thirty years or so."

"That's absurd! You're no longer getting paid anyway."

Captain Jerontis leaned back in his seat and smiled in a way that displayed an air of smug satisfaction. Then, he said, "You stated that you have two problems with my personnel change. What is the other one?"

"We want to talk to Mike Johnson about his reasons for leaving the mission, but we've been unable to locate him. What did you do with him?"

"I arranged with the Captain of the personnel shuttle to give him a ride back to Earth. Since he had been in space for six weeks working on this ship, I would assume that he is taking some time off before reporting back to work."

"He should have reported in beforehand. We need to know his whereabouts."

TIME: 48 Hours, 31 Minutes A.L.E.

Captain's Log Entry: "We've reached a velocity of 1,056 miles per second and have traveled a distance of 93 million miles, approximately the average distance between the Earth and the Sun. Earth now looks like just an ordinary bright star.

Captain Jerontis and Moose were reviewing operations data from the ship's propulsion and navigation systems when they were interrupted by a call from NASA Command: "Captain Jerontis! We have some disturbing news from an undercover FBI agent attending a national council meeting of Environment First. Council officials have assured the delegates that history is about to repeat itself. They said that the end of the ill-fated Challenger mission of a century ago would look like an exploding firecracker compared to the demise of the current Challenger mission. This announcement is ominous because it wasn't made to the press for the sake of gaining publicity, but at a closed, delegates only, meeting. If we take their statements seriously, then we have to conclude that they intend to cause an explosion involving the vast amount of antimatter fuel you are carrying."

"True, but the question is how?"

"The obvious way would be to disrupt the magnetic field in one of the antimatter containment tanks," interjected Moose. "The resulting matter-antimatter explosion would certainly make the Challenger accident of a century ago look like an exploding firecracker by comparison. A computer virus cleverly planted in the field control computers could cause a catastrophic malfunction."

"That's possible, but it would be extremely difficult to accomplish," commented Captain Jerontis. "To start with, it is a triple redundant system, each with an independent electrical power source. The virus would have to have been planted in three different computers and timed to act almost simultaneously. If a saboteur were able to accomplish that, there is still the final, fail-safe backup system that would have to be overcome. It is very simple, consisting of nothing more than a magnetometer connected to a switch. If the magnetometer detects a dangerous degradation in magnetic field strength, it instantaneously turns on a backup magnetic containment field that can only be turned off by restoring the primary magnetic field. By its simplicity, this system is nearly 100% reliable."

"That's all true," acknowledged Moose, "but I believe a determined saboteur that's a computer whiz could pull it off."

Captain Jerontis thought about the situation for a few moments. Then, he said, "A cleverly concealed computer virus would be difficult and time consuming to find, and I don't believe we have that much time. I think our best strategy would be to block that kind of sabotage by making sure that our final backup system has not been sabotaged. Moose I need an immediate inspection."

"We'll get right on it Captain," stated Moose as he got up and left in a hurry.

"I don't think that we should completely rule out the possibility of a bomb," declared NASA Command.

"With the stringent security procedures that have been in effect, I don't see how anyone could have transported a bomb to this ship."

"Transporting a bomb to your ship isn't the only way to get one onboard. Your ship's maintenance shop has some very sophisticated plastics manufacturing equipment in it. With the chemicals and other raw materials that you have onboard, an effective bomb containing plastic explosives could have been made in your shop. Planted in a critical area, next to an antimatter fuel line for example, devastating results could easily be achieved. Alternatively, such a bomb could be used to destroy your life support system or to kill key personnel, such as yourself. You are the only person on the ship who has been with the project since its inception, and that makes you a prime target for assassination."

"Using a bomb in that way would not produce the gigantic explosion required to make the earlier Challenger explosion look like an exploding firecracker."

"True enough, but we cannot limit ourselves to taking their pronouncement literally. If they are cunning enough to sabotage a starship, then we must assume that they are also shrewd enough to figure out that the FBI may have infiltrated their organization. Consequently, their declaration may have been made purely to throw us off track."

"If we had some bomb detection equipment onboard, it would sure make searching for a bomb quicker and easier."

"We are already working on that problem. Since we have a complete inventory of the chemicals, materials, and equipment that you have onboard, we can determine the kinds of plastic explosives that could be made in your maintenance shop. This is currently being done. We are also designing a simple detection device that you can build in your shop that will be capable of finding these particular kinds of plastic explosives. This design will be transmitted to you in just a few hours. It will be crude, but effective. In the meantime, all of your people should begin a systematic search of critical areas where even a small bomb could do devastating damage. A plan for a methodical search is currently being transmitted into your main computer.

Incidentally, we still haven't located Mike Johnson. If your ship really has been sabotaged, his last minute request to leave the mission, along with his disappearance, certainly makes him a prime suspect. Also, no one would be better qualified to sabotage a starship than its chief engineer."

"I have worked with Mike for many years," retorted Captain Jerontis. "I know him very well. I simply cannot believe that he would do anything to jeopardize this ship or the lives of the people on it. Surely, you must have other suspects."

"Security is working that problem. Mike isn't the only suspect. However, under the circumstances, we have initiated an all out effort to locate him. You must keep in mind that some of the best saboteurs in history achieved their success by appearing totally innocent and trustworthy. We are signing off for now. You have urgent work to do."

Captain Jerontis quickly assembled all available personnel, explained the situation, and organized them into bomb search teams. In addition, he instructed them to look for anything out of the ordinary that might indicate how the ship had been sabotaged, so that preventive action could be taken.

Captain Jerontis then turned to the pilot and said, "I want the antimatter engines gradually shut down and the fuel lines emptied."

"Yes sir," replied the pilot as he began entering the appropriate instructions into the flight control computer.

Captain Jerontis sounded several notes on the ship's warning klaxon to get the attention of all personnel. Then, he addressed them through the ship's intercom. First, he explained the bomb threat for the benefit of individuals not already working on the bomb search teams. Then, he said, "During the next few minutes, we are going to shut off all propulsive power. Prepare for weightlessness. It will continue until we've resolved the bomb threat."

Jerry had two reasons for shutting down the antimatter engines. To start with, the antimatter fuel lines were more readily accessible than the antimatter storage tanks, and therefore, an easier place to plant a bomb. A bomb that could rupture a fuel line would also disrupt the magnetic containment field in the fuel line. This would allow the antimatter in the fuel line to contact ordinary matter resulting in mutual annihilation and catastrophic energy release. The explosive energy released would be more than adequate to wreck the nearest antimatter fuel tank causing an explosion powerful enough to detonate all remaining antimatter resulting in instantaneous incineration of the entire starship. Even at this great distance, the flash from the explosion would be bright enough to be seen in the night sky back on Earth, quite adequately fulfilling the pronouncement made at the Environment First meeting. However, if the fuel line contained no antimatter, then the bomb would only damage the fuel line, which could easily be repaired or replaced.

The captain's other reason for shutting off propulsive power was simply to put the ship in a weightless condition. If a bomb were detonated near a load bearing structure, the ship would be far less susceptible to catastrophic failure than if it were under acceleration. A severe structural failure could also lead to the detonation of the antimatter fuel.

Jerry considered the ship's structure and compiled a list of areas where a bomb blast would have the most serious consequences. Further consideration in terms of accessibility allowed him to narrow down and prioritize the list.

Then, Jerry considered some other possibilities. Was there anyone on the personnel shuttle or on the Goliath with the capability of manufacturing plastic explosives and assembling a bomb with the equipment in the maintenance shop? If so, could this person have done this without being detected? Then, could this

31

individual have put on a space suit, gone outside, and attached the bomb to the hull close to an antimatter fuel tank without being detected? Not likely, but possible Jerry admitted to himself.

The Challenger's inventory of maintenance equipment included two robot repair vehicles for going outside the ship. These vehicles were equipped with a number of sensors and manipulator arms and could operate under computer control. Alternatively, they could be occupied and controlled by a one or two person crew, or they could be manually controlled from inside the starship. Since computer software was already in place for these robots to do a meticulous inspection of the ship's exterior, Captain Jerontis decided to dispatch them on this mission. Any bomb attached to the ship's exterior would show up as a deviation from specifications and thus be detected by the robots.

TIME: 72 Hours A.L.E.

Captain's Log Entry: "Our current speed is 1,085 miles per second and we've traveled a distance of 185 million miles, approximately the diameter of Earth's orbit around the Sun. Our antimatter engines have not been restarted.

Moose has verified that the final backup system to establish magnetic containment fields for the antimatter fuel tanks is fully functional. Our visual bomb search of critical areas has found nothing. The robot repair vehicles inspecting the starship's exterior have found only a few miniature craters caused by collisions with space dust.

Moose and two assistants are in the machine shop finishing the assembly of a bomb detector. Because of the urgent nature of the project, the design has been kept simple to allow for the use of off-the-shelf components. Even though crude, the device will be sensitive enough to detect the infinitesimal amounts of vapors and particles given off by plastic explosives. A small quantity of plastic explosive is being made to test the detector's capability."

Comfortably seated at the command console, Captain Jerontis was deeply lost in thought attempting to recall events of recent months in minute detail. He mentally searched for clues as to how his ship may have been put at grave risk. His thoughts were interrupted by the appearance of Dianne Dawson.

Captain Jerontis acknowledged her presence and she said, "You asked us to report anything out of the ordinary. I don't know how significant this is, but the composition of our air isn't quite what it should be. The oxygen percentage is slightly lower than normal, and the carbon dioxide level is a little higher than normal. Our environmental control equipment is performing well and is correcting for the imbalance, but it is operating at a level somewhat higher than it should be."

"Could this small aberration be the result of the increased level of activity on this ship?"

"I have considered that possibility and have factored it in as accurately as I can, and I still come to the conclusion that we are consuming more oxygen and generating more carbon dioxide than we should be."

"Do you have any explanation why this is occurring?"

"No, but I think I should investigate this and try to find the cause."

"I agree, and while you're doing that, I want you to also think about the possible ways that a saboteur could either wreck our life support systems or use them against us. For example, could toxic agents be released into these systems in sufficient quantities to be lethal to everyone onboard? For each sabotage technique that you think of, I want you to propose a course of preventive action. Perhaps, Doctor Nemard could work with you on this project."

"I'll ask her, and we'll report back to you when we have something of consequence."

TIME: 75 Hours, 30 Minutes A.L.E.

Captain Jerontis arrived in the machine shop to observe the first test of the new bomb detector.

Moose greeted him, "Two hours ago, we placed two ounces of plastic explosive inside that instrument cabinet. If this bomb detector works as advertised, it should easily detect the explosive. All we should have to do is open the small access panel in the back and insert this sensor probe."

"Let's do it," stated Captain Jerontis as he picked up a screwdriver and quickly opened the access panel.

With the bomb detector's sensor probe in hand, Moose reached toward the open panel. Before Moose could place the probe fully inside the cabinet, the red light on top the detector started flashing, the detector started chirping its audible warning, and the digital readout indicated strong signal strength.

"Wow! That thing is sensitive," exclaimed Captain Jerontis. "If a methodical search of the ship with this detector fails to find a bomb, then I think we can confidently assume that there's no bomb onboard."

"If there's a bomb onboard, we'll find it," declared Moose.

"If we have enough time," commented Captain Jerontis. "Here is a copy of the revised search plan. I suggest you get started immediately. Also, every three to four hours, you should test the detector against the plastic explosive you made just to make sure that it continues to function properly."

TIME: 76 Hours, 15 Minutes A.L.E.

Captain Jerontis went to the life support lab to consult with Dianne and Connie.

After greeting him, Dianne said, "We've examined the difficulties that a saboteur would face in an attempt to use our ventilation system to disperse a poisonous gas or other lethal agent throughout the ship. As you know, the system is equipped with some sensitive instrumentation in key locations. These instruments will almost instantaneously detect the presence of any foreign substance. The area in which the substance is detected is immediately closed off and isolated from the rest of the system until the substance is analyzed and removed. These safeguards were built in as protection against a localized fire or chemical accident.

For a saboteur to kill everyone on this ship, he would have to plant a toxic agent in a ventilation shaft and time its release with a shut off of the isolation equipment. To prevent the success of this kind of attack, we've programmed a backup computer to shutdown the entire system if a toxic substance is detected or if any of the sensing instrumentation malfunctions. Also, an alert will be sounded advising all personnel to wear oxygen masks."

"Let's conduct a simple test to make sure that everything is working," suggested Captain Jerontis.

"What do you have in mind?" questioned Doctor Nemard.

"Actually, a two-part test; first, we spill a foreign substance, such as ammonia, into the system and see if it does what it is supposed to do. Then, we simulate a malfunction by disconnecting one of the sensors."

"I don't have any ammonia handy, but I have some other harmless chemicals that should work just as well," commented Dianne.

"Good," said Captain Jerontis as he sounded a few notes on the warning klaxon and spoke into the intercom explaining the tests that were about to be conducted.

A short time later, after completing the tests, Captain Jerontis said, "I am satisfied that the basic system and the additional safeguards you've put into place are in good working order. But there is one more thing that we could do, and that would be to search the interior of the system for a canister of toxins coupled to a time release mechanism. For toxins to reach all parts of the ship, a chemical or biological bomb would have to be planted in the central duct before it starts to branch out. Such a bomb could be rigged to go off if tampered with. For self-protection, I'll wear my space suit while I conduct the search. Also, we'll turn off the air circulation and isolate the area. Doctor Nemard, I want you to monitor my progress from outside the area while I carry out the inspection."

"While you two are doing that, I am going to take another look at the problem of using more oxygen than we should be," stated Dianne.

After putting on his space suit and sealing himself in the central ventilation room, Captain Jerontis opened an access panel to the primary ventilation duct. Then, he placed a small remotely controlled inspection vehicle in the duct. As Jerry moved the vehicle down the duct, he used its video cameras and other sensors to search for suspicious looking objects. After searching the central part of the system for more than an hour and finding nothing, Jerry closed the access panel, but he left the remotely controlled vehicle inside.

Jerry emerged from the central ventilation room, took off his space suit, and said, "I am satisfied that this part of the ventilation system is clean, but I am going to have someone search the entire system."

Dianne and Connie nodded in agreement.

Then, Dianne said, "In regard to the oxygen/carbon dioxide imbalance, I've taken a close look at the data generated by our air regeneration system, and we are consuming about seven to nine percent more oxygen than we should be. It's almost as if we have 26 people onboard instead of 24."

Captain Jerontis commented, "Supposedly, everyone not going on this voyage left the ship with the departure of the Goliath and the personnel shuttle. If there are any extra individuals onboard, I would think that we would've discovered them during our preliminary bomb search."

"What if they're determined to stay hidden?" asked Connie.

Captain Jerontis briefly considered the question and replied, "Well, this is a very large ship, so I suppose that is possible. But what prompted you to ask that question?"

"Something that we haven't talked about is the possibility that one or two terrorists on a suicide mission might be stowed away on this ship patiently waiting for an opportunity to strike."

Silence filled the room as Jerry intently thought about Connie's comment. After a few moments, he said, "It just doesn't seem very likely that we have terrorists onboard. After all, security was extremely tight during those final months of checkout. But under the present circumstances, all possibilities must be checked out, however remote they may seem. I will report this to NASA Command and ask them to locate everyone who had access to this ship in recent months, and I will get someone to tell everyone on this ship to be alert for the possible presence of terrorists. I don't want to use the intercom for this because if there are terrorists onboard, I don't want to let them know that we're looking for them.

Getting back to life support, we've taken steps to protect our air, but what about the possibility of toxins being released into our food or water?"

"That possibility is the object of our next investigation," stated Dianne.

TIME: 78 Hours, 30 Minutes A.L.E.

Captain Jerontis returned to the command console to converse with NASA Command. Normal conversation, however, was becoming increasingly difficult because of the Challenger's great distance from Earth. A radio message traveling at the speed of light now took nearly nineteen minutes to reach Earth, which was 210 million miles away. Captain Jerontis transmitted his report. He waited thirty-eight minutes for a response.

TIME: 79 Hours, 8 Minutes A.L.E.

"Captain Jerontis! This is NASA Command. We've received your report and have started the investigation that you requested. One thing I can tell you right now though is that we still haven't located Mike Johnson. The captain of the personnel shuttle, along with some of the media, observed him boarding the shuttle. The shuttle's passenger log recorded the exact time at which he boarded. However, no one on the shuttle recalls seeing him during its descent to Earth. Also, he was not seen getting off the shuttle when it arrived at the spaceport terminal. We think everyone on the shuttle was so preoccupied with events leading up to your departure that Mike was able to quietly slip off the shuttle unnoticed by anyone and sneak back onto your ship. If this is what he did, we have no explanation for it. However, we seriously doubt that he is the terrorist that you're looking for because this activity on his part does not fit the profile of a terrorist. Anyone planning the destruction of your ship would not have engaged in any kind of activity that would've attracted our attention in a suspicious way. Since he was already assigned to your crew, he didn't have to do anything to be on the Challenger, especially something that would've aroused so much suspicion.

On another matter, the FBI has arrested all the top officials of Environment First for questioning. The arrest was based on a law passed in the latter part of the twentieth century that permitted the arrest of individuals who made bomb threats against airliners. In an attempt to discover if and how your ship has been sabotaged, these officials will be forced to submit to brain wave analysis while undergoing intensive interrogation. Under normal circumstances, this would be a gross violation of their civil rights and would not be allowed, but the President declared an emergency and issued an executive order that it be done. The WWCLU (World Wide Civil Liberties Union) will have a field day challenging this in the courts. As you know, they have a very long history of being more concerned with protecting the rights of criminals than with protecting the rights of the victims of crime. Hopefully, the FBI will be able to ferret out some specific information for you.

On a lighter subject, a source at SNS has informed us that TV viewers have sent Sam a total of 139,455 books on human anatomy, most of which explain in explicit detail how human reproduction works and how it is dependent on normal sexual activity. Needless to say, Sam is more than just a little chagrined at this huge response to the comments made by Doctor Nemard during your press conference. Since Sam has always been a nagging antagonist toward us, I thought you might find some humor in the embarrassing situation he now finds himself in. You could probably use a good laugh right about now. This concludes our transmission."

A smile of satisfaction filled Captain J.J.'s face as he visualized the avalanche of books that had descended on Sam at his SNS office.

Captain Jerontis then leaned back in his seat, closed his eyes, and mulled over the contents of the rest of the message just received. He was pleased with the drastic action ordered by the President and hoped and prayed that the FBI would be able to get the information that he needed to save his ship and crew from destruction. The arrests were perfectly legal thought Jerry, but forcing the suspects to submit to brain wave analysis during intensive interrogation was probably illegal and would subject the President to some political risk during the after-the-fact court battles that were sure to occur.

Captain J.J.'s thoughts shifted to Mike. Is it true that he is onboard as a stowaway? That would partly explain our excessive oxygen consumption. Is it possible that I also have a terrorist onboard? If so, that would fully account for the oxygen/carbon dioxide problem.

As Captain Jerontis continued to reflect on the situation, one question kept coming up: was there anything peculiar about Mike's behavior during the last few days before departure? Jerry dropped ever more deeply into thought as he focused his mind very specifically on that question. After a few minutes of being almost totally oblivious to his surroundings, it came to him. Although Mike kept it well hidden, for several days, he seemed to display a subtle underlying mood indicative of sadness.

His mood underwent a sudden change for the better when I informed him that a reporter named Michelle wanted to see him. Also, they did seem overly comfortable with each other, as if they had known each other for quite some time.

Mike's distant mood could have been the result of having to make a choice between going on an interstellar voyage that had been his dream for many years and staying on Earth with the woman he loved. Is it possible that Mike figured out a way to stay on the mission and bring Michelle along? The probability of this being the case brought a smile to Captain J.J.'s face.

Jerry was abruptly jarred out of his trance-like mental state by Doctor Nemard who said, "What are you so happy about? This is the first time I've seen you smile in days."

"How long have you been standing there?"

"I arrived here about a minute ago. I saw you deeply lost in thought and decided not to interrupt. Anyway, what are you smiling about?"

"Two things: first, I think I've figured out why Mike put in his replacement request, and I think I know where he is. Second, the last part of the message from NASA Command gave me something to laugh about and may be of interest to you."

Captain Jerontis told Connie about the embarrassing situation Sam was now in at SNS because of her comments at the press conference.

Connie laughed, "It serves him right. Maybe some large scale embarrassment will have a therapeutic effect on his obnoxious personality, but I doubt it. Anyway, what about Mike?"

Captain Jerontis related his thoughts to Connie who said, "Your conclusion seems valid and offers a good explanation for Mike's behavior, as well as, the oxygen/carbon dioxide problem.

In regard to Michelle, going back to the press conference, she asked the kinds of questions appropriate for someone who was trying to decide if she wanted to be part of this mission. First, she tried to get into your mind by trying to discover your deepest feelings regarding this mission. Then, she became very interested in our life support systems, in particular, how many people they could support before being overloaded. After the press conference, she asked me the kinds of questions that she needed answers to in order to assure herself that we will make a success out of this mission. It appears that sometime after that, she agreed to whatever plan Mike had devised to bring her along."

"That would explain why Mike was in such an elated frame of mind the next day," commented Jerry.

"I like Michelle and Mike. I hope they are onboard. Where do you think they might be hiding?"

"We've been on our way for several days now, and there's only one place where they could be comfortable for this long a time and have a reasonable chance of not being seen, and that's inside one of the shuttles down on the hangar deck. Why don't we go down there and welcome them to the mission. Besides, I could use Mike's help investigating the possible sabotage of this ship."

Connie hesitated for a few moments, as if lost in thought. Then, her cheerful mood was replaced by a look of worried concern, and she asked, "What if we're wrong, and instead of Mike and Michelle, we find a couple of armed terrorists comfortably living in one of the shuttles?"

"That's possible, but what led you to ask that question?"

"If Mike is down there, it seems he would've come out of hiding by now to help us with the bomb search; whereas, a terrorist would remain in hiding."

"Mike might not know that we're conducting a bomb search."

"But you announced the bomb search on the intercom."

After a moment of thought, Captain Jerontis said, "That's true, but the intercom does not have speakers inside the shuttles. Both the warning klaxon and intercom come through speakers on the hangar deck, but if Mike and Michelle were sound asleep inside either shuttle, they would not have heard me. Those shuttles have thick hulls that are well insulated. Very little sound passes through them."

"But we've been weightless for more than thirty hours. It seems like that would've attracted Mike's attention. It seems like his curiosity would have caused him to investigate this."

"If he thought that we were in critical danger, I'm sure that he would have. However, there are many non-critical reasons that could lead to shutting down the engines for a day or two."

"So you're not the least bit concerned that we might find a couple of armed terrorists hiding in one of the shuttles?"

"I'm not trying to say that. I'm only saying that it's possible that Mike and Michelle could be hiding in one of the shuttles and not know anything about our current situation."

"I hope you're right. I haven't known Michelle very long, but I like her. I hope she and Mike are with us."

"I believe that we're going to find them in one of the shuttles, but under the present circumstances, we'd better take some weapons with us and proceed with caution."

Captain Jerontis decided to take the additional precaution of issuing weapons to three crew members and taking them along for backup. When they arrived at the hangar deck, Captain Jerontis said to Connie, "Since you are the only doctor we have, I want you to stay safely out of sight until we find out if this area is safe."

After searching the personnel shuttle and finding it deserted, Captain Jerontis quietly entered the big cargo shuttle and went directly to the flight deck. Although deserted, he spotted a skirt that he recognized as the one Michelle had worn at the press conference. Quietly and cautiously, he approached the hatch leading to the cargo hold. Very slowly, he opened it as quietly as he could. Jerry peered into the dimly lit cargo hold. After a few moments, Jerry's eyes adjusted to the darkness, and off to one side, he spotted Mike and Michelle sound asleep.

Jerry smiled in happy satisfaction that his trusted friend was onboard. He glanced at his communicator and punched in the prearranged signal that it was safe for Connie to join him. When she arrived, Jerry pointed at the innocent looking stowaways and whispered, "Would you like the honor of waking them?"

"Sure," replied Connie as she drifted over to the two sleeping figures. After adjusting the alarm on her wrist watch, Connie held it close to Mike's and Michelle's ears and turned it on. The ringing chimes startled them out of their sound sleep. Both looked around, investigating their surroundings with sleepy eyes. Realizing that they had finally been discovered, Mike made eye contact with Captain Jerontis and said, "Captain! I've changed my mind. If it's not too late, I would like to withdraw my replacement request and rejoin the mission."

"Since we are now more than 200 million miles from Earth, I don't have much choice, do I?"

"I was hoping you would see it that way, and since you're in such an agreeable mood, is it okay if I bring my wife along too?"

"Wife?" questioned Doctor Nemard as she smiled at Michelle.

"Yes! We were married during Mike's last trip down to Earth.

"Having two additional people onboard won't be a problem," stated Captain Jerontis as he looked at Mike and Michelle. "Besides, we can use your skills."

Displaying a mischievous smile of satisfaction, Michelle looked at Captain Jerontis and said, "Actually, there are three of us, because I'm pregnant."

"Congratulations!" Captain Jerontis exclaimed. "This ship's life support systems will not have any difficulty supporting the lives of three additional people. The only problem we have is finding you a place to live. The 24 apartments on this ship are all occupied."

"I have an idea," said Mike, looking at Captain Jerontis playfully.

Seeing Mike's expression, Captain Jerontis said, "I'm almost afraid to ask, but let's hear it."

"This is only a suggestion, but I am thinking that if you were to take a good look at Doctor Nemard and work on developing an appreciation for her feminine beauty and warm loving personality, it's possible that an apartment could become available soon. Also, it might be more romantic to call her Connie occasionally instead of always addressing her as Doctor Nemard."

Doctor Nemard's expression indicated obvious personal pleasure and satisfaction with Mike's remark. She was, however, caught off guard as was the captain by Mike's totally unexpected suggestion and its implication. She looked at Captain Jerontis curiously searching for a reaction and was surprised to see him blushing and speechless. He seemed uncomfortable with everyone staring at him in anticipation of his response. I have never seen him like this before thought Connie with some degree of amusement. With his total commitment to this mission, is it possible that he's never thought about me except in a strictly professional way? Mike has put him on the spot in my presence.

After a few moments, Captain Jerontis recovered his wits and briefly gazed at Connie affectionately. Connie noticed and thought, maybe he has looked at me in more than just a professional way. The possibility caused a warm feeling of excitement to well up in her.

Connie's hopes were raised still further when Captain Jerontis turned to Mike and said, "As appealing as your suggestion is, it will have to wait until another time. We still have the urgent problem of finding the sabotage to this ship or proving that it doesn't exist. I have a bomb search team that is nearing the point of exhaustion. Since you are well rested, I want you to take over that job for a while."

Appearing puzzled, Mike asked, "What bomb search are you talking about?"

Seeing that Mike and Michelle did not know anything about the bomb threat, Captain Jerontis quickly briefed them on pertinent recent events. When the briefing was finished, Mike left to take over the bomb search.

Captain Jerontis said to Michelle, "I am going to put your reporting skills to work by having you transmit regular reports to Earth on the activities onboard this ship. Make an effort to include all of our personnel. In the event that we are destroyed, the video you transmit will be the last images that surviving friends and family back on Earth will see of their perished loved ones. Your first story will, of course, contain an explanation of your presence, as well as, Mike's presence on this ship."

"I'll get started right away. My first report will go out in just a few minutes."

TIME: 96 Hours A.L.E.

Michelle's latest news dispatch to Earth:

"We have been underway for exactly four days and have traveled a distance of approximately 278 million miles. During the last 48 hours, the people on this ship have had little or no sleep and are reaching the point of exhaustion. However, their tenacious resolve to survive seems to be giving them a superhuman strength that allows them to overcome their extreme fatigue and keep the sabotage search moving forward at an intense pace. The question is how much longer can they continue before reaching the point of collapse. Stopping for much needed sleep, however, is not an option. Not knowing how much time we have makes it imperative to continue the effort to the point of collapse.

To those of you who were paid to sabotage our ship: I ask you to reconsider your actions. I ask you to send an anonymous message to NASA Command telling them what you have done to undermine our mission before it is too late for us to take preventive action to save our lives. You have your money. The people who paid you are in custody, and you have nothing to gain by killing us. You might stop this mission, but you cannot stop human expansion into the Universe because the technology to carry it out is here, it does exist. Throughout history, human exploration and habitat expansion have always gone as far as allowed by imagination and ability. It is human nature, and you cannot change it. If we are killed, your leaders will be put on trial for murder, and if convicted, they will be executed. This will also happen to you, for you will be pursued until found. I urge you to come to your senses while there is still time to prevent your own executions."

TIME: 98 Hours, 20 Minutes A.L.E.

"Captain Jerontis! This is NASA Command. The FBI investigation has not yet revealed any specific information. Apparently, Environment First officials have cleverly established a system of code words to conceal the details of their plot. Only these code words were used when communicating with the individuals hired to do the actual sabotage. Given enough time, the mind probing interrogation techniques used by the FBI in conjunction with brain wave analysis will break through the code. They estimate 12 to 16 hours to accomplish this. I hope this won't be too late.

WWCLU attorneys have won a restraining order from a liberal minded judge to stop the FBI. Only problem is, they don't know where to deliver it, since the interrogation is being carried out at a secret location.

I have just been handed the latest information from the FBI. They do not yet have concrete proof or specific details, but they have strong reason to believe that the sabotage is in one of your flight control computers. We will send you additional information as soon as we have it."

Captain Jerontis thought about this. The entire flight control system including the computers had already been searched for the presence of a bomb. In addition, the computers had been searched for the presence of a virus. Nothing had been found. But, as tired as everyone is, we could have missed something. I will have both searches carefully redone.

Meanwhile, in the cafeteria, Michelle and Doctor Nemard finished eating their first meal in a long time. "I feel much better now," stated Michelle. "I guess I should have eaten sooner."

"Food is the fuel the body runs on. It's not good to run on empty, especially when you're busy and not getting enough sleep."

After a moment of silence, Michelle asked, "Do you think our ship really has been sabotaged, or do you think the whole thing is just a cruel hoax?"

"Unfortunately, I believe that it has. The people who have threatened us are the worst kind of fanatical extremists. They have sick minds and are psychologically unable to accept the will of others. They will stop at nothing to achieve their ends. Killing innocent people means nothing to them as they have shown with their terrorist attacks on NASA facilities. Even though they are mentally sick, they apparently are quite intelligent. And this combination makes them very dangerous and capable of doing whatever it takes to stop us."

"It just seems so tragic that a few psychos could thwart the will of a great nation."

"They haven't stopped us yet. Captain Jerontis is exceptionally intelligent and capable, as are the rest of us. I am confident that we will prevail."

"I hope you're right. With a wonderful husband and a child on the way, I am not ready to die yet. I want to see what kind of life we can make for ourselves in our new home on Alcent. I just wish I could do something to help."

"I think you already have. I heard your last report to Earth. The appeal that you made to the saboteurs may get a positive response. Explaining to them the futility of what they are trying to do along with the consequences might cause one of them to crack. Sick minds can be unpredictable."

"But these are fanatics who are passionately trying to achieve their goal of stopping us. Before I made that appeal, I decided that I didn't have much of a chance to get a positive response, but I had to try anyway."

"One other thing that I've been doing is praying for guidance," Michelle continued, "I've been a practicing Christian my entire life, and I've always prayed for guidance in times of crisis and whenever faced with a difficult decision."

"Has praying for guidance helped you?"

"I believe that it has. I've always made the right choices whenever I've been faced with difficult decisions. Anyway, praying for guidance can't hurt anything, so why not do it."

"Well, this is most definitely a time of crisis," responded Doctor Nemard. And with that statement, Connie bowed her head for a few moments of silent prayer. Seeing this, Michelle decided to join her.

When they finished praying, Doctor Nemard left the cafeteria and went to the medical lab.

Feeling a need for solitude, Michelle decided to return to the cargo shuttle to rest and think about her next report. A few minutes later, she arrived on the hangar deck and headed for the large cargo shuttle, which had served as a rather spacious apartment for her and Mike since leaving Earth. As she was about to enter it, she stopped, turned, and looked at the personnel shuttle.

Viewing its sleek design brought some thoughts to the forefront of her mind. I wonder if I will ever ride it down to our new home. What will it be like to navigate the atmosphere of Alcent and land on its surface? Will we find a place where we can live in comfort and security among the dinosaurs, some of which will be carnivorous?

With her mind pondering the possibilities of the distant future, Michelle became aware of a growing desire to explore the personnel shuttle. Very strange, she thought, that I should feel so compelled to enter it, almost as if I am being directed by an outside force.

Puzzled by the way in which she felt so strongly drawn to the personnel shuttle, Michelle approached it with a great deal of suspicion and cautiously peered into the passenger compartment. Not seeing anything of a threatening nature, she entered it and looked around. Nothing unusual here thought Michelle. I think I'll take a look at the flight deck.

Michelle slowly opened the hatch to the flight deck and cautiously looked in. Michelle thought, there's no one here and nothing looks out of place, so why did I feel such a strong compulsion to come here? While she considered the question, Michelle entered the flight crew's compartment and comfortably seated herself in the pilot's seat.

Is it possible that the sabotage to our mission is in this shuttle, and I was guided here to discover it? But what am I supposed to look for? Everything looks perfectly normal to me. Perhaps, if I put myself in a state of total relaxation, clear my mind of all anxiety, and leave it open to outside suggestion; maybe, just maybe, the same force that compelled me to come here will guide me to the sabotage. To avoid the possibility of being disturbed at a critical moment, Michelle turned off her communicator. Then, she proceeded to practice her relaxation techniques, and after a few minutes, she became so relaxed that she fell sound asleep.

TIME: 100 Hours, 45 Minutes A.L.E.

Moose, Dianne, and Captain Jerontis were in the cafeteria devouring their first meal in a long time. Speaking to Captain Jerontis, Moose said, "I checked in with Mike a few minutes ago, and I promised to relieve him as soon as we've finished eating. He's making good progress. We think that we'll be finished with the bomb search of all priority one and two areas in about two hours."

Captain Jerontis nodded in acknowledgment.

After a few moments, Moose asked, "How far do you plan to go with this bomb search before we restart our engines? What I'm getting at is that in order to be 100% sure that there's no bomb onboard, we will have to open every floor, wall, and ceiling panel, and that will take several weeks."

"I don't think we'll have to do that. The FBI believes that it will have some specific information for us sometime during the next several hours. If they fail to do that, and if we fail to find the sabotage, then I don't think that we'll be alive twenty-four hours from now."

"What leads you to that conclusion?" asked Dianne.

"For sensational publicity and to satisfy their egos, I believe that our saboteurs wanted the explosion to occur close enough to Earth to be an almost blinding flash in the nighttime sky. Quite frankly, I am surprised that the explosion hasn't already taken place. At the present time, we are nearly 300 million miles from Earth. Exploding all of our antimatter fuel at this distance would look like an extremely bright star back on Earth for a few seconds. Although brilliant, it could hardly be considered spectacular."

"But if the explosion is far brighter than anything else in the nighttime sky, it might be spectacular enough to satisfy their egos," commented Dianne.

"That means that if there is a bomb onboard, it will explode very soon," stated Captain Jerontis.

While nodding in agreement, Moose said, "We can complete the search of priority three areas in the next twenty-four hours. If we haven't found a bomb by then, and if we're still alive, I think we should consider ourselves the victims of psychological terror and restart our engines."

"I concur with Moose's recommendation," remarked Dianne. "I've been completely through our life support systems, and I am confident that there is no sabotage there. In regard to a bomb, unless we tear this whole ship apart, there's no way that we can be 100% sure that a bomb doesn't exist. Once all mission critical areas have been searched, we should resume acceleration to cruise velocity."

"If there aren't any new developments in the next twenty-four hours, that would seem to be a reasonable course of action," agreed Captain Jerontis.

"It's time for me to replace Mike," stated Moose as he got up to leave.

"Tell him to come to the cafeteria, so I can talk to him about our current situation. He has worked on this ship for so many years that he has a very detailed knowledge of it. I am going to ask him to think like a saboteur and see if he can come up with something we've overlooked."

"Good idea," said Moose as he left.

A short time later, Mike arrived, and Captain Jerontis briefed him on everything that had already been done. Then, he asked Mike to think like a saboteur.

"My mind works much better when I'm not starving," responded Mike. "I'll get some food and think this over while I'm eating. Then, I'll go down to the cargo shuttle and put myself into quiet isolation, so that I can sink my mind totally into this problem."

After ordering his food, Mike asked, "Have you seen Michelle recently?"

"No! Why? Do you have reason to be worried about her?"

"When Moose relieved me, I tried to reach her on the communicator, but she has it turned off for some reason. Thinking that she might be taking a nap, I stopped by the cargo shuttle, but she wasn't there."

Captain Jerontis reached for his communicator, dialed in the intercom number, and paged Michelle. After waiting a brief period and not getting any response, he sounded a few attention getting notes on the warning klaxon. Then, he said, "Attention all personnel! If anyone has seen Michelle recently or knows where she is, please report immediately."

No one called in except Doctor Nemard who said, "I ate with her in the cafeteria about three hours ago. She said she was going to the cargo shuttle to relax and prepare her next report. I haven't seen her since then. Is there any indication that something may have happened to her?"

"Mike has just been to the cargo shuttle, and she's not there. She hasn't responded to my page. Also, her communicator is turned off, and apparently, no one has seen her in the last three hours. Since we cannot rule out the possibility of an armed terrorist being hidden away somewhere on this ship, we have to consider the possibility that Michelle may have fallen victim to foul play. If that's the case, finding her might lead us to the terrorist. We need to begin an immediate search of the ship."

"I just lost my appetite!" exclaimed Mike. "I will lead the search!"

Without waiting for a response from Captain Jerontis, Mike got on the intercom and said, "Attention all personnel! Search your immediate and surrounding area for Michelle and report to me!" By a process of elimination, Mike would discover those areas that would need to be searched.

Meanwhile, down on the hangar deck, totally oblivious to the consternation Mike was going through, Michelle was sound asleep and in the midst of a vivid dream that seemed real. In her dream, she was orbiting Alcent, and after seven long years in space, the big day had finally arrived. It was landing day, the day that all had awaited for so long, when humans would finally descend to the surface and begin the adventure of building a new society.

In her dream, she wondered, am I dreaming, or is this real? It seems so real, but I must be dreaming, for we haven't yet left the Solar System. Still, this must be real because I just heard the warning klaxon signal the beginning of countdown to engine ignition. Also, the instrument panel is all lit up and countdown has now started, so this must be real and not just a dream. But if this is real, why am I sitting in the pilot's seat? I am not a pilot. I don't know how to fly this shuttle. I cannot land this bird on Alcent. There must be some mistake. Lord, please help me. If I am dreaming, please wake me up. But this can't be a dream, it's just too real ... too real ... too real ... .

All of a sudden, Michelle awoke with a start and instantly realized that it wasn't totally a dream. The instrument panel really was alive with lighted displays, and a digital countdown clock was ticking down with only eleven minutes and thirty-three seconds to ignition. Being a science reporter and knowledgeable in how nuclear thermal rockets function, Michelle knew immediately that if the reactor came to full power without any propellant flowing through it to keep it from overheating, there would very quickly be a total meltdown and a tremendous explosion. If propellant did flow through the reactor and out the rocket nozzle, it would quickly over pressurize the hangar deck and blow the ship apart. In either case, all antimatter fuel would be detonated.

Michelle urgently grabbed her communicator, sounded the ship-wide warning klaxon, accessed the intercom, and shouted, "Mike! Captain Jerontis! Moose! Come to the personnel shuttle immediately! I've found the sabotage! The NTR is eleven minutes away from ignition and meltdown!"

In the cafeteria, Mike and Captain Jerontis looked at each other with the kind of eye contact wherein each instantly acknowledged to the other a full awareness of the urgency of the situation. Instantaneously, they sprung into action, heading for the hangar deck with almost reckless speed.

"Looks like we've found Michelle and the sabotage," exclaimed Mike as they left the cafeteria.

"Yes! And what we do during the next eleven minutes will determine whether we live or die."

Captain Jerontis and Mike set a new speed record, arriving at the personnel shuttle in less than a minute. Moose arrived just a few seconds later. Turning to Michelle, Captain Jerontis commanded, "Begin transmitting to Earth a live report on what we are doing. Include every little detail. If we're unsuccessful, I want the FBI to have this information to help bring the saboteurs to justice."

Captain Jerontis then gave his attention to Mike, who was busy entering a shutdown command into the flight control computer.

"Something is wrong here," cried out Mike. "The computer isn't responding. They've either bypassed it, or they've instructed it to ignore us."

"If we disconnect its power, the countdown should stop," stated Captain Jerontis as he hit the power shut off switch. Again, there was no response as the countdown continued without interruption.

Mike commented, "Evidently, they've installed an auxiliary power source for this computer. The question is: Where?"

"Finding something that small could take more time than we have," remarked Jerry. "Let's go to the reactor room and disconnect all power and control lines leading into the reactor."

"That should work, unless they've found a way to bypass them," commented Moose.

"That's a possibility," stated Jerry. "If we fail to shut this thing down by four minutes to ignition, we will need to jettison this shuttle, ignite our engines, and pull away from it in a hurry."

While Mike and Moose raced to the reactor room, Captain Jerontis contacted the flight deck and gave appropriate instructions to the pilot and flight engineer to deal with this contingency. When Captain Jerontis arrived in the reactor room, Mike and Moose were already busy disconnecting the power and control lines to the electric motor that would soon begin withdrawing the control rods from the reactor's core, if allowed to do so. Noting that they were making rapid progress and didn't need his assistance, Captain Jerontis checked the control rod safety pins and said, "It looks like the saboteurs would have failed because the safety pins are still in place."

After a moment of thought, Captain Jerontis said, "It makes no sense that they would've overlooked such an important detail. Therefore, the safety pins must have been tampered with."

"I will inspect them," stated Moose as he selected a wrench from his tool kit and began extracting one of the pins.

When he had the safety pin head removed, he held it up for inspection. The saboteurs had neatly cut the safety pin from the pin head. Then, they turned the pin head back into the safety pin hole. To outward appearance, the safety pin was in place, but in reality, only the pin head was in place.

Moose pulled a heavy duty screwdriver out of his tool kit, inserted it into the safety pin hole, and said, "That should take care of this one for now."

Moose then inspected the second safety pin, found the same problem, and made the same quick fix. While Moose did this, Captain Jerontis returned to the shuttle's flight deck.

Captain Jerontis was greatly relieved to find that the countdown had discontinued at six minutes, thirty-seven seconds. On a display screen, he found the message: "Electric power to control rod drive motor has been interrupted. Countdown cannot resume until power is restored."

Via the shuttle's intercom, Captain Jerontis announced to Moose, Mike, and Michelle: "We've defeated the sabotage. I am going to the cargo shuttle's reactor room. If it has also been sabotaged, we don't have much time. To be effective, its destruction would have to be timed to coincide with the sabotage we just foiled. Meet me there without delay."

While passing through the cargo shuttle's flight deck, Captain Jerontis noted that all was quiet. He grabbed a tool kit from the shuttle's maintenance closet and headed for the reactor room. It too was devoid of any activity.

As a precaution, Captain Jerontis immediately began disconnecting the control rod drive motor. While he was doing this, Moose and Mike arrived, inspected the safety pins, and found the same situation as on the personnel shuttle.

After the temporary fixes were in place, Moose commented, "It seems strange that they would sabotage these safety pins without also sabotaging the computer."

"How do you know that they haven't?" asked Jerry.

"I am just assuming that it hasn't. Like you said a few minutes ago, to be effective, it would have to have been timed to coincide with the sabotage on the personnel shuttle. The saboteurs should have been smart enough to figure out that if we were fortunate enough to discover the sabotage in the personnel shuttle, we would immediately check this shuttle for the same tampering. Are we giving them too much credit, or are we overlooking something?"

"Whoever was responsible for destroying the safety pins had the quick easy job," commented Mike. "We haven't yet discovered how they sabotaged the flight control computer as effectively as they did, but I have to believe that it was a time consuming task. Because of tight security, they may not have had an opportunity to get that part of the job done on this shuttle."

"I suspect that your reasoning is correct," remarked Captain Jerontis. "However, as soon as we have the time, we are going to thoroughly check out the computer situation in both of these shuttles. But for the time being, we are going to rely on some new safety pins to prevent possible disaster. Mike, I want you to take care of making them and installing them. Moose, you will complete the bomb search of critical areas."

It shouldn't take more than an hour or two to accomplish that," stated Moose.

"I will have new pins installed in less than an hour," declared Mike.

Jerry said, "I am going to assume that the emergency is over and that we've defeated the sabotage. I am going to declare a twelve-hour rest period, so we can get some much needed sleep."

TIME: 4 days, 18 hours A.L.E.

"Captain Jerontis! This is NASA Command. The latest information from the FBI confirms your conclusion that the crisis is over. Until just a few hours ago, the brain wave patterns exhibited by the suspects during questioning were representative of an arrogant attitude based on a firm belief that we were powerless to stop them from destroying your mission. These patterns underwent a dramatic change when we forced them to listen to a recording of Michelle's broadcast of the details of you thwarting their efforts. With the full realization that they had failed to blow up your ship, the brain wave patterns of all suspects became a classic textbook example of what you find in people who have suffered defeat. Additional questions and probing comments by FBI interrogators failed to cause any change in the brain wave patterns, which continued to typify a state of hopelessness."

THREE

Romance and Near-Disaster on a Seemingly Endless Journey

TIME: 6 Days A.L.E.

Michelle's latest mission update to Earth:

"Our antimatter engines have been restarted. Our current speed is 1,656 miles per second, but we are continuing to gain speed at a steady acceleration of 1g. We've traveled a distance of 492 million miles, Jupiter's approximate distance from the Sun. In the early days of the space age, it took several years for a spacecraft to travel to Jupiter. We've covered the distance in just six days."

Still feeling burned out from the intense life-threatening experience of recent days, Michelle and Connie were lazily enjoying lunch in the cafeteria. "It seems like I've done nothing but sleep since the end of the crisis, and I still feel tired," Connie said.

"That's understandable" commented Michelle. "It was a long nerve-racking experience."

"It's definitely an experience that I'm happy to have behind me."

"Now that it's over, maybe, we can all fall into some sort of normal day-to-day life."

"Having a comfortable daily routine would make our long voyage a lot easier."

"And, life on this starship might even have a sense of normalcy about it," added Michelle.

"We are currently traveling faster than 1,600 miles per second, and we're still accelerating. What's normal about that?"

"*What's normal about that* is that it feels normal. There's no doubt in my mind that the number one benefit of accelerating at 1g is *that it feels normal*. It feels exactly like Earth's gravity, and that creates the illusion that everything is perfectly normal, yet in just nine months, we'll reach a velocity of about three-fourths of light speed."

"Even at these tremendous speeds, our journey will still take more than six years," remarked Connie.

"And we're only going to the Alpha Centauri System, our nearest interstellar neighbors."

"I'm glad that we're not going to a more distant star system. Six years in space is more than enough for me."

"Me too," declared Michelle with conviction.

After thinking about it for a few moments, Michelle said, "We do have a very long journey ahead of us. Being confined to this starship for more than six years could become monotonous and difficult to tolerate."

"We can make it tolerable, even fun. First, each of us must accept the fact that this starship is going to be our home for a long time. Second, each of us must develop a comfortable daily routine that is a balanced mixture of work and play."

"What if we succeed in making this starship such a comfortable home that we won't want to go down to the surface when we arrive at Alcent?"

"I've never considered that possibility," stated Connie. "Six years is a long time to be confined to a starship. When we arrive at Alcent, I believe that everyone will have an undying thirst for the wide open spaces on the planet's surface. I won't be surprised if each individual invents a very important reason why he or she should be the first to go down to the surface."

"But if we succeed in developing a comfortable daily routine, this starship will offer a safe secure home that will be a dramatic contrast to the savage life-threatening conditions that exist on Alcent."

"I hope that we do succeed in making our lives so comfortable that people won't mind living out their lives on this ship. That will make our long voyage enjoyable, and there's always the possibility that we won't be able to land on Alcent. We might find that life there cannot tolerate microorganisms from Earth."

"That would be a terrible disappointment," stated Michelle. "Despite the concerns I just voiced, I don't seriously believe that anyone would choose to live on this ship rather than on the planet."

"I had the feeling that you were just arguing for the sake of debate."

"That is fun sometimes, especially when you defend an absurd position and the other person thinks that you're serious. In fact, it might even qualify as one of those playful activities you said we need."

Michelle noticed that Connie was laughing softly. "What are you giggling about?" she asked.

"I was just thinking about how Moose takes pride in his ability to be a jokester and how funny it would be if we could pull some sort of gag on him while convincing him that we're serious."

"That would be funny. Let's watch for an opportunity. Maybe, he'll even set himself up for us."

"Moose is rather outgoing in a boisterous sort of way. I'm sure he'll give us an opening."

After a brief pause, Michelle said, "Getting back to Alcent, what do you think our lives will be like if we land and attempt to build homes there?"

"Knowing what we know about that planet, I believe that our life will be a wild challenging adventure. I think that we'll have experiences far beyond our wildest dreams."

"It's probably going to be a big challenge to stay alive when we're having those experiences, but perhaps, an even greater challenge will be to find a way to build comfortable secure homes without destroying the life that's already there."

"Evidently, you believe that we'll be able to meet both of those challenges, or you would not have joined this mission, practically at the last possible moment."

"I have tremendous respect for my husband's capabilities, and I have the same respect for Captain Jerontis. I also have great confidence in all the people on this ship. I know what all of you had to go through to be here. There is no doubt in my mind that we will be successful. Besides, I am a science reporter. How could I pass up an opportunity to be a part of the greatest scientific expedition ever?"

"You could have if you thought that we wouldn't survive and have a good life."

"Okay, I admit that I did need a little convincing, but Mike was able to meet that challenge."

"I get the feeling that he didn't have to work very hard to convince you," teased Connie.

Without saying anything, Michelle smiled in a way that indicated her deep love for Mike and the happiness that she experienced in her relationship with him. Seeing this, Connie nodded indicating she understood. She had a sense of longing, a wish that she had the same kind of relationship with the man that she loved.

Connie's mind drifted back to the sabotage crisis and she said, "Speaking about survival, there's something that I've been thinking about, and that is that all of us are still alive, seemingly, just by chance."

"What do you mean, *just by chance*?"

"Consider for a moment, if you will, what would've happened to us if the chain of events that led to your presence on this mission had been disrupted in some way. Then, you would not have been here, and it is very unlikely that anyone else would've been in the personnel shuttle when the unexpected NTR countdown started. Consequently, we would've all been incinerated in the ensuing explosion. It's ironic that after the expenditure of billions of dollars and twenty years of meticulous planning, the mission ends up being saved by something totally unplanned, namely, the presence of a stowaway."

"Even the best-laid plans cannot possibly account for all contingencies," commented Michelle in a rather matter of fact way. "I'm happy that I happened to be in the right place at the right time."

"You make it sound as if it wasn't any big deal, but we are very fortunate that you found a way to outwit security and be on this ship. How did you do that?"

"There was only one avenue open to me and that was to apply to NASA to be part of the media team covering your departure."

"It seems like that was a long shot at best."

"Not really! Being a nationally recognized science reporter with a record of wholeheartedly supporting NASA projects made it quite likely that my application would be approved, and it was. By the time I arrived here, Mike had everything planned."

"Even though he had everything planned, you still had a big decision to make. You've already told me that Mike was up to the challenge of convincing you to come with us, but if you don't mind telling me, I would like to know how you made such a big decision. What was the final deciding factor? What kinds of feelings did you have?"

"*The final deciding factor* was that I am deeply in love with Mike. Also, I am carrying his child, and I want to be with him."

"But you didn't have to go with us to live with him because he'd requested that he be replaced, so that he could stay on Earth with you."

"That's true, but Mike had his heart set on being on this mission long before he met me. It has been a dream of his to go to Alcent ever since Star Voyager revealed the kind of life that is present there. About a year and a half ago, Mike's life became more complicated when he met me during an interview about this project. When the interview was over, he invited me out to dinner. A whirlwind romance started, and we fell in love. Then, a power struggle began. I wanted to stay on Earth where we could have a comfortable secure life without having to worry about being eaten by a dinosaur. He wanted to figure out a way for both of us to go to Alcent. Because of the way things worked out, both options were available to us."

"So how did you reach the decision to go with us?"

"I have a feeling that you're not going to let this go until I tell you the whole story."

"I am curious, and as you know, I am not just the ship's doctor, I am also the mission psychiatrist. It is my job to get into people's heads and try to understand what makes them tick."

"That's true, but I get the feeling that there might also be something personal involved here."

Connie thought about Michelle's comment for a few moments. Then, she said, "You might be right. I'll give that some thought, and we can talk about it later. But right now, I would like to find out how you reached the final decision to go with us."

Michelle collected her thoughts for a few moments. Then, she responded, "To start with, as I told you, I am a Christian. My spiritual life has always been important to me. Throughout my life, whenever I've been faced with a difficult decision, I've always prayed for guidance. I've always believed that the Lord would help me make the right choice. In this case, I was torn between a desire for a safe comfortable life on Earth with family and friends and a desire to please the man I love by accompanying him on a dangerous adventure. The night that Mike took me to the observation deck, I was inspired by the spectacular beauty of the Universe, and I felt that I had to experience another part of it. Somehow, at that moment in time, I knew that I had to be on this mission and that I would play an important part in it."

"Do you believe that you received the guidance that you prayed for?"

"Definitely, but it was still a difficult choice."

"Now that you're here, are you happy to be with us?"

"Yes, but at the same time, I am sad that I will never again see my parents, brother, and sister. We've always been a close family. What was bad for them is they had no advance notice that I would be leaving Earth or that I was even thinking about it. Out of necessity, I had to keep it a secret."

"They must have been shocked when you told them several days after leaving. How are they taking it?"

"They're unhappy at losing me, but they're also proud of me for finding a way to become one of Earth's first interstellar pioneers. They are supportive of my decision and are praying for our success."

"I believe that you will also find that the people on this ship will be very supportive of you. We're all good people and supportive of each other. All of us are dealing with the loss of family and friends, and out of necessity, we will turn to each other. I believe that as time goes on, we will become a very close-knit community, like a large family in many respects."

"That will help make our long voyage more enjoyable," commented Michelle.

"Another thing for you to consider is that we haven't totally lost the people back on Earth that we're close to. Even though we can't be with them, we can transmit videos back and forth that are really quite realistic when viewed in 3-D on a wall-sized screen. So, we can stay in close contact, at least for a while.

Once we arrive at Alcent, two-way communication will be rather impractical. It will take 4.35 years for a transmission to reach Earth and 4.35 years for the response to reach us. Videos sent back and forth will be like historical news bulletins by the time they're received."

"But they'll still be welcome."

"I will enjoy getting news from Earth, and I am sure they will be thrilled with some of the video we'll be sending them, especially if Alcent turns out to be like we think it is."

Michelle thought about how much time would be required for communication with Earth, and this put into true perspective just how far from Earth they would be. They would be farther away than any humans had ever traveled and would be truly on their own, truly isolated from Earth. They would be building a new civilization totally without assistance from Earth.

Then, Michelle thought about her unborn child. Successfully raising children will be the key to getting a new society off to a good start. It will be a big responsibility, and my child will be the first in the new generation. Mike and I will have to give our child all the knowledge and training needed to survive and prosper on a hostile planet.

Noticing Michelle's silence and her faraway look, Connie patiently waited for a facial expression that indicated that Michelle's thoughts had run their course. Then, she said, "You just looked like your mind was a million miles away."

"Actually, my mind was a lot farther away than that. I was thinking about Alcent, and the fact that my child will be nearly six years old when we arrive there, and I will have a family of my own to worry about."

"And right now, you have a husband who loves you so much that he was willing to give up the ultimate adventure of all time to stay on Earth with you."

"When I think about all the marriages that end in divorce or are dysfunctional in some important way, I feel very fortunate to have such a devoted husband. Being pregnant with his child gives me a deep joyful sense of fulfillment."

"Since you brought that up, if you don't have any plans for this afternoon, I'd like you to come to the medical lab with me. It's time to give you a physical and begin your prenatal care."

"With all the stress we've endured these last few days, I think that's a good idea."

Two hours later, in the medical lab, Connie gave Michelle some good news, "All tests indicate that both you and your child are in perfectly good health."

"Did you run a test to determine the sex of my baby?"

"Yes, I did. Do you want to know the result?"

"Sure, why not?"

"You are going to have a baby boy. I hope that's what you want."

"I really hadn't given it any thought. I just want a normal healthy baby, which brings up an important question: can a child develop in a normal healthy way when he does not have other children to interact with during his growing years?"

"That is something to think about. If no other children are born until after we land on Alcent, your son will be at least six years older than they are. That will socially isolate him in the sense that he won't have any peers. I don't think that would be a healthy situation. I think I will suggest to Captain Jerontis that at least one additional child be borne during our voyage."

Michelle lit up with a naughty grin as she gazed at Connie and said, "Are you going to suggest to him that he get you pregnant so that my son can have a playmate? Why Doctor Nemard! I think that would be doing the psychologist part of your job far beyond the call of duty."

Connie briefly laughed at the remark. Then, she turned away breaking eye contact with Michelle while considering whether to open up to her. A few moments later, Connie turned back to face Michelle and said, "As a matter of fact, I am in love with the Captain. I would like to be pregnant with his child. Unfortunately, he doesn't seem to have noticed me in anything other than a professional way."

"Perhaps, he's already involved with one of the other women."

"If he is, it's one of the best kept secrets on the ship."

"Maybe, he has avoided making a play for you or any of the other women because this would have made him vulnerable to sexual harassment charges. Imagine the consequences of such an accusation if some radical feminist group decided to pursue it in court and the press made front page headlines out of it."

"Sam from SNS could've had a field day with that story," laughed Connie. "He is so opposed to this mission that he would've seized the opportunity to antagonize Captain Jerontis simply because he has been a key individual in putting this mission together."

Michelle nodded in agreement and said, "Whether the charge was justified or frivolous, the end result would've been the same. At the very least, Captain Jerontis would have been faced with a severe distraction while getting this ship ready for departure. At worst, he could have been pulled from this mission, effectively ending a career that he has devoted twenty years of his life to. Even though the possibility of that happening was small, I believe Jerry would have avoided the risk because this mission is his life. However, we are now a half a billion miles from Earth, and lawsuits carried out for the purpose of destroying someone's career are no longer a threat to be concerned with."

"You may be correct in what you've just suggested. Jerry does try to anticipate all possible consequences before taking any action, especially when this mission and his career are involved. I think that it is very sad that American society has become so involved with *political correctness* and *being sensitive* that someone in a position of authority, like Captain Jerontis, must avoid pursuing an intimate relationship with a subordinate out of fear of putting his career in jeopardy."

"Of course, he wouldn't have had to be concerned about that if you had done something to indicate to him that you're interested in more than friendship."

"Because of our intense workload, I really haven't had any opportunities to do that."

"Are you sure that's the case?"

"What do you mean?"

"Is it possible that you are using your workload as an excuse to cover up the real reason, which might be that you fear rejection."

Connie thought about Michelle's comment for a few moments. Then, she responded, "For a science reporter, you have pretty good insight."

"To become a good science reporter, I had to also become a good investigative reporter. I've never taken anything at face value. In the process of preparing a report, I've always questioned the validity of everything that was presented to me."

"That is a good explanation, but I think that there's more to it than that. I think you have a natural talent of being able to see into other people's feelings. Have you ever considered a career in psychology?"

"No, I just like to have a good understanding of the people around me, especially those who are important to me. So let's talk about your fear of rejection."

Connie thought about the request for a few moments and decided that Michelle did care and wanted to be helpful, so she decided to trust her and be totally open: "To start with, I know I am deeply in love with the Captain. I want him. If I had made a pass at him and been ignored or outright rejected, I would've suffered extreme emotional pain."

"In view of all the training that you had to excel in to qualify for this mission, I am surprised that you would have a fear of rejection."

"Excelling in training made me a professional at what I do; it did not cancel out my emotions. I still have feelings just like everyone else."

"That makes sense, but is there more to it than that?"

"Had I made a pass at Jerry and been rejected, it undoubtedly would have put a strain on the relaxed friendly working relationship that we have. And we had a ship and crew to get ready for departure and really didn't need a source of tension between us."

"I sense that you're still not telling me everything."

"If you want the rest of the story, I'll have to go back in time to my childhood days."

"I would like to hear it."

"Okay, being a part of this mission is something that I've wanted since age eleven when mission planning was initiated. At that young age, twenty years ago, I had a very active imagination which took me on imaginary journeys to Alcent. The wild adventure I enjoyed during those fantasies fed an ever-growing desire to be a part of this mission. By the time I was in my early teens, I made it my goal to be on this mission. In my fantasies, I constantly envisioned myself being a doctor, so I set that as a career goal. Somewhere in my teenage years, I concluded that my best chance to be on this mission was to be a better doctor than all others who applied. I also decided that being healthy and in good physical condition was a must. I had such a passionate burning desire to achieve my goals that I spent virtually all of my time studying, exercising, and doing whatever I could to be in an excellent state of health. What I am getting at is that this didn't leave me with very much time to get involved in relationships with boys and later on, men. I decided that I had to give up many of the social pleasures enjoyed by girls and young women and devote all of my time to achieving my career goals. But now that I've achieved them, I would like to have an intimate relationship with the man I love, maybe, even marry him and have some children."

"That sounds like a challenge you can handle, but if you don't mind my assistance, I could give you a little coaching."

"What do you have in mind?"

"Your fear of rejection is something that you wouldn't have to be concerned with if you could entice him to make a play for you. Let him think that it's all his idea. That will put you in the driver's seat."

"You have my attention. Tell me more."

"We need to get him to see you as a passionate, desirable woman and not just the ship's doctor. If we can accomplish that, then, if he is a normal man, all you should have to do is send out the proper signals and let nature take its course."

"I have no doubt that he is 100% masculine. I've been through his psychological tests with a fine-toothed comb."

"So you have given this some thought, despite your intense workload?"

"At times, I've torn my heart out over this."

"I think it's time we get started, and the first thing we need to do is get rid of the NASA issue clothing that you're wearing. While it's loose fitting and functional, it doesn't do a thing to show that you are a woman."

"You're right about that. Apparently, my uniform was designed by the *politically correct thinking crowd* with the idea of making men and women appear equal in the work place by concealing their differences with clothing. They succeeded."

"We are going to undo their success. We are going to put you into something that will knock his socks off. Fashion design is something I've always done as a hobby. It was fun, and I was even good enough to win some of the contests I entered."

Connie looked at Michelle and then, at herself. "Your outfit makes you look very attractive and feminine; whereas, my uniform could be worn by a man who works in a machine shop. Now that we've left Earth, I think it's time to put my uniforms into the recycling bin. Our computer library has an immense amount of information stored in it including the more popular women's fashions. Also, we have equipment for designing and making clothing."

"Do you know how to operate that equipment?"

"I sure do."

"Good! You can teach me, and we'll make you a few beautiful, new outfits."

Continuously growing more excited as she thought about the possibilities, Connie enthusiastically exclaimed, "This is going to be the most fun that I've had in a long time! When can we start?"

"Why not right now; while we're both in the mood for it. Also, as long as we're doing this, I would like to make something for myself too. Because of the way I became a part of this mission, I wasn't able to bring much along."

"Good idea," replied Connie.

"Once we get new outfits for you, I want to style your hair into something more updated. Maybe we can even use some make-up tips. When we're finished, the Captain would have to be blind to not notice you."

"It almost sounds like you're planning to totally make me over."

"Not really, we're just going to fix you up in a way that accentuates your natural beauty. After all, you are an attractive woman. You have a beautiful face, enchanting blue eyes and that great blond hair. I can't tell because of your clothing, but I think you also have a good figure."

"I do, and thanks for the compliments. Hopefully, I will soon get those same compliments from the man I love. I wonder what would be the right occasion to present the new me to him."

"I think it would be most effective if you could be alone with him the first time he sees you. That way, you can turn on the charm without any distractions."

Connie displayed a naughty grin and said, "I think the recent sabotage ordeal subjected the Captain to a great deal of stress. As the ship's medical officer, I think the responsible thing for me to do would be to call him in for a complete physical."

"You would of course be doing this purely in the line of duty," remarked Michelle, slyly.

"Certainly! After all, the captain's health is important to the success of our mission."

Michelle thought about the encounter Connie was planning and said, "One of the things I like about this is that you will have the element of surprise working for you. He will be expecting to see you in standard NASA issue sexless clothing and will be caught off guard by what we have in mind for him. Observing his initial reaction should give you a fairly good indication if you will be successful in achieving the desired relationship."

"If the approach we've been discussing fails to achieve the desired response, I may have to use more direct tactics."

With her curiosity immediately aroused, Michelle asked, "What does the good doctor have in mind for the Captain?"

"When he comes in for his physical, if he doesn't properly react to the glamorous new me, I might suspect that the stress of recent events negatively affected his ability to respond to unexpected situations. In that event, to avoid medical malpractice, I will be forced to examine his nervous system to make sure that it's functioning properly. To do that, I will have to check his responses to various kinds of stimulation."

"Why Doctor Nemard! I am beginning to suspect that you might be planning to deviate from standard medical procedure."

Displaying a broad smile, Connie looked at Michelle and asked, "Whatever gave you that idea?"

Michelle laughed, "I sense that your fear of rejection has disappeared."

"Not really! Rejection would be painful and put a strain on our friendship, but not knowing his true feelings for me is putting a strain on me anyway. So, which strain do I want to contend with?"

"That's a pragmatic way to look at it."

After thinking about the situation for a few moments, Connie said, "I really appreciate the way you've taken the time to listen to me and give me the support I need. You have a good way of making me feel at ease, even when discussing my innermost feelings. I think we are going to become exceptionally close friends, and I am happy you decided to come with us."

"Thank you, I appreciate it, and I feel the same way about you. Having close friends onboard will help ease the pain of leaving loved ones back on Earth."

"It's the kind of medicine ordered by the doctor."

Feeling happy and content, Michelle beamed a warm smile at Connie and said, "Let's make you some sexy, new clothes, so the doctor will have the right medicine to get her love life in order."

"I like the way you put that."

"It seemed appropriate."

"Before we begin, let me tell you briefly about the machine that we'll be using. It's quite complex and very capable. It not only makes clothing, but it also manufactures the fabric, buttons, zippers, and whatever else that it needs to make boots and garments. Thanks to genetic engineering, we can grow plants that are prolific at producing the fibers the machine uses to make cloth and the polymers it needs to make tough plastics, and it's all 100% recyclable."

"A machine that does all of that must be difficult to operate," commented Michelle.

"It's actually quite simple, even though it is a very complex piece of equipment. It is computer controlled, and the program is easy to use. The first step is to give the computer complete data about your body. We can do that right here in the medical lab or from anyone's apartment. It simply involves giving the computer a three-dimensional view of your body. This can be done in a number of ways, but one easy way is to let the computer simultaneously view your body with three video cameras. Here in the medical lab, there is a video camera in the corner to your left, in the corner to your right, and up there near the ceiling.

I will demonstrate how the system works. First, I press the program menu switch, and then select the New Clothing Program. As you can see, the computer has turned on the cameras. Now, I simply step into view of the cameras and remove all of my clothing. Next, I do a few simple poses, allowing the computer to see my nude body in different positions and from different angles. Finally, I do some basic range of motion exercises. The computer should now have exact measurements of all parts of my body, so that whatever clothing we make for me should be a perfect fit."

Connie stepped out of the cameras' field of view and reached for her clothing. As she began putting it on, she looked at Michelle and said, "Now, it's your turn."

Displaying an expression of concern, Michelle said, "I'm not sure that I want all those explicit views of my naked body in the computer for just anyone to look at."

"You are the only person who can access the data," responded Connie. "Once you've gone through the simple procedure that I just did, the computer will have enough physical data about you so that it can identify you. It simply won't allow anyone else to access your personal file."

"Are you sure about that?"

"Absolutely positive!"

Accepting Connie's assurance, Michelle stepped into the camera's field of view, removed her clothing, posed in different positions, and then did some stretching exercises. When the computer stated that it had enough information, Michelle put her clothes back on.

"Specifications for all the basic styles of clothing worn on Earth in recent years are stored in the computer's memory," explained Connie, as she began displaying them in 3-D on the wall-sized video screen. "When we find a fashion design that we like, I simply instruct the computer to show us what I would look like wearing it."

"What do you think about the evening gown that we're looking at?" asked Michelle?

Connie entered the *Display* instruction into the computer, and a life-sized, 3-D image of her wearing the gown appeared on the video screen. It showed her gracefully walking, turning, and doing the appropriate poses that a professional model would use to sell the dress.

"I like it, but I'm not sure that it's what we're looking for. If I am to meet Jerry here in the medical lab, I don't think a party dress is the right outfit."

"True," stated Michelle, "but I really do like that particular shade of blue. It looks really good on you. Apparently, the computer decided to match the dress color to your blue eyes."

"Color recommendation is one of the features of this program. Based on the colors of my eyes, hair, and skin, the computer will select the shades of the various colors that look best on me. For example, if I wanted to wear this dress, and I wanted it in red, I simply request that of the computer, and presto, there I am, wearing the same dress, only now, it's red. However, it isn't just any random shade of red; it is the optimum shade of red that looks best on me."

"With equipment like this, coming up with the right outfit for you is going to be easier than I thought. Let's see what you would look like in a blue jump suit."

Connie entered the appropriate instructions into the computer, and a life-sized, 3-D image of her wearing a blue jump suit promptly appeared on the screen. Again, the computer showed her gracefully walking, turning, and doing the kinds of poses that a professional model would do to sell the outfit.

"Let's try some alterations to that basic design," suggested Michelle. "It fits too loose. Let's change the fabric to an interlock knit. Also, let's change the v-neckline to a scoop neckline, and instead of being sleeveless, let's add sleeves that extend about half way to your elbows."

When the new image appeared on the screen, Connie exclaimed, "Wow! The way it hugs my body from top to bottom certainly does reveal every line and curve in my figure, but I'm not sure that I would call it an elegant outfit."

"That's true, it's not, but I think we can turn it into an exquisite outfit by adding the right kind of trim to it, starting with the neckline and sleeves. Also, a belt around your waist of the appropriate width, color, and design might be helpful. In addition, wearing the right kind of jewelry will always add a bit of class. With a little experimentation, which is easy to do with this computer, we'll create an outfit that you could successfully model at a high society fashion show back on Earth. Judging from the way you looked in that party dress and now, in this jump suit, I think you could've had a very successful career as a professional model, if you had chosen to do that."

"Thank you. That's the nicest compliment I've had in a long time. Imagine how different my life would be if I had selected that for my career."

Meanwhile, another discussion is taking place in the captain's quarters between Captain Jerontis, Mike, and Moose.

Captain Jerontis leaned back in his comfortable chair, stretched out, and yawned. "With the sabotage ordeal and the intense schedule of recent months now behind us, I am finally starting to feel relaxed, kind of like being on vacation."

Moose instantly responded, "Well, if I hadn't allowed you to talk me into going with you on this interstellar voyage, I would be on vacation right now. Imagine me laying on a warm sandy beach in the South Pacific surrounded by bikini-clad scenery. I would be faced with the difficult, but pleasant, task of deciding which one to choose."

Mike turned to Captain J.J. and asked, "Is it just my imagination, or is it true that Moose's mind wanders off into sexual fantasy land whenever he isn't busy working?"

"Either that, or he's trying to decide what kind of pizza to eat next," laughed Jerry.

"Aw come on, you guys are just ridiculing me because I like to enjoy life."

"We all like to enjoy life, but some of us have a broader field of interest and consequently, have more options open to us," teased Mike.

"It isn't a question of having a broad field of interest," retorted Moose. "It's simply a matter of getting your leisure-time priorities in order. I enjoy life in lots of ways, but I put exciting women and tasty food at the top of my list. Anyway, you are lucky to have a beautiful wife to live with."

"True, I do have a beautiful wife. But she isn't the only attractive woman on this ship. Specifically, in addition to my wife, there are six women with ages varying from 29 to 33. Also, there are six in the 18 and 19 age group, making a grand total of twelve. With all the stories I've heard from Jerry about how adventuresome you are, I am wondering why it's taking you so long to get together with one of them."

"How can you tell if they're attractive?" questioned Moose. "All they ever wear are those NASA uniforms that make them look like they're ready to go to work on a factory assembly line somewhere. Appearance-wise, they're not very exciting to my way of thinking."

Mike turned to Jerry and said, "Apparently, Moose has never developed the masculine art of mentally undressing women."

Much to Moose's displeasure, both Mike and Jerry laughed at Mike's suggestion that Moose lacked imagination. Moose glared at Mike, then, at Captain Jerontis; then, he said, "I am beginning to think that this is *Pick-On-Moose Day*. I make a legitimate comment about the bland, totally without style, uniforms that women who work for NASA are required to wear, and what response do I get? You guys decide to have fun at my expense by insulting my imagination. I simply cannot believe that women who are proud to be women, and want to look like women, could find any pleasure in wearing their NASA uniforms."

Captain Jerontis said to Moose, "You're probably right. During recent months, recent years for that matter, we've all been so preoccupied with making this mission a success that we haven't had much time to be concerned with clothing. And even if we had been, it probably wouldn't have mattered because our uniforms are a product of the politically-correct-thinking NASA bureaucracy. But since we're no longer under their control, I am going to post an order that allows all individuals to recycle their uniforms and dress any way they want to. It will be interesting to see what the women decide to wear."

"Evaluating them will be a good project for me," volunteered Moose. "Since I am currently on vacation, I'll have ample time for the task. Whoever comes up with the most exciting clothing will receive a prize, namely, the pleasure of my companionship."

"I think all that pizza you've been eating has given you a fat head," declared Mike.

"What makes you think you're on vacation?" questioned Captain Jerontis. "This isn't a pleasure cruise on the Caribbean, it's an important mission to start a new society on an alien planet."

"Well, the way I have it figured out, you canceled my vacation to the South Pacific when you coerced me into coming with you to be your chief engineer. But since Mike is still here, I am not needed in that capacity, and that leaves me free to pursue some of the finer pleasures in life, just like I would have on the vacation that I had planned. Actually, it is probably a good thing that I am on this mission. I can help you develop a much needed social life for yourself."

"Thanks for the offer," said Jerry, "but now that I'm no longer working 24 hours per day, I think I can take care of my social life quite adequately on my own. If you'll kindly think back to our college days, I think you'll recall that my social life was every bit as active as yours. While it's true that you're no longer needed in the position of chief engineer, I am happy to have the luxury of having two individuals onboard who are fully qualified for the job. I would like you and Mike to share the responsibilities of the position. This will allow both of you to have ample time off to pursue other activities, such as training for the responsibilities that you will have on Alcent."

"I am confident that Moose and I can work out a schedule that will allow him sufficient free time for his female fashions evaluation project," Mike responded. "As for me, since I will be in charge of geological research on Alcent, I intend to get started with my geology education. I have six years to become an expert in the field. This will be much easier now that Moose is here to share my engineering duties with."

"Since I am quite talented at evaluating female fashions, that project shouldn't take too much of my time," boasted Moose. "But I still have a great deal to learn about the intricate details of this ship. I intend to continue studying it before I start preparing for a research project on Alcent."

"I agree," responded Captain Jerontis, "but I would like you to be thinking about what area of research you would like to be involved with. Being an unplanned member of the crew, you were never assigned an area of responsibility. Therefore, you are free to select a field of study that is of interest to you. The only requirement is that the knowledge gained through your research has to have practical application and increase the probability of this mission being a success."

"I think I can tell you that right now," stated Moose. "I would like to study plant and animal life with the objective of determining what is edible and what its nutritional content is."

Mike laughed, "You were right. When he isn't thinking about sex, he's thinking about food, but at least his interests are broadening to include other things besides pizza."

"Someone needs to think about food," retorted Moose. "After all, it is necessary for survival. For example, what if our food synthesizers were damaged beyond repair in some sort of accident. Then, it would sure be nice to know what's edible and what isn't. I would love to discover several species of edible fish. Sport fishing is something that I've always enjoyed. On an unspoiled virgin planet, the fishing should be absolutely great."

"That's an exciting possibility," agreed Captain Jerontis, "but at this point, we don't know what kind of aquatic creatures have evolved on Alcent."

"But fish were present on Earth during the Dinosaur Age," argued Moose. "Why shouldn't they be present on Alcent?"

"There might be fish there," replied Jerry. "All that I'm saying is that we don't know. However, more than half of Alcent is covered with water, so there is ample habitat there for fish to have evolved in. Since so much of Alcent is covered with water, a large amount of our research effort will be devoted to underwater exploration. For this purpose, we've brought with us a small research submarine that is capable of comfortably carrying four people."

"What an adventure!" declared Moose. "We have no idea what kind of life exists in the oceans of Alcent. We could find underwater monsters capable of destroying our research submarine."

"That's true," agreed Jerry, "but we might also find an abundance of fish that are edible and exciting to catch."

"That possibility along with the challenge of facing and surviving unknown dangers excites me," declared Moose. "I definitely want to be involved in our underwater exploration project."

Captain Jerontis said, "Operating that research sub will be one of my responsibilities. However, since this appeals to you so strongly, I will be more than happy to share that responsibility with you. As far as finding food sources on Alcent is concerned, that will be an important project. It will be one of our top priorities. Dianne will be in charge of biological research, and Doctor Nemard has the skills to do nutritional analysis as well as search for toxic substances. If you want to work in this area, you will be working with them. I am sure they will appreciate your help."

TIME: 6 Days, 18 Hours A.L.E.

Dianne Dawson was in the cafeteria eating breakfast when Doctor Nemard walked in, scanned the menu of the day, made her selection, and placed her order. Then, she approached Dianne, and said, "You look deeply lost in thought. Do you mind if I join you, or do you need some time for yourself?"

Upon hearing Connie's remark, Dianne snapped out of her trance-like mental state and replied, "Please do join me. I could use some company right about now."

Connie sat down and made herself comfortable. She looked at Dianne, "I sense that something is troubling you. Would you like to tell me about it?"

"I was just thinking about some of the people I was close to back on Earth."

"We haven't even been gone a week yet, and you miss them already?" Connie asked, sympathetically.

"I know we've only been gone a few days, but the finality of our departure is hitting me hard at the moment. I feel a lonely sense of loss because I will never again be able to do anything with the people I've left behind."

"That's a normal reaction to our situation."

"Even though I understand that it's normal, what I am feeling right now is still painful. In recent years, I've worked so hard at getting a position on this voyage that I never dwelled on the fact that we won't be coming back. But now that we've left Earth, it has really started to sink in that the past is gone. Cherished memories of events that happened in my growing-up years have been pouring through my mind. The things that I did with my family and friends, the places that I enjoyed visiting; all of that is now part of the past, never again to be revisited, except mentally."

"You've just done an excellent job of describing all the symptoms of an age old disease commonly called homesickness. How do you plan to deal with it?"

"Well, to start with, I can't go back home, not even for a short visit. For the next six to eight years, this ship is going to be my home, so I am going to do whatever I can to turn it into a home filled with warmth and comfort. Maybe, in the process of doing that, I will develop some new relationships to help offset the loss of family and friends. But right now, more than anything else, I need some vacation time. It seems like all I've done for the past several months is work and sleep. I need some leisure time to just have fun."

"Now that we're finally underway, your workload should be greatly reduced, and you should be able to do that."

"I think so. I think I'll start by organizing some teams for competitive games. We do have a fairly large gym. I think it's time to put it to good use."

"That should be fun. If you're going to do volleyball and tennis, include me."

"Okay, you're number one on the list. How about basketball?"

"I'm not very good at that, but I'll try it."

"I was on the starting team in high school. I can teach you some techniques, and then, it'll be up to you to practice them."

"I think you'll find me to be an eager student. I like your idea of forming teams to play athletic games. They'll not only be fun, but they'll help us maintain our physical condition, and that will help promote health and happiness."

"That's true, but I am looking for more than that."

"Like what?"

"I am interested in the social aspects of team sports. I've always enjoyed participating in group activities for social reasons, but now that we've left Earth, I am especially interested in social activities. I need to find new personal relationships."

"That's something that all of us need to do, and in the process of doing that, we'll build a new society to replace the one we left behind."

"As small as this ship's population is, our new society might resemble a large extended family in many respects," commented Dianne.

"Our people are very supportive of each other in the work environment. If that carries over into the non-work environment, then our society will be very much like a large family."

"When we get to Alcent, we'll be giving birth to a new civilization, and that job will be a lot easier if we build a strong society before we get there."

"A strong supportive society will also make our long voyage easier."

"Pursuing interesting hobbies might also be a good way to make our long voyage more enjoyable; especially, hobbies that can be shared with others."

"What are you thinking about doing?" asked Connie.

"I like to be surrounded by living organisms. Maybe, that's what got me into a career in biology. Anyway, I managed to convince NASA to allow me to bring along 3,000 pounds of potting soil and seeds for several hundred different kinds of plants."

"Three thousand pounds is a big pile of soil. What are you going to do with all of that?"

"I am going to put my imagination to work and see what kind of artistic designs I can come up with for pots to grow plants in. Then, I am going to turn my apartment into a lush garden."

"It seems to me that 3,000 pounds is a lot of soil for just one apartment. If you use all of that, there might not be any room left for you."

"It's not all for me. I intend to share it with whomever wants it. I am sure there are others who will want plants in their apartments. The soft lines and contrasting colors of healthy plants have a soothing effect on the people who nurture them. Their presence in an apartment can turn a cold, sterile environment into one that is warm and alive."

"I love fresh tomatoes that are allowed to ripen on the vine. Did you happen to bring along any tomato seeds?"

"Yes, I did. In fact, I have seeds for several fruits and vegetables. Part of the justification for bringing along so much soil was to be able to produce some fresh food to supplement that produced by our food synthesizers. As for tomatoes, they are one of my favorite foods. I brought along seeds for three varieties."

"I think I can find room in my apartment for a couple tomato plants as well as some decorative plants. Could I look at what you have and select some that appeal to me? I would appreciate your help in getting them started and in properly caring for them."

"I would be more than happy to. I love working with plants. In regard to the tomatoes, I can even genetically alter them to give you the degree of flavor and sweetness that you like."

"I like them super sweet with lots of flavor."

"One of the varieties I have fits that description, so genetic altering won't be needed. Maybe, sometime tomorrow, we could get together and get this project started."

"That sounds good to me," responded Connie. "Changing the subject a bit, but still talking about seeds, have you ever thought of this starship as nothing more than a giant seed pod?"

"What exactly do you mean?"

"To explain what I mean, I will use an analogy. In the natural life of a plant, there is a sequence of events that begins when a seed germinates. The seed sends roots down into the soil and a tiny plant up through the surface of the soil. The tiny seedling grows and develops until it reaches maturity. Then, it produces seed to begin the cycle all over again. Compare the human species to a plant, and we can see a similar chain of events on a much larger scale. Through a process of evolution, the human species was born on Earth eons ago. Over the past several hundred thousand years, it has evolved and grown to a level of capability where it has ejected a seed pod. This ship is that seed pod, and we, the inhabitants of it, are the seed. When we land on Alcent, a new civilization will be born, which will grow and evolve."

"I've never really thought of myself as a seed inside a seed pod," stated Dianne. "But I like your analogy. To continue it a bit further, when a seedling springs forth from a seed, it can only develop into a strong mature plant, if it has a strong root system firmly embedded in fertile soil. Likewise, if we want our new society to grow and evolve into something great, we must establish a strong root system to support it. I believe that a key element in a strong foundation for a new society is the continued quest for knowledge and practical skills, especially survival skills. A system of government that promotes personal freedom and responsibility is also essential. Also, it is important to establish an effective education system to teach all of this to our children."

"I agree, but I think it is also important to have a spiritual life based on a belief in God. I've found that a great deal of happiness, contentment, and peace of mind can be achieved through the pursuit of a positive spiritual life. I believe that religion should be a part of our new society, but it must be a matter of individual choice."

"I've never been a member of any religion," responded Dianne, "but I do believe in God, and I have a very good sense of right and wrong that was instilled into me by my parents. When I have children of my own, I will probably handle the subject with them the same way that my parents taught me. Basically, I agree with you; this will be an important aspect of our new society."

Dianne paused for a moment. Then, she said, "Getting back to the subject of personal freedom, what do you think about the notice posted by Captain Jerontis stating that we are no longer required to wear our NASA uniforms?"

"I think it's great. I would like to dress the way I feel like dressing. I have no need to wear this uniform."

"What do you think motivated him to issue that directive?"

"I think the Captain would like us all to work together as friends in a relaxed informal atmosphere. Requiring everyone to wear a uniform denotes a sense of formality that I think he would like to dispense with. Also, the uniforms are a product of the NASA bureaucracy, and when it comes to bureaucrats with their multitudes of rules and regulations, the Captain tends to be a rebel."

"What you're saying is probably true, but I think there is something else involved here."

"What?" questioned Connie.

"I think his friend Moose was the instigator of that order. He has quite a playboy reputation, and I think he enjoys being around women who are nicely dressed, even suggestive."

Connie nodded, "You might be correct, but how do you feel about wearing your uniform? Wouldn't you like to get rid of it and wear something more stylish?"

"I am going to use any free time that I have today to design and make myself some clothing that is comfortable and feminine."

"You wouldn't be trying to look appealing to Moose, would you?"

"What makes you say that?"

"A moment ago, when you were talking about Moose's playboy reputation, I detected a sparkle in your eyes. I don't think it was there out of interest in me," commented Connie, laughing.

"You're very observant. But then, I guess you should be; after all, you're the psychiatrist."

Dianne thought about Moose for a few moments and her pulse sped up as a degree of excitement flooded her system. She admitted, "It is true. I am attracted to him. I especially like his jovial, fun-loving personality. And despite his playboy reputation, I believe he has a solid character and a good set of values. He is obviously a very intelligent individual, who can be very serious and hard working when he needs to be. Without these characteristics, he could not have advanced as far as he has."

"It appears to me that you have been thinking about him more than just a little bit. Has it occurred to you that a close relationship with him might be exactly what you need to cure the symptoms of the homesickness that you are suffering?"

"I haven't thought about it from that perspective, but I think there might be some merit to that theory. Am I to understand that the ship's doctor is prescribing a relationship with Moose as therapy for my homesickness?"

"Well, I am responsible for the health and psychological well-being of all individuals on this ship. If you need a prescription to get started, I will be more than happy to write you one."

Dianne laughed, "I appreciate your desire to be helpful, but I think I can do this without written instructions."

At that moment, Moose and Captain Jerontis entered the cafeteria. Noticing the presence of Dianne and Connie and that they were both laughing, Jerry turned to Moose and said, "They're certainly in a good mood. I wonder what they are so happy about."

"It's probably a jubilant reaction to that order you posted about wearing NASA uniforms," Moose responded.

Moose, having a rather loud booming voice, was easily overheard by both women. Connie and Dianne looked at each with a devious expression. Both understood what the other was thinking. They looked up at the men, who were now close to their table. Having established eye contact with Moose, Dianne was the first to speak, "What order are you talking about? Is there something wrong with our uniforms?"

"Captain J.J. issued an order that says we're no longer required to wear our uniforms. We can dress any way we like," Moose replied.

"But these uniforms are loose and comfortable," protested Dianne. "They're functional and easy to work in."

"She's right," stated Connie in quick agreement.

Surprised and disappointed by their comments, Moose shifted his gaze back and forth between the two women while he considered what to say next. Before he could say anything, Dianne smiled at him and said, "I see that you're still wearing your uniform, so can I assume that you agree with us?"

"I like this uniform," responded Moose. "I think I look pretty good in it,"

"It sounds like he agrees with us," stated Connie.

"Yes, and he even thinks the uniforms look good," noted Dianne. "So, why would anyone want to dress differently?"

"I think they look reasonably good on men," remarked Moose.

Looking Moose in the eye and doing her best to display a genuine expression of chagrin, Dianne asked, "Are you implying that we don't look very good?"

Captain Jerontis silently observed the three-way conversation with a great deal of amusement at the ease with which the two women maneuvered Moose into a delicate situation. He wondered what they were up to and how Moose would tactfully talk his way out of this one.

With both women and Captain Jerontis expectantly staring at him, Moose began to feel uncomfortable as he thought about what to say next. Being a quick thinker, Moose figured out what to say after just a few moments, and he politely said, "I wasn't trying to be uncomplimentary. I just like to see good looking women dressed in an attractive way, and these uniforms leave a lot to be desired in that regard."

"That almost sounds like a compliment. Thank you," Dianne said.

Dianne turned to Connie, "It took a little detective work, but I think I've established that my earlier assertion was correct, wouldn't you agree?"

Connie nodded in agreement.

Curious about what they were discussing, and suspicious about whether or not it applied to him, Moose asked, "What assertion are you talking about?"

"Oh, just something we were discussing earlier," responded Dianne.

Moose concluded that he wasn't likely to get an undisguised answer and decided to drop the subject.

Connie changed the subject. She directed her attention to Captain Jerontis and said, "I am concerned about the health of our personnel. It is possible that we could have some medical problems because of the intense pace of activity leading up to our departure and the high stress levels and lack of sleep during the recent sabotage ordeal. As a precaution, I've decided to give everyone a routine medical exam."

"That's a good idea," responded Captain Jerontis.

"I am glad you agree, because I want to start with you. How about tomorrow at 9:00 A.M.?"

"But, I am in perfectly good health. I really don't think I need a medical exam."

"You just said that it's a good idea, and since you are the Captain, your health should be closely monitored. Also, you need to set a good example for the crew. Besides that, if you are in such good health, you have nothing to worry about." Displaying a faint sly smile, Connie added, "Who knows, you might even enjoy it."

Jerry noticed the subtle smile, thought about the remark, and wondered why Doctor Nemard would think that a medical exam would be such an enjoyable experience. He figured she must enjoy her job a great deal. "Okay, I'll be there tomorrow at 9:00 A.M."

"On another subject," continued Captain Jerontis, "Moose has indicated a desire to learn the skills needed to evaluate natural sources of food on Alcent."

Dianne looked at Connie, "I think the Captain would like us to educate and train Moose in the field of Nutritional Biology."

Dianne said to Moose, "If you could stop by the life support lab tomorrow morning, I will help you get started in your area of interest."

TIME: 7 days, 18 hours A.L.E.

Captain Jerontis arrived at the medical lab for his physical. He entered the front room and announced his presence. From one of the back rooms, he heard Doctor Nemard say, "I'll be right there."

A few moments later, Captain Jerontis looked in the direction of the medical lab interior and saw Connie gracefully walking toward him in her new outfit. Alertly watching him for his first reaction, Connie noticed his eyes light up and a subtle change in his posture that indicated it was a pleasant surprise. Knowing she had his full attention, she did a graceful turn similar to those she had seen herself do in the computer video. The broad smile of approval that spread across the Captain's face told Connie what she wanted to know, but she decided that she would also like to hear it.

"How do I look to you?" she asked, with a warm smile.

"Sensational!"

"Thank you. Are you sure there's nothing else?"

Captain Jerontis quickly came to realize that Doctor Nemard had captivated his full attention. She was so appealing that he simply could not take his eyes off her. It was obvious that she did not want him to. His body flooded with a desire that had been subdued for far too long, and he wondered what kind of physical Doctor Nemard had in mind.

In a sweet sounding voice, Doctor Nemard asked, "Are you going to just keep silently staring at me, or are you going to answer my question?"

"You are beautiful, and I might add, that's a very sexy outfit you have on. Has anyone else seen you looking like this?"

The possessive note that Connie detected in Jerry's voice when he asked that question made her feel wanted and filled her with happiness. "Michelle helped me design this outfit. She also styled my hair and helped me with make-up and jewelry. You and she are the only ones who have seen me like this."

"Have you done all of this to please me? That certainly would make me feel special."

"You are special to me. Whenever my mind's not busy with work, it seems to find you."

Jerry was quiet, then said, "I'm happy you feel that way. By the way, you were right yesterday."

"Right about what?"

"When we were discussing my medical exam, you suggested that I might enjoy the occasion, and you were right."

"I would probably be in tears right now if it had turned out that I was wrong. Should we get started?"

A couple minutes later, while checking his pulse, Doctor Nemard said, "Your pulse and blood pressure are unusually high this morning. Have you been doing anything that would explain these high numbers?" she asked teasingly.

Being as obvious as he could, Jerry allowed his eyes to roam over her body with admiration and desire. "You don't need to sound so innocent! You know full well why I am so excited this morning!" he exclaimed.

Toying with him a bit, she said, "Please explain."

To comply with Connie's request, Jerry stood up and put his arms around her in a warm embrace. Finding her eagerly responsive, he kissed her passionately. While holding her in his arms, he said, "I've been wanting to do this for a long time, but for a number of reasons, I've had to keep my feelings suppressed. Now that we are safely underway, none of those reasons exist anymore. I love you Connie and have for a long time."

After kissing her again, he said, "I had feelings for you on the day that we met, and since then, my feelings for you have grown steadily stronger. It makes me feel really good to be close to you like this."

The Captain, having just done everything that she had hoped he would do, aroused Connie's penned up feelings of passion and desire to such a degree that she had difficulty controlling them. Attempting to meld her excited, trembling body even tighter against his, she said, "I feel the same way about you, Captain."

"When we are together like this, maybe you could call me Jerry instead of Captain."

"If you promise to call me Connie instead of Doctor Nemard."

"I can live with that. I know that I came here for a medical exam, but I am not exactly in the mood for that anymore."

"Your pulse and blood pressure feel much higher now than they were earlier. We need to lower them before we can continue with your physical."

"What medical procedure do you plan to use to do that?" teased Jerry.

Connie tilted her head back, looked up into his eyes, and said, "We need to deal with what's causing the high numbers."

She kissed him, seductively and whispered, "There's a bed in the patient recovery room that we can use, and I believe that you are familiar with the procedure. I've never heard it called a medical procedure before, but since it can be quite therapeutic, I guess we could call it that."

Doctor Nemard hung a sign on the medical lab door that said:

INTENSIVE MEDICAL PROCEDURE IN PROGRESS
DO NOT DISTURB UNLESS YOU HAVE AN EMERGENCY

She then closed the door and locked it.

Meanwhile, in the life support lab, Dianne was comfortably seated at her computer console and completed a review of the life support system's previous twelve hours of performance data. She found no problems and no evidence indicative of future problems.

Satisfied with the system's smooth operation, Dianne decided to move on to her next project: the development of an instruction program to help Moose acquire the knowledge and skills needed for food research on Alcent. Dianne was having a difficult time putting this program together because Moose kept entering her mind. She couldn't help wondering how he would react when he saw her wearing feminine clothing.

Hoping to excite him, Dianne made a determined effort to display her femininity. Her new outfit consisted of a knee-length full skirt made from soft, colorful material and a tan, somewhat see-through, long-sleeved blouse allowing visibility for the dainty bra under it. Courtesy of Michelle, Dianne wore a flattering, new hairstyle and a subtle touch of make-up. She completed her look with some jewelry and even a little perfume.

Unable to get her mind into Moose's training program, Dianne stood up, walked across the lab, and stood before a large mirror. Dianne looked at herself in self-appraisal. She gazed at her hips and slim waistline. Then, her eyes moved up to her breasts. This is just enough to stimulate Moose's imagination. I hope he thinks I'm attractive. At least I have a good figure from all the exercise I do.

Dianne took another look at her new hairstyle. "I like it!" she said to herself, "Michelle did an excellent job."

Dianne thought about her maternal grandmother who had given her the jewelry she was wearing to take with her to Alcent. She treasured the jewelry as a very special gift because her grandmother had worn it on her wedding day. She knew how special this jewelry was to her grandmother and how difficult it must have been for her to give it away. Dianne thought, this may have been my grandmother's way of giving me a part of herself to always remember her by. Maybe, she even intended this jewelry to be a tie between the family I will have on Alcent and the family I left behind on Earth. Since this jewelry is likely to be a conversation piece far into the future, it should accomplish that purpose.

Lost in thought, Dianne was startled by the sudden beeping of her communicator, which she immediately picked up and answered: "Life support lab, Dianne speaking."

Almost instantly, she received an exuberant response, "Good morning Dianne! This is Moose. Are you ready to begin the process of turning me into a human nutrition expert who is fully capable of evaluating biological organisms on Alcent to determine their suitability for human consumption?"

Hearing Moose speak in his high-spirited tone made Dianne tingle with excitement. This constant cheerful attitude was one of the characteristics that she really liked about him. She laughed at his long-winded way of asking a simple question, and said, "You sound like an eager student with an active imagination, and I am definitely ready to stimulate your imagination."

"Good! I'll be there shortly."

Dianne took one last look at herself and decided that she was ready for Moose. So she turned away from the mirror, walked across the lab, and sat down to await his arrival.

A few minutes later, Moose arrived at the life support lab. Dianne stood up to greet him, not just out of courtesy, but also, to gracefully present herself to him. Total surprise and fascination with the stunning attractiveness of the woman greeting him left Moose speechless. He intently looked at her in silent appraisal, then in sincere admiration.

Dianne was greatly pleased at Moose's reaction, so she did a little turn for him. In a soft, affectionate tone, she said, "Judging from the way that you're staring at me, I could almost get the feeling that you've never seen me before."

"I've never seen you looking like this! After that little masquerade that you and Connie put on in the cafeteria yesterday, which I naively took at face value, I concluded that I would never see you in anything other than a NASA uniform. I'm glad I was wrong."

Dianne chuckled at Moose's admission that he had been completely fooled by their ruse.

"What are you giggling about?" he asked.

"In view of your reputation for being a lady's man with a talent for understanding how women think, I am amused at how easily Connie and I misled you into thinking we were happy with our sexless appearance in our uniforms."

"Well, I don't know either of you very well. I've only been on this ship a few days, and I've been extremely busy. I just haven't had any opportunities to get acquainted with either of you. So how could I've known that you weren't serious and were just playing with my mind?"

"That's a good point," Dianne responded, "I don't know you very well either, except for hearsay. Before we get started with work, maybe, we should take a coffee break and talk for a while."

"Good idea! Let's go to the cafeteria. I haven't had breakfast yet, and it's been a long time since I last enjoyed a meal in the company of a lovely woman."

"Thank you for the compliment."

A few minutes later, in the cafeteria, Dianne said, "Except for you and Michelle, all of us on this mission had several years to think about whether we wanted to permanently leave Earth and go to Alcent. Michelle had a few months to consider the possibility. You made the choice in just a few hours. Would you mind telling me how you made such an important decision so quickly?"

"I love adventure, and I think living on Alcent will be the ultimate adventure."

"I can understand how your desire for adventure would motivate you to want to go, but in making your decision, weren't you bothered by breaking your ties to Earth, by leaving family and friends?"

"Not really. I have no wife or children, my parents are both deceased, and my best friend is on this ship."

After a moment of thought, Moose added, "I sense that you are feeling some distress because of leaving family and friends."

"Is it that obvious, or are you just that sensitive to other people's feelings?"

"Maybe, a little of both, but mainly, I don't think you would've asked that question the way you did unless it's a problem that you are troubled with. How are you dealing with it?"

"I started years ago when I committed myself to this project. Because of a total commitment to be on this mission, I avoided intimate long-term relationships that could have resulted in marriage and children. That would have put me in an impossible situation. But even though I avoided that problem, I've still left my family and some close friends. The fact that I will never again be able to do anything with any of them gives me an empty feeling."

"The loss of loved ones is a normal part of life. When I lost my parents in a car accident, I grieved for a long time. It happened so suddenly. They were in their late forties, very healthy, and should've had many years of life ahead of them. Losing them was completely unexpected and was very difficult for me to cope with."

"The grief that you felt must have been almost overwhelming. How did you handle that?"

"Initially, spiritual counseling from their pastor was helpful. The passage of time also helped. But, I've never stopped missing them. I wish they were still alive, so that I could share the excitement of being on this mission with them."

"What you just told me puts a different perspective on my situation. Instead of thinking about the vast distance that separates me from my family, I should be happy that they are alive and healthy and that I can share my experiences with them," Dianne said. "As far as close family is concerned, you are alone. That must be difficult for you. Do you ever feel lonely?"

"I am not entirely alone. Jerry and I have been close friends since our college football days. After I lost my parents, he insisted that I accompany him on a vacation trip to Australia. He helped me recover from my grief, and in the process, he became more than just a friend. In many ways, he is like a brother to me. I was an only child, and my parents are dead, so our friendship has evolved to the point where he has filled an important void in my life."

"I knew that you two are exceptionally close friends, but I didn't realize that you thought of yourselves as brothers. With him being white and you being dark, I think it's great that you could think of yourselves as brothers, but it does seem kind of unusual."

"What's so unusual about that? What goes on in a man's brain should not be influenced by the color of his skin."

"I agree, but unfortunately, too many people allow their thinking to be ruled by their skin color or ethnic background. In many places on Earth, serious social problems are caused by this, even fighting and killing. A study of world history shows that many wars have been fought because of this phenomenon."

"If I allowed my thinking to be shaped by my ethnic background, my mind would be in a continuous state of confusion."

"What do you mean by that?"

"My ancestry is somewhat complicated. One of my great grandfathers emigrated to America from Nigeria to do his doctoral work in Nuclear Physics. The woman he married was predominantly French and Native American of Creole descent. One of my grandmothers was Hispanic and Native American of Seminole descent. Her husband was English. If I were to allow my thinking to be ruled by my ethnic background, which of my ancestral cultures would I choose to be the dominant one?"

"That's an interesting question. Have you ever given it any thought?"

"Not much."

"You must have given it some thought, or you wouldn't know your family tree as well as you do."

"Let's just say that I've never made any attempt to live my life in accordance with what was acceptable in any of the cultures in my ethnic background. I've always just thought of myself as an American. I live in the present, and I plan for the future."

"I like that attitude," commented Dianne. "I also have several cultures in my family tree, and like you, I've never made any attempt to preserve any of them. Most of my life has been devoted to achieving the goals that I've set for myself, and that hasn't left me with very much time to be concerned about preserving the cultures of my ancestors."

"Which cultures are you talking about?"

"My African heritage is primarily from the Zulu Nation, and I also have French and Creole ancestry."

"I see that we have something in common in our ancestral past, but as complicated as mine is, I would be surprised if we didn't share some ancestry."

After a few moments, Moose noticed that Dianne was grinning at him mischievously. Wondering what it was about, he asked, "Is there something humorous in what I just said or are you thinking about something else?"

She leaned back into a somewhat enticing posture and responded, "It just struck me that since you don't have any close family, and since we share a few branches in our respective family trees, you might be tempted to start thinking of me as your sister and pursue a brother/sister relationship."

Surprised by Dianne's comment, Moose looked at her with an obvious expression of desire, "It would be very difficult for me to have that kind of relationship with you. Besides, I don't think it's what you want either."

"You're right," Dianne said. "I have no desire to have a platonic relationship with you. You excite me too much for that to be very satisfying."

"That's encouraging," said Moose, eagerly.

Dianne looked into Moose's eyes, "Before you get involved with me, I would like you to understand that I am much more interested in having a long-term relationship than in short-term pleasure. Like I said earlier, I've had to avoid long-term intimate relationships because they would've interfered with the commitment that I made to achieving the goal of being part of this mission. But now that I've achieved that goal, I would like to have the kind long-term relationship that I could not have before."

"I appreciate your honesty. Because of my career and other reasons, I've never had a long-term relationship with anyone either. But I think it's probably time I do."

"Why do you think that?"

"Sometimes, I feel alone in my life. I don't have anyone. There is a void in my life that needs to be filled. Recent encounters that I've had with women back on Earth, although exciting, have not relieved the loneliness that I feel more and more often. I need to belong to someone. I need a constant companion that I can share the ups and downs of my life with. Someone that I can be intimate with."

"Now, you are being very open with me. I like that."

"I've never revealed these feelings to anyone before, but I feel comfortable with you."

"Because of your reputation for having a jovial attitude toward life most of the time, I would never have guessed that you frequently feel lonely. But I guess I should have because as far as being dedicated to our careers is concerned, we have much in common. I frequently experience the feelings you've just revealed to me. Sometimes, one's personal life suffers because of dedication to a career. It just can't be avoided."

"Especially, when you have a very time-consuming career," added Moose. "But now, we have partially matching careers, and that will give us time together. En route to Alcent, you'll be helping me learn the skills that I will need to work with you after we arrive there."

"We'll have more than six years in space, and that will give us plenty of time to complete your training. It should be a pleasant experience."

"Also, we should have plenty of time for leisure activities. Perhaps later today, we could go down to the gym, play some tennis, and work out on some of the equipment. I haven't had enough exercise in recent weeks, and I am starting to feel the effects."

"Great!" stated Dianne. "I'd love to beat you."

"You're on! The exercise will feel good."

"I feel happier right now than I've felt in a long time."

"Good, me too. Let's go down to the gym."

After agreeing, Dianne seemed reluctant to move.

Noticing this, Moose asked, "Are you OK?"

Dianne stood up and faced Moose, "I put a lot of time and effort into looking like this. It seems a shame to get out of this and into gym clothes so soon."

Moose slipped his arms around Dianne, "I love what you've done. You are a beautiful woman."

His embrace made her realize things were happening very fast. "Thanks for the compliment. And I do think we should go play tennis for a while."

Not wanting to push Dianne into something that he sensed she wasn't yet ready for, Moose released her and said, "That's a good idea."

"I'll need a little time to change into gym clothes. Can you meet me in the gym in about twenty minutes?"

"Sounds good," responded Moose.

TIME: 15 Days, 18 Hours A.L.E.

Michelle's latest mission update to Earth:

"Nearly 16 days have passed since we left Earth. During that time, we have accelerated to a velocity of nearly 7,000 miles per second and have traveled just over 4 billion miles. To put this in perspective, we have traveled a distance slightly greater than Pluto's average distance from the Sun. The first spacecraft sent to Pluto required eight years to make the journey. We have traveled an equivalent distance in less than 16 days. As fantastic as our speed is, it is only about five percent of the velocity that we will reach in about eight and one half months.

From this great distance, Earth is no longer visible without a telescope. Although the Sun is still the most brilliant object visible from our observation deck, it is no longer dangerous to view without eye protection. It casts only about as much light into our observation deck as the full Moon did when we were in low Earth orbit.

Doctor Nemard has completed medical exams of all personnel, and everyone is in perfectly good health. Life onboard this starship has settled into a basic routine of work, continued training, and leisure time. Even though it is more than six years in the future, everyone is excited about building a new home on Alcent and is working hard at acquiring additional knowledge and skills to increase our probability of success when we arrive there.

All of the Challenger's systems are functioning smoothly, which makes our daily life quite easy and relaxing. For this, we express our sincere gratitude to the project scientists, engineers, and technicians for the excellent job they did in the design, construction, and testing of this starship."

TIME: 22 Days A.L.E.

Michelle's latest mission update to Earth:

"After 22 days, we have reached a speed of 10,085 miles per second and have traveled just over 8.6 billion miles. Less than an hour ago, we traveled through a region in space called Heliopause. It is a mild shock wave in which the solar wind interacts with the interstellar medium producing low-frequency radio emissions. Heliopause marks the boundary between the solar system and interstellar space. When we passed through it, we gained the distinction of becoming the first humans to enter interstellar space.

Going back in time to late summer, 1976, Voyagers 1 and 2 were launched from Cape Canaveral on a mission to explore the giant outer planets. In 2010, long after completing their basic missions and traveling in different directions, both spacecraft passed through Heliopause into interstellar space. A journey that required 34 years for the Voyagers has been accomplished by our starship in just 22 days."

TIME: 85 Days A.L.E.

Michelle's latest mission update to Earth:

"With the continuous, flawless performance of our antimatter propulsion system, we continue to gain speed at a steady acceleration of 1g. Our current velocity is 43,273 miles per second. This is approximately 23% of the speed of light. We have achieved 30% of our planned cruise velocity. Since leaving Earth, we have traveled a distance of 153.8 billion miles. We are now so far away that this message will not reach you until 9-1/2 days after I've transmitted it.

At this distance the Sun appears only as an exceptionally bright star in a cosmic background filled with magnificent beauty. Earlier today, on our observation deck, surrounded by a panoramic view of the universe, we carried out our first wedding ceremony. Captain Jerontis and Doctor Nemard were joined in holy matrimony. John Moosebeck and Dianne Dawson served as best man and bridesmaid. I was asked to conduct the ceremony, and I did so with great pleasure. This solemn occasion spawned a celebration filled with festivities that has emotionally charged everyone with joy and happiness. The party is still going on and will probably last for several more hours."

TIME: 112 Days, 61 Hours A.L.E.

Michelle's latest mission update to Earth:

"We are currently 272 billion miles from Earth traveling at a speed of 57,497 miles per second, 30.9% of light speed. Our antimatter engines were shut down about six hours ago, shortly after we collided with a small meteor. Because of our high speed, the meteor instantaneously vaporized upon impact with the shield mounted in front of our starship. This explosive release of energy blasted a large hole through several layers of our impact shield. Fortunately, the explosive impact energy was absorbed and dissipated by the multiple layers of the impact shield, so that our starship's hull was not damaged. The shield is currently being inspected and repaired. We expect to resume acceleration in just a few hours.

Because of our tremendous speed, collisions with objects as small as a particle of space dust cause the explosive release of a large amount of energy. Some parts of the Milky Way Galaxy are so filled with space dust that a journey similar to the one we are undertaking would be extremely hazardous, if not impossible. The part of the Milky Way that we inhabit, however, is relatively free of dust. This is the result of a colossal supernova explosion of a dying star located less than 200 light-years away in the constellation Orion approximately 300,000 years ago. The enormous shock wave created by this gigantic explosion swept through interstellar space like a galactic snowplow carrying with it nearly all the gas and dust particles that it encountered. In effect, a relatively gas-free, dust-free bubble was created in our part of the galaxy. This bubble is commonly referred to by astronomers as the Local Bubble. The Local Bubble is shaped much like a wind sock and measures some 600 light-years across. This bubble will continue to expand for the next 600,000 years or so before all the energy contained in the shock wave has been dissipated. Then, it will begin its collapse. The Solar System, the Alpha Centauri System, and a few thousand other nearby stars are contained within the Local Bubble.

All that remains of the star that died in the supernova that created the Local Bubble is a pulsar named Geminga. It is the burned out core of the dead star. Even though it is less than ten miles in diameter, its mass is comparable to that of the Sun. Composed entirely of neutrons, it is so dense that a single cubic inch of it has a mass of several thousand tons.

To our hominid ancestors of 300,000 years ago, the supernova looked far brighter than the full moon. Had it appeared in the nighttime sky, Earth's landscape would have been brightly illuminated, and for a few days, it would have seemed as though Earth had two suns.

I am astounded by the fact that our journey is relatively safe because of an event that occurred roughly 300,000 years ago. Relative to a human life span, this is a long time. But on a cosmic time scale, 300,000 years isn't much."

TIME: 185 Days A.L.E.
Michelle's latest mission update to Earth:
"We are currently traveling at a velocity of 95,756 miles per second, approximately 51.5% of light speed. We are continuing to gain speed at a steady acceleration of 1g. At present, we are about 754 billion miles from Earth.

Captain Jerontis and his wife, Doctor Nemard, joyfully announced today that they are expecting to give birth to a baby girl in about seven months. Mike and I are delighted by this news. We are expecting the birth of our son in four weeks and are happy that there will be another child onboard for him to grow up with.

Jerry and Connie made history two months ago when they became the first couple to conceive a baby onboard a starship. Our speed at that time was roughly 64,000 miles per second. So theirs would most definitely qualify as a high speed conception. Clearly a stellar performance by any stretch of the imagination.

There probably will not be any other children born until after we arrive at Alcent. However, Captain Jerontis has directed Dianne Dawson and our engineering staff to investigate ways to increase the capability of our life support system. The objective is to determine the maximum capability that our life support system can be expanded to. If other couples decide to be married, they will need to know if they can have children before our arrival at Alcent.

Because of our great distance from Earth, it will take 46.9 days for this transmission to reach you. By then, my son will have been born and will be several days old."

TIME: 220 Days A.L.E.

Michelle's latest mission update to Earth:

"We are now just over one trillion miles from Earth and moving at a speed of 114,194 miles per second, approximately 61.4% of light speed. We are pleased that our antimatter propulsion system is continuing its flawless performance.

Mike and I are the proud, happy parents of a healthy, baby boy who was born three days ago. He has light brown hair and light brown eyes. His weight at birth was nine pounds, five ounces. We've decided to name him Matthew in honor of my favorite Gospel writer. By the time you receive this broadcast, Matthew will be 70 days old."

TIME: 261 Days A.L.E.

Michelle's latest mission update to Earth:

"We have achieved a major milestone in our voyage to Alcent. We have just reached our cruise velocity. A few moments ago, our antimatter propulsion system was shutdown. We are currently 1.51 trillion miles from Earth and are moving at a speed of 135,793 miles per second, approximately 73% of light speed.

To have a greater fuel reserve, the decision was made to coast at a velocity of 73% of light speed instead of 77% as originally planned. This will increase the length of our journey from 6.40 years to 6.67 years, about 98 days. We believe that the increased travel time is a reasonable price to pay for the added safety and flexibility provided by a larger fuel reserve.

Because of the nearly perfect vacuum that exists in interstellar space, we will experience very little loss of velocity even though our propulsion system has been shut down. The only force that will slow us down is the pull of the Sun's gravity. However, because of our great distance from the Sun, its gravitational pull is very feeble.

We are currently in a weightless condition because we are no longer accelerating at 1g. Since it would be unhealthy for us to be in a weightless state for the next several years, we will use centrifugal force to create artificial gravity. To achieve this, we will detach stage one of our propulsion system, and move a short distance away from it. Then, we will make a 180-degree turn, so that the front end of our starship faces the top end of the propulsion stage. Next, we will connect the starship to the propulsion stage with a tether that is ten miles long. After slowly backing away from the propulsion stage until the tether is tight, we will spin up this configuration to the appropriate rotational speed to give us an artificial gravity of about 1g.

There are two reasons for using such a long tether: First, our starship has several decks, and the use of a long tether will reduce the variation in artificial gravity between the top deck and the bottom deck. Second, the use of a very long tether allows us to achieve an artificial gravity of 1g with a much lower rotation rate than would be required with a short tether.

After coasting through interstellar space for about 5 years and three months, we will dock with the first stage of our propulsion system, and begin 1g deceleration. It will take nearly nine months to lose the immense speed that we have gained since leaving Earth. If we are unable to cancel out the tremendous speed that we are traveling at, we will be unable to orbit Alcent. Then, we would be forced to live the rest of our lives onboard this starship. This could happen if we accidentally lose part of our fuel during the next five to six years, or if after our long coast period, our antimatter propulsion system fails to operate at peak efficiency. The serious consequences of these possibilities led to the decision to increase our fuel reserves by traveling at a lower cruising speed.

If we do not experience any significant problems during the remainder of our voyage, we will arrive at Alcent with a substantial amount of fuel. This will give us additional flexibility. For example, the interstellar probe, Star Voyager, detected planets around Alpha Centauri B, but was unable to ascertain detailed information about them because its course was optimized for the study of Alpha Centauri A. A large fuel reserve will allow us to study these planets to determine if one of them would be a more suitable place than Alcent for us to establish a home.

Because of our great distance, 94 days will have elapsed by the time you receive this transmission."

TIME: 365 Days A.L.E.
Michelle's latest mission update to Earth:

"We are currently 2.73 trillion miles from Earth traveling at 73% of light speed. Today, we are celebrating the second marriage on our starship. About three hours ago, Dianne Dawson and John Moosebeck exchanged vows in a joyful, wedding ceremony. Also, today marks our one year anniversary of leaving Earth. We are very thankful for the safe journey that we have had so far. These two events have created a festive, holiday atmosphere onboard our starship. Everyone seems determined to fill this day, and probably tomorrow, with recreational activities. Because of our great distance, 170 days will be required for this brief message to reach you."

TIME: 1 Year, 27 Days A.L.E.
Michelle's latest mission update to Earth:

"We are currently 3.05 trillion miles from Earth traveling at 73% of light speed. Nearly 190 days will have passed by the time you receive this broadcast. All starship systems continue to function in a problem free manner.

Today is another joyful occasion for our society. Just a few hours ago, Captain Jerontis and Doctor Nemard became the proud parents of a lovely baby girl. Her name is Denise. She has light blond hair, blue eyes, and weighs eight pounds, seven ounces. She is the first baby to be conceived and born on a starship in interstellar space.

My son is almost six months old now and is a happy, healthy, playful child. He is a popular child and loves all the attention that he is getting from everyone. We never have any difficulty finding a baby sitter when we need one."

TIME: 1 Year, 217 Days A.L.E.
Michelle's latest mission update to Earth:

"We are currently 5.28 trillion miles from Earth traveling at 73% of light speed. It will take 328 days for this transmission to arrive at Earth.

We continue to have a smooth, trouble-free flight. For this, we are grateful to those who designed, built, and tested this ship. Their pursuit of excellence has made this ship and all of its systems so reliable that only a minimal amount of maintenance is required. This allows ample opportunity for our personnel to pursue advanced education and training to acquire additional skills to meet the challenges we will face on Alcent.

Today, Mike and I put on a birthday party for Matthew. He is one year old. The light brown hair he was born with has gradually changed to a darker brown, and his light brown eyes have slowly become hazel. He has developed an almost insatiable curiosity making it necessary to watch him constantly, because he has learned to walk and loves to explore.

Denise is now six months old. Her beautiful blue eyes, golden blond hair, and facial features make her a living image of her mother. Denise is a happy, content child who thoroughly enjoys all the attention she constantly receives from everyone.

Despite being on a starship moving through interstellar space at great speed and living with artificial gravity, both children are developing normally and are in excellent health."

TIME: 2 Years, 27 Days A.L.E.
Michelle's latest mission update to Earth:

"I am beginning to develop a deep appreciation for the truly immense size of the universe. We have now been in space more than two years, and for well over a year we have been traveling at a speed of nearly 135,800 miles per second. We are now approximately seven trillion miles from Earth, a distance so great that this message traveling at the speed of light will require 436 days to reach you. Yet, after all of this time and speed, we have covered only 27.5% of the distance to the Alpha Centauri System, the Sun's nearest interstellar neighbors. Imagine how much time would be required to travel to the more distant stars in the Milky Way Galaxy. Then consider the fact that the universe contains hundreds of millions of galaxies, many of which are much larger than the Milky Way, and you will begin to appreciate the enormous extent of the cosmos and what an insignificant part of it we humans are. But someday in the far distant future, perhaps a few million years from now, there may be human civilizations thriving throughout the Milky Way. Our voyage to Alcent is the first tiny step in accomplishing this.

Life onboard the Challenger is comfortable. We have adequate space, privacy when we want it, and all basic essentials. But we are confined. Imagine living in a hotel where different functions are done on different floors. Then, imagine that within this hotel you have everything that you need for a comfortable life. Next, tell yourself that you cannot leave this hotel for seven years. That is what our life is like. We are comfortable, but we are confined, and will be for several more years.

Denise is one year old today, and there was a birthday party for her. She is a very pretty little girl and continues to enjoy all the attention she is getting from everyone. She has learned to walk, and like my son, enjoys exploring her surroundings. Both children display an inquisitive alertness to the activities that go on around them. Also, even at this early age, they are very much aware of each other and enjoy playing together."

TIME: 3 Years, 124 Days, 7.2 Hours A.L.E.
Michelle's latest mission update to Earth:

"We are now 12.75 trillion miles from Earth moving at a velocity of 73% of light speed. Today is an important event in our lives because we are halfway to the Alpha Centauri System. From this day forward, we will be closer to our new home on Alcent than the homes we left on Earth. We have decided to make today a special day of thanksgiving, much like the Thanksgiving holiday that is celebrated in the United States every year. We are thankful that the first half of our voyage has been safe, and that we are all in good health. We are grateful that Matthew and Denise are developing normally in this interstellar environment. In fact, they seem quite advanced for their ages. They've learned how to talk and are rapidly learning new words because of constant attention and tutoring from everyone."

TIME: 4 Years, 233 Days A.L.E.
Michelle's latest mission update to Earth:

"Today, we are 18.3 trillion miles from Earth and 7.2 trillion miles from our destination. We continue to travel at 73% of light speed. This transmission will require 3 years and 44 days to reach you. By the time you receive it, we hope to be on Alcent.

Just a few hours ago, our voyage nearly came to a tragic end when we passed through a cloud of interstellar asteroids. Because of the large size of the cloud and our great speed, there wasn't enough time to maneuver around the cloud, so we had to go through it. The asteroids, composed mostly of rock and some ice, ranged in size from a few feet across to as much as a few hundred yards. Because of our high velocity, a collision with even the smallest of these objects could easily have destroyed us. We estimate that there were several thousand of these small rocky bodies. Fortunately, they were spread out over a large volume of space so that our defensive systems were not overwhelmed and were able to destroy those that we would otherwise have collided with.

This ship is equipped with radar systems that are so powerful and sensitive that they are able to detect objects out to a range of a hundred million miles or more, a distance that we traverse in just over twelve minutes. Data from this equipment is fed into a fire control computer, which tracks all detected objects and determines if we are on a collision course with any of them. If we are, the computer aims and fires our antimatter particle beam gun at the threatening object. When the high-density beam of charged antimatter particles hits the ordinary matter in the targeted object, a powerful sustained explosive reaction occurs which either annihilates the target, or in the case of a large object, changes it's course so that we do not collide with it.

In all the trillions of miles that we've traveled to date, today was the only time that our particle beam gun was used. But if we didn't have this defensive equipment, we would no longer exist. The three asteroids that we destroyed were each about the size of a compact car. Colliding with any of them would most certainly have destroyed us. We owe our lives to those who insisted that defensive equipment be installed on this starship.

Because of our great speed, only about a half hour transpired from the time that we detected the asteroid cloud to the time that we passed through it. Needless to say, this was the most nerve-racking half hour in my life. Not knowing from one second to the next whether my life was about to end left me physically and emotionally drained. Every time the computer fired the antimatter particle beam gun, my mind was filled with anxiety for a few suspenseful moments while I wondered if it would be successful in destroying or deflecting its target. Making the whole experience even more hair-raising for me was the fact that I could not see any of the asteroids. We were just moving by them too fast. When whizzing by an object at a velocity of 135,800 miles per second, the human eye simply isn't able to see it. Our lives were totally dependent on the extremely quick reaction capability of our defensive equipment. Its flawless performance saved us from certain destruction. Once again, we applaud the excellence achieved by those who designed, built, and tested this starship."

TIME: 5 Years, 352 Days A.L.E.
Michelle's latest mission update to Earth:

"Right now, we are 23.99 trillion miles from Earth and 1.52 trillion miles from Alcent. This message will require 4 years and 33 days to reach you. By the time you receive it, it will almost be ancient history.

Today marks the achievement of another milestone in our journey to Alcent. Our long coast period at 73% of light speed is finally over. It has been a seemingly endless time period of more than five years that we have been traveling at this enormous speed. Although it has been and still is a comfortable home, almost everyone is tired of living on the Challenger. We thirst for the wide open spaces that you have on a planet as opposed to being confined in a starship.

Two exceptions are Matthew and Denise. They have never known any other home. Both are happy children who enthusiastically enjoy ordinary everyday life onboard this starship. But they are still very young and possessed with boundless curiosity. Each day brings a new discovery, new knowledge to be absorbed. Won't they be surprised by the huge new world that will greet them when we land on Alcent. The only concept they have of what it is like to live on a planet is derived from watching movies that were filmed on Earth.

During our long coast period, we added some degree of normality to our lives by providing ourselves with artificial gravity about the same as on Earth. This was accomplished with centrifugal force. The Challenger was secured to its first stage with a long tether, and this configuration was accelerated to the appropriate rotational velocity to provide 1g of artificial gravity. I believe that I would have found this long voyage unbearable if I'd had to float around in a weightless condition for more than five years.

A short time ago, we reduced our rotational velocity to zero and released the long tether that connected us to the first stage of our propulsion system. Then we carried out a sequence of maneuvers that has resulted in successful docking with the stage. Its antimatter engines have been ignited, and we are now losing velocity at a steady rate of 1g giving us an artificial gravity equal to that on Earth's surface. Almost nine months of deceleration will be required to reduce our present velocity of nearly 135,800 miles per second down to approximately five miles per second, which will be our orbital velocity around Alcent."

TIME: 6 Years, 1 Day, 3 Hours A.L.E.
Michelle's latest mission update to Earth:

"We are currently 24.15 trillion miles from Earth and 1.36 trillion miles from Alcent. The past two weeks of deceleration has reduced our velocity to 128,350 miles per second, approximately 69% of light speed.

Early in our voyage, the decision was made to cruise at 73% of light speed rather than the originally planned 77% of light speed. This left a fuel residual in the first stage, which has now been expended. We have separated from stage one and have resumed deceleration with propulsion stage number two. Its antimatter engines are performing normally. Stage one has been discarded and will continue to move through interstellar space at 69% of light speed until it collides with something and is destroyed."

TIME: 6 Years, 63 Days A.L.E.

Michelle's latest mission update to Earth:

"We are currently 24.75 trillion miles from Earth and 760 billion miles from Alcent. Our present velocity is 95,757 miles per second, approximately 51.5% of light speed. We continue to decelerate at 1g.

At the moment, we are 941 billion miles from Alpha Centauri C, the smallest and coolest of the three stars that make up the Alpha Centauri System. This is as close as we will get to Alpha Centauri C. Early in the mission, it was decided to not make any attempt to explore this star. Since it is a red dwarf of spectral type M5, Alpha Centauri C is too dim and cool to provide the amount of light and heat needed to support life on any planet that it might possess. Also, like many red dwarfs, it is a flare star. Occasionally it has explosive outbursts that double and sometimes even triple its energy output. Any planet close enough to the star to have life during normal times would certainly be torched to death by these explosive outbursts. Definitely not a place where we would be interested in trying to build a home.

In contrast to Alpha Centauri C, the Sun is bright, hot, and stable in its energy output making life on Earth not only possible, but comfortable. Alpha Centauri A is like the Sun in many respects. Both are bright yellow main sequence stars of spectral type G2. Only about 4% of the stars in the Milky Way are spectral type G, whereas about 70% are red dwarfs. The Sun and Alpha Centauri A are not average stars; they are members of a small special group where all the conditions are right to support planets filled with an abundance of life."

TIME: 6 Years, 217 Days A.L.E.

Michelle's latest mission update to Earth:

"We are currently 25.493 trillion miles from Earth and 17.551 billion miles from Alcent. Our present velocity is 14,630 miles per second, approximately 8.15% of light speed. We continue to decelerate at 1g.

Today is a special occasion for Matthew. It is his sixth birthday. Mike and I put on a birthday party for him, which almost everyone attended. Although everyone had a good time, Matthew and Denise were the center of attention and had the most fun. Hopefully, Matthew's next birthday party will be on Alcent.

Even though we are tired of living on this starship and would like to arrive at Alcent as soon as possible, we have decided to swing by Alpha Centauri B. One of its planets is in the star's life zone. We plan to do a brief orbital exploration of this planet to find out if it is capable of supporting life, if it has any life on it, and if it would be a more suitable home for us than Alcent. We have adequate fuel reserves, and this detour will delay our arrival at Alpha Centauri A and Alcent by only a few weeks.

Alpha Centauri B is an orange star of spectral type K2. Its mass is about nine-tenths that of the Sun, and its surface temperature is about 8.6% cooler than on the Sun. Although the star's light and heat output are not high enough to be ideal for life, they are intense enough to support life if the right kind of planet is located at the optimum distance from the star. The planet we are going to investigate seems to satisfy these conditions, but we won't know for sure until we get much closer.

Orange, spectral type K stars make up about 15% of the stars in the Milky Way. Only the largest, hottest, brightest stars in this group are capable of having planets with an abundance of life on them. Alpha Centauri B satisfies these requirements."

FOUR

Rescuing a Planet

TIME: 6 Years, 245 Days A.L.E.

Michelle's latest mission update to Earth:

"We have just completed our first orbit of Alpha Centauri B's second planet. To facilitate planetary exploration, we have maneuvered the Challenger into a circular polar orbit at an altitude of 230 miles. In this orbit, we will circle the planet once every 90 minutes. As the planet rotates on its axis, our instruments will have observed every part of it under both daytime and nighttime conditions by the time the planet completes one revolution (23 hours, 37 minutes). For lack of a name, the planet has been designated A.C.B.#2, or simply, B-2.

After being in interstellar space for more than six years, a planet that displays all the clues indicative of the presence of life has created a festive mood of eager anticipation of the future among the Challenger's personnel. The near-term possibility of living on a planet and no longer being confined to a starship has become very real. Nearly all off-duty personnel are on the observation deck gazing down on B-2, which seems to be an earth-like planet. With the Challenger currently approaching B-2's equator from the north, the observers see a vast ocean that extends to the north and south polar icecaps and to the eastern horizon. The ocean is dotted with numerous islands, some of which are quite large. To the west, two major land masses are visible that extend nearly to the western horizon. One of the continents is located north of the equator, and the other is located south of the equator. The continents are connected by a substantial land bridge that is estimated to be 50 to 60 miles wide at its narrowest point."

While Michelle did her mission update, Dianne was on the observation deck studying B-2. Fascinated by what she has seen, Dianne allowed her mind to become captivated by the panoramic view of a planet that resembled Earth in many important ways. The planet looked so appealing to her that she wondered if it might be a better place to live than Alcent with its multitude of dinosaurs. It just seemed so peaceful and inviting. Was this planet filled with an abundance of life or was it barren? As she pondered the question, a strange feeling gradually pervaded her senses that not only did life exist on this planet, but that it also included intelligent life. The sensation was so strong that Dianne became convinced that it was caused by something other than her imagination.

This unique sensation troubled Dianne and raised a few questions: What kind of life could it possibly be so that she could sense its presence from a distance of at least 230 miles? Did these life forms have brains that generated such strong energy fields that she could sense them at such a great distance? Were these life forms doing something to make their presence known? If so, why? Would these life forms prove to be congenial or hostile? So deeply lost in thought was Dianne that she failed to notice Moose sneak up behind her.

Moose silently gazed over her shoulder for a few moments. Then, he startled her out of her mesmerized mental state asking loudly, "Well, what do you think of it?"

Dianne flinched at the unexpected disruption of her thoughts, then turned toward Moose and said, "You sure like to sneak up and scare me. You just never seem to miss an opportunity."

"What do you mean? All I did was ask you a question," declared Moose, innocently.

"It wasn't the question that startled me. It was the way you crept up behind me."

"I did that out of love for you," stated Moose with utmost sincerity.

"Seems like a strange way to express love," retorted Dianne. "Would my dear sweet husband mind giving me an explanation?"

"Simple! It's all part of your training."

"Training?"

"Alcent will be a dangerous place, and you need to develop a greater awareness of your immediate surroundings."

"I am continually amazed at the way your mind always seems to find a way to justify the things that you do to satisfy your overactive sense of humor. Implying that I need to keep my guard up here on the observation deck, a place that I've always found to be perfectly safe."

"It almost sounds like my lovely wife no longer appreciates my fun-loving nature."

"On the contrary, your lighthearted attitude is one of the reasons I fell in love with you. It is one of the reasons I enjoy being married to you, but maybe you could avoid making me the object of your practical jokes for a while."

"I think I can comply with that request," replied Moose, giving her a kiss.

Dianne gave Moose a big hug and said, "I'm glad you're here, because I want to share my feelings with you. This planet reminds me of Earth in so many ways that it really intrigues me. It excites me to the point that it has my imagination running wild."

"So, what has your wildly excited imagination come up with?"

"I have a very strong feeling that there is intelligent life down there. Wouldn't that be exciting? Think about it: We've just completed a seemingly endless voyage through the lifeless void of interstellar space, and now, we are face to face with a planet that might have intelligent life on it. I can't help being wildly excited about that. I'd like to go down there and explore the place."

"That's an adventure I'd like to go on too, but what makes you so convinced that there's intelligent life down there?"

"Call it intuition if you want, but I can just sense that this planet is inhabited by intelligent life. I know it sounds weird, but I sense its presence. Also, the basic essentials for life as we know it are there; namely, an earth-like atmosphere, an earth-like climate, and an abundance of water."

"But how can you sense the presence of life that is 230 miles below us?"

"I don't know, but we are orbiting an alien planet. Life could have evolved into forms that have mental powers that are much different than ours."

"Are you suggesting that there might be intelligent life down there that is trying to communicate with you telepathically? If that's the case, they know that we're here."

"I wish I could answer your question, but I simply don't know. All I can say with certainty is that I strongly feel the presence of life. Anyway, the data that we accumulate and analyze during the coming hours and days should give us some answers to the life-question."

Moose was silent for a few moments while he thought about the possibilities and their implications; then, he nodded in agreement.

While gazing down on the planet, Dianne pointed out the two large continents and said, "They remind me of North and South America."

After looking at them in silence for a few moments, Moose said, "I see what you mean. They're even connected by a land bridge, and the deep green color of the land bridge sure looks like dense vegetation. It's possible that we're looking at a tropical rain forest."

"It appears that way to me too. One essential ingredient for a rain forest is lots of rain, and that heavy cloud cover lying just offshore to the west looks like it could deliver exactly that. As soon as we look at the high resolution images and other data that our instruments are gathering, we should be able to determine if there really is a thick rain forest there."

Directing Dianne's attention to another area, Moose said, "Speaking of weather, have you noticed that large storm system approaching the southern shore of the northern continent? Doesn't it have the ominous appearance of a hurricane?"

"It sure does."

"If this planet is as filled with life as you think it is, that storm is going to do some severe damage to it if it moves inland."

"We should track it and see what kind of damage it does. How plant and animal life responds to severe weather can give us an indication as to how hardy they are."

"I've never felt hardy enough to want to face a storm as powerful as that one looks," said Moose.

"I wouldn't want to either. Violent storms are usually very destructive to plant and animal life, but how quickly they recover does give us an indication as to how resilient they are."

"That may be true, but fortunately for the life down there, most areas that we're looking at seem to be experiencing fair weather, either completely clear air or air that contains scattered clouds."

A few minutes later, while passing over the south polar icecap, the Challenger entered B-2's nighttime hemisphere. However, with Alpha Centauri A currently the dominant star in B-2's nighttime sky, nighttime on B-2 just wasn't very dark. At its present distance of 2.45 billion miles, Alpha Centauri A flooded B-2 with far more light than a full moon in Earth's nighttime sky.

Observing this phenomenon, Dianne commented, "Having a second star so close that nighttime isn't really dark seems kind of strange, almost eerie. The amount of light down there appears to be comparable to what you have on Earth a few minutes after sunset. Imagine having the brightness of twilight all night long."

"Whether we live on this planet or on Alcent, we will be faced with that situation. Part of the year, the more distant of the two stars will be in the nighttime sky, and it just won't get very dark. But when we get use to that, it will probably seem normal, and we won't give it much thought."

A few minutes later, Moose said, "It looks like this hemisphere has only one continent, and it is fairly close to being centered on the equator. It appears to be a couple thousand miles short of reaching either polar icecap."

After a few minutes of silent observation and reflective thought, Dianne exclaimed, "Wow! Look over there! Judging from the size and frequency of those lightning bolts, this planet has thunder storms just as large and awe-inspiring as any back on Earth."

"That's a large system," commented Moose. "I would estimate that line of thunder storms to be close to a thousand miles long."

Preoccupied with their thoughts, Moose and Dianne silently observed the powerful lightning bolts light up the clouds far below them. Dianne wondered if life existed on this continent; and if present, how was it being affected by the awesome forces of nature being unleashed by this storm system. As she pondered the life-question, a dreadful feeling of cold fear flooded her senses. The strength and nature of the feeling alarmed Dianne so much that she shook from head to toe as an involuntary tremor passed through her body. She immediately grabbed Moose with a sense of urgency and cried out, "Moose! It's happening again, and I feel like it wants to torture me."

"What's happening again?"

"I sense the presence of life down there!"

"Are you positive?"

"Definitely!"

"Why do you think it wants to subject you to pain and suffering?"

"I don't know why. I don't even know if it has the means to harm me, but it evidently has some capability to communicate telepathically. For some reason, it used that ability to hit me with a wave of cold-hearted hatred so intense that it felt like a vicious attack."

"I wonder why it did that. Since this is its first encounter with humans, it can't possibly know much about us, so why would it hate us? I am especially puzzled that it would express hatred toward you."

"Why is that?"

"Because you have a warm personality and no desire whatever to plunder alien life."

"Maybe, that's the problem."

"What do you mean?"

"Maybe, this creature lives according to a philosophy that is based on cold-hearted hatred and consequently, finds my kindhearted personality repugnant."

"If that's the case, it isn't going to like any of us because we're all kindhearted. So, how much danger do you think we're in?"

"I don't know. We know nothing about this creature except that it's down there and has some sort of telepathic ability. We don't even know if I'm being targeted by a lone individual or by a large group. It's possible that I am being tormented by a hateful individual with a twisted mind who is a member of an otherwise benevolent society. It would seem like that would put us at less risk than facing an entire society that is evil. But whatever the case may be, we don't know what they're capable of doing with their telepathic powers."

Moose thought about the situation for a few moments; then, he said, "We've never had to deal with a species possessing a telepathic ability. What if they are able to use it against us?"

"In what way?"

"What if they have a very advanced telepathic ability, so advanced that they're able to get into our minds and read our thoughts and memories? Then, our knowledge would become their knowledge."

"I think that's very unlikely. To start with, this is their first contact with humans. They cannot possibly understand our language, and if they can't understand the language that our thoughts and memories are in, I don't see how they could pick our brains."

"I hope you're right," said Moose. "When we passed over the other two continents and you first became aware of the presence of life, did you sense any danger?"

"No, I didn't. To the contrary, it was more of a feeling of an awareness of our presence. I felt like we were simply being investigated. Perhaps, it was an effort to find out if we posed any kind of threat."

"Suppose it reached the conclusion that we do pose a threat to its well-being. What would it's response be?"

"Again, that question is almost impossible to answer. We don't know what kind of life we're dealing with; let alone, what its capabilities are."

"The only thing that we seem to be reasonably certain of is that we are dealing with a life-form that possesses telepathic capabilities to some degree. In addition, it seems safe to assume that it is probably intelligent," said Moose.

"Until we get more information, that's about all we can say."

"For the sake of discussion, let me speculate a bit," offered Moose. "To me, it seems likely that the life-form that contacted your mind in a non-threatening way may be of the same species as the one that projected hatred and a sense of evil to you. It may be that they differ only in religious philosophy. On the first two continents we passed over, the species may be living in accordance with a religious philosophy that promotes love, trust, benevolence, and tolerance. On the continent below us, the species may be living in accordance with a religious philosophy that advocates hatred, distrust, and intolerance of all who disagree with its teachings. They may even be carrying it to the extreme of tormenting or even killing those who don't accept their philosophy."

"What you're saying is that even though we mean them no harm, they may want to destroy us anyway, just because our philosophy is different from theirs."

"That's exactly what I am saying. However, wanting to destroy us and being able to destroy us are two different things. We could be in a great deal of danger or in no danger at all."

Dianne started to look worried, "If there really are beings down there with an advanced telepathic ability, we could be in grave danger. Suppose they are so advanced in its use that they can telepathically enter our minds and implant suggestions or even take control. At the very least, we could see some strange behavior on this ship. In a worst case scenario, they could cause one of our people to do something that could destroy us."

"Like you said earlier, they have never been exposed to our language, and not understanding our language should greatly limit what they can do."

"What if they find a way around the language barrier?"

"That is a scary possibility," responded Moose. "You've just suggested how a race of intelligent beings possessing advanced telepathic ability could seriously harm us, or even destroy us, without the use of high-tech weapons. But if they have high-tech weapons and use them in conjunction with their telepathic ability, we could find ourselves in an extremely serious situation. I think we should talk to Captain Jerontis about this."

A short time later, Moose and Dianne found Captain Jerontis and Doctor Nemard on the flight deck where they were busy viewing computer enhanced, high-resolution, three-dimensional images of small sections of the planet's surface. The sharply detailed images displayed on the large video screen gave the false impression of being very close to the planet's surface. The computer was programmed to display the image of a large area measuring as much as several thousand miles across. From this image, the viewer could select a point of interest, and by simply circling it with a small indicator beam, the computer would then expand the elected area to the size of the screen. Then, a small area of interest could be selected from this image and again expanded to the size of the screen. This process could be continued to the limit of the system's resolution capability. From its current orbital altitude of 230 miles, areas directly below the flight path as small as a few yards across could be displayed with details as small as one-fourth to one-half inch discernible.

Without taking the time for any sort of cordial greeting, Moose, in an urgent tone, said, "Captain! Sorry to interrupt you, but we may be in serious danger from the beings living on this planet, and we should take immediate precautions."

Alarmed by the sense of urgency displayed by the normally carefree Moose, both Doctor Nemard and Captain Jerontis quickly turned to face him and Dianne. Captain Jerontis asked, "What beings and what danger are you talking about? Connie and I have been looking at large-area images and high-resolution images of small points of interest for nearly two hours now, and we've seen no evidence of animal life, only lots of lush vegetation."

"Intelligent life that does not want to be seen could certainly conceal itself in a jungle of vegetation," countered Dianne who proceeded to report her experiences and the conclusions that she and Moose had reached. Captain Jerontis and Doctor Nemard listened intently to Dianne's report without interruption.

A few moments of silence ensued while Captain Jerontis and Doctor Nemard thought about what Dianne had just reported. Then, Captain Jerontis commented, "If they don't want to be seen and are attempting to conceal themselves, the question is: who are they trying to hide from? Is there an ongoing war between opposing philosophies that would cause them to camouflage themselves from each other, or did they detect us before we arrived here? If they detected us, they could've decided to hide from us while they attempt to discover our intentions. If that's the case, then in order to have sufficient time to conceal themselves and all evidence of their existence, they would've had to discover us long before we arrived here. But how could they've done that? We haven't detected any radar emissions, and we haven't alerted them to our presence by using our radar. All of our communications transmissions have been beamed toward Earth, directly away from them. In other words, it is unlikely that they could've discovered us by detecting any of our electronic emissions. If they detected us far out in space purely with telepathic ability, then they have an awesome mental power that is far beyond anything we've ever seen."

Doctor Nemard briefly considered Jerry's closing remark. Then, she said, "I find it difficult to imagine that any creature could possess telepathic ability so powerful that it could be effective at distances of hundreds of millions of miles."

While facing Jerry, Moose said, "I think your suggestion of an ongoing war is a plausible explanation for most of what we've experienced so far, especially if it is a worldwide war that has been going on for centuries. If these creatures have any factories and homes, it is possible that they may be underground. Perhaps, they are simply protecting themselves from their enemies and are not hiding from us at all. Furthermore, they might not have discovered us until we entered orbit around this planet; at which point, they could have detected us visually."

"It is possible that they detected us visually," admitted Dianne, "but the feelings that I had were very strong. I believe that these creatures do possess a telepathic ability and that it has an effective range of at least a few hundred miles."

"Until we know otherwise, I think we should assume that you are correct," stated Captain Jerontis. "But whether we were discovered visually or telepathically doesn't matter, the important thing is: they know that we are here. Consequently, we face the ominous possibility that opposing forces in a major war are visually and telepathically investigating us in an attempt to determine if we are a new weapon invented by the other side or an alien military force recruited by the other side. If either side decides that we are, then we could come under attack at any moment by whatever weaponry they possess."

"But we might not be attacked by weapons," commented Dianne. "It is possible that they might use their telepathic ability in an attempt to manipulate one or more of our personnel to destroy us from within."

Responding directly to Dianne, Moose said, "As you pointed out earlier, our language has to be totally alien to them. Because of this language barrier, it seems to me that it would be very difficult for them to telepathically enter our minds and hypnotize or control us in any way."

"The human mind is very complicated," commented Doctor Nemard. "In addition to words and numbers, it contains visual images, some of which are quite vivid. By using telepathic visual images, an alien should be able to find out how our ship is defended. For example, it could project into your mind an image of a large missile on an intercept course with our ship. Your mind might respond by forming an image of our anti-matter particle-beam gun destroying the missile. The alien would then know that for a missile attack to be successful; the particle beam gun would first have to be disabled."

"If they can use telepathically transmitted images to bypass the language barrier, we might be in real trouble," commented Moose.

Looking into Doctor Nemard's eyes with an expression of deep concern, Captain Jerontis said, "What if their telepathic ability is so advanced that they can enter our subconscious minds and explore the images stored in our memories; then, they would be able to obtain a wealth of information about us, perhaps even figure out our language. If they can do this without us being aware of it, our survival might be at risk. How do we defend against it?"

"In normal everyday life, it is the conscious mind that inputs information into the subconscious mind to be remembered for later use. In other words, the normal path to the subconscious mind is through the conscious mind. I think it is very unlikely that an alien being could explore our subconscious minds without us being aware of it, especially, if we are alert to the possibility that this might be tried. A danger period would be when we are asleep and the conscious mind is resting and not on guard."

"We need to alert everyone to the risk we are now facing," stated Captain Jerontis. "Also, I want all personnel to stay awake and mentally on guard until we leave this planet or determine that there is no threat to our security. That means we will have to complete our exploration in less than 24 hours, because it is difficult to stay awake longer than that. During that time, I want to find and identify the species with the telepathic powers. I want to determine if they have the ability to disturb or endanger us when we are living on Alcent. Since Alcent will never be closer than about a billion miles to this planet, I don't think it's very likely that they will be able to bother us. But I don't want to take that for granted. We will face enough dangers on Alcent without having to be concerned about telepathic attack from creatures on this planet."

Next, Captain Jerontis sounded three notes on the ship's warning klaxon to get everyone's attention. Since most of them were already there anyway, he directed them to assemble on the observation deck for an urgent meeting. Then, he asked Dianne and Doctor Nemard to conduct the meeting to alert everyone to the current danger and to find out if anyone had been contacted telepathically. In addition, he asked Dianne and Doctor Nemard to immediately report the names of any personnel not present at the meeting. These individuals would have to be located immediately and investigated to make sure they weren't under alien control.

As they were leaving, Connie said, "I will ask Michelle to keep the children mentally occupied, because they might be easy targets for mind tampering."

"Good idea, and could you send Mike up here when you are finished with your meeting?"

"Sure can."

Turning to Moose, Captain Jerontis said, "I would like you to stay here and help me find these creatures. Since we don't know the full extent of their telepathic powers, I believe that it's imperative that we find them before anyone needs sleep. That doesn't give us very much time, so we need to do this methodically. The question is, where is the best place to start looking?"

"That's a tough question, when you consider that we know virtually nothing about them except that they may have mental powers with enough range to harm us at this altitude. We don't even know if all of them have this ability, or if it's limited to a few special individuals. For that matter, they might even be using some specialized high-tech equipment to accomplish telepathic communication."

"That's a possibility, but if they are a high-tech society, we should be able to detect electronic transmissions. Since our arrival here, we've been conducting extensive electronic eavesdropping, and we've detected nothing. Therefore, either they are in a total electronic blackout, which would seem almost impossible to accomplish, or they are a primitive civilization and have not yet discovered electricity."

Looking at the dense jungle displayed on the large video screen, Moose said, "However advanced or primitive they are, they're going to be difficult to find under that."

"We might be able to find evidence of their location with our radar, such as buildings concealed by vegetation. Since they already know that we're here, there's no longer any reason for us to maintain electronic silence, so why don't you put our radar to work and see what you can find."

"Perhaps land areas bordering rivers, lakes, and oceans would be the best place to look. On Earth, even ancient civilizations tended to build their villages and cities near water for various practical reasons. Unless these creatures are primitive nomadic savages who just happen to have telepathic powers, we should find villages or encampments of some sort near water," Moose said.

"That sounds reasonable. While you're doing the radar search, I'll study high-resolution images of whatever rivers we happen to be passing over. Even primitive creatures might have canoes for fishing and transportation. And if we're dealing with a somewhat more advanced society, maybe I'll find a bridge or two."

A few minutes later, Captain Jerontis received a call from his wife who reported the names of three individuals not present at the meeting. Captain Jerontis noted that all three were currently on duty and asked Connie to contact them after the meeting.

About an hour later, with the Challenger beginning its fourth orbit of B-2, an obviously excited Mike Johnson arrived on the flight deck and reported to Captain Jerontis: "Dianne's opening statement at that meeting sure got everyone's attention, including mine. What happened these past few hours is truly a milestone in human history: the first contact with an apparently intelligent alien life-form has occurred. Dianne's experience wasn't unique either. Three other people recounted experiences similar to hers. Doctor Nemard and Dianne are currently meeting with them trying to find some reason why only four of us have been contacted. In particular, what do the four contacted individuals have in common? They'll report to you as soon as they can."

"Thanks for the update," replied Captain Jerontis, who then explained to Mike what he and Moose were doing.

"Have you found any physical evidence to confirm the existence of these creatures?" Mike asked.

"So far, we haven't found any indication of any animal life, just lots of lush vegetation."

"A crazy idea just entered my mind," stated Mike. "Is it possible that this planet's plant life has evolved some type of collective intelligence?"

"To me, that doesn't seem very likely, but I will ask Dianne. Maybe, she can concoct some wild genetic scheme of events that would allow plant life to develop intelligence. In the meantime, I want you to review the infrared data that we are recording about this planet. Search for something that can only be explained by the presence of intelligent creatures. Even though we haven't found any animal life, I believe that it is there, and that it is simply hidden from view by the dense vegetation that is just about everywhere."

For the sake of easier communication, Captain Jerontis decided to give B-2's three continents descriptive names. The two continents connected by a land bridge that reminded one of North and South America would be referred to as the Northern Continent and the Southern Continent. The continent that was approximately centered on the equator and located on B-2's opposite hemisphere would be called the Equatorial Continent.

A short time later, Moose exclaimed, "Captain, you have to see this!"

When Captain Jerontis joined Moose at his computer screen, Moose said, "I think I've found a city, but it's the strangest city I've ever seen. There is a circular area about ten miles in diameter that has almost no buildings on it, but around the circumference of this circle, there are various kinds of structures that extend outward for about two to four miles."

"That is very peculiar," agreed Captain Jerontis. "Let's instruct the computer to enhance these radar images for maximum detail."

The Challenger's radar had several features that enabled it to achieve exceptional detail. Being a multi-frequency radar, it could probe its target with radar signals varying from short wave (millimeter wavelength) to long wave (wavelength of several meters). The numerous radar images recorded could then be overlaid and compared by the computer to extract maximum detail. Also, the computer could determine the height of a building by measuring the difference in time for a radar signal to return from the top of the building and from the street alongside the building. In addition, because of the Challenger's orbital motion, radar images of the same target could be taken from different angles of perspective. By comparing these images, the computer could provide minutely detailed three-dimensional pictures of the target area. An additional benefit of a multi-frequency radar is that radar signals of the appropriate wavelength could penetrate a forest to reveal buildings concealed by it.

Captain Jerontis directed Mike to do a detailed infrared map of the area, while he went back to his screen to study the area with visual images.

A few minutes later, Captain Jerontis said, "My visual images show nothing except a jungle of vegetation."

"My infrared data isn't revealing much either. There just simply isn't very much temperature variation over that area," Mike said.

"Our radar systems are doing an excellent job of seeing through the vegetation," stated Moose. "To me, this looks like the remains of city that was destroyed by a thermonuclear bomb a long time ago, perhaps even centuries ago. All structures have been obliterated inside a circle about six miles in diameter. For an additional two miles outside of this circle, the wreckage of some buildings still exists. Outside of that circle, we start to find structures with less and less damage the farther out we look. Even though they are concealed by vegetation and partly buried by debris, we can see some of the streets in the long-dead city and some of the highways leading into it."

A few moments of silence ensued while Mike and Captain Jerontis studied the images and thought about Moose's analysis of them. Then, Captain Jerontis said, "If you are correct, and it looks like you are; then, there must be other bomb-destroyed cities. Using this set of data as a guide, let's instruct the computer to do a planet-wide search and find them."

"I guess we can scratch the *primitive society theory*," declared Moose.

"Not necessarily," countered Captain Jerontis. "We know only that there was a high-tech society here at the time this city was destroyed, assuming that it was destroyed by a nuclear bomb. If there was a planet-wide nuclear war, and if there weren't many survivors; then, it might be a very primitive society that is living on this planet at the present time."

"If we find numerous bomb-destroyed cities all over this planet, then you might very well be correct," stated Mike.

"If there was a planet-wide nuclear war, how were the bombs delivered?" questioned Moose. "If they were delivered by ballistic missiles, then these creatures would've had the capability to launch satellites; however, we haven't found any."

"We haven't made a dedicated search for satellites," replied Captain Jerontis. "But if they had satellites and were involved in a planet-wide war; then, they would've tried to destroy each other's satellites. If any of the weapons they used for that purpose are still around, we could be in more danger than we realize. Especially, if the weapons were automatically activated under computer control and fired against any satellite that didn't have the proper identification code. We might look like a fat juicy target to that kind of weapon system. The only defense we have is our antimatter particle beam gun, which would certainly protect us from any kind of missile attack; however, if we were attacked by a powerful laser, we would have no defense except to flee as fast as we could."

"If anti-satellite weapon systems existed at the time this city was destroyed, it is difficult to imagine that they could still be functional after all these years," commented Mike.

"We don't know how much time has passed since the war," argued Captain Jerontis. "We only know that one city was destroyed and that it has been overrun by vegetation. We are assuming that it would have taken at least several decades for plant life to overrun a radioactive wasteland, but that is only an assumption."

"Are you suggesting that plant life on this planet is so tough and aggressive that it could overrun a radioactive wasteland in just a few years?" questioned Moose.

"Look at the evidence. Every part of the planet we've passed over so far is covered with lush vegetation. It's even possible that the radiation released in a planet-wide nuclear war could have spawned genetic mutations in plant life that resulted in plants so aggressive, and rapid-growing that they quickly took over the planet. They simply overran everything. My point is that we can't assume that a nuclear war was fought centuries ago. It may have been fought only a few years ago, and anti-satellite weapons might still exist."

Captain Jerontis turned to Mike and said, "I want our defenses on full alert, and I want our engines ready for instant ignition in case we have to flee."

Then, Captain Jerontis turned to Moose, "I want you to have someone initiate a search for satellites or satellite-debris that might be orbiting this planet."

Mike and Moose immediately got on their communicators and issued appropriate instructions to subordinates to carry out Captain J.J.'s orders.

Captain Jerontis sounded the warning klaxon. Then, using the intercom, he explained the possibility that a laser attack could occur and that the engines could be brought to full power with no warning, whatever. With the Challenger currently in a stable orbit, its engines had been shut down since the time the orbit was achieved. With the starship not being subjected to any acceleration, its personnel were currently in a weightless condition. If the engines were ignited and instantly brought to full power, personnel not prepared for the resulting acceleration could be seriously injured or even killed.

Captain Jerontis also ordered all personnel to leave the observation deck. The walls of the observation deck were made of transparent plastic to provide observers with an unobstructed 360-degree view of the universe. If the Challenger were attacked by a powerful laser and the beam hit the observation deck, personnel present on the deck could be killed or suffer serious burns as well as permanent blindness. By evacuating the observation deck, Captain Jerontis sought to prevent a laser beam not quite powerful enough to destroy the ship from wreaking serious havoc by inflicting permanent injury to exposed crew members.

"Captain! There is a strong possibility that our particle beam gun would be effective against a ground target, such as a laser that was attacking us," stated Mike. "It is true that the gun was developed for use in space where the antimatter particles that it fires can travel without interference because of the vacuum that exists in space. However, there is a theory that claims the particle beam could penetrate a planet's atmosphere all the way to the planet's surface."

"But that theory has never been tested," countered Captain Jerontis. "The problem is very simple: when the antimatter particles fired by the gun contact the ordinary matter in a planet's upper atmosphere, they are destroyed in a process of mutual annihilation. The atmosphere acts like a layer of armor protecting surface targets."

Mike responded, "Granted, when antimatter particles hit the atmosphere, there is an explosion in which the antimatter and the contacted ordinary matter are totally converted into energy. In effect, for a brief period of time, a rapidly expanding sphere of pure energy is created: a sphere which contains no matter, only energy. Since it contains no matter, this energy sphere is similar to the vacuum in space. According to the theory, the follow-on antimatter particles in the beam will pass through this energy sphere and strike atmospheric molecules on its other side. Then, the particles will explode and create a second energy sphere, through which following antimatter particles will pass and contact atmospheric molecules to create a third explosion. Theoretically, this chain of explosions will create energy spheres all the way to the planet's surface. Since the antimatter particles in the beam are traveling at 90% of the speed of light, the chain of energy spheres is formed so fast that it is in effect an energy tunnel extending to the planet's surface. So in just a few milliseconds, our antimatter particle beam gun could punch a hole through the planet's atmosphere: a hole that could best be described as a vacuum tunnel filled with energy. A beam of antimatter particles could then pass through this tunnel to the planet's surface to hit and destroy its target. To an observer on the ground, it would look like an extremely powerful lightning bolt coming down from space, and it would be very loud, sounding much like the cracking boom of thunder. When the particle beam gun was turned off, the energy tunnel would collapse with a thunderous boom that would be much louder than the thunder heard in electrical storms."

"I am familiar with that theory," replied Captain Jerontis. "The critics of the theory argue that the energy field in the tunnel would be so intense that it would tend to scatter the following antimatter particles in the beam and prevent the formation of a tunnel extending to the planet's surface. To use the lightning bolt analogy, a tunnel with bends and turns might form, which would make targeting impossible. Unfortunately, the gun was never tested against surface targets because of political reasons. This lack of testing is a direct result of the treaty that banned the testing of space based weapons against targets on Earth's surface."

"So, because of politics, we are in a situation wherein we do not have complete knowledge about how a critical piece of equipment will perform," declared Moose. "Now that there aren't any politicians around, maybe we should test it here. We could shoot at a deserted iceberg in one of the polar seas; then, we will know whether or not the gun is effective against surface targets."

"I don't believe that will be necessary," responded Captain Jerontis. "We know that the particle beam gun is nearly 100% effective against an attack carried out with missiles and projectiles in the vacuum of space. If we are attacked by any kind of space vehicle, we could destroy it. The only uncertainty is an attack from the planet's surface with a powerful laser weapon. But a laser can destroy us only by burning a hole through the ship's hull in a critical area. This can be accomplished only if they are able to lock their laser beam onto the targeted area for however many seconds are required to melt down the hull. It seems to me that they would have an extremely difficult time maintaining lock-on if we instantaneously bring our engines to full power and go through a series of erratic maneuvers. Another argument against conducting a test is that they might observe it, and I don't want to give them any information about our capabilities."

Both Moose and Mike nodded in agreement. Then, Mike said, "If we are attacked by laser fire, for added insurance, we could fire the particle beam gun at the attacking laser. In just a few milliseconds, the computer would know if a straight energy tunnel formed all the way to the target. If not, we could fire antimatter particles in a scatter pattern in the upper atmosphere between us and the attacking laser. The resulting continuous explosion pattern would create a large, intense energy field that would give off brilliant light, intense heat, and a broad spectrum of radiation. I believe that this powerful energy field would totally mask us from them, making it impossible for them to track us while we make our escape."

"Kind of like creating a smoke screen," commented Moose.

"I like that strategy," stated Captain Jerontis to Mike. "I want you to get to work immediately and modify the fire-control program, so that it will do exactly what you just proposed."

As Mike left the area, Moose looked at Captain Jerontis and said, "You and I both know that all of this potential danger could be avoided if we just pointed our noses at Alcent, fired up our engines, and hightailed it on out of here. After all, Alcent is going to be our new home."

Doing his best to show Moose an expression of exaggerated bewilderment, Captain Jerontis said, "I am puzzled by that comment. My memory tells me that early in this mission you said that you were happy to be a part of it because you have a solder of fortune mentality. You said that you enjoy facing a dangerous challenge and conquering it. Now, you're suggesting that we leave immediately because of the potential danger here. Is old age catching up to you, or has life in space softened you?"

"Aw come on Captain, you know I haven't lost my courage. I was merely presenting that as an option for discussion. But I would be lying if I said that our long interstellar voyage has had no effect on me. I am getting tired of living on a starship, and I have a wonderful wife. We are ready to settle down on Alcent and start building our new home. Old age hasn't caught up to me just yet, but I would like to start having children before it does."

"I understand how you feel, but I think it's very important to understand what's happening on this planet before we leave. As you know, Alpha Centauri A and Alpha Centauri B are in a long elliptical orbit about their common center of gravity. Their distance from each other will vary from about a billion miles to about 3.25 billion miles. It takes about eighty years to complete a journey around this orbit. So once every eighty years when the two stars are closest to each other, if this planet and Alcent happen to be between the two stars, then they will only be about 850 million miles apart. That is less than the distance between Earth and Saturn. Even with the old fashioned rocket technology that existed in the early days of the space age, it was possible to get a probe to Saturn in just a few years."

"You don't need to convince me. I understand the importance of finding out what kinds of creatures live on this planet and what their capabilities are before we leave here. I'm just ready to settle down. I'm tired of being in space."

"I am too. I'm sure we won't be here for more than a few days; then, in less than three weeks, we will arrive at Alcent. Speaking of those wonderful women that we want to settle down with, here they are now. I hope they have some new information for us."

Moose and Captain Jerontis turned to face Dianne and Doctor Nemard expectantly awaiting a report on the results of their meeting. Dianne was the first to speak, "In addition to me, three others experienced telepathic contact by the non-threatening creature. What is interesting about this is all three of them are students of mine. I've been teaching them biology since we left Earth. Also, Doctor Nemard has been teaching them the practice of medicine."

After a few moments of thoughtful silence, Captain Jerontis commented, "That raises several questions. First, why only individuals skilled in biology and medicine? Second, how did they know which individuals have this knowledge? Third, Doctor Nemard has in-depth knowledge in both fields; why wasn't she contacted?"

"All contacted individuals were on the observation deck at the time of contact," responded Doctor Nemard. "I was here on the flight deck with you."

"Why would that make a difference?" questioned Moose.

"I don't know," replied Doctor Nemard. "I was only making an observation."

After thinking about these comments for a few moments, Captain Jerontis said, "The observation deck's hull is almost entirely clear plastic; whereas, the rest of the ship's hull is a combination of metal and fiber reinforced plastic. Is it possible that their telepathic messages are unable to reach an individual surrounded by metal?"

"If we knew how their telepathic power works, we could answer that question," responded Doctor Nemard.

"Give me an educated guess," requested Captain Jerontis.

After a few moments of thought, Doctor Nemard said, "To have telepathic ability, they must be able to tune into another creature's brain waves and also be able to project their own brain waves into the other creature's mind. As you know, a normally functioning brain generates an energy field that is detectable because of the energy waves created.

On Earth, the science of brain wave analysis is still in its infancy, but analyzing brain wave patterns does enable us to determine when an individual is lying or telling the truth. Also, the brain wave patterns that go with most human emotions have been identified; for example, we can tell when a person is happy or sad.

Perhaps, the creatures on this planet are way ahead of us in the science of understanding brain waves. Maybe, they can even tell what an individual is thinking when language isn't a barrier. It's even possible that they've developed equipment to transmit the brain waves of one individual directly into the brain of another individual, or maybe, their brains can do this unassisted by equipment. In any case, if this transmission is anything like a radio transmission, it would not pass through our ship's metal hull, but it would pass through the plastic windows of the observation deck."

Captain Jerontis said, "If your conjecture is correct, then we would only be at risk to mental tampering if we are on the observation deck. A tired crew member should be able to sleep in his quarters without being concerned about having his subconscious mind rearranged. It would also explain why you weren't contacted, but it doesn't explain why only individuals with medical and biological knowledge were contacted."

Moose declared, "I would like to point out that I also have been training in both biology and medicine, and that I was on the observation deck for a while, but I wasn't contacted."

"But you were conversing with me during the entire time that you were there," countered Dianne. "In contrast, the first time that I felt the presence of life, I was gazing at B-2, and I was intently wondering if it has intelligent life on it. Also, I was in a quiet, relaxed state of mind that I believe was very open to outside suggestions. I believe that the creature that contacted me picked up on this and made its presence known to me. The other three contacted individuals were in a mental state similar to mine and were also pondering the life question."

"Surely, other people on the observation deck were in a relaxed, mental state and wondering if life exists on this planet," stated Captain Jerontis. "Why weren't any of them contacted? Why only individuals deeply involved in the medical and biological sciences? How did they know which of our personnel have extensive knowledge in the medical and biological sciences?"

"People with careers in these two fields would think about life in a different way than those with other careers," answered Doctor Nemard. "If the aliens are very advanced in the science of brain wave analysis, they might be able to detect and understand the difference in brain waves generated by this difference in thinking. As to your other question, is it possible that they have some horrendous problems that people with comprehensive knowledge in the medical and biological sciences could help them solve?"

Captain Jerontis displayed radar images of the bomb destroyed city that Moose had discovered. Then, he briefly summarized and explained the conclusions that had been reached in his earlier discussion with Moose and Mike.

"A planet-wide nuclear war would certainly create some horrendous medical and biological problems," commented Doctor Nemard.

"There's no longer any doubt in my mind that a planet-wide nuclear war was fought," stated Moose. "I now have radar images of thirty-seven bomb-destroyed cities, and we've only completed one orbit since I started the search."

"Chemical and biological weapons can be even more dreadful than nuclear weapons," commented Dianne. "If these kinds of weapons were used along with nuclear weapons, survivors could be facing problems so horrible that continued survival is next to impossible."

Captain Jerontis thought about the situation for a few moments. Then, he turned to Dianne and said, "It seems quite likely that the creature that made its presence known to you in a friendly way was trying to get acquainted with you with the objective of eventually finding out if we can help them. If that's true, this creature will try to contact us again. Perhaps, it will try to gain some basic information about us, such as who we are, where we came from, what our capabilities are, and what our intentions are."

"When do you think it will try to contact me?"

"In about six hours, we'll be over the area of the Northern Continent where you were first contacted, but it will be in the middle of the night, and they might be asleep. A little less than twelve hours after that, we will again be over that area, and it will be in the middle of the day. Our best opportunities to learn about these creatures will be for you to be on the observation deck at those times."

"That sounds dangerous to me," objected Moose. "We know nothing about these creatures, except that they've fought a big war. We don't know what their intentions are, and we know nothing about their capabilities."

Captain Jerontis replied, "You are correct, but I don't believe that it would be wise to go to Alcent until we find out what is happening on this planet."

Then, Captain Jerontis turned to Dianne and said, "Attempting to communicate with these creatures will be risky. If we've guessed wrong about their need for help, we might be attacked. On the observation deck, you will be naked to the hazards of a possible laser attack against this ship. You could be permanently blinded, severely burned, or even killed. Also, your brain will be open to possible telepathic assault."

"I think I will have to assume the risk; there's just too much at stake," Dianne responded quietly. "I believe that if there were going to be any kind of attack, it would come from the creatures on the Equatorial Continent that expressed so much hatred toward me. I have no desire to assume the risk involved in further contact with them. Just thinking about the possibility sends a cold shiver up and down my spine."

Noticing that his wife trembled as she finished speaking, Moose said, "I sense that you were more deeply affected by that experience than you realize."

"I've never been a victim of rape, but my experience with the creature on the Equatorial Continent makes me feel like I suffered that kind of brutal personal attack," Dianne said.

"If these creatures can affect you so deeply using nothing more than telepathic powers, I really do not want you to be on the observation deck contacting one of them," Moose said.

Dianne gazed into her husband's eyes and said, "I understand how you feel, but this is something that I have to do. Besides, I will be trying to contact the one who was friendly."

"But we don't know what his intentions are. He could be a lion disguising himself as a lamb."

"I didn't get that feeling, but even though you could be right, this is something that I must do."

Moose thought about the situation for a few moments; then, he reluctantly nodded in agreement and said, "If you're going to expose yourself to possible risk on the observation deck, I want to be there with you. If anything were to happen to you, my life would be empty; especially now, when we're on the verge of realizing our dream of building a home and raising a family. We've waited a long time for this."

"I appreciate how you feel, but I see no reason why both of us should be exposed to possible risk. I think this is something I have to do alone. Also, by being alone, I will have no distractions, and I will be better able to focus my mind totally on the communication that I will be trying to achieve."

"Your reasoning is difficult for me to challenge. So even though I am worried about this, I must agree with you."

Speaking to Dianne, Captain Jerontis said, "I think the best chance to achieve contact is for you to physically and mentally do exactly what you were doing the first time you were contacted. If you are contacted, the first step will be to get acquainted and to establish our peaceful intentions. Since language is a barrier, this will have to be done with images. Since we don't yet know how advanced they are in their ability to use telepathic communication, we don't know if it's even possible to achieve two-way communication. But if we assume that they are advanced enough so that they can read your mind to the point of being able to see what you see, then it becomes an easy problem. We simply take a large computer video screen to the observation deck and use it to fill your mind with the image you want to convey. For example, ask the computer to display an image of you. Then, clear your mind of all else and focus entirely on the image of you on the screen. Hold the image in your mind long enough for the creature to see it. Then, remove the image from the screen, and stare at the blank screen. This will help you clear your mind, so that it is totally blank. If the creature truly wants two-way communication and is able to do it, then it should respond by projecting an image of itself into your mind. If this can be accomplished, then we can go back and forth with images until we understand each other."

Dianne listened attentively and carefully considered what Jerry was suggesting. Then, she said, "The possibility of achieving two-way communication with telepathically transmitted images seems rather far-fetched, like something out of a science fiction movie."

"It seems that way," replied Captain Jerontis, "but reality always seems to catch up with science fiction when given enough time. Only a few decades ago, interstellar travel was science fiction, now we've turned it into reality."

"If the alien does communicate with me using images, then the question is, what images do I present to him?"

"The first step will be to simply get acquainted," replied Captain Jerontis. "So I recommend that you keep it personal. You might present an image of yourself with your parents when you were a baby. Then, you might show some scenes from your growing-up years. A careful selection of images would also give them information about life on Earth. For example, images of you on a camping trip with your parents could include some beautiful mountain scenery. From your teenage and adult years, you might show scenes that would document your education and training; in other words, establish your professional credentials. After you've done this, present them the blank screen image and see what the response is."

"I like that approach, but to do that, I need to do some preparation. So unless there is more for us to discuss, I am going to my office to put together a good sequence of images."

Everyone exchanged glances and nodded in agreement, and Dianne left.

Five and one-half hours later, after passing over the eastern shore of the Equatorial Continent, Mike reported, "My infrared data has revealed something very unusual: six volcanic peaks venting jets of hot gas from openings near their peaks."

"What's unusual about that?" questioned Captain Jerontis.

"The gas jets are all at the same temperature, 115 degrees Fahrenheit."

"That does seem strange."

"Especially, when you consider their locations. The northernmost mountain is located on an island about a hundred miles north of the Equatorial Continent. The southernmost peak is on an island located about two hundred miles south of the Equatorial Continent. The other four mountains are about a hundred miles inland along the continent's east coast. How could six volcanic peaks spread out over a distance of several thousand miles be venting gas at exactly the same temperature?"

"The probability of that happening because of natural causes has to be close to zero," commented Captain Jerontis. "This has to be the result of activity being done by intelligent beings. But what are they doing inside those mountains that would result in the venting of gas at exactly 115 degrees?"

"Maybe, there's some type of power plant or industrial manufacturing facility inside each of those mountains that was put there before the war for protection from attack," suggested Moose.

"That's a possibility," responded Mike, "but I don't think that dormant volcanoes are a wise choice of locations for underground factories. Dormant volcanoes have a nasty habit of sometimes becoming active."

"That's true," agreed Moose, "but wartime urgency sometimes requires the acceptance of high risk to achieve a desired goal."

With the southernmost mountain still in view, Captain Jerontis instructed the computer to obtain high resolution optical data of it, while Moose requested radar data. A few moments later, Moose said, "The jet coming out of this mountain is giving a strong radar return. It either contains ionized gases or some type of fine dust that is radar reflective. I am also getting a Doppler Shift that indicates an exit velocity of about 900 feet per second. Also, the jet is coming out of the highest point on the mountain."

Quickly examining optical images, Captain Jerontis found what he was looking for. On his computer screen he displayed the image of a pipe approximately five feet in diameter rising nearly 100 feet above the highest point on the mountain. A grayish-black jet of gas was spewing out of it. Turning to Moose, Captain Jerontis asked, "What is the altitude of this mountain top?"

Moose quickly entered the question into the computer and received an immediate answer, which he gave to Captain Jerontis: "My radar data indicates that it is 33,644 feet above sea level."

"Are the other five peaks that high?"

Moose displayed a radar topographical map of the area, scanned it, and said, "All six volcanic peaks are between 31,000 feet and 36,000 feet."

Turning to Mike, Captain Jerontis said, "We now have a fairly complete infrared map of this planet. Have you detected any mountain top gas jets similar to these?"

"No! But, I will request the computer to do a data search just to make sure that I haven't missed any."

"Those mountains have two things in common: they all tower high into the stratosphere, and they're all located on the eastern edge of the Equatorial Continent," stated Captain Jerontis. "If the prevailing high-altitude wind at this location blows from west to east, then they could be using these chimneys to get rid of a toxic by-product of a manufacturing process. Perhaps, chemical and biological weapons are being manufactured inside those mountains."

While speaking, Captain Jerontis instructed the computer to display a weather map of the area. After briefly checking it, he said, "As I suspected, we have strong westerly winds blowing across those mountain tops. The wind velocity varies from 110 to 175 miles per hour."

"If chemical and biological weapons are being manufactured inside those mountains, the war must be still going on," commented Moose. "However, if that's the case, why hasn't our radar detected aircraft in flight or ships at sea?"

"I don't know," Captain Jerontis replied. "Maybe your wife will be successful in her attempt to communicate with the aliens on the Northern Continent, and we'll gain some additional clues to help solve this mystery. After she completes her communication attempt, I am going to adjust our orbit so that we will travel directly over these mountains on our next pass over this hemisphere. I want complete data on those exhaust plumes; in particular, I want detailed spectrographic data. If we can determine the chemical composition of the plumes, then we may be able to figure out what is going on inside the mountains."

"Speaking about my wife, I am worried about her being exposed to possible harm," commented Moose. "In her attempt to achieve telepathic communication with the aliens, she will be at the mercy of whatever mental powers they possess."

"That concerns me too. I wouldn't have asked her to assume the risk involved if there were any other way. But since it is important for us to contact these aliens, we need to compliment her for courageously volunteering to accept the risk, and we need to support her in any way we can. The video cameras that we installed on the observation deck will allow us to monitor her activities. We'll be just outside the area, so if something threatening happens, we can rush in and take action to break the telepathic link. Since my wife will be with us, immediate medical attention will be available, if a need for it develops."

After thinking about the situation for a few moments, Moose said, "I think we've taken all the precautions we can, and I do understand the need for contacting the aliens. I just wish that someone other than my wife would be making the attempt."

A short time later, the Challenger passed over B-2's equator approaching the Northern Continent from the South. Dianne was on the observation deck hoping to achieve telepathic communication with the aliens living on the Northern Continent. Even though it was nighttime, the planet was fairly well illuminated because of the nearness of Alpha Centauri A. Dianne was viewing the lush green land mass that the Challenger was rapidly approaching and wondered what kind of life was present and what kinds of problems it was facing in the aftermath of the nuclear war. She experienced a mixture of conflicting emotions. She was very excited about the possibility of becoming the first human to achieve two-way communication with an intelligent extra-terrestrial. However, she was also apprehensive about this, because to achieve telepathic communication, she had to open her mind to the probing of an alien she knew nothing about. Even though she was a skilled professional and a tough minded survivor, the possibility that the alien could do irreparable damage to her brain was frightening. Despite this possibility, Dianne carefully put her mind into a state of relaxation open to outside suggestion.

While pondering the question about what kind of life existed on the planet 230 miles below, a feeling of being alone pervaded her senses. Even though she had insisted on being alone on the observation deck so as not to expose other crew members to possible risk, the quiet emptiness that now surrounded her served to enhance her feeling of vulnerability. Dianne appreciated the presence of her husband and two closest friends just outside the observation deck, but wondered if they could rescue her quickly enough to prevent permanent injury if the alien decided to attack and damage her mental ability. Despite this risk, Dianne was tingling with excitement in anticipation of possible communication with an alien.

Dianne had always felt that if mankind ever discovered another race of intelligent beings, the first communication would be accomplished by a group of humans facing a group of the aliens; or perhaps initial contact would be by unmanned spacecraft. She never once dreamed that the first two-way communication would be attempted by a lone human or that she would be that lone individual.

The Challenger was almost over the area where Dianne first became aware of the existence of life, and she was not yet aware of any attempt to contact her. She wondered if the alien was sleeping or distrusted the personnel on the Challenger and did not wish further contact. She decided to focus her mind very intently on the question of what kind of life existed on the planet below her and to surround this intense mental focus with feelings of love, a desire for peace, and a desire to be helpful. So intense was her mental focus that her mind entered an almost trance-like state in which all else was blocked out. She had achieved the mental state that her mind was in when the aliens first made their presence known to her.

A few moments later, Dianne became aware of the alien probing her mind. She waited for perhaps a half minute for the feeling to become strong. Then, she looked at the large computer screen that displayed a three-dimensional, life-sized image of her, and she intensely focused her mind on it to form a vivid mental image of herself. She held this image in her mind for about a half minute. Then, she removed her picture from the computer screen and intently stared at the blank milky-white screen. She closed her eyes and held the blank screen image in her mind.

In just a few seconds, an image of the alien appeared in her mind. Without losing her mental trance, Dianne spoke softly into a small microphone that she was wearing: "I have achieved contact with one of the aliens. Although there are several small differences, he is humanoid in appearance. His skin color is golden-bronze. He has blue eyes, dark blond hair, and the beginning of facial lines that would indicate late middle age. He has a muscular build and a masculine appearance. He looks relaxed, healthy, friendly, and intelligent."

A few seconds after Dianne stopped her oral description of the alien, his image faded from her mind. Dianne surmised that the alien was aware that she was orally describing him and kept his image in her mind until she had concluded the description. As the image of the alien faded, it was immediately replaced by a star map showing Alpha Centauri A, Alpha Centauri B, and twenty nearby stars. Dianne spoke softly into her microphone: "He is showing me a star map of local interstellar space. I think he wants to know where we are from."

Outside the observation deck, Captain Jerontis looked at Moose and Connie and said, "I think we should show him. I don't think they can harm the people on Earth. I think he simply wants to know who we are and where we came from."

Moose and Connie both nodded in agreement; then, Captain Jerontis turned on his microphone and spoke softly to Dianne: "Have the computer place a star map on the screen that is oriented the same way as the map he is showing you. Then, draw a line from the Sun to Alpha Centauri B."

Dianne did what she was instructed to do. Then, she studied the video screen intently to form a vivid image of it in her mind. Almost immediately, Dianne experienced a feeling of acknowledgment that she interpreted to mean that the alien had received the image, so she switched to a blank screen and held an image of it in her mind. In just a few seconds, the alien projected an image of the star map into her mind, but it now contained new information. It showed an arrow heading directly back to the Sun, an arrow heading to Alpha Centauri A, and three arrows heading toward other stars. Along with this image, Dianne experienced a sense of alarm, a feeling of danger. The image of the star map was quickly followed by scenes of birds and animals drinking water from lakes and rivers and then, dying. The final scene showed members of the alien's species drinking water and then, dying.

While the alien was presenting these images to her, Dianne described them to her colleagues outside the observation deck. She concluded by saying, "I think the alien is trying to tell us to go somewhere else, because this planet is filled with death. I sense that he is genuinely concerned about our safety."

"Are you convinced that he is sincere, or do you think he is just trying to get rid of us?" questioned Captain Jerontis.

"I believe he is sincere."

"In that case, show him a star map containing only Alpha Centauri A, Alpha Centauri B, and their planets. On this map show him an arrow extending from this planet to Alcent. Then, show him a sequence of images from your childhood to the present time. A proper selection of scenes from key points in your life will put you on a personal basis with him and establish your professional credentials. Perhaps, this will lead him to give us additional information in regard to how the consumption of water is killing animal life."

Realizing that their orbital speed was rapidly moving them away from the alien, Dianne proceeded immediately to carry out Captain J.J.'s orders. Less than ten seconds after forming each image in her mind, Dianne received acknowledgment from the alien that he had seen the image. Dianne was surprised at how rapidly the alien could see the images in her mind. After completing her sequence of images, Dianne switched to the blank screen image.

The alien was very quick to respond. Dianne detected a sense of urgency on his part and surmised that the alien realized that she would soon be beyond the range of his telepathic powers. The alien rapidly presented to her a sequence of images from his childhood to the present time. Then, as he started to get into the subject of death caused by water consumption, the images abruptly ceased. When the images were cut off, Dianne immediately made an entry into the computer, so that the exact time and orbital position would be noted. Then, she said, "I am no longer receiving any images. I believe communication is over until our next orbit over this location."

Then, she left the observation deck and drifted right into Moose's welcoming embrace. Both Moose and Dianne rejoiced in the fact that communication with the alien had been accomplished without any harm being done to her. Captain Jerontis and Doctor Nemard also expressed their happiness at the outcome of the event. Their immediate conclusion was that this alien was friendly, needed their help, and would be providing them with additional information about the problem of death caused by water consumption. All four returned to the flight deck to analyze the results of their communication with the alien.

Upon their return to the flight deck, Captain Jerontis sounded three notes on the warning klaxon and announced: "All personnel prepare for acceleration. In three minutes, we will maneuver the Challenger into a new orbit."

After the orbital maneuvers were completed, Captain Jerontis said to Dianne, "Please give us all the information you can about the alien."

"First, I am happy that the individual I communicated with was friendly. He was so congenial that I never felt threatened. I felt totally at ease with him. Before the communication began, there were a few moments when I felt alone and vulnerable. He may have detected my apprehensiveness and made a special effort to be warm and friendly to put me at ease. He conducted his part of the communication in a courteous way."

"Based on what you just said, I would tend to agree," commented Doctor Nemard.

Dianne continued, "Also, he did show concern for our safety when he warned us not to land on this planet."

"You said that he is humanoid in appearance, but that there are some differences," stated Doctor Nemard. "What differences were most obvious to you?"

"The first thing I noticed was his forehead: it is somewhat larger than ours. With the additional volume in his skull, he may have a larger brain than we have. Perhaps, those additional brain cells are what gives him his telepathic ability. The second thing I noticed was that his ears are a bit larger than ours, which may indicate a more sensitive sense of hearing. The third obvious difference was his hands: he has four fingers like we do, but he has two thumbs opposing the four fingers. He has one thumb on either side of each hand."

"How tall do you think he is?" questioned Doctor Nemard.

"Since I didn't see him next to anything of known size, I have no way to judge that."

"You keep referring to him as he," commented Moose. "How do you know that he is masculine?"

"I noticed that he had a nicely balanced muscular build like you see in a man who is in good shape. Also, his clothing was nicely tailored and fit him quite snugly. He had the familiar masculine bulge in his groin area, and I saw no indication of breasts on his chest."

"From the tone of your voice, I almost get the feeling that you were turned on by him," commented Moose, dryly.

Dianne gave Moose a teasing smile, "He may have been sexually aroused by me."

"What makes you think that? Did you do something to excite him?"

"In one of the images I showed him, I was standing on a sandy beach wearing a skimpy bikini. But I showed him that image for purely scientific reasons. I wanted him to see what the human female looks like. That was just to be informative and should not have been especially arousing to him."

"Why not? After all, you do have a pretty nice figure," retorted Moose.

"Thank you," replied Dianne.

Doing her best to display a naughty grin, Dianne said to Doctor Nemard, "Isn't it wonderful that my husband is so in love with me that he even worries that I might be sexually arousing to an alien?"

"I wasn't worried about that," interrupted Moose, "I just think you may have been a little too personal with an alien that we know very little about."

"I was only trying to show him who we are and what we look like. Also, to indicate to him part of our basic social structure, I showed him a picture of us getting married and some scenes to indicate that we live together. In one of them, you were wearing only your jockey shorts. I believe the alien got the message."

"Again, I hope you weren't too personal with an alien we know very little about."

"I agree with her approach to the alien," commented Doctor Nemard. "I believe that the best way to speed up the exchange of information is to become somewhat personal. By being open with the alien, Dianne may have gained his trust. If he also finds Dianne pleasing to look at and pleasant to communicate with, then he may feel at least some affection for her. It seems to me that this set of circumstances would make the alien less likely to censor the information that he communicates to us."

"That's why I was personal with some of the images I presented to him. After I showed him a sequence of images from my life, he showed me a sequence of images from his life, some of which were also quite personal. One of the things that amazed me about him, was the speed with which he was able to see the images that I held in my mind. At first, I held images in my mind for about thirty seconds before I went to the next one, but after we got started, he only needed about ten seconds to read my mind. He let me know when he was ready for the next image by giving me a little mental prod. I was impressed by his ability to carry out telepathic communication via the use of mental images. I wish I understood the mental mechanism that he used to do this. This form of communication seems to be as easy for him as it is for us to sit here and talk."

"We may never understand how this is accomplished, because we probably won't be here long enough to research that question," commented Doctor Nemard. "But let's be thankful he has that ability; because with it, he can give us a great deal of information about this planet. One thing that strikes me about what you've said is that if he finds you attractive; then, the females in his species must look a lot like us. Were there any females present in any of the images he showed you?"

"Yes, the sequence of images he presented to me contained a summary of the major events in his life from the time he was born to the present. His parents were present in some of the images, and except for the differences peculiar to his species, his mother had the same basic anatomy as human females. One of the images showed that his parents were both killed in the nuclear war. Apparently, the war occurred shortly after he graduated from a university. I believe he is a veterinarian. If he is currently in his fifties, then the war would have occurred about thirty years ago. He also showed me what I think is a current family portrait, which indicates that he has a wife who is considerably younger than he is and three children who look like teenagers."

"Did he show you any scenes from the war?" questioned Captain Jerontis.

"Yes! There were several. When he showed them to me, I strongly felt his deep sadness. In fact, he communicated emotions along with most of the images that he placed in my mind. Knowing his feelings shed additional light on the images and made them easier to understand."

"Tell me about the war images," requested Captain Jerontis.

"Like I said, I believe the war started about thirty years ago. There was a massive exchange of nuclear bombs. They were delivered primarily with missiles and aircraft. Some were launched from ships and submarines. Apparently, all major cities and military bases were destroyed. In addition to the nuclear exchange, chemical weapons were used. Then, to make the death complete, biological toxins and several kinds of lethal microbes were released by the remnants of the opposing forces. This final act was tantamount to committing suicide, because these poisons were so potent and long-lived that they poisoned the environment on the entire planet for several years. If I have correctly interpreted the images that he showed me, this war and the poisoned environment that followed it killed approximately 99% of all living organisms.

Shortly after the war, plant life began to overrun everything. Apparently, several new species of plants resulted from genetic mutations caused by the radiation released by the nuclear weapons. Evidently, these plants thrive on radiation, because they are growing most vigorously in the areas with the greatest radioactivity.

Images from the alien came to an abrupt end at the time that I noted in the computer. I believe that our orbital motion dropped us below the horizon from his viewpoint. Perhaps, he can only communicate with us telepathically when we are on a direct line of sight. If that's the case, we can calculate an approximate location for him from our location at the time of communications cutoff. On our next pass over that area, we can take detailed radar and optical data and see if we can find any evidence to pinpoint his location."

"That's a good idea," agreed Captain Jerontis who turned to Moose and asked him to estimate the alien's location and review existing data to see what the area looked like.

Turning his attention back to Dianne, Captain Jerontis said, "There are three things that strike me about your account of the war. First, I am awestruck by the horrible, nearly complete death and destruction caused by this war, which would explain why we haven't seen any ships at sea or aircraft in flight. Second, I am surprised by the rapid growth of vigorous plant life that has overrun this planet in the aftermath of an all out nuclear war. Third, I am amazed by all the detail you are able to recall from a sequence of images that were rapidly run through your mind."

"That amazes me too. Apparently, the alien not only placed these images in my conscious mind, but also strongly implanted them in my memory, because I am able to recall them vividly. It is unfortunate that the science of brain wave analysis is still in its infancy. How convenient it would be if we could have a computer tune in to my brain waves and analyze and interpret them accurately enough to portray the images that the alien transmits into my mind. If we could do this while it is happening, then everyone could see the images, and we could record them for future reference."

"That would be a convenient capability for us to have in our current situation," agreed Captain Jerontis. "But since we don't have it, I think it would be prudent for you to go to your office and enter into the computer memory the best description you can of each of the images the alien showed you along with your interpretation. Being alone and quietly thinking about the scenes the alien showed you may give you some additional insight into what he tried to communicate to you."

"As vivid as those mental images were, I don't believe I will have any difficulty entering accurate detailed information into the computer library. Also, this alien needs to have a name, so that it will be easier for us to discuss him. For the sake of convenience, let's just call him Rex."

"That'll work," commented Captain Jerontis. "In less than an hour, you will have another opportunity to communicate with him. If he needs our help in some critical way, perhaps, he will tell us what it is that he thinks we can do for him."

"I will be ready for that," stated Dianne with a degree of excitement in her voice as she turned to leave the flight deck to go to her office.

"Hold on a second," said Moose to his wife. "I think I have an image of Rex's location. If we assume that his telepathic powers are limited by line-of-sight, then he should be living in the area I have displayed on the screen. This image is of an area that measures about fifteen miles by fifteen miles. There is a fairly good sized river flowing right through the middle of it, and there are also two lakes that are about a mile across. Besides all that water, there are several high hills that would make it easy to have an underground home, if there's still a need to live underground."

"That does look like a convenient area to live in," commented Dianne.

"During your next communication with Rex, you might show him this image," suggested Captain Jerontis. "If Rex is living in this area, and if he wants us to know his exact location; he can simply place an X or some other symbol on the image to mark his position."

"If Rex does give us his exact location, that would indicate that he trusts us," stated Doctor Nemard.

"Or he might be in such desperate need of our help that he has no choice but to trust us," commented Captain Jerontis. "In any case, we will meticulously explore that area during our next pass over it."

Realizing the conversation was over for the time being, Dianne left the flight deck and went to her office.

"Captain! We are approaching the northernmost volcanic peak on the eastern edge of the Equatorial Continent," announced Mike as he displayed an optical image of it on the large video screen. "Whatever that stuff is, it is still being vented from the mountain top at a temperature of 115 degrees. Radar data indicates an exit velocity of 900 feet per second. The wind across the mountain top is blowing from west to east at 160 mph."

"Do we have any spectroscopic data on that exhaust plume," asked Captain Jerontis?

"I am just now getting the first readout on that," replied Mike, "and it indicates an absence of carbon dioxide, carbon monoxide, sulfur dioxide, oxides of nitrogen, and water vapor. Therefore, we are not looking at exhaust from the combustion of organic fuel."

"That tells us that the large pipe at the top of the mountain is not a smokestack for a power plant that provides energy for an underground industrial complex," stated Captain Jerontis. "I had suspected that this would be the case. Even though the grayish-black color of the exhaust makes it look like smoke from a coal burning power plant, there simply isn't any logical reason why a power plant chimney would be at the top of a high mountain. Is there enough information in the spectroscopic data so that the computer can identify the chemicals in that plume?"

"The computer has concluded that the exhaust jet contains two distinct organic chemicals," replied Mike. "Both are composed of large complex molecules. The computer has determined which elements are present and their approximate proportions, but it is unable to determine the precise geometry of these molecules. It is saying that the spectral signatures of these chemicals are different from the spectral signatures of any of the chemicals cataloged in its library. In other words, these two chemicals have never been found on Earth."

"It will be interesting to see if the exhaust plumes coming out of the other five mountains contain the same chemicals as this one" commented Captain Jerontis.

"I think something sinister is happening down there," stated Mike.

Captain Jerontis said, "I agree. I can think of only two reasons to eject chemicals into the stratosphere when there is a high velocity wind blowing them away from the Equatorial Continent: either the chemicals are a toxic by-product of a manufacturing process and they want to get rid of them, or the chemicals are being used in a chemical warfare attack against the other two continents. Such an attack can only work if three conditions exist. First, the strong high-altitude winds must blow all the way to the other continents. Second, a significant percentage of the chemical toxins must remain airborne until the other two continents are reached. Third, most of the toxins must precipitate out of the atmosphere once they reach the other two continents."

"Let me interrupt you for a moment," requested Mike. "We now have the second volcanic peak in view. It is putting out an exhaust plume at 900 feet per second with an exit temperature of 115 degrees. Spectroscopic data is identical to that of the exhaust plume from mountain number one. Also, there is a westerly wind at 165 mph."

While Mike reported data for mountain number two, Moose displayed a weather map for the area east of the Equatorial Continent. He looked at it briefly and said, "The high-altitude wind not only extends all the way to the other two continents, but blows all the way across them before it finally dies out. Also, there are a few thunderstorms over parts of both continents. That is significant, because the tops of some of these storm systems are above 45,000 feet. Those storms are certainly capable of milking chemicals out of the stratosphere and depositing them on the land mass below."

"That leaves only one question unanswered: are the chemicals still in the stratosphere when the wind arrives over those continents?" Captain Jerontis said.

"Now that we have the spectral signatures of these chemicals, we can check for their presence in the atmosphere during our next pass over them," stated Mike.

"Suppose we find that these chemicals are there, that still doesn't prove that chemical warfare is in progress," commented Doctor Nemard. "I can't think of any logical reason for a chemical attack to be taking place. After all, the war that was fought thirty years ago was so horrible that there simply isn't much animal life left to kill."

"That's true," agreed Captain Jerontis, "so let me propose a sequence of events that could lead to an illogical attack. Suppose the aliens on this continent started the war with the expectation of winning, but were themselves destroyed by the ensuing retaliation. For whatever reason, suppose that the chemical warfare complexes inside these mountains escaped destruction. Furthermore, let's suppose that for the most part, the only aliens on the Equatorial Continent to survive the war were the ones who were inside these mountains. Now, let's suppose that even though their country started the war, they are blaming their enemies for their own devastation. It is possible that these survivors are so totally consumed by hatred that they now have a fanatical compulsion to continue the war until nothing is left alive on the other continents. Perhaps, they've even formed a religious cult based on hatred in which they actually worship the chemical warfare machines inside these mountains. If that's the case, then keeping these machines functioning may be the sole purpose in their lives. They may be so fanatical that they aren't even concerned that an unexpected change in wind direction could cause the poisons they are producing to come raining down on what's left of their continent. Their only purpose in life might be to kill the few remaining living creatures on the other two continents no matter what the cost."

"Sick, deranged minds could fit into the scenario you just outlined," agreed Doctor Nemard. "It's almost like the murder-suicide theme you sometimes find at a crime scene; only here, it is being done on a global scale."

"Your theory about what's happening here could be right on," commented Moose, "but how do we prove it?"

"I have an idea," stated Mike.

"What?" asked Moose.

"Simple, let's enlist Rex's help."

"How do you propose to do that?" questioned Moose.

"We have Dianne show him a sequence of images to reveal to him what is happening here," replied Mike. "The first image would be a picture of one of these mountains with its exhaust plume. The second image would be a weather map that would show the locations of all six mountains and the wind direction at their tops. The third image would be a close-up of one of the exhaust plumes with spectrographs along side of it to show the spectral signatures of the two chemicals in the plume. Dianne thinks Rex is a veterinarian. Because of problems caused by the war, he may also be a research scientist. If that's the case, and if these chemicals are raining down on him, he might know what they are. He might even recognize their spectral signatures. If these chemicals are causing problems, I am certain Rex will find a way to tell us that."

"Suppose he confirms that these chemicals are toxic agents being used in a chemical attack against all living creatures on this planet; then, what do we do about it?" questioned Moose.

In a strong tone, Doctor Nemard said, "If that's the case, I don't think that we will have any choice except to destroy those mountains and the poison factories that they contain. We used our antimatter particle-beam gun to save our lives when we passed through a cloud of interstellar asteroids on our way to here. Certainly, we could use the gun to give life on this planet a chance to survive and recover. It's like those mountains are cancerous tumors that need to be surgically removed."

"While I agree with you," Captain Jerontis replied, "I think we should discuss all of our options and their consequences before we attempt to take out those mountains. We should definitely show Rex some images of what we are planning to do and see how he reacts."

"We've passed over the third mountain, and we now have the fourth one in view," announced Mike. "The data for these two are the same as for mountains one and two."

"It is beginning to look like the same process is going on inside all six of these mountains," commented Doctor Nemard.

"If that's the case, I wonder if they are operating independently, or if they are under the control of one individual," questioned Captain Jerontis. "If they're under the control of one individual, then there must be open communication. Which means that if we attack one of these chemical warfare machines, the aliens operating the others will know about it and will put themselves on full alert. This will be a problem if they have any defensive systems capable of attacking us at this altitude."

"During their nuclear war, some of the bombs were delivered with intercontinental ballistic missiles," stated Moose. "That being the case, they definitely had the ability to launch satellites and to launch nuclear-armed anti-satellite missiles. This might explain why we haven't found any satellites or satellite debris orbiting this planet. Any satellite incinerated by a nearby nuclear blast would have been reduced to radioactive ash that we might no longer be able to detect. Perhaps, they also possessed nuclear-armed anti-missile missiles. Maybe, these poison factories survived the war not only because they are buried deep inside mountains, but also because they were very well defended."

"Your analysis might be correct," remarked Captain Jerontis, "but as far as we are concerned, the big question is: do they still have functional nuclear-armed anti-satellite missiles?"

"I think we should assume that they do and develop an attack strategy that makes their missiles impotent against us," stated Mike. "For example, we could attack from geosynchronous orbit. This would place us at an altitude of about 22,000 miles. Even if they have anti-missile missiles capable of reaching that high an altitude, the travel time would give us ample opportunity to detect and destroy them. As far as our attack is concerned, a narrowly focused beam of antimatter particles fired from a high-altitude orbit will be just as lethal as a beam fired from a low-altitude orbit."

"In addition to our safety, there is another advantage to attacking from geostationary orbit," commented Captain Jerontis, "and that is it will give us time to experiment with the particle-beam gun. First, it has never been tested against a surface target, so we will have to experiment with that. Second, we need to find the best way to attack these mountains to efficiently destroy the poison factories they contain. We don't want to expend any more antimatter than is necessary. Being stationary over our target area will give us all the time we need."

"We are now over the fifth mountain, and I am getting basically the same data as we recorded for the first four mountains," stated Mike.

"Do we have any data that reveals the presence of concrete slabs on or near any of those mountains?" questioned Captain Jerontis. "That kind of concrete construction could indicate the presence of underground missile silos."

"I will see what I can find," replied Mike.

Then, Captain Jerontis turned to Moose and said, "I want you to discover how the aliens are getting their raw materials into those mountains. The more we know about our targets; the more efficiently we will be able to put them out of operation."

Moose nodded and started working the problem.

Speaking to her husband, Doctor Nemard said, "It sounds like you've already concluded that a chemical warfare attack is being conducted from within those mountains. It also sounds like you've already decided to shut them down."

"An ongoing chemical warfare attack is what best explains the information that we have. I will have Dianne present a summary of our data to Rex. If he is awake, this communication will take place in about forty minutes. Hopefully, his reaction will shed some light on the validity of my conclusion. If his reaction supports my conclusion, then I will have Dianne show Rex some images of us destroying the poison factories. How he reacts will have a bearing on whether or not we attack."

"Would you like me to prepare the images for her?" asked Doctor Nemard.

"That would be helpful. Thank you for offering."

Then, Captain Jerontis buzzed Dianne's office, and when she answered, he said, "Dianne! I need you to come to the flight deck in about fifteen minutes for a meeting about your next contact with Rex."

"I'll be there."

A few minutes later, Mike said, "A computer search of our radar data does reveal the presence of numerous concrete missile silos located in and around all six of these mountains. Most of them are open and empty, but there are a few that still have their concrete lids in place. It's impossible to tell if the closed silos contain operational missiles."

"I think we should assume that at least some of them are functional," replied Captain Jerontis.

"Judging from the size of the open silos, it appears that they did contain defensive missiles," commented Mike. "They don't appear large enough to have housed intercontinental weapons."

"They could have contained small ICBMs, but until proven otherwise, we have to assume that the closed silos contain functional defensive missiles that are nuclear armed and able to reach us at this altitude. I trust that you've already programmed the fire control computer to deal with that possibility."

"I have, and they can't hurt us with a missile attack, unless there's a malfunction in our defensive systems. To guard against that possibility, I have my engineering crew checking out our defensive systems to make sure everything is in perfect working condition."

Satisfied that Mike had the possible missile problem under control, Captain Jerontis said, "Perhaps, the biggest danger we face is from a laser attack."

"They could certainly damage us with a laser attack," agreed Mike, "but I don't think they can destroy us unless they're able to detonate our antimatter fuel."

"That's probably true, but that fuel will be hard to reach with a laser. They will have to burn through our meteor shields to get to those tanks, and if we're doing erratic maneuvers, I don't think they can lock on to a spot long enough to burn through it. But a laser attack could still lead to our destruction if they score a lucky hit that cripples our defenses to a missile attack. For example, a direct hit on the particle beam gun could put us in a serious situation."

"That's the beauty of attacking from geosynchronous orbit. If they even have missiles that can reach that altitude, it will take them so long to get there, that we can simply leave before they arrive."

"That attack strategy leaves us vulnerable only to laser attack, and we don't know if they even have lasers, but we must assume that they do until we know otherwise."

"I think that's a wise assumption," agreed Mike. "If all those empty silos did contain defensive missiles, then these mountain complexes were heavily defended, and that means that their owners placed great value in them and were determined that they survive the nuclear exchange. If they have lasers, they probably put some of them here too."

"I think the fact that they were so determined to have these mountain complexes survive lends additional credibility to the conclusion that they contain chemical weapons systems. Perhaps, they thought that if all else failed, they could eventually win the war with chemical weapons."

"Chemical weapons are definitely potent weapons of mass destruction and capable of eventually winning a war."

"But since the two sides have already destroyed each other, there is no longer any need to be conducting a chemical attack. If that is what is going on, it can only be seen as a hideous crime against an entire planet."

"If we're able to determine that that is what is happening, we'll have a big decision to make," commented Mike.

"The data that we gather during our next pass over the other two continents along with what Dianne learns from Rex during her next meeting with him should help us with that decision."

"I hope he's still up. It is nighttime where he lives, and he could be in bed, sound asleep."

"We'll know in a half hour."

Thirty minutes later, Dianne was on the observation deck preparing for her next meeting with Rex. Captain Jerontis, Doctor Nemard, and Moose were outside the observation deck monitoring Dianne's activities.

Observing the planet far below her, Dianne couldn't help noticing how peaceful it looked. Then, she thought about the horrible tragedy endured by this planet's creatures as a result of the war and wondered how many species had been made extinct. Then, she thought about the creatures presently engaged in a desperate struggle for survival and how this struggle for survival might be doomed to failure because of a planet-wide chemical attack conducted by sick, demented minds. Recalling the cold hatred and evil that she felt during the Challenger's first pass over the Equatorial Continent sent an involuntary tremor through Dianne's body.

Noticing the approach of the southern shore of the Northern Continent, Dianne started to clear her mind of the sadness that she felt for this planet's creatures. She filled her mind with thoughts of Rex and the things she wanted to accomplish in the hoped for contact with him.

A few minutes later, Dianne achieved a state of total relaxation and entered a trance in which all was blocked out except for a vivid mental image of Rex. In just a few moments, she felt a mental prod and immediately replaced Rex's image with a sharp mental image of herself. When she felt a second mental prod, she replaced her self image with a blank screen image. It had been decided to let Rex open this communication, because it was felt that this would be the best way to discover his top priority problem.

Dianne did not have to wait long, for Rex immediately began placing images in her mind. Dianne spoke softly into her microphone and described the images as they occurred. "I have just achieved contact with Rex. He is showing me what I think is a temperature scale. On one end of it, there is a block of ice, and on the other end, there is a pot of boiling water. At about the point on the scale that would represent our normal body temperature, he has placed a green mark and the pictures of several creatures, including his picture.

"Now, I am looking at an image of an animal drinking water. I now have the image of the temperature scale back in my mind; only now, the animal that just drank water is pictured considerably above the green mark. Evidently, something in the water caused its temperature to go up drastically. Now, Rex is showing me an image of the animal drinking more water. Now, we're back to the image of the temperature scale, but the animal has moved still higher on it. A new image shows the animal drinking still more water.

"I see this doomed animal having convulsions and suffering a painful death. Apparently, it was killed by chemicals that caused its rate of metabolism to run wild and at the same time blocked its natural ability to control its body temperature, which rose so high that critical internal organs started to fail. What a cruel way to kill a creature. The natural thing for an animal with an elevated body temperature to do is to drink water, which in this case caused it to ingest more poison and make the problem worse.

"I see an image of Rex analyzing water samples in a laboratory. He is showing me two test tubes full of dark solutions. I think he's trying to tell me that he has isolated two chemicals responsible for the deaths of creatures that drink water containing them in sufficient concentrations. I see an image of this planet in orbit around Alpha Centauri B. Pictured next to this planet are the two test tubes with the dark chemicals. I see a new image showing that this planet has moved half way around Alpha Centauri B; only now, the dark solutions in the test tubes are gone. I believe Rex is telling me that these two poisons are not stable, and that they deteriorate in about half a year.

"I see an image of a spectroscope. I now have an image of a test tube containing a dark solution and next to it is its spectrograph, and now the other dark chemical and its spectrograph. I see a map of this planet with the spectrographs slowly moving around on the map. Rex knows that, since these chemicals deteriorate in half a year, they must be continuously pumped into the environment. He is asking us to find the source. The spectrographs he showed me depict spectral signatures that look identical to what we measured for the chemicals in the exhaust plumes that we've been studying, thus confirming a chemical warfare attack. If I show Rex the source of these poisons, what will the response be? Is it possible that his country may have held a few intercontinental missiles in reserve for this kind of emergency?"

"If they did, that would save us from having to do the job," commented Captain Jerontis. "Show him the sequence of images about the mountains."

Dianne presented the mountain images to Rex, and after a few moments received a response. "I see Rex in a state of hopelessness. I feel his emotions. He is in a state of despair. I believe he is helpless in this situation. I believe that what's left of his country lacks the capability to stop the injection of these poisons into their environment. Members of his species can probably survive by drinking distilled water, but they will be unable to save the wild animals."

"Show him the sequence of images of us destroying the poison factories," ordered Captain Jerontis.

Dianne did as directed, and received an almost immediate response. "I see an image of Rex wearing an expression of renewed hope, and I feel strong, heartfelt appreciation coming from him."

"Do you have any reason to disbelieve any of the information or emotions that Rex has transmitted into your mind?" questioned Captain Jerontis.

"His story about chemicals killing animals confirms the conclusion that we had already reached regarding the chemicals spewing out of the mountains. His spectroscopic data seems to match ours. He gave us this information before we presented our data to him. The probability of Rex fabricating his story and showing us two complicated spectral signatures that match the ones we recorded is nil. Also, for whatever it's worth, my intuition tells me that Rex is a sensitive, benevolent individual who is working hard to promote the survival of his species and what's left of the animal life in his vicinity."

"Your reasoning agrees with mine, and I have a healthy respect for your intuitive judgment. I am going to place a sequence of images on your computer screen that I want you to show Rex."

The first image Captain Jerontis put on the screen showed a picture of B-2 and the Challenger's current orbit around it. It also showed a geosynchronous orbit and a dashed line indicating the Challenger's transfer into this much higher orbit. The second image showed the east coast of the Equatorial Continent and the Challenger firing its antimatter particle-beam gun at the poison spewing mountains. The third image showed the Challenger returning to its present orbit. The fourth image showed the Challenger doing a data gathering pass over the destroyed mountains. The fifth image showed B-2 making one-half revolution on its axis of rotation. The sixth image showed a communication scene between Dianne and Rex. Captain Jerontis hoped that the fifth image would tell Rex that approximately one-half day would pass before his next communication with Dianne. After the sixth image, Captain Jerontis switched to a blank screen to indicate the end of his transmission.

Almost immediately, Dianne reported, "I see an image of Rex nodding his head up and down. I think he is trying to tell us that he understands your message. Also, I am detecting feelings of hopefulness and sincere appreciation on his part. There is now a new image entering my mind. I see Rex and his family on their knees with their heads bowed. Either they are praying for our success, or they are humbly expressing their gratitude to us for what we are going to do for them." This image stayed in Dianne's mind for a full minute, then it faded away. Feeling the absence of mental energy from Rex, Dianne realized that this communication session had ended, so she and her colleagues returned to the flight deck.

Immediately after their arrival, Mike reported: "I've done a spectroscopic study of the atmosphere under our flight path over the Southern Continent and the Northern Continent. I've recorded the spectral signatures of both of the chemicals that are pouring out of the volcanic peaks on the Equatorial Continent. Evidently, the strong high altitude wind has enough turbulence in it to keep a substantial percentage of these toxins airborne until they reach these continents. I've also found these poisons present in lakes by doing a spectroscopic analysis of light reflected from their surfaces.

"Also, I had one of my assistants record high resolution optical images of the shores of these lakes. We've located several dead animals lying next to the water indicating that they were poisoned by the water. In addition, we have a video showing two large animals in the final minutes of their lives."

Mike displayed the video on the screen for all to see. It showed the two large animals lying on the lake shore with convulsive tremors surging through their bodies. The agony continued for several minutes, and then, both lay still. In appearance, the animals had a basic resemblance to elephants. "Our infrared data indicates that these animals had body temperatures above 110 degrees at the time of their deaths."

"Your data strongly validates the testimony Rex just gave us," commented Captain Jerontis. "I believe we now have a conclusive body of evidence that a chemical attack is in progress against these two continents that seeks to kill all living creatures. We have no way of knowing how long it has been going on or how long it will continue. Perhaps, it has been going on intermittently since the nuclear exchange in the opening phase of this war. Maybe, every time they have a strong westerly wind, they eject these poisons into the stratosphere. Most likely, they will continue this insanity for as long as they are capable of continuing it. Maybe, it is their intention to kill all life on this planet, and then come out of their mountains and repopulate the planet with life forms of their choosing. In order for life on these two continents to have any chance at all to survive and prosper, this evil plan must be thwarted. The chemical warfare machines must be shut down, and we are going to do exactly that."

Captain Jerontis sounded three notes on the Challenger's warning klaxon, then announced: "In five minutes we will begin acceleration into a geosynchronous transfer orbit. During the two hours following engine shutdown, there will be additional engine ignitions to adjust our speed and direction to achieve the desired orbital position."

Five minutes later, the Challenger's antimatter engines ignited on schedule. With the desired orbital parameters entered into the Challenger's flight control computer, there was little for Captain Jerontis and his crew to do except to monitor the starship's progress. This left them free to relax for a while and to plan an attack on the chemical warfare machines.

Gaining her husband's attention, Doctor Nemard looked into his eyes and said, "I agree with your decision to take immediate action. Aren't you glad that we don't have instantaneous communication with Earth that would make it possible for government bureaucrats to be in charge of this mission?"

"Do you think that they would handle this situation differently than we are?"

"Well, first they would have to appoint a commission to study the problem for at least three months. Then, they would appoint a second commission to study the findings of the first commission. After all of this studying had been completed, there would of course be the requirement to file an environmental impact statement which would also have to be studied by a commission to insure its validity. And let's not forget the rights of the killers who are manning the poison factories; after all, we've just imposed a death sentence on them, and they should have the right to at least ten years of legal appeals before we execute them. How much additional death took place on the Southern Continent and the Northern Continent during this long drawn out process wouldn't be as important as making sure that all bureaucratic and legal requirements were met before any substantive action was taken."

Captain Jerontis looked at his wife in amazement, chuckled, and said, "We are 4.35 light-years from Earth and have been in space for well over six years. After all this time, I am surprised that you still harbor all this deep-seated hostility for bureaucrats and their multitudes of costly time-consuming regulations and for a legal system that frequently seems more concerned with the rights of criminals than with the suffering of their victims."

"I don't feel any hostility. I'm just happy that we don't have to contend with multiple layers of bureaucratic nonsense anymore and that we can take prompt action when we need to."

"She makes a valid point," commented Moose. "What if we needed congressional approval before we could take action. How many months would we have to sit here in orbit waiting for all those endless debates to take place? I like our current situation. We are free to get the job done promptly and move on to Alcent, where we can get started with the project of building a home."

"I am beginning to think that I have a ship full of anti-establishment renegades who are happy to be free from bearing the burden of a bloated government bureaucracy," commented Captain Jerontis. "I wonder what kinds of political systems existed on this planet at the time the war started, what part they played in starting it, and if any of them have survived."

"Considering the almost total destruction of humanoid life that has taken place, it seems almost impossible that any kind of centralized government could still exist," noted Dianne.

"It's possible that the authority in charge of the chemical warfare machines is the largest political and military power base remaining on the planet," remarked Captain Jerontis.

"Maybe, each little pocket of life that has managed to survive has formed its own small self-sufficient social group," speculated Connie. "I wonder how large a social unit Rex is part of."

"Maybe, after we take care of the immediate problem of putting these chemical warfare machines out of operation, we can explore some societal questions with him," suggested Dianne. "I would like to know more about the community he lives in. Simple things, like how many are in his community, and how they provide themselves with the basic essentials of life. Also, I would like to get some basic information about the plants and animals that live down there."

"If he will show us his exact location, we could land a robot probe near him that would deliver a couple of video cameras equipped with microphones," stated Captain Jerontis. "Whatever he records with the cameras, he could transmit to us using the robot lander's communication equipment. The probe would also contain a viewing screen so we could broadcast to him."

"I like that idea," replied Dianne. "Communicating that way would be much faster and more convenient than the telepathic images we've been using."

After a brief pause in the conversation, Moose decided to change the subject and asked Captain Jerontis, "What do you think is going to be the most efficient way to shut down the chemical warfare machines?"

"As I see it, there are two approaches we can take. We can attempt to shut them down with minimal loss of life, or we can hit them with massive firepower with the intention of trapping and killing all the creatures who are inside the mountains operating those machines.

"In the first option, we hit the top of each mountain with a short burst of antimatter to create a powerful enough explosion to seal up the pipes that are spewing out the poisons. I believe a one-half-second burst should do the job. In less than twenty seconds, we can easily close all six of them. Then, we wait an hour to give the operators of the equipment an opportunity to leave. After that time has passed, we deliver a forty-second burst of antimatter to one of the mountain tops. The total explosive power delivered to the mountain top should be roughly equal to that of a five-megaton hydrogen bomb. This should be enough power to remove several thousand feet of the mountain top and cause massive avalanches of molten rock, hot mud, rocks, ice and snow. The lower levels of the mountain will be totally buried. A deep crater will be left in the top of what remains of the mountain. Then, we wait an hour to give the occupants of the remaining mountains a second chance to escape. When this time has expired, we blast the remaining five mountains in rapid succession.

"In the second attack option, we give them no chance to escape. In rapid succession, we simply hit all six mountains with a forty-second burst of antimatter. The rationale behind this kind of attack is that the creatures operating the chemical warfare machines are so totally evil in their philosophy towards life that they must be eliminated. Allowing them to escape destruction would simply give them the opportunity to find other destructive ways to express their hatred. The objective of this attack is to destroy both the machines and their operators.

"The objective of the first attack option is to destroy the chemical warfare machines and not their operators. There are some valid reasons to take this approach. First, our reconnaissance indicates that their society has been destroyed and that they can no longer produce weapons of mass destruction. These poison factories are all that remain from the terrible war: destroy them and the war is over. Second, it's possible that some of the creatures operating the chemical warfare machines are there against their will. Perhaps, they were forced to serve by an authoritarian government. Why not give them a chance to escape. Third, there has already been enough killing. If we destroy their ability to attack the rest of the planet, maybe, they will come to their senses and devote their energy to building a better life for themselves."

"I am not sure they are capable of devoting their energy to constructive activities," commented Doctor Nemard. "If we judge them by their current activity, it is difficult to reach any other conclusion except that they are insane in a very cruel, sadistic way. They must be aware that the chemical agents they are pumping into the stratosphere will indiscriminately kill exposed water-drinking creatures on two-thirds of this planet. Not to mention that an unexpected change in the wind direction would be hazardous to life on their continent. Since there is no possible gain for them in carrying out this attack, we must conclude that they are insanely cruel. That being the case, if we allow them to live, they will find cruel ways to prey upon their fellow humanoids, perhaps, even subjugating them and using them as slaves. Their current activity indicates that they would be extremely cruel slave masters. I believe that their demonstrated insanity is so deeply ingrained that they are incapable of change. We must not only destroy their chemical warfare capability, but we must also kill them."

"It almost seems paradoxical to hear a medical doctor recommending death for six large groups of humanoids," commented Captain Jerontis.

"On the contrary, if you put a medical perspective on this, I believe it is analogous to using radiation therapy to destroy six cancerous tumors that would otherwise destroy whatever normal life still remains on this planet. In regard to the possible presence of innocent individuals forced to serve against their will, if we allow them an opportunity to escape, the insanely cruel will also be able to escape, and this must be avoided. To put this in medical terms, when a malignant tumor is killed, it is sometimes necessary to kill some perfectly healthy tissue along with it to insure that all malignant tissue has been killed."

"I agree with her," stated Dianne. "The monstrous cruelty being committed here is almost unimaginable. What they are attempting is the genocide of several species including the genocide of a large percentage of their own species living on the other continents. I don't see any benefits that they can gain by doing this. Therefore, I believe this genocide is being attempted purely to satisfy an insane, hateful desire for revenge. In my mind, what they're doing qualifies as the ultimate war crime ever committed. It is an atrocity on a global scale. The penalty for a war crime of this magnitude should be death."

"I didn't realize our wives could be so blood thirsty," commented Moose to Captain Jerontis.

Staring directly into her husband's eyes, Dianne said, "I still cringe when I recall the cold hatred and evil that was transmitted into my mind when I was on the observation deck during our first pass over those mountains. The expression of that intense hatred for me at a time when I had no desire whatever to harm them tells me that these creatures will never be beneficial to this planet. They will always be insanely cruel predators intelligently looking for ways to satisfy their sadistic desires. We must eliminate them and their poison machines."

"I was with you on the observation deck," recalled Moose. "That was the only time I've ever seen you visibly shaken with fear."

"Given the intensity of the hatred that was expressed, why didn't they attack us at that time?" questioned Captain Jerontis.

After a few moments of thoughtful silence in which no one volunteered an answer, Captain Jerontis spoke in answer to his own question: "There are two obvious possibilities: either they have no way to attack us, or their defensive weapons are few in number and are reserved for use only when they are attacked."

"I think it might be partly the later possibility," commented Mike. "Our radar exploration did locate a number of missile silos with their concrete lids still in place. They may contain functional defensive missiles or even powerful laser weapons. Perhaps, they no longer have any ability to manufacture missiles and want to conserve what they have."

"Given the degree of hatred expressed, if they have powerful laser weapons, why didn't they attack us with them?" questioned Captain Jerontis.

"We could assume that they don't have laser weapons, since they didn't attack, but I think that would be a dangerous assumption," responded Mike. "I don't know what they're trying to gain with the chemical attack they're conducting, but it may be very important to them; so important that they were unwilling to risk an attack on us because they fear that we may be able to shut them down. Also, they may have concluded that we've come here from another planet. They may have reasoned that if we were from one of the other continents on this planet, we most certainly would have attacked them by now to shut down their chemical attack. Not knowing where we are from would add a huge uncertainty to their ability to estimate our capabilities. Uncertainty about the potency of our retaliatory capability does have a great deal of deterrent value. It's possible they've decided to leave us alone hoping that we won't interfere with their chemical attack and that we will eventually leave. Now, it must look to them like we are leaving, because we are rapidly accelerating away from this planet. Won't they be surprised when we launch our attack. But even if we catch them by surprise, we must expect prompt retaliation by whatever weapons they possess."

"The risk for us is that we simply don't know what their capabilities are," continued Mike. "It would be a tragic ending to our mission if we were destroyed in our effort to save this planet. It took twenty years to design and build this starship; and more than six additional years for us to get here. We and the people who made this mission possible have put so much into it that I think we should either attack with the strategy that has the lowest risk for us, or we should simply leave and not interfere with what is happening on this planet."

"Your reasoning and conclusions are difficult to disagree with," commented Captain Jerontis. "However, in view of everything that we've seen since arriving here, I don't think I would feel very good about myself if we left here without destroying these poison factories. I think life on this planet deserves a chance to have a good future. I've never enjoyed killing, but I think we need to forget the possibility that some of the humanoids inside those mountain fortresses might be there against their will and simply take them out as quickly as we can. I think the best way to do this would be to ... "

Captain Jerontis could not finish his statement, because he was interrupted by Mike: "Captain! Our infrared instruments have detected the sudden appearance of two hot spots next to the northernmost mountain. They are rising rapidly, and are without question the exhaust plumes of missiles. The computer has calculated their acceleration to be 37g. They are on course to intercept us, and with that high acceleration, they will reach us in just a few minutes. Our fire control computer has already aimed our particle-beam gun at the lead missile.

Captain Jerontis said, "They must have taken a look at our flight path and concluded that we are heading for geosynchronous orbit, and they must be convinced that we plan to attack them once we are on station. Their missiles do not have enough speed to attack us in a timely manner at that altitude. Therefore, they are attempting a preemptive strike against us. I don't think they will launch additional missiles until they find out how we deal with these two. Let's not fire on them until they reach their maximum speed. I want to know what their performance capability is, and I want to gain some additional altitude before they fire more missiles. However, since they might be nuclear armed, I don't want them getting any closer to us than about fifty miles. Immediately after we destroy these missiles, I want to attack the mountain fortress that fired them."

"Understood," responded Mike. "These missiles should be soft targets and easy to destroy. I've programmed the fire control system to hit each one with a ten-millisecond burst of antimatter. But we need to decide how much explosive power to deliver to the mountain fortress that fired them. Also, this gun has never been fired through a planet's atmosphere. I believe it will work, but we don't know that for sure."

"Captain! We have another potential problem," reported Moose. "Our radar has just detected a satellite near the orbital position we are headed for, but I am not detecting any electronic emissions from it. It could be a dead satellite, a relic from the beginning of this war, or it could be dormant and waiting for an activation signal. The fact that it's positioned directly over the mountains in a geosynchronous orbit makes me suspicious. Whatever its purpose, it could be armed with defensive weapons that could be used to attack us."

After a few moments of thought, Captain Jerontis said, "I think our lowest risk attack option is to destroy the two incoming missiles and then, immediately attack all six mountain fortresses in rapid succession. If we hit the top of each mountain with an eight-second burst of antimatter, this will be the equivalent of a direct hit from a one-megaton hydrogen bomb. Allowing two seconds for the fire control system to re-target successive mountains means that all six will be attacked in about a minute. This attack may not cause enough destruction to put them out of action permanently, but it should inflict enough damage to prevent additional attacks against us. This will give us all the time we need to deliver permanent destruction to these facilities."

While Captain Jerontis was speaking, Mike entered the attack instructions into the fire control computer. Then, he said, "The system is ready, and the missiles fired at us have reached their maximum velocity. They are closing on us at eight miles per second and will intercept us in seventy seconds."

Captain Jerontis sounded three notes on the warning klaxon and announced: "Our attack will begin in thirty seconds."

Twenty seconds later all hatches between adjoining compartments were closed and sealed to minimize air loss in the event the ship's hull was pierced. Then a ten-millisecond burst of antimatter particles hit the lead missile causing it to disappear in a blinding fireball followed immediately by the annihilation of the second missile in a brilliant fireball.

Two seconds later, a high-density beam of antimatter particles pierced B-2's atmosphere looking like a blazing lightning bolt from outer space. With awesome destructive power, it struck the top of the northernmost mountain instantly stopping its outflow of poisonous chemicals. The booming, thundering roar of the powerful, continuous explosion lasted for eight seconds. The enormous explosive release of pure energy from the mutual annihilation of matter and antimatter caused part of the mountain top to rise into the atmosphere and begin forming a huge mushroom shaped cloud. Additional massive amounts of mountain top material began cascading down the sides of the mountain in powerful avalanches that swept away and buried everything they encountered. In just a few seconds, several hundred feet of the mountain top was removed.

Mike exuberantly exclaimed, "The theory is correct: the beam does penetrate a planet's atmosphere exactly as predicted. Also, those missiles were nuclear armed, and the antimatter explosions were powerful enough to trigger their nuclear warheads. At least fifty times more energy was released than would have been from the antimatter we delivered to the missiles proving that they had nuclear warheads."

Two seconds after the northernmost chemical warfare complex was blasted, the second mountain-contained poison factory was bombarded with a high-density beam of antimatter particles for eight seconds. Then, two seconds later, the third one was attacked. Four seconds into this attack, the Challenger was hit by a powerful laser beam fired from a weapon located near the base of this mountain. The fire control computer immediately broke off its attack on the mountain top and blasted the laser, instantly putting it out of action. While this was taking place, eight more lasers fired on the Challenger: four from mountain number four, and two each from mountains five and six. During the next twenty seconds, all eight of the lasers were hit with short bursts of antimatter and blasted out of existence. Then, the fire control computer resumed the attack on the chemical warfare machines.

"Captain! We've sustained some damage as a result of the laser attack," reported Moose. "Four of them were able to melt holes through our micro-meteor shield before we disabled them. Two of these succeeded in burning holes through our hull."

With the aid of surveillance cameras, Moose displayed the damage on a video screen, and said, "The observation deck took a direct hit: that hole is about two feet across. Also, the hangar deck took a solid hit: that hole is about three feet across. The cargo shuttle has a large hole melted through its fuselage. It appears to be far enough forward so that the shuttle's nuclear reactor escaped damage. Had either of those laser beams hit one of our antimatter fuel tanks we would no longer exist. As it is, I don't think we've suffered any fatalities or injuries because there weren't suppose to be any personnel in the damaged areas."

"There are a total of thirty-nine missiles headed in our direction," reported Mike. "These are probably all that they have. They've probably concluded that they cannot prevent us from destroying their mountain fortresses, and they are making a final, desperate attempt to destroy us in retaliation for destroying them. By launching every missile they have, they are hoping to overwhelm our defenses."

"We've now shut down all six chemical warfare machines," stated Captain Jerontis. "Let's start taking out those missiles."

Mike punched in the appropriate instructions, and the fire control computer immediately began targeting and destroying the incoming missiles.

"So far, every missile we've hit has resulted in the detonation of a nuclear warhead," reported Mike. "Apparently, they're all nuclear armed."

"It was no accident or stroke of good luck that these poison factories survived the war," commented Captain Jerontis. "They were extremely well defended. Apparently, these aliens placed the highest priority on the survival of their chemical weapons, so that they could rain lethal toxins down on their enemies long after the war was over. By subjecting their enemies to a continuing rain of death for many years after the war was over, they probably hoped to rebuild their society while denying their enemies the same opportunity. They evidently believed that even if the nuclear phase of the war ended in a stalemate, they could still eventually be the victors if their poison factories survived."

Doctor Nemard commented, "If that's the case, I wonder what factors were involved that would cause a political system to become so insanely malicious that it would be willing to destroy all life on the rest of the planet so that it could become the only remaining power."

"You are the mission psychiatrist, what do you think would motivate people to do something like that?" asked Captain Jerontis.

"I can only speculate, but it's possible that some fanatical religious cult gained power. Perhaps, it was a cult that practiced total intolerance of all who refused to accept its doctrines. Maybe, the humanoids on the other two continents completely rejected this religion and its teachings. Unable to tolerate rejection, the only way the cult based political system could achieve 100% membership was to kill or enslave all that could not be coerced to join it. On a smaller scale, there are examples of this in human history."

"There isn't any way that we can prove your theory, but it is at least a possible explanation for what has happened here," commented Captain Jerontis.

"Maybe, after this battle is over, we can establish better communications with Rex, and he can inform us about this planet's recent history," commented Dianne.

"Captain! We've completed the destruction of all the missiles that were launched against us," reported Mike.

"Good! Let's finish the destruction of these mountain fortresses, starting with mountain number four. Since it was the most heavily defended, it might be their command center. Hit it with a sixty-second burst, and hit the other five with forty-second bursts. When the smoke clears, we will survey the damage and decide if any additional attacks are needed."

"Understood," replied Mike as he entered the instructions into the fire control computer, which immediately began the process of carrying out the attacks.

"Captain! We are still on course for geosynchronous orbit," stated Moose. "Our plan was to attack from there, but our attack will be over by the time we arrive in that orbit. Are you planning to investigate the satellite that our radar search discovered up there?"

"Since we've already expended most of the fuel needed to reach geosynchronous orbit, we might as well take a look at it," replied Captain Jerontis. "You and I can do that while Mike and his engineering staff are busy repairing the damage to this starship. By taking a look at the equipment on that satellite, we can discover its purpose. Its mass will tell us how much booster power they once had. Studying its instrumentation, electrical power source, and construction materials will give us an indication of the level of technological advancement achieved by the aliens. Who knows, there may be something there that we can use."

Moose responded, "There is some risk involved in investigating that satellite. It could be armed with defensive weapons, or it could be carrying a bomb designed to go off if the satellite is tampered with. In view of the damage we've already suffered, I think we should avoid additional risk, and just go to Alcent. We will face plenty of danger once we arrive there."

"I don't want to take any unnecessary risk either, but we need to learn as much as we can about these aliens before we leave here," asserted Captain Jerontis. "Since you are worried about risk, I want you to devise a plan to investigate that satellite that will reduce our risk to an absolute minimum. Figure out a way to determine if that satellite is armed; if it isn't, I would like to capture it and take it with us."

Moose stared at Captain Jerontis in disbelief for a few moments. Then, he said, "You aren't joking! You are serious! You do want to take it with us, don't you?"

"Only if we can determine beyond a reasonable doubt that it is safe to do that, and if our on-site investigation reveals that we might gain some significant knowledge by having additional time to study it."

"I will develop a plan to achieve those objectives with zero risk," declared Moose with conviction.

Captain Jerontis made eye contact with Mike in a way that Mike interpreted as a silent request for a progress report. In response, Mike simply stated, "Three down and three to go."

"You are removing a big chunk of material from the top of each mountain and creating massive avalanches that even contain molten rock. In addition, you are blasting a deep crater in the top of what remains of each mountain, and you are acting like doing all this is a simple routine matter. You seem to be enjoying yourself."

"The capability of the fire control system coupled with the astounding power of the antimatter particle-beam gun makes the job easy, and the flawless performance of this equipment does make the task rather routine. Having this tremendous power at my fingertips and using it to rescue a planet from genocide gives me a feeling of exhilaration. Having and using the power to determine a planet's future is almost like playing God."

"I can understand how you could feel that way," commented Captain Jerontis.

Mike asked, "Can you imagine the horrible consequences, if a weapon system like this fell into the wrong hands? A military power possessing a spaceship armed with this system could hold an entire planet hostage, yet it was essential to our survival when we passed through that large constellation of interstellar asteroids a few years ago."

After a few moments of thought, Captain Jerontis said, "The U.S. presumably developed this gun for the sole purpose of increasing our probability of survival, but now that they have this technology, I wonder if they've built more of them to guarantee national security. During its multiyear test and development period, this gun was used to annihilate all the unwanted space junk orbiting Earth. This must have made many politicians and military leaders aware of the system's potential. A benevolent power possessing this system could truly become the world's police force."

"At the moment, we are the police force for this planet," declared Mike, "and we've just completed the job of permanently shutting down the largest scale criminal activity I've ever seen."

A short time latter, with the Challenger approaching geosynchronous orbit, Moose reported: "We are about four hundred miles from the alien satellite, and I have some pretty good images of most of it. From the way that it is slowly tumbling, it appears to be out of control, and that would indicate that it is no longer a functional satellite."

Captain Jerontis looked at the images on the video screen and said, "While that could be true, it's also possible that it is simply in a dormant state awaiting an activation signal."

"To cover that possibility, let's aim the particle beam gun at the satellite and have the fire control system maintain the lock-on," stated Moose. "Then, if it does anything threatening, we can instantly destroy it."

Captain Jerontis looked at Mike, who said, "Already programmed in."

"If it is an armed, functional satellite that is currently in a dormant state, maybe we can trick it into activating itself by making it think that it is about to be attacked," suggested Moose. "We can direct an intense radar beam at it to make it think that it's being targeted. We can go through the full range of frequencies available to us and find out if there's any response to any of them."

"That's a good idea," agreed Captain Jerontis, "but before you do that, let's illuminate it with a laser beam so that we can get more detail out of our optical images. Part of that satellite isn't very well illuminated and it is difficult to see very much detail in the dark area."

Moose aimed a laser at the satellite and turned it on, brightly illuminating the satellite's dark side.

After studying the enhanced optical images for a few moments, Captain Jerontis said, "There isn't any obvious physical damage, so if it's no longer operational, it must be the result of internal problems. Most likely, it was launched thirty or more years ago before the war started. If that's the case, old age could certainly have shut it down by now. Judging from the antenna configuration, it may have been a communication satellite, perhaps for military use. Also, it has enough cameras on it, so that it may have been used for surveillance. One of its functions may have been to monitor the weather in this hemisphere."

Speaking to Moose, Captain Jerontis said, "Proceed with your radar assault, and let's see if there is any response."

Moose did as directed. After a couple of minutes of trying various frequencies, Moose said, "There has been no attempt to jam our radar; in fact, there has been no response of any kind."

"So, do you think that it's safe to move in and do a hands-on investigation of that satellite?" questioned Captain Jerontis.

"No! I don't think we should expose ourselves to possible risk. I think we should close to a distance of about fifty miles. Then, we should launch one of the robot external-repair vehicles to the satellite and use it to do the investigation. With it, we should be able to determine if this is a dead satellite and if it is worth taking with us."

"That sounds like a more reasonable course of action."

A short time later, the Challenger reached geosynchronous orbit and took up a position about fifty miles away from the alien satellite. Shortly thereafter, Moose dispatched one of the robot repair vehicles on a course to the alien spacecraft. Mike and his engineering staff used the other one to begin the task of repairing the holes in the Challenger's hull.

In less than an hour, Moose's robot arrived at the alien satellite. Moose directed the robot to slowly circle the satellite and send back minutely detailed images of all parts of it. Next, he aligned the robot with the tumbling satellite's axis of rotation. Then, using the robot's control rockets, Moose gave it a rotational velocity equal to that of the alien spacecraft, thereby eliminating all relative motion. Finally, using the robot's grappling arms, he attached the robot to the alien spacecraft.

Moose turned to Captain Jerontis and said, "We've captured it. Now, we can take a look inside."

"Good work," acknowledged Captain Jerontis.

Moose directed the robot to drill a small hole through a side panel in the satellite's main body. Then, a tiny video camera equipped with a lamp was passed through the hole into the satellite's interior.

After viewing detailed images of the spacecraft's interior for a few minutes, Captain Jerontis said, "I don't see anything unusual or threatening in this area. I wonder what the rest of its interior looks like."

"We'll soon find out," responded Moose as he began drilling an access hole into another compartment. I don't know about you, but I am thrilled about being the first human to investigate a high-tech piece of equipment that was designed and built by an intelligent extraterrestrial species."

"You've undergone quite a change of heart. Earlier, you wanted to ignore this satellite's existence and move on; now, you are excited by the possibility of learning about the aliens."

"Earlier, I felt fortunate to be alive; after all, we'd just had a couple holes burned through our hull. Had one of those laser beams hit one of our antimatter fuel tanks, we would've instantaneously ceased to exist. My hopes and dreams of the last few years would have vanished in an instant. I am ready to move on to Alcent, build a home, and raise a family. I don't want to take any additional potentially deadly risks."

"I didn't realize that our near catastrophe affected you so deeply, but I understand how you feel. We should be able to finish up everything we need to do at this planet in just a couple days, and then, we can move on."

"Thanks for your understanding," replied Moose. "I appreciate that."

"We've now penetrated another compartment," announced Moose as the images began appearing on the video screen.

After viewing the images for a few minutes, both men agreed that everything looked normal and harmless.

About an hour and a half later, Moose and Captain Jerontis completed their investigation of the satellite's interior. Captain Jerontis stated, "From everything that we've seen, I believe this satellite is exactly what it appears to be: a communications and surveillance spacecraft that has been inoperative for a long time. The fact that its control gyros are not operative combined with the fact that its station keeping fuel tanks are empty is enough all by itself to convince me that this is a long-dead satellite."

"Those empty fuel tanks point to a fact that we haven't considered, and that is that this spacecraft has an easterly drift of about twelve miles per day," commented Moose. "If that drift rate was imparted to it at about the time it ceased to function, and if we assume that this satellite has been inoperative for about twenty years; then, this satellite may have been located over the other two continents during its operational lifetime. They could have used it as a communications link between the two continents and for weather information. If this satellite belonged to them, and was a non-military satellite; then, it is unlikely to be armed with any kind of weapon system. This possibility tends to substantiate the fact that we haven't found any."

"Does this mean that you are ready to declare that it is safe for us to take this satellite with us, so that we can do a detailed analysis of its components and the materials used in its construction?"

After pondering the question for a few moments, Moose asked, "Is there any possibility that this satellite could be harboring viable toxic microbes after all these years in the harsh environment of space?"

"To me, that seems almost impossible, but I think we should have our wives answer that question. Do you have any other objection to taking this satellite with us?"

"None that I can think of," replied Moose.

"Good! Let's attach both the satellite and the robot repair vehicle to external hard points on our hull until our wives have had a chance to investigate them for viable toxic microbes. Even finding and examining dead microbes would be educational."

"I will begin the process of bringing back the historical artifact that we've so bravely captured," jested Moose in a playful tone.

"You're quite cheerful all of a sudden."

"We're almost home. In just a few weeks, we'll arrive at Alcent. Who knows, we may find a warm, exotic, sandy beach that we can build our homes next to. As I recall, it was just a little over six years ago when I was about to go to just such a beach for a much needed vacation. But, it wasn't to be. Why? Because, you boldly caused me to cancel my plans by convincing me that it would be in my best interest to accompany you on this trip. Out of loyalty to you, based on our long-term friendship, I scrapped my vacation plans and accepted your offer. Why? Because, I knew that you desperately needed my engineering talents and a little social guidance from time to time. In repayment for my professional support all these years, I think that the least you can do would be to make sure that I get my long-delayed vacation, perhaps, on a nice warm sandy beach on Alcent, preferably, one that is perfectly safe for humans."

Doing his best to fake an expression of disgust, Captain Jerontis responded, "Some sense of appreciation you have. I put my career on the line when I sneaked you on this ship, so you could be part of the ultimate adventure of all time. And now, more than six years later, the only thanks that I get is that I still have to listen to you snivel about a missed vacation trip to some partially submerged patch of sand."

"Somehow that just doesn't seem fair," replied Moose in a jovial tone, followed by a bit of laughter.

"And now, you're actually laughing at my need to be appreciated. You're being very insensitive. I think I will consult Doctor Nemard about you and find out if she is interested in giving you some sensitivity training. But, who knows, she might say that you are a hopeless case and that there is nothing she can do to help you."

"Or she might decide to participate in our silliness and get a few laughs for herself."

After a few moments of silence, during which both men enjoyed their own relaxed thoughts, Moose said, "In all seriousness, I have been and still am deeply grateful to you for the way you gave me a chance to be on this mission when the opportunity arose. Literally speaking, we've come a very long way since then."

"That's almost a severe understatement of reality. Along with the rest of the Challenger's personnel, we've traveled infinitely faster and farther than anyone else in history. What we've accomplished existed only in science fiction just a few years ago. Right from the beginning, there was never any guarantee that we would be successful, but our long journey is almost over. In just a few weeks, we will begin exploring the planet that will become our home."

"With an entire planet at our disposal, we should be able to find some rather choice real estate on which to build our homes. We may even end up living next to a partially submerged patch of sand as you so unromantically described my dream vacation spot."

"That's almost guaranteed. Since both of our shuttles are equipped with hydrofoils, we must live on the shore of a body of water that is large enough for us to land on and takeoff from. Like you, I am excited about the possibilities."

Before either man could make another comment, Mike reported in with his communicator: "Captain! We have completed the repair of the hole through the hangar deck hull. In about an hour, we will be finished with the repair of the hole in the observation deck hull. The hole in the cargo shuttle's fuselage will be easy to repair. We are very lucky that none of the shuttle's critical systems were destroyed."

"Thank you for the progress report," replied Captain Jerontis.

Turning to Moose, Captain Jerontis asked, "How long before your project is complete?"

"The robot repair vehicle will arrive here with our trophy in about twenty minutes. I will need an additional half hour to secure them both to the hull."

A little over an hour later, Mike arrived on the flight deck and reported: "We've completed repairs to the hull, and both areas have been pressurized. They are now safe for our personnel to enter. We plan to repair the shuttle on the way to Alcent."

"I assume that you did a good job," stated Captain Jerontis. "Do I get any kind of guarantee?"

"I would stake my life on it. By that, I mean that I would be willing to roll out a sleeping bag next to either of the repaired holes and camp out for a while; in case of failure, I would be sucked into the vacuum of space."

"So you're telling me that there is a life-time guarantee on your repair work?"

"Absolutely!"

"Moose! Do you have the alien satellite and the robot repair vehicle secured to the hull?" questioned Captain Jerontis.

"Sure do!"

"I think it's time to drop down to a lower orbit and do a reconnaissance run over those chemical warfare complexes that we shut down," stated Captain Jerontis. "Before we move on, we need to be certain that they are permanently out of action."

Captain Jerontis sounded three blasts on the warning klaxon, and announced: "In three minutes we will begin 1 g acceleration to move into a polar orbit at an altitude of 230 miles."

Three minutes later, the Challenger's antimatter engines ignited on schedule to begin the orbital transfer that would require about three hours.

Directing his attention to Moose and Mike, Captain Jerontis said, "During the past hour, I've done a computer analysis of the data gathered by our instruments during our attack against those mountains. Each mountain is now about a half mile shorter than it was. Even though the crater in the top of what's left of each mountain is only a quarter of a mile deep, there is a high probability that the beam of antimatter particles penetrated each mountain to depth of several miles during the attacks. The computer has concluded that the tremendous release of energy in the attacks resulted in a temperature above one million degrees at the leading edge of the particle beam. Massive amounts of rock simply melted, reached the boiling point, and evaporated causing extremely high pressure to build up. This extremely hot, high-pressure mixture of liquid and gaseous rock gushed upward around the incoming particle beam and poured out of the top of each mountain looking like an erupting volcano. When the particle beam gun was shut off, the eruptions continued until the pressure was dissipated. Then, the sides of the vertical tunnels, being in a super hot state of plasticity, collapsed inward filling the tunnels to the point that they now look like craters that are only a quarter of a mile deep. If the computer is correct in its analysis of the data, then the hollowed out chambers that contained the chemical warfare equipment must have collapsed. The computer has concluded that the seismic energy rumbling through those chambers was more than adequate to have caused chamber collapse and complete destruction of all equipment."

"Is it possible that the particle beam may have penetrated all the way to the chambers containing the chemical warfare equipment?" questioned Mike.

"I don't know at what level in these mountains the chambers were located, but based on the data we have, the computer has calculated that the particle beam penetrated to a depth of three to four miles. If the manufacturing chambers were located near the base of each mountain, the particle beam probably did not reach them, but there is a high probability that molten rock may have poured into and flooded those chambers. The extremely high temperatures and pressures generated by the incoming beam of antimatter particles may have sent a high speed jet of liquid and gaseous rock down the same pipes that the aliens used to pour poisonous chemicals into the stratosphere."

"That would be true justice if the pipes they built to carry poisons into the atmosphere served to transport the fires of hell into their poison manufacturing complexes," commented Moose. "If this did happen, then in a matter of a few seconds, they and their poison manufacturing equipment were melted into a liquid state. I don't see any way that they could have survived our attack."

"I don't either," agreed Captain Jerontis. "But I want our defenses on full alert anyway."

"The programs I put into the fire control computer earlier are still there," stated Mike.

Three hours later, the Challenger began its low altitude pass over the target area. Reviewing high definition optical images, Captain Jerontis commented, "The massive avalanches have deeply buried everything around the base of this mountain. All the snow and ice we melted has caused some destructive floods. It looks like a massive volcanic eruption has just occurred. The mountain and the area around its base look like a volcanic wasteland. I wish we could have shut them down without inflicting so much destruction on such a scenic area."

"We did what we had to do," stated Doctor Nemard.

"In many respects our attacks were like natural volcanic eruptions," stated Dianne. "As destructive as they are, nature always recovers. Life is not fragile: it is tenacious. Life around these mountains will recover, and so will life on the rest of this planet, now that the poison factories no longer exist."

Turning to Dianne, Captain Jerontis said, "In about an hour, you will have an opportunity to communicate with Rex. Let's show him images of this destruction, so that he will know that the era of poisonous rain will end once the atmosphere has cleansed itself."

"That should make him and his family very happy," stated Dianne.

"Also, we need to tell him that we'll soon be leaving for Alcent, probably in less than a day. Tell him that if he'll give us his location, we'll send down a robot lander that will contain communication equipment. Tell him that we'll station a satellite in geosynchronous orbit over his location that will be capable of relaying communication between him and us when we are on Alcent. This satellite will also provide him with weather information. We will also put a surveillance satellite in a polar orbit at an altitude of 350 miles. These two satellites are mainly for our benefit, because I want to monitor activity on this planet. Also, I believe that Rex will be a friendly and reliable source of information. Giving him access to the data from these satellites will put him in the position of being able to help us interpret the data, if the need arises."

"Communicating all of this with nothing more than telepathic images is going to be a challenge," commented Dianne. "I am going to my office to generate the computer images I will need to accomplish this."

A short time later, Mike said, "We've now taken a close look at all six of our targets, and I see nothing that would indicate anything other than complete and permanent destruction of the poison factories. The job is done."

FIVE

Pioneer Island

TIME: 6 Years, 250 Days A.L.E.

Michelle's latest mission update to Earth:

"We have left B-2 and are on course for Alcent. Having been under acceleration at a steady 1g for 24 hours, we have reached a velocity of 527 miles per second and are currently 22,760,000 miles from B-2. Our flight plan calls for acceleration to continue for two more days reaching a velocity of 1,581 miles per second. We will coast for about 15 days, followed by three days of deceleration at 1g. Even though Alcent is 2.45 billion miles away from B-2, we will be there in less than three weeks."

After transmitting her mission update, Michelle went to the cafeteria to relax with Dianne and Doctor Nemard.

"How does it feel to be the first human to have communicated with an intelligent alien?" Michelle asked Dianne.

"Pretty good."

Michelle was incredulous, "*Pretty good*! You've done something that no other human has ever done, in a unique way, and all you can say is a rather matter of fact, *Pretty good*?"

Surprised by the strength of Michelle's reaction, Dianne answered, "I wasn't trying to sound like the experience was just another routine day at the office. It's just that right now, I feel relaxed and laid back, like I'm on vacation."

"I think you deserve a vacation. You've been involved in some very intense mental and emotional activity, but how do you feel about it?"

"It was a thrilling experience, especially for me, because I've always believed that we aren't the only intelligent species in the universe. But, even in my wildest dreams, I never thought that I would be the first person to communicate with an intelligent alien, and prove that we aren't alone."

"If we had gone directly to Alcent without swinging by B-2, we would've never discovered them. As eager as we are to start building our homes on Alcent, we could easily have skipped visiting B-2," Doctor Nemard commented.

"But if we'd done that, we would've always had that unanswered question about the possible existence of life on B-2," Michelle said.

"That question would have tugged at my mind a lot," declared Dianne. "I've devoted my life to the study of life, and having an earth-like planet nearby would've always made me wonder if life exists there."

"I would've been curious about that too," commented Michelle. "Then again, I've often been accused of having an overly abundant supply of curiosity. That's undoubtedly what motivated me to become a science reporter. Constant exposure to the latest scientific discoveries has always been exciting to me and has served to both satisfy and stimulate my curiosity. Being in a starship with the capability to visit a nearby earth-like planet and not taking advantage of that capability would've been disappointing."

"When we're busy building our homes on Alcent, we will have the satisfaction of knowing that we aren't alone in our little corner of the galaxy," added Doctor Nemard. "Also, I like the idea of having intelligent nearby interstellar neighbors. Once we overcome the language barrier, communicating with them will be much easier."

Directing her question to Michelle, Doctor Nemard asked, "How do you like having the responsibility of teaching the aliens our language and learning theirs?"

"Those satellites we placed in orbit around B-2 and the ground equipment we gave Rex will make the job easier. Now we're able to transmit large volumes of information back and forth or do nothing more than just socialize."

"Do you like that kind of responsibility?"

"I like it! It will be challenging, but it will be fun. I will be working with Rex's wife, Shannon. We've already started the project, and I've found her to be a warm, intelligent individual filled with enthusiasm. She has such a positive attitude. In view of the horrible tragedy inflicted on their planet by the long devastating war, I think her upbeat personality is truly remarkable. I really like working with her."

"Much of her positive outlook might be a direct result of us destroying those chemical warfare complexes," stated Dianne.

"That's definitely true," agreed Michelle. "The first words that she taught me from their language is their equivalent of the English phrase, *Thank you.* She has been very emotional in its use. I think they view us as the saviors of their planet. They seem very comfortable with the fact that we will be living nearby on Alcent."

"Perhaps, they think that we are willing and able to come back if they need us," stated Doctor Nemard.

Dianne added, "Also, they know that we have advanced high-tech capabilities, and they're probably hoping that we'll help them solve the critical medical and biological problems created by the war."

"That might be one of the reasons why Shannon is so eager to learn our language," speculated Michelle.

"True," agreed Dianne. "But, I think they're just as excited about getting acquainted with us as we are about getting acquainted with them. Finding out that they're not the only intelligent species in the universe has to be an astounding event in their lives."

Facing Dianne, Michelle asked, "How did you feel at the exact moment when you first became aware that an alien was attempting to contact you?"

"It caught me completely by surprise. I was totally unprepared for it. I was on the observation deck observing B-2, and I was wondering if any kind of life existed on it. In answer to my question, an awareness of the presence of life flowed into my mind. It felt like my mind was being gently touched, sort of like a mental caress. I guess you could call it a mental handshake that was done in a warm friendly manner. It was like of someone saying: Yes! I do exist; let's get acquainted."

"What was your reaction to that?" asked Michelle.

"I was puzzled by it. I strongly felt the presence of life, but I didn't understand how I could sense its presence. Since this was my first experience with telepathic communication, it didn't immediately dawn upon me that this was what was happening. After all, we've never been able to scientifically prove the existence of a human ability to communicate telepathically. So there I was, strongly convinced of the presence of life, but troubled by the fact that I didn't understand how I could know that."

"Since we are in an alien environment, I can understand how such an inexplicable mental experience could be cause for concern," stated Michelle.

After a brief pause, Michelle continued, "About twelve hours after that experience, you must have been very excited when Rex transmitted a sharply detailed image of himself directly into your mind. During that single moment in time: the existence of an intelligent alien species was confirmed, communication with it was achieved, and the existence of the ability to telepathically transmit images became known. It was truly an epic moment in human history, and you were directly involved."

"I feel very good about that," admitted Dianne. "When I was a teenager, I made it my goal to be a part of this mission. I studied very hard to become the best that I could possibly be, but I never dreamed that all of my intense studying and dedication would eventually result in me becoming the first human to communicate with an intelligent alien."

"You must feel a great deal of personal pride," commented Michelle.

"I do! It was very gratifying and definitely a high point in my career."

"Your experience confirms a belief that I've held for a long time, and that is that an individual who relentlessly strives to achieve excellence will always find unexpected rewards," Michelle commented.

Directing her remark to Michelle, Doctor Nemard said, "Your presence on this ship also tends to confirm that concept."

"What do you mean by that?" questioned Michelle.

"Very simple! Your pursuit of and achievement of excellence in your career is largely responsible for you having been selected to be a part of the news team that covered our departure from Earth. I'm referring to that press conference that took place on this ship nearly seven years ago. Your part in it gave your husband an opportunity to hide you on this ship. I would be willing to bet that you never dreamed that your achievement of excellence in your career would result in you becoming a part of this mission."

"That's definitely true," admitted Michelle.

"Your achievement of excellence in your career has also had an unexpected reward for the rest of us," declared Dianne.

"What do you mean?" questioned Michelle.

"Because of your presence, we are all alive. You discovered the sabotage to our ship only a few minutes before we would've been annihilated. And because of that, Rex and his people will no longer have to endure poisonous rain. All because you achieved excellence in your career."

Michelle looked at Dianne and Doctor Nemard, "I appreciate your recognition. Coming from my best friends makes it more meaningful to me than all of the *Excellence In Reporting Awards* I received during my career back on Earth. Now that we are on the final leg of our journey to our new home, the career that I devoted myself to back on Earth seems very distant. In less than three weeks, we will begin exploring Alcent in search of an ideal location for our new home. Won't that be exciting?"

TIME: 6 Years, 269 Days, 23 Hours, 15 Minutes A.L.E.
Michelle's latest mission update to Earth:

"We are currently 29,000 miles from Alcent and are approaching the planet at a velocity of 21.5 miles per second. Losing speed at a steady 1g, our velocity will be reduced to five miles per second in forty-five minutes. At that time, we will enter a polar orbit around Alcent at an altitude of 210 miles."

After transmitting her brief message, Michelle joined Doctor Nemard, Matthew, and Denise on the observation deck. Filled with joy, Michelle announced to the children in an exuberant tone: "That planet will soon be our new home."

Never having been on a planet and not aware of the distance involved, Matthew said, "It doesn't look very big. Will our new home be smaller than our starship home?" he asked.

Recognizing how sincere her son was in asking such a question, Michelle wondered how to answer it so that the children could get a true appreciation for the enormous difference in size between Alcent and the Challenger. Quickly deciding that this was impossible and that they would not comprehend the vast open spaces on Alcent until they actually experienced them, Michelle simply explained, "Our new home will be much larger than our starship."

"How will we get inside of it?" questioned Denise.

"We are going to live on its outside surface," responded Connie.

Being only five years old, and having lived all of her short life inside a cylindrical starship, this concept presented quite a large problem to Denise. A problem compounded by the fact that she had never experienced planetary gravity or the wide open spaces that exist on a planet. Displaying a very obvious puzzled expression, Denise gazed at the small sphere, seemingly suspended in empty space, and then said, "But it's round like a ball. What will happen if we fall off of it?"

Connie patiently grasped her daughter's hand, and both sat down on the observation deck. Interested in the same problem, Matthew sat down next to Connie and anxiously awaited an explanation. Giving her attention to both children, Connie asked, "Do you remember a few days ago when we were weightless, and we were able to float around in our starship?"

After both children said yes, Connie continued, "Right now, we cannot float around, can we?"

After both children said no, Connie said, "That is because we have artificial gravity. It holds us against this floor."

Then, she asked both children to stand up and jump as high as they could. After both children had done this several times, Connie said, "Even when you jump as high as you can the gravity pulls you back down. Our new home on Alcent will have gravity as strong as you feel now. No matter how high you jump or how fast you run, you will never fall off."

After thinking about it for a few moments, the children seemed to grasp the concept and accept the reassurance from Connie. Both now stood up, leaned against the crystal-clear plastic hull, and gazed at Alcent.

Observing the children deeply lost in thought about their future home, Michelle wondered if they would have any emotional problems with leaving the comfort and security of the only home they had ever known. Since there would be several months of exploration before a manned landing took place, Michelle decided that there would be ample time to prepare the children for the big event.

Recalling an event from history, Michelle thought about the fact that back in 1492, Christopher Columbus had been warned that the Earth was flat and that when he and his ships reached the edge of the Earth, they would fall off into a bottomless abyss. Seeing Alcent from 29,000 miles away and observing it grow in apparent size as they approached it, Matthew and Denise would have the true nature of their new home indelibly impressed into their minds along with an understanding of gravity and weightlessness.

Michelle's thoughts were interrupted by her son who asked, "Is Alcent like the Earth where you came from?"

Matthew's question stimulated Michelle to mentally recall fond memories from the distant planet Earth, a planet that she would never see again. Michelle remembered the pleasant experience of a passing rain shower on a mild summer day followed by warm sunshine and the fragrance of clean, fresh air accompanied by the sound of wild birds happily singing. In sharp contrast to this were the winter snow storms that turned the countryside into a winter wonderland that on a clear, cold night seemed so bright, quiet, and peaceful under the light of the full moon. Then, she thought about the backpack camping trips through forests over mountainous terrain bordering the vast Pacific Ocean. The pleasant memories flooding through Michelle's mind served to heighten her desire to leave the confinement of the starship that had been her home for so many years. Even though grave danger would always be present on Alcent, she longed for the pleasant experiences derived from living on an earth-like planet.

Michelle was jogged out of her mesmerized mental state by her son who had lost his patience, grasped her hand, and tugged on it while saying, "Mother, is Alcent like the Earth that you came from?"

Looking into her son's eager upturned face, Michelle said, "I didn't mean to ignore you, but I was thinking about Earth. It was my home for a long time, and I miss it. In many ways, Alcent is like Earth. Living there will be fun and exciting. You will see many of the things that you've only seen in movies from Earth."

Recalling scenes from a movie that he had seen just the previous day, Matthew asked, "Will our new home have big trees?"

"Yes, it will."

"Will there be a tree big enough for Dad to build a tree house in?" questioned Matthew.

"Some of the trees on Alcent are huge," replied Michelle.

"But will Dad and uncle Jerry have time to build a tree house for Denise and I to play in?"

Michelle looked at Connie and asked, "What do you think about the possibility of that happening?"

Connie gazed at the eager faces of both children and said, "I think your fathers will find the time to build you a tree house. In fact, there just might be lots of volunteer help on the project. I think some of the adults will enjoy such an undertaking, just for the sake of reliving childhood fantasies. The tree house just might end up being large enough for adults to relax in."

"I think that's quite likely," agreed Michelle.

Denise asked, "Will there be birds in the trees to sing pretty songs like the birds in the movie we saw yesterday?"

"We don't know if there are songbirds on Alcent," responded Connie.

Matthew looked worried, "Will there be monster bears by our new home that can climb the tree all the way up to our tree house?"

Matthew's question brought a look of fear to Denise's face. Noticing this, Connie sought to allay both children's worries by acknowledging the danger and assuring them that they would be protected: "We don't know if there are any tree-climbing bears on Alcent, but we do know that there are many wild animals. We don't know if any of them can climb trees, but some of them are very big and very dangerous. But you don't need to worry about them, because we have powerful guns, and we will protect you."

Accepting Connie's reassurance, both children again leaned against the transparent plastic hull to resume gazing at the now much larger appearing Alcent. After a few moments, Matthew exclaimed, "Look Mom! It's getting bigger!"

Michelle responded, "It's not getting bigger; it only looks like it's getting bigger because we are rapidly moving closer to it. We'll soon be close enough so that you will begin to understand how large it really is."

While Matthew was busy thinking about what his mother had just told him, Denise noticed the beautiful deep blue color of a large part of Alcent and the dark green color of a large area bordering the blue area. She also noticed brilliant patches of white overlaying parts of both areas. Turning to her mother, she said, "I like the blue part. It's the same color as my eyes. Will our new home be on the blue part?"

Connie smiled at the pure innocence and sincerity of the question and wondered how to instill in her five-year old daughter the concept of a vast ocean in view of the fact that the largest quantity of water that Denise had ever experienced was in the bathtub. Connie decided to save the size lesson for a later time and simply said, "The blue area is a huge body of water. We might build our home next to it but not on it."

"Is the dark green area where trees grow?" questioned Denise.

"Yes, and there are also many other kinds of plants growing there," Connie replied.

"What are the bright white areas?" asked Matthew.

"Those are clouds," answered Connie.

"But, they look different from the clouds in the movies," objected Matthew. "These clouds are brighter and more white."

"That's because we are above the clouds, and we can see the brilliant light from Alpha Centauri A that they are reflecting," Connie said, "The people in the movies were below the clouds looking up at them. When clouds are thick, not very much light can pass through them. That is why they looked so dark."

Reflecting on what Connie had just said, both children returned to staring at Alcent. Denise again turned to her mother and asked, "What are those clouds made out of? What do they do?"

Directing her attention to both Matthew and Denise, Connie answered, "Both of you always help us water our plants. Do you know why we give them water?"

"Because plants will die without water," the children replied, almost in unison.

"The trees and the other wild plants growing on Alcent need water too," Connie explained, "The clouds are made out of tiny droplets of water. Sometimes the clouds have more water than they can hold, and some of it turns into rain and falls out of the clouds. The rain waters the trees and all the other wild plants."

"I saw rain in the movie we watched yesterday!" Denise proudly exclaimed.

"I saw the rain too," stated Matthew. "When it started raining, the children went into their tree house, so they wouldn't get wet. After the rain, they had fun running through small pools of water. I think our new home will be fun. When can we go there?"

Detecting the eagerness in Matthew's voice, Michelle recognized that her son would not have any emotional problems leaving the comfort and security of the starship. She responded to his question by saying, "In a few minutes, we will be in orbit; and by the time we complete one orbit, you'll see just how big Alcent really is. It is so big that we'll have to explore it for several months with our telescopes and other instruments, so that we can find a safe place to live. Then, we'll go down and start building our new home."

"Will you show me pictures of the plants and animals that you find with the telescopes?" asked Matthew.

"Yes, we will," responded Michelle.

Denise quickly asked, "Will you show me too?"

"Yes!" replied Michelle.

Pleased with how inquisitive the children were being, Connie looked at Michelle and said, "I think our children want to help us explore Alcent and find a good place to build our new home."

Before Michelle could respond to the comment, both children enthusiastically said, "Yes! When can we start?"

"We've already started," answered Michelle. "After we circle the planet a couple times, we'll start taking detailed pictures of the areas that we are interested in. We'll show them to you, so you can learn what is down there."

Satisfied with the answer, both children continued to gaze at Alcent, which was now less than 500 miles away. Looking from left to right, the children were awestruck by the immense size of Alcent, which now totally dominated the view from the observation deck. Matthew exclaimed, "It really is big! How long will it take us to go all the way around it?"

"About an hour and a half," answered Michelle. "That's about how long the movie you watched yesterday lasted."

Turning to Connie, Michelle remarked, "This hemisphere has only one continent, and it extends from the south polar icecap to the north polar icecap. It looks like it's at least 3,000 miles across at its widest point and no less than 2,000 miles across at its narrowest point."

"It appears to be close to 3,000 miles wide at the north polar icecap," commented Connie. "I would guess that the icecap is about 1,500 miles in diameter. That means that animals from this hemisphere could migrate to the other hemisphere without having to traverse the icecap. I wonder how far this continent extends beyond the icecap."

"We'll soon know," stated Michelle. "In less than fifteen minutes, our orbital speed will take us well beyond the icecap, putting us over the other hemisphere. However, it is probably dark now, since Alpha Centauri A and B are both over this hemisphere."

A few minutes later, Matthew asked, "What is that big, round white area? It looks different than the clouds."

"That is the north polar icecap," replied Michelle.

"But, what is it?" questioned Matthew.

"It is ice that is covered with snow," answered Michelle. "When it is too cold for clouds to make rain, they make snow. When it doesn't get warm enough to melt all the snow, it eventually gets so deep that some of it turns into ice."

Thinking about how cold ice cubes are, Matthew said, "I don't think the icecap would be a good place to live. It would be too cold."

"I want to live someplace where it is warm," said Denise in quick agreement.

"I don't think anyone wants to live on either icecap," commented Connie.

A few minutes later, the Challenger was beyond the north polar icecap and over Alcent's nighttime hemisphere. Having completed its deceleration to five miles per second, the Challenger's antimatter engines were shut down, and the big moment had finally arrived. The Challenger and its occupants were now in a polar orbit around Alcent; 6 years, 270 days after leaving Earth.

No longer being subjected to 1g deceleration, the Challenger's occupants were again experiencing weightlessness. Matthew exclaimed, "This is fun! I like to float around."

"Me too!" Denise laughed. Pushing off with her legs, she went floating off in pursuit of Matthew.

Watching the children joyfully playing self-invented games to take advantage of the weightless environment led Connie to remark, "Isn't it amazing how well they've adapted to weightlessness. They relish it."

"It's definitely a delightful experience for them," agreed Michelle. "It's something that they'll remember long after we're settled on Alcent. Perhaps, it's a memory that will be with them for the rest of their lives."

Noticing that Alcent's nighttime hemisphere wasn't completely dark and that the observation deck was softly illuminated, led Connie to comment, "Considering that it's nighttime, it sure isn't very dark in here. Where is all this light coming from?"

Pointing across the observation deck, Michelle said, "It's coming from over there."

Suddenly, both women realized that they had forgotten that Alcent had two moons. Almost simultaneously, they pushed off and floated across the observation deck to look at them. Connie exclaimed, "They look just as big as the Moon did back on Earth. What a uniquely impressive sight it is to have two moons that look that large."

"With two nearby stars and two moons, we aren't going to have very many dark nights on Alcent," remarked Michelle.

"Imagine having a home on a lake beach and, during the evening twilight, sitting on the beach and listening to the water lapping against the shore. Imagine feeling a warm gentle breeze flowing through your hair and caressing your body," Connie said. " Perhaps, the breeze might even be carrying the fragrant scent of wild flowers. While enjoying all of this, you look out across the lake and view a moonrise, followed shortly by a second moonrise."

"What a wonderfully romantic setting. If you're there with Jerry. You could end up being the first woman to get pregnant under the light of two full moons."

"I would like to have more children, and I wouldn't mind getting pregnant in such a romantic setting."

"Well, it is possible that your romantic evening on the beach could be interrupted by a hungry dinosaur," commented Michelle.

"You've just given me the verbal equivalent of a cold shower."

"I didn't mean to destroy your fantasy, but we will be living on a dangerous planet."

"Hopefully, we'll find a place to live that will be relatively free of carnivorous dinosaurs," stated Connie. "I believe that a small island in the middle of a large lake might be just such a place. It seems reasonable to assume that a small island would not be able to provide enough prey to support large predators; therefore, there should not be any present."

"Unless Alcent has carnivorous dinosaurs that enjoy swimming, the island home you just described might be ideal for us," agreed Michelle. "In any case, we'll have to live near water, because our shuttles are equipped with hydrofoils. A large inland lake would be good for the shuttles to operate from. Who knows, you may have a chance to live the romantic fantasy you have just described."

"After nearly seven years in space, I am ready for that."

"Me too!" exclaimed Michelle.

During their conversation, Michelle and Connie drifted across the observation deck to resume visual exploration of Alcent. Even though Alcent was only illuminated by moonlight, its major features were still readily visible.

"The continent we observed earlier not only extends past the north polar icecap, but also extends southward as far as we can see," Connie commented. "And as was the case in the other hemisphere, its width appears to vary from 2,000 to 3,000 miles. I wonder if it extends all the way to, and even beyond, the south polar icecap."

"If it does, that would mean that this planet has one giant continuous continent that encircles the globe from pole to pole like a huge belt."

"If that's the case, then the majority of this planet's water is contained in two giant oceans."

Michelle thought about the situation for a few moments, "It seems strange that a planet could have only one continent that encircles it like a giant belt. If that's what we have here, it is definitely a unique geological configuration. My husband has devoted the last six and one-half years to becoming an expert in geology. Perhaps, he can figure out what geological processes resulted in the formation of this kind of continent."

"That will be an interesting problem for him."

"I have a feeling that this planet will provide each of us with an ample supply of challenging problems no matter what our individual area of expertise is. It's possible that our biggest challenge will be that of simply staying alive."

"You might be right. From a medical perspective, I expect to be challenged by bacterial and viral diseases that I've never seen before."

"When I think about the dangers that we'll be confronted with, the first thing that usually comes to my mind is the threat posed by the large predatory animals," Michelle said. "However, they'll probably be much easier to deal with than harmful microorganisms."

"Large carnivores will certainly be easier to locate and identify than harmful microbes. But when we get some robot laboratories on the surface, we can start finding out what kinds of microbes are present and how they compare to the microbes that live on Earth. That will, at the very least, give us an indication of the potential for contracting any life threatening diseases."

Before Michelle could respond, Matthew came to her and said, "I'm getting hungry. Can we go to the cafeteria and get some pizza?"

Michelle started to answer Matthew's question, but she was abruptly interrupted by Denise who said, "I am hungry too!"

Michelle turned to Connie and said, "Care to join us?"

"That sounds good to me," replied Connie, following them.

Meanwhile, on the flight deck, Captain Jerontis, Mike, Moose, and Dianne are beginning the task of reviewing and analyzing the data that is rapidly being accumulated by the Challenger's instruments.

"I sure hope we don't find any unpleasant surprises like we encountered at B-2," Dianne said, somewhat anxiously.

"What do you mean?" asked Moose. "We dealt with that problem quickly, and in the process, we did a great service to that planet. Rex and his people, along with the animal life, will now have a chance to multiply and prosper."

"I can't deny that," responded Dianne. "I am proud of what we did for them. In addition, we now have friendly nearby interstellar neighbors."

"So, what is it that you are worried about?" questioned Moose.

"I'm really not worried. I just hope that we don't find anything that would greatly delay our landing, or worst case scenario, prevent our landing entirely. We've been in space for a long time, and I think that it is time for us to have the opportunity to multiply and prosper. To put it bluntly, we've been married for more than five years, and I would love to have some children. But we can't do that until we establish that it is safe to go down there."

Giving his wife a tender look of understanding, Moose said, "I share your feelings, and I have some good news for you. Keep in mind that this isn't conclusive because we haven't yet completed one orbit, but a computer analysis of the radar data that we have does not show any evidence to indicate the presence of an advanced intelligent species. In fact, I haven't found any kind of construction, not even the kinds of simple huts that primitive creatures might build to live in."

"That tends to corroborate the conclusions reached through a detailed analysis of the data returned by Star Voyager," commented Mike. "The primary conclusion being that Alcent is a primitive earth-like planet inhabited by dinosaurs. If that is a valid conclusion, then we're not going to be arriving in the aftermath of a nuclear war and in the midst of a genocidal chemical attack."

"The conclusions based on Star Voyager's data may or may not be correct," commented Dianne. "Let's not forget that Star Voyager whizzed by this planet at 20% of the speed of light, and that didn't give it very much time for exploration. It was purely a matter of luck that a few of the limited number of high-resolution photos just happened to find dinosaurs. Also, Star Voyager passed over Alcent's northern hemisphere and returned no data at all for the south polar region."

"That's all true," agreed Mike. "We have very little detailed information about Alcent, and we cannot rule out anything until we have data that allows us to. The next few days should give us a pretty good idea about what's down there."

Captain Jerontis nodded and said, "In view of what we discovered on B-2, I would be perfectly content to find that this is a primitive planet on which dinosaurs are the dominant life form. Also, after nearly seven years in space, I long for some of the simple pleasures available from living on a planet, something as simple as diving into a lake and going for a good swim, or catching some fish and grilling them over an open campfire."

After a brief pause, Captain Jerontis continued, "Our mission plan calls for the exploration of this planet from orbit and with robot landers for up to two years before we land on it. As you know, this plan was developed by the best bureaucratic brains in the multiple layers of government bureaucracy; and as such, it satisfies all the stifling regulations that would apply if we were still on Earth. But since we're no longer subject to the absurd rules that they've come up with, we are free to just get the job done. I think it may be possible to shorten this exploration period to as little as six to eight weeks.

As I see it, there are three objectives that we must accomplish before we can land. First, we must achieve an understanding of the immune systems of the most common creatures on Alcent to make sure that microorganisms from Earth are not a serious threat to them. Second, we must identify the most common microbes on Alcent and determine whether they pose a lethal threat to us. Third, we must find a relatively safe place to live that is located next to a body of water large enough for our shuttles to operate from."

As he finished speaking, Captain Jerontis made eye contact with Dianne fully expecting that she would be the first to comment. His expectation proved to be correct when she said, "Our robot landers are equipped to achieve the first two objectives. I think we have a good chance to accomplish them in six weeks, if we quickly find optimal locations to land the robot labs and don't encounter any unexpected difficulties."

"What do you consider an optimum location to be?" asked Captain Jerontis.

"An optimum location is one where a robot laboratory will encounter the greatest abundance of diverse life forms. Time-wise, I would like to drop the first lander within forty-eight hours. Then, I would like to work with it for a few days before we drop additional landers. Depending on what we find, we may want to make some modifications to the follow-up landers.

During our long voyage, I trained three assistants. They are nearly as competent in my field as I am. Working as a team, we should be able to operate our remotely controlled laboratories continuously, thereby greatly reducing the time required to complete our research."

"I like your plan ," remarked Captain Jerontis. "During the next 48 hours, we will select a landing site and drop one of your labs on it."

"I will start working on site selection immediately," stated Dianne.

Speaking to Captain Jerontis, Moose said, "I have an idea on how we can speed up the process of determining what dangers may be present at the site that we select for our first manned landing. What I have planned will be especially helpful with our final evaluation of the site."

"What do you have in mind?"

"Once we make our final selection of a site to build our homes on, we send in Charlie. We have him roam around during the day and sleep next to a campfire at night. If he survives, we pick him up after two or three days and give him a thorough examination to determine if anything has happened to him."

Giving Moose a puzzled expression, Captain Jerontis said, "I personally know everyone on this ship, and I can assure you that we don't have a crew member named Charlie."

Moose grinned and said, "Charlie's not a real person. He is a human replica, an artificial man of sorts. He doesn't exist yet, but I've figured out a way to build him. All of his key components would either be off-the-shelf equipment or easily manufactured in our shop. I believe I can have him operational in less than six weeks."

Being somewhat skeptical, Captain Jerontis commented, "That seems like a rather complicated project to accomplish in just six weeks. How do you plan to do it?"

"When I first got the idea, I thought that it would be a difficult, time-consuming project, but the more I looked into it, the more convinced I became that I could do it in just a few weeks. The first question that came up was: How do I make his legs so that he will be able to walk around easily? As it turns out, the technology for manufacturing artificial limbs is very advanced. Our medical library contains designs for both arms and legs that are almost as good as real arms and legs. They contain artificial muscles that expand and contract like real muscles and are powered by electrical energy from battery packs."

"How do you plan to control the artificial limbs in a way that allows Charlie to maintain his balance when he's walking around?" asked Captain Jerontis.

"I will install an inertial guidance system in the upper part of his body. The design used in our robot landers should be capable of handling the job. All I will have to do is change the software so that it will control the movement of arms and legs instead of firing control thrusters and moving aerodynamic control surfaces.

Charlie's eyes will consist of video cameras. Information from them will be fed into his inertial guidance system's computer to prevent him from walking into trees and stumbling over rocks."

After thinking about it for a few moments, Captain Jerontis said, "It sounds feasible. What is the rest of your plan?"

"Since the primary purpose of building Charlie is to evaluate the dangers to us, we need to convince potential attackers that he is human. For that reason, I want to cover him with artificial human skin that has been coated with natural human skin oil and perspiration. Since many predators respond to scent, we want Charlie to smell like a human.

Also, stinging insects and venom injecting creatures of any kind are a potential problem. Charlie can help us evaluate this threat if he is properly designed. Some of these creatures find their prey by being able to see in the infrared portion of the spectrum, especially those that hunt at night. To attract them, we need to maintain Charlie's body temperature at about ninety-nine degrees. We can do this by covering his frame with an electric temperature control unit like the ones used in our space suits. We cover this with a one-half inch thick layer of fairly rigid, but pliable plastic foam to simulate flesh. This will be covered with artificial human skin. If Charlie is bitten by a venom injecting creature or stung by a venom injecting insect, the plastic foam will absorb the venom. Then, we can retrieve the venom from Charlie and analyze it."

"You have this design very well thought out," remarked Captain Jerontis. "Apparently, you've been working on this for quite some time, but you've never mentioned it. Why all the secrecy?"

"I've only been working on it for a few days, and I wanted to convince myself that the project is feasible before discussing it."

Captain Jerontis exclaimed, "I like the concept! Small creatures that are able to produce and inject lethal venom could pose a greater threat to our survival than the large carnivores. We definitely need to find out if they exist, how numerous they are, and what they look like. Charlie is probably the perfect way to do that. Besides the batteries in his artificial limbs, I would suggest that we also fill his body with batteries to give him additional operating time and range."

Mike added, "If we use Charlie in conjunction with a robot lander, then he could periodically plug himself into the lander's power plant to recharge his batteries. Also, the lander could give us video of Charlie's activities when he's near the lander."

Captain Jerontis said, "I think we should put microphones in Charlie's ears and equip him with a transmitter, so we can get video and sound directly from him to complement what we get from the lander."

"I like that idea," stated Mike, "but I think we should also equip Charlie with a radio receiver and install speakers on his chest and back. Then, we can subject the area around him to the sounds that people normally make."

"Those are all good ideas," commented Moose. "But, there is one more thing that we might do to increase Charlie's effectiveness at discovering predators, and that is to give the predators a scent that they can't refuse. It seems to me that there is one scent that almost always provokes predators, and that's the scent of blood. Somewhere in Charlie's body we need to make provisions to carry a small amount of human blood. That will enable us to run an experiment in which we send Charlie on a long walk and have him drip droplets of blood on his trail as he walks. To properly conduct this experiment, we need to give Charlie a third eye in the back of his head, so that we'll be able to see anything that follows him and observe the method of attack. We might also have him smear some blood on one of his forearms to find out if that attracts anything."

Obviously pleased, Captain Jerontis said to Moose, "You've come up with a marvelous concept. Charlie will be invaluable to us in discovering and evaluating some of the threats that we'll face. I want you to use all available personnel to expedite the design and construction of Charlie. I would like to have him ready for use in no more than five weeks. By then, I expect that we will have selected the site of our future home. I want one of the robot landers modified to deliver and support Charlie, so that we can use him to do the final evaluation of risks at the site."

TIME: 6 Years, 272 Days A.L.E.

Captain Jerontis and his colleagues were in the cafeteria discussing possible locations for their new home. They had considered numerous sites, but all except one were rejected for various reasons. That location was being discussed and appeared to be ideal.

Looking at the area on a wall-sized video screen, Captain Jerontis said, "This location seems to satisfy all of our requirements. The lake is large enough to facilitate shuttle operations, and the island near the middle of the lake is spacious enough for us to comfortably live on. Also, there is an abundance of life in the region around the lake for us to study."

"I like this area's potential for sports fishing," commented Moose.

"I'm not surprised about that being the first thing on your mind," remarked Jerry.

"You can't tell me that you're not excited about the possibilities. You and I have had some pretty good fishing trips."

"That's true, but we don't even know if this planet has any fish on it."

"I can't argue with that," stated Moose, "but if fish do live here, a lake that is 15 miles across and 47 miles long has to have fish in it. It's not only a big lake, but it's also connected to other large bodies of water. The river flowing out of the lake's south end enters a huge river in about 13 miles. About 40 miles downstream from there, this huge river flows into the ocean. With slow currents, no rapids, and no waterfalls; both of these rivers are easily navigable, which also gives us access to ocean fishing."

"Those rivers will also give our research submarine easy access to the ocean," added Captain Jerontis.

"That's great, but what really excites me about those rivers is the possibility of ocean fish migrating to fresh water spawning areas," remarked Moose. "All the cold clear streams flowing into the lake from the mountains to the east may be very attractive to fish in search of a place to spawn."

Dianne patiently listened to her husband and Captain Jerontis discuss fishing possibilities. Then, she said, "If you guys are done fantasizing about future fishing trips, I would like to point out that the abundant diversity of life forms living in the region around the lake will greatly simplify my job. There are so many species living in this area that using our robot labs to study just them should allow us to reach valid conclusions about whether life from Earth is compatible with life anywhere on Alcent."

"That's especially true when you consider that many of the species in this area aren't unique to this area," commented doctor Nemard. "We've seen some of them on the other side of the planet."

"Evolution takes place over a long period of time, millions of years, sometimes even hundreds of millions of years," Dianne said, "Given that much time, individual species can travel great distances, even to the other side of the planet and back."

Doctor Nemard explained, "This planet's unique geological configuration makes that easy. It has only one continent, which encircles it like a giant belt. Neither polar icecap gets any closer than seven hundred miles to ocean beaches, so animals can easily migrate entirely around Alcent over a long period of time."

"That freedom to migrate lends additional credibility to my supposition that if life from Earth is compatible with Alcent life in this region, it should be compatible with life anywhere on the planet."

"That sounds reasonable," commented Doctor Nemard, "but I think we should drop robot labs in some other areas anyway, just to make sure."

"I agree," stated Dianne, "but depending on what we learn in this area, we may be able to put that off for a while, thereby shortening the research time needed before we can land."

"I am ready to land now!" stated Moose.

"You're just all fired up about going fishing," commented Dianne.

Moose smiled at his wife and said, "That's true."

"I am ready to go down there too," admitted Dianne. "Once we've selected the area, we'll get the research done as quickly as we can."

After a few moments of silence, Michelle said, "One of the things that I like about this area is the pleasant climate that it appears to have. Being located at about 33 degrees north latitude, it is close enough to the equator, so that winters will be mild. However, it is still far enough north so that summers won't be unbearably hot."

"I don't believe that I'll have any trouble adjusting to year 'round pleasant weather," commented Doctor Nemard.

"I think that constant warm weather is boring," stated Captain Jerontis. "I enjoy having a changing climate. I like to have definite seasons. There is something special about each season that adds interest to daily living."

Speaking to Jerry, Michelle said, "Since this planet's axis of rotation is tilted 23.7 degrees relative to its orbital plane, we will have definite seasonal weather variations, but all seasons should be quite pleasant."

"Mild winters are important for shuttle operations," commented Mike. "Since we will land and take off on hydrofoils, we simply cannot live on a lake that freezes over in the wintertime."

"My intuition tells me that we could live on the big island in the middle of the lake and never see any ice on it," Michelle said.

"I'm not sure how your intuition arrived at that conclusion, but I agree with it," Mike said, "Using the computer, I've plugged data into several different climate models for this planet, and I've reached the same conclusion."

Michelle smiled at her husband and did not offer any explanation for her ability. Instead, she said, "I've taken a good look at that big island in the middle of the lake, and I believe I would enjoy living there."

"Did your intuition tell you that?" asked Mike in a teasing way.

"No! I don't need intuition for this. That island has several appealing features. It's very picturesque. It has several miles of sandy beach, lots of trees, and a pleasant climate."

"It does sound like a great place to live," replied Mike, "and that island also has some characteristics that make it ideal for shuttle operations. First of all, it is about four miles long and most of it is approximately three-fourths of a mile wide. The length is important for wind protection. When the wind is blowing from the west, the water on the east side of the island will be calm and easy to land on. It will be a four-mile stretch of calm water. When the wind is blowing from the east, the water on the west side of the island will be calm and easy to land on. A second feature that facilitates shuttle operations is the way the island narrows to only about a hundred yards across approximately three-fourths of a mile from its south end. This would provide us with a small sheltered bay on both sides of the island in which to anchor the shuttles after landing. A small island just outside each bay shelters them from strong winds."

Captain Jerontis said, "This location seems so ideal for our needs that I believe we should concentrate our exploratory research on it. If everything goes the way we hope it will, it is possible that we could be ready for a manned landing in as little as four weeks. After we've built our homes, we can explore the rest of the planet in a more leisurely manner."

Turning to Moose, Captain Jerontis asked, "How long will it be before Charlie is ready to go down and roam around on the island?"

"We have a group of highly motivated individuals working on that project. I believe Charlie will be ready in about three weeks."

Turning to Dianne, Captain Jerontis asked, "Have you been able to locate an ideal landing site for the first robot lab?"

"Across the water directly east of the island, there is a meadow that extends several miles inland from the lake shore." While speaking, Dianne placed a three-dimensional image of the area on the large screen for all to see. Then, she pointed at a hill and said, "If we could place our robot lab on top of this hill, its video cameras would give us an unobstructed view of the forests to the north and south, the open meadow to the east, and the lake shore to the west. When we see something of interest, we can dispatch RPVs (Remotely Piloted Vehicles) from the laboratory to collect specimens for analysis."

"I like the area," commented Captain Jerontis. "It looks like a good place to start our research. There are several distinctly different species of animals grazing in that meadow. Apparently, they are no threat to each other judging from the way they are peacefully grazing together. Also, there must not be any predators in the vicinity."

"Perhaps, the carnivores have had their fill for the day and are sleeping until they get hungry again," suggested Moose. "With that much prey available, predators can't be too far away."

"It is a peaceful scene at the moment," commented Dianne. "I wonder if bringing a robot lab in for a landing will spook any of them."

"The lab will make its final approach suspended from a wing-type parachute," stated Captain Jerontis. "The para-wing will be deployed at an attitude of about 5,000 feet, and will circle the area as it slowly descends to the targeted hilltop. Just before landing, the para-wing will be pitched up into a stall to kill most of its forward velocity, and the laboratory will descend vertically for the final few feet. The entire approach and landing will be silent."

Dianne thought about Captain J.J.'s comments for a few moments and said, "That silent gliding approach might mimic that of winged predators."

"That's true," replied Captain Jerontis, "but many of the animals grazing in that meadow are so large that I don't think they could be used as prey by the winged predators. Therefore, I wouldn't expect them to be spooked into a stampede by our lander."

"While that's true, we need the small animals to stick around too, or if they are spooked, we need them to return to the area. I think we should paint the lander with a camouflage paint scheme with the colors present in that meadow. Then, it will look natural to the area, like it belongs there. But we need to get rid of the para-wing. A large collapsed parachute lying on the ground next to the lander will certainly look unnatural."

"I think I have a way to do that," stated Mike. "The lander is already programmed to release the parachute immediately after landing. All we need to do is pack a balloon and a bottle of hydrogen in the lander and attach them to the para-wing's suspension lines. When the para-wing is released, the hydrogen bottle will inflate the balloon, which will carry away the para-wing."

"Good," stated Dianne.

"How long will it take you to make that modification to the lander and give it a camouflage paint job?" asked Captain Jerontis.

"I don't think it will take us any longer than a day or two," replied Mike.

"Get started immediately and do whatever you can to expedite the job," ordered Captain Jerontis.

Turning to Dianne, Mike asked, "Would you like to help me select the colors and layout of the camouflage paint scheme?"

"Yes, I would. In fact, I could do that part of the job while you design and make the modification for the balloon that will carry away the parachute."

"Thank you! I appreciate the help."

TIME: 6 Years, 274 Days A.L.E.

A mood of excitement and exhilaration, tempered by some degree of anxiety, pervaded the personnel of the Challenger. After nearly seven years in space, a robot laboratory was in the final phase of its descent from the Challenger to its eventual resting spot on Alcent. The people of the Challenger would soon have specific information about what they hoped would be their new home.

Their euphoric mood was tempered only by the possibility that the laboratory might find that life from Earth was incompatible with life on Alcent. This would be the case if the microorganisms on Alcent were fundamentally different from microorganisms on Earth. A great variety of diseases are caused by microorganisms. Microbes that cause diseases are usually referred to as germs. Some germs are bacterial, others are viral. With immune systems developed over hundreds of millions of years of evolution, animal life on Alcent was able to cope with the germs present on Alcent.

If the Challenger's personnel landed on Alcent, microbes from Earth would land with them, because it is impossible to totally cleanse microorganisms from the human system. If the various species of microbes from Earth were basically similar to the various species of microbes on Alcent, then the immune systems of animals on Alcent would be able to effectively deal with them. If microbes from Earth were basically different from microbes on Alcent, then the microbes from Earth could pose a lethal threat to animal life on Alcent with entire species potentially being wiped out by disease. Likewise, the immune systems of the Challenger's personnel might not be able to cope with Alcent's microbes either, and exposure to them could result in serious disease and even numerous fatalities.

So, after nearly seven years in space, whether or not the Challenger's personnel would be able to inhabit Alcent would be determined by living organisms too small to be seen without a microscope. The big question would soon be answered by a robot laboratory now in the final phase of its descent, a robot laboratory that had been meticulously sterilized to protect Alcent's animal life from potential danger from Earth's microbes.

"The para-wing has just deployed," stated Mike. "So far, I am really pleased with the flawless performance of this lander's flight control system. If the para-wing will now do its job, the robot lab should land precisely on the top of that hill."

"We couldn't ask for better weather," stated Captain Jerontis. "The sky is free of clouds, and the wind speed on the surface is no more than five miles per hour."

With the Challenger's powerful optical instruments trained on the site, a sharply detailed image of the slowly descending robot lab was displayed on large video screens throughout the starship. The para-wing's snow-white upper surface made it easy to see from space. To make it less visible to the grazing animals below, the para-wing's lower surface was dyed a shade of blue that it was hoped would be close to the color of Alcent's sky.

"That sure is a smooth graceful descent," remarked Michelle. "I like the way it is slowly circling its hilltop destination."

"There is a reason for the circling descent," remarked Mike. "Using data from its flight control instruments, the robot's computer is continuously calculating wind velocity during its circling descent. From this, the computer will calculate the altitude and the distance from its destination from which it will need to begin its final approach glide for what we hope will be a perfect, on-target landing. To minimize forward velocity on impact, the final approach will be made directly into the gentle wind on the surface. Also, the para-wing will be pitched up into a stall just prior to impact. That should kill nearly all forward velocity and give the lab a gentle landing."

"It's amazing how you can take a robot probe that is moving five miles per second in orbit at 210 miles and land it at a specific location on Alcent's surface," commented Michelle.

"That hasn't yet been accomplished, but it looks like it soon will be," stated Mike. "Although, I'll have to admit that we did pick a difficult target in that it is very small."

"That hill doesn't look all that small to me," joked Michelle.

"That hill isn't all that small," stated Mike.. "But what we're trying to do is land on top of that rock at the top of the hill."

Mike pointed at the rock displayed on the video screen and said, "That rock formation rises about 35 feet above the hilltop and has a fairly flat top that measures approximately 35 feet by 60 feet. I know that it's a small target, but if we succeed in placing our robot lab on top of it, the lab will be protected from being run over by charging dinosaurs attempting to escape a predator."

"That is a small target. Do you really think the robot will be successful at landing precisely on top of that rock? If the approach is too low, it will crash into the side of the rock and be wrecked."

"Using its radar altimeter and its forward distance measuring radar, the flight control computer will make continuous calculations to determine if it will be successful at landing on top of that rock. If it concludes that it will fail, then it will turn to either side to avoid a collision. The lab is now on its final approach, so we'll soon know where it will land. Barring a sudden change in wind speed or direction, I believe it will land right on target."

A few seconds later, a unified cheer resounded throughout the Challenger as the robot lab made a perfect landing. At the instant of touchdown, the lab released its para-wing, and the bottle of hydrogen began inflating the attached balloon. In a matter of seconds, the balloon gained enough buoyancy to begin its ascent into the atmosphere to carry away the discarded para-wing.

Feeling a great deal of admiration for him, Michelle turned to her husband and said, "What a perfect landing. Everything had to work flawlessly from the time the probe left this ship to the time it landed. I marvel at the way that you always seem to find a way to do things that seem to be almost impossible."

"We did have a little luck," responded Mike. "All I did was make sure that the flight control system was in perfect working order and properly programmed. We were lucky that the wind didn't play any tricks on us."

Overhearing the conversation, Dianne turned to Mike and said, "You're being too modest. You did an excellent job. Now that you've delivered my lab to a perfect landing; it's time for me to put my skills to work. But before I start identifying and classifying microorganisms, let's put the lab's video equipment to work and do a 360-degree scan of the area around the lab."

"That should be interesting," remarked Michelle. "These will be our first ground-based views of the plants and animals living in the area where we hope to live."

A few moments later, a telescoping pole supporting two video cameras and directional microphones started extending itself above the robot lab. In just a few seconds, the cameras reached their maximum height of 20 feet above the top of the lab. Using one of the video cameras, Dianne devoted the next several minutes to surveying the top of the rock. After determining that it was devoid of life except for lichens, moss, and grass that had established a foothold in cracks and crevices; Dianne turned to Mike and said, "You've delivered my lab to what appears to be a very safe, secure area. It will be nice to be able to conduct our research without being disturbed by the creatures that live down there."

Mike smiled warmly at Dianne and nodded in silent acknowledgment of the sincere appreciation that she had just expressed to him for a job well done.

Next, Dianne raised the camera angle a bit and started a panoramic scan of the area around the rock. But Dianne halted the camera's rotational movement only seconds after she started it because an absolutely breathtaking view filled video screens throughout the Challenger. The camera had spotted a giant sauropod calmly lumbering out of the forest to the north of the lab.

"Look at the size of that creature! He must be at least a hundred feet long!" Dianne exclaimed.

"He must weigh nearly a hundred tons! What a gigantic animal," Captain Jerontis added.

The giant sauropod stopped and swung his head from side to side surveying the open meadow for signs of danger. Then, he repeated the scan of the open meadow more slowly, and this time, he moved his rather large ears around as if to cup them in an attempt to hear indications of danger. After doing this, he pointed his head in the direction of the lake, flared his nostrils, and took a deep breath of the gentle breeze blowing towards him. Apparently satisfied that there wasn't any danger present, the giant sauropod bent his long neck completely around, so that his head was facing the forest; then, he let out a soft call that sounded like: "hoot, hoot, hoot." After this, he turned toward the lake and resumed walking.

Immediately following the soft hooting sound, an infant sauropod emerged from the forest with its mother walking directly behind him. Behind them, two more infants emerged from the forest staying close to their mothers. Bringing up the rear of this column was a large male, although not as large as the leader.

The people of the Challenger were totally fascinated by what they were watching. Mesmerized into a state of silence, they watched the herd of sauropods calmly make its way to the lake where they drank large quantities of water. All were drinking except the male at the rear of the herd. He stood guard, alertly watching for danger. After the dominant male had quenched his thirst, he took up a position of guard duty while the subordinate male drank.

The only sounds heard on the Challenger were sounds from Alcent. The camera's directional microphone enabled the Challenger's personnel to listen to the herd of sauropods. These sounds were heard against a background of other sounds from the surface picked up by the lab's other microphones. The scene and its sounds had a profound effect on the Challenger's personnel as they considered the reality of living with creatures so large and powerful that they could effortlessly knock down even a stoutly built house.

Finally, Moose turned to Captain Jerontis and said, "Even though we knew that creatures of such enormous size might exist on this planet, I must admit that this foreknowledge did very little to prepare me for the reality of actually seeing them. I hope that I am never standing between them and wherever it is that they want to go.

"Just from the few minutes that we've observed these creature's behavior, three things are immediately obvious. First, the fact that one of them is always on guard and fully alert indicates that carnivores live in this area. Second, these carnivores must be truly awesome if creatures as large as these respect them to the point that one of them is always on guard. Third, these sauropods' behavior indicates that they are quite intelligent, disciplined, and able to communicate effectively."

Captain Jerontis added, "Not only are these creatures huge, but they're also very well equipped to defend themselves. They have three horns growing out of their heads: one on each side and one on top.

These must be deadly effective weapons when you consider how long and strong their necks are. In addition, they have three horns near the ends of their long, strong tails, which also must be deadly effective weapons. What kind of carnivores could these creatures possibly fear? I doubt that even the ferocious Tyrannosaurus Rex from Earth's Cretaceous period could overcome this group's leader."

"If this planet does have predators that are similar to the Tyrannosaurus Rex, that would explain why these creatures are constantly on guard," conjectured Moose. "Even though these creatures are gigantic, if a charging T-Rex caught one them off guard and managed to clamp his huge teeth-filled jaws onto the sauropod's neck, I would think that death would be inevitable. But if they are constantly on full alert, the T-Rex never has an easy opportunity."

"There are a couple of other things to consider," stated Dianne. "First, they have three infants to protect, and parental instinct could be causing them to be extra wary. Second, the degree of caution they are exhibiting could be the result of intelligence, perhaps even thinking."

"Are you suggesting that these animals might be capable of analytical thought?" questioned Doctor Nemard.

"To answer the question, Dianne narrowed the field of view to just the herd leader and showed him on half of the video screen. On the other half of the screen, she showed an image of a sauropod from Earth's dinosaur age. Then she said, "When you compare these two images, it becomes immediately obvious that this herd leader's head is proportionally much larger than the head on the sauropod from Earth. This raises the possibility of a much larger brain, which increases the probability of intelligence."

"What level of intelligence do you think they might have?" asked Doctor Nemard.

"I don't know. I am only suggesting that head size relative to body size indicates that there is potential for a considerable amount of intelligence. Simply knowing the difference between eight objects and six objects would put these creatures a step above animal life on Earth. I certainly would not expect them to have any kind of technical knowledge, but an understanding of simple numbers is definitely possible."

"They might even be smarter than that," speculated Doctor Nemard. "We must keep in mind that the Alpha Centauri System is about five hundred million years older than the Solar System. With all that additional time for evolution to proceed, some of the animals on this planet could be quite intelligent."

"That herd leader might even have a good enough memory to remember the various ways that different predators like to attack," speculated Captain Jerontis. "In addition, he may even be able to think about those attack methods and devise defensive strategies to defeat them."

"If he is capable of all of that, then he is much more intelligent than any animal on Earth," remarked Dianne.

Captain Jerontis said, "Given the enormous size and potential intelligence of these creatures, I think that we should ..."

Captain J.J.'s comment was interrupted by an extremely loud bloodcurdling roar that blasted from every speaker on the Challenger because they were all tuned in to the broadcast from the robot laboratory. The terrifying scream reverberated throughout the Challenger with such intensity that it caused nearly everyone's heart to skip a beat.

After recovering from the unexpected horrifying roar, Dianne directed the lab's computer to aim the second camera on top of the long telescoping pole at the source of the scream, which came from a creature that had just emerged from the forest south of the lab. The scene picked up by this camera was displayed on a video screen next to the one displaying the sauropods.

Captain Jerontis was the first to comment, "In case anyone had any doubts about predators being here, they don't have to speculate any longer. There they are. They are monstrous, and they look like extremely capable killing machines."

"They certainly do," agreed Moose, "and they look very similar to the Tyrannosaurus Rex."

"What is disturbing about this is that there are three of them," commented Mike. "If they hunt in packs, the danger posed by them is tremendously increased. If one of us were alone down there and encountered a pack of these killers, death could be the end result, even with the kinds of guns that we have."

"I don't think this group is hunting," speculated Moose. "You'll notice that all the creatures which had been peacefully grazing next to that forest are now madly fleeing the scene. If these T-Rexes were hunting, I think that they would've used stealth to sneak up on a doomed victim. That bloodcurdling scream may've been an arrogant challenge, as if to exclaim: We are here! We are coming through! And you can either flee and stay alive or remain and be killed!"

"Arrogance is an attitude found primarily in the human species, especially among politicians and government bureaucrats," remarked Doctor Nemard. "Are you suggesting that this high-and-mighty, better-than-thou attitude might also exist among animals?"

Pointing at the video screen showing the three T-Rexes proudly and fearlessly stomping through the open meadow, Moose declared, "There is my proof."

"Take a look at what the sauropods are doing," directed Captain Jerontis. "This is very interesting."

Not intimidated by the challenge from the T-Rexes, the herd leader was confidently walking away from his herd and toward the T-Rexes as if to give himself some fighting space. Then, while swinging his head from side to side, he bellowed out some sounds that sounded very crisp, almost like a drill sergeant issuing orders. Almost immediately, the largest of the females stepped forward, taking up a position on his right. The other male took up a position to her right. The remaining two females kept the three infants between them and stood guard over them.

Looking at the other screen, Captain Jerontis noted that the three T-Rexes had halted their march and had turned to face the sauropods. The largest T-Rex was at least fifty feet long and was apparently the leader. The other two were slightly smaller and looked like immature adults, or perhaps, they were females following a large male.

Without removing his eyes from the screen, Captain Jerontis stated, "I believe some of our questions have been answered. I have no doubt whatever, that these sauropods are able to think and devise defensive strategies. Furthermore, they are able to effectively communicate, and the subordinates in the herd have the discipline to follow orders."

"I wonder how intelligent the T-Rexes are," questioned Moose. "Are they smart enough to know that the sauropods are ready for them? If they know this, will they attack anyway? Did they even come here to attack? Is it possible that they're intelligent enough to be here for no other reason except to scout the defenses of this herd of sauropods?"

"That would be a scary situation, if they are that smart," remarked Captain Jerontis.

What happened next came as a complete surprise to the people on the Challenger. In total amazement, they watched as the 100-ton leader of the sauropods reared up on his hind legs and let out an absolutely deafening, deep-throated roar that froze the inhabitants of the Challenger with a spine-chilling effect. Then, when the huge sauropod's front feet slammed back onto the ground, he lowered his head and charged with the seven-foot horn on top of his head now horizontal and pointed directly at the T-Rex leader. Quickly reaching a speed of thirty miles per hour, the stout horn backed by 100 tons of bone and muscle suddenly became an extremely deadly weapon. Both the female and the male to her right participated in the charge.

Quickly realizing that they were in a deadly no-win situation, the T-Rexes turned and fled. The sauropods gave chase for about a quarter of a mile; then, they gradually lumbered to a halt. After stopping, the herd leader again reared up on his hind legs and issued an extremely loud deep-throated roar; as if to say, don't come back. The sauropods watched the fleeing T-Rexes for a few moments, then returned to the rest of the herd.

The eerie sound of silence permeated the Challenger as all were deeply lost in thought about the implications of the awesome scene they had just witnessed. To observe a scene in which such massive animal power and ferocity were in play only a few minutes after their first robot lab had settled down on the surface of Alcent provided a very sobering display of what they would face in their efforts to survive and prosper on this planet.

After nearly a minute of sober thought, the silence was finally broken by Moose who exclaimed, "I can't believe that we are seriously planning to go down there and live among those brutes! We must be crazy!"

Doing his best to present Moose with a genuine expression of bewilderment, Captain Jerontis said, "I am extremely surprised that you would say something like that. You must be just kidding."

"How could I possibly be just kidding? It's going to be extremely dangerous down there."

Faking the most sincere tone he could come up with, Captain Jerontis said, "Ever since we left Earth, you've been constantly reminding me about how I coerced you into canceling your exciting, adventurous vacation trip to an exotic, warm, sandy beach in the South Pacific. Right down there on the shore of that lake is a warm sandy beach, and it's definitely exotic. I am willing to bet that time spent on it would be a very exciting adventure. I am surprised by your reluctance to take advantage of the opportunity."

Having overheard the conversation, Dianne was enjoying the brief diversion from the serious situation they had just observed and now had to evaluate. Also, she wondered with a some degree of amusement how her husband would respond to these playfully provocative comments from his best friend.

Having good peripheral vision, Moose noticed without looking in her direction that his wife was attentively listening to the conversation. Choosing his words carefully, he responded to his close friend, "Captain J.J., old buddy, you're joshing me again. You're comparing apples to oranges. Obviously these two kinds of beach adventures are very different. Besides that, I am now a happily married man looking forward to becoming a father in the near future. Consequently, I am much more cautious about the kinds of adventure I get involved in."

"Are you sure you're not just getting soft with age?" Captain Jerontis asked, playfully.

"Those monsters we just observed are capable of causing anyone to lose his courage," responded Moose. "We have to respect their capabilities and use extreme caution when dealing with them."

Happy that her husband said all the right things, Dianne contentedly went back to work.

Michelle reflected on the awesome display of brute power that she had just witnessed. The thought of living among these creatures caused her entire body to briefly shiver. Then, she looked into her husband's eyes and said, "I remember a peaceful evening on the observation deck when you showed me the wondrous beauty of the universe and convinced me that we should leave the comfort and security of Earth to live on this planet."

"Are you having second thoughts?" asked Mike.

"The scene we just witnessed was rather frightening. On Earth, I never gave much thought to animal life while going about my daily activities. On this planet, I doubt that there'll ever be a routine day. All activities will have to be carefully planned to account for the possibility of encountering these animals."

"That's definitely true. Ordinary everyday life on this planet will be a constant challenge, but I welcome that challenge, and am glad we are here."

"So am I," agreed Michelle. "Every day will be an exciting adventure filled with new discoveries."

"It's quite possible that we've just seen the largest herbivore and the largest carnivore that this planet has," commented Mike.

"They are so big that it's difficult to imagine finding animals that are even bigger. Even though, we had reason to believe that dinosaurs as large as these would be here, I really wasn't prepared for what we just watched."

"That incredible display of brute power and ferocity would have been awe-inspiring no matter how well prepared we were. I wonder what Matthew thinks about those dinosaurs."

"He and Denise are with their tutor of the day," stated Michelle. "But her lesson plan was undoubtedly interrupted by the dinosaur scenes. I think I'll check on them and find out how they're doing. Also, I think I'll share the excitement of what we just saw with Rex and Shannon. During my next communication with then, I will transmit the video with full sound effects. I'm sure they'll be fascinated by it."

As Michelle left the flight deck, Captain Jerontis turned to those remaining and said, "I am impressed with the degree of intelligence shown by those sauropods. When faced with a potential threat from the big T-Rexes, they reacted to it like a well-disciplined army. They demonstrated tactics, communication, discipline, and confidence. Also, they may have an understanding of simple numbers, as was shown by the fact that three sauropods charged three T-Rexes. If they are the biggest and most intelligent creatures on this planet, then, they are probably the dominant species. If that's the case, we should devote a great deal of time to studying them."

"We can start by getting a blood specimen, a fecal sample, and a urine specimen and running them through the robot lab for analysis," suggested Dianne. "Our RPVs are so small relative to the sauropods that I doubt they'll even pay any attention to them."

As she was speaking, Dianne launched an RPV from the robot lab and guided it on a course that would take it to the sauropods. The robot lab was equipped with six small remotely piloted vehicles (RPVs) that were designed for the specific purpose of collecting samples and bringing them back to the lab for analysis. Each of the six RPVs was designed for a specific mission. The one launched by Dianne looked like a flying saucer. It was quite small, having a diameter of only eighteen inches and a maximum thickness of only five inches. The counter-rotating propellers were mounted in a twelve-inch diameter opening through the middle of the RPV. The propellers were powered by electric motors receiving electricity from rechargeable batteries. The RPV was capable of taking off and landing vertically, hovering, and flying in any direction.

Silent operation was one of the key features of the RPVs. This was achieved with electric motors that made a barely audible hum and propellers that were specially shaped for quiet efficient operation. With its camouflage paint scheme made up of dull browns and greens and its nearly silent operation, the little RPV mimicked a large, wind-blown, falling leaf as it quietly soared around in flight.

Using images returned by the little RPV's miniature video cameras, Dianne guided it to a gentle landing on the back of the herd leader. With small pincers, the RPV immediately anchored itself to the thin bristle-like hair on the giant sauropod's back. The RPV then deployed a small arm equipped with a sensitive microphone at its end. Using the arm to place the microphone in contact with the enormous sauropod's skin and then to slowly move it around, Dianne listened for the sound of flowing blood. After a few minutes of exploration, Dianne found a vein just under the animal's skin that was appropriate for her needs. Then, she deployed a second arm, and used it to apply some antiseptic to the area and to insert a tiny needle through the animal's skin and into the vein. After withdrawing a small quantity of blood, she flew it back to the robot lab for analysis.

While Dianne monitored the robot lab's examination of the blood sample, Moose flew a second RPV to the area. After patiently waiting for nearly an hour for the herd leader to relieve himself, Moose was able to collect a fresh urine specimen and a fresh fecal sample to return to the lab for analysis.

Speaking to Mike, Captain Jerontis said, "I think it would be interesting to follow these sauropods around for a few days to observe their day-to-day behavior and see their territory."

"After what we've seen today, I am not about to volunteer for the job," responded Mike rather quickly.

Captain Jerontis laughed, "I wasn't implying that you should. What I had in mind is using a modified RPV to attach a small instrument package to the herd leader. Two or three video cameras, a couple of microphones, and a transmitter should be sufficient to gain a large quantity of information."

"Where on the animal do you want to attach the instrument package?"

"I think the ideal location would be near the base of that big horn on top of his head. Then, as he moves his head around to investigate things of importance to him, we'll be able to see and hear what he sees and hears. In effect, we'll learn about his world from his perspective."

"I like your idea," Mike exclaimed. "The video and the sound effects should be fascinating."

"I think so," agreed Captain Jerontis. "Over a period of time, the herd leader will show us his territory. Perhaps, these creatures are migratory and wander over great distances. If so, we'll see a great deal of real estate and many of the plants and animals that live on it. We'll find out if predators are a serious problem for the sauropods. We'll learn how the members of the herd intermingle on a day to day basis. By observing how various members of the herd react to the different sounds that the leader makes, we'll begin to understand the meanings of the various sounds. Also, we'll learn how extensive a vocabulary these animals have. That should help us determine how intelligent they are."

"So, in effect, what we are going to do is recruit the biggest creature we've ever seen to show us his world and teach us his language," commented Mike.

"That's exactly right. How long will it take you to put it together?"

"It shouldn't take more than a few days. I think we should send this down by special delivery, rather than wait for the next robot lab to take it down. This offers a quick way to gain some special information about the planet we plan to live on."

"Attaching the instrument package to that horn is going to be a bit tricky, but he has to sleep sometime, and that will be the time to do it," Mike continued. "As quiet as our RPVs are, I don't think the sound will wake him; but it might, so I will design an attaching clamp that will quickly grapple the horn, allowing the RPV to accomplish its mission in seconds and leave."

"I like the special delivery idea. Let's package it and send it down as soon as you have it ready to go."

"I think I've seen enough exciting scenes from the surface for one day, so I'll start on this right away."

TIME: 6 Years, 278 Days A.L.E.

Mike designed, constructed, and delivered to the surface an instrument package that he hoped to attach to the base of the horn located on top of the sauropod herd leader's head. To accomplish this, he joined two small RPVs with the instrument package secured between them.

Speaking to Captain Jerontis, Mike said, "For the last four days, that herd has shown up in the early evening to drink at the lake. Shortly after that, they lie down in an open area and sleep for the night, with one of the adults always awake and on guard. The remaining adults always surround the infants."

"Even while sleeping, all that bone and muscle makes a formidable protective enclosure for the infants," commented Captain Jerontis. "I continue to be impressed by the intelligence and discipline the adults demonstrate while protecting themselves and their young."

"I would like to find out if their behavior is instinctive or the result of reasoning."

"That instrument package you put together will enable us to constantly monitor their activities, and that should help us determine just how intelligent they are."

"I hope they return to the lake again this evening, so we can install our instruments."

"I wouldn't expect them to leave the area as long as there is plenty of food and water for them," Captain Jerontis said. "I wonder if they always drink from that same location because there is good solid footing there."

"Their feet are so large that they seem to be able to get around on any kind of ground, even though they are very heavy. I think they drink from that same area every night and morning because of the large open meadow. I think they come to the meadow to sleep. Since there is no cover for predators to use to sneak up on them, they only need to post one sentry. The guard has unobstructed visibility for more than a mile in all directions."

"Your explanation for their behavior is too logical for the behavior to be purely instinctive. I am willing to bet that it is the result of intelligent planning."

"It looks that way," agreed Mike.

"Once we get that instrument package attached and have had the opportunity to observe them for a while, we should be able judge the extent of their ability to think."

"If all goes according to plan, we will attach the instruments sometime tonight," stated Mike. "On another subject, do I need to launch any additional satellites?"

"The three that we've deployed should be adequate to handle our needs for the time being."

The three satellites referred to by Captain Jerontis had been placed in geosynchronous orbit, and as a result, each would indefinitely remain over a point on Alcent's Equator. The three satellites were equally spaced around Alcent, with one of them placed over the equator directly south of the robot lab's landing site.

The satellites had two primary functions: communications and weather observation. The satellite in orbit above the robot lab was used to receive the lab's transmissions and relay them to the Challenger, either directly or through one of the other satellites. The three satellites allowed the Challenger to be in continuous communication with ground experiments regardless of its orbital location.

The sophisticated weather observation instruments on the satellites provided detailed global data about Alcent's weather systems. This information would be a consideration in the selection of a site at which to live and would help in understanding the planet's ecosystem.

TIME: 6 Years, 278 Days, 9 hours A.L.E.

It was nighttime over the meadow where the robot lab was located. The sky was relatively free of clouds, and the meadow was illuminated by light from two moons. The meadow was currently peaceful, for the predators had already made their kills. The sauropods retired for the night and were sleeping under the watchful eyes of one of the females, currently the lone sentry.

Michelle joined her husband on the flight deck, because she wanted to watch his attempt to attach the instrument package to the sauropod herd leader. Mike was busy explaining to her that the task would be easy.

Pointing to an image on the computer screen, Mike said, "As you can see, I have joined two RPVs, and the instrument package is mounted on the platform that connects them. The wide open clamp at the front of the instrument package will grasp the sauropod's top horn. There is a trigger at the base of the clamp. When that trigger crashes into the animal's horn, the clamp will snap shut. Then, the RPVs will detach from the instrument package and fly back to the lab."

"You are going to attach an instrument package to a 100-ton dinosaur, and you make it sound like a simple routine task," remarked Michelle.

"All I have to do is fly the RPVs to the vicinity of the animal's head, and then gently crash the base of the wide open clamp into the horn at a point on the horn that is a few inches above his head. Keep in mind that Dianne has already collected three blood samples from this creature, and she has also used ultrasound to take a look at the creature's internal anatomy. Installing this instrument package will be no more difficult than those tasks. Even though these RPVs are somewhat larger than the ones Dianne uses to collect blood and do ultrasound research, they are still very quiet in flight and should not disturb the animal."

"It's the advanced technology that has been incorporated into these RPVs that makes these seemingly impossible tasks appear so routine," concluded Michelle. "They truly are amazing little machines."

"For what we need to accomplish, the RPVs are essential pieces of equipment. Even after we're living on Alcent, we'll continue to use them for a multitude of tasks. Something as simple as scouting the territory around us when we're on an exploratory trip will greatly reduce our risk."

Speaking to Michelle, Captain Jerontis said, "I think it's time for your husband to put his piloting skills to work before something disturbs that herd leader and wakes him up."

Since Mike already had everything checked out and ready to go, he immediately launched the connected RPVs and guided them to the giant sauropod. The linked RPVs quietly approached the sauropod head-on. After hovering for a few moments to verify the final approach parameters, the RPVs slowly soared forward and gently crashed into the horn as planned. The clamp immediately snapped shut, and the RPVs detached and began their return flight. The whole procedure was so quiet and gentle that the giant sauropod never even stirred.

Mike turned away from the controls, smiled at his wife, and said, "It was a simple task, and we now have a 100-ton tour guide, one of the many benefits available to those contemplating a move to Alcent."

"This is amazing!" Michelle exclaimed. "Think about it! As these gigantic creatures go about their normal everyday activities, we are most certainly going to get some priceless imagery and sound effects. I will select some of the more dramatic scenes and include them in my daily transmissions to Earth. I am sure they will find them fascinating."

"After they see that spectacular video of the incident between the sauropods and the T-Rexes, I am sure they will be prepared for anything," remarked Mike. "In that video, the sound effects alone are rather spine-chilling."

"More than four years will go by before they get to see that. Even though I traveled and actually experienced the vast distance between here and Earth, it still boggles my mind to realize that my transmissions traveling at the speed of light require 4.35 years to reach Earth. By the time they see the sensational scene that we saw a few days ago, we will probably have forgotten about it; yet for them, it will be the news event of the day."

"I think our long journey has given all of us a new concept of space and time," remarked Mike. "And now that we're here and have seen some of the huge animals that we are planning to live among, the whole setting is almost surreal. It's almost as if we're characters in a science fiction movie rather than real people with real lives."

Michelle laughed, "So that's how you make all these difficult tasks look so easy, none of this is real, we're all just part of a movie."

TIME: 6 Years, 291 Days A.L.E.

Michelle's latest mission update to Earth:

"It has been seventeen days since we landed our first robot laboratory on Alcent. To determine as rapidly as possible whether the human immune system is capable of defending against attack by Alcent's microorganisms, Dianne and her assistants have maintained a very intense pace of research with the robot lab. Also, they are attempting to answer an equally important question: Will the immune systems of Alcent's animal life be able to defend against microbes from Earth?

Using the robot lab's sophisticated equipment to analyze specimens delivered by our RPVs, Dianne and her assistants are isolating, identifying, and cataloging Alcent's microbes. In the search for microorganisms, the RPVs have collected numerous water samples from the lake, from streams, and from stagnant pools. Rainwater has also been analyzed. A broad variety of soil samples have been investigated. The RPVs have also managed to locate and return fragments of decaying flesh missed by predators and scavengers. Numerous air samples have been investigated in the search for microbes. Samples of both living and decaying plant life have been investigated.

As each new microorganism is discovered, its identifying features are fed into the Challenger's computer, which then searches its memory to determine if a similar microbe exists on Earth. Then, using a model of the human immune system, the computer determines the microbe's potential danger to humans.

The other part of the project is to learn as much as possible about the immune systems of Alcent's animal life. To that end, the RPVs have collected several blood, urine, and fecal specimens from each of twenty-three species of animal life. Locating antibodies in a creature's blood gives an immediate insight into the capabilities of the creature's immune system, because specific antibodies are produced by a healthy immune system to attack and kill specific invading microbes. By isolating an antibody and doing a detailed description of it, the researcher can draw some conclusions about what the targeted invading microbe looks like. Also, the degree of sophistication of the antibody indicates how capable the immune system is. Immune systems that are able to design and produce complicated antibodies are capable of defending against a broad variety of microorganisms.

Preliminary conclusions based on the research done to date indicate that microbes from Earth will not pose a serious threat to Alcent's animal life and that Alcent's microbes will not be an insurmountable challenge to the human immune system. Needless to say, we are very encouraged by these results.

Dianne decided that it is time to send down a second robot laboratory. This one will be landed on the large island in the middle of the lake. The site selected for the landing is, once again, the top of a rock formation."

TIME: 6 Years, 291 Days, 3 Hours A.L.E.

The second robot lab began its final approach glide. Having continuously monitored flight parameters, Mike said, "Everything looks good for a perfect landing."

"This is very exciting," commented Michelle. "We are about to take a close look at the island that we hope to live on."

"That's true only if we achieve a safe landing," stated Mike. "Even though everything looks good, we are still at the mercy of the wind. If the para-wing gets hit by a sudden large change in wind direction or velocity, the robot lab's landing could be fouled up, and it could be seriously damaged. I don't expect that to happen, but it is possible."

"You always express a note of caution, yet you always seem to accomplish the things that you set out to do," commented Michelle.

"I simply try to anticipate all contingencies and plan for them as best I can."

About a minute later, an enthusiastic cheer echoed throughout the Challenger as the robot laboratory made an excellent landing. Michelle beamed an admiring smile at her husband and exclaimed, "Nice work!"

The robot lab had landed on a plateau located near the south end of the island. The plateau was about 300 yards wide by 700 yards long. It was located at the top of a nearly vertical rock formation that rose approximately 150 feet above the surrounding land. Only the north face of the rock formation deviated significantly from the vertical. It was a rock slide with a slope of about forty-five degrees.

Mike immediately put one of the lab's surveillance cameras to work viewing the area around the lab. While he panned the area, everyone viewed the scenes from the plateau with utmost interest. These scenes were of the precise area where the people of the Challenger expected to build their homes. Even though all had already seen detailed images of the area which had been provided by the Challenger's powerful optical instruments, the images originating from on-site equipment were of keen interest, because they provided more detail and an entirely different perspective. Now, for the first time, the people of the Challenger were seeing the area as they would see it when they were living on it. After all, the robot lab had landed on a spot that could conceivably be in the middle of someone's front yard in the very near future.

After Mike finished scanning the area around the lab, he raised the camera to view the distant lake shore. Then, he did a 360-degree sweep to survey the island's picturesque surroundings. The spectacular scenic beauty and vast openness of the area fanned the flames of desire in the Challenger's inhabitants to leave the starship and live in traditional homes.

Michelle joyfully exclaimed, "What a dream location!"

"What do you like about it the most?" asked Mike.

"Everything!" exclaimed Michelle.

"It seems to me that a professional reporter could be more specific," bantered Mike.

"I do like everything about it," declared Michelle with enthusiasm. "But if you want me to be specific, let's start with the view. To the east, there are eight miles of open water against a backdrop of meadows, forests, and snow-capped mountain peaks. To the west, there are seven miles of open water against a backdrop of meadows, forests, and low-level mountains. Directly north of the plateau, there is the rest of the island, which extends for three miles, and it is covered with dense forest. South of the island, there are twenty miles of water against a backdrop of meadows and forest land, which is so far away that it just blends into the skyline."

"It is definitely picturesque," agreed Mike. "But one of the things that I like about this island is that its shoreline provides twelve to fifteen miles of waterfront property. Plus, the four small islands lying just offshore from the main island are large enough to live on. In short, each family will have a choice location on which to build a home and more than one hundred acres of land to go with the home. That's what I call spacious living."

"That will be a refreshing change from the city living I knew back on Earth," stated Michelle. "I sure hope that we don't discover anything that prevents us from living there."

"Everyone is probably anxious about that possibility," commented Mike. "But we must think positively and hold the expectation that this island will become our home."

Captain Jerontis remarked, "Of all the locations we've looked at, none is more ideal than this one. This island is large enough to give us plenty of living space, but too small and too isolated to provide enough prey to support large carnivores. Therefore, there shouldn't be any present."

"On Earth, some carnivores are good swimmers," commented Mike.

"We could live on the plateau," responded Captain Jerontis. "Then, any large carnivore that manages to swim across several miles of water will be faced with the difficulty of climbing to the plateau. On three sides, there is a 150-foot rock cliff. On the north side, there is a rock slide with a 45-degree slope. Some large carnivores might be able to climb that rock slide, but it should be easy to set up a warning system. It seems like we should be quite secure in homes built on that plateau. It should be a place where we can relax and enjoy life."

"I agree," Mike said. "The plateau is the safest place to build our homes, but I hope that we will discover that we can live anywhere on the island in comfort and safety."

"I believe that will prove to be the case, but I think we should live on the plateau until we find out if large carnivores ever visit the island."

"That sounds like a prudent approach," agreed Mike.

"I have an image in my mind of a spacious log cabin," declared Connie. "With all those tall trees growing on the island, it should be easy to build a roomy, comfortable cabin. On the inside, it could be finished and furnished with the best that our technology has to offer, but on the outside, it would always remind me of those rugged, self-sufficient, early American pioneers."

Captain Jerontis gazed into his wife's eyes for a few moments and noted how sincere she was. Then, he said, "So you really have your heart set on living in a log cabin."

"Well, it does fit right in with what we are. In every sense of the word, we are pioneers. We will be living in a heavily forested area, and we must be rugged and self-sufficient."

"A sturdily constructed log home would be symbolic of all that and would look like a natural part of the setting. It's also practical in terms of available construction materials. I like the idea. Let's plan on it."

Moose and Dianne looked at each other for a few moments, then, almost in unison, they turned to Captain Jerontis and said, "We like the idea too."

Bubbling over with excitement at the prospect of soon having a real home to live in, Connie asked, "When can we go down and get started?"

Captain Jerontis said, "During the next couple weeks, we're going to thoroughly investigate the island. If we fail to find anything that would prevent us from living there, we'll send Charlie down for a final look. If he wanders the island for a couple weeks without anything of consequence happening to him, then we'll carry out our first manned landing."

"I wish we could speed up that process," Connie said, "We've been in space for such a long time, and I am ready for something as simple as watching the clouds drift across the sky."

After a few moments of silent daydreaming by everyone present on the flight deck, Connie declared, "I think the crew for the first manned landing should definitely include a doctor in case a medical problem arises."

"I think the chief engineer should be part of the crew in the event there is an unforeseen equipment problem," Mike asserted quickly.

"I think an expert biologist should be present to do an on-site evaluation of the threat posed by the life forms that inhabit the area," stated Dianne with conviction.

"Since this will be an epic event in human history, it seems to me that there should be a reporter present to cover the news aspects of the occasion," commented Michelle.

Captain Jerontis looked at Moose and said, "I believe everyone on this ship is going to express an important reason to justify inclusion in the crew for the first landing. What's your excuse?"

"Well, I am sure that everyone already realizes that my broad variety of skills and talents would come in handy to cope with whatever problems happen to arise," stated Moose with complete sincerity. "But the main reason I would like to be a part of the first landing is just simply for the pure excitement of it. Think about it. This will be the first time ever that mankind will set foot on an alien planet that is abundantly filled with life, what an adventure. No matter how much research we do with the robot labs, the element of risk will still be present."

"Despite his lack of humility, he is being truthful," commented Dianne.

"I wasn't trying to be boastful, I was merely pointing out that I would be a valuable addition to the landing party," retorted Moose.

"I already knew that. It was just your way of stating it that caught my attention," replied Dianne.

"I haven't yet decided how many people are going down on the first landing, let alone who," commented Captain Jerontis. "Until we complete our research with the lab that we just sent down, we won't be able to define all of our objectives for the first landing. Also, what happens to Charlie while he is wandering around on the island will help determine our personnel roster. I am just as excited about going down there as all of you are, but we must be patient."

Pointing at the video screens, Captain Jerontis noted, "Even though the island scenes look very peaceful, we must keep in mind that they are only of the plateau, and the rest of the island could prove to be a very dangerous place. I suggest that we get started exploring it."

Responding to Captain J.J.'s directive, Moose and Dianne each launched a small RPV. Both RPVs were equipped with video cameras and microphones. Moose planned to explore the island's east coast and south end while Dianne explored the island's west coast and north end. After this, they would begin exploring the island's interior.

Mike launched the largest of the lab's RPVs. Its payload was a neatly packaged marine explorer consisting of a deflated pontoon equipped with underwater exploration instrumentation. He skillfully piloted the RPV out over the lake to a point about 100 yards off shore. There, he brought the RPV to a halt and had it hover motionlessly over the water. Using the RPV's winch, Mike lowered the deflated pontoon about ten feet below the RPV and about three feet above the water. Then, he inflated the pontoon and lowered it onto the water.

The marine explorer's battery pack, electric motor, and instrument package were attached to the bottom side of the pontoon. With the bulk of its weight attached to its underside, the pontoon was very stable and could not easily be tipped over. Except for two small video cameras and a transmitting antenna the topside of the pontoon was covered with solar cells to recharge the marine explorer's batteries.

The marine explorer would be used to accomplish the critical objective of ensuring the safety of shuttle landings and takeoffs. To that end, Mike would explore the underwater world around the island in a meticulous search for hazards to shuttle operations. In addition, the marine explorer's underwater cameras and sonar would be used to search for fish and other marine life.

TIME: 6 Years, 298 Days A.L.E.

One week after landing a robot lab on the island's plateau, Captain Jerontis and his colleagues were discussing some of the discoveries made to date.

"I've made numerous RPV flights all over this island," stated Moose, "and I've been unable to find any large creatures. Apparently, this island is inhabited primarily by small mammals, reptiles, birds, and insects."

"Have you concluded that none of those creatures are large enough to pose a serious danger to us?" questioned Captain Jerontis.

"None of them are large enough to be a physical threat to us; however, some of the reptiles could have a poisonous bite. Also, some of the insects appear to have stingers. We can evaluate the potential danger from these creatures when we send Charlie down."

"How long before Charlie will be ready to go?"

"We could send him down now, but there are some additional capabilities I would like to give him that will expand his usefulness. Specifically, I am attempting to give him the ability to run at speeds up to twenty miles per hour. Also, I am installing an infrared video camera and a simple radar to enhance his nighttime reconnaissance capability. If we could delay sending him down for about three days, these improvements will make him even more useful to us."

I think those capabilities are worth the delay," agreed Captain Jerontis. "Have you learned any additional information about those flying dinosaurs you discovered two days ago?"

"In some respects, they are the most remarkable creatures I've ever seen," commented Moose. "I am going to show you a video that I just finished making about an hour ago."

Moose entered the appropriate instructions into the computer, and almost immediately a fantastic movie showing the dinosaurs in flight appeared on the large video screen accompanied by full sound effects. Moose narrated, "I made this video by flying one of the RPVs with the creatures. As you can see, in some ways they resemble the pterodactyls that flew in Earth's atmosphere back in the dinosaur age. But there is one big difference, these creatures have feathers. Also, their feet are interesting. They are webbed like duck feet, but they have talons like an eagle."

Moose paused for a moment and then said, "I think the most impressive thing about these creatures is their size. Two of them have wing spans of about forty-five feet. The other two have wing spans of about twenty feet. I think we're looking at two adults and their offspring. It appears that the adults are teaching the youngsters how to feed themselves as you will see in the next part of the video.

"At this point, one of the adults went into a high-speed dive, and I followed him down with the RPV," Moose said, a few moments later. "When he reached the lake's surface, he immediately sank his talons into a large fish that was swimming too close to the surface. Then, he made a quick pull up from the dive.

"What happens next is most interesting. First, he transfers the fish from his talons to his teeth-lined jaws. Then, he taunts the juveniles with it by going from one to the other and acting like he's going to feed them, but then pulling away. Now that he has their attention, he closes his jaws tightly, biting a piece out of the middle of the fish. While he eats this, the tail end and the head end of the fish start falling towards the water. Apparently, the juveniles haven't yet mastered all their flying skills, because they are quite clumsily making their way down to the water in pursuit of the pieces of fish. Evidently, the adult has intentionally given the juveniles an incentive to learn diving techniques, which is exactly what they'll need to eventually feed themselves."

"That's an amazing video you put together," commented Captain Jerontis. "I am impressed with your skill in flying that RPV. You stayed with those pterodactyls through some rather fancy maneuvers."

"Our RPVs have some remarkable flying capabilities, and they are easy to fly."

"Why is it that you didn't include these pterodactyls among the creatures that you earlier said inhabit this island?" questioned Captain Jerontis.

"It is spring in this area, and these pterodactyls came to this island from the south. I observed their arrival. After that feeding scene we just watched, I saw them fly off to the north. Even though I can't prove it, I believe that they are just passing through on a migration flight."

"Whether they live here or are just passing through, they do pose a danger to us," commented Captain Jerontis. "If this island is a resting point for migrating predators with fifty-foot wing spans, it might not be the ideal place to live that we hoped it would be."

"With talons and teeth like they possess, they could easily kill an adult human," stated Moose. "I don't know what their maximum lifting capability is, but I believe that the adults could carry away one of us. Our children would definitely be easy prey for them."

"We may want to set up a radar station to warn us when they are around," remarked Captain Jerontis. "If they turn out to be the only detriment to living on this island, I will have to vote in favor of living there. This island just simply has too many advantages to pass up."

"I agree with that," stated Moose. "Plus, I have just discovered another advantage; namely, the presence of a multitude of large fish. That school of fish the pterodactyls feasted on is very large. Take a look at this video and you'll see what I mean."

Moose replayed selected parts of the video they had just seen, and Captain Jerontis remarked, "There must be thousands of fish in just that one school. I wonder if they are ocean fish migrating to mountain streams to spawn."

"That's a possibility," said Moose. "They sure are big. They look like their weight ranges from sixty to ninety pounds. I haven't been fishing for a long time, and the sight of all those fish is giving me the fishing fever. I am ready to go. I hope they are still around after we land and get settled down. If they're good to eat, we aren't going to starve anytime soon."

"Even if they aren't, a lake that large must have other fish in it," remarked Captain Jerontis. "Something else revealed by your video is the exceptional clarity of the water in that lake. I don't know how far below the surface those fish are swimming, but we aren't having any trouble seeing them."

"The clearness of the water caught my attention too," remarked Mike. "In the process of exploring the water around the island, I've put together some spectacular videos of underwater scenery and marine life. Thanks to the remarkable clarity of the water, I've discovered several species of fish, including shell fish."

Looking at Moose, Mike said, "I can assure you that the lake contains an ample supply of fish, so you will have lots of exciting fishing trips. If half the species of fish I've seen are edible, it will be a long time before we are hurting for something to eat."

Turning to Captain Jerontis, Mike said, "In regard to shuttle operations, there is no reason why we can't land and take off on either side of the island. The water is deep, and there are no obstacles lying below the surface."

"I am happy about that," declared Captain Jerontis. "Deep water that is free of obstacles and sheltered from the wind will make landing and taking off on hydrofoils a simple matter. However, there is another possibility that we should consider, and that's the possible existence of large marine animals. If they exist and if they swim from place to place in groups, they could present an unpredictable hazard to shuttle operations."

"That's a possibility," agreed Mike. "I will expand my underwater exploration to greater distances from the island in a search for large marine creatures."

"Also, because of the remarkable water clarity, we might be able to spot them with the RPVs if they exist and if they ever swim near the surface," added Moose.

"I trust that you gentlemen will make a determined search for large marine animals," stated Captain Jerontis.

Both Moose and Mike nodded in acknowledgment of Captain J.J.'s directive.

Turning to Dianne, Captain Jerontis asked, "Have you discovered any potentially lethal microorganisms?"

"I haven't found any microbes that would pose a greater danger than what our immune systems had to contend with back on Earth," replied Dianne.

"I don't know if I should take comfort in that or not," Captain Jerontis commented. "After all, some of Earth's microorganisms are quite dangerous. Would you mind elaborating a bit?"

"The most dangerous microbe that I've found so far is a strain of bacillus similar to the bacteria that produces botulin. Botulin is the toxin that causes botulism, a disease of the nervous system. Although it is potentially deadly, it will be no more difficult to deal with here than it was back on Earth. Following basic sanitary procedures in the preparation and preservation of food should eliminate the danger posed by these bacteria."

"If that's the most dangerous microbe you've found so far, we don't have much of a problem," Captain Jerontis responded.

"Have you found anything else that might cause medical problems?"

Dianne established eye contact with Doctor Nemard, and using the silent communication that they had become quite proficient at, a mutual decision was reached for Doctor Nemard to answer the question.

"Specimens that we took from a small squirrel-like mammal living on the island showed it to be carrying a virus that fits into the family of viruses that cause influenza in humans," she said. "Detailed information about the virus has been entered into the computer, and it is developing a vaccine to counteract the virus. It should be ready in a few days. As a precaution, I recommend that we vaccinate all who are going down."

"That sounds reasonable," commented Captain Jerontis.

After a few moments of silence, Captain Jerontis asked, "Can anyone think of a legitimate reason that would prevent us from establishing our home on this island?"

During the silence that followed the question, Captain Jerontis established eye contact with each of his colleagues and received no verbal response. Then, he said, "I am going to interpret your silence to mean that you have no reason to delay going down."

Then, Captain Jerontis turned to Moose and said, "Send down Charlie as soon as you have him ready. During his first week, I want him to visit every part of the island. If nothing of consequence happens to him, we will make our first manned landing."

Moose nodded in acknowledgment of Captain J.J.'s order. Then he left the flight deck to go to the shop to assist the personnel working on Charlie. Moose was determined to expedite the final improvements being made to Charlie.

Captain Jerontis addressed those remaining on the flight deck, "I've been thinking of a name for the island. I would like to call it Pioneer Island. I think this would be an appropriate name for our home. By any definition of the word that you choose to use, we are pioneers."

"That's most definitely true," stated Connie, "but there is another reason why we should name our home *Pioneer Island.*"

After a pause during which Connie waited to make sure she had everyone's attention, Captain Jerontis lost patience and said, "Well, are you going to share that reason with us?"

"Yes! And I hope you won't think I sound like I'm preaching, but I feel strongly about this. Getting directly to the point, I have studied the early history of the United States, especially the lives of the pioneers. For the most part, these people were rugged individuals. They were survivors. Most of them were self-reliant and proud of it. They didn't look to government or anyone else to do for them what they could do for themselves. They loved their freedom and independence too much to allow themselves to become dependent on others, especially government. Their freedom and determined can-do attitude was largely responsible for the United States eventually becoming the greatest nation on Earth. If they hadn't laid the foundation for this great nation, we probably would not be here. In honor of them and what they achieved, I strongly feel that we should name our home *Pioneer Island.*"

Several moments of thoughtful silence followed Connie's speech. Then, Captain Jerontis said, "If we surpass their strengths and avoid their mistakes, we should be able to build the foundation for an even greater nation. In any case, I agree that *Pioneer Island* is a fitting name for our home."

"The thought of living in a large log cabin on *Pioneer Island* appeals to me. It's romantic!" Connie said.

"Since we are on the subject of names, I would like to propose that we name the lake Clear Lake," Mike remarked.

"That's definitely a fitting name," commented Captain Jerontis,

"I believe the meadow where we landed our first robot lab should be named Sauropod Meadow," Dianne said. "Since the herd of sauropods sleeps there every night, they apparently consider the meadow to be theirs."

"If they think that meadow is theirs, I don't think we should disagree with them," remarked Captain Jerontis.

TIME: 6 Years, 301 Days A.L.E.

On the flight deck, Moose was watching the large video screen with a deeply felt personal interest. What he saw on the screen was a real-time motion picture of the final approach glide of a robot lab suspended from a para-wing. This robot lab was modified to deliver Charlie to the surface and to support his activities while on the surface. What made this video so filled with detail was that it originated from cameras on the robot lab already on Pioneer Island.

"I like this," Moose said. "I feel like I am standing on the plateau watching Charlie being delivered. I feel like the para-wing and lab are heading directly towards me, which means they are heading directly for the lab that's already on the plateau."

Turning to Mike, Moose said. "You aren't going to crash Charlie into the lab that's already there are you?"

"Don't worry, we're only going to land near the lab," Mike responded. "The flight control system is homing on a signal from the lab, but Charlie will land a short distance beyond it and a little to the right."

"I hope you're right," commented Moose. "I wouldn't want Charlie damaged in a crash landing."

"You remind me of an expectant father, who is nervously awaiting the birth of his first child," said Mike. "You have to relax and remember that Charlie isn't a real person: he's just a robot."

"Charlie is more than just a robot," replied Moose. "He's my creation. I want him delivered safely and in good working order."

Pointing at the video screen, Mike said. "As you can see, the para-wing has just veered slightly to the right. We should have touchdown in just a few seconds."

Several seconds later, the lab carrying Charlie made a gentle landing approximately fifty yards away from the lab already on the plateau.

After letting out a big sigh of relief, Moose said. "I guess I really didn't need to worry. Once again, you've achieved a soft landing that is right on-target."

"That almost sounded like a compliment," remarked Mike. "Thank you!"

"You're welcome!" replied Moose, who immediately initiated the sequence of events that would get Charlie out of the lab and into action.

A short time later, Charlie was standing next to the lab. Moose turned on the video cameras that made up his eyes and the microphones that made up his ears. Moose instructed Charlie to slowly turn his head from side to side. Moose observed the video coming from Charlie and listened to the sounds that Charlie's ears were hearing.

"It's almost as if I'm standing on Pioneer Island," Moose declared. "By looking at the video screen, I can see exactly what I would be seeing if I were standing where Charlie is standing. Not only that, but I can hear what he hears."

Next, Moose instructed Charlie to walk toward the other lab. While Charlie walked the fifty yards, Moose observed him from the front and from the back using the video cameras on the labs. "He sure walks smoothly. A casual observer could easily mistake him for a real person."

When Charlie reached the lab, Moose instructed him to walk around the lab and visually inspect it. Then, Moose had Charlie stand up straight and face the distant mountain range to the east. Turning on Charlie's speakers and speaking into a microphone, Moose exclaimed loudly, "Hello Alcent! My name is Moose! I am from Earth!"

When Moose's voice boomed out of the speakers on Charlie's chest and back, the microphones on the labs picked it up and broadcast it back to the Challenger. This enabled the people on the Challenger to hear Moose's voice as it sounded on the plateau.

Captain Jerontis turned to Mike and said, "I think Moose is acting like a kid with a new toy."

"It sure looks that way," commented Mike with a chuckle.

"You guys shouldn't be making fun of me, just because I'm having fun while I check out Charlie to make sure that all of his systems are functional. Even though I'm having fun, I am serious about what I'm doing."

"Don't be offended by my comment," Captain Jerontis responded. "I am enjoying this as much as you are. And Charlie is exactly the right kind of new toy for us to have at the moment."

Acting more like a proud father than the inventor and builder of a robot, Moose went back to checking out Charlie. Moose turned on Charlie's radar and instructed him to use it to measure the distance to the lab that had delivered him. Charlie's quick response was: 50.4 yards.

Next, Moose instructed Charlie to run back to the lab. Watching Charlie run, Moose said, "I like the way he runs with such apparent ease. Those long, graceful strides give him the appearance of a long-distance runner."

Then, Moose checked out Charlie's infrared vision and found it to be functioning properly.

Turning to Captain Jerontis, Moose declared formally, "Charlie is ready for duty sir."

Reflecting on Moose's declaration, his comments and possessive attitude in regard to Charlie, and on the degree of concern shown during Charlie's landing approach; Captain Jerontis decided that Moose felt a great deal of pride for having conceived the concept of Charlie, and then, completing the design, development, and construction in a timely manner. Captain Jerontis also concluded that Moose felt very attached to Charlie even though Charlie was just a robot. Captain Jerontis complemented Moose, "You've done an excellent job in the design and construction of Charlie. I am impressed by the way you've completed such a complicated project in such a short time."

Feeling a great deal of satisfaction in his achievement and happy with the recognition given to him by his closest friend, Moose displayed a broad beaming smile and said, "Thank you for the compliment. I hope that Charlie fulfills our expectations."

"During the next few days, we'll put him to work and find out what he can do for us," said Captain Jerontis. "For the next few hours, let's have Charlie explore the area within 100 yards of either lab. Within this distance, the cameras on the labs can easily show us any insects or other creatures that investigate Charlie. Then, we'll use his support lab to give him a thorough inspection for stings and bites."

As Moose started Charlie walking in the direction of a clump of bushes, he said, "There sure aren't very many trees on the plateau."

"The openness of the plateau is one of the reasons why it is such an attractive place to land our labs," commented Mike. "It's possible that the soil on most of the plateau isn't deep enough to physically support tall trees. The fact that some small areas are exposed rock tends to support my speculation. There are fewer than one hundred tall trees on the plateau, and nearly all of them are grouped in three small areas. It is my guess that we'll find deep soil only in those areas. On the rest of the plateau, I believe that the soil is only deep enough to support shrubs, grass, and other kinds of small plants."

TIME: 6 Years, 301 Days, 3 Hours, 30 Minutes A.L.E.

"Charlie has been exploring the area around the labs for about three hours now," Moose said. "Apparently, nothing of consequence has happened to him."

"Let's use his support lab to recharge his batteries and give him a thorough inspection," directed Captain Jerontis. "I am especially interested in finding out if he has suffered any bites or stings."

A short time later, Moose said, "The lab has inspected Charlie and he hasn't received any bites or stings, not even from insects. Wouldn't it be nice if it turns out that there's nothing dangerous on the plateau?"

"Seems like that would make it a rather boring place to live," joked Mike.

"If you need danger to make your life exciting, you could always visit Sauropod Meadow and wait for the T-Rexes to arrive," suggested Moose.

"I don't think I need that much excitement," Mike quickly responded.

"Let's have Charlie hike through the groves," Captain Jerontis said. "I want to find out if there's anything living in them that might attack him."

A few minutes later, Charlie reached the first group of trees. He stopped and looked up in a determined search of their branches for living creatures. There weren't any present, except for a few birds and insects.

"These trees remind me of pine trees and fir trees," Moose remarked.

Charlie walked into the group of trees. He stopped and looked around. Then, he looked up and searched the branches. Part way up the trunk of a dead tree, he spotted a small hole with insects entering and leaving. Moose directed Charlie to use his zoom lens capability to obtain close-up imagery of the insects.

"Those insects look like honey bees. I wonder if that's what they are," Moose commented.

"It is springtime in this area, and there are a multitude of blossoming plants on this plateau," said Captain Jerontis. "When Charlie leaves this grove, let's have him check out the nearest group of flowers in search of these insects. If they are an Alcent-version of Earth's honey bees, it should become readily apparent from their behavior."

"I hope they aren't an Alcent-version of Earth's killer bees," commented Mike.

"Perhaps, we should find out how aggressive they are in defending their nest," suggested Moose.

"I think that's an excellent idea," stated Mike.

Moose directed Charlie to walk directly to the tree. When Charlie reached the tree, he stopped, tilted his head back, and looked up at the small hole, which was about eleven feet above the ground. So far, the insects were entering and leaving without concern for Charlie's presence.

Next, Moose instructed Charlie to walk around the tree. Still no reaction from the insects.

Then, Moose had Charlie pick up a small stone and lightly tap on the tree several times. This resulted in several dozen of the insects exiting the nest and excitedly buzzing around the immediate vicinity of the nest.

"If this were on Earth and if these were killer bees, Charlie's artificial human skin would have suffered several hundred bee stings by now," asserted Mike. "It's beginning to look like it would take a direct assault on their nest to provoke them to attack."

"I think we should find out," stated Moose as he directed Charlie to pick up a stick that was laying on the ground nearby. Moose had Charlie tap the tree with the stick, starting at ground level and gradually moving up toward the nest entrance. As the tapping got closer to the entrance, more insects exited the nest. They buzzed around in a frenzy as if seeking direction. When the tapping stick came within two feet of the nest entrance, several of the insects attacked Charlie, stinging the arm with the stick, his neck, and his face. As Charlie stopped tapping on the tree and backed away from it, a few more of the insects stung him. Then, Charlie turned and ran away with a small swarm of the insects in pursuit. Only two of the pursuing insects stung Charlie. All broke off pursuit by the time Charlie was fifty yards away from the nest.

"Apparently, these insects won't attack unless their nest is directly threatened," remarked Mike.

"Let's give them about a half hour to settle down, and then, let's have Charlie return to their tree and walk around it a couple times without doing anything threatening," Captain Jerontis said. "I want to find out if they now recognize Charlie as an enemy and attack him simply because he is near their nest or if they will ignore him when he isn't doing anything to provoke them.

"In the meantime let's have Charlie investigate some of the nearby flowers," he continued. "If we find some of these insects gathering nectar, then we should take a look inside that tree and find out if they're making honey with it. If they are, we should get a sample of it for analysis and call these insects honey bees."

A short time later, Charlie approached a large flowering shrub. As expected, several of the insects were buzzing around the shrub, going from one blossom to the next. Using Charlie's close-up lens capability, Moose zoomed in on one of the blossoms and observed one of the insects contentedly gathering nectar. Apparently, the nectar in this blossom was as much as the insect could carry, because when it left the blossom, it flew off in the direction of the nest. After seeing several more of the insects do the same thing, it was decided to have Charlie follow them to verify their destination. Charlie's ability to run at speeds up to twenty miles per hour allowed him to easily keep up with the nectar-laden insects.

When Charlie reached the trees, he slowed down to a leisurely walk. He could now see the dead tree with the nest in it and could see that this was the insect's destination. Charlie approached the tree at a pace comparable to that of a human being out for a relaxing walk. By having Charlie approach the tree in a non-threatening way, Captain Jerontis hoped to find out if the insects would consider him and hence humans to be enemies because of their earlier experience.

About five feet from the tree, Charlie stopped and looked up at the nest entrance. The insects were entering and exiting without showing any concern about his presence. Next, Charlie walked around the tree. Then, he stepped up to the tree, reached out, and gently put a hand on it. Then, he leaned against the tree like a human stopping to rest. Throughout this activity, the insects paid no attention to him.

"Evidently, these insects are quite docile and won't attack unless directly threatened," commented Captain Jerontis. "I think it's time to march Charlie back to the lab, so we can extract and analyze the venom from the stings he received earlier. Hopefully, it will prove to be non-lethal to humans."

Several hours later, it was nighttime on the plateau. Charlie was wandering the plateau under the light of a full moon and a half moon. Dianne and Moose were currently the only individuals on the flight deck, and they were directing and monitoring Charlie's activities.

"The plateau sure is quiet and peaceful," remarked Moose.

"The light from two moons adds a pleasant romantic touch to the scene," commented Dianne.

"Let's pretend we're down there right now going for a walk in the moonlight. Using Charlie's eyes and ears, we can do that fairly realistically."

"Sounds like fun. Let's go to the south end of the plateau and look down at the lake and the moonlight reflecting off the water."

"Walking around in the moonlight with Charlie should help us determine if there are any nighttime predators around that have managed to stay hidden from us during the daytime."

"Are you trying to add an element of risk to our make-believe romantic walk in the moonlight?"

"Since it's make-believe, all the risk will be to Charlie," replied Moose. "But in the very near future, we may actually go for a romantic walk in the moonlight. In fact, we may be doing that in less than ten days. So, let's use this make-believe journey to evaluate the risks."

"Finally, after all these years in space, we are about to achieve our goal of settling down on Alcent for what we hope will be a long happy life filled with peaceful prosperity. It's a life-long dream that's about to come true; and the best part of it is, I am here with you. Two months from now, I might be pregnant with our first child."

Moose gave his wife a warm, loving hug and said, "That would be wonderful. Pioneer Island appears to be an ideal place to raise a family."

"I am happy that those nectar gathering insects aren't going to be a threat to our children. They turned out to be docile, and their venom is very similar to what bees produce back on Earth. If it turns out that they are making honey with the nectar, then I think we should try to increase their numbers by providing them hives to live in. Perhaps, we could harvest part of the honey. Wouldn't it be a pleasure to eat some warm, honey-covered, freshly baked bread made from our very own homegrown grain?"

"Yes, it would! And I must admit that the way you're talking is filling me with conflicting desires. I don't know if we should be heading for the bedroom or for the cafeteria."

"If talking about living on Alcent in conjunction with a make-believe walk in the moonlight has that kind of effect on you, then I am really going to enjoy living there," Dianne responded.

"Stop Charlie and get a close-up to his left!" she exclaimed, urgently.

Moose did as directed and near the center of the video screen was a small rodent running as fast as he could. Moose immediately zoomed in on the creature for increased detail. Then, out of nowhere, a diving bird of prey suddenly entered the scene. The bird's sharp talons instantly dug into the rodent's back and neck followed immediately by a crisp blow to the rodent's head delivered by the bird's sharp beak. The hapless rodent died instantly in the sudden attack by the extremely efficient feathered predator.

"Nothing like sudden death to take the romance out of a stroll in the moonlight," remarked Moose as he directed Charlie's sensors to follow the retreating bird. Since his video cameras were equipped with light intensifiers, Charlie's nighttime vision was excellent. This in combination with his radar and infrared vision made it very easy for Charlie to track the flight of the bird.

"It looks like the bird's destination might be that group of tall trees near the south end of the plateau," speculated Dianne. "Perhaps, this bird has a nest in one of the trees and the rodent will be fed to its chicks."

"Let's head Charlie in that direction and look for a nest," said Moose as he sent Charlie toward the trees at a fast walk.

"While you're busy controlling Charlie's activities, I will take a close look at that bird and the rodent," stated Dianne as she entered instructions into the computer to recall the video of the attack. Dianne displayed the video on the screen next to the one that Moose was using to control Charlie's activities. Dianne picked up the video at the instant that Charlie had zoomed in on the rodent. Running the video in super slow motion and freezing selected images, Dianne was able to study the rodent in detail.

"This creature would fit quite nicely into a family of animals called ground squirrels back on Earth," commented Dianne.

"Specifically, it looks very much like a gray gopher," remarked Moose.

Dianne continued running the video in slow motion, freezing key images of the bird's attack and of it carrying away its prey. "On Earth, I believe this bird could be fit into the owl species," stated Dianne. "It has a broad head and large forward facing eyes. These are the distinctive features of owls. It probably has excellent night vision and is primarily a nocturnal hunter."

"And it is a very skilled hunter, if the attack we just witnessed is typical of what it can do."

"If this bird were on Earth, it would be one of the larger members of the owl family. From this video, I would estimate its wingspan to be slightly more than three feet."

"Charlie has just arrived in the grove," stated Moose as he directed Charlie to search for the bird and a possible nest.

After several minutes of searching individual trees, Charlie's infrared camera located a warm body above a branch. Even though the body was fairly well concealed by foliage, its temperature of approximately one hundred degrees made it easily detectable in the infrared.

"I think we have located our bird," stated Moose. "I am going to simplify this image by having the computer subtract out everything with a temperature outside of the ninety-nine to one-hundred-one-degree range."

A few seconds later, Dianne said, "That image is rather sketchy. Too much is missing because of having been blocked out by foliage, but it does look like our bird. I am entering a request for the computer to compare this sketchy image to the detailed images it has of the bird to find out if it can make a positive identification."

Several seconds later, the computer responded: "The probability is .973 that this is the same bird."

"I think we can assume that this is our bird," stated Moose. "Now let's look for evidence of a nest."

A few minutes later, Moose and Dianne discovered the nest several feet below the bird and in the tree to its left.

"It looks to me like the bird is guarding the nest while its mate is hunting," Moose said. "It is my prediction that this bird will not leave until its mate returns."

"Let's watch for a while and find out."

About twenty minutes later, the bird's mate arrived with a small reptile firmly clutched in its talons. "I wonder where that came from?" questioned Moose.

"It looks like a lizard. If it came from this island, we need to find out if it has a poisonous bite. Even though it's only about fifteen inches long, it could still be dangerous if it has a poisonous bite and aggressively defends itself."

"Not to change the subject, but have you noticed that the bird that had been standing guard has already left?" Moose said, "Now, I am going to make another prediction, and that is that the bird that just arrived with the lizard will not leave until its mate returns."

"If that's the case, it implies that there are predators around that these birds fear."

"That might be true, but it doesn't take much of a predator to kill and eat baby birds. A carnivorous mammal no larger than a squirrel could raid an unguarded nest."

After a few minutes of additional observation, Dianne said, "It seems like our romantic walk in the moonlight has turned into a bird-watching expedition."

"When we are living on this planet, many of our plans are likely to have unexpected outcomes," remarked Moose.

"Is that another prediction?"

Sensing that his wife might be teasing him, Moose searched her eyes, "It does sound like I did nothing more than state the obvious, doesn't it?"

"Yes, but it is nevertheless an important point, because our survival will surely depend on us always being ready for the unexpected."

"Even though our romantic walk in the moonlight has been interrupted, I think it was a worthwhile interruption. I think we should always take advantage of unexpected opportunities to learn about our environment. The more that we know about it; the more able we'll be to live in harmony with it. That will make our lives easier and more relaxing than the alternative of continuously clashing with it."

"I agree," nodded Dianne. "Also, I think that our long-term survival and prosperity depends on living in harmony with our environment."

"The rapid acquisition of knowledge about it is the key. One quick way to gain this knowledge is to observe predators like this family of owls. Simply observing them for several weeks and keeping track of the prey that they feed their young will quickly make us aware of many of the small creatures that live in this area."

"Speaking about the owls, the other parent has just returned with a fish," announced Dianne.

"These birds are certainly versatile predators. I wonder how he managed to catch a fish."

"Perhaps this fish was sick or injured and was floundering around on the surface, and the bird recognized it as a meal of opportunity."

"That's a possibility."

After a few moments of silent observation, Moose said, "I think we should launch an RPV, fly it to the grove, and land it on the branch of a nearby tree. Observing these owls with its video cameras will allow us to use Charlie to continue our romantic stroll."

"Good idea!"

Several minutes later, Dianne said, "I've secured the RPV to a branch in a good location to observe the nest and its immediate vicinity. The video from it is good, so let's resume our romantic walk in the moonlight."

A short time later, Charlie was standing near the southern edge of the plateau. Sounding concerned, Dianne said, "You've marched him almost to the edge. If he takes one more step, he'll fall 150 feet and crash into the sandy beach. Simply losing his balance could topple him over the edge."

"Don't worry about Charlie; he has a very good sense of balance."

"But, his feet are less than a foot from the edge."

Moose decided to repeat what Mike had told him earlier in the day: "You must keep in mind that Charlie isn't a real person; he is just a robot."

"But I am starting to become attached to him. He may be just a robot, but he is your creation, and he is serving us very well. I would feel sad if he fell to his destruction."

"Well, if it will relax your worried mind, I'll have him back up a couple steps."

"You are a good actor, but you're failing to convince me that you're unconcerned about Charlie. I know that you are just as attached to him as I am."

Moose chuckled, "It's becoming increasingly difficult to fool you. It seems like every time I try to mislead you, purely in fun of course, you see right through it."

"Well, we have been married for a few years, and I do know you very well."

Now that Charlie had stepped back from the edge of the plateau, Moose directed him to drop down into a prone position and peer over the edge. Displaying the view from Charlie's video cameras on the largest screen on the flight deck gave Moose and Dianne a very realistic sensation of actually being on the edge of the cliff.

"What a beautiful scene," remarked Dianne. "It is so peaceful and inviting. I would dearly love to set up a tent and camp for a few days on the sandy beach at the base of the cliff. With the tall trees on both sides of the bay, the beach is sheltered from the wind from every direction except the south. And the whole scene is softly illuminated by the light from two moons that are now high in the sky."

"Even the sounds are soft and peaceful. All that I hear is the whispering sound of a gentle breeze flowing through the trees, the splashing sound of small waves lapping the beach, and the sounds made by small nocturnal creatures busily living their lives."

"It's truly amazing that such a peaceful place could exist on a planet inhabited by a multitude of creatures with awesome size and power."

"We may have found the most ideal place on all of Alcent on which to build our homes. With intelligent planning and hard work, Pioneer Island might become our island paradise."

"I wish we were down there right now," stated Dianne. "I would love to make love on that warm sandy beach and then go for a midnight swim in the moonlight."

"I would too," Moose said and moved into a position behind Dianne. He put his arms around her in a loving embrace.

After a few moments of silence during which Dianne and Moose soaked up the view and the sounds from their future home, Moose said, "We can't go swimming in the moonlight tonight, but we can go to our apartment and make love with that view covering one entire wall. With the only sounds in our apartment coming from Pioneer Island, we should be able to pretend quite realistically that we are down there on that beach."

"What a wonderful conclusion to an imaginary romantic stroll in the moonlight," responded Dianne, somewhat passionately.

Upon hearing the desired response from his wife, Moose left a note on the control console stating that Charlie was doing an important extended period of observation of the bay and was not to be disturbed. Then, he and Dianne left the flight deck and went to their apartment.

About an hour later, Moose and Dianne returned to the flight deck. They were greeted by Connie, who looked at them and said, "You two certainly seem to be in a buoyant mood. Have you made some discovery that I should know about?"

Moose and Dianne looked at each other and chuckled. "I think you've already discovered the procedure responsible for our uplifted moods," Dianne said.

Instantly realizing that she had innocently asked a rather personal question, she offered, "I didn't mean to pry into your private life. I just thought you might have discovered something wonderful about Pioneer Island."

"Actually, we have," responded Moose. Pointing at the large video screen, he said, "When we viewed this scene from our bedroom, we discovered that it had a rather erotic effect on us. It was very stimulating, and the overall experience was exquisitely satisfying. Being a medical professional, perhaps you could explain how this exotic scene from an alien planet could have had such an amorous effect on us."

While considering what Moose had just said, Connie silently gazed at the scene and listened to the peaceful sounds coming from it. After a few moments, she asked, "How long has Charlie been transmitting the sights and sounds from this area?"

"For about an hour," replied Moose.

"Is the entire transmission stored in the computer?" questioned Connie.

"Yes, it is," answered Moose.

Attempting to sound both sly and innocent, Connie said, "I am going to ask Jerry to review it with me from our bedroom. Perhaps, we will make the same discovery that you and Dianne made. If we do, and if you really do need an expert evaluation of it, I will analyze it and give you a professional explanation from a medical perspective."

"I appreciate your offer," Moose responded, "but since I am already quite knowledgeable on the subject, I must decline."

"That's the kind of response I expected from you," stated Connie as she turned and left the flight deck.

Moose made eye contact with Dianne, "I wonder what she has on her mind."

"As if you don't know," replied Dianne while displaying a naughty smile of self-satisfaction.

Moose returned the smile, and gave his wife an affectionate hug. He turned to face the video screen, "When we're living on the plateau, there is one small problem that we'll face whenever we want to swim in that bay; and that is, we'll have to climb down a nearly vertical cliff of 150 feet to get to the water. If we're serious about living on the plateau, we'll have to devise some easy means to get on and off it. It seems like a simple elevator consisting of pulleys, cables, a cage, and an electric motor would be rather easy to design and build."

"I like that idea; however, on the north side of the plateau, we should be able to construct a trail between the plateau and the land below it. Even though the 45-degree slope is quite steep, we should be able to handle it by building a number of switch-backs in the trail."

"That shouldn't be all that difficult."

"Which brings up a question. How do you plan to get Charlie off the plateau, so he can explore the rest of the island?"

"He will tie a rope to a tree and while grasping the rope for support, he will make his way down the slope. After each exploration trip, he can use the same rope to climb back up to his support lab."

"When do you plan to have Charlie begin exploring the rest of the island?"

"Tomorrow morning, about an hour after Alpha Centauri A rises into the sky, Charlie will begin his descent off the plateau. Then, he will explore the forest around the plateau."

"How much longer are we going to leave Charlie stranded at the south end of the plateau?"

"I think it's time to return him to the vicinity of his support lab. Then, we'll have him lie down for the rest of the night to simulate a sleeping human. The lab's video cameras will be trained on him to record anything that might happen to him, such as an attack by pterodactyls. If nothing that tragic occurs, then tomorrow morning, we'll give him a thorough inspection for insect bites and stings, or bites and stings of any kind for that matter."

"Your idea of designing and building Charlie was sure a good one," said Dianne with obvious pride in her husband. "By the time we land, we'll have a much better understanding of potential risks than we would've had without him."

"I am pleased with the way he turned out. I expect that he will be a valuable asset long after we've landed and built our homes. For example, Charlie will probably lead the way whenever we explore new territory. Using him in conjunction with RPVs should help us avoid deadly confrontations with the danger-ous animals that inhabit Alcent."

"That's a good example of a way to harmonize with our environment rather than clash with it."

After a few moments of silence, Dianne noticed that her husband was deeply lost in thought, so she asked, "In what far away place is your mind?"

"Actually, my mind was back on Earth. I was thinking about the environmental extremists who tried to kill us to prevent us from coming here. It just occurred to me that anyone who would honestly evaluate the facts would have to conclude that we are being responsible in regard to Alcent's environment. We are doing, and will continue to do, everything within reason to protect it."

"Yes, but our commitment to that policy wasn't good enough for them. In their view, the human species is a form of environmental pollution. According to them, our very presence on Alcent pollutes the environment. In their view, the human species does not have the same right to evolve and expand its terri-tory that other species have."

"They are, of course, entitled to speak their point of view, but they do not have the right to force others to listen to it."

TIME: 6 Years, 307 Days, 2 Hours A.L.E.

Captain Jerontis was conducting a meeting in the cafeteria, which was being attended by all off-duty personnel. Captain Jerontis declared officially: "The event that we've all been waiting for and preparing for is now less than 24 hours away. Tomorrow, our first manned landing will occur. I will pilot the personnel shuttle to a landing on the east side of Pioneer Island. My crew for this mission will be Doctor Nemard, Moose, and Dianne."

Our primary objective will be to conduct medical research. Doctor Nemard will do a daily medical examination of each of us. If none of us experience any medical problems of consequence during a period of thirty days, additional personnel will be landed on Pioneer Island.

A second objective will be accomplished by Dianne. She will be searching for dangerous microorganisms. Also, she will be investigating insects and other life forms to determine their potential to harm us.

Moose will begin the project of finding local sources of food. It is my prediction that he will begin by looking for tasty, nutritious fish."

Much to Moose's chagrin, a round of laughter greeted this matter-of-fact statement of the obvious. Then, Captain Jerontis said, "I plan to continue the exploration of the island that has been started by Charlie. Although we've learned a great deal with the RPVs and with Charlie, there is still much to be done. Moose will now give us a brief summary of the results of Charlie's activities."

"During the past several days Charlie has wandered the length and breadth of Pioneer Island," Moose reported. "Each night he slept in a different location. He has slept on the beach, in the forest, on the plateau, in open meadows, even in a tree. Please excuse my use of the verb slept. Charlie didn't actually sleep; he imitated a sleeping human. While simulating a sleeping human, he was not molested except by insects, and none of them injected any venom into him. The only insects to ever inject venom into him were bees, and their venom was no more dangerous than bee venom on Earth. This attack occurred during daylight when Charlie threatened their nest.

On three occasions, Charlie dripped droplets of blood on his trail. On two of these occasions, he was trailed by a small mammal that looked very much like an extra large weasel. In both cases, these mammals stopped following Charlie when they got close enough to become aware of his size. Apparently, Pioneer Island is home to carnivorous mammals the size of a large weasel. But Charlie's experience and the lack of large prey strongly indicates that there aren't any large predators living on the island.

The only large predators we've seen there are the pterodactyls, and apparently, they don't live on Pioneer Island, but only stop there to rest while on their way to somewhere else. On two occasions, they were flying over the island while Charlie was wandering around in open areas. Both times, they ignored him. Either they weren't hungry, or they didn't recognize him as potential prey."

After Moose's concluding remark, Captain Jerontis turned to him and said, "Thank you for your report."

Facing the assembly, Captain Jerontis said, "Our next report will be presented by Dianne."

Dianne moved to a position in front of the group and delivered her report: "As you know, we've been engaged in a very intense research program to learn as much as possible about the immune systems of the creatures living on Alcent. You are all familiar with the details of the research, so I am not going to expound on that. I am simply going to say that we've concluded that Alcent's animals have evolved immune systems that are fully capable of guarding against attack by any microbes from Earth that we inadvertently introduce into their environment.

"Part of our research involved an intense effort to find and identify as many of Alcent's microorganisms as possible. We've isolated and catalogued well over a thousand. Doctor Nemard has evaluated them from a medical perspective and has concluded that the human immune system should be able to protect us from them. Of course, we cannot be 100% sure of that until we go down and live on the planet for an extended time, and that is what we plan to begin doing tomorrow."

After pausing for a few moments to allow the assembly to digest her comments, Dianne said, "On another subject, I would like to propose that the site of our first homes be named Stellar Plateau. Since we are the first interstellar pioneers from Earth, I believe this is a suitable name."

Noting that nearly everyone was nodding in agreement, Captain Jerontis declared: "Stellar Plateau it is."

After a brief pause, Captain Jerontis continued, "When we land on Alcent tomorrow, a new era will begin; an era in which a new civilization will be built. Tomorrow will be the reference point in time for all future generations. When they look back in time, tomorrow will be seen as their genesis day. Tomorrow will be Day One on a new calendar.

"There is, however, one remaining key event that must be accomplished before tomorrow's landing can take place. This afternoon, Mike will land a large capsule on Stellar Plateau that contains everything that we'll need to survive and accomplish our objectives during the next thirty days."

Turning to Mike, Captain Jerontis said, "Your skill in landing capsules precisely on target has been demonstrated repeatedly. I am confident that you will not have any problem delivering this one on target."

"Thank you," replied Mike. "The capsule is ready to go. Its flight control program and equipment have been checked and rechecked."

The capsule referred to by Captain Jerontis and Mike was very similar in design to the Apollo Capsules used in America's first manned lunar exploration program. However, with a maximum internal diameter of twenty-two feet, this capsule was much larger. It had two floors in it that would be used for living space and for research. It was packed with food, research equipment, survival equipment, construction materials, basic tools, and Moose's fishing tackle. The capsule would make its final approach and landing suspended from a very large para-wing. If all went according to plan, Mike would land it within fifty yards of the two robot labs already on Stellar Plateau.

The meeting continued for nearly two hours giving everyone an opportunity to discuss the first landing. But the meeting didn't come to an abrupt end; rather, it gradually evolved into a party, a party to celebrate what all had waited such a long time for. After nearly seven years in space, the eve of the first landing had finally arrived.

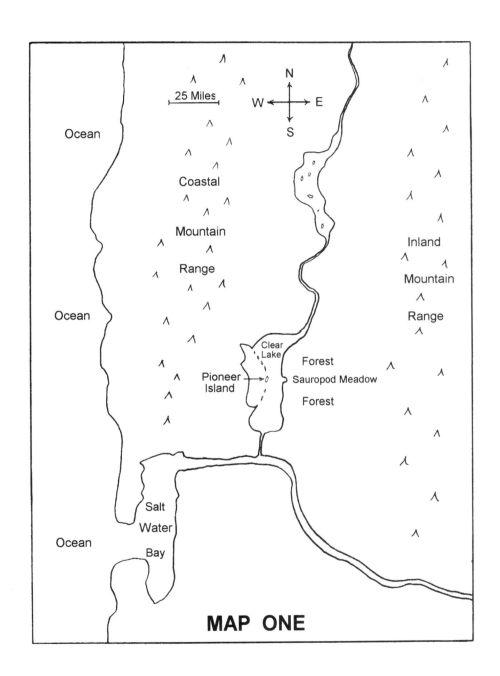

Ocean

25 Miles

N
W — E
S

Ocean

Coastal

Mountain

Range

Ocean

Inland

Mountain

Range

Clear
Lake

Pioneer
Island

Forest

Sauropod Meadow

Forest

Salt

Water

Bay

Ocean

MAP ONE

141

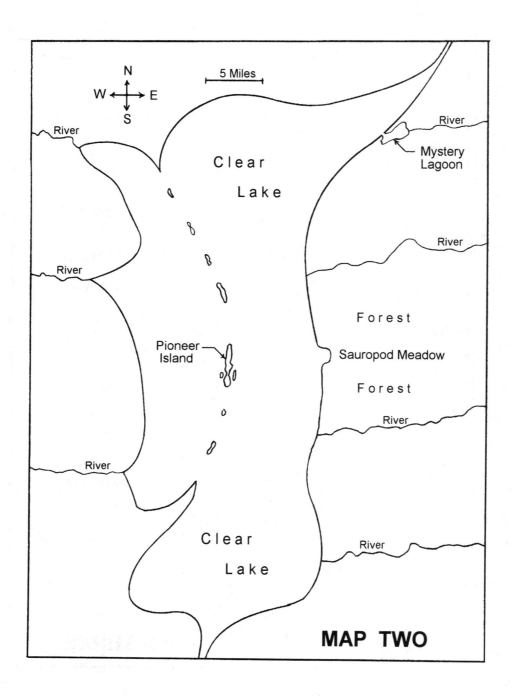

N

W ← → E

S

5 Miles

River

Clear

Lake

River

River

Mystery
Lagoon

River

Forest

Sauropod Meadow

Forest

River

Pioneer
Island

River

Clear

Lake

River

MAP TWO

142

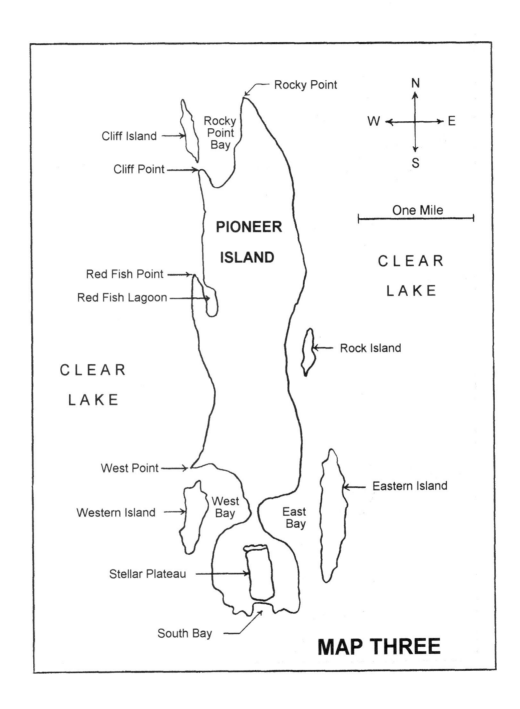

Rocky Point

Rocky
Point
Bay

Cliff Island

Cliff Point

PIONEER

ISLAND

Red Fish Point

Red Fish Lagoon

N

W   E

S

One Mile

C L E A R

L A K E

Rock Island

C L E A R

L A K E

West Point

Western Island

West
Bay

East
Bay

Eastern Island

Stellar Plateau

South Bay

MAP THREE

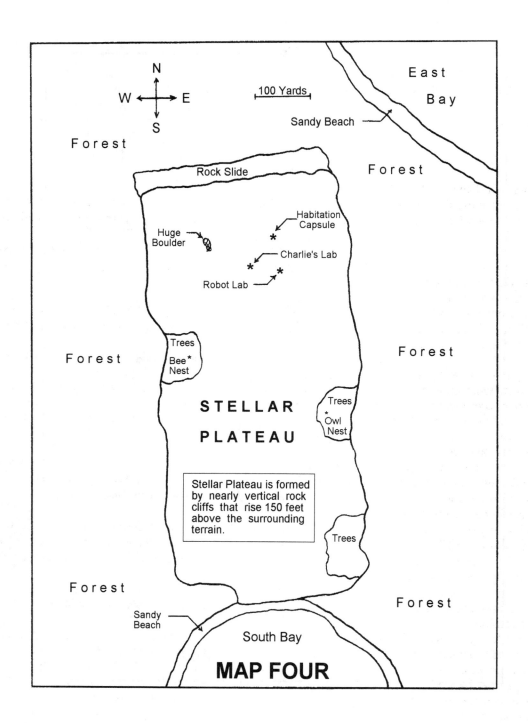

N
W ← → E
S

100 Yards

East
Bay

Sandy Beach

Forest

Rock Slide

Forest

Habitation
Capsule

Huge
Boulder   *

Charlie's Lab
*

Robot Lab   *

Forest

Trees
Bee *
Nest

Forest

STELLAR

PLATEAU

Trees
*
Owl
Nest

Stellar Plateau is formed
by nearly vertical rock
cliffs that rise 150 feet
above the surrounding
terrain.

Trees

Forest

Forest

Sandy
Beach

South Bay

MAP FOUR

144

SIX

The First Day of a New Era

TIME: 6 Years, 308 Days, 1 Hour A.L.E.

Captain Jerontis, Doctor Nemard, Dianne, and Moose were in the personnel shuttle flying north about a mile off the west coast of Pioneer Island. They were in a steep gliding descent and dropped below 35,000 feet.

While observing the scene through an observation port, Connie said, "Pioneer Island sure looks small, and its dark green color looks rather drab."

"You don't sound very excited about going there," commented Dianne.

"What do you mean?"

"This is our big day! I am so excited that I can hardly contain myself! But the way you sounded when you described Pioneer Island, I could almost believe that you're not very thrilled about going there. I know that's not the case, so I'm wondering if something's troubling you."

"I don't know why I am so unemotional about it. Considering that a dream that has driven my life since my early teens is about to come true, it seems like I should be wildly excited; but instead, I feel subdued and somewhat apprehensive. Perhaps, my subconscious mind is harboring a fear that something might yet happen to prevent my dream from coming true."

"This kind of anxiety isn't normal for you. Maybe, it's the result of fatigue. After all, we have been working at a feverish pace for several weeks now."

"That might be, and besides that, I didn't get much sleep last night. As you know, yesterday's party lasted well into the night. And when I finally did get to bed, thinking about today kept me awake. Eventually, I did fall asleep, but my sleep wasn't very restful; it was filled with wild dreams about today."

"Yesterday's party was fun, but it looked to me like you were quite restrained."

"I was worried about today."

"Well, today is here. You don't need to worry about it anymore. It is time for you to unwind and let go. Relax! Enjoy yourself! This is our big day! We've waited a long time for this event, and we'll remember it for the rest of our lives. So, set your anxiety aside and enjoy the excitement of our arrival. Forget about your fatigue and lack of sleep. Just tune it out."

"That's quite a pep talk. I can see that you really are fired up."

"Yes! I am! And I suggest that you forget whatever it is that's been bothering you and get with the mood of the occasion."

Connie thought about Dianne's pep talk for a few moments. Then, her mood showed dramatic improvement as she warmly smiled and said, "Thank you. I needed that."

At that moment, the personnel shuttle rolled 25 degrees and began a 180-degree right turn.

A short time later, Connie said, "Take a look at this view. We've lost enough altitude so that I am beginning to appreciate the immense size of Clear Lake. It totally dominates the scene."

"It's easy to see how well Clear Lake isolates Pioneer Island from the surrounding countryside and the huge dinosaurs that live there."

"Maybe, Pioneer Island really will be the safe secure home that we are hoping it will be."

"All of our exploration and research indicates that it will be. Are you worried about something?"

145

"Pioneer Island has more than three square miles of thick forest that we've only partially explored. We really don't know for sure that it doesn't contain any serious dangers."

"That's true," agreed Dianne. "Thoroughly exploring that forest is one of our top priority projects, and not knowing what we are going to discover makes that an exciting adventure. Our survival might depend on us being continuously alert for dangers of any kind."

"If I'm going to be keenly alert, I guess I'd better start getting more sleep. I could start by taking a short nap this afternoon. If I have Jerry cover me with suntan lotion, I can do some sunbathing while I nap. That is something that I haven't done in years. But, maybe I should call it Alpha Centauri bathing."

"I think that most of us will continue to call it sunbathing; even though, the radiant heat will be coming from Alpha Centauri A. But I'm wondering how much of a nap you're going to get if you're planning to have Jerry massage your nearly nude body with suntan lotion."

"Well, I could always take a nap afterwards. Anyway, just a few moments ago, you said that I should relax and enjoy myself. I think your exact words were: *Unwind and let go! Relax! Enjoy yourself!*"

"That's true, but I wasn't thinking about sex when I made those suggestions."

"Well, I wasn't thinking about sex when I mentioned sunbathing. You suggested that."

"Yeah, I guess I did. But now that the subject has come up, it does seem like a good idea. Can you think of a better way to celebrate our arrival?"

"Not at the moment."

"I can't either, so sometime today, I might just hand Moose a bottle of suntan lotion and ask him to cover me with it. I could probably seduce him and even make him think that it was all his idea."

"You sound rather cunning."

Dianne laughed, "Moose never seems to mind."

"It would be rather disappointing if he did."

During the next several moments, Dianne and Connie silently gazed at the picturesque surroundings of their new home, each totally lost in thought. Dianne broke the silence by pointing directly east and exclaiming, "Look at that huge volcanic peak! The summit must be well above 25,000 feet."

"I noticed it from the Challenger's observation deck, but seeing it from a 200-mile high orbit didn't do it much justice. Seeing it from this perspective makes it look enormous. It rises well above the surrounding range."

"As tall as it is, that snow cap is probably permanent. In fact, it might be more than just snow. The upper levels of that mountain might be home to several large glaciers."

"Perhaps one of the rivers flowing into the east side of Clear Lake originates on that mountain," commented Connie.

"If that's the case, maybe someday, an exploration party will follow it to the mountain and even climb the mountain part way."

"Considering the kind of animal life living in the area, that would be a perilous adventure."

"That's true," agreed Dianne. "But after having been confined to a starship for nearly seven years, many of the men and women on this mission are hungry for such an adventure. They'll welcome the challenge of facing the dangers, outwitting them, and surviving."

"Before any dangerous exploration trips take place, I think that it would be wise to build our homes and get firmly established on Pioneer Island, maybe even have some children."

"I can't disagree with that."

Meanwhile, in the cockpit, Captain Jerontis turned to Moose and said, "It won't be long now old buddy; we're almost there. You'll soon have an opportunity to enjoy an exotic beach with your lovely wife. I am sure you'll find just as much excitement on Pioneer Island as you would've had on that vacation to the South Pacific that I interrupted nearly seven years ago."

"I have no doubt about that. I'm glad that you found a way for me to be here."

"I am too."

A few seconds later, Moose confirmed, "Our hydrofoils are down and locked in position."

"We should have contact with the lake in less than thirty seconds," remarked Captain Jerontis. "It's been a long time since I landed on hydrofoils, but our flight control computer makes the job easy."

"We're on course, and our speed is 195 mph, just as it should be," noted Moose.

A few seconds later, Captain Jerontis said, "Our stab-con-foils (small stability and control hydro-foils) have just entered the water and the entry was barely perceptible."

A few moments later, Moose announced, "Our large hydrofoils are now in the water. What a soft landing! We've made an absolutely smooth transition from atmospheric flight to gliding on the water. We are here! And we've arrived without even a small jolt."

As Moose finished exclaiming, the shuttle's hydro-drogues automatically deployed, causing it to rapidly lose speed. When its speed diminished to the point that the hydrofoils could no longer support it, the shuttle settled into the water and floated on its hull. Captain Jerontis then deployed the shuttle's propeller, which was powered by a steam turbine using high pressure steam generated by the shuttle's nuclear reactor. Maintaining the shuttle's speed at about ten mph, Captain Jerontis guided it into East Bay, where he brought it to a halt about fifty yards offshore and dropped anchor in water about thirty feet deep.

Finally, the excitement that she had been restraining reached the bursting point, and Connie exclaimed, "We are on Alcent! And there is someone standing on the beach waving to us!"

"That's Charlie!" said Dianne. "I should've known that Moose would have him standing there waiting to welcome us."

Moose opened a hatch and looked around East Bay for anything that might pose a danger. Not seeing anything that looked threatening, he pushed out a plastic boat that immediately inflated. Then, Moose deployed a short ladder, picked up his rifle, climbed down the ladder, and stepped into the boat. Dianne and Connie immediately joined Moose. Captain Jerontis handed Moose several guns before stepping out of the shuttle. After closing the hatch, Moose and Captain Jerontis picked up the oars and began rowing to the nearby shore.

Moose, Dianne, and Jerry were so preoccupied with the sights and sounds of Alcent that no one noticed Connie quietly removing her hiking boots. With her boots removed, she was wearing only snug fitting shorts and a halter top.

Connie stood up in the front of the boat and announced: "All of our research and underwater exploration indicate that this water is perfectly safe. So, I am going swimming."

Before anyone could offer a word of caution, Connie took a deep breath and dove into the cool, clear, refreshing water.

Caught completely by surprise, Captain Jerontis exclaimed, "Why did she do that!"

While quickly removing his shirt and boots, he said, "I wish that she had waited until we've had a chance to more thoroughly explore this lake before jumping into it."

Dianne commented, "She is obviously very happy to be here, confident the water is safe, and eager to enjoy it; in other words, she has decided to unwind and enjoy herself."

Grabbing one of the spear guns and strapping it to his back, Captain Jerontis said, "That may very well be true, but I am concerned about her safety, and I wish that she had waited."

Then, Captain Jerontis dove into the water and swam straight down to a depth of about fifteen feet, where he searched the surrounding water for anything that might pose a threat to his wife. He quickly noted that the incredible cleanliness of the water allowed him to see for quite some distance in all directions. Much to his relief, he was unable to spot anything that looked threatening. In fact, the water looked very peaceful with small schools of fish lazily swimming around. He noticed that he was behind his wife and surmised that she was unaware of his presence.

A few seconds later, Connie surfaced about twenty feet from the boat and exclaimed, "This is the most refreshing experience I've had in years! And it looks perfectly safe down there."

Then, Connie let out a terrifying scream, as she felt her ankles firmly grasped from behind and felt herself being pulled down. Almost immediately, her ankles were released. Then, Connie noticed that her husband wasn't in the boat, and she instantly realized what had just happened. A moment later, Jerry surfaced next to Connie, looked into her eyes, and waited for her to speak.

"I guess scaring me was your way of reminding me that we are on a dangerous planet," Connie responded.

Captain Jerontis smiled and asked innocently, "Did I use an effective method of communication?"

"Since you were underwater and didn't hear my scream, you have no idea how truly effective it was."

"I didn't hear your scream, but I felt you tremble."

Seeing that her husband was armed, and recognizing how quickly he had joined her in the water, Connie realized that she must have worried him greatly, so she apologized: "I didn't mean to worry you, but based on our data, I really did think that swimming in this bay would be perfectly safe. Even so, I appreciate how quickly you entered the water to protect me, if that became necessary."

"The loving relationship that we've had for so many years has made you the treasure of my life. If I lost you now, my life on this planet would be filled with sorrow. Today is the beginning of the future that we've dreamed about, and I want to share with you the joys and excitement of that future."

Deeply moved by her husband's sincere expression of love for her, Connie said, "You make me feel so special and so very happy. You are the most wonderful husband a woman could ever have."

After a few moments of silence, Connie asked, "Do you think we could go back underwater and take another look around?"

"I didn't see anything that looked threatening down there, so let's enjoy ourselves, but let's stay alert."

Connie and Jerry filled their lungs with air and swam straight down about fifteen feet. After looking around and not seeing any danger, Jerry turned and swam toward his wife. Seeing her husband approach, Connie met him with open arms. Captain Jerontis accepted her invitation, embraced her tightly, and then gave her several intimate caresses. Passionately affected by her husband's erotic touch, Connie responded by caressing him. After a few moments of intimacy, they broke their embrace and headed to the surface for a breath of air.

As they broke the surface, Moose yelled out: "Well, what's it like down there?"

"Very stimulating," replied Captain Jerontis.

"That's a rather vague answer," responded Moose.

"To the contrary, it's right to the point," countered Captain Jerontis. Then, he and Connie filled their lungs and went back into the alien underwater world to do some additional exploration.

Moose looked at Dianne and said, "There must be some exotic scenery down there in order for the Captain to describe it as very stimulating."

"Well, we are on an alien planet. Whatever they see and do down there could have a special air of excitement about it, especially when you factor in the possibility of grave danger unexpectedly showing up."

After looking around and digesting the sights and sounds of the immediate area, Moose commented, "It seems rather calm and peaceful here. I wouldn't mind going for a good swim myself."

"That would be fun, but I don't think that more than two of us should be in the water at the same time until we know for sure that it is safe."

"I have no disagreement with that."

About a minute after they had gone under, Moose said, "It seems like they've been down there for a long time. I wonder if anything has happened to them. If it weren't for the light breeze and the ripple that it is putting on the surface of the lake, we might be able to see them."

Almost as if in answer to Moose's concern, Captain Jerontis and Connie surfaced just a few feet away from the boat. "You've been down there a long time. I was starting to worry about you. What is down there that is so fascinating?" Moose asked.

Connie established eye contact with Dianne, displayed a sly expression, then turned to Moose and said, "The underwater scenery is enchanting, but what kept us down there for so long is that we were warming up for sunbathing."

Before Moose could comment, Connie turned to Captain Jerontis and said, "Let's head for the shore."

"Okay, but let's make the swim in three or four underwater segments, so that we can get better acquainted with the underwater world."

After Jerry and Connie went back underwater, Moose turned to Dianne and said, "I've done a lot of swimming and sunbathing in my life, but I fail to understand how swimming warms a person up for sunbathing. My experience has always been the exact opposite. Sunbathing always made me so hot that I usually went swimming to cool off."

"This sure is a mysterious planet," Dianne teased.

Moose looked at his wife and remarked, "Perhaps, there's something that you could tell me that would clear up part of the mystery."

"What makes you say that?"

"I saw the sly expressions that you and Connie exchanged. Would you mind letting me in on the secret?"

Deciding not to tease her husband any longer, Dianne told him about the earlier conversation with Connie concerning suntan lotion and Jerry. Moose immediately understood what had been going on underwater and laughed at himself for not figuring it out sooner. Then, in a hopeful tone, he asked, "By chance, did you happen to pack some sun screen in your travel bag?"

"I sure did," Dianne replied warmly.

"Maybe, sometime this afternoon, we can take a break from work and find a comfortable secluded spot where we can relax and enjoy the radiant heat from Alpha Centauri A."

"What a wonderful idea," Dianne answered.

As Moose resumed rowing, Dianne asked, "Have you noticed how clean this lake smells?"

"Yes, I have. It reminds me of how fresh and clean the air smells after a rain shower. It's a scent I haven't been exposed to in a long time, but I still remember it. I like that fresh, clean smell. We must never harm this lake's pristine state."

"We certainly have the technology to avoid polluting it."

A few minutes later, Moose and Dianne stepped into shallow water and pulled the boat onto the sandy beach. Shortly thereafter, Jerry and Connie joined them.

During the next few minutes, the four lone humans silently surveyed this small region of their new world. They gazed up and down the sandy beach, watching and listening to the water gently lapping the shore. They looked across East Bay to the one-mile long island that sheltered the bay from easterly winds. They looked at the forest and listened to the gentle breeze whisper through the trees. They wondered if the forest contained any undiscovered dangers. They looked at the deep blue sky with its broadly scattered fluffy white cumulus clouds and appreciated its serene beauty. To the north, they noticed four pterodactyls several thousand feet above Pioneer Island soaring beneath one of the clouds, apparently riding the thermal that supported the cloud.

"Evidently, these creatures sometimes fly purely for pleasure," Moose commented. "What other reason would there be for them to be at such great altitude? Surely, they aren't hunting for food way up there."

Fascinated by the pterodactyls, the new arrivals from Earth continued to observe and admire the huge creatures. Watching them fly in large circles as they rode the thermal to greater altitudes led Moose to remark, "Standing here and watching them gives me a totally different feeling than watching video of them while onboard the Challenger."

"In what respect?" asked Captain Jerontis.

"Now that we are a part of their world, their size and killing capability makes me feel small and vulnerable. To use an analogy, I've seen fascinating movies about the Great White Shark, but I've never had the courage to go swimming with them."

"Are you suggesting that living here is analogous to swimming with sharks?" questioned Captain Jerontis.

"No! I am only saying that studying pterodactyls from the safety of the Challenger was like visiting the local library; whereas, studying them while living with them is dangerous, even a small mistake could be life threatening. And what is particularly worrisome is that they might be quite intelligent. The more intelligent a predator is: the more dangerous it is."

"What leads you to think that they might be fairly intelligent?" asked Captain Jerontis.

"Take a good look at them," replied Moose. "It appears that they are flying purely for the joy of flying. They could just as well be lazily sleeping somewhere. Apparently, they are intelligent enough to have made the choice between taking a nap for relaxation and flying for enjoyment. As further evidence of intelligence, they are flying in a manner that requires very little expenditure of energy. Specifically, they are using their huge wings to ride a thermal. With their apparent intelligence, they could easily make the choice to dive upon us in a group attack. Their fifty-foot wingspans would make me feel like I was under attack by a squadron of fighter aircraft."

"That would be an alarming experience," commented Captain Jerontis.

"That's an understatement," declared Moose. "I would be more than alarmed. My adrenaline would be flowing, and my ability to shoot accurately would be tested."

"I think it's important to keep in mind that we don't have any evidence that they will ever make a group attack on us, or even attack us at all," stated Captain Jerontis. "We've never seen them eat anything except fish, and they haven't damaged Charlie or even approached him during the week that he has been wandering this island. At this point, we simply don't know if they will ever look upon us as potential prey."

"It's possible that they prefer fish, and don't prey on land animals as long as fish are easily available," commented Dianne. "An obvious advantage to them is that fish are low risk prey in that they don't defend themselves the way many animals do. Why should these pterodactyls risk injury while obtaining their food, if they don't need to."

"If what you're suggesting is true, do you think that's an intelligent choice on their part or purely instinctive?" asked Connie.

"I don't know the answer to that question," replied Dianne. "However, considering that this planet is approximately 500 million years older than Earth, these creatures have had ample time to have evolved intelligence."

"How intelligent they are is certainly an important question, but of more immediate concern is whether or not they will ever try to eat us," Captain Jerontis said. "It is imperative that we find that out as soon as we can."

"How do you propose to do that?" asked Moose.

"Very simple. We use ourselves as bait."

"That sounds dangerous," remarked Connie.

"There will certainly be an element of risk, but with proper planning, the risk should be minimal," Captain Jerontis responded. "Anyway, whatever the risks are, we must not forget that the primary reason we're here is to evaluate the hazards of living here before we bring more people down. Defining the threat posed by the pterodactyls seems to me to be of most immediate concern."

"What do you have in mind?" asked Moose.

"Movement will usually attract the attention of predators, especially the kind of movement that indicates that the potential prey might be injured. So, sometime when there are pterodactyls above us, you and I will get into an open area and engage in vigorous activity designed to get their attention. Once we have their attention, we'll move around as though we are crippled. Dianne and Connie will observe the pterodactyls and record their reactions to the various things that we do. We will all be armed. Of course, we will be near shelter that we can quickly retreat to. Also, Charlie will be with us. If they approach, you and I will quickly retreat to shelter while Charlie stays in the open. If and how they attack him will give us a great deal of information."

"If they attack Charlie, they will learn something too," said Moose.

"What's that?" asked Captain Jerontis.

"The ones that attack Charlie will learn that he isn't a very tasty meal, and hopefully, those particular creatures will leave us alone."

"That's a possibility," agreed Captain Jerontis. "But I don't think Charlie is durable enough to teach all the pterodactyls that pass through this area that we aren't good to eat."

"That is one thing that bothers me about your plan," stated Moose.

"What do you mean?"

"I put a lot of time and effort into designing and building Charlie, and I really don't want to lose him by allowing these creatures to carry him away."

"Sounds like you have become quite attached to him," commented Captain Jerontis. "Need I remind you that he isn't a real person, that he is just a piece of equipment."

"But he is a very valuable piece of equipment," countered Moose. "Before we conduct your experiment, I think we should equip Charlie with several canisters of highly irritating chemicals that we can release the instant he is attacked."

Facing Dianne, Moose said, "It seems like our chief biologist should be able to formulate something that would be extremely irritating, but not do any lasting damage."

"I think I can do that," replied Dianne.

"It's a good idea," stated Captain Jerontis. "If the irritating chemicals work, we not only get to keep Charlie, but we can equip some of our RPVs with canisters of these chemicals and use them to chase away any pterodactyls that get too close to us. Hopefully, we will be able to avoid killing any of these magnificent creatures."

"Another thing to consider is that there may not be another species on this planet that looks like us," commented Dianne. "If that's the case, and if these pterodactyls have enough intelligence to recognize that we are something new in their environment. It's possible that they may be curious enough to want to investigate us. In other words, if they approach us, we should not assume that it's only because they're hungry, they might simply be just curious."

"That's possible, but right now, they seem to be having so much fun flying that they aren't the least bit interested in anything else," Captain Jerontis replied. "But you do bring up an interesting point. If there isn't another species on this planet that resembles us, then all the creatures that we encounter will not have any pre-learned ways to react to us. Some animals might be very tame, since they haven't learned to fear us. For the same reason, some predators might be fearlessly aggressive toward us."

"It will be interesting to see how each species reacts to us," commented Dianne.

Watching the large soaring pterodactyls, Connie said, "Confronting some of these creatures to find out how they're going to react to us could prove to be very dangerous."

"That's true," agreed Dianne, "but it will be a thrilling experience each time we do it. And finding out which creatures are dangerous and which are docile is one of the reasons we are here. On Earth, this information is taken for granted, but for us, it is something that must be learned."

"Hopefully, we can do that learning without anyone being killed or seriously injured," commented Connie.

Captain Jerontis said, "We will use reasonable caution, but it is impossible to eliminate all risk. During the next thirty days, we'll introduce ourselves to as many species as possible and learn what we can, but right now, it's time for us to go to Stellar Plateau. We have a large capsule to unpack and a camp to set up."

A few moments later, after belting on her pistol and shouldering her rifle, Connie said, "Packing around all this artillery is going to take some getting use too."

"Having those huge pterodactyls in sight makes getting use to it a lot easier," remarked Dianne.

"I can't argue with you on that point," answered Connie.

With Charlie and Captain Jerontis in the lead, and Moose doing rear guard duty, the small group of humans began its trek to Stellar Plateau. After hiking across 25 yards of sandy beach, they reached the forest. They stopped and peered into its darkly shadowed interior looking for signs of danger. Being on an alien planet, they weren't sure what form danger might take. Any insect, snake, mammal, or lizard-like creature could be capable of injecting deadly venom. Therefore, until they knew otherwise, contact with any living creature would have to be avoided.

After intently searching for any indication of danger, Captain Jerontis said, "I don't see anything threatening, do any of you?"

"Even though we don't see anything threatening as far as animal life is concerned, let's not overlook the possibility of hazardous plant life," Dianne said. "Some plants protect themselves with toxic, irritating chemicals, and contact with them can be very painful. I realize that it's impossible to avoid all contact with plants, but I recommend that we avoid it as much as possible."

"This forest is quite thick, but I think we can pick our way through it with minimal contact with plants," remarked Captain Jerontis. "In a little over a hundred yards, we'll be at the rock slide on the north face of the plateau, and there isn't much growing on it."

Captain Jerontis sent Charlie into the forest along the chosen path. All intently observed Charlie and his surroundings. After Charlie walked about ten yards without incident, Captain Jerontis entered the forest. Connie, Dianne, and Moose followed him at about five-yard intervals.

A short time later, they reached the base of the rock slide. One by one they climbed it using the same rope for support that Charlie had been using. When all were on Stellar Plateau, they marched directly to the large capsule that would serve as their home for a while.

They put down their packs and rifles and took a few minutes to just look around in spellbound silence as the stunning scenic beauty of the location fully gripped them. They slowly drifted around the capsule checking out the picturesque view in every direction.

Finally, Connie exclaimed, "I am absolutely going to enjoy living here! Everywhere I look; I see a spectacular vista! I am happy that there aren't enough trees on this plateau to block very much of our view."

Recalling Connie's earlier remark, while onboard the personnel shuttle, led Dianne to ask, "So, am I to assume that you no longer think this island is too small and too drab?"

"Yes! You can most definitely assume that. I am thrilled to be here."

"My feelings exactly," agreed Dianne. "Would you like to do some exploring with me?"

"What do you have in mind?" asked Connie.

"Nothing too dramatic. I just want to take a look at the plant life in this area. Also, I would like to see what we can find by way of insects, birds, rodents, whatever."

"In other words, anything that's alive," remarked Connie.

"That's right. Since this island is now our home, I want to become familiar with every living thing on it. So, let's take a look around."

"We could start with those flowering bushes over there," suggested Connie as she pointed at them.

"It sounds like there might be some happy birds in those shrubs."

"I wonder what they look like."

"I don't know, but they sound happy," Dianne said. "All that chirping could be part of a mating ritual. It is springtime in this area."

"Let's go see what we can find out."

As Dianne and Connie started walking toward the bushes, Captain Jerontis yelled out, "Aren't you two forgetting something?"

"What do you mean?" asked Connie.

"Your rifles!" exclaimed Captain Jerontis.

"We aren't going very far," protested Connie. "We'll be close enough, so that you and Moose can protect us."

"Moose and I are going to be busy unpacking the capsule and won't be able to watch you continuously. Until we know that it's not necessary, I want all of us to be armed at all times."

Nodding in agreement, Dianne and Connie shouldered their rifles and Connie said, "It's so quiet and peaceful here that it's easy to get lulled into a false sense of security. At the moment, there aren't even any pterodactyls in sight, but I guess they can arrive unexpectedly at any time."

"Either them or some other creatures that we don't yet know about," remarked Captain Jerontis.

Turning to Moose, Captain Jerontis said, "Let's open it up and get started. The first thing that we need to do is remove and assemble our storage shed."

A short time later, Moose remarked, "These prefabricated panels sure make this job quick and easy. We simply snap them together, and they lock in place."

During the next hour, Captain Jerontis and Moose completed construction of the storage shed. With a floor area measuring 12 feet wide by 24 feet long, the shed would provide ample space to store the equipment and supplies currently packed in the capsule.

The shed had a single plane roof set at an angle of 30 degrees. Covered with solar cells and facing in the southerly direction, the roof would provide part of the electrical power needs of the small encampment.

Captain Jerontis and Moose walked a few yards away from the new shed and sat on some outdoor chairs to drink a cup of coffee and admire their handiwork. They were joined by Dianne and Connie who had just returned from their exploration walk.

Connie looked at the storage shed and thought about its implications. Then, she said, "That little shed really makes me feel good. Even though it's just a simple little building, it is our first building, and it represents the beginning of the process of turning this island into our home."

"Admittedly, it is a rather humble beginning, but I feel good about it too," replied Captain Jerontis.

"The first thing that we need to turn into our home is the capsule," remarked Dianne.

"Are you suggesting that we should get busy and transfer our supplies from it to the storage shed?" asked Connie.

"That would give us a comfortable secure place to sleep tonight," replied Dianne.

Turning to Moose, Jerry said, "I think our wives are in a homemaking mood at the moment."

Before Moose could respond, Dianne said, "Actually, I feel more like I am on a camping trip. That capsule reminds me of a recreational vehicle. But, it is full of supplies and equipment that we have to remove before we can camp in it."

"It would be difficult to imagine being on a more exotic camping trip than this," commented Moose. "We are camped on an island in the middle of a huge lake that no one has ever fished in. The lake is surrounded by land inhabited by huge dinosaurs. We have creatures with fifty-foot wing spans soaring over our heads. We are on a planet that currently has two suns in its daytime sky and sometimes has two moons in its nighttime sky."

"I can't think of any camping trip that I would rather be on," commented Captain Jerontis.

"It's simply amazing how far you have to travel these days to find good camping," remarked Connie innocently.

Everyone chuckled, Moose looked at her and said, "Thanks to your husband, I was able to make the trip."

"I hadn't thought of our first thirty days here as a camping trip," admitted Captain Jerontis, "but I like the idea. This site is wilder, more isolated, and more pristine than any place I've ever camped at on any backpack trip back on Earth."

"Calling our first thirty days a camping trip sounds more romantic than calling it a scientific expedition," commented Connie. "I like it too."

"I think we should finish setting up our campsite," remarked Captain Jerontis. "While the rest of you are transferring our supplies to the shed, I will deploy the capsule's legs and adjust them to level it."

The capsule had landed on its heat shield, which was backed by shock absorbing material to cushion the landing impact. Since the capsule would almost always come to rest at an angle other than perfectly level, it was equipped with legs that could be deployed and adjusted to level it. The legs would also be securely anchored to the ground and serve as a solid foundation to ensure that the capsule would be a sturdy home even during a wind storm.

Finishing their jobs after about an hour of continuous effort, the interstellar pioneers sat down to enjoy their first meal on Alcent. It was only a simple prepackaged meal, but because of the festive mood of the occasion and the spectacular scenic beauty that surrounded them, it seemed very much like a Thanksgiving day feast.

Looking at her husband, Connie asked, "Do you know what I like most about this meal?"

"What?"

"The fact that we are eating it here on Pioneer Island. Think about it! We are the first humans to have ever completed an interstellar voyage. We've traveled a vast distance at fantastic speeds, and we've arrived here in good health. I think that is a very good reason for some joyful celebration."

"I do too," agreed Jerry.

"In addition to feeling good about that," Dianne remarked, "I have another very big reason to be happy and excited. I am now living among a multitude of alien life-forms that I can study firsthand. This planet is a biologist's wonderland, and I intend to explore the wonders of life to the fullest degree possible."

"I think you will have lots of help from the rest of us," commented Doctor Nemard.

"I'm counting on that," said Dianne. "It is a big, interesting project. Everything here is something new that we need to study."

"There is one big question that we need to answer for each life-form that we encounter, and that is: Does this life-form pose any kind of danger to us?" Captain Jerontis asked.

"Except for our brief stay at B-2, that question hasn't concerned us at all in the last seven years," Dianne said.

"Today marks the end of that part of our life," declared Moose. "Today is a significant turning point in our lives. It marks the end of the challenge of getting here, and it marks the beginning of the challenge of surviving and prospering now that we are here."

"That may present us with even greater challenges than those we overcame to get here," remarked Captain Jerontis. "Perhaps, our greatest challenge will be to simply stay alive."

"Staying alive and prospering in an alien environment is a multifaceted challenge," remarked Dianne. "One important aspect of that challenge is finding a way to provide ourselves with an abundant supply of nutritious food."

"That shouldn't be very difficult in view of the abundance of plant and animal life that exists here," commented Captain Jerontis.

"Also, we have an extensive inventory of seeds for the basic food plants grown on Earth," stated Dianne. "I plan to analyze soil samples and experiment with growing some of these plants. Since it is springtime in this area, I will begin this project as soon as I can."

Connie commented, "It will be interesting to see how well Earth plants grow in this alien environment, and how they react when they encounter plant diseases and parasites that don't exist on Earth."

"With a little genetic engineering, I should be able to give them defenses against most diseases and parasites," remarked Dianne. "But it's quite possible that most of our plants won't have any problems. We'll just have to grow them and find out."

"Speaking of food, I can't think of anything more wholesome or nutritious than delicious fresh fish," declared Moose. "With that indisputable fact in mind, I plan to begin my research on the various species of fish in Clear Lake tomorrow morning."

Being as obvious as she could, Dianne stared at Moose's fishing tackle neatly displayed in front of the shed, she teased Moose, "I never would've guessed that you were planning to go fishing."

Moose smiled at his wife and replied, "I admit it. I am eager to go fishing. Imagine the thrill of fishing where no one has ever fished before."

"That will be exciting," agreed Dianne.

"But I won't be doing it just for fun; it is a serious research project. After all, fish are an immediate source of food. Unlike plants, we don't have to plant them and wait for them to grow up before we can eat them; they are already here. We just have to do some lab work on each species to make sure that they are nutritious and non-toxic."

"As far as time is concerned, your fish do have an advantage over my plants," admitted Dianne.

"Another thing that really excites me about my fish research is its immense potential because of the sheer size of Clear Lake. Think about it! We are living in the middle of nearly 700 square miles of water, and it is connected to a huge ocean by a large river!"

"Your fish research might end up being far more exciting than you are expecting it to be," commented Captain Jerontis.

"Are you saying that because of something that you saw underwater this morning?" questioned Moose.

"No, I was thinking about the pterodactyls. We've never seen them eat anything except fish. After you hook a fish, it might splash around on the surface while you're landing it. That will certainly get the attention of any pterodactyls that happen to see it. What happens next could be extremely exciting for you."

Looking a bit chagrined, Moose said, "Seeing a fish flopping around on the surface might be a bigger temptation than they can resist. It seems to me that at least one of them would dive in and grab it."

"And then, you might end up hooking a pterodactyl," remarked Captain Jerontis. "That's one fish story that you could take to your local tavern back on Earth and not be concerned about being outdone by another fish story."

"OK, I admit that your fish research could turn out to be a lot more exciting than my plant research," laughed Dianne.

"You people are raising the possibility of a lot more excitement than I had in mind," Moose objected. "I was hoping to just take the boat out early tomorrow morning and enjoy catching a few fish. Then, if they check out okay in the lab, we can have fresh fish for dinner."

"Whether we like it or not, the pterodactyls are part of our everyday life," declared Captain Jerontis. "Sometimes they will inconvenience us, because their presence will force us to delay a planned activity. However, I think that having the opportunity to study them is well worth the price of a little inconvenience."

After nodding in agreement with Jerry's comments, Moose suggested, "Why don't you come fishing with me tomorrow morning. Then, when either one of us is preoccupied with landing a fish, the other can be on alert."

"I was already planning on asking myself along," replied Captain Jerontis.

"If there are any pterodactyls in the area, we might look for a spot where we can fish from the shore. A place with dense forest close to the water would be ideal. If the pterodactyls decide to join us, we can quickly take shelter in the forest."

"That's a good plan," agreed Captain Jerontis.

Sensing that Moose and Jerry were finished making their fishing plans, Connie said, "Sitting in this warm sunshine after a big meal is making me sleepy. I think I need a nap."

"As little as you slept last night, you should be sleepy," commented Jerry.

"You're right, I didn't get much sleep. Yesterday's party lasted well into the night, and then, I had a difficult time falling asleep because I was excited."

"Well, the capsule has been unpacked, and our bed is ready for use. If you're too tired to walk over there, I could carry you."

"I'm not disabled, I'm just sleepy. Besides, I don't want to nap in our bed. I feel like enjoying the outdoors. This is my first day outside in nearly seven years."

"What do you have in mind?" asked Jerry.

"I would like to combine my nap with some sunbathing. The radiant heat coming from Alpha Centauri A really feels good, so does the gentle breeze. An outdoor nap would be most pleasant."

"Sounds like a recipe for a bad sunburn," commented Jerry.

"I have a bottle of sunscreen. Maybe you should take a break and massage some of it into my skin. I will do the same for you."

Jerry thought about his work schedule for a few moments. "I guess I have time to sit in the sun with you for a while."

Pointing at Alpha Centauri A and Alpha Centauri B, Jerry said, "I've never been sunbathing with two suns."

"That alone will make this a novel experience," commented Connie.

Connie pointed at a large rock, "There's a thick carpet of grass on the other side of that huge boulder. If we put down a couple of air mattresses and cover them with beach towels, we should be both comfortable and secluded."

Jerry looked at his watch and said, "I'm sure we'll be comfortable, but I don't know about secluded. If I'm not mistaken, the Challenger should be passing overhead right about now, and they do have some very powerful optical equipment."

"By the time we get comfortable, they will have disappeared over the horizon and will no longer be able to watch us," replied Connie.

"True," agreed Jerry. "So, let's get our rifles and the other things that we need and go relax for a while."

Shortly after Connie and Jerry disappeared behind the gigantic boulder, Moose said, "Just in case they become preoccupied with each other and forget where they are, I think you and I should stay alert for danger."

Displaying a sly grin, Dianne remarked, "That is part of the plan."

"What plan are you talking about?"

"The one Connie and I put together when we were out walking around," replied Dianne.

"I thought you were out looking at the things that live in this area."

"We were, but we were also looking for a safe place to sunbathe. Safety is essential in order for one to be completely relaxed and carefree. So we included armed sentries in our sunbathing plans."

"So, when they return, are they going to stand guard for us?"

"What did you have in mind that will require the services of armed guards?" teased Dianne.

Moose grinned and replied, "I would love to be a part of the erotic fantasy that you and Connie dreamed up."

"I am happy we think alike."

After a few moments of silence in which Moose allowed his mind to drift into fantasy-land, he asked, "How did you and Connie decide which couple would be the first to enjoy the pleasures of nude sunbathing?"

"We flipped a coin."

"How could you flip a coin? We don't have any coins."

"We had to improvise. We found a fairly flat pebble with distinctly different coloration on its two sides. I flipped it. Connie correctly called it and elected to be first."

"I wonder if Jerry knows that what he's doing at the moment was determined by the toss of a rock."

"It seems to me that both you and Jerry should be comfortable with that method of determining who makes the first play."

"What do you mean?"

"Back in your college football days, your games were always started with a coin toss."

"That's true, but at the moment, I don't think Captain J.J. is scrambling around trying to throw a touchdown pass."

"That's undoubtedly correct, but since he doesn't have to overcome any defense, I'm sure that he will score quite easily."

Moose chuckled, "I'm glad you and Connie dreamed up a way to put some pleasurable activity into our first day here. What a wonderful way to enjoy this wild, scenic wonderland. Just thinking about it is getting me quite aroused."

"I can see that," Dianne smiled mischievously.

"You aren't supposed to be looking at my groin. After all, we are on guard duty."

"That's why I am so alert to everything that's going on around me."

"You sure are quick-witted today. I can't seem to get ahead of you on anything."

"I seem to be in an elevated state of well-being with my emotions running in several different happy directions all at once. I simply cannot contain myself. My happiness reservoir is filled to the brim and is overflowing every which way, obviously, because a lifelong dream has finally come true. Reasonable cause for being in a state of ecstasy, don't you think?"

"How could I possibly disagree? I, too, am experiencing a wildly excited state."

"From what I can see, that is certainly true!"

"You're not going to miss an opportunity today, are you?"

"No! I'm not! I am happy, and I feel like having fun."

"So, that's why you and Connie planned this erotic outdoor activity?"

"Well, can you think of a more delightful way to have fun and welcome ourselves to our new home?"

"Going fishing could be very exciting," Moose replied.

"Are you suggesting that we go fishing instead of nude sunbathing," Dianne teased.

"No! I'm not!" Moose quickly exclaimed.

"I'm glad we cleared that up."

"Maybe we should try to conceive our first child in an outdoor setting, perhaps on a moonlit beach on a warm, pleasant evening," Moose suggested.

"I like that idea. If nothing of consequence happens to us after living here for a couple months, I think we should do that."

"We've been waiting for a long time to have children, but I believe that it was worth the wait. I think this island will prove to be an ideal place to raise a family. Two months should give us ample time to determine if it really is the relatively safe place that we think it is."

During the next hour, Dianne and Moose continued discussing their new home and plans for the future. Their discussion was interrupted by the appearance of Jerry and Connie from behind the huge boulder. Eager for their turn, Moose and Dianne began walking toward them. When they met, Dianne looked at them and smiled, "You two sure look blissfully content."

Jerry and Connie looked into each other's eyes and, for a few moments, silently shared the deep love and happiness that was an integral part of their marriage. Jerry said, "Thanks for standing guard and giving us the opportunity to relax and enjoy ourselves. We really appreciate it."

"It was just a flashback in time," responded Moose.

"What do you mean?" asked Captain Jerontis.

"Back in our football days, I was pretty good at protecting you."

"I can't argue that point, but I can return the favor by protecting you. So, why don't you and Dianne relax and enjoy yourselves."

Faking formality, Moose turned to his wife, "You heard the Captain's orders!"

They both faced Captain Jerontis, stood rigidly at attention, smartly saluted, and marched off in the direction of the large boulder. Jerry and Connie laughed at the sight of Dianne and Moose rigidly marching in unison.

"In view of that bit of clowning around, I believe they are in the perfect mood to enjoy themselves," commented Connie.

"I think so too," agreed Jerry.

On alert for danger, Jerry and Connie slowly walked back to the habitation capsule. Arriving at the capsule, Jerry did a panoramic scan of Stellar Plateau looking for anything that might pose a threat, but the plateau was peaceful. Jerry then searched the sky for pterodactyls, but he found only a beautiful blue sky containing a few fluffy cumulus clouds.

Jerry turned to Connie and feasted his eyes on her scantily clothed body, "You sure look happy."

"I am happy! I am glad to be here, and I am still basking in the afterglow of the loving you just gave me. I think my pleasure was magnified because of where we are."

"We were sharing the joy we feel at finally arriving here after a very long journey. The risk factor of unknown danger showing up unexpectedly added some extra excitement."

"That very real risk of danger made me feel like we were engaging in hot, forbidden sex," commented Connie.

"Now that you put it that way, I did feel like we were getting away with something." Jerry gave his wife an affectionate hug and said, "Speaking of risking danger and getting away with it, that was quite a stunt you pulled when you dove into the lake this morning."

"But, it really wasn't an irresponsible, impulsive act. Mike and his assistants did a thorough job exploring the water around this island with the marine explorer, and they did not find anything that appeared threatening."

"*Appeared* is the key word in that statement," countered Jerry. "Piranha don't appear very threatening either when they are peacefully swimming around."

"OK, you make a good point."

"However, now that the point has been made, I must admit that it was fun, refreshing, and just plain exciting."

"Are you suggesting that by diving into the lake, I put fun and excitement into your life by just being myself?"

"You sure did!" Jerry recalled how happy and satisfying his marriage to Connie had been over the years, "In fact, you almost always make me happy by just being yourself. Adding joy and happiness to my life seems to be a natural talent of yours."

"I'm glad you feel that way," replied Connie. "All the love and respect that you've always given me, and the thoughtful consideration that you've always shown for my feelings, has made me feel so secure in our relationship that I just always have a strong desire to please you. Pleasing you makes me happy."

"So, you're saying that by just being myself, I not only make you happy, but I also stimulate your natural talent to make me happy."

"That about sums it up," responded Connie.

"That's one of the things that I really like about being married to you. I can just be myself, and you are happy with me as I am. I don't have to try to be something that I'm not."

"Being true to oneself, especially in a marriage, is essential to achieving personal happiness."

"Is that your professional opinion, Doctor?"

"I do sound rather formal at times, don't I?"

"Yes, you do."

"I don't mean to, but it is sometimes difficult to separate my professional life from my personal life."

"I wasn't suggesting that you should. I was just teasing you a little bit."

"Despite your teasing, I do have some strong opinions on marriage and family."

"I would never have guessed that."

"You're teasing me again, but that's okay, because I know that your thoughts about marriage and family are basically the same as mine. I also know that our society will be off to a very good start if all the people on this mission end up in marriages as good as ours. The traditional family will be the basic social unit in our society. If these families are filled with love, security, and mutual respect, then, our society will have a solid foundation on which to grow."

"A professional opinion again, Doctor?"

"Most definitely! And it's valid too. You only have to look at the history of the U.S. to find out about the problems that can occur with the breakdown of the traditional family."

"There can be little doubt that children have a much easier time growing up and becoming responsible adults when their parents have a peaceful, loving relationship based on mutual respect."

"Of course, children do thrive on security and happiness."

"Denise and our future children will get plenty of both."

"Speaking of our future children, I would like to have a fairly large family. I see no reason why we can't, since I have at least a dozen child-bearing years left. Also, I am in excellent health."

"Since you are the doctor in the family, I am assuming that is a valid professional opinion."

"It is."

"I wonder how Denise will react to having some brothers and sisters to contend with."

Thinking about Denise, Connie said, "She has been the center of our attention for a long time, but if we share the excitement of the arrival of a baby with her so that she feels included, I'm sure she'll do just fine."

"She might even be as excited about it as we'll be."

"Can you image how excited she'll be when we bring her down here in a couple of months?"

"With her overly active curiosity, it's going to be a full time job just to follow her around and answer her questions," commented Jerry. "But, before we bring the children down, we have to be very sure that it is safe for them to be here. Big creatures, like the pterodactyls, aren't that much of a concern, because they are easy to see and can be dealt with by armed sentries. What does concern me very much are small creatures that are able to inject painful or even lethal venom. How do we guard against them when we don't know what they are or if they even exist?"

"People on Earth have that knowledge because it was learned by the painful experience of thousands of generations. If we are to have the long, happy marriage and the large family that we want, we must gain this essential knowledge quickly."

"That's a big job, but if we're going to bring the children down in sixty days, we have to learn in two months what our ancestors learned in millions of years."

"Basically, we have to capture every new organism that we find, take it to the lab, and check it out," explained Connie. "Even though this is a small island, there are probably hundreds, maybe even thousands of different species of bugs living here; plus all the small mammals, reptiles, and birds."

"Biological research is definitely our number one priority for the immediate future."

"Besides doing the research, we are also part of it by virtue of being here. During the next thirty days, each one of us will get a daily medical evaluation from me. We can make my medical research more meaningful, if we experience this environment to the greatest degree possible."

"Is that why you dove into the lake this morning?"

"No! I just had the urge to go swimming, something I haven't done in a long time. But that is a good example of soaking up this environment. Microorganisms in the water were given an opportunity to enter our bodies. But in view of the kinds of microbes our robot lab tests have discovered in that water, I will be surprised if we suffer any ill-effects."

"That water seemed so fresh and clean. In fact, it even tasted good."

"You swallowed some of it?" questioned Connie in an incredulous tone.

"I admit that it wasn't a wise thing to do, but I accidentally got some of it in my mouth, and it tasted so good that I decided to swallow it. I'm really not too worried about getting sick; after all, I am living with a competent doctor."

"But I think we should run more tests on it before we start drinking it."

"Perhaps, more testing and exploration should have been done before we went swimming in it," suggested Jerry.

"I guess we were both a little too hasty. Probably the result of suddenly being confronted by the great outdoors after being confined for a long time. However, there is an advantage to all this, it does make my medical research on us quite meaningful as far as the lake water is concerned."

Jerry nodded in agreement.

"I would like to go swimming for a little while every day," said Connie. "Whatever risk there might be from microbes should not be a deterrent, since we have already exposed ourselves to that risk. If we keep our marine explorer in East Bay for the next few weeks and keep track of the underwater world, I should be able to swim in reasonable safety."

"We have no way of knowing that for sure."

"This is now our home, and if we are going to enjoy it, we have to be able to experience everything that it has to offer."

"I agree, but in regard to swimming, we have to find out if Clear Lake contains any fish with voracious feeding habits like the piranha. It is impossible to defend against an attack by huge numbers of this kind of fish. I realize that we didn't have any problems this morning, but maybe, we were just lucky."

After considering Jerry's comments for a few moments, Connie said, "I have an idea how we can discover if any of the fish in East Bay are voracious feeders."

"What do you have in mind?"

"It seems reasonable to expect that voracious feeders would go into a frenzy if we present them with the scent of blood. I do have a supply of each of our blood types in my medical inventory, and I think I can safely spare some of it for a potentially life-saving experiment. If you will design and build a blood dispenser that we can suspend ten to fifteen feet below our marine explorer, the rest will be easy. Whenever the marine explorer drifts over a school of fish, we simply squirt out a few cubic centimeters of blood and observe their behavior. If they become wildly excited and seek out and attack the source of the blood, then swimming in the lake could be very dangerous. If the blood has no effect on them, I wouldn't expect them to attack us when we're swimming."

"Your reasoning seems valid, and the experiment will be easy to conduct. When would you like to do it?"

"As soon as we can. I enjoy swimming, and I've only been once in the last seven years."

"It should be quite a simple device. It's essentially nothing more than a remotely operated squirt gun. I will improvise something after tomorrow morning's fishing trip. By tomorrow afternoon, we should be able to begin experimenting."

"It shouldn't take more than a few days to tempt every species of fish in the bay," commented Connie. "If we don't get any meaningful reaction from any of them, I will feel quite safe going swimming."

"It may not be totally safe, but I don't know of any risk-free way that we can discover all possible dangers. At some point, we simply have to dive in and take our chances. However, I don't want you to go swimming alone. I want to be with you. And until we know that it's not necessary, we will be armed when we are swimming."

"Carrying weapons while swimming will be a bit cumbersome and will take some of the fun out of it."

"That's true, but I don't see any way to avoid it. Clear Lake is large, deep, and connected to an ocean. It seems like large marine predators must exist somewhere in all that water. The question is: do any of them ever come near Pioneer Island?"

"It will probably take at least a year to answer that question with any degree of certainty, especially, since many animals have seasonal migration cycles."

"Unfortunately, I think your time estimate is correct," agreed Jerry.

"It's not completely unfortunate. There is a benefit to this."

"What is it?"

"I will have you with me when I go swimming, and that will be a lot more fun than swimming alone."

"It'll be fun for both of us, and I'm sure Moose and Dianne will want to join us. For added safety, we can take ... "

Connie interrupted Jerry, in an urgent tone, "Two pterodactyls are over East Bay!"

As Jerry turned to look at them, Connie spoke with a fired up sense of urgency, "They appeared above Eastern Island so suddenly that they must have approached it flying low and fast. Then at the last instant, they popped up to get over it. Now, they're gliding back down toward the water. Why are they flying so low and fast?"

"I don't know, but it looks like they're going to pass right over our shuttle. With their size and strength, they could damage it if they choose to."

"I hope they don't decide to head directly at us!" exclaimed Connie. "As fast as they are flying, they could be on top of us in just a few seconds."

"They are flying fast, at least sixty mph, maybe even seventy."

As the two pterodactyls popped up to clear the narrow neck of land separating East Bay from West Bay, Connie said, "I guess they weren't the least bit interested in our shuttle."

Watching them fly over West Bay, Jerry commented, "Apparently, they aren't interested in us either."

"You sound disappointed."

"We humans have become accustomed to thinking of ourselves as the dominant species, the center of everything. Being totally ignored by these creatures is a little deflating."

"I don't mind being a little deflated, and I hope they continue to ignore us," Connie quickly responded. "I wonder if they would've ignored us if we'd been in the water. The suddenness with which they appeared is tending to dampen my desire to go swimming."

"Why? The possibility of their sudden appearance just adds a little extra adventure to it."

"But I don't need all that adventure. I just want to enjoy a good swim now and then."

"I do too, but the possibility of being eaten by airborne creatures in addition to the possible existence of marine predators does turn swimming into quite an adventure."

"It's a dramatic contrast to my childhood days when my mother used to warn me about the risk of drowning," commented Connie dryly.

"The possibility of drowning seems to be the least of our worries."

"The fact that pterodactyls can appear so suddenly is frightening."

"The potential danger that we face from them might be greater than we thought," stated Jerry. "Their low-level, high-speed flying ability combined with their ability to instantly pop up and over obstacles in their flight path is impressive. A stealth approach based on these capabilities would allow them to attack prey on the far side of a hilltop with little or no warning. This reminds me of fighter aircraft in a terrain following mode to escape radar detection."

"But how would they know that there's prey on the far side of a hilltop?"

"They spot it while they appear to be innocently circling at high altitude. Then, they leave the area, but while they're leaving, they mentally map the attack route to their prey. Within minutes of leaving an area, they could return and attack their prey with virtually no warning."

"Do you think they're intelligent enough to do all of that?"

"I don't know, but if they are, they present a very serious danger to us."

160

"I wonder if we'll ever be able to go swimming, or do anything for that matter, without the presence of very alert armed guards."

"Until we've been here long enough to understand all the dangers that might confront us, we don't have any choice. We have to always be armed and alert."

Her gaze intently fixed on the pterodactyls, Connie said, "Despite the possible risk they pose, I don't mind having them around. They are fascinating creatures to observe."

"They certainly are. What do you think this pair is up to?"

"Judging from the way that they're circling Western Island, I think that they're looking for a place to land."

"The obvious place would be at the top of that rock cliff near the island's north end. Rather than looking for a place to land though, it looks more like they're investigating the area around their potential landing site. The question is why? What are they looking for?"

"There are two possibilities that come to mind," commented Connie. "Either they're hungry and are searching for prey, or they're preparing to land and are searching for enemies."

"It doesn't seem like they could be searching for enemies. These islands just don't have enough prey on them to support a predator that is large enough to be a serious threat to pterodactyls. Also, we haven't seen anything big enough to make a good meal for a pterodactyl, and we've never seen them eat anything except fairly large fish. So, I don't think they're searching for prey either."

"Your argument that they don't have enemies on these islands sounds reasonable, but they are doing a very thorough inspection of that cliff top. The degree of caution that they're using indicates that they are concerned about something. If they're not searching for an enemy, what do you think they're doing?"

"The high speed way in which they flew directly to Western Island raises another possibility," commented Jerry. "Maybe, it's their home, and they've been gone for a while and are now returning. Maybe, they are inspecting it to see if anything has changed since they left. Maybe, they are going to build a nest over there or use a nest they built last year. Maybe, the reason for their inspection is to determine if another pair has laid claim to their nesting site."

"If you're correct, what are the implications for us? What if they decide to lay and hatch some eggs over there? Are we going to be comfortable having a family of pterodactyls that close to us?"

"That will depend entirely on their attitude toward us. Until we know what that is, their continuous presence will certainly require us to always be very alert."

"In other words, they will do us a favor by forcing us to do what we should be doing anyway," remarked Connie.

"Also, they will provide us with an opportunity to study the family life of pterodactyls, if we can avoid killing them in self-defense."

"I'm starting to hope that they will raise some young over there. Having a family of pterodactyls so close to us will certainly speed up our acquisition of knowledge about the species. Since our long-term prosperity depends on the attainment of knowledge, it would be tragic if we end up having to kill these creatures and lose this learning opportunity."

"If they decide to nest on Western Island, we'll devise a way to attach a radio transmitter to each adult. Then, we'll each carry a receiver that will set off an alarm whenever they get too close."

"That's a good idea," remarked Connie. "But how do you know that they lay eggs? Maybe, their young are born alive."

"Obviously, we don't know. That is something that we'll find out."

After a few moments, Jerry said, "It looks like they've finally completed their inspection of the island."

"Yes, and they're landing at the very top of the cliff."

"There is one other reason why they may have been flying so low and fast and that is simply for the thrill of it," Jerry speculated. "Flying sixty to seventy mph a few feet off the water would give them a sensation of speed that they wouldn't have at an altitude of several hundred feet."

"Seeing how close they can get to obstacles before popping up and over them would also be a thrilling thing to do."

"The pterodactyls we saw riding a thermal this morning appeared to be flying purely for pleasure. Now, we have a second incident where the way in which they were flying may have been purely for the thrill involved. It is beginning to look like these creatures might be quite intelligent and fun-loving."

"I wonder if they're intelligent enough to recognize that we're something new in their environment, and if they'll then try to determine if we pose a threat to them," asked Connie.

"I hope the answer to that question is more important to them than whether or not we are good to eat."

"I hope that's the case too," Connie stated quickly.

"I wonder if they're cunning enough to send one or two of their kind to distract us while others attack from a different direction?" questioned Jerry as he turned to do a 360-degree scan.

"Whatever the answer to that question is, I doubt that these two are part of any such plan. They're too busy inspecting their surroundings."

"Even so, until we fully understand pterodactyls, we have no choice but to give them credit for any capability that we can reasonably expect them to have."

A few moments later, Moose and Dianne returned feeling relaxed and content. Noticing that Connie and Jerry weren't paying much attention to them, Moose asked, "What are you two so preoccupied with?"

To answer the question, Connie handed Moose the binoculars she had been using and then pointed at the pair of pterodactyls. While Moose and Dianne took turns using the binoculars, Connie and Jerry briefed them on the activities of the pair.

After a short period of discussion, Captain Jerontis said, "I think it's time to finish making our home livable."

"In other words, it's time for us to hook up our water supply," remarked Moose.

"Yes, and our wives will accompany us and do guard duty."

Jerry and Moose removed two rolls of collapsed, lightweight hose from the shed. Even though the hose was quite light, it was tough and durable because it was made from high-tensile-strength fibers embedded in tough pliable plastic. Each roll contained six hundred feet of hose.

Two water tanks were located above the capsule's second floor: one for hot water and one for cold water. The smaller of the two tanks had been used as a storage compartment for the capsule's high-speed parachute and would now be used for cold water storage. The larger of the two tanks had served as a storage compartment for the capsule's large para-wing and would now be used as a hot water tank.

After connecting one end to the capsule, Moose and Jerry laid the hose to the edge of the plateau, down the rock slide, through the forest, and across the sandy beach. They took great care to lay the hose in such a way as to minimize the risk of it being accidentally punctured.

Then, with Dianne and Connie standing guard, Moose and Jerry pushed the small inflated boat into the water and rowed out to the shuttle. They entered the shuttle and removed their water supply system's pump, its solar power plant, and its inlet filtration system. After rowing back to the beach, they set up this equipment.

Next, they turned on the pump's radio receiver, which would receive on/off signals from the habitation capsule. With a transmitter, Jerry sent a command to the capsule to turn on the water system. The capsule immediately sent a signal to the pump. The pump's electric motor hummed to life, and fresh clear lake water entered the collapsed hose. The pioneers watched the collapsed hose swell to its full 1.25-inch diameter as the water progressed up it toward the capsule.

"Looks like we'll be able to take hot showers tonight," Dianne remarked.

"I don't know how hot they'll be," remarked Jerry. "The hot water tank is fairly large and it will take time to heat that much water. It is getting so late in the day that the solar heat exchanger won't get much heat from Alpha Centauri A until tomorrow. And, we can't run the hot water tank's electrical heating coils for very long until we get the rest of our electrical power plant operational."

"Sounds like we'll be taking lukewarm showers tonight," amended Dianne.

"That's a reasonable guess," stated Jerry.

"Right now, I am more concerned about food than taking a shower," remarked Moose. "All the excitement and activity since lunch time have made me hungry."

"You're always hungry," noted Jerry.

"Lunch was more than four hours ago. I should be hungry."

Faking an air of disbelief, Jerry silently stared at Moose. After enduring the stare for a few moments, Moose said, "If you're trying to convince me that I shouldn't be hungry by acting surprised, it's not working."

Jerry chuckled and said, "Actually, I'm hungry too, but there's one more thing I think we should do before we eat."

"What?" asked Moose.

"I think we should remove the few remaining things that we still have in the shuttle, and then, we should send it back up into orbit."

"That will leave us stranded here with no quick way to leave, if we need to," Connie said.

"That's true," agreed Jerry. "But there are creatures on this planet that are large enough to wreck our shuttle, and I don't believe that it would be very wise to leave it anchored here and exposed to that risk. It is a rather critical piece of equipment."

The small party considered Jerry's proposed action and all reluctantly nodded in agreement. Then, they entered the boat and rowed out to the shuttle.

While Moose and Jerry were in the cockpit preparing the shuttle for takeoff, Dianne and Connie transferred the few remaining supplies and personal items to the boat. After about a half hour, they returned to shore.

The shuttle now rested low in the water, because its propellant tanks, which had been empty, were now full of water. The water would be pumped through the shuttle's nuclear reactor where it would be instantly converted into extremely high temperature, high pressure water vapor that would expand out the shuttle's rocket nozzle. If run at full power, the shuttle's nuclear thermal rocket could accelerate it to orbital speed and altitude in less than ten minutes.

While the interstellar pioneers stood on the beach and watched, the personnel shuttle came to life under the direction of its flight control computer. Both anchors were lifted into the fuselage, and their hatches were closed. With a high-pitched whine and a muffled roar, the steam turbine came to life and its power fed into the shuttle's propeller, which immediately began churning the water under the shuttle's tail. At a speed of about ten miles per hour, the shuttle taxied out of East Bay and into open water. Then, with full power delivered to the propeller, the shuttle rapidly gained speed, rose up on its hydrofoils, and glided above the water at a speed of about sixty mph. Suddenly, the powerful NTR boomed into action with a loud thundering roar and quickly accelerated the shuttle to takeoff velocity. In less than a minute, the shuttle reached the cold upper atmosphere where the water vapor from the NTR condensed into a white cloud-like trail brilliantly lit by the light of Alpha Centauri A.

As the shuttle continued its climb into orbit where it would rendezvous with the Challenger, Connie said, "It's gone."

Noting that his wife sounded like she felt abandoned, Jerry said, "We can bring it back anytime."

"I know," replied Connie. "But that's not the same as having it anchored right out there in the bay. Maybe, it's just a psychological thing, but I feel like the umbilical cord has been cut and that we are now dependent on this planet. In other words, this is now our home!"

"Watching the shuttle leave certainly does reinforce that feeling," agreed Jerry.

"Food would reinforce my feeling that this is our home," emphasized Moose.

Turning to Dianne, Connie said, "I think your husband is hungry, and it seems like we just had lunch."

Before Dianne could comment, Moose blurted out, "Lunch was five hours ago, and I'm starving!"

"Has it really been that long?" teased Dianne.

Looking at his wife, Moose said, "I suppose you're going to try to convince me that you're not hungry either."

Dianne smiled and said, "Actually, it has been a long exciting afternoon, and my stomach is rumbling on empty at the moment."

"So what are we waiting for? Let's go eat," said Jerry, as he began hiking in the direction of the plateau.

A short time later, they were comfortably seated around a table in front of their home, and Dianne said, "I like eating outdoors. It makes me feel like we're camping, and after our long voyage, I am ready for some outdoor living."

"Outdoor living is easy to enjoy with the kind of weather that we're having today," commented Connie.

"Our high of the day was seventy-nine degrees, and it's currently a comfortable seventy-two," reported Moose.

"What a pleasant temperature range," remarked Dianne.

"The huge lake that surrounds us is probably going to have quite a moderating effect on the temperature swings that we'll experience," commented Jerry.

"Warm summers that don't get unbearably hot, and mild winters that rarely ever have temperatures below freezing; that's my kind of climate," declared Connie.

"Moderate climate is one of the big reasons we selected this area," stated Moose.

Jerry stood up, looked to the west and said, "We're going to experience a peculiar event relative to our past, but one that will be common place in our future."

After waiting a few moments for everyone to look to the west and wonder what event he was referring to, Jerry continued: "This evening, we'll see our first double sunset. In a few minutes, Alpha Centauri A will disappear below the horizon. However, it's not going to get dark, because Alpha Centauri B won't set for nearly two hours."

"That's going to feel strange and take some getting use to," stated Connie. "It's quite deeply ingrained in human experience that when the Sun sets; it soon gets dark."

"It's going to seem weird for a while," agreed Jerry.

While the intersteller pioneers gazed in silence, Alpha Centauri A slowly slipped below the horizon. The brilliant yellow fireball that had dominated the sky and brightly lit the day was now out of sight. A much smaller appearing orange fireball, Alpha Centauri B, now dominated the sky. Even though it was currently about twenty-five times more distant from Alcent than Alpha Centauri A, its soft orange light was still many times brighter than the full moon in Earth's nighttime sky.

"It's been such a long time since I've enjoyed the simple pleasure of experiencing a splendid sunset that I've almost forgotten what it's like," remarked Connie.

For several moments, the group silently gazed at the sunset, each lost in thought. Feeling quite emotional about the scene, Connie said, "A beautiful sunset has a special aura about it. It's a time of transition. The harsh, brilliant glare of daylight is replaced by the soft glow of twilight. The heat of the day slowly surrenders to the coolness of the night. The sounds of the daytime creatures are gradually replaced by the sounds of the nocturnal creatures. Watching this brings back some fond memories from Earth, a planet that we'll never see again."

While they shared nostalgic memories from the distant planet, Earth, Alpha Centauri A slipped so far below the horizon that the soft glow of twilight became so dim that it was no longer noticeable. Then, Alpha Centauri B became the only light source of consequence, and some very unearthly lighting effects became quite prominent.

"This is eerie," remarked Dianne. "All the colors of the landscape, that we became familiar with today, have now taken on an orange tinge. This strange light sort of gives everything a mysterious sense of unreality. I wonder how long it's going to take for this to feel normal."

Looking at her arms and hands, Connie said, "Even my skin has taken on a strange orange hue, almost as if I've contracted some sort of skin disease."

"You should probably see a doctor about that," suggested Jerry.

"You seem to have developed the same condition," replied Connie. "Perhaps, we should see the same doctor."

"I've never had orange tinted skin before. Do you think it might be a serious allergic reaction to our new environment?"

"One thing I learned early on in medicine is that things aren't always as serious as they appear. Once we get use to this condition, I doubt that we'll even notice it."

"When you two are finished with your verbal trivia, perhaps we could all go for an after-dinner walk and explore this plateau," suggested Moose.

Jerry and Connie looked at each other puzzled, "Apparently, Moose is in a serious frame of mind and isn't able to appreciate the fun we are able to have with silly small-talk," Connie said.

"He has always been rather serious and restrained when confronted by a strange new situation," remarked Jerry. "It just seems like he has never really been able to relax and have fun with something new and unexpected."

"What do you mean?" objected Moose. "I've always been fun-loving and adventurous. That's why I would like to explore this plateau while we have this strange, weird kind of light pouring down on it. It'll be like an exotic stroll in the moonlight, only this light is much brighter than a Full Moon, but still so subdued that it has a romantic sense of unreality about it. That orange glow just makes everything look weird. Even the sky has an orange tint to it, and the clouds that have been white all day are now a creamy orange."

"Sounds like you're really emotional about this," observed Jerry.

"I've waited a long time to arrive here, and now that I am here, I plan to enjoy it to the fullest," declared Moose.

"Well, if you feel that strongly about something as simple as going for a walk, I suppose we could do it," remarked Jerry.

"That nonchalant attitude that you're trying so hard to display doesn't fool me a bit. You're just as excited about being here as I am!" exclaimed Moose.

Having gotten all the expected reactions from Moose, Captain Jerontis chuckled with satisfaction and asked, "Do you have any particular objectives in mind for this exploratory walk?"

"On Charlie's first night here, Dianne and I used him to make an imaginary walk in the moonlight. I know that we don't have moonlight now, but I would like to retrace his steps."

"In other words, you would like to turn an imaginary stroll in the moonlight into the real thing," commented Jerry.

"That's what we want to do," stated Moose and Dianne in unison.

"So this is an experiment to find out if the real thing is more fun and exciting than the imaginary walk was," commented Jerry.

"Is there any doubt that the real thing will be better?" questioned Moose.

"Sometimes, anticipation combined with imagination makes an imaginary experience better than the real thing," remarked Jerry.

"Well, I guess it's up to us to make reality as good as the fantasy was," stated Dianne.

"That shouldn't be too difficult," commented Moose. "The first time that we do anything here will have a special air of excitement about it, simply because we're doing it here."

"Part of that excitement stems from the risk posed by known and unknown dangers," added Dianne.

"And there's always the possibility of making an exciting new discovery," added Connie.

"So, let's go make some discoveries while we enjoy the evening," suggested Jerry.

After picking up their rifles, the group headed toward South Bay with Charlie in the lead. They walked at a relaxed pace, occasionally pausing to investigate a shrub, a wild flower, or a peculiar kind of grass. Birds and insects received similar attention. Even the texture and coloration of rocks were discussed in speculation of their mineral content.

"I like the openness of this plateau," commented Connie. "It doesn't give predators very many places to wait in ambush."

"As far as we know, there aren't any predators on this island that are large enough for us to worry about except for the pterodactyls," noted Dianne.

"Until we've thoroughly explored it, I don't think we should rule out the possible presence of dangerous animals," remarked Connie. "For example, omnivorous creatures like the black bears that live on Earth could be quite content on the islands in this lake, particularly if they enjoy swimming and have some fishing skills."

"Pregnant females in the species might even swim to an isolated island to raise their young away from the huge T-Rexes and other large predators," Dianne said.

165

"A bear-like creature probably wouldn't have any trouble climbing the rock slide at the north end of this plateau," remarked Moose.

"Like I said a few moments ago, I am glad this plateau is so open," reiterated Connie.

"Your point is legitimate," agreed Jerry.

"The three small groves on this plateau are the only hiding places of consequence," stated Moose. "Perhaps this would be a good opportunity to explore them."

"I would rather do that during the full light of day," stated Captain Jerontis. "This dim orange light is adequate in open areas, but I believe it is too dark in those groves to safely explore them."

"I think we should just walk to the south end of this plateau and enjoy the view out over the lake while we still have enough light to do that," commented Dianne.

"I like that idea," declared Connie.

"I guess my grove exploration proposal has been unanimously overruled," stated Moose.

A few minutes later, they arrived at the south end of the plateau. Looking out over the water, Connie remarked, "The south end of the lake is so far away that it's virtually indistinguishable from the land and sky. It all just seems to blend together."

"It is nearly twenty miles away, and this lighting is rather subdued," commented Jerry.

"This viewpoint makes it dramatically obvious how large this lake is and what an important part of our lives it's going to be," noted Connie.

"Hopefully, it will provide us with an abundant supply of seafood and some very exciting sports fishing for a long time to come," remarked Moose.

"Equally important is the way that it isolates us from a multitude of large, ferocious creatures," noted Captain Jerontis.

"But a bear-like creature that enjoys swimming could still reach us," stated Connie. "Especially, if it's smart enough to swim from one island to the next. That way, it wouldn't have to swim more than two to three miles at a time. Give this hypothetical creature fur consisting of hollow hair with sealed ends, and it would have the ability to float. That would make swimming very easy."

"Why are you so convinced that this kind of creature might exist in this area?" questioned Captain Jerontis.

"I keep thinking about how meticulously that pair of pterodactyls investigated Western Island before they landed. The existence of bear-like creatures would explain their caution."

"Such a creature would have to be fairly large to be a serious threat to the pterodactyls," commented Captain Jerontis. "I think the adults would have to weigh at least 400 to 500 pounds."

"That would make them large enough for us to worry about," remarked Moose, "and females protecting their young would be especially dangerous."

"Even though we don't have any direct evidence that such a creature exists, I think we should assume that it does until we prove otherwise," commented Dianne. "Life does seek to be ubiquitous, and if given enough time, evolution will usually develop a life-form to fill every possible niche."

Speaking to Dianne, Captain Jerontis said, "I want you to have one of your assistants take a good look at all the animals we've discovered so far to see if any of them might fit into the role we've been discussing."

Making eye contact with everyone in turn, Captain Jerontis said, "If large animals have been visiting these islands regularly over a long period of time, we should be able to find clues to indicate that. Let's be alert for them."

"If pregnant females come to these islands to bear and raise their young, this might be the time of the year that they do that," speculated Connie. "It is springtime, and using Earth's animals as a guide, many do deliver their young during springtime. Also, earlier today, those pterodactyls were searching for something, and they would certainly be in a position to know what time of the year large creatures come to these islands."

"In other words, we may soon meet these creatures, if they exist," commented Jerry.

"I think that's a reasonable assumption," agreed Connie.

"Is it possible that such a creature might already be here?" asked Jerry.

"Let's keep in mind that I've marched Charlie the length and breadth of this island during the past week, and he wasn't bothered by anything except insects," commented Moose.

"A female with babies probably would've avoided him unless he'd directly confronted her," countered Connie.

After thinking about the situation for a few moments, Captain Jerontis said, "There is a way that we might answer the question without searching every part of this island. It's a fact that most large animals need water. Unless pools or springs exist in the forest for them to drink from, they have to use the lake, and most of this island's shoreline consists of sandy beaches. If we walk these beaches, we should be able to find tracks to the water's edge and back into the forest, if there are any large animals here. I think we should delay for one day the things that we'd planned to do tomorrow and walk around the island instead."

"We might take some surveillance cameras with us and set them up at key viewpoints to monitor long stretches of open beach," suggested Connie.

"Good idea," commented Jerry.

"I think it would be interesting to make some short exploration trips into the forest at selected points around the island," stated Dianne.

"I like that idea too," remarked Jerry.

"Even though I won't get to go fishing tomorrow, the day could turn out to be quite an enjoyable adventure," commented Moose. "Who knows, I might even find some good places to fish from shore."

After a pause in the conversation, Dianne and Connie wandered off to investigate a flowering bush. A gentle breeze had carried the blossoming bush's perfume to them. It reminded them of the rich pleasing fragrance of a lilac in full bloom.

Meanwhile, Captain Jerontis silently gazed out over the lake deeply lost in thought. Noticing the reflection that had engulfed his best friend, Moose commented, "It certainly does have an adventurous appeal to it."

"Yes, it does. I was just thinking about how much fun it would be to be out there in a sailboat when there's a good stiff breeze. It's been a long time since I've heard the pop of a sail and felt the wind whip through my hair while the sun beats down on my back."

Jerry's comments and the enchanting appeal of the huge lake brought memories of sailing adventures among the islands of the South Pacific to the forefront of Moose's mind. After a few moments of reveling in these fond memories from the distant planet Earth, Moose said, "I wish we could spend the next few days roaming around this lake in a sailboat."

"I do too, but unfortunately, we have higher priority things to do, and we don't have a sailboat."

"Our research submarine converts into a sailboat," remarked Moose. "We could have it put on the cargo shuttle and sent down."

"It's scheduled to be brought down in thirty days with the next group of people coming down. Are you proposing that we bring it down sooner on an unmanned shuttle flight just so we can start having fun with it?"

"There are other immediate advantages to having it here besides having fun."

"Such as?"

"It would definitely aid me in my fish research. I could go anywhere in the lake without being exposed to the danger that I face in our small open boat. That little submarine is a very rugged vessel. If pterodactyls were to suddenly show up, I could retreat to the sub's interior and close the hatch. Also, if we had the sub here we could begin exploring the 700 square miles of underwater world that surrounds our island."

"You make a good case for bringing it down earlier than scheduled. But before we do that, I think we should explore this island thoroughly enough to convince ourselves that it doesn't have any hidden dangers."

"How long do you think that will take?"

"Three square miles of thick forest will take some time to explore, but the only question we need to answer immediately is whether or not any dangerous animals live here."

"It shouldn't take more than a few days to accomplish that," remarked Moose.

"Then, we'll need a few days to finish setting up the rest of our equipment; the highest priority item being the wind powered electrical generator."

"Assembling it shouldn't take more than a day."

"Also, we should work with our wives for a few days to help them with their medical and biological research."

"Adding it all up, it seems like we should be ready to bring that sub down in about two weeks," concluded Moose.

"Perhaps, even a few days sooner than that."

"Wouldn't it be exciting to ride the sub over to Sauropod Meadow and watch those huge creatures come to the edge of the lake to drink?"

"That would be an awesome experience, like a scene out of a science fiction movie, only this will be real."

"I wonder how close to them we could get without alarming them?"

After pondering the question for a few moments, Jerry replied, "A field mouse looks upon a house cat as a mortal enemy, but a deer totally ignores a house cat."

"Are you trying to say that a 200,000-pound creature would ignore a 250-pound creature no matter how close it got?"

"I think that's a pretty good possibility. On Earth, humans are the dominant species. Almost everything else fears us. Here on Alcent, that's not the case. I don't think those sauropods would be alarmed no matter how close we got to them. In fact, we could probably wander among them and they wouldn't bother us as long as we didn't act threatening."

"That sounds like a reasonable theory. When are you going to test it?" questioned Moose.

"Not much over an hour ago, you adamantly claimed to be an adventurous person. So, I thought you might eagerly jump right into this opportunity for some real adventure."

"I like exciting adventure, but I haven't yet lost my mind," retorted Moose.

"But you just said that my theory sounds reasonable."

"Agreeing with your theory shouldn't be interpreted as volunteering to test it."

"But can you imagine what it would be like to be the first human to wander in the midst of 100-ton dinosaurs? What a trip that would be!"

"It would definitely be a thrilling trip, but I don't think I could get the approval of my travel agent," commented Moose.

"Travel agent?"

"The one standing over there next to your wife."

"She seems to be a reasonable person," commented Jerry. "I think you could convince her, if you use the right approach."

"Why don't you show me how it's done by convincing your wife that it would be safe for us to wander among the sauropods, and then tell her that you're thinking about trying it."

"I think I'll wait until we're observing the sauropods from the submarine," replied Jerry. "Then, when our wives start exclaiming how huge those creatures are, I will throw out the suggestion that we go ashore to find out if we can wander among them and be ignored by them because we're so small compared to them."

"It could be fun to see how they react to that proposal."

After chuckling in anticipation of the reaction they expected to get from their wives, Moose and Jerry returned to silently viewing various points of interest in their new world, each lost in thought. Their wives returned to their sides to enjoy with them the few remaining minutes of the strange, eerie light that preceded the second sunset of the day.

Alpha Centauri B now hung low over the horizon casting a straight path of reflected orange light off the surface of the lake. This pathway of reflected light seemed to form a soft glowing avenue connecting the south end of Pioneer Island to the western shore of Clear Lake. To complete the exotic scene, the orange light of Alpha Centauri B also colored a large part of the western sky with a soft orange glow that reflected off the lake on either side of the radiant avenue.

As if this eerie light weren't already enough to create an unearthly scene, a pair of pterodactyls arrived and began skillfully performing aerial maneuvers. Pulling out of steep dives at the last instant, performing vertical loops, barrel rolls, and banking into tight turns; the pterodactyls playfully demonstrated their skills. At times, their fifty-foot wingspans were fully silhouetted against the soft orange background light, readily revealing their immense size.

"What a wild primitive scene!" exclaimed Connie. "It's absolutely spectacular! And filled with danger! I feel small and vulnerable! Those pterodactyls could be on us in seconds, if they choose to attack."

While speaking, Connie flicked off the safety switch on her rifle and held it firmly in a position that would allow her to respond quickly to an attack.

"Even though they're big and fast, we certainly have adequate firepower to defeat them if they attack," stated Jerry.

"Yes," agreed Connie. "But today is the first time in my life that I've had to face such awesome creatures, and it's a bit frightening."

"At the moment, they don't seem to be interested in us," observed Captain Jerontis. "So, let's just stay alert and enjoy the show they're putting on."

"And what a show it is," commented Moose. "I'm almost convinced that they're engaged in some sort of stunt flying competition. But if they're smart enough to plan and carry out something that complicated, then we're dealing with some pretty intelligent creatures."

"It's possible that they're doing nothing more complicated than playing *Follow-The-Leader*, a simple game that young children play," remarked Dianne.

After thinking about it for a few moments, Moose responded, "You might be correct, but I get the feeling that intelligent planning is behind the sequences of maneuvers that they're executing. There seems to be a purpose to them."

"That's a possibility," admitted Dianne. "But, it's also possible that it's nothing more than instinct. They might just be doing something that their ancestors have been doing for millions of years."

"In any case, I am amazed that such large creatures could have such remarkable flying agility," remarked Moose.

Jerry said, "In order for them to do these complicated aerial acrobatics with such skill and precision, they must have tremendous physical strength, an excellent sense of balance, and a superb flight control system."

"In biological terms, that would be a highly capable brain and an excellent network of nerves that are able to rapidly carry messages between brain tissue and muscle tissue," stated Dianne.

Jerry chuckled, "I don't believe I've ever heard a flight control system described quite that way, but it definitely applies to these creatures."

"In an indirect way, you just agreed with me that these pterodactyls are intelligent," Moose said, looking at this wife with an air of smug satisfaction.

"What do you mean?" questioned Dianne.

"Saying that they have highly capable brains is nearly the same as saying that they're intelligent."

"Having brains that are capable of controlling intricate muscle movements doesn't necessarily mean that they're intelligent," responded Dianne.

"I am willing to bet that they are," retorted Moose. "Would you like to make a wager that they aren't?"

"Before I can accept that offer, you have to tell me what level of intelligence you think they have."

"I think they're capable of planning activities in advance," Moose responded. "I believe they're capable of elementary analytical thought to solve simple problems. And I think they can handle simple numbers. For example, if they saw seven animals enter a forest and five of them leave the forest, they would know that two remain in the forest."

"There's a reasonable chance that they do have that level of intelligence, so I'm not going to bet with you."

Moose smiled silently feeling like he'd won the argument.

"We don't have proof yet," Dianne said, noting his expression.

Observing that Moose and Dianne's debate had run its course, Jerry said, "If pterodactyls are intelligent enough to think and solve problems, then we face a very dangerous enemy if they decide that we are a menace to them and must be eliminated."

"If that's the case, then we'll have to use our weapons to teach them to respect us and leave us alone," declared Moose.

"But if they are intelligent, they might also prove to be good-natured and fun-loving," remarked Connie. "Every time I've seen them flying, they've appeared to be having fun."

"Creatures that enjoy living tend to be good-natured," stated Dianne. "If pterodactyls are good-natured, then the ones that get to know us should end up trusting us if we never give them a reason not to. To gain and keep their trust, we might even provide them with some valuable benefit."

"It would be wonderful to have them be allies rather than enemies who respect us," remarked Connie. "Imagine how much easier it would be to raise children in this hostile environment if one of them decided to perform the role of guard dog."

"Having a flying guard dog with a fifty-foot wingspan would take some getting use to," remarked Dianne, "but it certainly would be preferable to the alternative."

Making eye contact with Moose and chuckling a bit, Jerry remarked, "I think our wives have fantastic imaginations."

"It does sound like a wild fantasy," admitted Connie. "But, you can't deny that it is possible."

Moose and Jerry looked at the huge creatures skillfully performing aerial acrobatics; and then, they looked at their wives, smiled and shook their heads in disbelief. Almost in unison they said, "It's definitely a wild fantasy."

"But it is possible," insisted Connie.

Reluctantly, both Moose and Jerry nodded in agreement. "If you really feel that way, why are holding your rifle so firmly?" Jerry countered to his wife.

Connie quickly gave a serious response, "Because their capabilities are so awesome and we don't yet know what their intentions are."

Then, upon seeing the smug grin displayed by her husband, Connie instantly realized that she had just fallen for his bantering remark. "You got me that time," she laughed.

"Saying that their capabilities are awesome is almost an understatement," declared Moose. "Even their endurance is almost unbelievable. They're performing one high-energy maneuver after another. Aren't they ever going to get tired?"

"To have such remarkable endurance, they must have very strong, efficient cardiovascular systems and a high metabolic rate," remarked Connie.

"They are truly amazing creatures," stated Dianne. "They're definitely a tremendous improvement over the cold-blooded, dimwitted pterodactyls that lived on Earth during the Mesozoic Age."

"I don't mean to bring this discussion to a close, but that dim orange sun is about to slip below the horizon, and it's not going to take more than a few minutes to get very dark. Until we get a lot more familiar with this environment, I think we should avoid being out after dark," Jerry said.

After taking one last look at the exotic scene, they began the return trip to their campsite. Even though walking at a brisk pace, they stole occasional glances at their second sunset of the day and at the pterodactyls.

By the time the interstellar pioneers reached their campsite, Alpha Centauri B had set and the darkness of night was quickly settling in on Pioneer Island. Also, the pterodactyls were circling Western island preparing to land.

Tired from the day's activities, they entered their habitation capsule, anticipating a good night's sleep. Jerry and Connie would sleep on the capsule's first floor, and Moose and Dianne on the second floor. They would sleep in relative security for the capsule had been constructed of durable material and was rugged enough to withstand considerable punishment. Also, using the capsule's night vision surveillance cameras, the crew in the Challenger would be on full alert for any dangerous creatures that might approach the capsule.

Having worked up quite a sweat with all the physical activities of the day, even cool showers would feel good. Afterward, the day's activities would have to be discussed with the people on the Challenger.

With their elevated levels of excitement and curiosity, this discussion had the potential to last well into the night.

But there was one person who Jerry and Connie wanted to share the day with in a special way, and that was their daughter. However, Denise would not be alone; she would be with her close friend Matthew. And the children would be with Mike and Michelle. Both Jerry and Connie wanted to make sure that the children received some special attention on this special day.

After all of these activities had run their course, the two couples would retire for the night and share their aspirations with each other while drifting off into a deep sleep. The first day of a new era would finally come to a close.

SEVEN

Exploring Pioneer Island

TIME: Day Two.

After sleeping soundly for about six hours, Jerry awoke feeling refreshed and happy that his first night of sleep on Alcent had not been disturbed by anything. He sat up and looked around the interior of the capsule, which was softly illuminated by the dim light of early dawn entering through a large eastward facing window. Noticing that Connie was still sleeping, and remembering how little she had slept the previous night, Jerry was careful not to awaken her. He slipped out of bed and dressed as quietly as possible.

He silently moved around on the capsule's first floor and gazed through all six of its large, rugged, crystal-clear, plastic windows. After satisfying himself that there was nothing dangerous in the capsule's immediate vicinity, Jerry picked up his rifle, quietly opened the door, stepped outside, and silently closed the door.

Jerry stood straight and tall and took a deep breath of the cool, fresh, early morning air. He was immediately struck by its clean pristine scent and the invigorating feeling that came over him. Feeling fully alert, he intently took another look around the area. Not seeing anything threatening, he started walking away from the capsule toward the large boulder that he and Connie had made love behind on the previous day.

About half way to the boulder, Jerry stopped and looked at both robot labs and at the capsule where his fellow pioneers were still sound asleep. Seeing that two video cameras were tracking his progress and that other cameras were panning the area, Jerry appreciated that people on the Challenger were concerned for his safety. Facing the nearest of the cameras, he displayed a broad happy-to-be-here smile, gave a thumbs-up signal, and then continued walking toward the large boulder.

When he reached it, he climbed to its top. This put him a full sixteen feet above the surrounding terrain. In the dim light of dawn, he again visually inspected the surrounding area. Then, facing the slowly brightening eastern sky, Jerry sat down to enjoy his first sunrise since leaving Earth.

Pioneer Island had an aura of quiet peacefulness about it. Most nocturnal creatures had already retired for the day, and most daytime creatures had not yet begun their activities. Even the air seemed still, as Jerry could not even feel a gentle breeze. He marveled that such quiet peacefulness could exist on a planet so abundantly inhabited by large dangerous creatures. He wondered if Pioneer Island would always be this peaceful. It seemed almost too much to hope for.

Deeply lost in peaceful thought, Jerry was startled by the sudden beeping of his communicator. Mike's voice came through with a sense of urgency: "The two pterodactyls that slept on Western Island last night are awake and are stretching their wings. It looks like they might be getting ready to take off."

"Thanks Mike," replied Captain Jerontis as he turned to face Western Island. Using binoculars, he took a close look at the pterodactyls and said, "With all the energetic flying they did last night, they're probably hungry for a good wholesome breakfast."

Sounding concerned, Mike said, "I hope they don't have you in mind."

"They seem to prefer fish to red meat," Jerry jokingly responded.

Mike laughed and said, "I hope you're right."

A few minutes later, as Alpha Centauri A peaked over the eastern horizon, the pterodactyls launched themselves from their cliff top. Flying east, they passed over Pioneer Island a little to the north of Stellar Plateau. Over East Bay, they turned and flew to the southeast.

About three-fourths of a mile away from Jerry, they circled an area of the lake. Then, one of them folded its wings tightly against its body and, straight as an arrow, swiftly dove into the lake with hardly a splash. In less than a minute, large fish were swimming near the surface, some of them leaping out of the water. The airborne pterodactyl quickly swooped down and grabbed a fish with its talons. While pulling out of its shallow dive, it transferred the fish to its beak, then circled back, swooped down, and seized another fish with its talons.

Then, the pterodactyl that was underwater broke the surface and made a running, wing-flapping takeoff. When it became airborne, it joined its companion, who tossed it the fish it was carrying in its beak. Then, both pterodactyls returned to Western Island, where they landed and leisurely ate a seafood breakfast.

"Wow! What deadly efficient teamwork!" exclaimed Mike. "It sure didn't take them long to catch their breakfast."

In an incredulous tone, Jerry exclaimed, "Did you notice that creature's diving technique? It entered the water so cleanly that there was hardly even a splash. I'm astounded that such a huge creature could accomplish that."

"That dive was definitely impressive, but the fact that it was even made came as a total surprise to me."

"I certainly wasn't expecting anything like that either. Yesterday, these creatures amazed me with their flying skills. Is it possible that they are equally at home in the water?"

"Evidently, they are comfortable and competent in the water," replied Mike. "But apparently, they don't have enough speed and agility to catch fish underwater."

"Either that or they prefer to get under a school of fish and drive them to the surface where the airborne pterodactyl can more easily seize them."

"Perhaps, the underwater pterodactyl is trying to catch a fish, but with the knowledge that if it fails, it will probably receive a meal from its mate."

"That just might be their strategy," commented Captain Jerontis. "Diving deep and approaching the fish from the depths has several advantages. In the dim light of dawn, a large dark predator coming up from the depths will not always be seen, whereas, the school of fish will be silhouetted against what little light there is. If the approaching pterodactyl isn't seen, it will probably catch one of the fish; if it is seen, the fish will probably panic causing some of them to flee to the surface where the airborne pterodactyl will make the kill."

"That's a strategy that should usually result in the catching of fish."

"I'm amazed by the ease with which this pair executed the strategy. They made it look like they were doing nothing more complicated than just going for a walk in the park."

"How do you think they came up with such an effective strategy?"

"I don't know, but I'm struck by the fact that pterodactyls don't have to expend very much time to obtain their food. And that leaves them with lots of free time to enjoy life and investigate things that they're curious about. If they've had this much free time for thousands of generations, and if they've used very much of it to inquisitively investigate things that have excited their curiosity, then it's possible that they may have developed a considerable amount of intelligence."

"How smart do you think they are?" asked Mike.

"It seems quite likely that they have enough intelligence to think about and fine-tune a fishing strategy that has probably been passed from parents to offspring over many generations."

"For them to do that, they not only have to be able to recognize a problem and think it through to a solution, but they also have to be able to communicate that solution to each other, so that it can be included in the plan for the next fishing trip."

"Those are rather advanced thinking and communication skills, but it appears that they do have them."

"That would make them far more advanced than most of Earth's animals."

"And potentially far more dangerous than most of Earth's animals," added Captain Jerontis. "If they decide that we are a threat to their way of life, it is possible that they could devise tactics to make our lives quite miserable, even though we are well armed."

"If they have as much intelligence as you are speculating that they might have, then the big question is: have they formed any sort of society in which members can call upon each other for assistance to achieve a common goal, such as preventing us from colonizing their planet?"

"If they have, they could almost certainly overcome our weapons by overwhelming us with sheer numbers. Especially, if they are cunning enough to cleverly use guerrilla warfare tactics. Even if we were able to achieve a one hundred-to-one kill ratio over them, they would still win, albeit at a terrible price."

After a few moments thoughtful silence, Jerry continued, "We haven't even been here a full twenty-four hours, and I've only observed pterodactyls four times, but I'm almost ready to conclude that our success or failure in establishing a home here will be greatly affected by what kind of relationship we have with them."

"That's a pretty good possibility," agreed Mike. "Even if it turns out that they aren't as intelligent as we think they are, their physical capabilities alone are an awesome force to be reckoned with."

"That's putting it mildly! They weigh more than most of Earth's most efficient carnivores, they can easily fly seventy miles per hour, and they can swim fast enough to chase fish."

"But they might be mild-mannered rather than mean-tempered. If that's the case, they might even turn out to be fun to live with."

"That would be wonderful," stated Captain Jerontis, "but until we know that, we have no choice but to respect their capabilities."

"The wise thing for us to do would be to learn as much about them as we can, as quickly as we can."

"I agree, and with that in mind, I want you to put the Challenger's instruments to work searching the area within 150 miles of Pioneer Island. Try to determine approximately how many pterodactyls live in this area. If you find any large concentrations, you might land some RPVs near the largest group and study them up close. Attempt to determine if they're functioning as a closely knit social group or if they all just happen to be living in the same place. Also, let's devise some non-threatening experiments that we can conduct to determine how intelligent they are."

"I will get that project started right away," stated Mike.

"You might also have someone continuously monitor the activities of the pair living on Western Island. They're the ones of most immediate concern to us, but we are going to be busy exploring Pioneer Island and won't have time to constantly watch them."

"I'll land a small RPV on that cliff top, so we can observe and listen to them. If they have an audio method of communication, I would like to record it and decipher it."

"I like that idea. If they have a language that our computers are able to decipher, then listening to them will speed up our effort to gain an in-depth understanding of them. But until we do thoroughly understand them, I think the best policy is to avoid doing anything that might appear threatening to them. We certainly should not provoke them in any way that would cause them to become our enemies."

"That, in itself, might eventually produce some information about their intelligence and attitude," commented Mike.

"What do you mean?"

"If they start observing your daily activities on a regular basis when you haven't done anything to provoke them or gain their attention, I believe that would indicate that they have enough intelligence to have recognized that you are something new in their environment. It would also demonstrate that they have an inquisitive nature."

"But it wouldn't prove that they have the ability to think and solve problems."

"That's true, but being inquisitive about you would indicate a desire to acquire knowledge."

"Looking at us from their perspective, what do you think they would be most interested in learning?"

"Since they're predators, I think that they would want to know if you're easy to kill and good to eat."

"That's not a very comforting thought, so if they start showing lots of interest in us, I will have to give them something to think about."

"What are you planning to do?"

"I will demonstrate the power of my rifle by firing an explosive bullet into a small dead tree. Hearing the explosion and seeing the tree fall down should be enough to let them know that they should leave us alone."

"It will be interesting to see how they react to that."

"If they're able to think, they might conclude that it would be advantageous for them to be our allies."

"It almost sounds like you're admitting that your wife's idea about having a flying guard dog with a fifty-foot wingspan wasn't such a wild fantasy after all," Mike jokingly commented.

"How did you find out about that conversation?"

"From my wife, who else? She and the children had an endless series of questions for Connie last night."

"Speaking of my wife, I think it's time I return to the capsule and awaken her and Moose and Dianne. I'm starving. It's time to eat breakfast and start exploring this island."

About an hour and a half later, they left their campsite carrying weapons and light packs. After climbing down the rock slide, they hiked through the forest to East Bay and then headed north along the east coast of Pioneer Island.

"What a beautiful morning," stated Connie. "The temperature is pleasant, the air smells fresh and clean, and it's quiet and peaceful. The only sounds I hear are a few birds chirping in the forest and the gentle lapping of the water on the beach. It also appears that there's nothing dangerous around. There aren't even any pterodactyls in sight."

"When they aren't present, this area doesn't look much different from some of the remote wilderness areas that I've hiked into back on Earth," remarked Jerry.

"I'll bet those remote wilderness areas never had a lake as big as this one," commented Connie.

"No, but some of the lakes I hiked in to were far enough into the wilderness to isolate them from crowds of people, and camping next to them was peaceful and relaxing. Being here reminds me of some of those trips."

"Well, we certainly are isolated from crowds of people."

"That's one of the things that I like the most about being here."

"That doesn't surprise me, since getting away from people was one of the big reasons you did so much backpacking back on Earth."

"True, but besides that, I enjoyed the adventure of exploring remote wilderness areas. The more remote, the more I liked it."

"Little wonder you're so happy to be here. This island is as remote as it gets as far as humans are concerned."

"No doubt about that."

"And there's also no doubt that we're going to find plenty of adventure here, and it will most likely be more dangerous than the adventure that you enjoyed on previous backpack trips."

"I can't argue that, but I did have three very dangerous bear encounters in Alaska."

"Maybe, those encounters helped prepare you for some of the dangerous adventures that we're sure to have here."

"Those encounters taught me to be very aware of my surroundings when in the wilderness."

"I think you enjoy the natural high of a dangerous adventure," Connie said.

"That's true, but for as far back as I can remember, I've always enjoyed the adventure of exploring wilderness areas, even areas that held no dangers of consequence."

"How far back can you remember?"

Jerry consider the question for a few moments, "I was only four years old when my parents took me on my first backpack trip. After that, we went backpacking so often that camping in wilderness areas was an integral part of my childhood. Sometimes, I feel like I grew up with a pack on my back."

"I'll bet your parents never dreamed that they were preparing you for life here on Alcent."

"They couldn't have, because when I was a kid, we didn't even know that Alcent existed."

"Just the same, all that backpack camping you did must make you feel at home here on Pioneer Island."

"Glancing at the dense forest, Jerry said, "This is definitely a wilderness area, and yes, I do feel comfortable here. I am happy to be here, and excited about turning this island into our home."

About a mile and a half north of East Bay, they came upon a large log lying on the beach. They decided to sit on it and relax with a cup of coffee. Jerry faced the forest; alert for danger, while the others faced the lake and a small nearby island.

Commenting on the island, Moose said, "It sure does look like nothing more than a rock pile. I think *Rock Island* would be a suitable name."

"Other than one small grove of what look like palm trees, there isn't much large vegetation growing over there," remarked Dianne. "A few bushes, grasses, and an assortment of other small plants are all that have managed to find a foothold among the rocks."

"It might be fun to go over there sometime and climb around on those rocks," stated Moose. "Who knows, we might find some useful minerals."

"If we had our boat here, we could make a quick little side trip right now, and I could take a close look at the plants growing over there," commented Dianne.

"It's only a couple hundred yards. I could easily swim that far," remarked Connie.

"I hope you're not planning to," Jerry instantly responded. "We haven't yet done any experimenting to find out if any of the fish have voracious feeding habits. Also, after what I saw those pterodactyls do this morning, I don't think swimming is a very good idea until we understand their feeding habits a little better."

Connie chuckled, "What a quick response. I wasn't planning to go swimming. I only made that remark to find out if you were listening."

"I'm glad you're happy with my reaction."

"If you two would like to get serious for a few moments, I want to point out that I've spotted something of interest on top that island's cliff," remarked Dianne who was viewing it through binoculars.

While handing the binoculars to Connie, Dianne continued, "At first glance, it looks like a small brush pile. However, after inspecting it more closely, it's easy to see that it was carefully constructed from rocks, driftwood, and brush. I wish we could investigate it from up close and maybe determine its purpose."

"We can," said Moose, who stood up and walked over to Charlie. Moose reached into Charlie's backpack and pulled out a small RPV and two headsets equipped with video goggles and ear phones. He handed the headsets to Dianne and Connie and then gave the RPV's control unit to Dianne.

"While you two are investigating that brush pile, I will help Jerry stand guard."

The headsets were equipped with a separate video screen for each eye. Each screen showed the image detected by one of the RPV's two cameras. The RPV would aim the two cameras at the same point in the same way that human eyes focus on the same point. Thus, individuals wearing the headsets would see a three-dimensional view of whatever was in front of the RPV and have the illusion of riding in the RPV.

"It was nice of you to bring this equipment along," remarked Dianne. "Knowing how exercise stimulates your appetite, I thought that maybe you'd use Charlie's pack to stash some extra food."

"The thought did cross my mind, but I thought the RPV might come in handy."

After Connie and Dianne put on and adjusted their headsets, Dianne launched the RPV and flew it low and fast to Rock Island. Waiting until the last possible instant to pitch up and climb to the cliff top elicited a cry of alarm from Connie: "Pull up! We're going to crash!"

Hearing Dianne's loud laughter above the sounds from her earphones, Connie exclaimed, "You did that on purpose, just to startle me."

"Thrilling, wasn't it?"

"It was so real! You shocked me right out of my laid-back frame of mind. Thanks to you, I now have a better appreciation for the thrill those pterodactyls must have felt yesterday when they flew low and fast, popping up and over Eastern Island at the last possible instant."

Basking in the afterglow of the adrenaline rush, Dianne piloted the RPV to the apparent structure, slowly circled it, and climbed above it for a top-down look. Then, she said, "At first, I thought that it might be a pterodactyl nest, but it certainly does not look like a nest of any kind. It looks more like a crudely built shelter of some sort."

"Yes, and it even has a rock foundation," remarked Connie. "The rocks are more than a foot across and are arranged in a circle approximately eight feet in diameter. Pieces of driftwood have been carefully placed on the rocks to build a roughly circular wall. As the wall gets higher, each piece of driftwood is placed closer to the center of the circle gradually bringing the top to a close, shaping it roughly like a dome."

"It looks like the whole thing has been tied together with long, pliable branches and vines that have been woven into the structure. That's why it looked like a brush pile at first glance."

"The key questions are: who or what built it, and what is its purpose?"

"The most obvious answer to the first question would be that it was built by pterodactyls," replied Dianne. "For one thing, that cliff top is at least forty feet above the surrounding rocks. Pterodactyls are the only creatures that we know of that have the ability to get to that cliff top and to carry those large rocks and pieces of driftwood up there."

"But why would they build it?" questioned Connie. "It's obviously not a nest."

"There's a small opening on the north side. I will try to fly the RPV through it, so we can see the interior. Maybe, that will give us a clue."

A few moments later, Dianne said, "It sure is dark in here. They've done a good job of closing most open spaces in this dome. I feel like I'm inside of a den used by a wild animal to rear its young."

"Maybe, that's the explanation," Connie said. "Maybe, pterodactyls don't lay eggs. Maybe, their young are born alive. Maybe, a pair of pterodactyls built this dome to shelter their infants in."

"That's a possibility, however, this shelter would be quite leaky during a rain storm."

"But if the rain were accompanied by wind and hail, an infant pterodactyl would be protected from the storm's worst effects."

"That's true," agreed Dianne. "Even though it is crude, it is rather stoutly built, and it would withstand a brisk wind and an intense hail storm."

"That's one kind of extreme weather. Another kind of extreme weather is intense heat. On a hot day, that bare rock cliff top could become very uncomfortable."

"Are you suggesting that an infant could find shade inside the shelter?"

"Either that, or it could climb to the top of the shelter and roost there rather than on the hot rock."

"Both possibilities make sense."

Dianne continued inspecting the crude structure. After a few moments she said, "This definitely is a sturdy structure and that raises another possibility."

"What?"

"Pterodactyls could use this structure to protect an infant from predatory birds. If both parents wanted to leave for a while, they could push their infant into this shelter and shove a large rock against the entrance to close it. A bird comparable in size to the Golden Eagle would find an unguarded infant pterodactyl to be easy prey, but it would have a difficult time ripping this shelter apart to get to it."

Dianne piloted the RPV out of the shelter. Just outside the entrance, a little to one side, she found a large rock that appeared to be about the right size to block the shelter's entrance. Between the rock and the shelter's entrance, Dianne found numerous scratch marks in the rock surface of the cliff top. Then, she said, "It certainly looks like that rock has been pushed against the shelter's entrance many times."

After Connie agreed with her, Dianne landed the RPV and handed the control unit and her headset to Moose. Connie gave her headset to Jerry. While Dianne and Connie stood guard, Moose and Jerry inspected the shelter. After examining it for a few minutes, they came to the same conclusions as their wives.

While Moose flew the RPV back from Rock Island, Jerry removed his headset and watched the returning RPV. Speaking to Moose, he said, "Pass it to me."

As directed, Moose flew the RPV directly to Jerry, who reached out and caught it. "This RPV's close resemblance to a Frisbee reminds me of when we use to compete in Frisbee tournaments in college."

"Back then, even in my wildest dreams, I never imagined that I would someday use Frisbee-like RPVs to help me explore an alien planet inhabited with monstrous creatures," Moose responded.

"I don't think anyone else in those tournaments had that in mind either."

After returning the RPV and headsets to Charlie's backpack, the interstellar pioneers resumed hiking north along the water's edge. Walking at a leisurely pace and taking time to investigate things of interest, it was nearly lunch time when they arrived at Rocky Point.

"So far, we haven't found any evidence to support your theory that this island is periodically visited by animals large enough to be a threat to pterodactyls," Jerry said to his wife.

"We don't have any direct evidence, such as tracks on the beach, but we do have additional indirect evidence," she responded.

"What do you mean?"

"I'm referring to that shelter we found on the cliff top on Rock Island. Why haven't we found one or more similar shelters on Stellar Plateau? After all, Stellar Plateau is nothing more than a large cliff top. Perhaps, it's because the cliff top on Rock Island is accessible only by air; whereas, Stellar Plateau can be reached by large predators able to climb a rock slide."

"While your conjecture might be correct, it doesn't seem like enough to base a conclusion on. First, we don't know if the shelter on the Rock Island cliff top was built by pterodactyls. Second, even if it was, they may have built it there simply because they prefer small cliff tops."

Sounding genuinely worried about the possibilities, Connie said, "I can't refute what you're saying. However, I strongly feel that this island is visited regularly by large creatures that the pterodactyls are wary of, and if that's the case, we need to be wary of them too."

Jerry noted his wife's uneasiness. After thinking about how she rarely felt this way, he said, "I am going to trust your feelings on this. So until we can prove otherwise, I am going to assume that these creatures exist and that they pose a serious threat to us."

Connie appreciated the way that her husband responded to her anxiety. She turned her mind back to the problem of identifying the creatures that she believed existed. "If these creatures swim from one island to the next, they could come to Pioneer Island either from the north or the south. Unfortunately, if they come here from the north, we aren't going to find any tracks on this rocky terrain. This point is larger than a football field, and it's nothing but rocks."

"Tracks on the beach are only good until the next rainstorm," commented Jerry. "We might find some longer-lasting clues here in this field of rocks."

"Like what?"

"Take a look at this flowering bush. It's a lot like the wild rose bushes back on Earth. Not only are it's blossoms delicate and fragrant, but it's branches are covered with thorns. Since there are lots of them growing among these rocks, a creature passing through here might accidentally rub against some of these bushes and leave behind some hair or a bit of skin. Let's inspect them and try to find some."

Not wanting to interrupt them, Moose and Dianne had been silently listening to Jerry and Connie. But now that their conversation had reached a conclusion, Moose said. "Can we eat lunch first; I am starving."

"That doesn't surprise me," commented Dianne.

"I don't think I can relax enough to eat lunch until after I've had a good close look at those bushes," stated Connie.

"I don't think I can put my mind into the investigation until after I satisfy my hunger," commented Moose.

"Why don't you and Dianne eat and stand guard, while Connie and I examine these bushes. When you're finished eating, we'll switch roles."

"I can be comfortable with that," remarked Moose.

"Before you two start poking around in those bushes, you should let me test them for toxicity," advised Dianne.

"Those bushes don't look very dangerous to me," remarked Connie.

"Poison Ivy looks perfectly harmless too, but contact with it causes severe skin irritation," remarked Dianne. "Anyway, it'll only take me a few minutes to do the tests."

Dianne reached into her pack and removed a small kit. After putting on plastic gloves, she cut a small branch from one of the bushes. Then, she removed one of six bottles of chemicals from the kit, and placed a few drops of its contents on the stem, on a leaf, and on the blossom. Not seeing any reaction, she proceeded to the next bottle of chemicals. After testing with all six chemicals and not getting any reaction, she said, "It tests negative for all the surface toxins that we think plants are capable of producing."

Grinning at Dianne, Jerry asked, "Can I send you my medical bill, if I develop a severe reaction because of contact with these bushes?"

"Well, I don't know about paying the bill, but I could recommend a good doctor for you."

Connie smiled at Dianne and Jerry and said, "That sounds like a deal I can live with."

With Moose already sitting on a rock eating lunch, Connie and Jerry walked to the nearest clump of bushes and started examining them. After fruitlessly searching the bushes for several minutes Jerry said, "This is taking too much time. There are so many bushes here that this is going to take all day. We need to narrow down the search."

Connie glanced at all the bushes and asked, "Do you have any ideas on how we can do that?"

Jerry considered the question for a few moments. "If a large creature swam to this island from the north, where would it be most likely to come ashore? What would be the first thing it would do after coming ashore? And what direction would it go when leaving the water's edge?"

"If we could answer those questions, we would know where to look for clues."

"And we could save some time. We still have the entire west side of this island to explore, and I would like to be back at our campsite by first sunset."

"So would I. By then, I'm going to be tired, ready for a hot shower and dinner."

"Let's assume that an animal coming to this island from the north would either come ashore at its earliest opportunity or swim directly to its destination on some other part of the island."

"Its first opportunity would be the very tip of Rocky Point," said Connie.

"If you were this animal, what's the first thing that you would do after coming ashore?"

"If I were a fur covered animal, I would vigorously shake myself to rid my fur of water, like dogs do when they come out of water."

"That vigorous shaking might cause your fur to lose any strands of hair that are loose. Perhaps, we should search the rocks near the point."

About ten minutes after beginning a meticulous search among the rocks near the tip of Rocky Point, Connie exclaimed, "Look what I found!"

Jerry went to her side and looked where she was pointing. Stuck to the east face of a rough rock was a single strand of brown hair about four inches long. After looking at it for a few moments, Jerry said, "In order for that hair to be stuck to a nearly vertical surface like that, it would have to have been put there very recently, or wind and rain would have removed it by now."

"The last rain was ten days ago. It was a fairly substantial storm, dropping about two inches in less than twelve hours."

"That would certainly have washed that hair off that rock," stated Jerry. "So whatever put it there passed through here since that rain storm."

"If it was put here by an animal shaking water out of its fur, the animal must've been standing a little to the east of this rock in order for the hair to end up on the rock's east face," reasoned Connie. "Maybe a little bit farther east, we'll find some hair on the west faces of rocks."

After a few moments of searching, Jerry and Connie found four-inch long strands of brown hair on the west faces of two rocks. Noting that these two rocks were about eight feet east of the rock with hair on its east face, Jerry said, "It looks like your mystery animal is small enough to stand between rocks that are eight feet apart."

"That's not a very comforting thought. A grizzly bear weighing twelve hundred pounds is small enough to walk between rocks eight feet apart."

"An animal as small as forty to fifty pounds vigorously shaking itself could easily have put that hair on those rocks."

"While that's true, it seems to me that hair that is four inches long would come from an animal much larger than that."

"I think so too. If you were this animal, what would you have done after shaking the water out of your fur?"

"That would depend on where I came from."

"Assume that you came from the next large island north of here."

"That island is more than three miles away. After swimming that far, I would be tired and looking for a place to lie down and rest for a while. Considering rocks to be uncomfortable to lie down on and wishing concealment while resting, I would find the forest very appealing and head directly to it along the path of least resistance."

After collecting the hair for laboratory analysis, Jerry and Connie started walking toward the forest following the easiest most direct route. They were joined by Moose and Dianne, who had just finished their lunch. Jerry and Connie briefed them while they were walking.

About three-fourths of the way to the forest, the route they were following passed between two clusters of bushes. At the point where their route passed between the two clumps of bushes, there were two bushes separated by only thirty inches. Pointing at the opening between the groups of bushes, Jerry said, "Unless our mystery animal detoured around all these bushes, it would've had to pass through that opening. Let's inspect those bushes for clues."

After examining the bush to the right for a few moments, Connie said, "The thorns on this bush have snagged lots of hair, and it looks like what I've already collected."

"There's a considerable amount of hair on this bush too," stated Dianne after investigating the other bush.

"Apparently, our mystery creature is considerably wider than the space between these bushes," remarked Jerry. "Anyone have a tape measure?"

"I do," answered Dianne. "I brought one along in case I wanted to record the dimensions of interesting plants."

After locating two branches directly across from each other, Jerry measured the distance between the farthest points on which hair could be found. Then, he said, "Unless our mystery animal sways from side to side a lot when it walks, the part of its body that left this hair is forty-two inches across."

Next, Jerry measured the distance to the ground from the highest hair on any of the branches, then he said, "The part of the animal that left this hair was fifty-four inches above the ground. I don't know what this animal looks like, but these numbers indicate that it is fairly large."

"Definitely big enough to be very dangerous," stated Moose.

"Look at this leaf!" exclaimed Dianne.

"What about it?" asked Captain Jerontis.

"It's broken loose, and it's hanging from the branch by only a thin thread of bark. I believe that it was broken away from the branch by the animal which left this hair and that this happened this morning. Even though this leaf is limp, it still contains a lot of moisture. It isn't dried out like it would be if it had been broken loose a few days ago. In fact, this leaf could've been torn loose as recently as an hour ago."

Captain Jerontis asked, "How do you know that the hair was deposited here at the same time the leaf was torn loose? How do you know that the hair wasn't left here several days ago, and then something else, a bird for example, tore the leaf loose this morning?"

"Look closely," directed Dianne. "As you can see, when the leaf was torn loose, a thin strip of bark was torn from the cane. The leaf is now hanging on the end of that thin strip of bark. But what is important here is that there's a strand of hair laying across the part of the cane where the bark was torn away. That hair could only have been put there after the bark was torn away. I believe that our mystery animal plowed through here rubbing this branch hard enough to tear this leaf loose. Then, this thorn snagged this strand of hair and left it draped across this injury."

"If you are correct, our mystery creature passed through here within the last couple of hours," commented Captain Jerontis.

"And if he found a spot just inside the forest to lie down and take a nap, he might still be there," suggested Connie.

"If that's the case, I doubt that he would still be sleeping, in view of all the talking we've been doing," remarked Captain Jerontis. "If he's still around, he's probably watching us very closely trying to figure out what we're up to and if we're good to eat."

Assuming himself to be the one still responsible for guard duty, Moose took a few steps toward the forest to position himself between his colleagues and the forest. Flipping off the safety switch, he held his rifle in a quick-response position and intently stared into the forest searching every shadow for movement, however slight.

Feeling totally confident in Moose's ability to protect them, Dianne and Connie collected additional hair for laboratory analysis. They also inspected the longer, sturdier thorns for traces of skin, flesh, and blood that could be collected for analysis.

While they were doing this, Captain Jerontis reached into Charlie's pack and retrieved the RPV, its control unit, and a headset. Then, he walked over to Moose and said, "I would like to get a good look at our mystery creature. If it's still here, I would like to get behind it and watch it observe us. Since it won't know that it's being watched, we can learn its natural reactions to us. From its posture, I might be able to determine if it's just curious, or if it's preparing to attack."

"If the creature's still here, it's doing a very good job of concealing itself," remarked Moose. "I can't see any indication whatever that it's still present."

"I will search the first forty to fifty yards of the forest with the RPV."

After putting on the headset, Jerry launched the RPV and flew it straight up about 150 feet. Then, he flew it over the forest for about fifty yards before dropping down into the forest. Slowly flying the RPV among the trees, Jerry systematically searched the forest directly ahead of Moose. Then, he searched to the right and to the left. Jerry said, sounding disappointed, "Apparently, it's no longer here."

After landing the RPV and removing the headset, Jerry said to Moose, "In case I missed something, I would like you to repeat the search while I stand guard."

Feeling a tap on his left shoulder, Jerry turned and saw Dianne who said, "Why don't you let me repeat the search, so that you can eat lunch with your wife."

"Thanks! I am hungry."

After finding a couple of rocks with fairly flat tops, Jerry and Connie sat down to enjoy their lunch. Connie asked, "When you think about our mystery creature, does any image of what it might look like form in your mind?"

"We don't know very much about it; other than, it's big, covered with brown fur, and can swim at least three miles. We can speculate that it probably walks on fairly large padded feet, since the gravel areas that it walked over weren't disturbed in any obvious way. A large animal walking on hooves, or small feet, would've left obvious tracks in the gravel."

"But what do you think it looks like?"

"The image that keeps forming in my mind is that of a bear, and that worries me. Depending on the shape of its body, this creature could weigh up around a thousand pounds, or maybe even a lot more. Grizzly bears that big are very powerful animals and sometimes mean-tempered. I wish we could've gotten a good look at this animal."

"Do you think it knows that we're here?" asked Connie.

"What little breeze we have at the moment is blowing from north to south, so if it has a good sense of smell, it knows we're here."

"Do you think we should follow it into the forest and try to get a look at it?"

"Only with the RPV. I don't want to follow it on foot with the breeze blowing in its direction. It would surely know that it's being tracked, and we wouldn't get to see it unless it wanted us to see it. More likely, it would probably circle around and stalk us from behind or lie in ambush somewhere. Tracking it on foot in its domain would be very dangerous. I think we should fly the RPV into the forest for a few hundred yards, searching from side to side as we go; and then, follow a different route on the return trip. If we don't find it, we should put off the search until tomorrow. I would like to use this afternoon to explore the west side of this island."

"Knowing that creature's roaming around this island will give me something to think about tonight when I'm trying to sleep peacefully," commented Connie. "Imagine waking up in the middle of the night with that thing staring in one of the windows."

"That would be a bit alarming."

"*A bit alarming*? To me, it would be more like a bad dream, a very realistic nightmare."

"It might be frightening," conceded Jerry. "But I doubt that we would be in any danger. As strong as that creature probably is, I doubt that it could break into our capsule. It is a very rugged shelter designed to withstand severe physical punishment. It was designed and built with dinosaurs in mind. Even the plastic windows are thick, strong, and tough."

"I realize that, but it would still be very distressful to wake up to a large animal looking in the window wondering if we would make a good meal for it."

"When we go to bed tonight, I want you to totally forget about our mystery creature and sleep soundly. With all the video cameras that we have on top of our capsule and robot laboratories, our friends on the Challenger will have our campsite under continuous surveillance."

"Are those the Captain's orders?"

"Yes, they are!"

"Will the Captain be there to make sure that I follow those orders?"

Displaying a naughty smile, Jerry said suggestively, "I think the Captain's looking forward to being there and to giving you something else to think about."

"That sounds quite promising," Connie responded happily.

After a few moments of pleasant daydreaming, Jerry said, "I think we should get our minds off tonight's pleasures and get back to the problem of the moment."

"You're throwing cold water on the fantasy I was just starting to get into."

"Making love with the knowledge that dangerous creatures are hanging around just makes the experience more exciting for you," commented Jerry.

"That combined with the excitement of being here does seem to magnify my erotic nature."

"Being here seems to be affecting me that way too. So, if you'll keep your fantasy tucked away in a corner of your mind, maybe tonight, we can turn it into reality."

"I like that idea."

"Let's get back to thinking about our mystery creature. While it's not going to be able to break into our capsule, it could sure make a shambles out of our supply shed and its contents. Also, it could probably seriously damage our robot labs."

"The pterodactyls could probably wreak the same havoc if they wanted to," commented Connie.

"While that's true, I don't sense that they pose that threat because of the way that they obtain their food and the ease with which they keep themselves well-fed and content. In comparison, our mystery creature might be a bear-like animal; and as such, it might aggressively rip into anything that smells like it might contain food. Some of the scents emanating from our labs and supply shed might make it think there's food inside."

"We need a way to protect those facilities when we aren't there."

"An easy way to do that would be to ring each facility with an electric fence. A single wire about thirty inches above ground and about six feet out from the facility should work. We can make the voltage and amperage high enough to give the creature a painful jolt, but low enough so that it's not likely to be seriously injured."

"There is one other thing we could do," suggested Connie. "We could put some of our skin oil and perspiration on those wires every morning and evening. If our mystery creature has a keen sense of smell, it will detect the scent before it receives a painful electrical shock. Perhaps, it will associate pain with the human scent and be motivated to leave us alone if it picks up our scent when we're out wandering around the island."

"That's a clever idea! In fact, we might carry that idea a step farther. So far, we've been following the same path up and down the rock slide. If this creature decides to stalk us by following our scent, it will climb the rock slide along the route we use. Near the top of the rock slide, we could install an electric wire across our route and cover it with our skin oil and perspiration. If the creature follows our scent, it will certainly sniff that wire. As a result, it will receive a painful electrical shock to its sensitive nose."

"That might cause it to quit stalking us."

"Or it might decide to bypass the fence to avoid the painful shock. If it does that, it will certainly have a decision to make when it arrives at our campsite and finds wires with the same scent on them."

"Is it possible to set up these electric fences this evening?"

"We don't have the materials to do that, but Mike could put the things we need into a small capsule and send them down. Besides the electric fence materials, I'll ask him to equip a couple of RPVs with spray canisters of irritating chemicals and send those down too."

"How soon do you think he can get all that stuff together and sent down?"

"Mike's able to get things done in a hurry when it's important. I won't be surprised if he has these things in our campsite before we arrive there this evening."

"We sure are going to great lengths to avoid killing this mystery creature," commented Connie.

"Do you disagree with that policy?"

"No, I like it. For one thing, we don't know if this animal is a threat to us. It might be a very reclusive creature. Second, if we track it down and kill it to avoid possible risk to us, we lose the opportunity to learn about it and its species."

"I believe everyone on this mission shares those feelings," commented Captain Jerontis as he reached into his pack to retrieve his communicator. Then, he punched in Mike's number and received an immediate response. Jerry briefed Mike and then gave him his shopping list.

"The requested items will be in your campsite waiting for you when you return this evening," Mike replied. "Would you like us to use the robot lab's RPVs to search the forest for your mystery creature?"

"In particular, I would like you to search the forest along the waterfront on this island's west side, both ahead of us and behind us."

"We'll make sure that you aren't stalked or ambushed," declared Mike.

Before Jerry could say another word, Connie grasped his wrist and pulled it toward her. Then, she spoke into his communicator: "Thanks Mike! I appreciate that."

At the conclusion of the conversation, Jerry looked in the direction of the forest and saw Moose and Dianne returning.

"I carefully searched the immediate area and failed to find the creature," Dianne reported. "Then, I flew the RPV a couple hundred yards farther into the forest and found some footprints in a wet area next to a small pool."

"I would like to see those footprints," stated Jerry.

Dianne handed him the headset and said, "I have its memory recall set at the beginning of the footprint sequence."

Jerry put on the headset and pressed the replay switch. Looking at the images of the footprints, he said, "In some respects, these look similar to bear tracks."

After studying them for a few moments, he took off the headset and handed it to Connie. While she studied the tracks, Jerry briefed Moose and Dianne about the planned electric fence and his discussion with Mike. Then, he said, "I don't think there's anything more to be gained by searching this area for additional information about our mystery animal."

"There's one more thing that I would like to do, before we move on," remarked Dianne as she removed binoculars from her pack. "That little island over there looks a lot like Rock Island, except that it has a higher cliff. I am going to look at that cliff top and see if I can find another of those rock and driftwood shelters."

While Dianne inspected the cliff top, Moose looked at the island and said, "I think we should name it Cliff Island, since that cliff is its most prominent feature."

"OK," Jerry agreed.

"Large parts of the cliff top are sloping toward the west, and I can't see those areas from here," noted Dianne.

"I'll fly the RPV over there and take a look," stated Captain Jerontis as he picked up the control unit and put on a headset. In less than a minute, Jerry had the RPV flying low above the cliff top.

Still wearing the other headset, Connie decided to join him and switched from memory recall to live action.

A few moments later, Jerry announced, "There is one of those structures here."

After examining its exterior, Jerry flew the RPV through the small entrance and investigated the interior. Upon leaving the dome, he said, "This shelter very closely resembles the other one. There's even a large rock next to the entrance and scratch marks in the cliff top to indicate that it has been used to close the entrance."

Before returning, Jerry circled the cliff and said, "As we saw on Rock Island, there is no easy access to this cliff top except to fly there."

"When we get back, let's check the cliff top on Western Island for the presence of one of these shelters, and let's find out if the cliff top is only accessible by flight," Connie suggested.

"If there's one there, it will be interesting to see what our resident pterodactyls are doing with it," commented Jerry.

A few minutes later, the group began walking south on the western shore of Pioneer Island. When they had hiked about one-fourth mile, they noticed a pair of RPVs circling them. They waved at the RPVs, which waggled return greetings before heading into the forest.

"Somehow, I feel much safer with our friends searching the forest in our vicinity," commented Connie.

"I do too," remarked Jerry. "But let's not allow their presence to reduce our state of alertness. We are on an alien planet, and there might be grave dangers here that our friends won't discover with their RPVs."

"The discoveries of the past hour have served to intensify my degree of alertness," stated Connie. "If we hadn't suspected the existence of the mystery creature and been specifically looking for evidence to confirm its presence, we probably would've made a short lunch stop on Rocky Point and then continued on our way without even knowing that it's here. Which makes me wonder what we should be looking for the rest of the day. How do we recognize the signs that might warn us of possible other dangers?"

"All we can do is carefully observe our surroundings and investigate everything that attracts our attention no matter how small or insignificant it might seem," replied Jerry.

"Right there, next to that rock, is something that interests me," remarked Connie.

"Are you referring to those seashells?"

"Yes! Look how big they are! They are as big as large dinner plates! Evidently, something had a seafood dinner next to that rock. The question is, what?"

After examining a few of the shells, Jerry said, "Apparently, the creature that feasted on these clams was fairly large."

"What leads you to that conclusion?"

"A small creature would've had to smash the shells on this rock, but the creature that ate these clams only broke away the edge of the shell. It apparently had enough strength to pry the shells open."

"A bear-like animal could do that," remarked Moose. "Once it had the edge of the shell broken away, it could stick its front feet claws into the shell and pull it open."

"Perhaps, these shellfish were eaten by our mystery creature on a previous trip to this island," commented Connie.

"Or another member of its species," suggested Dianne.

"I like seafood," remarked Moose. "I wonder if these things are good to eat."

"I can't think of any kind of food that you don't like," commented Dianne dryly.

Connie and Jerry laughed at Dianne's remark. Moose simply smiled and said, "I can't deny that, but I especially like good fresh seafood."

"If these shellfish taste anything like abalone, I would consider them a delicacy," commented Connie. "When we have time, we'll have to do some lab work on them and find out if we can safely eat them."

"I wonder if they live on the lake bottom or if they dig themselves into it," questioned Dianne. "If they live on it, rather than in it, they should be very easy to find and harvest."

"If they turn out to be a delicacy and are also plentiful, they will provide us with an abundant source of food," commented Moose.

"We may be in competition with our mystery creature's species for this delicacy," remarked Jerry.

"If they're prolific, that shouldn't be a problem," commented Dianne.

"But they may not be all that abundant," said Connie. "I don't recall seeing any large shells along the east coast of this island."

"Maybe, they live in those waters but are too deep for our mystery creature to reach," commented Jerry. "It's possible that our mystery creature lacks diving skills and can only harvest shellfish in water that is shallow enough so that it can reach the bottom."

"Maybe, they prefer a rocky, gravely bottom," speculated Dianne. "If the lake bottom here in Rocky Point Bay is like the beach we're walking on, then it's definitely rocky and gravely."

"We have lots of underwater imagery taken with the marine explorer," remarked Connie. "Someone on the Challenger could review it and find answers to some of our questions."

"That sounds like a good job for one of my assistants," stated Dianne as she punched a number into her communicator.

"Perhaps tomorrow or the next day, I will have time to do the lab work on one of these shellfish," stated Connie. "If they check out, maybe we can build a campfire and have this planet's version of an abalone feast."

"Great idea," remarked Moose.

"Sounds like fun," commented Jerry as he resumed walking south along the waterfront of Rocky Point Bay.

Upon reaching Cliff Point, Jerry said, "Judging from all the shells we've seen, it appears that there is an abundant supply of shellfish in this bay. Also, it is evident that lots of them are accessible to the species of our mystery creature."

"You're assuming that those are the animals that have been eating them," remarked Connie.

"They are the prime suspects," stated Jerry. "If there is an abundance of large shellfish living near each of the islands in this lake, it would give these creatures an easy source of food and a reason to swim from island to island."

"If that's the case, large numbers of them might be frequent visitors to this island and present us with a constant threat," Connie said, sounding concerned.

"As time goes on, we'll learn about these creatures and discover how serious a threat they are," stated Jerry. "The first thing we need to do is find out what they look like. I think we can do that by installing one of our surveillance cameras right here on Cliff Point. The second thing we need to do is attach a radio transmitter to the back of each animal we locate, so we can track them."

Looking up the rocky slope of Cliff Point, Jerry said, "The top of that large boulder up there would be the ideal place to locate a surveillance camera. From there, it could scan nearly all of the shoreline of Rocky Point Bay."

"How do you plan to get to the top of that boulder?" asked Connie.

"I don't think I can get to the top of that boulder. It looks like it's just a little beyond my reach. However, I can lift you high enough so that you can scramble the rest of the way to the top. After you set up the camera, I will help you climb down."

"I'm sure happy to here that last part of your plan," Connie laughed.

"I like that part of the plan too. I couldn't possibly leave the most wonderful part of my life stranded here on top of a boulder," Jerry said, giving his wife a hug.

She started scrambling up the rock strewn slope with her colleagues closely following her. When they reached the large boulder, Moose and Dianne stood guard, while Jerry boosted his wife up the side of the boulder, so she could climb to the top. There, she took a few moments to enjoy the view and said to Jerry, "You were right. This vantage point does provide an unobstructed view of nearly all of Rocky Point Bay's waterfront. This is an excellent location for a surveillance camera."

Connie set up the camera's tripod and glued it to the boulder. Next, she installed the camera with its electric motors. Then, she deployed the camera's antenna and solar power plant. After contacting Mike, she put the camera through a sequence of operations to verify that it was functioning properly. Mike confirmed that a strong signal, carrying clear images, was being received on the Challenger.

After taking a few moments to again enjoy the scenic view, Connie said, "I really can't believe that we're finally living here. I feel like this is all part of some fantastic dream. The picturesque beauty that surrounds us is breathtaking."

"Since you're enjoying the scenery so much, does this mean that the last part of my plan is no longer important to you?" questioned Jerry.

"No!" Connie said quickly, "I'm not implying that I want to stay up here. You can help me down now."

Jerry reached up and helped his wife scramble down off the boulder. Then, the small party resumed their southward march.

"I think we should bring our research submarine down very soon," commented Connie. "I would like to do an underwater cruise around this island. It would not only be fun, but our future well-being depends to a great degree on what lives in this lake, and the sooner we start exploring it, the better off we'll be."

"Can you imagine how exciting it will be to make an underwater cruise in this clean water with a submarine that has a transparent plastic hull. The scenery just might be fantastic, and we will undoubtedly make some important discoveries," Dianne added.

"Exploring the underwater world around this island is important and will be an exciting adventure," acknowledged Jerry. "But before we do that, I think we should spend a few days exploring the dense forest on this island."

"We explored these forests rather extensively with RPVs for more than two weeks before we landed here," noted Dianne. "What do you hope to discover that we haven't already found?"

"Although our RPVs are very valuable exploration tools, there are still things that can best be accomplished by a human presence. For example, this morning, we located three strands of hair that put us on the trail of a large creature that may, or may not, prove to be dangerous, but at least, we know it's here. If there are any serious dangers in this forest, I want to find them and study them so that we can account for them when planning our daily activities."

"In other words, you're hoping to make our lives safer," commented Dianne.

"That's my primary goal, but I also want to become more familiar with this island's terrain. Walking on the land and feeling it underfoot gives me a totally different perspective than looking at it with an RPV."

"Studying plants and animals in person is also better than using an RPV to collect samples and deliver them to a robot lab," added Dianne.

"I agree with both of you," stated Connie. "That's why I think we should bring our submarine down as soon as possible. With it, we can spend long periods of time in the underwater world that we need to explore. This will allow us to gain knowledge more quickly than studying video from the marine explorer. Plus, it will be exciting and lots of fun."

"I can't disagree with what you're saying," commented Jerry.

"So when can we bring the sub down?" questioned Connie.

"We should finish setting up our camp and do what we can to make it safe and secure before we bring our sub down. Two important jobs that need to be done are: setting up our electric fence and assembling our wind-powered generator."

Speaking to Connie, Dianne said, "I think we can talk him into bringing it down in about five days."

"That sounds reasonable to me," commented Connie.

"I think our wives are getting pretty good at arm-twisting," Moose remarked to Jerry.

Connie and Dianne looked at each other and smiled. "Well, what do you think? Can we bring the sub down in five days?" Connie persisted.

After thinking about it for a few moments, Jerry said, "That seems like an attainable schedule."

Moose chuckled, "It appears that our wives have much more influence over you than I do."

"What do you mean by that?"

"Last night, when I talked with you about bringing the sub down, you didn't think we could do that for about ten days to two weeks. When they talk to you about it, it can be done in five days."

Jerry glanced at Moose, then, he looked at Dianne and Connie. After a few moments, he said, "It seems quite obvious why they should have more influence over me than you do."

"That's an unfair advantage," remarked Moose.

"We can't help it that we are beautiful women: God made us that way!" Connie said quickly.

Jerry stared at Moose and patiently waited for a reaction.

Feeling like he was on the proverbial hot seat, Moose responded, "If you think I'm going to disagree with that assertion, you're crazy!"

Dianne and Connie looked at each other, silently expressing an air of smug satisfaction. Then Dianne decided it was time to get back to the project of the day, "I wonder if there are any trees or bushes on this island that produce edible fruit or nuts."

"Since we left our campsite this morning, I've noticed quite a number of trees that resemble palm trees," stated Connie. "I wonder if any of them bear fruit or nuts that are edible and nutritious."

"Why don't we investigate the next one we see," suggested Dianne. "And for lack of a better name, why don't we call them palm trees."

"There's a small grove of palm trees directly ahead," Connie said a few minutes later. "And they're growing right to the water's edge. This is the perfect opportunity to investigate them."

As the interstellar pioneers entered the rather open grove of palm trees, she remarked, "The answer to the first part of my question is pretty obvious: these trees do bear nuts. Pieces of nut shells are scattered all over the place."

"They look a lot like coconut shells," remarked Dianne.

"And there are husks laying around too," noted Connie. "Apparently, these nuts were encased in husks when they developed high up in these trees."

"I wonder if our mystery creature and its peers ate these nuts," asked Dianne.

"We don't have any other suspects," replied Jerry. "But whatever ate them was strong enough to remove the husks from the nuts and then crack open the shells. After we've spent a few days exploring this island, we'll be in a better position to determine what ate them."

"I would like to find a nut that's still intact and take it with us for analysis," stated Dianne. "They may be a source of food for us."

After searching the grove for a few minutes, Moose found a nut still encased in its husk. After removing most of the husk, he placed the six-inch diameter nut in his backpack.

"I'm amazed at how closely it resembles a coconut," remarked Connie. "In fact, I am amazed by the way that so many of the plants here resemble earth plants."

"We are on an earth-like planet," commented Dianne. "When you consider the seemingly infinite variety of plants that nature has evolved on Earth, it seems perfectly reasonable to expect that many of the plants we find here will look like copies of earth plants."

"It seems like that should also be true for animal life," remarked Moose.

"It probably is," agreed Dianne. "There are many designs a creature can take, but inefficient designs usually become extinct as they are crowded out by designs that are better equipped to survive and prosper. The features that allow an animal to survive and prosper here probably aren't that much different than on Earth. In other words, the laws of evolution apply here as on Earth, and we end up with many plants and animals that look like copies of plants and animals from Earth."

As the interstellar pioneers resumed their southward march, Moose said, "The fish that I looked at in video taken by the marine explorer didn't look much different from the fish on Earth."

"There's a limit to the number of variations in shape and color that fish can have," remarked Dianne. "Evolution dictates that only the efficient designs will survive and prosper. It seems reasonable to expect that two earth-like planets would evolve many similar species of fish if the process of evolution is allowed to run for hundreds of millions of years like it has here and on Earth. However, it is also reasonable to expect that there will be many species that are unique to each planet to fill the special niches that exist on each planet."

"In any case, I am still eager to do some fishing," insisted Moose.

A few minutes later, they arrived at a lagoon that they had previously named Red Fish Lagoon. Video from the marine explorer had revealed an abundance of fish in the lagoon shaped much like the fresh water bluegill, but with most of its body colored a vivid scarlet. The species was given the name redfish, hence the name: Red Fish Lagoon.

"If redfish are as tasty as bluegills and as much fun to catch, we're going to have some pleasant fishing trips to this lagoon and some excellent seafood meals," commented Moose.

"Since our submarine is also a good surface vessel, we will have a sturdy boat to fish from once we have it down here," remarked Jerry.

"In view of where we're living, it might turn out to be one of our most valuable pieces of equipment," commented Moose. "Consider its uses: a research submarine, a fishing boat, a recreational sailboat, and a means of transportation."

"It is definitely a versatile piece of equipment," agreed Jerry, "but in time, it won't have to fill all those roles. After we've determined that it's medically safe to be here and our equipment and people have been brought down, we'll be able to build quite a variety of boats. Then, we'll use the submarine primarily for research."

"And for underwater sightseeing trips," remarked Connie.

"Our little submarine's transparent hull is what I like the most about it," stated Dianne. "That will allow us to enjoy the underwater scenery that must exist in a lake as large and deep as this one."

"Plus, the water is so incredibly clean that a person should be able to see for great distances," added Connie.

"Imagine how romantic it will be to go on an underwater cruise, alone with your favorite man," Dianne suggested to Connie.

Obviously excited by Dianne's comment, Connie smiled at Jerry, "It does have a romantic appeal to it, doesn't it?"

"The idea has potential," Jerry replied, calmly.

"I hope I'm the man in your fantasy," Moose smiled at his wife.

"Of course you are," responded Dianne. "I was just thinking about how unique it would be for us to conceive our first child on such a romantic voyage."

"That would be unique," agreed Moose. "But if our research submarine is going to be used for numerous romantic voyages, we might have to start calling it the Love Boat."

After chuckling at Moose's suggestion, Jerry said, "I think our wives are really getting good at conniving. If they keep this kind of talk going, they'll have us bringing that submarine down tomorrow."

"That's a wonderful idea," said Dianne and Connie in unison. "Whatever made you think of that?"

After thinking about it for a few moments, Captain Jerontis said, "Perhaps, we could bring it down in three days instead of five. We could spend tomorrow setting up our wind-powered generator and electric fences, if we don't get to them today. Also, we can explore the groves on the plateau. While we're doing that, our friends on the Challenger can search the island with RPVs for our mystery creature. The next day, we can explore the south lobe of this island. The day after that, we can explore the forests on the main part of this island. If all goes well, we can bring the 'Love Boat' down the day after that."

"I think we can make that plan work," commented Moose.

Dianne and Connie also expressed their approval.

After completing their hike around Red Fish Lagoon, they resumed their southward journey. Late in the afternoon, they arrived at West Point.

"I don't know about you, but I am hungry and tired," Connie said to her husband.

"That's understandable," remarked Jerry. "We've been on our feet all day. I think we've hiked about ten miles, much of it over sand and gravel. In addition to all of our other activities, that's enough to tire most anyone."

"I still have some food left in my pack. Perhaps, we could stop for a short rest and a snack."

"I think that's a good idea. We could sit on that log over there and enjoy the view out over the lake for a while."

"I don't feel all that hungry at the moment," remarked Dianne. "While you two are eating, I'll fly the RPV over Western Island and search for those dome structures."

"I'll stand guard," announced Moose.

A few minutes later, Dianne said, "The pterodactyls we watched yesterday aren't on the island at the moment, but I think I know why they made such a thorough search before landing. The wreckage of one of those dome structures is scattered around on the cliff top."

"I can understand how that would've gotten their attention," commented Connie. "Especially, if they're the ones that built it and used it to shelter their young."

Dianne continued reporting her observations of the scene: "The west side of the cliff top is much lower than the east side. In fact, it's only about forty feet high, and there's a large tree leaning against it that extends well above the cliff top. It's my guess that the tree was tipped against the cliff during a recent storm. Then, a large animal arrived on the scene, climbed the tipped tree to the cliff top, and tore apart the dome structure. Perhaps, it was looking for an easy meal, or maybe, it just felt like being destructive. Evidently, the pterodactyls that arrived yesterday hadn't been here for a while, and when they saw the wreckage, they decided to investigate before landing."

"Maybe, the storm that tipped the tree destroyed the shelter," suggested Moose.

"That's a possibility," agreed Dianne. "But the fact that the pterodactyls thoroughly investigated the scene before landing implies that they experienced this kind of devastation at the hands of creatures that they fear. Why else would they verify that the creature was no longer present before landing?"

"If your theory is correct, it tells us several things about the creature," commented Moose. "First, it has to be capable of seriously injuring or even killing adult pterodactyls. In addition, it must be a good tree climber and very good at stealth."

"The tree leaning against the cliff is at an angle of about forty-five degrees," noted Dianne. "An animal wouldn't have to be a good tree climber to scramble up it."

"Perhaps, a member of our mystery creature's species is responsible for the devastation," suggested Moose.

"We currently think that our mystery creature is a large, bear-like animal," commented Dianne. "But the creature the pterodactyls fear could just as easily be a cat-like animal. A feline weighing as little as two hundred pounds could probably kill a pterodactyl. It could silently climb the tipped tree, quietly sneak up on a sleeping pterodactyl, leap on its back, and bury its fangs in the creature's neck. Give this feline feet that are larger than a cat would normally have, put webs between its toes, and you have an animal that would be a good swimmer."

"Almost sounds like a huge, overgrown sea otter," remarked Moose.

"That's also a possibility," stated Dianne.

"Although a cat as small as two hundred pounds could kill a pterodactyl in the scenario you outlined," said Moose, "I don't think that it's likely to happen except to a lone pterodactyl. In the case of a mated pair, I doubt that the mate of the dead pterodactyl would allow the cat to feast on the kill unless it was much larger than two hundred pounds. A pterodactyl could kill a 200-pound cat by simply burying its talons in the animal's body. To insure death, it could strike it in the head with its beak, or it could lift it to an altitude of a few hundred feet and drop it."

"The only point I'm trying to make is that once we've located our mystery creature, we should not assume that we've found the creature that the pterodactyls fear," remarked Dianne. "Whether they weigh two hundred pounds or six hundred pounds, dangerous cat-like creatures might also be visiting Pioneer Island."

"I think we should investigate the scene and see if we can find some clues to indicate what kind of creature wrought the destruction," commented Captain Jerontis.

"What if the pterodactyls return while we're doing that?" questioned Connie.

"I wasn't implying that we do the investigation in person. This search for clues could be done effectively with our mechanical bugs. We could carry four of them over there with an RPV and have two of them crawl around among the pieces of wreckage. We use the other two to crawl around on the tree. Our friends on the Challenger could control the bugs and monitor their instruments."

"We may not find any clues," remarked Dianne. "We don't know if this destruction occurred a few days ago or several months ago. All clues could be washed away or blown away by now."

"That's true for hair, blood, and footprints," agreed Jerry. "But since it would require lots of force to rip apart one of these dome structures, we may find some claw marks in the driftwood. How far apart the claw marks are combined with the width and depth of individual marks would tell us something about the animal responsible for the destruction. Also, the creature may have left claw marks in the tree while climbing it."

Dianne nodded in agreement. "We shouldn't rule out the possibility of finding some hair. The tipped tree is still alive and growing. If it suffered any injuries during the storm that tipped it, sap oozing out of them would have been sticky enough to trap some hair if an animal rubbed against it before it dried."

"If we find any hair, do you have the right equipment down here to determine if it's from the same species as the hair we've already collected?" asked Captain Jerontis.

"With the equipment that we've brought down, I can not only determine if it's from the same species, but I can also determine if it's from the same animal."

"I would sure like to have that information," remarked Jerry. "It would be advantageous to know if more than one species of large animals visit this island."

"If there's any hair there, I am confident that our colleagues on the Challenger will find it," stated Dianne. "I believe they will enjoy searching the scene with mechanical bugs. With stereoscopic headsets, they will see what their bugs see and have the illusion of crawling around on Western island, and we know how eager they are to come down here. With four people running four bugs, they may even make a game out of it with a prize for the one who finds the most clues."

"I would be surprised if they don't make a contest out of it," commented Jerry.

"I don't mean to change the subject," interrupted Connie. "But look up there! It's still quite high, but if I'm not mistaken, that's a para-wing circling Stellar Plateau."

"It looks like Mike has kept his promise, and the materials for our electric fences will be waiting for us," remarked Jerry. "Unless something really grabs our attention, let's make a nonstop hike to our campsite. I would like to set up part of that fence yet today."

About forty-five minutes later, the interstellar pioneers arrived at their campsite. They found the newly arrived capsule less than a hundred yards from their habitation capsule. As they approached it, Connie's communicator started beeping. Upon answering it, she received a cheerful, "Hi! How are you?" from Michelle.

"Other than being exhausted from the day's activities, I feel pretty good," replied Connie.

"That's good news!"

"You think it's good news that I am exhausted?" Connie joked.

"I wasn't referring to your fatigue. I was just happy that you feel good, and haven't contracted any mysterious illness after two days on Alcent."

"I thought that was the case, but I couldn't resist teasing you a little bit," admitted Connie. "Medically speaking, it is much too soon to conclude that we aren't going to have any problems as a result of being here. However, it is encouraging that we all feel good and haven't had any adverse reactions to anything. Tomorrow, I will do some blood analysis to see if anything has changed since we left the Challenger."

"Hopefully, you won't find anything that appears ominous. I am eager to join you as soon as possible. After seven years in space, I am ready for some outdoor living. Something as simple as a backyard barbecue in a scenic setting would be a lot of fun."

"That does sound like fun, and this island certainly does have an abundance of scenic settings."

"I'm glad you like the idea. If you'll look inside the capsule we just sent down, you'll find some thick juicy steaks, a grill, and a bag of charcoal. I hope you're hungry, because we also packed several side dishes to go with your steaks."

"What a wonderful surprise!" exclaimed Connie. "I am famished, and a barbecue will be fun. Thank you for being so thoughtful."

"It was Mike's idea, but we worked out the menu together. Also, Denise let us know what kind of pie you like, and she insisted on helping our chef make it for you. So, you do have some dessert to go with your dinner."

"That was thoughtful of her. I will be sure to thank her when I visit with her this evening."

"She'll appreciate hearing from you. Enjoy your dinner!"

"We will, and once again, thank you."

Turning to Dianne, Connie said, "I would really like to take a shower and put some clean clothes on before we eat."

"I would too," agreed Dianne.

Having overheard the part of the conversation about steaks and charcoal, Moose could not resist the temptation to play the part of an expert. Using a boastful, high-spirited tone, he said, "I would like to point out that back on Earth, I was a respected gourmet chef when it came to outdoor cooking."

"I don't know if he's trying to impress us, or if he wants to volunteer to cook our steaks," Dianne said to Connie.

"I don't know either, but I think we should go take our showers and give him the opportunity to show us how skilled he is."

Dianne nodded in agreement. Then, she and Connie silently stared at Moose and patiently waited for him to react.

After enduring the combined stare for a few moments, Moose said, "It appears that I just volunteered to get the charcoal going and cook the steaks."

"How sweet of you to offer," remarked Dianne as they started walking toward the large habitation capsule.

Amused by the whole episode, Jerry quietly chuckled to himself, "I guess they have considerable influence over you too."

"What do you mean by that? I enjoy outdoor cooking. I just wanted them to think that they coerced me into doing the cooking; and guess what, they fell for my ploy."

Jerry shook his head in disbelief, "That's not how it looked to me."

"My acting was really good. I even sold you on the idea that I only meant to offer some helpful tips on how to make the steaks come out to perfection."

Appearing unconvinced, Jerry said, "Whatever the case may be, you now have the opportunity to demonstrate your expertise. And I think the steaks had better turn out pretty good, or you will never hear the end of it."

"You're right. Let's open up that capsule, so I can get the charcoal started. I don't know what they sent down to go with our steaks, but while I'm cooking them, I might as well prepare the entire meal."

"They packed enough food for a real feast. I'm glad, because I am hungry and ready` for a big dinner," Jerry said, a few minutes later.

"This is going to be fun," said Moose as he grabbed the grill and the bag of charcoal. "I love the aroma of steaks sizzling over a bed of charcoal."

"I hope our mystery creature doesn't find it appealing too. What little breeze we have is now coming from the south. The scent from our sizzling steaks is likely to drift out over the entire island to the north of us. If he has a good sense of smell, he may decide to investigate."

"We'll have to be extra alert this evening," declared Moose.

"Also, I would like to set up our electric fence along the entire north end of this plateau before we retire for the day. It's only about a thousand feet and shouldn't take us more than a couple hours. All we have to do is drive a plastic stake into the ground every fifteen feet or so, roll out and attach the wire, hook it up, and turn on the power."

"There isn't much soil in some areas along the edge of the plateau," commented Moose. "We may have to support some of those stakes with rocks. Even so, we should be able to complete the fence in less than two hours."

"I'll get the project started while you're playing backyard chef."

About a half hour later, Dianne and Connie emerged from the habitation capsule looking quite refreshed. When they approached Moose, Dianne said, "Those steaks really smell good. How long before they're ready?"

"Probably, about five minutes."

"Is there anything we can do to help?" asked Dianne.

"Everything is on the table except the steaks and something to drink," replied Moose.

"I'll take care of the beverages," offered Dianne as she turned and went back to the habitation capsule.

A few minutes later, the interstellar pioneers sat down around their outdoor table to enjoy their second dinner on Alcent. The mouth watering aroma from the charbroiled steaks with their special sauce and spices served to intensify their ravenous hunger. Warm garlic toast, baked potatoes, steaming vegetables, and a mixed green salad made up the main part of the dinner. Dessert consisted of Denise's cherry pie topped with whipped cream.

A pleasant atmosphere for the feast was provided by mild temperatures, a gentle breeze, and a blue sky containing a few widely scattered cumulus clouds. The perfect weather seemed to enhance the effect of the panoramic view of Clear Lake with snow capped mountains in the background to the east.

Hanging low in the western sky, Alpha Centauri A blazed brilliantly. Higher up in the western sky was the much dimmer orange star, Alpha Centauri B. Appearing between the two stars were both of Alcent's moons, which looked like double crescents. The side of each moon that faced Alpha Centauri B appeared as a dim orange crescent; whereas, the side of each moon that faced Alpha Centauri A appeared as a much brighter creamy-yellow crescent.

As they began eating their dinner, Connie exclaimed, "What a feast! This steak is twice as big as what I would've eaten when we were on the Challenger, but all that strenuous activity and outdoor living has made me so hungry that I will probably eat all of it."

Dianne tasted her steak and said, "This steak is so delicious and tender that it's difficult to believe that it's an imitation steak made by a food synthesizer."

Moose smiled in self-satisfaction and silently shifted his gaze back and forth between Connie and Dianne. After a few moments, Dianne said, "That almost looks like an *I am a good cook* expression. But you deserve a compliment. My steak is cooked exactly the way I like it. You did an excellent job."

"My steak is also done to perfection. Thank you!" Connie added.

"Perhaps, Moose should be permanently in charge of our outdoor cooking," commented Jerry.

"Outdoor cooking is fun," said Connie. "I think we'd all like to take a turn at it."

"This steak is good," stated Moose, "but I wonder what barbecued dinosaur steak would taste like."

"Which species of dinosaur do you have in mind?" questioned Dianne.

"There are several species of small dinosaurs that resemble flightless birds that might taste really good if properly prepared. One species in particular has adults that weigh about 500 pounds. I've observed them a number of times. They are herbivores that roam around in small herds. Being fast runners, they use their speed to escape predators. As numerous as they appear to be, we should be able to take one for food occasionally without doing the species any harm."

"These imitation steaks are excellent," commented Dianne. "I don't see how dinosaur steak could possibly be this good."

"We won't know until we've tried some," countered Moose.

"I can't argue that," replied Dianne. "But, I'm wondering if it's possible that you might be eagerly anticipating the excitement of a hunting expedition sometime soon."

"That would be an exciting challenge," remarked Moose. "But there is a consideration that I think is more important than the excitement of a hunting trip, and that is: we need to identify as many food sources as possible. Even though our food synthesizers have served us well during our long voyage, now that we're here, I think we should acquire the knowledge to be independent of them. The more options that we have to satisfy our basic needs: the greater the probability that our civilization will be successful."

"It almost sounds like you're implying that we should develop the capability to survive and prosper without our technology," commented Jerry.

"Only in regard to such basic needs as food, shelter, and self-defense, most especially, food. I feel very strongly that we should seek to become independent of our food synthesizers as soon as possible," Moose said. "However remote the possibility is, it is still possible that we could lose them in some tragic accident. On a planet as abundantly filled with plant and animal life as this one is, we should not get into a position of not having anything to eat simply because we don't know what's edible and what isn't."

"It seems like food is never very far away from my husband's mind," Dianne said to Connie.

"I've noticed that about him," responded Connie, "but he has made a good point."

"That's true, but I still like to tease him a little bit anyway. He loves the attention, and it makes him feel like I still love him."

"I agree with your reasoning," Jerry said to Moose. "Finding our what's edible is an important project that we need to begin as soon as we've done enough exploration to ensure our safety."

The lively group continued to discuss things of concern to them while they leisurely enjoyed their dinner and the pristine scenery around them. Being the first to finish eating, Jerry resumed setting up the electric fence and was soon joined by Moose.

Dianne and Connie stayed in the campsite to wash dishes and put away leftover food. After a half hour, they were satisfied that the campsite was tidy, so they joined their husbands to assist them with setting up the fence. All four made a special effort to rub the wire over their skin to deposit skin oil and perspiration on it. This would ensure that the electric fence carried a strong human scent.

Upon completing the fence across the north end of Stellar Plateau, the pioneers installed an electric fence around their supply shed. When this was complete, they turned on both fences and verified that they were working.

"I feel good about this," commented Jerry. "If our mystery creature decides to follow our scent up the rock slide tonight, it will receive a painful jolt if it sniffs the fence wire. Hopefully, it will remember the pain the next time it encounters our scent and stay away from us."

"That would be the best possible outcome," agreed Moose. "But another possibility is the pain could fill it with rage that might cause it to charge through the fence. Then, we will have an animal filled with fury charging around here on the plateau."

"That is also a possibility," agreed Jerry. "But if that happens, we have the means to deal with the problem. In the meantime, I am tired, and I'm heading for the shower."

"I'll be in there as soon you're out," Moose called after him.

About two hours later, after discussing the day's activities with their friends on the Challenger, the interstellar pioneers retired to their beds in a happy state of exhaustion.

EIGHT

Neighbors Drop in for a Visit

TIME: Day Three.

It was early dawn with the eastern sky just barely beginning to brighten while the rest of the sky was still dark and filled with a multitude of stars. The sky was clear except for a few low clouds over the north end of Clear Lake, a pleasant breeze was blowing from the south.

As on Day Two, Jerry quietly slipped out of the habitation capsule leaving his wife and friends behind, still sound asleep. First, he carefully inspected his surroundings with night vision goggles; then, he walked to the large boulder that he had sat on the previous morning. After climbing to its top, he made himself as comfortable as possible and prepared to enjoy some peaceful solitude during the dawn of a new day.

Jerry was thankful that once again they had all slept peacefully without being disturbed by anything. He wondered where the mystery creature was, what it was doing, and why it apparently hadn't tracked them. He reached this conclusion because there wasn't any evidence to indicate that any large animal had encountered the electric fence during the night. Perhaps, today's RPV search of the island would locate it.

Even though he was deeply lost in thought, Jerry was still alert for activity around him and noticed the movement of a dark shape near the habitation capsule. Using his night vision binoculars, Jerry saw that Moose was outside the capsule. Staying motionless, Jerry continued to silently observe him. It became apparent to Jerry that Moose's destination was the boulder he was sitting on and that Moose was unaware of his presence.

When Moose was about sixty yards away, he stopped and slowly turned to search his surroundings. Then, he resumed walking at a slow, cautious pace while alertly looking from side to side. When he was about twenty-five yards away, he again stopped and slowly turned to inspect his immediate vicinity.

Jerry decided to make sure that Moose was truly awake, so he picked up a baseball-sized rock and threw it so that it landed about ten yards behind Moose. The rock struck the ground with a forceful thud and bounced into a shrub imitating the sound of an animal crashing into a bush. Moose instantly spun around with his rifle ready to fire. Then, Jerry lobbed another rock, which again, landed behind Moose with a resounding thud. As with the first rock, Moose quickly spun around, ready to fire his rifle.

Jerry waited several seconds to give Moose's imagination a chance to run wild. Then, he laughed in a loud boisterous way and yelled out, "You remind me of a kitten chasing tossed pebbles."

Instantly realizing that he wasn't surrounded by predators, but was instead, the butt of a joke, Moose felt greatly relieved and laughed too. "That's the best one that anyone's ever pulled on me. For a few seconds, you had me convinced that a couple of wild animals had me in mind for their breakfast."

"Did you have a mild adrenaline rush?"

"I don't think *mild* is the right description. I was instantly ready for action."

"Well, you certainly impressed me. Your reaction time is pretty good for an old man. I think you're definitely ready for a dinosaur hunt."

"What do you mean, *old man*? I'm only forty-eight, same as you. If I am an old man, so are you."

"Well, maybe you're not that old after all."

194

"I'll bet you could react pretty fast too, if you thought you were about to become a meal for some wild animal," commented Moose.

"I have no doubt about that. Perhaps, my reaction time will be tested when we get around to going on a dinosaur hunt."

"I am sure that will be the case. No matter how well we plan the hunt, it is going to be an adventure that I don't think I'm ready to go on just yet. I am ready to go fishing, however."

"Maybe we should do that right now," suggested Jerry.

"What about the danger from pterodactyls? Being out in that small open boat with no place to quickly retreat to will leave us totally exposed to danger."

"That is true, but I watched pterodactyls fish yesterday morning, and I was amazed by the ease with which they caught them. When they can catch fish so easily, I don't think that they would have much interest in contesting us for our fish, if we catch any."

"What about the possibility that they might look upon us as an easy meal?"

"We've been out and about for two days now with pterodactyls frequently in sight, and they haven't paid any attention to us, but if they threaten us, we have enough firepower to deal with them."

"What about our wives? Don't you think they might be alarmed if they wake up and find both of us gone?"

"As tired as they were last night, we'll probably be back before they wake up. But if we aren't, they can always beep us on our communicators."

"It's still quite dark. Aren't you concerned about being ambushed by our mystery creature when we walk through the forest in this darkness?"

"You have so many objections that I am beginning to wonder if you are serious about wanting to go fishing," teased Jerry.

"Well, I wonder why that is! Just a few minutes ago, you had me convinced that I was about to be attacked and possibly eaten. That put quite a scare into me. It really drove home the fact that we are on an alien planet that we really don't know much about."

"Are you suggesting that those rocks I lobbed in your direction might have the effect of keeping you alive because you're now going to be overly cautious?"

"I don't think that I will ever be too cautious, but you definitely got my attention. It will be some time before I get lax about being cautious. Which brings me back to our fishing expedition, have you considered the possibility of being ambushed by our mystery creature in the darkness of the forest?"

"There'll be a lot more light in about fifteen minutes," replied Jerry. "By the time we pick up our fishing gear, walk to the north end of the plateau, and scramble down the rock slide, there should be enough light to safely walk through the forest to the beach. Charlie will lead the way, and we will be alert for anything that might be trailing us. Plus, I do have these night vision goggles."

"OK, we'll be able to row out into the middle of East Bay before sunrise."

A short time later, Moose and Jerry were at the bottom of the rock slide and ready to enter the darkness of the forest, when Moose said, "I think we should wait for more light. It's still very dark under the canopy of foliage formed by these trees."

"We only have to go through about 150 yards of forest to get to the open beach," stated Jerry. "If you'll stand guard, I'll put on a headset and march Charlie to the beach and back. That will give me a chance to scout our route. Also, if there's a dangerous creature present, perhaps it will reveal its presence by attacking Charlie."

"By the time you get Charlie out and back, there will also be more light."

Less than fifteen minutes later, Charlie emerged from the forest unscathed, and Jerry announced, "It looks perfectly safe between here and the lake."

"What are we waiting for? Let's go fishing," Moose said.

Moose and Jerry cautiously followed Charlie through the forest. When they reached the open beach, they noted that sunrise was only minutes away. After searching the sky for pterodactyls, they placed their rifles and fishing gear in the boat and pushed it into the water. A few minutes later, they were well out into East Bay.

Moose remarked, "It's been a long time since I've been fishing, and it's really exciting that we're the first humans to ever fish this lake."

"What kind of fish are you hoping to catch?"

"Before we came down here, I spent a considerable amount of time reviewing video from the marine explorer. One species that kept catching my attention is a game fish that looks very much like a northern pike, except that its coloration resembles that of a rainbow trout. So I decided to call it a rainbow pike. I would like to catch one of them because they look like they would put up a good fight, and they might be quite tasty."

"How do you plan to catch a rainbow pike to the exclusion of other fish?"

"Rainbow pike were present in much of our video. They are fairly numerous around this island. On three occasions, I saw one of them strike another fish and eat it. I've made some lures that I'm hoping will excite their appetites enough to provoke a strike. I am going to try this one first."

Moose showed Jerry a double-jointed lure with a small shiny metal spinner in front of its nose. It had an additional spinner that revolved around the shaft of the triple hook attached to its tail. The body of the lure was painted blue-green on the top and silver-gray on the bottom with a scarlet stripe running down the middle of each side. The lure was nine inches long counting the fore and aft spinners.

"That's a fairly large lure," commented Jerry.

"I am hoping to catch a fairly large fish. This lure is about the size of the fish that I watched rainbow pike strike and eat. I've given it the same body colors, and the small spinners are there to attract attention."

"Where would you like to try your luck?"

"I've seen rainbow pike here in East Bay, but they seem to be especially numerous in the channel between Eastern Island and Pioneer Island. I thought maybe you could row us east along the south shore of this bay. If we don't catch one by the time we get into the channel, we could pick up a northward drift from the southerly breeze. When we get to the north side of this bay, we should row back into the bay, so we don't end up having to row the boat against the wind."

"It seems like your plan has me doing all the work, and you doing all the fishing."

"After the way you scared the hell out of me this morning, I think you owe me something."

"That was all your fault."

"What do you mean by that remark?"

"Well, if you didn't have the habit of sleeping in, you would've been outside before I was."

"When I got up, it was still dark out. How can you consider that sleeping in?"

"I was outside before you were; so relative to me, you slept in."

"That's pretty weak, but I'll make a deal with you. If I don't catch a fish during the time that we go out to the channel, fish the channel, and circle back into the bay; then, I will take over the rowing, and you can fish while you tell me what course to row the boat on."

"That sounds fair. Let's go."

With the lighthearted negotiations complete, Moose dropped the lure into the water and pulled it along at different speeds to check its action. Then, he tested it with abrupt stopping and starting movements, during which a small weight ahead of the lure caused it to make shallow dives from which it abruptly recovered when pulled forward.

"I like that lure's action," commented Jerry. "It looks very much like a swimming fish except that all its movements are exaggerated. And when you apply irregular motion to the lure, it looks like an injured fish. Add the effect of the spinners, and there is more than enough action to attract the attention of any large fish looking for a meal."

"I hope that's the case," said Moose as he lifted the lure out of the water. Then, he cast it toward the center of the bay. After it splashed into the water about thirty yards away, Moose began reeling it in, and said, "Now, we'll find out how the fish react to it."

After Moose retrieved the lure without success, Jerry rowed the boat forward about twenty-five yards. Then, Moose again cast it toward the center of the bay. "You can't believe how excited I am! I feel like a kid with a new toy," he exclaimed.

"You should feel that way! You're fishing in a huge lake where no one has ever fished before. We know that this lake has lots of fish, some of which are quite large."

"When I was a kid, I used to dream about fishing in a remote wilderness lake that had never been fished in, but those kinds of lakes don't exist on Earth anymore."

"Relative to where you were living when you were a kid, this lake is definitely remote and in a wilderness area."

"Another one of my childhood dreams has come true," declared Moose.

Again, Moose retrieved his special lure without success, and Jerry rowed the little boat about twenty-five yards farther east. Then, Moose cast in the direction of Eastern Island and said, "I will try reeling it in with nothing but the erratic, stop-start, jerking motion."

"That will make it look like an injured fish."

"Hopefully, that will make it especially tempting to a large, hungry rainbow pike."

While Moose patiently worked his lure, doing his best to make it look like a wounded fish, Jerry said, "I wonder how many sports fishermen back on Earth would love to trade places with you right at this moment."

"Probably, just about all of them. What's especially exciting to me is that this lake is so large that it's going to take us several years to explore all of it."

"And if we want some additional adventure, we can go sixty miles upriver to the north and there's another huge lake to fish in and explore," commented Jerry.

"And don't forget that there's a huge river south of us that leads directly into the ocean," added Moose.

A few moments later, Moose's casting rod bowed sharply as a large fish struck the lure and began rapidly pulling out line. "Wow! I think I've hooked a whale!"

Moose quickly tightened the drag a bit hoping to turn the fish around before it pulled all the line off his reel. The increased drag turned the fish around after it swam straight out for about fifty yards. Moose quickly reeled in the slack line in preparation for the fish's next run. But before Moose could reel in all the slack line, the fish started another high speed run directly away from the boat.

"This reminds me of a twenty-five-pound albacore I caught back on Earth!" exclaimed Moose. "I don't know what I've hooked, but it's big."

At that moment, the fish leapt straight up completely out of the water, shook itself vigorously, then dove back into the water and swam in the direction of the boat. "It's a large rainbow pike!" yelled Moose as he rapidly reeled in slack line.

On its next run, the fish didn't go quite as far before it tired and changed directions. A few minutes later, Moose managed to pull the tired fish close enough to the boat so Jerry could capture it with a landing net.

"What a catch! It must weigh at least twenty pounds," remarked Moose. "And to think, our wives slept through all the excitement."

"I don't think so. There's been an RPV circling us almost from the moment the fish struck. I didn't tell you, because I didn't want to distract you. Apparently, when our wives woke up, they looked outside for us and noticed that your fishing gear was gone, and they decided to investigate. Anyway, I think we've been on candid camera."

"When Mike and the boys see that video, they'll be ready to come down right away!" Moose proudly exclaimed.

"They're already eager to come down, but I'm sure this will add a little fuel to the fire."

At that moment, the RPV swooped down and hovered close to the boat with its cameras focused on Moose's trophy. Then, via a speaker on the RPV, Dianne said, "That's quite a catch. It was thrilling to watch you guys bring it in. In fact, it was so exciting that I'm ready to go fishing too."

"All the excitement has made me hungry!" Moose declared, "I haven't had breakfast yet. If I knew for sure that it would be safe, I would have fish fillets for breakfast."

"When you bring it home, Connie and I will begin our research on it. If all goes well, we can have fresh fish for lunch."

"Great!" responded Moose.

While looking at the RPV, Jerry said, "Since you're here, would you mind scouting the forest around our trail. If our mystery creature's in the area, it might be tempted by the scent of fish."

"Can do," responded Dianne. With that, the RPV sailed off in the direction of the forest, and Jerry started rowing the boat in the same direction.

A short time later, Moose and Jerry arrived in camp without incident and put their fish in an ice chest with a generous covering of ice. Then, they sat down at the outdoor table to enjoy breakfast with their wives.

After breakfast, Dianne and Connie carried the ice chest with the fish in it into the habitation capsule. Except for the small area that Jerry and Connie used for sleeping, the capsule's entire first floor was devoted to research equipment. The facilities and appliances needed for comfortable living were located on the capsule's second floor.

"Lets start by dissecting this fish and examining all of its internal organs along with the contents of its digestive tract," Dianne said.

"When we're finished with that, let's identify the chemicals and biological structures present in its various body fluids and tissues and compare them to earth fish" commented Connie.

"That information should give us a pretty good idea whether or not this fish is safe to eat."

"I think we can get all this done by lunch time. What do you think?"

"I think you are ready for some fresh fish."

"Is it that obvious?"

"Between you and my husband, I'm not sure who is the most eager for a seafood meal," stated Dianne.

"Aren't you ready for a change in our menu?" Think about it. For seven years, we've been eating products produced by our food synthesizers with raw materials grown on the Challenger. If it's safe to eat, this fish will be our first meal that is from Alcent. That's a big step toward making Alcent our home."

"While all of that is true, I still think you just want to eat fish."

"OK! I admit it! But you haven't answered my original question."

"Getting back to that, yes, I think we can get our research done fast enough to determine if this fish is safe to eat for lunch. Especially, if we use the sophisticated equipment in the robot lab for part of our research."

"That's a time saving idea," agreed Connie.

Meanwhile, out by the supply shed, Moose and Jerry were busy attaching mechanical bugs to an RPV while listening to Mike comment, "As soon as you playboys get those bugs attached, we can start investigating the destruction scene on Western Island."

While displaying an air of contentment, Moose looked at Jerry and asked, "What do you think he's referring to when he uses the term playboys?"

"I don't know," Jerry replied, sounding puzzled. "We've been working hard ever since we arrived here. Why just this morning, we got up when it was still very dark, so that we could begin our research into native food sources."

"I watched the video of that research," commented Mike. "It looked to me like the only searching you guys did was for a good spot to catch fish. I just don't know how you can handle all the stress you're subjecting yourselves to."

"It's not easy," remarked Moose. "But we're in such good physical condition that we can endure constant strenuous activity without any debilitating fatigue. Also, we have such rock-solid emotional control that we can be continuously alert for potential danger without getting stressed out."

"Moose's degree of alertness is so fine-tuned that earlier this morning he was spooked by bouncing pebbles," Jerry commented.

"Spooked by bouncing pebbles? That doesn't sound like rock-solid emotional control to me," Mike said, trying to sound incredulous.

"It was dark out, and I couldn't instantly see what was happening," Moose quickly retorted.

Moose proceeded to give Mike the details of what had happened, concluding with, "I would be willing to bet that you would've reacted the same way I did."

"I probably would have," agreed Mike. "But I think it was hilarious just the same. This may go down in our history as the Bouncing Pebble Incident."

After a brief pause in the conversation, Jerry said, "The bugs are attached and ready for operation. I hope your investigative team can find some clues. It's important to find out what sort of animal tore apart that dome structure."

"If there are any clues to be found, we'll find them," declared Mike. "Since the pterodactyls aren't there anymore, we can do a meticulous search without being interrupted by them."

"Did you see them leave?" questioned Jerry.

"Yes, I did. Yesterday morning, I flew an RPV to Western Island to observe them and listen to them. I'd hoped to begin the process of deciphering their language, if they have one, but they left shortly after I arrived."

"Did they do anything before they left, or did they just simply spread their wings and fly away?" asked Jerry.

"Before leaving, they surveyed the wreckage of the dome structure and examined the tree leaning against the west side of the cliff. They even tugged at it in an attempt to dislodge it, but they quickly discovered this to be futile and gave up. Then, they took off, circled the area twice, and left. It looked like they were reluctant to leave."

"I wonder if they'll be back anytime soon?" asked Moose.

"I think that depends on a number of factors," remarked Jerry. "If we assume that they're a mated pair looking for a place to raise their young, then whether or not they return will depend on how successful they are at finding another suitable location. If they were just passing through, then we probably won't see them again."

"I don't think they were just passing through," commented Mike. "When they tried to dislodge that fallen tree, it looked like they were trying to reclaim their home."

"I wonder if pterodactyls are possessive about their nesting sites and attempt to reuse the same one every time they raise more young?" questioned Moose.

"That is something we can only speculate about," commented Mike. "But I can say with certainty that this pair was very reluctant to leave Western Island. For reasons known only to them, they seemed quite attached to it, and it wouldn't surprise me a bit to see them return."

"There is a personal consideration in all of this that none of us has mentioned, and that is that we are planning to live in log cabins," stated Jerry. "It seems reasonable to ask two questions. Is the creature that tore apart the dome structure strong enough to tear apart a log cabin? If so, how sturdy do our homes need to be so that we will be secure inside of them?"

"Getting valid answers to those questions and building accordingly will have a direct influence on how soundly I sleep at night," declared Moose.

"You're not the only one with those feelings," stated Jerry.

"Perhaps, our search for clues on Western Island will yield some information to help answer the questions you raised," remarked Mike. "Also, we are going to do a thorough RPV search of Pioneer Island today, and hopefully, we will find the mystery creature."

After briefly discussing some other topics with Mike, Moose and Jerry removed the components of the wind-powered electrical generator from the supply shed.

"Where do you think we should set it up?" asked Moose.

"I think we should put it on top of the big boulder that provided us with some pleasant seclusion our first day here. The telescoping pole that supports the turbine is thirty-six feet long when fully extended. Putting it on top of the big rock will add sixteen feet to that."

"I think that's a good location. Including the height of this plateau, our wind turbine will be more than 200 hundred feet above the lake. Most of the time, the turbine should encounter a higher wind velocity the higher up it is."

"Not only that, but that rock is as large as a two-story house and will provide a solid foundation on which to bolt the turbine's support pole."

"I'm glad we have this wind powered generator," stated Moose. "It will provide us with a good backup source of power in case we get an extended period of rainy weather that reduces our solar power to very low levels."

"Hopefully, that kind of weather system will have enough wind with it to keep our wind turbine spinning."

"It won't take much wind to get three to five kilowatts out of this generator, and that's enough power to keep us going indefinitely."

Working intently, Moose and Jerry completed assembly of the windmill in only three hours. After scrambling down off the boulder and walking a short distance away, they gazed up at the windmill to admire their handiwork.

"I feel good about this," remarked Jerry. "It's only the second structure that we've built here, but it's another significant step in the long process of turning this island into our home."

"It is so firmly anchored to that large boulder that it does have a real sense of permanence about it. Symbolically, it seems to say that we are here to stay."

"It's too bad that we don't have a little more wind, so that we could give it a good test."

"Let's turn it on anyway and find out what it will do with the little breeze that we do have."

Jerry turned on the windmill, and its wind direction vane swung the turbine so that it faced directly into the wind. The turbine immediately started rotating causing Jerry to say, "Apparently, the wind is blowing a little harder up there than here on the ground."

"This is great!" exclaimed Moose. "Even though we don't have much wind, we're still generating two-and-a-half kilowatts. On windy days, we're going to have more power than we know what to do with."

"We'll find a productive way to use it. Also, don't forget that more people are coming down in four weeks, and everyone is coming down thirty days after that."

"That's only if we don't encounter any medical problems of consequence."

"My intuition tells me that we won't," commented Jerry. "This is only our third day here, but I'm already starting to feel at home. I just don't sense that we're going to encounter any problems that we can't solve."

"I'm starting to feel at home too. I like it here. If our wives determine that the fish I caught is safe to eat, I am going to feel even more at home."

"Let's find out how they're doing with their research," suggested Jerry.

As they approached the habitation capsule, Moose sniffed the air a couple times, smiled in satisfaction, and said, "I think we're going to have fresh fish for lunch. Evidently, their research has shown it to be safe to eat."

"I smell it too, and it smells good. Apparently, they decided to pan-fry it, rather than charcoal broil it."

"Maybe they're fixing a special lunch for us, and they want it to be a surprise," commented Moose. "If they'd cooked the fish outdoors, we would've immediately known that it passed all of their tests."

When Moose and Jerry entered the capsule, they were greeted by the sizzling sound and mouthwatering aroma of frying fish. They ascended the stairs to the second floor, and found their wives busily setting the table and putting the finishing touches on a gourmet seafood lunch. Both looked up from their work and cheerfully greeted their husbands.

"I hope you guys are hungry, because we've prepared a feast," Connie said.

"I am hungry, but even if I weren't, this meal smells so good that it would quickly make me hungry," Jerry responded quickly. "All I need to do is wash my hands, and I'll be ready to eat."

"It's been a long time since I last enjoyed home-cooked fish," commented Moose. "The sizzling sound and pleasant spicy aroma bring back childhood memories of my mother's home-cooking."

"I hope our cooking measures up to what you remember of your mother's cooking," remarked Dianne.

"I have no doubt that it will," stated Moose.

A few minutes later, all were comfortably seated around their small dining table. Connie looked at the feast laid out before them and was so moved by it that she said a special prayer of thanksgiving. She was especially thankful for the fact that the meal's main course was from Alcent. Since this was their first such meal, it represented a special occasion.

After tasting the fish, Moose said, "This is delicious."

"I don't recall ever eating fish this good," stated Jerry.

Speaking to Connie, Dianne said, "I think they're complementing us on our cooking."

"We sure are," stated Moose.

"The flavor is excellent," remarked Jerry. "What did you do to make it taste so good?"

"We really didn't do all that much," replied Dianne. "When cooking seafood, it helps to start out with something that's really fresh. Cooking fish a few hours after it's caught is about as fresh as it gets."

"All we did was fry it in butter-flavored oil and give it a light sprinkling of Cajun spices," explained Connie.

"Not only did they do a superb job on the fish, but they also came up with some excellent side dishes," Moose said to Jerry. "This is definitely a feast."

"Even better than the dinner that you fixed for us last night?" questioned Dianne.

After pondering the question for a few moments, Moose decided to subdue his ego and give a safe answer, "Even though I cooked an excellent meal last night, I think this one is even better."

Realizing what had just transpired in Moose's mind, Dianne gave him a look of loving appreciation.

Jerry observed the exchange between Moose and Dianne with some degree of amusement. "Since we're sitting here enjoying delicious fish fillets, I am assuming that your research found this fish to be perfectly safe to eat," he said to Dianne and Connie.

"Chemical analysis of its tissues and fluids didn't reveal any significant differences from earth fish," remarked Connie.

"Also, the anatomy of this species is nearly identical to that of earth fish," commented Dianne.

"Did that surprise either of you?" questioned Jerry.

"No," replied Dianne. "Keep in mind that Earth and Alcent are very similar planets and that evolution has been going on for hundreds of millions of years on both planets. Evolution allows only the most efficient creatures to survive. Inefficient creatures must evolve, or they become extinct. As on Earth, the fish that exist here are the end result of eons of evolution. Since Earth and Alcent are similar, it's reasonable to expect evolution to produce similar fish."

"If your reasoning is valid, then many of the creatures we find on this planet should be similar to creatures that exist or have existed on Earth," commented Jerry.

"As time goes on, I believe we will find that to be the case," stated Dianne. "But I also expect to find many creatures here that are very different from any that have ever existed on Earth, because Alcent is older than Earth and has had a different history. Both of these factors can affect the evolutionary process."

"For whatever reasons, I'm glad that evolution has given us fish to eat," stated Moose. "There's something about a delicious home-cooked meal that makes me feel at home."

"Makes me feel at home too," agreed Jerry.

Dianne and Connie established eye contact, and for a few moments, seemed to be reading each other's thoughts. "We're glad you men feel at home with our cooking. We wouldn't want you to run off with other women simply because they cook better than we do," Connie chuckled.

Both men laughed. "Do I sense a feeling of smugness because you are the only women on the entire planet?" Jerry asked.

"There are some advantages to that," replied Connie.

After a couple of minutes in which everyone was lost in thought, Connie said, "I would love to go swimming sometime this afternoon. It is a beautiful day, and it looks like the temperature will get into the low eighties. "

"That does sound like fun," agreed Jerry. "But before we do that we need to run the blood experiment on the fish in East Bay to find out if any of them are voracious feeders, like piranha. I don't want to become a meal for fish right after we've had a meal of fish."

"That would be a turnabout of events," commented Connie.

"I had Mike make a blood dispenser for us, and he sent it down with the fencing materials yesterday," stated Jerry. "After lunch, Moose and I will install it under the marine explorer. Then, while we explore the south lobe of this island, you and Dianne can expose the fish in East Bay to the scent and taste of human blood. Hopefully, that won't provoke any frenzied reactions from any of them, and when Moose and I get back in a couple hours, we can all go swimming."

"Sounds like a good plan," declared Moose.

201

"To me, it sounds like fun," remarked Dianne. "I haven't been swimming since we left Earth."

"We'll take turns swimming and standing guard," stated Jerry.

A few minutes later, the interstellar pioneers finished their meal. While Dianne and Connie put away the leftover food and washed the dishes, Moose and Jerry went to East Bay to install the blood dispenser under the marine explorer.

About an hour later, Jerry called in and said, "Your blood dispenser is installed and ready for action."

"Good!" responded Connie. "We'll begin exposing fish to human blood right away."

"We'll check in with you a little later and find out how the experiment is going. Right now, we're going to take a look at the south end of this island."

"Be careful. I don't want anything to happen to you guys."

"Don't worry about us. We're not about to become a meal for anything."

"I sure hope not," stated Connie. Then, she turned to Dianne and said, "Let's find out how our local fish react to human blood."

"Let's start close to shore in the area where we plan to swim and then move out into the bay," Dianne suggested.

A few minutes later, Dianne and Connie were comfortably seated and wearing video headsets to view imagery from the marine explorer's underwater cameras. These cameras covered the complete field of view beneath the marine explorer. The images from the various cameras were smoothly joined by a powerful computer, making them look like a single continuous image. The video headsets worn by Dianne and Connie were equipped with motion sensors to detect their head movements. These motion detectors told the computer which direction the wearer of a headset was looking. The computer then showed the wearer the scene in that direction. This gave the wearer of a headset the illusion of sitting inside a transparent capsule suspended beneath the marine explorer.

Since Connie was piloting the marine explorer, she was viewing forward-downward imagery while Dianne was viewing rearward-downward imagery. Connie switched on the explorer's electric motor and slowly headed out into the bay.

About twenty yards offshore, in water about fifteen feet deep, they spotted a school of sunfish. These fish were shaped much like small dinner plates equipped with heads, tails, and fins. Even though the fish were multicolored, the dominant color was golden yellow. Since these fish looked much like Earth's freshwater sunfish, they had been given that name.

Connie slowly lowered the blood dispenser into the midst of the school and then ejected a small quantity of human blood. Dianne and Connie observed the blood as it slowly dispersed into the lake water. As the blood spread out into a larger and larger volume of water, some of the fish came into contact with it.

After observing the fish for a short time, Connie said, "They seem to be completely oblivious to the fresh blood present in their environment."

"Either they can't taste or smell it, or they aren't flesh eaters and don't recognize it as an indication that food might be close by," commented Dianne. "In either case, I doubt that this species would bother us when we are swimming, so let's move on."

As the peaceful afternoon wore on, Dianne and Connie became ever more engrossed in their experiment. The panoramic imagery developed by the marine explorer's video system made them feel like they were actually in the alien underwater world with the fish that they were exposing to human blood. Even though it was just an illusion, the feeling that they were underwater was so real that it added excitement and a sense of danger to their experiment. It gave them a very real feeling of what it would be like to be underwater and bleeding from a small cut with fish around picking up the scent of blood. Each time they exposed fish to human blood, they felt anxiety while wondering if the fish would attack the source of the blood. Each time they exposed fish to human blood without getting a reaction made them more confident that swimming in Clear Lake would be safe.

Suddenly, they were jolted out of their underwater world by the beeping of a communicator. Dianne answered the call while Connie continued to observe the fish she had just exposed to human blood.

202

Michelle greeted Dianne and said, "You may want to avoid going outside at the moment, because a pair of pterodactyls have just landed a short distance north of your capsule. They are now cautiously approaching you."

"Thanks for the warning," responded Dianne.

"I need to observe these fish a bit longer," remarked Connie. "Perhaps, you can check out those pterodactyls."

"Okay," replied Dianne as she removed her headset and turned to look out the north window. Dianne's pulse suddenly quickened at the sight of the slowly approaching pterodactyls that were now only about fifteen yards away. Even though she had been warned of their presence, the very nearness of the large creatures made their size and power instantly obvious and sent a chilling tingle up and down her spine.

About ten yards away, the pterodactyls stopped, peered intently at the capsule, and then made some squawking sounds back and forth. This activity led Dianne to remark, "It looks to me like they're having a discussion about what to do next."

While continuing to observe the scene with the video camera on top of the capsule, Michelle said, "It appears that it has finally dawned upon them that there are some alien structures in their environment that they need to investigate."

"In spite of their size and strength, they sure are wary," commented Dianne.

"I can't fault them for that," remarked Michelle. "They are investigating something that is totally different from anything that they've ever seen before. The fact that they're even doing this demonstrates some degree of intelligence, curiosity, and courage on their part."

Without coming any closer than about ten yards, the pterodactyls slowly circled the habitation capsule and the storage shed. While they were doing this, Dianne went from window to window to observe them and said, "They're staring at this capsule from top to bottom. I wonder what there is about it that they find so interesting."

"Since they've never seen one before, they might simply be trying to figure out what it is," commented Michelle. "Specifically, they may be trying to determine if it poses any danger to them."

"Or they might be trying to find out if this capsule contains anything that they can eat."

"Obtaining food doesn't seem to be much of a problem for them, so I don't think that's the case."

"If you're convinced of that, I guess I could safely step outside and introduce myself to them."

"I don't recommend that you do that," Michelle quickly replied. "I was just stating an opinion."

By this time, Connie finished observing the most recent school of fish that she had exposed to human blood, so she joined Dianne. After a few moments, Connie said, "I wonder if these are the same pterodactyls that we saw on Western Island."

"I was wondering about that too, so I had the computer make an image comparison, and it confirmed that they are the same creatures," stated Michelle.

"It's possible that they're thinking about rebuilding the wrecked shelter on Western Island in preparation for a baby and have decided to investigate us first," commented Dianne.

"We don't know if they're capable of that kind of advanced thinking," remarked Connie.

"While that's true, it certainly looks like they're thinking and communicating," noted Dianne. "As you can see, they've returned to their starting point, and they're standing there squawking back and forth while looking at this capsule."

"How close to the windows did you stand when you followed them around this capsule?" asked Connie. "What I'm getting at is were you close enough so that they could see you?"

"I think so. These windows are large, and there's lots of light in here, so they must be aware that this capsule is inhabited."

"Let's stand very close to the north window, wave at them, and see how they react," suggested Connie.

Dianne stepped forward to within a few inches of the window and waved at the pterodactyls. Then, Connie joined her and did the same thing. The pterodactyls intently stared at them in silence for a few moments; then, they resumed their squawking-sounding communication.

"I don't think there's any doubt that they know this capsule's inhabited," remarked Connie.

"Let's move from window to window and find out if they will follow us around the capsule," suggested Dianne.

Connie moved to the next window to the west. Then, while standing very close to the north window, Dianne pointed at Connie. After Dianne saw that the pterodactyls had shifted their gaze to Connie, she joined her. Following a few moments of back and forth squawking, the pterodactyls also moved to the west, apparently in response to Dianne's actions. By repeating this procedure, Dianne and Connie moved the pterodactyls from window to window until they were on the south side of the capsule.

"It looks like you have established an elementary form of communication with them," remarked Michelle. "It appears that they interpreted your hand signals to mean that you wanted them to follow you around the capsule. However, I am wondering why they have so willingly followed you from window to window."

"Apparently, they've decided that we aren't any threat to them, and they couldn't think of any reason to not follow us," commented Dianne.

"But what do they hope to gain?" questioned Michelle.

"Perhaps, it's a matter of curiosity," replied Dianne. "They might be very inquisitive creatures who are hoping to learn something about us. Maybe, they think that we're trying to tell them something and are following us hoping to gain that information. Maybe, they want to meet us."

"The window we're looking through is right next to our front door," stated Connie. "I think I will slowly open the door and step out onto the front porch."

"That could be rather dangerous," remarked Michelle.

"I thought it was your opinion that they're not interested in eating us," replied Connie.

"I did say that, but I wasn't implying that you should put my opinion to the test."

"Eventually, we are going to have to find out how these creatures are going to react to us in a face to face meeting," declared Connie. "Right now, we are being presented with a perfect opportunity to do that."

"Admittedly, there is some risk in this, but Connie is right," stated Dianne to Michelle.

"I think the risk is minimal," commented Connie as she picked up her 10.5-millimeter semiautomatic handgun and selected a ten-round clip containing ammunition with explosive projectiles. "They've maintained a distance of about ten yards, and if they decide to attack from that distance, I will have ample time to deal with it."

"It would be a shame to have to kill these magnificent creatures," remarked Dianne.

"I won't unless I have to," stated Connie. "I plan to stay very close to the front door, so that I can quickly jump back inside and slam the door shut. The gun is only my last resort."

"In case you need assistance, I'm ready," stated Dianne as she picked up her handgun, which was similar to Connie's.

With Dianne standing against the window and intently observing the pterodactyls, Connie unlatched the front door and slowly began opening it.

"You have their attention," stated Dianne. "They are staring directly at the door."

Connie continued to slowly push the door open with her left hand while she held her gun in her right hand ready for instant use. In a few moments, she had the door wide open. Then, she stood straight and tall in the doorway and faced the pterodactyls, which were only about twenty-five feet away. Since the pterodactyls seemed to be a bit nervous and uncertain about what to do, Connie did not make any sudden movements that might be interpreted as threatening. Instead, she stood still and shifted her gaze back and forth between the large wild creatures. Then, in a soft, soothing voice, she said, "I don't know what you guys are so nervous about. Both of you are much bigger than I am, and you can leave anytime you want to."

The largest most colorful of the two pterodactyls made some squawking sounds, and the smaller, plainer colored pterodactyl stepped backwards a few yards. Then, the larger one also stepped backwards and the two began squawking back and forth while keeping an eye on Connie.

"I think they're talking about you," commented Dianne.

"It sure looks that way," stated Connie.

About a minute later, Dianne said, "I don't know what all that squawking means, but they seem to be losing some of their nervousness."

"Now that they appear to be more relaxed, I think I will give them a better view of me," stated Connie as she slowly stepped forward onto the front porch while grasping the door with her left hand and her gun with her right hand.

The larger of the two pterodactyls noticed this, and as if to mimic Connie, slowly stepped forward a couple yards. Then, he stopped, stood in what appeared to be a relaxed posture, and gazed at Connie with eyes that seemed to be searching for information.

Observing this, Connie said, "You sure look like a wise old bird to me. If I could squawk in a way that you could understand, I would answer your questions, but I can't. So, how do I go about telling you that we would like to be friends with you and your mate?"

Meanwhile, Moose and Jerry were sitting on the sandy beach at the foot of South Bay discussing the construction of an elevator to facilitate getting on and off the south end of Stellar Plateau. This discussion was prompted by the fact that when they arrived at South Bay, the temperature was eighty degrees and the water looked so inviting that both removed their hiking boots and waded out a few feet. After discovering how warm the sheltered water in the south-facing bay was, they decided that it was better for swimming than the cooler water in East Bay and that some sort of simple elevator was in order. Being a couple of practical minded engineers, they soon became preoccupied with how best to build one.

Both men were so relaxed in their pleasant surroundings that when Jerry's communicator started beeping, it was almost an unwanted intrusion, and Moose asked, "Are you going to answer that or just let it beep?"

"I'd better answer it. It's probably Connie calling to check on our progress. She and Dianne do have their hearts set on going swimming this afternoon."

"That's true, and they might also be worried about our safety. After all, we are out here in the open exposed to possible danger."

"I'm glad our wives are inside the capsule, and we don't have to worry about their safety," commented Jerry.

"Me too," remarked Moose.

When Jerry finally answered the call and discovered that it was Mike, he said, "Hi Mike. I'm surprised it's you. I thought my wife was calling me."

"She's rather busy at the moment," Mike responded. "She's standing on the front porch having a conversation with a pair of pterodactyls."

"SHE'S DOING WHAT!"

"She's standing on the front porch having a conversation with a pair of pterodactyls," repeated Mike.

After a few moments of silence, Mike asked, "Do you have a hearing problem?"

"No! I heard you, but you're so matter-of-fact about it that I'm trying to decide whether you're serious or just kidding."

"I'm not kidding."

"I wish that she weren't exposing herself to so much risk."

"She seems to have the situation under control. If you will put on your video headset, I will beam you the imagery that we are watching. Everyone here on the Challenger who isn't doing a pressing job is watching this drama unfold wondering how it will end."

A few moments later, Jerry was wearing his video headset. He watched Dianne join Connie on the front porch and heard her say, "Since we can't squawk in a way that these creatures will understand, maybe we should indicate our desire to be friends by offering them a gift of some sort."

"That might work," agreed Connie. "But what can we give them that they would appreciate receiving?"

"We have raw and cooked fish, and we know that they like fish," commented Dianne.

"But they can easily get all the fish they want. I think we should offer them something that they've never had before."

"Those cinnamon rolls that you baked this morning were delicious, and I think we still have about a dozen of them," remarked Dianne.

"Why don't you get some of them. We'll each eat one, and depending on how they react, we might throw them one or more."

The pterodactyls watched with interest as Dianne disappeared into the capsule and then reappeared a few moments later. Dianne handed Connie a cinnamon roll and both proceeded to eat their rolls under the watchful eyes of the pterodactyls.

"It's encouraging that they haven't yet made any menacing moves towards us," Connie remarked.

"Maybe they're trying to lull us into lowering our guard in preparation for an attack."

"Although that's possible, I don't get that feeling," remarked Connie. "But they sure are observing us closely. I think they've figured out that these rolls are something good to eat, so would you like to toss one to the big guy in front?"

Dianne held up a roll and stepped forward two steps. Then, she extended her arm out as far she could reach. The pterodactyl looked at it and stepped forward two steps and stopped. Now only about five yards away, he looked at Connie, then at Dianne, then at the roll.

"He seems reluctant to come any closer," commented Connie.

"He's not as reluctant about that as I am," Dianne quickly declared.

"Well, you have his attention, so toss him the roll."

Dianne gently tossed the cinnamon roll to the huge pterodactyl who with a quick head movement easily caught it with his beak. However, he did not immediately eat it. Tasting different from anything in his usual diet, he seemed intent on fully checking out its flavor. "I don't know if he's trying to prolong the enjoyment of an unfamiliar flavor or if he's trying to determine if the roll is safe to eat," Connie said.

"I think he just ate it, so it didn't take him long to make up his mind," remarked Dianne.

"He must've liked it, because he's looking at you like he's hoping you'll toss him another one," commented Connie.

"If he wants more rolls, what's keeping him from simply attacking me and taking them. He can't possibly know anything about guns, but he does know that he is big and fierce, so why is he treating us with so much respect?"

"We can debate that later," Connie quickly responded. "I'm not sure that this is the right time to test his patience."

"Perhaps not, but while I have his attention, I want to try some more sign language and see how he responds."

Dianne held up a cinnamon roll for the large pterodactyl to look at. Then, she pointed at his mate.

After a few moments, the large pterodactyl made some soft brief squawking sounds, and his mate stepped forward. Dianne, immediately tossed the roll to her, which she easily caught. After checking out its flavor for a few moments, she ate it. Dianne then tossed each pterodactyl one of the two remaining rolls.

After they ate them, Dianne asked, "Well, what do we do now?"

"I think we should go back to our fish research. I don't know that there's much more that we can accomplish with these creatures at the moment. We've had our first face to face meeting, and they now know who we are. I think you should step into the capsule while I watch them. Then, I will back into the capsule and close the door. That should indicate to them that the meeting is over. We'll find out how they react."

As the pterodactyls watched, Dianne and Connie entered the capsule and closed the door. Feeling a bit drained from the intensity of the encounter, Connie sat down and said, "Wow! I can't believe what we just did."

"It was incredibly exciting."

"It was also very dangerous, and if we'd thought about it a little longer, we might not have faced them outside."

"Despite the danger, we had to do it," commented Dianne. "We were presented with an opportunity to increase our knowledge about these creatures, and we had to take advantage of it."

"That's true, but I'm wondering why they gave us that opportunity. What motivated them to drop in and investigate us?"

"We can only speculate, but one possibility is that they're planning to rebuild the wrecked shelter on Western Island in preparation for an infant, and they decided to investigate us first."

"Are you suggesting that they have enough intelligence to not only think and plan, but to also recognize and investigate possible hazards to their plans?"

"Again, we can only speculate, but my impression of them is that they are quite intelligent."

"Apparently, they've concluded that their meeting with us is over," remarked Connie. "They seem to be leaving."

Dianne joined Connie at the south window and observed the pterodactyls walking south. Then, the large male in the lead started running, spread his wings over their full fifty-foot span, and took off. The smaller female immediately followed.

"What an amazing sight," commented Connie.

"It's hard to believe that we just had a meeting with those magnificent creatures," remarked Dianne.

"It might be difficult to believe, but I have a feeling that we'll be meeting with them again. In fact, it's possible that we might even play a crucial role in each other's lives."

Dianne wondered how that might happen, but she didn't say anything. She just silently watched the huge creatures fly away.

When the pterodactyls were out of sight, Connie said, "Let's finish our fish research. I'd still like to go swimming this afternoon."

Meanwhile, back at South Bay, Jerry said, "Our wives are back in the capsule, and the pterodactyls are flying this way."

"I wonder if they're going to land here and introduce themselves to us."

"I hope not," stated Jerry. "We're right out in the open here. With no place to retreat to, we'd have to kill them if they made any threatening moves."

Moose pointed up and said, "They're directly overhead right now."

As the pterodactyls turned west, Moose said, "Apparently, they aren't interested in us."

"Whatever they learned during their meeting with our wives must've satisfied their curiosity about humans for the time being."

"It looks that way."

"I think we should resume our hike and get back home before Connie and Dianne find some other dangerous activity to get involved in."

"What they just did caused some anxiety for us, but we do have to admire them for their courage," commented Moose.

"That's true, but I just hope that their courage never gets them into situations where there's too much risk involved, and they end up suffering the consequences."

"I don't think we need to worry about that; they do have pretty good judgment. For example, in their meeting with the pterodactyls, they did have their handguns ready for action. They are very quick and accurate with those weapons. I think they concluded that their risk was minimal, and I agree with that conclusion."

"Nevertheless, I'm glad the encounter had a successful outcome, and I am more comfortable with us taking the risks, instead of our wives."

"Me too."

A few minutes later, Moose and Jerry rounded the southwestern tip of Pioneer Island and headed north. By the time they had hiked about a hundred yards, Jerry's communicator started beeping. When Jerry answered it, he heard Mike exclaim: "Stop right where you are! We've located a large animal that might be your mystery creature. He's just inside the forest about 150 yards in front of you. You are upwind from him, and I believe he's picked up your scent, because he is sniffing the breeze with a great deal of interest."

"What does he look like?" questioned Jerry.

"He looks big, at least a thousand pounds. If he had white fur instead of brown, he could easily pass for a polar bear."

Turning to Moose, Jerry asked, "Would you like to calmly stroll up the beach and find out if we can pass by him without being attacked?"

"I think we should turn around and go back the way we came. If this animal is mean-tempered or hungry, he will almost certainly attack. Then, we'll have no choice except to kill it. And, as a consequence, we'll lose the opportunity to observe its daily living habits."

"I think that is the wise course of action," commented Jerry as he turned and started rapidly hiking away from the area.

Moose and Jerry heard some laughter come through the communicator. "Sounds to me like you guys aren't quite as adventuresome as your wives," Mike said.

Jerry thought about how Connie had dove into East Bay within minutes of landing on Alcent. Then, he thought about the pterodactyl incident and said, "It's possible that you're right, but in this situation, I think it's important that we learn as much as we can about this animal. And that means that we must avoid killing it. We need to attach a radio transmitter to it, so we can track its movements."

"I do agree with you, but I couldn't help making that remark," chuckled Mike . "We already have a small RPV approaching the animal from behind, and we should have the transmitter attached in a few moments."

"The tiny radio has been successfully glued to the animal's fur on its back between its shoulders, and it's transmitting a strong signal," Mike continued. "We also grabbed a few strands of hair for comparison to what you found yesterday and to what we found on Western Island earlier today."

"I wasn't aware that you found any hair on Western Island," remarked Jerry.

"We just completed the search about a half hour ago, and I haven't had an opportunity to talk to you about it until now. We did find some hair stuck to sticky sap on the tipped tree. We also found some claw marks in the driftwood from the wrecked shelter. We've returned the mechanical bugs and the hair specimens to the robot lab."

"It'll be interesting to see if all of our hair samples are from the same animal," commented Jerry.

"I think you guys should pick up the pace a little bit," stated Mike. "The animal we just tagged has stepped out of the forest and is heading south."

As Moose, Jerry, and Charlie broke into a slow run, Jerry asked, "Are you sure he's after us? Maybe, he's just going somewhere."

"He has just stopped to sniff the air, and he is now heading south again. I don't think there's any doubt that he has your scent and has decided to investigate. I don't know if he's just curious or if he's hungry, but whatever his intentions are, he does look determined."

"We aren't going to be able to outrun a bear," Jerry said, "so unless you can discourage him from following us, we are going to have to shoot it. This might be a good time to test those modified RPVs that you sent down yesterday."

"We've already launched them," replied Mike. "Also, the bear has not yet broken into an all out run; he's just trotting along."

"But once he catches sight of us, he's probably going to charge," remarked Moose.

"Especially, if he's hungry and thinks we might be good to eat," commented Jerry.

A few minutes later, Moose, Jerry, and Charlie were at the foot of South Bay and Mike informed them, "The bear will come around the point in a few seconds and will have you in sight. Even though you will be about 150 yards away from him, you might want to stop and face him. If he sees you running, you might look like escaping quarry, and he might decide to charge."

"Let's hide behind that huge log over there," directed Jerry. "We'll have our backs against the cliff, and we'll be able to observe the bear while being almost completely hidden."

When they were behind the log, Jerry supported his rifle on top of it and aimed at the point. He chambered a cartridge, turned on the laser spotter, and focused the telescopic sight.

The bear came lumbering around the point. Jerry immediately commented, "He is huge, well over a thousand pounds. And he is definitely following our trail."

"I would hate to be walking on the beach and have him come charging out of the forest with no warning," remarked Moose.

As the huge animal steadily came closer, Moose and Jerry's adrenaline started flowing causing their hearts to beat faster and their excitement to become intense. Finally, Jerry said to Mike, "This bear is close enough, I suggest you start discouraging him."

"I've been waiting for your command. I didn't want to spoil your excitement of a close encounter. When your wives tell you their pterodactyl story, you'll need to have a good story of your own."

"Our story's exciting enough! Start discouraging this brute before we have no choice except to kill it."

"Yes sir!"

At that moment, a piercing high-pitched scream filled the air as a pair of forty-inch-diameter RPVs came swooping down with their electronic sirens wailing with deafening intensity. The bear instantly stopped its advance and looked up at the diving RPVs. The first RPV pulled out of its dive and hovered ten feet in front of the bear at an altitude of twelve feet with its siren still screeching. The second RPV hovered twenty feet ahead of the bear at an altitude of six feet with its siren still screaming.

The bear stared at the RPVs, but because of their small size, was not intimidated by their loud screaming. After a brief pause, the bear resumed its advance, so a small smoke bomb was released from the nearest RPV. It landed about three feet in front of the bear and burst open releasing a cloud of irritating fumes. The smoke cloud was large enough to envelop the bear's head. Some of it got into his eyes and nose causing him to roar with rage at the painful irritation. He quickly backed out of the cloud, turned and charged into the water of South Bay. After washing his eyes and nose for nearly a minute, he came out of the water, shook himself vigorously, and resumed pursuing Moose and Jerry.

"It looks like he doesn't want give up," commented Mike. "Since he's not willing to respect our warning, we'll have to drop a larger, more-potent chemical bomb."

Again the RPVs came swooping down with their electronic sirens shrieking loudly. Both RPVs stopped and hovered side by side ten yards in front of the bear at an altitude of ten feet. The bear stopped and looked at them and then let out a loud terrifying roar.

"It looks like he did learn something from our warning bomb," commented Mike.

"It also looks like he's trying to scare away the RPVs with that loud roar of his," remarked Jerry.

As Jerry finished speaking, the bear stood up on his hind legs, pounded his chest, and repeated the bloodcurdling roar. Then, he took three steps forward, stopped, and again repeated the horrifying roar while pounding his chest.

"Instead of dropping a larger more-potent chemical bomb, I am going to try a different tactic," stated Mike. "I am going to drop several of the small smoke bombs, each one will be two to three yards closer to the bear. We'll find out if he's smart enough to get the message."

"Good plan," remarked Jerry.

Mike dropped the first smoke bomb, and when it exploded, the bear roared defiantly. Then, the second smoke bomb exploded about three yards closer, and again, the bear roared defiantly. When the third smoke bomb exploded, it was close enough so that the bear got a faint whiff of the irritating fumes. This caused just enough pain to remind him of his previous painful experience, and he turned, dropped down on all four feet, and took off running with a pair of screaming RPVs in pursuit. After running about fifty yards, the bear turned to the right and headed into the forest crashing through bushes as though they didn't exist. Pursuit with the RPVs was discontinued about fifty yards into the forest.

"I don't think he will bother us for a while," remarked Moose.

"I hope so, but I don't trust him," stated Jerry. "I am glad we have a transmitter on him, so we can keep track of where he is."

"I wonder if that's the creature that came to this island yesterday," questioned Moose.

"I've just been handed the lab report on the hair analysis," stated Mike. "This bear is not the animal that came to your island yesterday, but his hair does match the hair we found on Western Island. Analysis of hair from the animal that came ashore yesterday indicates that it belongs to the same species as the bear that just added a little excitement to your afternoon."

"That means that there are at least two of these brutes on this island, one we know the location of and one we don't," Jerry said.

"Considering what we've just experienced, I would sure like to know where the other one is," declared Moose.

"Our personnel are searching the forest with all available RPVs, and we haven't yet found it," stated Mike. "But we have several hours of daylight left, and we may still find it today."

After thinking about it for a few moments, Captain Jerontis said, "I don't think that we should explore the forest in person until we've located the other bear. There are just too many dense areas that would give a cunning hunter good cover from which to ambush us. I want you to continue a systematic search with RPVs until the missing bear and any others that might be here have been located and tagged."

"Whatever it takes, we'll find them," declared Mike.

"While you're doing that, we could begin our underwater exploration if we had our submarine down here," remarked Captain Jerontis.

"We've already loaded it on the cargo shuttle. We can send it down this evening or tomorrow morning, whichever you prefer."

"Tomorrow morning will be just fine."

"Good! We'll use this evening to give it one final checkout, so that it will be ready for immediate use. Also, if there's anything else you want sent down, let me know."

"We could use our portable sawmill, a chain saw, some basic wood working tools, and 300 yards of rope able to support at least 2000 pounds," Moose said immediately.

"Are you planning to lasso one of those bears and build a corral to put him in?" asked Mike.

After taking a few moments to visualize doing what Mike's inquiry had suggested, Moose said, "I've carefully considered your question, and I'm not able to envision a desirable conclusion to such a project."

"Once you have him in the corral, you would have an opportunity to study him up close," suggested Mike.

"You're not convincing me! I've already been as close as I care to get. The project we have in mind is to build an elevator to get on and off the south end of the plateau."

"And when we're finished with that, we will try our skill at building a small log cabin," added Jerry.

"Those projects don't sound as challenging as the one I just suggested," teased Mike.

"They're challenging enough for us," stated Moose. "We'll save your brainchild for you, so that you can have some exciting adventure when you get here."

I'll pass on it too. Just being down there will be exciting enough for me."

"I think it's time for us to return to our campsite," stated Jerry. "We're planning to take our wives swimming yet this afternoon."

"That sounds like fun! I wish I could join you."

"In just a few weeks, you will be down here," assured Jerry.

"I can hardly wait, but as busy as you guys are keeping me, the time will go by fast."

"There is something that you might do for us during the next couple hours," stated Jerry.

"What?"

"You might concentrate your RPV search in the forest that borders East Bay. We don't need any unpleasant surprises while we're swimming."

"Good idea," responded Mike. "Also, we'll keep the marine explorer between you and the open water and watch the underwater world."

"Thanks! I appreciate it. Also, we could use more surveillance cameras. If large bears occasionally visit this island, it would be nice to detect them when they arrive and attach transmitters to them."

"I'll take a look at a map of the island, determine how many cameras you need, and send them down in the morning," Mike responded.

Moose and Jerry made the return journey to their campsite without incident. Upon entering the capsule, they found their wives fully engrossed in their fish experiment.

Wearing a sly grin, Jerry looked at Moose and said, "I wonder if their afternoon was as exciting as ours."

"We had a lot more excitement than we were expecting," Connie exclaimed quickly.

She and Dianne removed their video headsets and eagerly told their husbands about their sensational pterodactyl encounter. Listening to their story, it became increasingly obvious to Moose and Jerry that their wives felt tremendous satisfaction with what they had accomplished. They were glowing with pride and excitement. They had calmly faced wild, fierce creatures and had confidently remained in control throughout the encounter, despite the danger. They have every right to be proud of themselves thought Jerry.

When they finished their story, Jerry asked, "Did you sense any hostility in the pterodactyls at any time during your encounter with them?"

"We were extremely alert, and we had our guns ready, but they kept their distance and never made any threatening moves," Connie replied.

"I never felt threatened either," commented Dianne. "Now that I've had a chance to think about it, I could almost believe that they made a conscious effort to make sure that we felt comfortable in their presence."

"If that's the case, I wonder why they would do that," Jerry said.

"Maybe, they have enough intelligence to have recognized that the structures we have here could only have been constructed by beings who are far more intelligent than they are," Connie speculated. "Maybe, they've decided that it would be better to be friends with such creatures than enemies."

"If we assume that your conjecture is true, then what do you think we should do next to continue our communication with them?"

"I think we should avoid doing anything that they might interpret as threatening and wait for them to come to us."

"That's my feeling too," commented Dianne. "As mobile as they are, they can meet with us any time they're interested in doing so."

After reflecting on their comments for a few moments, Jerry said, "In addition, I think we should be alert to the possibility that their friendliness was only an act. In other words, let's not lower our guard."

Everyone nodded in agreement. Then, Moose turned to his wife and said, "I would like to go swimming. Did your fish experiment find any man-eaters in East Bay?"

Dianne shot her husband a naughty glance and wondered if she should make a sexy comment in response to the easy opening that he had just given her. However, before she could say anything, Moose noticed the way she was looking at him and quickly rephrased his question: "I would like to know if you discovered any fish with feeding habits like the piranha?"

Dianne laughed softly, "That's a much more specific question."

"We didn't get any frenzied reactions from any of the fish we exposed to human blood. If there are any voracious feeders in East Bay, we haven't identified them," she finished.

"We didn't see anything that looked threatening," added Connie. "In fact, everything looked very peaceful and I am ready to go swimming."

"What are we waiting for!" exclaimed Moose. "Let's go!"

On the way to East Bay, Dianne asked, "Did you guys enjoy your stroll on the beach?"

"It was fun, and like you, we had an unexpected intense emotional experience," replied Moose.

"It sounds like you had an erotic encounter with some sunbathing mermaids, and that dashes my assumption that Connie and I are the only women on the planet."

"Our encounter wasn't quite that exotic, but it was intense and filled with some spine-tingling excitement."

"Was it more intense than our pterodactyl encounter?"

"Comparable."

"You guys had that much excitement, and you haven't told us about it yet?" exclaimed Dianne.

"You never asked," countered Moose.

"Well, now that you have my curiosity piqued, I would appreciate hearing about your adventure."

"We were stalked by a huge bear that I am convinced wanted to eat us for lunch, but Mike managed to convince him that following us wasn't that good an idea."

"That must've been quite exciting. What happened?"

By the time the interstellar pioneers reached the forest, Moose and Jerry finished the story about their bear encounter, and Dianne reacted by saying, "I don't feel all that comfortable about entering the forest."

"I don't think we have much to worry about," assured Moose. "This immediate area is buzzing with RPVs. Our friends on the Challenger are determined to find anything that might be a threat to us."

211

"Just the same, I intend to be ready," stated Dianne as she took her rifle off her shoulder and held it in a ready-to-fire position.

"I wasn't implying that we shouldn't be on guard. I was only saying that we aren't likely to be ambushed on our way to the beach."

A few minutes later, they arrived on the beach. Connie said to Dianne, "Since Jerry and I have already been swimming, why don't you and Moose go first, while we stand guard."

"Thanks," said Dianne as she stripped down to her swim suit. "Race you into the water," she said to Moose.

Dianne ran into the water with Moose in hot pursuit. After wading out to a depth of about four feet, she started swimming. About thirty yards from the beach, she did a surface dive and headed for the bottom with Moose only about two yards behind her.

About a minute later, both Moose and Dianne surfaced, took several deep breaths, and again, headed down into the underwater world.

When they surfaced again, they were about fifteen yards farther out. "It's only about sixty to seventy yards out to the marine explorer, why don't we swim out to it," Moose said. "When we get there, we can swim around underwater within view of its cameras and put on a show for our friends on the Challenger."

"Sounds like fun; let's do it."

Moose and Dianne leisurely swam out to the marine explorer and lazily circled it in view of its above water cameras. Then, they swam down to a depth of about fifteen feet, faced the nearest camera, smiled, and waved. After swimming around under the marine explorer for about a minute, they headed for the surface.

After several deep breaths, Moose said, "This is the cleanest lake I've ever swam in. I'm amazed at how clearly we could see the bottom from the depth we were at. It had to be at least thirty feet below us."

"It's incredibly clean, but I wish it were a little warmer."

"I don't think it's really all that cold," commented Moose.

"It's not cold enough to be uncomfortable, but it's not as warm as I would like it to be either."

"It is only early spring. Even though this is a deep lake, I think that it should be noticeably warmer by the end of the summer. In the meantime, I think we should be swimming in South Bay, it's significantly warmer than this. To make it more convenient, Jerry and I are going to build an elevator to get on and off the south end of the plateau."

"That sounds good to me. Let's do one more underwater swim for the cameras, and then let's head for the beach and let Jerry and Connie have their turn."

After their second underwater performance for their friends on the Challenger, Moose and Dianne spent the next ten minutes playfully frolicking around in the water as they made their way to the beach. Then, while Moose stood guard, Dianne stretched out on a beach towel to soak up some of the radiant energy pouring out of the twin stars, Alpha Centauri A and B.

Connie noted that Moose seemed to be standing guard with a special air of alertness about him. On the way to the water, she turned to Jerry and said, "That bear seems to have had quite an effect on Moose."

"It had quite an effect on me too. I think that it's going to be a long time before either one of us falls asleep on guard duty."

"That means we can relax and enjoy our swim, since Moose is on full alert."

For the next twenty minutes, Jerry and Connie enjoyed the pleasures of a refreshing dip in Clear Lake. Then, they laid out some beach towels and joined Dianne in some lazy sunbathing while Moose continued to stand guard. During the next half hour, they spoke very little, each content to be lost in thought. The setting was so quiet and peaceful that Connie and Dianne soon fell asleep.

Jerry got up, and speaking not much louder than a whisper, said to Moose, "I think it's my turn to pull guard duty."

"Okay, but rather than sunbathe, I am going to go for another swim."

About ten minutes after entering the water, Moose returned, "I'm hungry. It must be almost dinner time."

Both Connie and Dianne were now awake. "I would like to take another quick dip into the bay before we return to camp," Dianne said.

While Moose stood guard, Jerry and Connie entered the water with her.

A short time later, they returned feeling refreshed. "I'm ready to go home, and just as soon as we get back, I am going to put some fish in the frying pan," Connie said. "My stomach is growling."

"You mean I'm not the only one who is hungry?" asked Moose.

"I think we're all ready for dinner," remarked Dianne.

"Let my vote make that unanimous," stated Jerry.

Twenty minutes later, they were back in their campsite. Their plan for the rest of the day was to have a peaceful, relaxed evening followed by an early bedtime and getting some extra sleep.

At 10:00 P.M., all were ready to retire for the day, but decided to go outside and do some stargazing first. The nighttime sky was dominated by Alcent's two moons. The nearest moon, which journeyed around Alcent once every ten days, was high in the southern sky and appeared as a half moon. The more distant moon, which required seventeen days to travel around Alcent, was about forty-five degrees above the western horizon and appeared as a crescent moon. Since the more distant moon was considerably larger than the nearer moon, it appeared to be about the same size, despite its greater distance. Even though both moons were much smaller than Earth's moon, they appeared to be about the same size as Earth's moon because of their proximity.

Because of their familiarity with Earth's time keeping, it was decided to keep the same time system as existed on Earth. The fact that Alcent's day was twenty-four minutes longer than Earth's day was accounted for by having sixty-one minutes in each hour. One year on Alcent, the time required to make one journey around Alpha Centauri A, was 364 Alcent days.

"What a pleasant evening," remarked Connie.

"It really has been peaceful and relaxing," agreed Dianne.

"I like the pleasant weather," commented Moose.

"We have had really pleasant weather since our arrival here, but that might soon change," Jerry said. "Mike told me that there is a large low pressure system building out over the ocean that is heading this way. Perhaps, we'll have a windy rainstorm in a day or two."

"It's been eleven days since the last rain, so we do need some to keep all the plant life around here healthy," remarked Dianne.

"It's been seven years since I've experienced a windy rainstorm," remarked Moose. "I think I just might enjoy being out in that."

"I enjoy having two moons in the sky," stated Connie. "I wonder how long it's going to take to get use to that. It just seems so unreal."

"I think it's romantic," commented Dianne. "Think about it! Several times each year, we'll be treated to having two full moons. If Alpha Centauri B is also in the nighttime sky, it just simply isn't going to be very dark. Two full moons plus a dim orange sun, won't that be exotic?"

"All the vacations I took to exotic places in the South Pacific can't begin to compete with what we have here," remarked Moose.

"We should think about giving those moons names," suggested Jerry.

"I think we should give them romantic names," stated Connie.

"Do you have any names in mind?" asked Jerry.

"A full moon is romantic only because it occurs during the nighttime. Romance that occurs during the night can be called nocturnal romance, so why don't we name one of these moons Nocturne?"

"I like that name," commented Dianne. "It really is a fitting name, because the light of a full moon can be helpful for almost any nocturnal activity."

"We have two moons to name," remarked Jerry.

"In ancient Greek Mythology there was a goddess of love and beauty named Aphrodite," stated Dianne. "I think we should name one of these moons Aphrodite."

"Good idea," remarked Connie.

"It seems we have our names," commented Jerry. "Now the question is, which moon gets which name?"

"I can answer that question," declared Moose. "Since it is desirable to be as close as possible to a love goddess, I think we should name the nearest moon Aphrodite and the more distant one Nocturne."

"That kind of logic is hard to disagree with," remarked Jerry.

"Don't you just love the way our husbands think?" Connie asked Dianne.

Dianne displayed a subtle, naughty grin and said, "There are some advantages to the way they think."

They enjoyed the quiet peaceful evening for another half hour before going back inside their habitation capsule and retiring for the night.

At 11:50 P.M., Jerry was startled out of a sound sleep by the sudden beeping of his communicator. He answered it with a sleepy-sounding voice.

"I am sorry to wake you like this," Mike said, "but that bear you encountered this afternoon started tracking you about forty-five minutes ago. He is now climbing the rock slide."

Instantly, Jerry became fully awake. "I hope the shock from our electric fence will be painful enough to keep him off this plateau. If not, we'll probably have to kill him."

"I have my doubts about that," replied Mike. "The impression I got earlier today is that this is a very strong-willed animal who does not easily give up on what he sets out to do."

"Whatever it takes, we cannot allow that bear to roam around here on our plateau," declared Jerry. "He is too large and powerful. I am going to turn up the power on the fence. I hope the shock will be strong enough to knock him on his butt."

"It'll be interesting to see how he reacts to that. We've been following him with a small RPV, so you can watch him if you turn on one of your video screens. He is only about ten yards away from your fence."

Jerry turned on the screen and watched the bear approach the fence. The bear stopped, sniffed the wire, and detected the strong human scent. In response, the bear let out a soft menacing growl, as if to protest the presence of the fence.

"Come on a little closer and touch that wire with your nose," coaxed Jerry.

As Jerry spoke, the bear continued sniffing the wire without contacting it. Each time the bear sniffed the fence, he voiced a soft menacing growl.

"Apparently, these animals use scent as a means of marking territorial boundaries," Mike commented. "This guy sounds like he's upset by the fact that you've marked a territory. It looks like he's trying to decide if he should respect it."

"If he touches that wire with his nose, it might help him make up his mind."

Jerry barely finished his comment when the bear did exactly that. The intense electrical shock that entered his tender nose tissue caught him completely by surprise. The excruciating pain caused him to jump back several feet and to let out an extremely loud horrifying roar that split the quiet peaceful night with a bloodcurdling effect.

So loud was the roar that it instantly woke Moose and Dianne out of a sound sleep. Thinking the bear was just outside the capsule and about to break in, Moose practically flew out of bed, grabbed his rifle, and ran down the stairs to the first floor. Dianne quickly joined him with her rifle in hand.

The pain of the electrical shock passed, but the bear continued to roar defiantly as it walked along the fence sniffing it from a distance of a couple feet. Watching and listening to the bear, Jerry said, "I wonder if he's going to challenge the fence again."

"I don't know, but he seems very determined," Mike said.

"He has just had his second painful experience while following the human scent," commented Jerry. "I wonder if he's smart enough to accept the warning, or if he will need additional convincing."

"A couple of screaming RPVs would remind him of what happened this afternoon and might be all the convincing he needs," Moose said.

"We're ready to launch them on a moment's notice," responded Mike.

"Let's give him a chance to respect our territory before we launch them," suggested Jerry.

When the bear reached the west end of the fence and found that it went to the very edge of the plateau, he turned around and followed it to its east end. Upon finding that this end also extended to the very edge of the plateau and that he could not get around it, he roared in defiant protest. Then he turned around and walked along the fence in a westerly direction, occasionally stopping to sniff it from a distance of a few inches. Each time he stopped to sniff the wire, he let out an angry growl before continuing on his way.

"I think it's starting to sink into his brain that he cannot roam around here on the plateau unless he can solve the electric fence problem," commented Jerry.

"It looks that way," agreed Mike, "and it also looks and sounds like he isn't very happy about it."

"I don't think his objective is to roam around here on the plateau," remarked Moose.

"I don't think so either," agreed Jerry. "I think it's quite likely that our scent has convinced him that we might be good to eat. Why else would he track us at nighttime unless he's hoping to catch us sleeping and get an easy meal?"

"Pterodactyls sleep on cliff tops," remarked Connie. "Maybe he'd hoped to find some sleeping pterodactyls up here."

"I watched him follow Moose and Jerry's trail," stated Mike. "There's no doubt in my mind that it's them he's after."

"Maybe he's just curious and wants to find out who we are and what we look like, the way those pterodactyls did this afternoon," Dianne speculated.

"That's a possibility," conceded Mike, "but while watching him track Moose and Jerry, I got the distinct feeling that this is a hunter tracking prey."

"I wonder what he's up to now," remarked Jerry.

All looked at the video screen and saw that the bear had backed away from the fence a few yards and was facing it. Then, he began growling and pawing the ground.

"He reminds me of a bull trying to gather up enough courage to charge," Moose commented. "If he does charge, he will get a painful shock when he hits the fence, but his momentum will carry him through it."

"I believe it's time to call in our Air Force," Jerry said.

At that moment, Mike's assistants launched the chemical-bomb-carrying RPVs and turned on their sirens. However, rather than instantly hit the bear with full volume sound effects, a subtle psychological strategy was used. The sirens were turned on just barely loud enough for the bear to hear with the objective of making him think that enemies were slowly sneaking up on him.

The purpose of this strategy was to give the bear a chance to recall his previous painful experience at the hands of the RPVs and to retreat before having to face them. With the steep rock slide behind him, the bear could not quickly retreat, and a sudden confrontation with loudly screaming RPVs might have made it feel cornered. Since cornered animals sometimes charge out of desperation, and the goal was to keep the animal off the plateau to avoid killing it, the slow approach was judged to be the strategy most likely to succeed.

At the first faint sound of the sirens, the bear stopped pawing the ground. He became very still and his ears perked up as he attempted to pinpoint the direction the sound was coming from.

Observing that he had captured the bear's attention, Mike directed the RPV pilots to separate their aircraft by about one hundred yards. After this was done, the pilots flew their RPVs slowly toward the bear while gradually turning up the volume of the sirens.

The bear stared in the direction of each approaching RPV. Then, he intently listened to the RPV approaching from the left. Next, he sniffed the air in an attempt to identify a scent. After this, he gave the same attention to the RPV approaching from the right. Then, the bear slowly crept backwards. After backing over the edge of the plateau onto the rock slide, he stopped his retreat. With his eyes, ears, and nose protruding above the edge of the plateau, the bear tracked the advance of the RPVs.

"It looks like he does not want to face two enemies along with the electric fence. I think we've convinced him to change his plans," Mike said.

"Apparently, he has no desire to repeat his experience with the intense burning pain caused by our chemical bombs," commented Jerry. "Maybe, he did learn something from that experience."

"That might be, but it also looks like he's not yet ready to give up on tracking us," remarked Moose. "He has only retreated far enough to conceal himself from the approaching RPVs."

"Are you suggesting that he's hoping the RPVs won't find him and go away, so that he can then continue tracking us?"

"That is a possibility, or he might be hoping the RPVs will go away, so that he doesn't have to confront them while climbing down that steep rock slide."

"Let's bring back the RPVs and find out what he does," directed Jerry.

A few minutes after the RPVs had been returned, the bear cautiously raised his head, looked around, sniffed the breeze, and intently listened. Then, he climbed over the edge of the plateau and cautiously approached the electric fence. After carefully sniffing it from a distance of a few inches, he stood still for a few moments, apparently deciding what to do next.

"Should we turn on the sirens to help him make up his mind?" Mike asked.

"No!" replied Jerry. "I think he is going to leave. But if he doesn't, turn on the sirens to full volume and approach him at high speed. Hover a few yards away from him and drop some chemical bombs."

Second by second, time ticked away. Jerry proved to be correct. The bear turned and walked toward the rock slide, which he proceeded to scramble down slowly and cautiously.

"I think he has decided that he's up against a force that he's not equipped to defeat," commented Dianne.

"That might be true," replied Jerry, "but I believe that this is a strong-willed animal with a dogged determination to get what he wants. With his obvious size and strength and apparent cunning intelligence, he has the potential to be extremely dangerous. Living here is going to require continuous vigilance, especially if these creatures are frequent visitors to this island."

"It would be helpful to always know where they are," commented Connie.

"When our submarine arrives tomorrow morning, we will use it to travel around this island and install surveillance cameras at key locations, so that we can monitor all of our waterfront," Jerry said. "Then, we can immediately attach a radio transmitter to every animal that comes here and track its movements. In time, we'll learn how serious this problem is. But for right now, I am tired, and I'm going back to bed."

NINE

Feeling at Home

TIME: Day Four.

About a half hour after first sunrise, the interstellar pioneers were enjoying a hearty breakfast when they received a call from Michelle. After the usual greetings, she said, "Your favorite bear is currently eating a shellfish breakfast. If you would turn on one of your video screens, you could watch him via the surveillance camera on Cliff Point."

"Thanks for letting us know," replied Jerry as he turned on the capsule's largest video screen just in time to see the bear break the edge off a clam the size of a large dinner plate. After inserting his front claws into the shell, he pulled it open. Then, he completely ate the contents, even to the point of licking the shell clean.

The bear, which had been sitting, got up, wandered into the water, and swam out a short distance. Then, with only his rump and back legs sticking out of the water, he reached down to the bottom of Rocky Point Bay and grabbed a large shellfish. With the big clam in his mouth, he returned to the beach to eat it.

"That surveillance camera you set up on Cliff Point sure gives us an excellent view of exactly what he's doing," Jerry said to Connie.

"And since he doesn't know that he's being watched, we get to see his natural behavior," replied Connie.

"It looks like he might not have any diving skills and can only eat what he can reach," commented Jerry.

"I think that's true," agreed Dianne. "The hair that we analyzed is hollow with closed ends, so he might have too much buoyancy to be a good diver."

"As big as he is, I would guess that he can reach the bottom in water at least eight feet deep without any real difficulty," commented Jerry. "Being able to harvest shellfish out to a depth of eight feet should give him access to more than enough lake bottom to keep him supplied with food for quite some time."

"Apparently, he decided to have a seafood breakfast after he figured out that he couldn't have us for a midnight dinner," remarked Moose.

"When shellfish are so easy for him to get, I'm wondering why he was stalking us," questioned Jerry.

"Some foods smell better than others," Connie replied. "Your scent probably made the bear think that you guys would taste better than shellfish."

"That's not a very comforting thought," remarked Jerry. "Some foods smell so good that the aroma can make me feel like eating, even when I'm not hungry. If the human scent affects these bears that way, then they are going to be a serious problem for us."

"That's a possibility," agreed Connie, "but it's also possible that the human scent only affects this bear that way. We need to expose more of them to our scent before we'll know how serious the risk is."

"Once we get our network of surveillance cameras set up, we'll be able to monitor all of our waterfront and attach a transmitter to all bears that visit our island," Jerry said. "Knowing where they are, along with always being armed and alert, should reduce our risk of becoming a meal for a bear to almost zero."

Pointing at the video screen, Moose said, "I wonder how many of those shellfish he's going to eat. There are eight empty shells right there where he's sitting."

"Nine, counting the one he's eating," stated Dianne.

"I wonder how big those shellfish get at depths beyond what the bears are able to harvest," questioned Moose.

"When we pass through Rocky Point Bay with our submarine later today, we should check that out and pick up a few of them," suggested Dianne. "If they checkout in the lab, we can have them for dinner."

"Wonderful," exclaimed Connie. While looking at her husband, she asked, "What time are we expecting our sub to arrive?"

Jerry looked at his watch and said, "It should be here in about forty minutes."

The interstellar pioneers finished their breakfast while observing the bear and discussing their plans for the day. Then, they walked to the northeast corner of Stellar Plateau to await the arrival of the large cargo shuttle.

In just a few minutes, they spotted it high in the western sky heading north. About thirty seconds after it passed by, the stillness of the early morning was shattered by the loud thunderclap of a sonic boom. By this time, the shuttle was already several miles north of Pioneer Island, flying at subsonic speeds, and well into its 180-degree turn that would put it on the final leg of its landing approach.

"It's been a few years since I last heard a sonic boom," commented Moose.

Viewing the shuttle with binoculars, Jerry said, "Its flight is a thing of beauty. The turn looks very graceful, and it looks like it's right on course."

A short time later, the shuttle's small stability and control hydrofoils entered the water followed immediately by its large hydrofoils. Its hydro-drogues deployed, rapidly slowing it down to the point where its hull settled into the water. At a speed of about ten miles per hour, the shuttle cruised into East Bay. About 150 yards offshore, it came to a stop.

"Even though it's unmanned, I feel like we have a visitor," remarked Connie.

"That's the kind of comment I'd expect to hear from someone living out in the boondocks who hasn't had company in a long time," commented Dianne. "Surely, we haven't been here so long that you're already craving visitors."

"I guess I'm starting to feel at home, and I'm ready for some friends to stop by for a visit."

"We don't know for sure if they're friends, but we did have a couple creatures drop in to visit us yesterday afternoon."

"That was definitely the high point of my day. I don't believe that I've ever had an unexpected visit from humans that was anywhere near as exciting as the visit from those pterodactyls. I wonder if they'll stop by again sometime."

"It wouldn't surprise me if they do," replied Dianne. "They've started rebuilding that shelter on Western Island, even though the bear that destroyed it is still right here on Pioneer Island. Evidently, they believe that they can defend that site against this bear."

"I wonder why they're so attached to that site. Why don't they just use one of the abandoned shelters we discovered two days ago?"

"Maybe, they aren't abandoned, but just temporarily not in use," speculated Dianne. "Maybe these creatures have a sense of private property and respect each other's property rights."

"Until we know the answer to that question, I think we should respect their property too," stated Jerry.

Looking at each of his fellow pioneers, Moose said, "As soon as you people have resolved the issue of pterodactyl property rights, I think we should go down to the bay and unload our submarine, so we can take it on a checkout cruise."

"Let's do it," stated Jerry.

Twenty minutes later, the pioneers tied their boat to the shuttle and prepared to enter it. Once inside, Moose and Jerry went to the flight deck. They checked instrumentation read-outs to verify that the shuttle's essential systems were in a healthy state. Then, they deployed and inflated the shuttle's pontoons. Next, they opened the large clamshell type doors on the bottom of the shuttle's fuselage. Jerry lowered the submarine about three feet to provide additional space between it and the top of the cargo bay.

Jerry stood up and said, "I'm going into the submarine. When I'm ready, you can lower it into the water. I'll take it down and give it a brief checkout. When I've finished that, we'll unload our wood working equipment and send this shuttle back to the Challenger."

Appearing eager for the adventure, Connie said, "I would like to go with you on the submarine checkout."

Jerry nodded in agreement to his wife's request. Then, he and Connie headed for the cargo bay.

A few minutes later, they were inside the submarine with the hatch closed. Jerry sat at the sub's control console and turned on its systems. Then, he said, "I'm ready. You can lower us into the bay."

Moose turned on the winches that were supporting the submarine. As the winches fed out cable, the submarine slowly dropped out of the shuttle's cargo bay into the water. When the top of the submarine was about ten feet below the bottom of the shuttle's fuselage, Jerry released the support cables allowing the sub to continue falling away from the shuttle. He turned on the sub's electric motor and headed toward the mouth of the bay.

With an overall length of thirty-six feet and a maximum internal diameter of seven feet six inches, the little submarine could accommodate four people on an extended voyage of exploration. Additional people could be carried on shorter voyages.

Most of the submarine's batteries and ballast were contained in its keel, which had a maximum width of fifty-four inches and a depth of forty-six inches. The electric motor, essential equipment, facilities, and instrumentation occupied about half the space inside the main hull leaving the other half for human occupants.

The feature that had the most appeal for humans using the submarine was its transparent plastic hull. Advanced plastics technology made it possible to have a hull stronger and tougher than any that could be built from metal alloys of the same weight and at the same time be as transparent as the highest quality window glass available.

Sitting next to her husband in the submarine's nose, Connie exclaimed, "Wow! What a view! This hull is so clear that it's almost like there's nothing between us and the water."

"It is amazing that such a strong material could be so transparent," commented Jerry.

"I'm also amazed by how quiet this submarine is. I don't hear anything, except the underwater sounds of the lake."

"The capability to cruise silently was designed into this sub, so that we could move among the creatures we want to study without alarming them with lots of noise."

"That feature's also going to make underwater sightseeing trips very peaceful and relaxing," commented Connie.

"Until we become totally familiar with this lake, there's not going to be much difference between an exploration trip and a sightseeing trip."

"Whatever we call them, they are going to be fun."

"They're probably going to be so much fun for everybody, that this submarine is going to be the most popular piece of equipment we have."

"I have no doubt about that," agreed Connie.

After testing the submarine's controls and essential equipment, Jerry and Connie stayed in the underwater world for an additional fifteen minutes to enjoy the fascinating sights and sounds. Then, they surfaced near the cargo shuttle.

When Connie emerged from the submarine, she was greeted by Dianne who was standing on one of the shuttle's wings. Seeing Connie's beaming smile, Dianne remarked, "It looks like you had fun. What was it like?"

"I felt like I was inside a glass bubble submersed in a huge aquarium filled with exotic life-forms, and I was amazed by the remarkable clarity of the water. I could see the underwater landscape for great distances, and I loved its unique, scenic beauty. With the marine explorer, we had the illusion of being underwater, but actually being there is far more exciting. I felt like I was a part of the underwater world that I was viewing. I felt like I was visiting an alien world."

"We are on an alien world."

"But, I felt like I was visiting a separate alien world."

"You mean exploring the depths of this lake is going to be an exotic, scenic adventure," declared Dianne.

"It's a project that I'm eager to begin," stated Connie.

"I am too!" exclaimed Jerry. "Let's get our wood working equipment unloaded, so we can launch this shuttle. Then, we'll pack the equipment up to our camp and have an early lunch. That will leave us the rest of the day to explore the underwater world around our island and set up some of our surveillance cameras."

Two hours later, the interstellar pioneers were on the plateau looking down on the cargo shuttle, which now rested low in the water because its propellant tanks were filled with water. Moose and Jerry had prepared the shuttle for takeoff, and now, the flight control computer would do the rest.

Like a giant that had just awoken, the shuttle came to life and slowly cruised out of East Bay looking for enough open space to flex its muscles and demonstrate its immense power. Upon reaching the vast openness of Clear Lake, the shuttle's nuclear power plant flooded its marine propulsion system with an abundance of energy. Very quickly, the shuttle accelerated to speeds that allowed it to rise up out of the water and ride on its hydrofoils. Then, the powerful NTR thundered to life with an ear-shattering roar, and in a matter of seconds, the large cargo shuttle became airborne and began a steep climb through Alcent's atmosphere. While climbing through the cold upper atmosphere, the extremely hot water vapor pouring out of the NTR's exhaust nozzle condensed into a brilliant white vapor trail dramatically contrasted against the deep blue sky.

"What a spectacular sight, an awesome display of technology and power," Connie commented.

"And the best thing about it is that it's clean power," remarked Jerry. "We are living in a beautiful pristine environment, and I am happy that we have the technology to keep it that way."

"Let's have a quick lunch and go for a submarine ride," suggested Moose.

"That's the first time I've ever heard you suggest that we have a quick meal," commented Dianne.

Moose grinned and said, "I do like to take my time at the dinner table, but I am excited about taking the sub out for a cruise."

"I am too," stated Dianne.

"It won't take long to fry some fish fillets," remarked Connie. "I'll do that, and you can fix the side dishes. In less than an hour, we'll be on our way."

"It's a deal," replied Dianne.

"We should probably take some food with us," suggested Moose. "It might be late by the time we get back."

"That's quite likely," agreed Jerry.

An hour and twenty minutes later, they were in their boat rowing out to the submarine. "We need to build a dock to tie it up to, so we don't have to row out to it whenever we want to use it," Moose said, admiring it.

"With the power saws and tools that came down today, that shouldn't be all that difficult," commented Jerry.

Dianne gazed at Moose and Jerry and suggested, "Before we build a dock, I think we should build an easy-to-use trail up the rock slide to make it easier to get on and off the plateau."

"Good idea," commented Connie.

"It appears that the trail has a higher priority than the submarine dock," Jerry said to Moose.

Moose looked at Dianne and Connie, then at Jerry and said, "That's a valid conclusion."

While they were tying up to the submarine, Jerry said, "Since we have a new toy to play with, I think we should indulge ourselves for a few days before we build the trail and the dock. If the weather stays nice for one more day, I think we should sail over to Sauropod Meadow. I would like to be there waiting for them, when they arrive in the late afternoon to drink water."

Dianne and Connie looked at Jerry with a bit of anxiety written on their faces. Jerry immediately added, "We will, of course, be anchored a safe distance offshore. I just think that it would be extremely exciting to see those huge creatures up close."

"Maybe, we should go over there today, and set up our surveillance cameras tomorrow," suggested Moose.

"We could do that," conceded Jerry, "but our submarine is rather cramped for space at the moment. We have twenty camera packs onboard. If we deploy as many of them as we can today, then we should be able to finish the job tomorrow morning. That will leave the afternoon free for a trip to Sauropod Meadow."

"That is the best plan," admitted Moose.

"We need to tow this boat along for transportation to and from shore," remarked Jerry.

"That's going to put a limit on how deep we can dive."

"How deep do you want to dive?"

After thinking about it for a few moments, Moose said, "I guess we shouldn't have to dive more than fifty to sixty feet to see lots of scenery, since we will be staying close to the island."

"So, if we tow the boat at the end of a rope a couple hundred feet long, it won't interfere with us diving to those depths."

"How much rope did you bring along?" asked Moose.

"Eighty yards," replied Jerry.

A few minutes later, the interstellar pioneers were inside their submarine heading out of East Bay to the first camera installation site. They immediately put the little submarine into a shallow dive, so as to cruise about eight to ten feet above the bottom of the bay.

"This is fantastic!" exclaimed Dianne. "You could not have described it better when you said you felt like you were in a glass bubble submersed in a huge aquarium. That's how I feel. This is amazing!" she exclaimed to Connie. "Multitudes of colorful fish are everywhere, and I feel like there's nothing between us and them. And it's so quiet and peaceful."

"Based on our research with the marine explorer, we knew that it would be like this, but actually being here is much more exciting than the illusion of being here," commented Connie.

"If we're careful to manage the resource well, our new civilization will have lots of exciting fishing for a long time," commented Moose.

"That should be easy," stated Jerry. "All we have to do is not catch more than what we need and avoid polluting the lake."

In less than ten minutes, they arrived at their first camera installation site. After surfacing, they retrieved their small boat and rowed it to shore. While Moose and Dianne stood guard, Jerry and Connie set up the camera and tested it. Then, they went back to the submarine, took it down, and proceeded northward along the east coast of Pioneer Island to the next site.

By mid-afternoon, they arrived at Rocky Point. Since island-hopping bears coming from the north would most likely land here, two cameras were set up to continuously cover every foot of the waterfront.

Then, the pioneers took the little submarine into the depths of Rocky Point Bay. While exploring the bay, Moose commented, "There sure are a lot of those large clams all over the bottom of this bay. I wonder why so many of them live here and so few on the rest of the lake bottom that we've looked at today."

"Apparently, some special conditions exist here that they like," remarked Dianne. "The question is: what are they?"

"Perhaps in time, we will find other clam beds in this lake, and then we can try to determine what they all have in common," stated Moose.

"Do you still want to take a couple of them home with us?" Jerry asked Dianne.

"As late as it's going to be when we get back to our camp, we aren't going to be able to have them for dinner. However, I could do the lab work this evening, and if they check out, we could have them for breakfast. If they turn out to be similar to abalone steak, they are going to be a delicacy."

"I think she's trying to say that we should take a couple of them home with us," remarked Moose. "How do you plan to capture them?"

"I thought we could surface directly over a couple of choice specimens. Then, I will just dive in, swim to the bottom, and grab them."

"It looks like you're not going to have any problem finding choice clams," commented Moose. "Some of these guys are huge, easily two feet wide."

"Well, the water here is about forty feet deep, and apparently, the bears aren't able to reach them at this depth. Forty feet is also a little deeper than I care to go without diving equipment. Let's see what we can find in about fifteen to twenty feet of water."

About a minute later, in water nineteen feet deep, Jerry said, "I'm amazed at how numerous these shellfish are. On average, they're no more than three to four feet apart."

"I think this proves that the bears are unable to dive and can only harvest what they can reach from the surface," commented Moose.

"Well, I am able to dive," stated Jerry as he brought the little submarine to the surface.

"Do you think that it's safe to swim in this water?" asked Connie.

"I have been carefully observing the fish, and I haven't seen any species that aren't in East Bay. Have you?"

"No, I haven't, but I've noticed that the water's not as clear here as what we've explored so far today. I don't know that that's a risk factor; it's just something that I've noticed."

"Maybe that's why the clams are here," remarked Dianne. "The water in this bay might be rich in the organisms that they feed on."

After thinking about it for a few moments, Jerry said, "I don't think the risk is all that great. I am going to go down and get one of those clams. If I don't have any problems, I will go back down and get a second one."

Jerry turned to his wife, "If those tiny organisms make me sick, I will have to see a doctor."

Connie smiled, "I know where you can find a good one."

"Let's take back a bottle of this water, so we can study these organisms," stated Dianne. "Then, if there's a problem, the doctor will be better able to treat it."

"That's a good idea," agreed Connie.

Jerry climbed through the hatch onto the submarine's deck. Then, he pulled the small boat part way in and retied it, freeing up about fifty feet of the rope. Turning to Moose, who had joined him on deck, he said, "Those clams are going to be easier to bring up with this rope than for me to hold onto with one hand while I swim with the other."

After attaching the end of the rope to his waist, Jerry stepped to the edge of the submarine and dove into the water. Still inside the submarine, Connie watched her husband swim straight down to the bottom, select a large clam, and quickly tie the rope around it. Then, Jerry immediately swam back to the surface for air, while Moose hauled up the large shellfish.

"I am amazed at how big this thing is," stated Moose as he pulled a tape measure off his belt to measure the clam. "It is twenty-seven inches long, twenty-two inches wide, and has a maximum thickness of nearly eight inches."

Jerry commented, "I don't know how big the edible parts are, but my guess is that there is more than enough to make a feast for us. So let's not take any more until we find out if they're edible and taste good."

"If they are, we'll have another abundant source of food," remarked Moose.

After securing the clam to the submarine's exterior, the interstellar pioneers proceeded to their next destination and installed another surveillance camera. During the balance of the afternoon, they installed three additional cameras. Then, they returned to East Bay, arriving just as Alpha Centauri A set in the west. Twenty minutes later, they were back at their campsite.

After dinner, Connie, Dianne, and Moose proceeded to do the lab work on the clam and to take a look at the organisms in the water from Rocky Point Bay. Meanwhile, Jerry had a meeting with Mike to discuss the day's events and future plans.

"We still haven't located your mystery bear," Mike said.

"Maybe that bear has already left Pioneer Island," speculated Jerry.

"It's also possible that it's a female that has crawled into a very well concealed den and has given birth to one or more cubs. We don't know anything about these animal's reproductive methods, but it's certainly possible that she might stay with the cubs for a few days."

"Eventually, she will need to come out for food and water. If she goes to the beach for water, one of our surveillance cameras will spot her. After we attach a radio to her, we will find her den. Then, we can send in a little mechanical bug to investigate."

"If she does have cubs, the bug will give us some interesting video."

"In the meantime, we are going to delay going into the forest for the sake of exploration. We certainly don't want to stumble onto a female with cubs. She would probably attack; then, we would have to kill her. I would rather study her and learn how these animals raise their young."

"That's definitely preferable to killing her," remarked Mike.

"Delaying exploration of the forest until we find her isn't going to be a problem. We have plenty of other things to do."

"Your favorite bear spent most of the day sleeping after having clams for breakfast," stated Mike. "Right now, he's wandering south along the west coast of your island."

"It will be interesting to see how he reacts when he comes upon our tracks. Just a few hours ago, we did cross the beach in several places to install cameras."

"If he has any memory at all, your tracks and scent will remind him of the painful experiences he had yesterday."

"With that memory in mind, I would think that he would want to avoid further contact with us and quickly retreat from our spoor. But if he stays put and issues defiant challenging roars when he stumbles upon our spoor, then I will have to conclude that this is a fearless animal and consequently, extremely dangerous."

"If he continues on his present course, we'll soon know his reaction," stated Mike.

After a few moments of silence, Mike asked, "What are your plans for tomorrow?"

"In the morning, we're going to set up as many cameras as we can and hopefully, complete our surveillance network. Then, we're going to eat lunch and sail over to Sauropod Meadow for a close up look at those huge animals. Are we going to have nice weather for one more day?"

"The storm system that's moving in is a big one. It's going to be with you for a few days. You are going to get several inches of rain and some wind, perhaps gusting up to fifty mph. We don't think the rain will arrive before tomorrow night, but the wind is going to pick up sooner than that."

"At lunch time tomorrow, I will need your latest reading on this system."

"We'll have it ready for you," assured Mike.

"What have our pterodactyl neighbors been doing today?"

"They've been busy rebuilding the wrecked shelter. Watching them has been fascinating. They are fast, efficient builders. They know exactly what to do, and their teamwork is excellent."

"How much of it did they rebuild today?"

"They're almost finished, a couple hours in the morning ought to wrap it up. Dianne's colleagues have concluded that these creatures' young are born alive and that this female is nearly ready to give birth."

"That would explain their urgency in rebuilding that shelter."

"I wonder how they plan to defend that site if your favorite bear returns to destroy the shelter again."

"I think they are intelligent enough to have developed a strategy for defending the site, or they would not be rebuilding the shelter."

"That bear tested you twice yesterday. I think he's a very strong-willed creature. It wouldn't surprise me if he were to return to Western Island in search of a baby pterodactyl to eat."

"If he does, it's going to be interesting to see what the defense strategy is," commented Jerry.

At that moment, Michelle appeared on the video screen next to Mike and said, "Your daughter would like to ask you some questions."

Denise stepped in front of Michelle, "Hi Daddy! Is our new home fun? Is it safe? When can I come down?"

For the next half hour, Jerry visited with his daughter, patiently answering all of her questions. Then, Matthew joined Denise and repeated many of the same questions, which Jerry also patiently answered.

After concluding his visit with the children, Jerry stepped outside to enjoy the cool, fresh evening. Looking to the west, he noted the dim orange sun, Alpha Centauri B, hanging low above the horizon. To the east was Aphrodite, which would be in a full moon phase in one more day. High in the southern sky was Nocturne, currently in nearly a half moon phase. "What a bizarre scene," stated Jerry to himself.

For the next half hour, Jerry wandered around the campsite looking at things and pondering the future. Deeply lost in thought, his communicator suddenly started beeping. It was Mike, "Your favorite bear is about to wander upon your spoor. We have the surveillance camera at that location trained on him."

"I would like to see his reaction," stated Jerry as he headed for the capsule. Once inside the capsule, Jerry turned on the largest video screen and tuned in to the signal from the surveillance camera. The screen was filled by the image of a large bear wandering down the beach.

When the bear reached the fresh human tracks, the scent immediately caught his attention. Instantly, he came to full alert. His ears perked up, he intently stared at his surroundings, and he sniffed the breeze. Satisfied that he was alone, the bear followed the spoor to the water's edge. Then, he turned and followed it to the large boulder on which the surveillance camera was mounted. Upon reaching the boulder, he stood up to his full height sniffing the scent trail up the side of the boulder. With his head just clearing the top of the boulder, he stared directly at the camera.

After a few moments, he circled the boulder looking for a continuation of the trail. Unable to find it, he followed the spoor back to the water's edge. After staring out over the water for a few moments, the bear resumed his southward journey along the waterfront.

"What are your thoughts?" Jerry asked.

"I think he remembers and respects his painful experiences of yesterday," Mike responded, "but I don't think he's going to allow those experiences to intimidate him."

"The way that he investigated our spoor seems to support those conclusions. This bear appears to be a stubborn strong-willed creature that is every bit as intelligent as the smartest animals back on Earth."

"It wouldn't surprise me if these bears prove to be more intelligent than the smartest animals back on Earth," commented Mike.

"I wonder if he's going to revisit out electric fence and try to find a way to overcome it."

"I don't know what his destination is, but he is heading in your direction."

"I'm glad we have a radio on him," remarked Jerry. "In fact, it might be a good idea to attach a second radio to him. Since these radios are only glued to the bear's fur, they could be lost if a little fur were shed in that area."

"I'll take care of that the next time he takes a nap."

At this moment, Moose joined the conversation: "I have some good news on the shellfish. They are safe to eat, and I am going to sauté some right now and find out what it tastes like."

"I hope you people don't get fat with all the good things you're finding to eat down there," commented Mike.

Moose retorted, "Are you kidding? With all the physical work we've been doing, it's a struggle just to keep from losing weight."

"That must be difficult for you to deal with," commented Mike.

"What do you mean?" questioned Moose.

"The fact that you can eat all you want and not worry about gaining weight must be putting a real strain on you."

"Yeah, it's a tough situation, but I'm flexible enough to adjust to it," replied Moose.

A short time later, the interstellar pioneers sat down at the dining table to enjoy a bedtime snack of shellfish fillets.

"This reminds me of abalone steak," commented Dianne.

"I think it tastes better than abalone," asserted Connie.

"Since it's been a long time since any of us have had abalone steak, you must have a very good memory to make that claim," noted Dianne.

"Back on Earth, abalone was a delicacy for me. It was a rare treat that I enjoyed very much, but I think this is better."

"You're probably right," remarked Dianne after savoring another piece of the shellfish steak.

"I think it's time we give these creatures a name," declared Moose.

Dianne suggested, "Why don't we just call them abalone, since that's what they taste like."

They enjoyed the delicate flavor and tender texture, and everyone nodded in agreement to Dianne's suggestion. "We seem to have unanimous agreement that these shellfish be called abalone," Jerry said.

"Considering how tasty they are, we're very fortunate to have such an abundant supply of them," Connie commented.

"I agree," stated Jerry, "and I think we should do a thorough study of the conditions that exist in Rocky Point Bay and determine exactly what it is that allows these abalone to thrive there. Then, we need to make sure that we never do anything to jeopardize their environment."

"We've already started that research," stated Dianne. "This abalone's stomach contained the same kinds of organisms that we found in the water we took from the bay. If we can determine why these organisms are so abundant in that bay, then we'll know why the abalone thrive there."

"I wonder how many years it takes them to reach the size of the one that we harvested today," questioned Moose. "How fast they grow will determine the rate at which we can harvest them. We certainly don't want to deplete a resource as delicious as this one."

"That's an important question for the long-term, but from what we saw today, I don't think it's possible for us to deplete this resource in the near-term, if we take only what we need," Jerry commented.

"That's definitely true," agreed Moose. "Even after all of our people are here, we just won't be able to eat that much. We will get at least three meals out of the one we brought home today."

"I like the last part of what you just said," remarked Dianne.

"What do you mean?"

"You spontaneously referred to this campsite as home."

"It really is starting to feel like this is our home," stated Moose. "I guess I'm surprised that I feel like that after only four days."

"It's the food that makes you feel that way," said Jerry in a jovial way.

"I think that's part of it," commented Moose, while savoring a bite of abalone steak. "But as exciting as these four days have been, they are only the beginning. I can spend the rest of my life exploring, fishing, and hunting; and there will be no letup in the excitement. The element of danger will always be present, and the unknown will never be very far away."

"So, in other words, living in an area that fills your life with risk and adventure makes you feel at home," commented Jerry.

"That sums it up quite well."

"I like lots of adventure too, but I really don't need very much risk," remarked Connie.

"After that stunt you pulled with the pterodactyls yesterday afternoon, I believe that you also like taking risks," commented Jerry.

"You're right. That experience did give me an adrenaline rush, but I don't think I was in very much danger. Those pterodactyls never did anything threatening, and I did have my trusty handgun ready for instant action."

"I think we all thrive on some dangerous adventure," remarked Dianne. "There isn't a single person on the Challenger who isn't aching to come down here."

"There's no doubt about that," stated Jerry.

As the evening wore on, the interstellar pioneers continued their lighthearted conversation, deeply enjoying the cozy relaxing atmosphere in their new home. Eventually, fatigue from the day's activities caught up with them, and they reluctantly ended their party and went to bed. Feeling comfortable and secure in their home and optimistic about the future, they settled into a deep peaceful sleep.

TEN

Face-To-Face With Death

TIME: Day Five.

Late dawn, and the eastern sky grew bright in anticipation of Alpha Centauri A peeping over the horizon to begin a new day. Jerry and Connie stepped outside to enjoy the early morning air while Moose and Dianne prepared breakfast. With binoculars in hand, Connie surveyed the vicinity looking for anything of interest. With rifle in hand, Jerry watched the immediate area looking for anything of a threatening nature.

The early morning stillness was pierced by loud shrieks coming from the northwest. Looking in the direction of the shrill screeches, Jerry and Connie saw a pair of pterodactyls diving on and screeching at something in the water off the north end of Western Island.

Focusing in on the scene with her binoculars, Connie said, "It looks like there's a bear swimming towards the island, and the pterodactyls are extremely upset by this. They're making a determined effort to intimidate the bear into staying off the island."

"If that's the bear that's been giving us attention, I don't think he's going to be intimidated. The pterodactyls will need to use force, and despite their size, I don't think they can fight the bear and win, unless they have some clever strategy in mind."

"They just might have an effective strategy. I faced those pterodactyls the day before yesterday, and when I looked into there eyes, I sensed that I was making eye contact with intelligent creatures. I had the distinct feeling that they have advanced brains containing a great deal of wisdom. I also sensed that they aren't wanton killers. At the moment, I think they're making a determined effort to persuade the bear to stay off Western Island, before they resort to force."

"And if persuasion doesn't work, do you think they have a strategy in mind to defeat this bear?"

"I don't think they would've rebuilt the shelter without such a strategy."

"If they are as wise as you think they are, then it makes sense that they would try intimidation before putting themselves at risk in a battle with a large powerful opponent."

At that moment, Jerry's communicator beeped. Upon answering it, Jerry heard Mike say, "Good morning, how do you like the action so far?"

"It has the potential to turn into a savage battle," replied Jerry.

"I think that's a certainty, if your favorite bear continues on his present course. We're getting a good view of the action from the surveillance camera on West Point."

While Mike was talking, Dianne and Moose stepped out of the capsule with binoculars in hand. Moose said, "If there's a battle, I'm betting on the pterodactyls."

"I think that you're right, even though the pterodactyls weigh no more than about four hundred pounds and the bear weighs well over a thousand," Jerry said.

As the bear continued on course getting ever closer to Western Island, the pterodactyls switched from intimidation tactics to inflicting pain. The male swooped down and glided low over the water approaching the bear from the rear. When he reached the bear, he pitched up into a stall stopping his forward motion. Then, as he dropped down, he dug his talons into the bear's rump, inflicting intense pain. Very

226

quickly, the pterodactyl removed his talons and retreated as the bear howled with rage, rolled over, and attempted to grab him.

Undeterred by the painful attack, the bear continued swimming toward Western Island. In a well coordinated second attack, the female pterodactyl dove into the water behind the bear, swam beneath him, and quickly jabbed him in the back with her sharp beak when he rolled over to fend off an attack from the airborne male pterodactyl. Again, the bear howled with rage, but continued on course.

The female pterodactyl surfaced for air a short distance behind the bear. Upon seeing her mate bank into a tight diving turn, she dipped back underwater to swim beneath the bear. Again, she jabbed the bear in the back with her beak when he rolled over to defend against the airborne attack. Again, the bear howled with rage, but continued on course.

"That bear sure doesn't like to be told where he can't go," remarked Moose.

"He's definitely very strong-willed," stated Jerry.

"Apparently, the pterodactyls have decided that the tactics they've been using aren't going to work, because they've returned to the cliff top," observed Dianne.

"I don't think they've given up," commented Mike. "They're squawking back and forth like they're discussing a new strategy."

"I wonder what they're considering," commented Jerry.

"Whatever it is, we'll know shortly, because that bear is only a minute or two away from their island," replied Mike.

Since the Western Island cliff top sloped to the west, the pioneers could not see the pterodactyls directly, so they went into the capsule to watch them on the video screen. What they saw amazed them. The two pterodactyls were calmly walking around on the cliff top looking at rocks. When they found rocks of the right size and shape, each pterodactyl picked up a rock with each of its feet, took off, and flew in the direction of the bear.

The bear was now wading ashore. Once completely out of the water, he stopped on the rocky beach to shake water out of his fur. The pterodactyls circled the bear at an altitude of about five hundred feet.

"Those rocks must weigh at least fifty to sixty pounds each," remarked Jerry. "I don't know how accurately they can drop them, but if they hit the bear in the head, he is going to have a severely fractured skull. It seems like that kind of injury would kill the bear."

"We'll soon know," remarked Moose. "The female is ready to begin her bomb run."

Swooping into a shallow dive, the female pitched up into a stall directly over the bear. Satisfied with her position, she released both rocks. The rocks missed the bear by only a few feet, but one of them struck a large rock on the beach with such a hard impact that it shattered. A jagged softball-sized fragment hit the bear squarely in the side of the head, opening a gash, and momentarily stunning him.

Within seconds, the pair of rocks dropped by the male pterodactyl came crashing down. One of the rocks grazed the bear's ribs on his right side causing a painful abrasion. The other rock hit the gravel beach a few feet in front of the bear kicking sand and gravel into his face.

Unable to physically retaliate against his tormentors, the bear stood up on his hind legs, looked up at the circling male pterodactyl, and issued a loud defiant roar. The male pterodactyl screamed loudly in return.

Meanwhile, the female pterodactyl had quickly returned to the cliff top. There, she picked up a 100-pound piece of driftwood leftover from the shelter-building project. With a sense of urgency, she carried it over the roaring bear and released it.

Upon seeing the log falling toward him, the bear grudgingly accepted the precariousness of his position, dropped to all four legs, and charged into the forest. Pushing his way into an unusually thick clump of trees, the bear sought protection from the aerial bombardment. The male pterodactyl circled low over the thicket making sure the bear stayed put.

Already feeling mild early contractions indicating the onset of labor, the female pterodactyl returned to the cliff top. There, she made herself comfortable next to the nearly completed shelter and waited for nature to take its course.

Fascinated by the encounter, the interstellar pioneers reflected on the implications of what they had just witnessed. Moose commented, "I'm impressed by the way the pterodactyls warded off the bear without putting themselves in jeopardy."

"They aren't out of danger yet," remarked Jerry. "The tree that allows the bear access to the cliff top is still there, and the bear is on Western Island."

"Also, it looks like the female may be in labor," speculated Connie. "If she gives birth shortly, and the bear picks up the scent, he may sense the vulnerability of the situation and attempt to take advantage of it."

"He still has the male to contend with," stated Jerry. "While climbing the tipped tree to get to the cliff top, he will be exposed to attack. The male pterodactyl could allow the bear to climb most of the way to the cliff top and then attempt to knock him off the tree. A fall of forty feet would either kill or cripple him."

"And the bear would have to endure a bombardment of rocks while in route to the tree," commented Moose.

"If he's running fast and uses the forest for cover, he will be difficult to hit," countered Jerry.

"We could eliminate the problem by dropping that tree," suggested Connie. "These pterodactyls did stop by to investigate us the day before yesterday. While we can only speculate on their motives, it is possible that they would like to have a cordial relationship with us."

"Dropping that tree would solve an urgent problem for them and show them that it could be advantageous to be friends with us," stated Dianne.

"After what we've just seen, there's no doubt in my mind that it would be to our advantage to have them as friends," declared Moose. "Despite our weapons and technology, they could make our lives miserable through patient intelligent use of their capabilities."

"There's no longer any doubt in my mind that they are able to think and communicate," stated Connie. "With millions of them living on this planet, they could jeopardize our efforts to begin a new civilization if they decide that we are a threat to their way of life. I think we should demonstrate our desire to be friends with them by dropping that tree. Then, we should go about our normal daily activities and wait for them to make the next move."

"We could do it with an explosive charge delivered by an RPV," suggested Moose.

"The blast might be very nerve-wracking to the female currently giving birth," commented Dianne.

"To achieve our objective, we have to bring it down in such a way that the pterodactyls know that we are the ones who brought it down," stated Jerry. "That means that we have to go over there and be seen bringing it down. We could cut it down with a chain saw, or we could fire explosive bullets into it."

"The rifle shots and exploding bullets might be very alarming to the female," commented Connie.

"I guess that means we're going to cut it down with a chain saw," stated Jerry.

"That is a risky course of action," remarked Moose. "If the male pterodactyl decides to drop rocks on us, we will have to shoot the creature we're trying to help."

"If Dianne and I take the lead when we get to Western Island, I don't think that will happen," declared Connie. "After all, we did have a friendly encounter with them just two days ago. Besides that, both pterodactyls are preoccupied. One is busy giving birth, and the other is watching a known enemy."

"Let's not forget that we haven't yet explored Western Island, and we don't know what hazards we'll encounter in the forest on the way to the cliff," remarked Moose.

"There are risks involved," Jerry said quickly, "but we do have an opportunity to demonstrate to these pterodactyls that it will be to their advantage to be friends with us. Despite the risks involved, I believe we must go to Western Island and drop that tree, and we have to do it now before the opportunity disappears."

"How they react to us doing that will, at the very least, give us some insight into how their minds work," commented Connie. "Will they be appreciative and find a way to show their appreciation, or will they completely ignore the fact that we did them a big favor?"

"The answer to those questions will indicate to us if there's any potential for achieving a mutually beneficial relationship with them," remarked Jerry.

The interstellar pioneers quickly gobbled down their breakfast. Then, after picking up their electric chain saw, its battery pack, and their weapons, they headed for their submarine. Once onboard the submarine, they cruised around the south end of Pioneer Island and went directly to the west side of Western Island. While in route, Jerry put on a headset, launched an RPV, and investigated the forest between the tipped tree and their anticipated landing point.

Upon reaching their objective, they anchored the sub, stepped into their boat, and rowed to shore. The male pterodactyl, still circling above the thicket in which the bear had taken refuge, noticed this and flew over to investigate. Connie and Dianne stepped out of the boat onto the shore. Standing straight and tall they looked up at the circling pterodactyl and tried to appear friendly. After circling them only once, the pterodactyl returned to the bear.

"Apparently, he recognizes us as friendly," remarked Connie.

"With a known enemy to watch, I don't think he will bother us," commented Jerry.

After strapping the chain saw onto his back, Jerry picked up his rifle and led the small group into the forest along the route he had just explored. With the battery pack strapped to his back and rifle in hand, Moose performed rear guard duty. After cautiously making their way through about 150 yards of forest, they arrived at the tipped tree.

When they looked up the tree to determine how to bring it down, they saw the male pterodactyl perched on the edge of the cliff looking down at them. "Apparently, he doesn't completely trust us," commented Dianne.

"I think he's just being cautious," remarked Connie. "With his mate giving birth, I don't blame him; especially, since he's only had one encounter with us on which to base his judgment."

"Based on that encounter, he has no reason to believe we are anything other than friendly," stated Dianne.

"But he has no way of knowing what our intentions are," remarked Jerry, "and the sooner we start sawing, the sooner he will know why we're here."

"Unless we climb about half way up this tree, it's going to take several cuts to bring it down," commented Moose. "If we cut it off at the bottom, it will still be leaning against the cliff. If we cut it off about half way up, then I think it will dislodge itself from the cliff when it falls."

Looking up at the alert pterodactyl perched on the edge of the cliff, Jerry asked, "Are you brave enough to climb half way up this tree?"

"All things considered, I don't think that would be a wise thing to do."

"Well, let's start sawing then," stated Jerry as he plugged the saw into its battery pack. "While I'm sawing I want you to be alert for that bear. The thicket he took refuge in is less than two hundred yards north of here."

While Moose moved into position to guard approaches from the north, Jerry spoke to Dianne, "I would like you to guard us from the south." To Connie, Jerry said, "That leaves the west for you to watch."

"Who's going to keep an eye on the pterodactyl?" asked Connie.

"When I turn this saw on, I think he will figure out what's happening."

Jerry selected a point about six feet up the tree and started sawing. When the saw started biting into the tree spewing out copious amounts of sawdust, the pterodactyl came to full attention and watched with keen interest. In a matter of seconds, the saw sliced through the tree, and Jerry quickly stepped back as the tree slid down the cliff a few feet while its bottom end dropped to the ground.

The pterodactyl nimbly hopped backwards a few feet in surprised reaction to the tree's movement. Then, Jerry made a second cut about six feet up the tree and quickly stepped back when the tree again slid down a few feet. Now, it fully dawned on the pterodactyl what was happening, and he excitedly started hopping around the top end of the tree in anticipation of its disappearance from the cliff top.

After three more cuts, Jerry decided that what was left of the tree was in a very unstable position and that one more cut would bring it down. After determining where it would fall and warning the others, Jerry made the final cut and quickly stepped out of the way while the remainder of the tree fell away from the cliff.

The big male pterodactyl looked down at the fallen tree and the man with the chain saw. Then, he hopped around making some squawking sounds.

"It sure looks like he's dancing around in celebration of this tree being gone," commented Connie.

"He has reason to celebrate," declared Dianne. "The bear no longer has access to the cliff top, and his mate is giving birth."

"Now, he's looking at us and clapping his wings against his sides, and that sure looks like applause," remarked Connie.

"I get that feeling too," stated Jerry.

After watching the pterodactyl celebrate for a few moments, Jerry said, "With a young one currently being born and with a rain storm due to arrive tonight, I'll bet that they could use some pine boughs to finish up their baby's shelter. So I am going to cut a bunch of the smaller branches off the top end of this tree. Then, we'll find out if they make use of them."

While the big male pterodactyl watched with interest, Jerry quickly cut most of the branches off the upper part of the tree. When he finished this task, he looked up at the big pterodactyl. The creature stared directly at Jerry establishing eye contact. After a few moments in which he seemed to be searching for a way to communicate, he again clapped his wings against his sides.

Not knowing how best to respond, Jerry simply smiled broadly, raised his right hand, and waved at the big pterodactyl. Seeming to sense that Jerry was saying good-by and wishing him well, the big pterodactyl nodded his head as if to say he understood. Then, the pioneers picked up their equipment and returned to their submarine.

After using the rest of the morning to install surveillance cameras at key locations on the south end of Pioneer Island, they returned to their campsite for lunch. During lunch they discussed their options for the rest of the day.

"I think sailing over to Sauropod Meadow this afternoon is really going to be fun," stated Dianne.

"That would be fun, but we still have four cameras to set up," remarked Jerry.

"Do we have to set them up today?" inquired Connie while looking at her husband.

Jerry quietly read the facial expressions of each of his colleagues, then commented, "If I say yes to that question, it looks like I might have a mutiny on my hands."

They all laughed at Jerry's comment, then Moose said, "According to Mike, this afternoon is the last good weather we're going to have for several days. If need be, we can set up those four remaining cameras between showers, but rain would sure take a lot of the fun out of a sailing trip."

"I could not have said that any better myself," stated Jerry. "So, let's finish our lunch and go sailing."

"I wonder how long it will be before the pterodactyls visit us again?" questioned Connie.

"I think they're going to be busy with their infant for a while," commented Dianne while she turned on the largest video screen and tuned in to a camera that had been placed on the Western Island cliff top with an RPV. As Dianne panned the area, images appeared that showed the female resting in the sun with her infant snuggled against her. The male was busy finishing the shelter, meticulously weaving pine boughs into it from the bottom to the top.

"It didn't take him long to figure out what to do with all those branches you cut off that tree," Dianne remarked to Jerry.

"The way he's overlapping them, it looks like he's had roofing experience," commented Jerry. "There's no way that it's going to be leak proof, but he sure is making an effort to have it shed water. I wonder if he can sense the drop in atmospheric pressure and know that rain is on the way."

"That's possible," remarked Dianne, "but he may be just doing this because the infant has already arrived and you provided him with the materials."

"They sure look content," observed Connie.

"They should," declared Dianne. "They have what appears to be a healthy infant, and the bear is no longer a threat."

Jerry said, "I wonder what the bear is up to now."

"I checked on him a short time ago," responded Moose, "and he was still in the thicket nursing his wounds. In fact, he was sleeping. I think he will stay there until tonight and then leave Western Island."

"It wouldn't surprise me to find him eating abalone tomorrow morning," commented Jerry. "I wonder how long it will be before he leaves Pioneer Island."

"As long as he has plenty of abalone to eat, he will probably stay, unless he gets tired of eating them," remarked Moose.

"I wonder if there's anything else here on the island for him to eat," asked Connie.

"We've found lots of coconut shells but only one coconut," stated Dianne. "Something ate them."

"If these nuts ripen in the fall and drop off the trees during the winter, they would be a wintertime source of food for the bears," Connie said.

"If they eat them," remarked Dianne.

"If our bears are anything like Earth's bears, there isn't much that they won't eat," commented Moose, "but if they're like Earth's bears, they should be hibernating in the wintertime."

"If they have a year 'round food supply, they have no need to hibernate," stated Dianne.

"I am starting to think that bears might be permanent residents of the islands here in Clear Lake," commented Jerry.

"If these islands provide them with an ample supply of food besides security from T-Rexes, then they would seem to be ideal habitat for them," agreed Moose.

"I think the adult bears have enough speed and intelligence to elude the T-Rexes," commented Jerry.

"But on these islands, they wouldn't have to be concerned about T-Rexes," stated Moose.

"That makes these islands prime sites for females with cubs and for bears too old to run from the T-Rexes," commented Dianne.

"Does that mean that Pioneer Island might be both a retirement home and a maternity ward for bears?" questioned Connie.

"That's a possibility," remarked Jerry.

"When we were still in space, I had assumed that raising children here on Alcent would require constant vigilance," Connie commented. "But when we discovered Pioneer Island, I'd hoped that we would be isolated from all the large dangerous creatures and wouldn't have to be continuously on guard. A constant bear problem sure dashes that hope."

"In time, we'll learn how serious the problem is and take appropriate steps to deal with it," declared Jerry. "To start with, we can make this plateau inaccessible to bears. That will give our children a large area on which to run around in safety."

"You're assuming that the pterodactyls won't be a threat to our children," commented Moose.

"It looks like we may be able to develop a friendly relationship with the ones we assisted this morning," speculated Jerry.

"That may be," remarked Moose, "but let's not forget that while most humans are kindhearted, some are evil predators. I am assuming that pterodactyls also have varied personalities. The ones that we've made friends with might be benevolent toward us, but some of those that don't know us might try to prey on us."

"Until we have reason to believe otherwise, I think we should assume that to be the case," stated Jerry.

The interstellar pioneers finished their lunch, packed a generous supply of food and beverages for their sailing trip, and headed for their submarine. Once onboard, they decided to sail on the surface to enjoy the beautiful day.

One feature that helped make sailing on the surface enjoyable was the little submarine's spacious deck. Mounted just above the hull, the deck was eight feet across at its widest point and had a maximum length of twenty-eight feet.

Along each side of the submarine, just below the deck, were two plastic tubes that extended nearly its entire length. Each tube contained a deflated pontoon and was attached to telescoping booms mounted on top of the submarine. When the booms were extended to their full length, the pontoon-containing tubes would be twenty-one feet out from the submarine's hull. With the pontoons inflated, the submarine's telescoping mast could be extended upward and its main sail deployed, thereby converting the submarine into an outrigger-type sailboat.

However, if there was insufficient wind to operate a sailboat and if the sky was clear and sunny, then the submarine's solar sails could be effectively used. These were rolled up inside tubes mounted on each side of the submarine. To deploy the solar sails, they were simply unrolled and laid out horizontally along the tops of the booms supporting the outrigger pontoons. During the heat of the day, the energy radiating down onto the solar sails from Alpha Centauri A would produce forty to forty-five kilowatts of electrical power.

"I'm glad we're going to sail on the surface," commented Connie, "it will give us an opportunity to enjoy this beautiful day."

"And we'll have an opportunity to check this boat's capabilities as a sailboat," stated Moose.

"If Mike's weather forecast is correct, we'll have plenty of wind by late afternoon to do that, but right now, we have no wind, so let's use our solar sails," Jerry said.

Moose and Jerry deployed the outrigger pontoons and inflated them. Then, they deployed the solar sails. With a nearly clear sky and Alpha Centauri A almost directly overhead, the solar sails generated 43.6 kilowatts of electrical power.

"We have enough power to make a quick trip out of this," declared Moose. "But I think a slow quiet trip would be much more enjoyable."

"Let's cruise at about four miles per hour," stated Jerry. "That will give us a couple hours to be lazy while in route, and we can use the surplus electrical power to bring our batteries back to a full charge."

"A leisurely cruise on a large pristine lake; what a pleasant way to have a relaxing afternoon," remarked Connie.

"It sounds like you approve of my plan to cruise slowly."

"How could I possibly disapprove? I am ready to kick back and relax for a few hours, and I am going to begin the afternoon with some serious sunbathing. When I've had my fill of that, I'll go below deck and enjoy viewing the underwater world for a while."

"All that strenuous activity seems like too much of a burden for one person," commented Dianne. "I think I'll join you, in case you need help."

While Dianne and Connie made themselves comfortable on a couple air mattresses, Jerry piloted the vessel out of East Bay. Moose went below deck and entertained himself by observing the underwater world and devising strategies to catch some of the fish he was seeing.

When they were out of East Bay, Jerry turned control of the boat over to its navigation computer. Then, he made himself comfortable on an air mattress next to his wife.

For a few minutes, Jerry basked in the warm radiant energy pouring down on him from Alpha Centauri A. He listened to the gentle lapping of small waves against the side of the boat. This soft splashing sound had a relaxing hypnotic effect on Jerry that nearly put him to sleep. But the sudden screeching cries of a passing gull-like seabird snapped him out of his sleepy mental state. Jerry looked up at the bird and watched it soar out of sight; then, he turned his attention to his boat. He listened intently in an attempt to hear the boat's electric motor and propeller, but no matter how hard he strained his hearing, he was unable to hear the motor or the propeller. Jerry deeply appreciated the quietness of the boat and the sensation of just silently drifting along.

In the laziness of the afternoon warmth, Jerry became aware of a gentle breeze that was kicking up, and he enjoyed its pleasant caressing effect. Reveling in this pleasure, Jerry gazed upward and noted that the sky had a beautiful deep blue color. Against this deep blue backdrop, there were a few fluffy cumulus clouds floating around.

He closed his eyes and let his mind wander. The first thought that entered his mind was that he was deeply enjoying the pleasures of sailing. He thought about the fact that he was sailing on a huge lake, a lake with 700 square miles of water. He noted that he and his three colleagues were the only people on this lake, on the entire planet for that matter. He recalled sailing outings when he felt like he was hemmed in by all the other boats. What a contrast this was! Jerry loved the vastness of the lake, but for a few moments, the thought of being one of only four humans on the entire planet made him feel lonely.

Jerry lazily rolled over onto his right side. He lifted his upper body and supported it by leaning on his right elbow. "I am glad you're here," he said, facing his wife.

Connie looked at Jerry, puzzled, "What prompted that comment?"

"Look around you. What do you see?"

Connie did as directed, "I see mile after mile of open water."

"That's what prompted my comment. We are four lone humans. We are isolated. There is no one else here."

"You almost sound troubled by that."

"I'm not troubled by it. I was just thinking about how crowded Earth is. Billions of people live there. By contrast, there are only four people on this planet, which is about the same size as Earth."

"What motivated you to think about that at this time?"

"I was thinking about past sailing outings and how little space there was to maneuver on some of them. Those memories made me appreciate the vastness of this lake and the fact that we have it completely to ourselves. We don't have to compete with anyone for a share of a limited space."

"How did that prompt you to turn to me and say that you're glad I'm here?"

"The downside of being the only people here hit me hard for a few moments."

"Are you going to tell me what you were feeling during those few moments?" Connie asked.

Jerry looked into his wife's eyes and felt that she was sincere in her effort to understand what was going on in his mind. So, he collected his thoughts and said, "I need to back up a bit to give you a good explanation."

"Take your time; I'm not going anywhere."

"In recent days, recent weeks for that matter, we've been extremely busy. We've taken very little time off. This sailing trip is being done purely for recreation. We're enjoying the pleasures of sailing while going sightseeing. I am enjoying this very much. I was laying here thinking about how nice it is to have this whole place to ourselves, but then, I was struck by a scary thought: What if I were the only person here? The thought of not having anyone to share this with made me feel lonely. That is when I turned to you and said, 'I am glad you're here'."

Connie thought about Jerry's comments and tried to imagine herself living on Pioneer Island with the knowledge that she was the only human on the planet. "Being here alone would be a difficult and lonely life. I'm not sure that I could handle that," she said.

"On a lighter note, I am glad that recreational sailing stimulates your thinking in a way that makes you appreciate my presence, because I would like to spend a few days sailing around on this lake purely for the sake of fun."

"Your presence would definitely be appreciated on such a voyage."

Up to this point, Dianne had politely remained silent, because she did not want to interfere in Connie and Jerry's conversation, but now, she said, "That kind of sailing voyage would be fun. I hope I'm included."

"I think we could find a spot on the crew for you," Jerry said.

"Good! I would enjoy a few days of sailing, but I would like to do a much longer voyage."

"What do you have in mind?" asked Jerry.

"I would like to sail completely around this lake staying close to shore. I think such a voyage would be thrilling and interesting. It would give us an opportunity to see the many plants and animals that live in the countryside."

"This vessel is so quiet that it just might be ideal for observing wild animals along the waterfront," commented Connie. "It's possible that many of them wouldn't even be disturbed by our presence."

"It would be almost like driving through a large nature-land zoo and observing wild animals that are free to roam in a replica of their natural habitat," commented Jerry.

"This area might be a fairly accurate replica of a scene from ancient Earth," Connie said. "Many of the creatures that we'll see here will make us feel like we've traveled back in time to Earth's dinosaur age."

"We'll never have an opportunity to experience time travel to Earth's dinosaur age, but for the rest of our lives, we will have ample opportunity to observe and interact with dinosaurs," Jerry replied. "A cruise around this lake would be a good way to familiarize ourselves with some of them."

"And in just a few hours, we'll have our first opportunity to get close to what might be the largest and most intelligent land animals on this planet," stated Connie. "Think about it! We are going to approach animals that are many times larger than any that humans have ever seen."

"How close to them are we going to get?" asked Dianne.

"That will depend on how they react to us," replied Jerry. "If they aren't overly alarmed by our presence, we might sail quite close to shore, so that we can really appreciate their immense size."

"I think I would like to appreciate their size from a safe distance," stated Connie.

"That's a thought that I can relate to," remarked Dianne.

"After the fearless way both of you faced those pterodactyls two days ago, I wouldn't think that you would be afraid to get close to the sauropods," bantered Jerry.

"I don't think you should assume that we were without fear," remarked Dianne.

"Don't forget, we had a safe haven to quickly retreat to," added Connie. "Those sauropods are so big that you would need a well-built concrete bunker as a safe shelter to retreat to if they decided to attack."

"As small as we are relative to them, they'll probably think us to be insignificant and not a threat," commented Jerry.

"Being viewed as insignificant by members of the animal world could very well be a new experience for members of the human species," remarked Connie.

"That would not be very flattering to my ego," stated Dianne.

"It wouldn't be very flattering, but the practical consequences might be significant," commented Jerry. "If the sauropods think we are too small to be a threat to them, they might ignore our presence. Then, we might be able to move around the area in relative safety by simply staying in their midst."

"That would take some getting use to," stated Dianne.

"I'm not sure that I'm ready to go hiking with creatures that weigh up to one hundred tons," remarked Connie.

"But what an adventure it would be," declared Jerry.

"Sailing around the lake and observing the countryside from the safety of this boat would be adventuresome enough for me," stated Connie.

"Besides seeing the countryside, such a voyage would also give us an opportunity to study aquatic life," commented Dianne. "If the water in the rest of this lake is as clean as it is around Pioneer Island, then our transparent hull will make aquatic research easy."

"It sounds like both of you prefer the sailing voyage over a hiking trip with the sauropods."

Dianne and Connie looked at each other with incredulous expressions. "I can't believe he's serious about the hiking trip," Dianne said.

"Whether I'm serious or not, you'll have to admit that it is possible that we could make such a trip."

"It will be quite simple to test your theory," remarked Dianne. "When we arrive at Sauropod Meadow, we can send Charlie ashore and have him wander into the herd and watch how they react to his presence."

"I am planning to do that," replied Jerry.

"However that experiment turns out, I still prefer sailing," declared Connie.

"There's no doubt that exploring this lake's coastal regions would be a super adventure," remarked Jerry.

"And it would be a quick way to survey the countryside around our lake and the life that populates it," stated Connie.

"I don't know how quick it will be," commented Jerry. "This is a big lake with several hundred miles of coastline. An around-the-lake voyage could easily take a week, especially if we conduct the voyage in a leisurely way so that we have plenty of time to relax and enjoy it."

"I like the last part of what you just said," remarked Connie.

"I do too," agreed Dianne. "A slow, leisurely voyage is not only the best way to have the most enjoyment, but it is also the way that is most likely to result in us learning the most about the countryside and the life that inhabits it."

"From the way you two are talking, I think this voyage could easily take much longer than a week," Jerry said.

"Even if the trip takes longer than a week, I think we should make it anyway," commented Connie.

Jerry looked at this wife, "You seem to have your heart set on doing it."

"It would be an exciting adventure and lots of fun."

"I sense that there's more to it than that."

"There is."

"What?"

"I think such a voyage could aid our medical research."

"How?"

"Our primary reason for being here is to find out if the human immune system can effectively deal with the microorganisms that are here. It seems reasonable to assume that the more of this area that we are exposed to, the more microorganisms our immune systems will be exposed to. The more exposure we have, the more meaningful our medical research should be."

"You make it sound like we are lab animals taking part in a research project," commented Jerry.

"That is the reality of what we're doing," stated Connie.

Dianne said, "In addition to direct exposure, there is another way the voyage could help our medical research."

"What way is that?" asked Jerry.

"We could conduct a direct search for dangerous microbes by collecting water, soil, and air samples for later analysis. Also, if we see any sick animals, we can use an RPV to collect tissue and waste material specimens for analysis and attempt to isolate the germ that caused the illness."

"You're putting a lot of work into my pleasure trip," commented Connie.

"That's true, but the opportunity to gain information will be too good to pass up."

Connie nodded in agreement. "I'm ready to sail around the lake even though Dianne is trying to take all the fun out of it by filling it up with work," she said to Jerry.

"I'm not trying to fill the voyage with work; I'm just trying to sell your husband on the idea of making the voyage," Dianne answered.

"I don't think it's a tough sell," replied Connie. "I think he wants to go too."

"That's true, but he has everything on a prioritized list, and we just have to motivate him to put the sailing trip near the top of the list."

As Dianne finished speaking, she and Connie turned to Jerry and smiled at him expectantly.

Jerry switched his gaze back and forth between them as they silently waited for his reaction. After a few thoughtful moments, Jerry said, "If Mike's weather forecast is correct, we are going to have stormy wet weather for the next several days. After that, let's plan on cruising around this lake."

Dianne and Connie turned to each other glowing with expressions of satisfaction. They nodded to Jerry in acknowledgment of his proposal.

Jerry thought about the proposed sailing trip for a few moments. "To add to the adventure, Moose and I might find some safe looking areas where we can go ashore and look around for a while."

"That sounds too dangerous," commented Dianne. "I really don't want my husband going ashore. I could end up losing him."

Looking worried, Connie said, "I share Dianne's concern. The countryside is a dangerous place. Do you and Moose need to take that much risk?"

"We would be very cautious. Besides, we would only be doing this to aid your medical research."

"In what way?" asked Connie.

"Correct me if I am wrong, but I think you said that the more of this area that we are exposed to, the more meaningful your medical research will be."

Connie smiled at how easily her husband had used her words to make a point. She turned to Dianne and said, "He is right about that."

However, Dianne was not convinced, "I still don't like the idea of Moose going ashore. The very thought scares me."

Noticing how deeply worried Dianne looked, Jerry said, "I've known Moose for a long time, and he's not going to do anything stupid that could get him killed."

"You don't know him as well as I do. With his driving spirit of adventure, it wouldn't surprise me if he found a way to stumble into an unarmed confrontation with a T-Rex."

"Before going ashore, we would thoroughly scout the area with RPVs. T-Rexes are very big animals. I don't see how we could miss their presence."

"What you're saying is true, but I think Moose could unintentionally find a way to have a confrontation with one of those brutes."

"I think you worry too much," commented Connie.

"That might be, but we've waited a long time to build a home and have children. And I don't want to risk losing him now."

"So, that's it," Connie said. "You are on the verge of realizing a dream, and you fear that something might still happen to prevent that."

Dianne nodded silently.

"We live on a dangerous planet, but we must live our lives fully," Connie continued. "We must not take foolish unnecessary risks, but neither should we avoid all adventure because it might be dangerous. We must carefully evaluate the risks, plan for them, and then go forward."

Dianne thought about Connie's comments. "You are, of course, correct, but I will still be worried if Moose goes ashore."

With their travel plans decided upon, Jerry wandered around on deck and gazed out over the lake in all directions. The northern and southern shores were about twenty miles away and could not be seen. This gave Jerry an immediate appreciation for the vastness of Clear Lake and the knowledge that might be gained by exploring its waterfront. Jerry thought about how dangerous the now placid lake would become during a violent wind storm that would generate huge waves. This made Jerry appreciate the utility of the vessel he was sailing, for a powerful wind storm could be dealt with by simply retracting the sails and outriggers and diving to depths not affected by a storm on the surface.

As Jerry's gaze shifted eastward to Sauropod Meadow, he thought about the huge creatures that lived there. Realizing that a lifelong fantasy of standing in the immediate vicinity of dinosaurs was about to come true, Jerry's pulse quickened with excitement. For several minutes, he stared in the direction of Sauropod Meadow and wondered about the possibility of spending a day wandering around with the huge sauropods. Then, he went to his supply pack and removed a video headset. After stretching out on an air mattress, he put on the headset and tuned in to the signals coming from the camera pack mounted on the primary horn of the sauropod herd leader. Jerry soon became engrossed in the sights and sounds coming from the vicinity of the sauropods and imagined himself being with them. The fantasy seemed very real, because the sights and sounds coming into Jerry's headset gave him the illusion of sitting on the herd leader's head.

Meanwhile, Dianne and Connie were busy basking in the radiant heat pouring down from Alpha Centauri A. The warmth had an almost sensual effect, which was magnified by the gentle breeze caressing them. Taking advantage of the pure laziness of the situation, Dianne allowed her mind to wander through fantasies that seemed appropriate for the occasion. When she reached the point where her fantasies were no longer satisfying, she turned to Connie and said, "I'm going below deck to help my husband enjoy the underwater scenery."

Dianne winked at Connie, "Don't disturb us for a while."

Connie grinned, "I think we'll stay here on deck until one of you returns. We wouldn't want to interrupt a deeply penetrating research project at a critical moment."

"That would be a bit frustrating," replied Dianne as she disappeared below deck.

Having grown tired of lying down, Connie decided to wander around on deck and gaze out over the lake. She marveled at the quiet peacefulness that seemed to be everywhere. Starting with the vessel she was riding, she noted that it seemed to be just quietly drifting along. Try as she might, she could not sense even the slightest sound or vibration. So well designed and insulated for sound was the vessel's electric motor that its operation could not be detected by the human ear. Likewise, its large low-speed propeller was meticulously sculpted for silent operation.

Gazing out over the lake, Connie thought, what a contrast to lakes on Earth where on a beautiful day like this, the water would be crowded with boats of all types, thereby destroying the peacefulness of the afternoon. Here, there are only sea birds, and occasionally, a fish jumping out of the water.

Surveying the sky in all directions, Connie noted three widely separated pairs of pterodactyls at high altitude. Judging from the seemingly effortless way that they were soaring around like sail planes, they appeared to be flying purely for the pleasure of it.

I love the peaceful solitude of this area, thought Connie. We are very fortunate to have such a wonderful place to build our home. We must make every possible effort to maintain this area in its pristine condition. With our technology, we should be able to live a prosperous life and harmonize with our environment in such a way that we preserve all of its wondrous beauty.

For the next half hour, Connie continued to soak up the peaceful serene beauty of her surroundings while lost in thought. She was abruptly jarred out of her meditative mental state by Jerry who had removed his video headset, sneaked up behind her, and placed his hands on her waist.

Quickly recovering, she turned to him, gave him a big hug, and declared: "It's absolutely wonderful out here! Our new home is turning out to be everything that I'd hoped it would be."

"How is everything in the world of the sauropods?" she asked.

"When I removed my headset, they were peacefully eating virtually every kind of plant life that could possibly be edible. I wonder how much food a 100-ton animal needs to consume in a day to sustain itself."

"I don't have an answer to that question, but it's possible that an adult sauropod might eat as much in a day as a hundred head of cattle."

"Whatever the amount, as healthy as they look, they apparently aren't having any problem keeping themselves well-fed," remarked Jerry.

"Well, this area is filled with lush vegetation, and the climate is conducive to rapid growth of plant life. The plants they munch on probably generate new growth and restore themselves rather quickly."

At that moment, Dianne appeared from below deck closely followed by Moose, who said, "What a fascinating lake this is. I am amazed by the broad variety of fish that live here. I would like to be personally responsible for figuring out how to catch fish in each species."

"I really don't think that it's fair to expect you to do that entire project by yourself," remarked Jerry.

"I don't think so either," agreed Dianne. "That's just too much responsibility for one person."

"What you're trying to say is that it would be too much fun for one person," responded Moose.

Jerry looked at Dianne and said, "Your husband sure has good insight into what other people are thinking."

"He's always been very good at recognizing the obvious," said Dianne, good-naturedly.

"You people can tease me all you want," retorted Moose, "but the fact is, sports fishing is one of my areas of expertise. And out of the goodness of my heart, I am willing to share some of my fishing skills with the rest of you."

"That's certainly a generous offer on your part," replied Jerry. "Sign me up for some lessons."

"As numerous as these fish are, it shouldn't take very much fishing skill to catch all that we can eat," remarked Dianne.

"We could have a contest to find out whose technique is the best for catching a particular species," suggested Moose.

"I accept that challenge," Jerry quickly responded.

Connie made eye contact with Dianne and said, "Dianne and I will be the impartial judges in this contest. But what will be the prize for the winner?"

"I think ego gratification should be the winner's prize," suggested Dianne. "And the loser should clean the fish, cook the meal, and clean up afterward."

Jerry looked at Moose and said, "Well, what do you think of that?"

"Sounds good to me," Moose confidently replied.

"So far, the only fish that we know is safe to eat is the rainbow pike," stated Connie. "When we go on our around-the-lake cruise, it would be nice to have fresh fish to eat every day."

"We could have a daily contest on that cruise," suggested Moose.

"That will add some fun to the expedition," agreed Jerry.

"Before we go on that cruise, we need to test more fish to determine if they're safe to eat," stated Connie.

"When we get to Sauropod Meadow, we'll see what kind of fish are most numerous in that part of the lake," stated Jerry. "If there are different species than what live around Pioneer Island, we'll try to catch a member of each of the dominant species and take them home with us for testing."

"Some species may be unique to particular areas, but I would expect most species to be found throughout the lake," commented Dianne.

"Our cruise will give us an opportunity to find out," commented Jerry.

After a few moments of silence that seemed to indicate an end to the fish conversation, Jerry said, "I'm starting to feel hot and sweaty, and I'd like to dive in for a cool refreshing swim."

"I would too," remarked Connie. "Do you think that it would be safe to swim in this part of the lake?"

"Let's go below and look around," suggested Jerry. "If we don't see anything that looks threatening, let's dive in."

Jerry and Connie went below and observed the underwater world for a few minutes. "Most of the fish present here look like the various species we exposed to human blood in East Bay. The few strange ones look like the type that would prey on smaller fish rather than make a massive group attack on large prey," Connie said.

"But, you can't be sure about that. What I mean is, you can't always be certain of a fish's feeding habits just by considering its appearance."

"That's true, but pterodactyls dive into this lake every day to catch fish without themselves being devoured. Also, the bears seem to be able to safely swim from island to island. Those two facts alone seem to indicate that piranha-type fish don't exist here."

"That sounds reasonable. However, it's also possible that piranha-type fish are here, and that there is something about pterodactyls and bears that they don't like, and consequently, don't feed on them."

"Unfortunately, that is possible. But the water looks so clean and inviting. I really would like to go swimming. I just think it would be fun and refreshing. Isn't there some way that we can be sure that it's safe to swim here?"

Jerry thought about Connie's question for a few moments. "If there are piranha-type fish in this lake that fill their stomachs by making massive group attacks on animals, it seems to me that they would live close to shore in areas that thirsty animals frequently visit. If one of them happens to get bumped into the lake, it would become a prime target for a feeding frenzy. It doesn't make sense for this kind of fish to be present out here, miles away from the nearest animals."

"Unless they feed on other fish in massive group attacks."

"Well, we certainly don't look like fish."

"It almost sounds like you're about to conclude that it would be safe for us to go swimming."

"There's no way that we can be certain that it is safe, but we don't have any evidence to indicate the existence of such fish, and we haven't seen anything large enough to be dangerous by itself."

After doing a brief additional search of the underwater world, Connie said, "I sure don't see anything that looks threatening."

"I don't either, and our sonar data doesn't indicate any large creatures lurking beyond visual range. So let's cut power and let this boat drift while we go have some fun in the water."

Jerry and Connie went topside, walked to the front of the deck, and dove into the cool, clear, water. They were joined almost immediately by Moose and Dianne. After frolicking around in the water for about twenty minutes, the pioneers returned to their boat feeling refreshed and ready to lazily enjoy the warmth of the afternoon.

It didn't take long for the radiant heat from Alpha Centauri A to dry them off and warm them up. Being relaxed and carefree, all were content to let their minds wander into that marvelous fantasy land that the imaginative human mind is so capable of producing. Apparently, Jerry and Connie were mentally experiencing similar landscapes, for when Connie turned to Jerry and made eye contact with him, he seemed to know what was going on in her mind. When she quietly stood up and went below deck, he eagerly followed her.

Noticing this, Dianne said to Moose, "I don't think we should go below deck for a while."

Moose grinned, "I think I'll trust your insight on this one."

Not quite a half hour later, still below deck, Jerry and Connie were basking in the afterglow of successfully bringing a fantasy into reality. Casually looking at a small school of unusually colorful fish, Connie said, "Is it just me, or do you feel it too?"

"Feel what?"

"It seems like our lovemaking has had an added air of excitement to it ever since we arrived here. It's just so exquisitely satisfying."

"I think it's because we're on an alien planet that is just about as exotic as it could possibly be. Every day brings exciting new discoveries, and the element of danger is always present. Being here has put us into a heightened state of awareness that carries over into our love life."

"It's been so exciting that I feel like we're on our second honeymoon," commented Connie.

"I do too."

"We had our first honeymoon on a starship in interstellar space, and now, we're having our second honeymoon on an alien planet. Where do you suggest we go for our third honeymoon?"

"We really don't have much choice in that matter, but even if we did, I would chose to stay here. Every day is a fantastic adventure. This morning, we befriended a pair of pterodactyls. In no more than about an hour, we'll become the first humans to ever come face to face with huge dinosaurs, perhaps, the largest that have ever lived, here or on Earth."

At that moment, the computer called Jerry's attention to a significant change in the sonar data. Jerry looked at it, and said, "We've just had a large abrupt increase in depth. For the last couple of miles, the lake has averaged about three hundred feet deep, but now, we are over an area that is about sixteen hundred feet deep."

"That is a big drop-off."

"I wonder if this is just a deep hole, or if it's an underwater canyon that runs the length of the lake."

"An underwater canyon that long would be a large, deep-water ecosystem that might contain life forms very different from the shallower parts of the lake. To fully understand this lake, we will have to explore those depths."

"One more job for our little submarine," stated Jerry in a tone that denoted pride in the little vessel.

"Can we safely dive to a depth of sixteen hundred feet?"

"We can safely dive to about five thousand feet."

"I wonder if there are places in this lake that are that deep."

"I would be surprised if there are, but I didn't expect to find water as deep as it is right here."

About fifteen minutes later, Jerry said, "The depth has suddenly decreased to about 250 feet. If we have a canyon in the bottom of the lake, it's about a mile wide at this point."

"If it turns out to be an underwater crater, it's still large enough to have its own ecosystem."

"We're going to arrive at the east coast about two miles south of Sauropod Meadow. On the return voyage, we'll sail about two miles north of there before we turn west. If this deep hole exists four miles north of here, then it will begin to look like a canyon."

"We must be getting quite close to the coast," remarked Connie.

"We're only about a mile away. We'll be there in about fifteen minutes."

"I am going up on deck and scan the coast and countryside with binoculars. If I find something interesting, I'll call you."

"I will continue observing the underwater world. Perhaps, I will discover fish and other creatures that we don't have around Pioneer Island. I will call you, if I see something of interest."

When Connie appeared on deck, Dianne looked at her and said, "You sure look cheerful and content."

"Is my mood that obvious?"

"Yes, it is. It looks like your mood might be the result of doing some of that same sort of deeply penetrating research that Moose and I engaged in earlier."

Giving Dianne the most sly grin that she could come up with, Connie said, "We were able to probe to totally unexpected depths, and Jerry has assured me that we will look for the same depth during our return voyage."

Not expecting what appeared to be a very candid response, Dianne's mouth dropped open, but no words came out, as she stared at Connie in complete surprise.

Obviously pleased with the effect of her comment, Connie said, "I wouldn't have answered your question if I'd realized that you would lose your voice as a result."

"It isn't that I've lost my voice. It's just that your comment has raised so many questions that I don't know which to ask first, or even if I should ask any, since they are rather personal."

"I don't see anything personal about doing research that probes to unexpected depths. My husband assures me that such research is perfectly safe and should lead to the discovery of new life. In fact, you might want to join us; you could find it interesting."

"What! I can't believe that you're suggesting that I watch you."

Pleased that Dianne still hadn't caught on, Connie maintained her composure and said, "You might even help us if you feel up to it; after all, you are very well qualified."

Having overheard the conversation, Moose was beginning to suspect that Dianne was being misled and decided to join the ruse by saying, "I can vouch for the fact that she is definitely very well qualified."

Pleased by her husband's comment, but shocked by its implication, Dianne silently stared at him, then at Connie.

"If you're going to keep losing your voice like this, you should probably see a doctor," remarked Connie.

"It's the doctor who's causing me to be speechless, and I am starting to wonder exactly what it is that she's up to."

Realizing that the gag had run its course, Connie let out a burst of laughter.

"Now, I know I've been had!" Dianne exclaimed. "Would you mind telling me exactly what you've been talking about, and please use words that don't have double meanings."

"I was very specific in everything that I said. It's just that you've had sex on your mind all afternoon, and you chose to interpret my comments in that context."

"You certainly didn't do anything to discourage that interpretation."

"I couldn't do that; I was having too much fun."

"If I interpret your comments literally, I must conclude that you and Jerry found a deep hole in the lake bottom, and that you used sonar to probe these unexpected depths. Furthermore, you want to explore those depths to see what lives there, and you want me to help."

"You've just proven that I am easy to understand when you choose to listen to what I say instead of jumping to erroneous conclusions based on what's going on in your mind."

"Well, we are on vacation this afternoon, and Moose and I did have a delightful erotic experience, so I just assumed that you and Jerry did too, and that this was responsible for your vibrant mood."

"We did, and it was, but you gave me a marvelous opportunity that I couldn't pass up."

"I appreciate that, and just to prove that I am a good sport, I am going to put my imagination to work and find a clever way to get back at you."

Connie smiled, "I have no doubt that you will, but I'll bet it won't be as good as the way I just got you."

"That's a challenge I can't pass up. Now, I am determined to make it even better."

"That's the kind of friendly competition I can relate to," commented Moose.

Connie presented Dianne with a smug smile of satisfaction that seemed to say: I don't think that you can outdo me on this one. She turned, walked to the front of the boat, and started scanning the east coast with her binoculars.

In just a few moments, she spotted a herd of dinosaurs similar in appearance to the styracosaurus that lived on Earth during the late Cretaceous. As near as she could tell, the herd had about thirty members, some of which had waded into the lake. She focused her gaze on what appeared to be the largest member of the herd, a big male pacing back and forth along the waterfront, occasionally stopping to look inland and smell the air.

While Connie studied the large bull, Dianne joined her with binoculars in hand and immediately focused on the styracosaurus herd. The restive pacing of the large bull also caught Dianne's attention, and she said, "That animal sure looks nervous about something."

"Maybe, these creatures are nervous by nature," commented Connie.

"The rest of the herd seems quite relaxed," noted Dianne. Then, she handed her binoculars to Moose.

After observing the overall scene, and then, the large bull, Moose commented, "Perhaps there are other large bulls in the area who want to take over his herd, and he is anxious about an impending battle."

"That would explain why he's the only member in the herd who is restless," remarked Connie. "If there were T-Rexes prowling the vicinity, it seems like the whole herd would be anxiously on alert."

"Maybe, the rest of the herd is confident in that big bull's ability to defend them against a T-Rex," commented Moose. "I would guess that he is about thirty feet long, including his stout tail, and he must weigh at least eight or nine tons, perhaps even as much as ten tons."

"He definitely looks big and powerful," agreed Connie.

"But that's only part of the story," stated Moose. "Take a look at his fighting assets. He has a big rhino-type horn on his head, plus he has six large horns growing out of that large bony neck shield. Also, he's not totally defenseless when attacked from the rear. That stout muscular tail has a bony structure near its end. If that tail is as strong as it looks, that large bony blob makes it a lethal club."

"It looks like he is the only animal on guard duty," stated Connie.

"I think he's fully capable of doing the job," declared Moose.

"Perhaps, we were too quick to conclude that he's nervous about something," Connie commented. "He may simply be wary because he's taking guard duty seriously."

"With T-Rexes living in this area, it's hard to fault him for that," remarked Dianne.

"That such large animals, so well equipped for fighting, must maintain such a keen vigilance really demonstrates the fact that we are surrounded by a very savage world," Connie commented. "Can you imagine what it would be like to try to build a home among those creatures? Imagine how perilous everyday living would be."

"Survival would definitely be a daily challenge," declared Moose. "It would be a kill or be killed situation."

"I would rather live on Pioneer Island and just occasionally visit the wild countryside," stated Dianne.

Moose handed his binoculars back to Dianne, and said, "I am going below to take over fish watching, so Jerry can look at this herd."

A couple minutes later, Jerry arrived on deck, and Connie handed him her binoculars. While Jerry observed the styracosaurus herd, Connie and Dianne related their observations and thoughts to him.

"I would like to get a close look at those animals and find out how they react to us," stated Jerry. "Our present course puts us on a direct approach to them, and I don't think approaching them head on is a good idea. It might make them feel like we are challenging them for their space. They might even view us as a threat, and I would rather they see us as non-threatening."

Jerry continued to speak while changing course. "After we've gone south for several hundred yards, we'll turn toward shore. When we are only a couple hundred feet from shore, we'll head north and maintain that distance from shore. To them, it should look like we are simply passing by and not a threat."

Jerry belted on his pistol and shouldered his rifle and asked, "Have either of you spotted any predators that might be able to swim fast for short distances?"

Dianne and Connie both said no, but both armed themselves in reaction to Jerry's question. Then, Dianne said, "When you consider all the animals that come to this lake to drink every day, it seems like there would be predators that are proficient at pursuing prey that has been spooked into the water."

"Are you suggesting that we might look good to eat to such a creature?" asked Connie.

"I don't think we should ignore that possibility."

"Let's also be alert for pterodactyls," Jerry said. "We still don't know for sure that they only prey on fish."

"Given the abundance of land animals, it seems like there should be several species of pterodactyls that prey only on land animals," Dianne commented. "We could look like an easy meal for such a flying predator."

Several minutes later, the solar sailboat with its small group of humans turned north along the waterfront. All were now on deck, intensely excited in anticipation of their first encounter with dinosaurs.

As they drew nearer to the styracosaurus herd, Jerry reduced speed to less than two miles per hour. The solar sailboat appeared to be silently drifting along the surface of the lake. As the humans continued northward, the distance between them and the dinosaurs steadily decreased. Then, one of the adults in the water, the one closest to the humans, noticed the slowly approaching boat and sounded a warning. All the herd members immediately looked in the direction of the animal sounding the alarm and discovered the boat. They intently gazed at it and sniffed the air.

A few moments later, Jerry commented, "They're checking us out, but they don't seem to be very alarmed by our presence."

"Apparently, we don't look like any of their known enemies," remarked Moose.

"Even though they're not alarmed enough to retreat, they are intently looking at us," commented Connie.

"Evidently, the big bull that had been pacing the beach is more concerned about threats coming from the land, because he has returned his attention to that direction," noted Dianne.

"The rest of them sure are curious about us though," observed Jerry.

"Maybe that's why the big bull has wisely gone back to watching the land. He knows the rest of the herd is alert to anything that we might do," Dianne said.

"I wonder if they're aware of us, or if they only see our boat?" questioned Jerry. "We're still about a hundred yards away from them, and it may be that all they're able to see is our boat, which should look to them like an inanimate object slowly drifting by and not cause for alarm."

"Even if they are able to see us, we're so small compared to them that there still is no reason for them to be alarmed," speculated Moose. "Also, they've never had any bad experience with humans, or any experience at all for that matter, so they have no reason to view us as enemies."

"But wild animals survive by being wary of things they've never seen before," stated Dianne.

"We're now as close as we're going to get, and they still don't seem to be alarmed by our presence," Jerry said, "Some of them have even lost interest in us."

"It's not very flattering to my ego to have these animals consider us to be irrelevant," commented Connie.

"It might be that we're far enough away from them, so that we haven't infringed upon what they consider to be their space," speculated Dianne.

"That theory will be easy to test," stated Jerry. "After we are well past them, we'll turn around, come back, and pass by them at a distance of about a hundred feet. If that doesn't alarm them, we'll try fifty feet if the water's deep enough."

"To make the experiment realistic, I think we need to walk around on deck, so that there's no doubt in their minds that living creatures are approaching them," commented Dianne.

"That is a good experiment to do," remarked Moose. "Someday, we might want to do an overland hike, and we'll need to know which creatures will tolerate our presence."

A few minutes later, the interstellar pioneers completed their 180-degree turn and headed south. When they were about one hundred feet from the nearest styracosaurus, Dianne said, "All they're doing is just occasionally glancing at us."

"We now know that they aren't bothered by us being only one hundred feet away from them," remarked Moose.

"Let's briskly move around and find out if that stimulates any interest," suggested Connie.

While everyone followed Connie's suggestion, Jerry said, "It looks like they're not impressed by our activity."

After passing by, the interstellar pioneers turned around and passed by the herd at a distance of fifty feet. While all engaged in physical activity, Dianne said, "Other than occasional glances, they don't seem to have much interest in us."

"Apparently, they really do think that we are too small to be of any significance to them," remarked Connie. "Humans have dominated the animal world for so many centuries that this is going to take some getting use to."

"Does that mean they will ignore us no matter how close we get to them?" questioned Moose.

"Unless we go closer, we won't know the answer to that question, and the lake bottom right here is only a couple of feet below the bottom of our hull, so we really can't go any closer," Jerry responded.

Moose looked at Jerry, "We can't go any closer with this boat, but we can go closer; in fact, we can go right into their midst. How adventuresome do you feel at the moment?"

"I've always been willing to take reasonable risks when justified, but I'm not sure that what you're about to propose is justified."

"You haven't heard my proposal yet."

"I know you well enough to guess what it is. You're either going to suggest that we swim among these animals or that we get into our little inflated boat and row into their midst."

"We did bring it along in case we needed it," declared Moose.

"We brought it along in case we found a safe place to go ashore, but I don't believe that this is a safe place to do that," Dianne exclaimed.

"If these animals consider us to be irrelevant because of our small size, then there shouldn't be any problem," countered Moose. "Anyway, I wasn't considering going ashore in the middle of the herd; I just want to slowly approach those that are in the water to see how they react. On land, they could charge and kill me. Those that are ninety-five percent submersed in water can't charge, and they don't look like they can swim either. If I stay away from their tails, I should be safe."

"Your reasoning sure sounds good," stated Jerry in a skeptical sounding way.

"I'm not convinced either, but if you insist on doing this, I am going with you," Dianne said.

"Would you like to swim, or should we use the boat?" asked Moose.

After thinking about it for a few moments, Dianne said, "I can see advantages and disadvantages to either approach."

"I think we should use the boat. Then, if the styracosaurus that we approach decides to attack, we can dive in and swim for it, while he destroys our boat."

"That makes sense," agreed Dianne, "and it looks like there aren't any piranha-type fish here for us to worry about."

"If there are, they certainly aren't hungry at the moment," commented Moose.

Several minutes later, Jerry brought the solar sailboat to a halt about one hundred feet offshore and dropped anchor. Then, Moose hauled in the inflated boat that had been in tow. Dianne and Moose entered the small boat and began slowly rowing in the direction of the nearest styracosaurus.

With rifle in hand, Jerry was on full alert for possible trouble from any source. With video camera in hand, Connie sent a steady stream of imagery up to the Challenger, so all could observe the historic event about to unfold.

When Moose and Dianne were about twenty feet away from the styracosaurus, the animal started acting a bit uneasy. Then, it raised its head and bellowed out what sounded like a warning.

"I don't think it wants us to come any closer," stated Moose as he brought the boat to a stop.

"I'm surprised we got this close."

"As small as we are compared to it, I thought we'd get much closer. I wonder if it can differentiate between us and the boat, or if it thinks that we and the boat make up a single, fairly large, living organism. If so, that might explain the warning bellow."

"An animal that has never seen equipment with occupants could think that."

Moose backed the boat away from the styracosaurus a few yards. Then, he said, "Watch for a reaction. I am going to show it that we aren't one organism."

Moose gently entered the water without a splash and slowly swam away from the boat under the watchful eye of the styracosaurus. Then, Moose stopped, looked back at the animal, and then, at Dianne.

"I don't know what he's thinking, but whatever it is, he apparently doesn't feel in any danger from us, because he isn't making any move to leave the water," Dianne said.

"If you were as big as he is, would you feel any danger from creatures as small as we are?"

"Absolutely not!"

"Why don't you join me in the water. It's warmer than it was out in the middle of the lake. It's actually quite pleasant."

Dianne looked at the large styracosaurus, which was less than forty feet away. She thought about its awesome strength and fighting capability, but with ninety-five percent of the animal submersed, it certainly could not run or move very fast in any direction by whatever means. Then, she thought about the novelty of being one of the first humans to ever swim in the immediate vicinity of dinosaurs, and she quietly slipped over the side of the boat and slowly swam toward Moose.

"Now that we're no longer in the boat, and he can see how small we really are, I wonder how close we can get," Moose said.

"How close do you want to get?"

"I would like to become the first human to ever touch a living dinosaur."

"Are you crazy?" exclaimed Dianne.

"No! It's just something I'd like to do. I wouldn't try this on land, but here in the water, I don't think that I am in all that much danger, especially if I approach him slowly and back off if he sounds another warning."

"I think what you're planning to attempt is foolish, but I sense that you are determined to try it."

"Whether or not I can pull it off depends on these animals. If they're docile and mild-mannered when dealing with small, non-threatening creatures, I'll be successful. If they're mean-tempered, I won't."

"By the time you find out what their attitude is, you could be dead or crippled for life."

Determined to convince his wife, and perhaps himself, that it wasn't all that dangerous, Moose said, "Take a look over there, and you can see a pair of water fowl, the size of Canadian geese, swimming right next to a styracosaurus. Note that they are being totally ignored. Over there, a pair of birds that look like sea gulls are perched on the back of one of these brutes, and they are being ignored."

"I hope you're not planning to do that."

"Do what?"

"Climb onto the back of one of these animals."

Moose stared at the nearest styracosaurus for a few moments while he considered Dianne's comment. Then, he turned to Dianne as if to say something, but did not. Instead, he returned to looking at the large dinosaur.

"I shouldn't have mentioned getting onto his back, because I can see that you're seriously considering the possibility. And, you are daring enough to try it," Dianne said.

"You'll have to admit that it is an intriguing idea. Imagine being the first human to not only touch a dinosaur, but to also sit on one. When the video reaches Earth, it will be the most sensational news event of the day, and I will become an instant celebrity."

"There's no doubt about that, but these are wild animals, and the idea of sitting on one is just too dangerous. Besides that, I don't think they're going to allow you to do that anyway."

Pointing at them, Moose said, "Those sea gulls are being allowed to. I realize that I don't look like a sea gull, but if these animals prove to be mild-mannered, and don't see me as a threat, then sitting on one should be perfectly safe."

"I think that you will be taking too much risk to gain information that's not essential for us to have at the moment. Remember, all that we are trying to find out is if they'll tolerate us being close to them. Knowing which dinosaurs we can safely be close to does have practical value."

Displaying a mischievous grin, Moose said, "I wasn't serious, but when you mentioned the idea, it did sound like an exciting challenge, something worth exploring."

"You sure enjoy leading me on, and I actually thought that you were serious."

Moose laughed, "Trying to get close enough to touch one of them is all the risk I care to take."

"I am very glad to hear that."

Moose began slowly swimming in the direction of the big styracosaurus. When he was about ten feet away, he stopped and looked at the dinosaur's head. The first feature that caught his attention was the big horn located on its face a few inches below its eyes. With a length of about five feet, the horn would be a very formidable weapon. Moose then looked at the dinosaur's neck shield. Of the six horns growing out of it, the two at the top were the largest and appeared to be about four feet long. Those protruding to either side were only about three feet long.

Studying the dinosaur's massive head, neck shield, and horns, Moose noticed a large L-shaped scar on the right half of the neck shield. Moose looked into the dinosaur's eyes and in a soft voice said, "I wonder what kind of battle you were in when you got that scar. It's rather wicked-looking, but since you're here, you must have won the fight. Despite that scar, you seem peaceful, but you look so frightening that I'm not sure that I want to get any closer."

While Moose was speaking, the styracosaurus pointed his nose at Moose and sniffed. Using the same soft tone, Moose said, "Do I smell like a friend or like an enemy? Not having smelled a human before, I guess you probably don't know what to think."

Moose cautiously moved about a yard closer and slowly reached out with his right arm placing his hand only a few feet from the dinosaur's nose.

In response, the styracosaurus flared his nostrils and sniffed several times.

"You're going to have a difficult time identifying my scent, we're newcomers to your world. But we plan to be here for a long time, so why don't you get my scent firmly impressed into your brain, so that you can remember me."

Looking at the dinosaur's big nose horn, Moose decided that he didn't want to get close enough to touch the animal. The horn just looked too deadly, and he did not want to be within its range. However, Moose's decision turned out to be meaningless, because the big styracosaurus stepped forward and touched his nose to Moose's hand to get a stronger impression of his scent.

Moose was surprised by the big dinosaur's move, and now that he had achieved his stated goal of becoming the first human to touch a dinosaur, he wasn't sure that he really wanted that distinction. He wondered how to get out of the situation that he was now in. He quickly decided that his best move was to not make any sudden moves but to remain perfectly still. So even though his heart was racing, he did his best to not panic and to appraise his situation in a calm relaxed way. He took a good look at the big dinosaur's head and softly said, "Despite your fearsome weaponry, your touch is as gentle as that of a milk cow back on Earth. Even so, I'm now within the range of your nose horn, and I feel vulnerable. Maybe, I was crazy to have put myself into this position, but I'm here now, so what do I do next?"

After Moose pondered the question for a few moments, the big styracosaurus moved his head up and down a few inches to rub some of its soft nose tissue against Moose's fingertips leading Moose to say, "So, you have an itch that you need scratched. You're too big to argue with, so I guess I'd better start scratching."

Moose proceeded to gently scratch the area, and the styracosaurus reacted by moving his head in small amounts to place the annoying itch precisely under Moose's fingertips. Fully aware of the dinosaur's big horns, Moose said, "I sure hope you find this satisfying, because this is one time that I don't want to face an unhappy customer."

When the big dinosaur's itch had been alleviated, he moved his head away from Moose's hand and made some soft mooing sounds.

Looking into the creature's eyes, Moose said, "I wonder if you're expressing appreciation."

After a few moments, during which the styracosaurus seemed to be thinking, it slowly turned to the right, leaving its left side exposed to Moose. "If you're going to turn your weapons away from me like this, I guess you must have decided that I'm harmless. I wonder what your intentions are."

Behind the dinosaur's left shoulder, a few inches above the water line, Moose noticed that he was twitching his hide. "Are you trying to tell me that you have another itch that you want scratched? I don't think it would be very wise to disappoint you, so I guess I'd better scratch it."

When Moose moved closer to scratch the itch, he noticed a peculiar looking bug, about an inch long and a half inch wide, sitting on the dinosaur's skin. "I wonder if that bug is causing your irritating itch."

Moose reached out, grasped the bug between his thumb and forefinger and tried to remove it, but found that it was firmly attached. "This must be some sort of parasite, but as big as you are, I can't see that it's causing you much of a problem."

However, the styracosaurus continued to twitch its hide at the site of the parasite. "I guess I should try to remove it," stated Moose as he reached down to his belt to get his hunting knife. Moose gently slide the knife's sharp point under the parasite and with a prying motion caused it to release its pincers. Upon turning the bug over, Moose noticed that it was equipped with a suction tube that appeared to be about a half inch long.

After studying the bug for a few moments, Moose dropped it into the lake. It was then that he noticed other similar bugs floating in the water next to the styracosaurus.

Speaking to Dianne, who was anxiously watching from a distance of about twenty feet, Moose said, "I wonder if these parasites need to breathe and can easily be drowned. If so, entering the water would be an easy way for these dinosaurs to get rid of them."

"Except for the ones on their backs, that would work," replied Dianne, "and it's possible that those sea gulls are removing those. I see that they've moved to another animal, and they appear to be inspecting its back and occasionally pecking at something."

"This dinosaur must think I am related to those sea gulls, because he's twitching another part of his hide, and I see that there's another one of these parasites there."

Moose moved a little to his right, reached up with his knife, and gingerly removed the parasite. Then, he spotted another one just beyond his reach. Noticing that the styracosaurus was completely tolerating his presence, Moose decided to crawl partially onto its back, so that he could remove the parasite. After this, he spotted one between the dinosaur's shoulders. Moose positioned himself to remove it, and then realized that he had placed himself completely astride the dinosaur's back without having given it any thought. He sat upright, looked at Dianne, and said, "Sorry honey, I guess I've ended up doing what I was only kidding about."

"Well, that big brute doesn't seem to have any objections to your presence."

Moose looked at Jerry and Connie and, knowing that he was on camera, waved and smiled.

At that moment, a loud bellowing roar erupted from the throat of the big styracosaurus doing guard duty. The loud roar brought an instantaneous reaction from the styracosaurus that Moose was sitting on. It reared up on its hind legs and twisted its huge body toward shore. To keep from falling off, Moose instinctively grabbed a mane of hair growing along the dinosaur's backbone. When the dinosaur came down from its reared up position, it began a mad galloping rush toward shore, and Moose was now getting the wildest ride of his life.

Moose quickly thought about slipping into the water and swimming to safety, but discarded the idea out of a fear of being trampled to death. Wondering what the wild rush was all about, Moose looked toward shore and saw five T-Rexes rapidly approaching. Experiencing an instantaneous surge of adrenaline, Moose's mind instantly presented him with an image of being caught in the middle of a battle between dinosaurs. Now, the possibility of being trampled didn't seem quite as risky as it had a few seconds earlier and Moose decided to swim for it, but it was too late. There was a styracosaurus on either side of him, and Moose could not see any clear water to jump into. Quickly looking over his shoulder, Moose saw that there was even one behind him.

In just a few seconds, the styracosaurus that Moose was riding reached shore. It quickly bellowed out orders that caused the largest members of the herd to form a defensive line. With water no longer concealing its true size, Moose saw that he was riding the largest member of the herd, apparently the herd leader, for it confidently marched to the center of the defensive line.

Moose quickly said to himself, "How did I get into this mess? I have five hungry T-Rexes in front of me. A styracosaurus herd nervously primed for battle to either side and behind me. It looks like my safest choice at the moment is to stay right here and hope this face-off doesn't turn into a battle."

Moose looked straight ahead at the nearest T-Rex, which was only about ten yards away, and wondered: How did I ever get so close to one of those bloodthirsty killing machines armed with only a knife.

Moose's gaze was drawn to the T-Rex's massive jaws and teeth. Noting the abundant slobber falling from its lower jaw, Moose thought: With saliva flowing that freely, this animal is convinced that he is about to eat. Those teeth lining his jaws are as long as my hunting knife and look like daggers. It looks like he could eat me in two or three bites. What a monster, a ten-ton killer.

At that moment, the T-Rex's eyes focused on Moose for a few seconds, and it recognized that Moose was something different than it had ever seen on the back of a styracosaurus. Apparently, it considered him too small to be relevant, for it went back to inspecting the styracosaurus defensive line.

Nevertheless, during those few seconds, Moose felt the cold determination of a huge predator that was determined to eat. He felt like he had stared directly into the face of instant death, and he was filled with a cold, spine-numbing fear. But with an intense mental effort, Moose tuned out that fear, for he could not afford the luxury of entertaining it. To survive, he needed to keep his mind functioning freely.

Moose watched the big T-Rex look to the right and then to the left, apparently seeking a weak point in the styracosaurus defensive line, which was made up of the adult males. Behind the line, were the females and the juveniles. While the females had large nose horns, they were not equipped with neck shields and the additional horns growing out of them, but they appeared ready to defend their calves to the death if necessary.

Attempting to determine his chance for survival, Moose looked to the right and saw five males pawing the ground with their front feet and nervously moving their heads around while snorting. To the left, he also saw five males primed for battle.

The dominant T-Rex turned to the left and moved down the line looking for the weakest male. He occasionally sounded a challenging roar hoping to panic one of the styracosauruses, but they did not panic. They bellowed return challenges and pawed the ground with even more determination.

The remaining four T-Rexes followed their leader, anxiously primed for battle. All looked for a weak point in the styracosaurus defensive line and roared out challenges hoping to spook a nervous young styracosaurus into making a panic run from behind the line. Without the protection of the herd, it would then become easy prey.

The styracosaurus herd leader bellowed out some orders, and three of the males to the right moved forward, turned left, and followed the T-Rexes. Then the herd leader and the other two males from the right-side defensive line dropped back and moved to the left behind the left-side defensive line.

Observing what was happening, Moose thought, I like this strategy. We now have a five-man defensive front with three roving line backers, and the rest of the defensive line is pursuing the offense in the offensive backfield.

Unable to find a weak point in the defensive line and seeing additional defenders behind the line, the T-Rex leader was forced to conclude that he and his pack could not reach the cows and calves without fighting a fierce, costly battle. He then looked behind him with the idea of trying the other end of the defensive line, but he found that his pack was being pursued. The T-Rex leader roared out in protest at having to go hungry. Then, he and his pack turned inland and quietly left the area in search of weaker prey.

Boy am I glad this ended peacefully, thought Moose.

Moose looked at the retreating T-Rexes as did the styracosaurus herd leader. As the T-Rexes got farther and farther away, the styracosaurus herd started to settle down and engage in peaceful activities.

Moose thought, the herd has escaped death and injury, but I still have a big problem: how do I get out of here? He looked toward the lake and estimated it to be about eighty yards away, straight through the middle of the herd. Moose thought about some of the long touchdown runs he had made back during his college football days and recalled: I was very good at evading defenders on the way to the goal line, but they weren't big and lethal like these brutes. I wonder if I could zigzag my way through this herd? Would I be better off to run for it or to walk slowly? If I walk slowly and stay as far away from individual animals as I can, will they ignore me?

This herd leader seems to be totally unconcerned about having me on his back, or has he forgotten that I'm here? He couldn't possibly have thought about me during the T-Rex encounter. Maybe, he has forgotten me, and he can't see me, because I'm sitting behind his neck shield. If I sit still, he should remain unaware of my presence.

It seems like I shouldn't be in much danger as long as I sit still, but sitting still doesn't get me back to the boat. I wonder how he'd react if I were to slide off his back and head for the water. What if he attacks, am I quick enough to evade him? I used to be very good at evasive running. Should I slide off and make a run for it, or should I play it safe and stay put?

My problem would be solved if this big guy would go back into the lake, but he seems to have decided to do guard duty. Is it possible that I am trapped on the back of a ten-ton dinosaur?

I never dreamed I'd ever be in a situation where staying on the back of a dinosaur would be my safest course of action. But that does seem to be the case, so I might as well relax and enjoy this unique experience while I watch for an opportunity to escape.

Meanwhile, Dianne had returned to the solar sailboat. With binoculars in hand, she anxiously observed Moose doing what he had joked about doing. "Now that the T-Rexes have left, my husband doesn't appear to be in imminent danger, but how do I get him back?" she asked.

"I think all we can do is patiently wait," responded Jerry. "Eventually, that herd leader will put another animal on guard duty. Then, if we're lucky, he will come to the lake to drink. It is a warm afternoon, and he is active; hopefully, he will get thirsty soon."

"Also, these animals seem to enjoy being in the water," added Connie. "Some of them have already gone back into the lake. The herd leader may do that too."

"I hope you're both right," stated Dianne.

"There's always the possibility that Moose will make a run for the lake," commented Jerry.

"But that would expose him to possible attack," remarked Connie.

"We'll have to be alert for that possibility and shoot any animal that attacks," stated Jerry.

"But as big as those dinosaurs are, even if we inflict lethal wounds, they still might be able to kill Moose while they're dying," commented Connie.

"While that's a possibility, I believe the explosive bullets in our rifles have enough destructive power to immediately drop any animal we shoot."

"I think my husband has carefully considered his options and has decided to stay put."

"It seems his wisest choice at the moment," commented Jerry.

"He sure looks relaxed," observed Dianne. "How can he be so relaxed when he's in such grave danger?"

"I don't think he's in grave danger as long as he stays right where he is," commented Jerry. "The beast he's riding seems to have accepted him and will also protect him from predators. The danger will occur when he dismounts to return to us."

"I would sure like to talk to him," stated Dianne. "Maybe we could deliver a communicator to him with an RPV."

"I think we can do that without disturbing the styracosaurus, but carrying on a conversation might call his attention to Moose's presence," Jerry replied.

"Moose talked to that beast while they were in the water and the sound of his voice didn't seem to bother him," remarked Dianne. "As far as my voice is concerned, we can turn the speaker down, and Moose can hold it close to one of his ears."

"Let's attach a communicator to an RPV and send it to him," stated Jerry. "Then, we can plan his escape together."

"I'll take care of that," volunteered Connie.

"It's unfortunate that we don't have one of the big RPVs with us, then we could deliver some weapons to him," Dianne said.

"Had we known that your adventurous husband was going to ride a dinosaur into a confrontation with T-Rexes, we would've been better prepared," Jerry remarked.

"How do you plan for something as unexpected as that?" questioned Dianne. "That wild ride is the biggest surprise that he's ever had in his entire life. I wonder what thoughts raced through his mind at the moment that he realized what was happening."

"I don't know," commented Jerry, "but he came to this planet looking for exotic adventure, and it doesn't get much more exotic than riding a dinosaur that's preparing to battle T-Rexes."

"I've attached a communicator to this RPV," stated Connie.

"Fly it over to him, and then, let's wait until he contacts us," directed Jerry.

About a minute later, Moose saw the small RPV circling him. Then, the RPV came up from behind him passing slowly over his left shoulder. Moose reached up and caught it. He removed the communicator, then released the RPV.

Moose brought the communicator up to his mouth, but changed his mind and did not speak. Instead, he thought: If I speak, will this dinosaur associate my voice with the me that he saw in the lake? Will he figure out where the voice is coming from and realize that I am still on his back? If he does, will he even care?"

Moose surveyed the herd and noticed that there were sea gulls on the backs of some of the animals. Some of the gulls were actively looking for parasites; others were just perched and doing nothing. Then, he noticed some of the birds squawking at other gulls.

The presence of the gulls is accepted with a total lack of concern, Moose thought. Although I am much bigger than a gull, my weight is still only about one percent that of this styracosaurus. If these animals aren't concerned about gulls sitting on them, why would they be concerned about me. They've never had any bad experiences with humans to cause them to be wary of us. But, I think I'll be quiet for a while anyway and just wait for a good opportunity.

During the next half hour, the big styracosaurus paced back and forth along the inland side of his herd alertly surveying the countryside for signs of danger. Moose sat still on the big dinosaur's back and did some surveying of his own.

Then, what Moose had waited for and hoped would happen, finally did; the herd leader turned to one of the other adult males and bellowed out an order. The male got up from his resting position and joined the herd leader. For a couple minutes, both animals did guard duty; then, the herd leader calmly walked into the midst of the herd where he stopped and looked around.

Now, I'm only forty yards from the lake, thought Moose. I wonder why this big guy has stopped. What's he looking for?

While Moose pondered the question, the herd leader turned to his left and walked toward a female and calf resting near the edge of the herd. When he arrived, he made a soft mooing sound and the female answered in kind. Then, the herd leader gently rubbed his nose against the sleeping calf. He folded his legs under him and laid down with the calf between him and the female.

This is my chance, thought Moose. I am only twenty yards from the lake, and there's only one dinosaur between me and the water. Moose looked at the styracosaurus blocking his direct route to the lake and noted: he's lying down with his eyes closed. He appears to be sleeping. I think I'll try gently sliding off this big guy and calmly walking toward the lake. With a little luck, I won't disturb any of these dinosaurs, but if any of them are upset by my presence, I think I can easily dash into the lake before they can attack me.

I guess I should consider the possibility of predators lurking in the bushes that are too small to concern these dinosaurs, but big enough to kill me. Moose carefully searched the vegetation within fifty yards of the herd, but was unable to spot any movement that might reveal the presence of a hidden predator. Still not wanting to use his communicator, Moose looked out at the solar sailboat and saw his wife and friends alertly watching him. I only have a knife, but they have rifles, and they know what I am about to do.

Moving gingerly, Moose slid off the big styracosaurus without incident. Noting that the big dinosaur was undisturbed by his movement and presence, Moose stood within a yard of him and again, searched the surrounding area for evidence of hidden predators. Not seeing any, Moose calmly walked to the lake while watching the nearest dinosaurs and staying alert for predators.

In a matter of seconds, Moose reached the water's edge, waded in, and began leisurely swimming toward the sailboat. Seeing her husband in the water, Dianne dove in and swam out to meet him. When she reached him, she gave him a big hug and said, "Boy am I happy to have you back! The thought of losing you really filled me with an empty feeling. We're just beginning the most exciting phase of our lives, and I want you here to share it with."

"What happened this past hour is part of what makes the rest of our lives so exciting," Moose answered.

"I know, but I wish it weren't so dangerous. I want you around, so that we can enjoy building a home and raising a family."

"That's my dream too. I didn't plan what happened. I was a victim of circumstances. One thing just led to another, and I got carried away."

Dianne laughed and said, "You certainly did put some new meaning into that centuries-old cliché."

Before Dianne and Moose could say anything more, Jerry yelled, "If you two don't mind returning to the boat, we could still see those giant sauropods today."

"That sounds like a good idea. I'm ready to lie down on deck and relax for a while," Moose replied.

"Why do you need to lie down?" asked Jerry. "You've been sitting for most of the last hour."

"What choice did I have?"

A few moments later, Dianne and Moose were on deck, and Jerry said, "It looks like those sauropods will be at their favorite drinking spot in about fifteen minutes. By cruising at twelve miles per hour, we'll be there about five minutes ahead of them."

Looking at Moose, Jerry continued, "Since you're the most experienced person we have at contacting dinosaurs, you might want to go ashore and greet them when they arrive."

"No, thanks! I've had enough excitement to last me for a few days."

Moose laid out an air mattress. But before he could lie down and relax, Dianne grabbed his left arm and said, "You have one of those parasites on your back."

"Now that you've called it to my attention, I do feel a biting-kind of an itch below my left shoulder blade. Is that where it is?"

"That's exactly where it is."

"I hope it isn't poisonous."

"I don't know if it has injected any venom, but its suction tube has penetrated your body and may have placed some of Alcent's germs beneath your skin," commented Dianne.

"Let's try to remove this thing without killing it," Dianne said to Connie. "When we get back tonight, we need to do some lab work and find out what microbes it's carrying. Also, just to play it safe, we should take it apart and look for poison glands."

"And when we get back, I'll draw a blood specimen from Moose and examine it to determine if his immune system is developing the appropriate antibodies," Connie replied.

"Judging from those scratches and abrasions on your legs, you just might have been exposed to a multitude of Alcent's microorganisms," Connie said to Moose.

"My immune system's tough enough to fight off anything this planet has to throw at it."

"That may be true, but I am going to do some medical work on you anyway," asserted Connie.

Dianne and Connie carefully removed the parasite and placed it in a specimen container. Then, Dianne said, "Since this appears to be a bloodsucking insect, let's call it a tick."

"Since I discovered them on the big styracosaurus, I think we should call them styracosaurus ticks, which we can simplify to sty-ticks," Moose suggested.

Observing a couple droplets of blood oozing out of the tiny puncture wound in Moose's back, Connie opened her medical bag and retrieved a suction device to pick up the blood and suction the wound to obtain a bit more for later analysis. "Some of the microbes that sty-tick was carrying should be present in this specimen, and if it injected any venom, some of that should also be present."

"It's a bit ironic to think that organisms too small to be seen without a microscope might end up doing me more harm than the ten-ton brute I sat on," Moose commented.

"That's a possibility," stated Connie, "but I'm confident I can treat anything that your immune system has trouble with."

"It sure is nice to have a competent doctor onboard," stated Moose.

Jerry grinned at Moose and said, "I sure enjoy having her along."

"I think you're talking about something other than her medical skills," commented Moose.

"He's trying to say that I find lots of ways to fill his life with joy and happiness," Connie answered quickly.

Moose looked at Dianne with an obvious expression of fondness, "I am happy to say that I also find myself in that situation."

A few minutes later, the interstellar pioneers arrived at the sauropods' favorite drinking spot. Dropping anchor about fifty yards offshore, they awaited the arrival of the giant dinosaurs, which were currently about a quarter of a mile away.

"Even at this distance, it's obvious that they are huge," commented Dianne.

"They must be thirsty, because they sure aren't wasting any time getting here," observed Connie.

"They are marching along at a pretty good pace," agreed Dianne, "and their marching has a distinct majestic style to it."

"That style seems to indicate that they think they own this place and that all other creatures should step aside or be trampled," remarked Connie.

"There's no doubt in my mind that they are the dominant species as far as land animals are concerned," stated Jerry, "and apparently, there's no doubt in their minds either."

"As long as they're alert and avoid being ambushed, they certainly don't have to worry much about predators," declared Moose.

"You're willing to make that claim after staring into the eyes of a T-Rex?" questioned Jerry.

"The T-Rex I made eye contact with probably weighed around ten tons, and he was the biggest in the pack. This sauropod herd leader probably weighs around one hundred tons, has three large horns on his head, and three smaller horns on his tail. In my judgment, being ten times bigger, and well armed, makes him extremely difficult prey, even for the fierce T-Rex."

"That's probably true, but as big as these sauropods are, eventually, even they must become weak because of old age or serious illness. Then, they can be preyed on by the T-Rexes. Can you image what a feast a creature weighing between eighty and one hundred tons would be for them?"

"It certainly provides an incentive for a T-Rex hunting pack to occasionally challenge a sauropod herd to find out if there's a weak member," replied Moose.

When the sauropods reached the lake, they lined up along the water's edge to drink, except for one male who faced the open meadow watching for predators.

"What an impressive slight!" exclaimed Connie.

"We may be looking at the largest land animals that have ever lived, here or on Earth," commented Dianne.

Looking at Moose, Jerry said, "Sitting on the herd leader's back would put you higher than the peak of the roof on a two-story house."

"You seem to be implying that I should try it," remarked Moose.

"You did come to this planet looking for adventure, and you are an experienced dinosaur rider."

Before Moose could respond, Dianne said, "My husband's had enough adventure for one day, and I'd like him to stay alive for a while."

"It appears that your suggestion has been vetoed," remarked Moose to Jerry.

"Attempting to climb his tail to get onto his back could be dangerous," admitted Jerry. "As big as he is, you could fall off and break your neck."

"Falling off his back would result in lots of broken bones," remarked Moose. "It's difficult to imagine an animal so big that one could easily be killed by simply falling off it, but here we are looking at animals that are that big."

"Probably, the safest way to experience their size would be to walk through underneath one of them," commented Jerry. "I think we could do that without even ducking."

"We could try it," responded Moose. "I don't think it would be as dangerous as climbing onto one's back."

"I'll bet that if we walked under the herd leader, he would completely ignore us," speculated Jerry. "Think about it. We don't weigh much over about a tenth of a percent of what he weighs. That makes us extremely small in his mind. Relative to him, we would be like a pair of one-pound kittens wandering up to and under a 1,000-pound bull moose. Why would that big sauropod even pay any attention to us? We would have to look totally irrelevant to him."

"You aren't serious about trying this, are you?" questioned Connie.

"Don't you think that it would be exciting?" asked Jerry. "Imagine standing underneath a dinosaur that might be the largest animal that has ever lived."

"It would certainly be a novel adventure, but I think it's an unnecessary risk. We are finally in a position where we can start fulfilling our dreams, and it seems like we should avoid unnecessary risk taking."

"I don't think there's any risk of being attacked, but there definitely is the possibility of being stepped on and squashed."

"It's comforting to know that the possibility of being crushed is the only risk that you would face."

"In my younger days, I was the fastest quarterback in college football, and I'm still pretty quick on my feet. By being alert and ready to instantly react, I think I could get quite close to one of those animals with very little risk of being stepped on."

"I am confident in your ability, but the possibility of losing you is real. Just thinking about that possibility makes me feel sad. Is the novelty of being near one of those giants worth the risk?"

"This wouldn't be just a daredevil stunt. Since we're planning to live here for the rest of our lives, we need to find out how the animals living here react when they see humans approaching. In the not-to-distant future, we will make exploration trips into the countryside. Should the need arise, retreating into the midst of a herd of large well-armed herbivores that tolerate our presence might be a possible way to gain protection from some predators. This strategy might be an effective alternative to killing them. Also, it is even possible that this self-protection strategy could become a necessity. Suppose one or more humans were stranded in the countryside without firearms or were simply out of ammunition."

"There's no doubt that the more knowledge we have about the creatures that live here, the better off we'll be, if we stay alive while we're gaining that knowledge."

Displaying a gleaming smile, Jerry gazed into Connie's eyes and said, "You sound so different than the person who earlier this afternoon said that we must not avoid adventure because it might be dangerous. I think you said that we must evaluate the risks, plan for them, and then go forward. I think you also said that we must live our lives fully."

Connie thought about Jerry's comments for a few moments, "You're right. I did say all of that."

"Have you changed your mind, or do you still feel that way?"

Connie turned away from Jerry and observed the huge sauropods. "I still feel that way, but we've just had a rather harrowing experience. It started out in an innocent way, and all of a sudden, Moose's life was on the line. Going ashore is very dangerous. We just don't know all the risks. We can't evaluate risks that we don't know about."

"That's true, but risk-taking is now part of our lives. If my theory is correct, the risk should be minimal in this case."

"Even though I sense great danger, you may be correct, and if you insist on going ashore, I want to go with you. I've never played football, but I can move just about as quickly as you can."

"I'm not going to dispute that, and you're welcome to come with me. We'll take Charlie along and send him in first to find out how the sauropods react."

Turning to Moose, Jerry said, "You and Dianne can watch our backsides while we're preoccupied with those big dinosaurs."

A few minutes later, Jerry and Connie beached the small inflated boat about seventy yards south of the sauropods. After carefully scanning the immediate area for signs of hidden predators, they sent Charlie walking toward the sauropod herd. The closest sauropod was the giant herd leader, who was still standing at the water's edge and drinking occasionally.

When Charlie had approached to within twenty yards, the big dinosaur turned his head toward him, briefly looked at him, then went back to drinking. Charlie continued walking straight toward the dinosaur's mid-section. A few seconds later, he walked underneath the big sauropod and then turned around and passed under him again.

"It looks like my theory is correct," commented Jerry. "Apparently, that big brute decided after only a casual glance that Charlie's just too small to be any kind of threat."

"So, are you now ready to do what Charlie just did?"

"I think so, but before I do that, let's take another careful look around to make sure that we aren't being stalked by any predators."

After a brief, but intensive, visual search of the immediate area, Jerry said, "Let's station Charlie a few yards behind you and a little to your right and keep him slowly pacing back and forth. If there are any predators hidden in those thick patches of brush over there, Charlie will be between you and them."

With Charlie in position, Jerry began walking toward the big sauropod in as relaxed a manner as possible. Connie stood with her back to the lake, so she could easily make frequent glances inland while she observed Jerry. She held her rifle in the ready-to-use position with a cartridge in the chamber and the safety off.

When Jerry was about fifteen yards from the big sauropod, he stopped and studied the creature from head to tail for a few moments. Totally awed by the dinosaur's immense size, Jerry softly said to himself, "It's difficult to believe that an animal could grow so large. He's easily a hundred feet long."

Jerry studied the dinosaur's legs and marveled at the enormous bones and tremendous muscle power required to support and move such a huge animal. "Just one of those massive legs must weigh more than any land animal on Earth, except for maybe a full-grown elephant. They must be eight to ten feet in diameter with feet that are twelve to fourteen feet across.

I wonder how old this guy is. It must take several decades to grow up and become a full-sized adult. In much of the animal world, adulthood can last three to ten times as long as the growing-up time period. That means this guy could easily be well over one hundred years old."

At that moment, the big sauropod looked in Jerry's direction, and after glancing at Jerry for a few seconds, returned to sipping water out of the lake. "He sure doesn't have much interest in me, but why should he be concerned about me when I'm so tiny compared to him."

Encouraged by the sauropod's seeming lack of interest, Jerry decided to move closer, and a few seconds later, he was beneath the dinosaur's stomach. He stopped, tilted his head back, and looked up at the huge creature's underside, which was about a foot above him. "I can't believe I'm actually doing this. I am actually standing under a dinosaur that probably weighs about a hundred tons. But, I should get out of here; I've already proven my theory. But first, I have to touch this guy, so I can say that I've done it. I hope he isn't ticklish."

Jerry reached up and very gently touched his fingertips to the sauropod's stomach. He quickly removed them and began walking back to his wife. Even at a distance of about seventy yards, Jerry noticed that she seemed to breathe a sigh of relief.

About fifteen yards away from the giant dinosaur, Jerry stopped to look back at him, and thought: It may be a while before I ...

At that instant, Jerry's thoughts were abruptly interrupted by the sudden sharp report of a rifle followed instantly by an explosion. Jerry quickly spun around to the sight of a saber-tooth cat-like creature knocking his wife to the ground. The sight of a large cat pinning his wife to the ground horrified Jerry. Loud, ripping snarls added to the horror of the scene.

Jerry instantly decided not to fire his rifle at the cat, for it was armed with explosive bullets powerful enough to kill his wife when fired into the cat on top of her. Instead, he broke into an all-out sprint toward Connie. Before he reached her, he saw that a second cat had knocked Charlie down and was violently shaking him and snarling. The massive charge of adrenaline flooding Jerry's body caused his brain to race so fast that it seemed like everything around him was moving in slow motion.

The cat shaking Charlie seemed to be doing it very slowly. The cat pinning Connie seemed to be motionless. The image of Connie lying in a pool of blood with a saber-tooth cat on top of her engulfed Jerry's mind and brought a fresh flood of adrenaline, which added to the speed of Jerry's sprint. Useless in this situation, Jerry had already dropped his rifle, so he could run faster.

Even though looking directly at the cat on top of his wife, Jerry's peripheral vision saw that the cat shaking Charlie had dropped him and was also bounding toward his wife. Instantly, Jerry thought, I guess he didn't taste any blood in Charlie, so now, he's heading toward Connie. Simultaneously with that thought, he drew his 10.5-millimeter semiautomatic pistol and quickly fired three explosive bullets into the cat without even slowing his sprint.

Jerry holstered his pistol, drew his hunting knife, and a second later, dove at the cat on top of Connie. He quickly plunged his knife into the animal's chest behind its right shoulder. In that instant, Jerry also wrapped his left arm under the cat's neck. He stood up, jerked the heavy cat off his wife, and rapidly rammed his knife into it three more times before realizing that the animal was already dead.

Fearing for the worst, Jerry looked down at his blood-drenched wife lying in a pool of blood. Then he dropped to his knees at her side.

Before Jerry could say anything, Connie struggled to sit up. She smiled weakly, "Thanks for getting that thing off me."

Reaching toward Jerry, "Would you mind helping me up?"

The flood of adrenaline that had surged through Jerry's body was now replaced by an abundant flow of tears streaming down his face. Seeing this, Connie said, "If seeing me drenched with cat blood is going to make you cry, I guess I should get cleaned up."

"It was horrible! I thought that I had lost you! I am overjoyed that I haven't!"

"I feel weak and banged up, but you haven't lost me."

Jerry gently helped her up and put his hands on her shoulders, "I hope I never again see you lying in a pool of blood with a carnivore on top of you. Are you all right?"

"I think so, but I did suffer some bruises when that cat knocked me down and fell on top of me. He slammed me into the ground extremely hard."

"This attack sure happened fast."

"It was very fast! I was watching you stop to look back at the dinosaur, when out of the corner of my eye, I saw a rapid movement. I quickly turned in that direction to see a cat knock Charlie down and a second cat spring toward me. Instinctively, I instantly raised the end of my rifle and fired, from the hip so to speak. The last thing I remember seeing was the bullet explode and rip open the left side of the cat's chest. He must have been killed instantly, but he had already sprung and was only a couple yards away from me when the bullet exploded. Even though already dead, his momentum carried him forward, knocking me down. My head must have struck a rock. I must have lost consciousness, because the next thing I was aware of was you lifting the dead cat off of me."

"You're also bleeding from your left shoulder. It looks like one of that cat's saber teeth punched a hole in you when he crashed into you."

Connie looked at the wound, then at the dead saber-tooth lying next to her feet. As her gaze focused on the cat's open mouth and its prominent fangs, a cold shudder passed through her body, and she said, "It's frightening to think that those large daggers were headed for my neck. Except for a quick, lucky shot, I would have been killed almost instantly."

"It wasn't just luck. You were trained to react instantly and decisively to surprise attack. But what about this puncture wound?"

"It doesn't appear to be very serious, but I'm glad it's in my shoulder and not in my neck."

"Just the same, I want to get you back to the boat, so Dianne can examine you. All the medical training you gave her during our long voyage can now be put to good use."

"I'd like to get out of these bloody clothes and wash this blood off me."

"But not in the lake. All that blood could certainly attract marine predators, if there are any. I'll help you bathe when we get back on deck. Right now, I am going to help you into the boat. Then, I'm going to pick up our rifles and Charlie and get us out of here."

"OK," she agreed.

A short time later, when they got back on the sailboat, Dianne exclaimed, immediately alarmed, "You sure are a bloody mess! I hope that's not all your blood. Are you OK?"

"Most of it is from the cat I killed." Beaming with pride, Connie said, "I was pretty quick with my rifle, wasn't I?"

"It's fortunate that you were," agreed Moose. "We weren't able to shoot at the cats, because you were directly between us and them."

"That grueling survival training we went through sure paid off," commented Dianne.

"That's the reason I'm still alive, and I now feel like I've been combat tested."

"You have, and you passed in a colorful way—mostly red. Let's get you cleaned up, so I can examine and treat your injuries."

"Let's save some of this cat blood for analysis," said Connie.

Dianne collected cat blood samples from Connie; then, she bathed her and examined her injuries. "This puncture wound could cause you some problems. Since that saber-tooth never brushed his teeth, you could have some nasty microbes in your body. I need to suction this wound, and I'll save the fluid for analysis."

"If you'll give the wound a good cleaning, I think my immune system can handle the rest."

"Your immune system is definitely being tested. You and my husband will give us our first good look at how the human immune system handles the alien microbes that gained entry via your open wounds."

"The next several days are critical. What a confidence builder it will be if Moose and I don't develop any pathology."

"Listening to our wives talk makes me feel like a medical research animal," Moose said to Jerry.

"One of our objectives is to evaluate human reaction to Alcent's environment," commented Jerry, "so your feeling is soundly based in reality."

"I know, but in my younger days, I never dreamed that I would someday play the role of a medical research animal on an alien planet."

"You probably never dreamed that you would someday ride a dinosaur either."

"That's true, and I'll bet that none of your dinosaur fantasies ever included standing beneath a 100-ton sauropod and reaching up to touch his stomach."

"You're right, but now that we're here, I had to prove a point; namely, that animals as big as these would consider creatures as small as us to be irrelevant. I believe that we will never be attacked by these giants and that the only danger we face from them is that of being stepped on if we're ever standing between them and wherever it is that they want to go."

"That would yield the same result as a human stepping on a beetle: Squish!"

"That sums it up very well," remarked Jerry.

At that moment, Connie approached Jerry, "Do I look better now?"

"Definitely! Red never was a good color on you. How do you feel now that your injuries have been treated?"

"My head aches, my left shoulder hurts, and I have several bruises. But, if I ignore those things, I feel very fortunate that I'm still alive. My aches and pains will pass. The pain killer I took should take effect shortly."

Jerry gave his wife a gentle hug and said, "You handled yourself very well in the face of such an ordeal. I am proud of you."

"As vigilant as I was, I am amazed by how quickly those saber-tooth cats just seemed to appear out of nowhere."

"They've convinced me that they are masters of stealth. And their stealth ability is greatly aided by their camouflage color schemes, allowing them to be nearly invisible when they are in the right vegetation and under the right lighting conditions."

"Their stealth capability and size relative to us makes them extremely dangerous predators," contended Moose.

"I would guess they might weigh 350 to 400 pounds," commented Jerry, "and you're right, our size should make us look small enough to be an easy kill, but big enough to be a pretty good meal."

"I could use a pretty good meal myself," declared Connie. "I'm starving!"

"I am hungry too," stated Jerry. "Let's begin our return voyage and eat dinner."

"There's a fairly heavy cloud front moving in from the west," remarked Moose. "In a matter of minutes, Alpha Centauri A will be behind those clouds and we're not going to get much power out of our solar sails."

"But the wind is starting to pick up," commented Jerry. "This might be a good time to try out our wind sails."

"I think the rainy weather that Mike's been talking about will be upon us in no more than an hour or two, perhaps even before we get home," Moose remarked.

"If the system contains some strong wind, our sailing could become very exciting," speculated Jerry. "Let's get these solar sails rolled up and put away. Then, let's deploy our wind sails."

A short time later, Moose and Jerry had the solar sails put away and had put up the tall telescoping mast and main sail. "I love the sound of a sail flapping in the breeze and then snapping taut when it's properly oriented to the wind. It's been a long, long time since I've enjoyed hearing those sounds," Jerry said.

"This does bring back memories," commented Moose. "But the last time I went sailing, there were too many other boats. This time, we have a huge lake all to ourselves, and that really appeals to me."

"I hope the wind gets a lot stronger in front of the incoming storm, so we can really have some fun," said Jerry.

"Let's talk to Mike and find out what his forecast is," suggested Moose.

While Moose was talking to Mike, Dianne and Connie appeared from below deck with dinner in hand. The sight and scent of food motivated Moose to cut short his conversation with Mike and head for the picnic table set up on deck. Soon, all were seated and enjoying a delicious meal of abalone steak and rainbow pike. With the navigation computer in control, Jerry was free to relax and enjoy dinner with his wife and friends.

"Mike said not to worry, the wind will be much stronger before we get home," Moose reported. "He said he wished he could be here to take part in all the excitement that we're having. From the tone of his voice, I think he's counting the days until he can join us."

"Everyone up there has been following our day-to-day adventures with utmost interest," remarked Connie. "They're all eager to come down, and I can't blame them. They've been inside the Challenger for nearly seven years. Even Denise wants to come down, and she doesn't even know what it's like to be on a planet. She just knows how exciting our lives are and wants to be here with us."

"On her first day here, I think we should plan on spending lots of time with her," said Jerry. "As active as her curiosity is, showing her around and answering her questions is going to keep us busy for a while."

"But it will be fun," remarked Connie. "Watching her wide-eyed reactions to the simple things that children born and raised on Earth take for granted will give us some precious moments to remember for a long time."

"We should put much of her first day on video, so she can enjoy it when she is older," suggested Jerry.

"That will also provide us with some priceless future enjoyment," added Connie.

While Jerry and Connie talked about Denise, Moose and Dianne made silent eye contact. They read each other's minds as surely as if they had spoken to each other. "Would you mind sharing those thoughts with us?" Connie asked them.

"We're thinking about getting pregnant when our thirty-day quarantine is over, if we get through it without any medical problems of consequence," Dianne responded.

"We've been patiently waiting for a long time," added Moose.

"Promise me that you'll let me give both of you a thorough physical before you do that," requested Connie.

"I think we could submit to that," responded Dianne.

"This whole month is one continuous medical exam," commented Moose. "By the end of it, there won't be much about us that you won't know, but I guess one final checkup won't hurt anything."

"I assure you that it won't hurt," remarked Connie.

Jerry said, "Getting back to our thirty-day quarantine, if we get through it without any significant medical problems, I wonder if we really need a second thirty-day quarantine involving a few additional people. Maybe, we can safely skip that and just bring everyone down."

"I think we should keep that option open, but let me make a thorough evaluation of our medical situation at that time," replied Connie.

Looking at Jerry, Moose said, "Looks like you got the same answer we got in regard to getting pregnant."

"Now and then, there comes a time when the doctor should have the final word," commented Connie.

"I don't know about the final word, but at least a strong recommendation," remarked Jerry.

Realizing that she may have claimed a little too much authority for herself, Connie said, "That is a better way of saying what I meant."

At that moment, a call came in from Mike, who said, "I have a weather update for you."

"Is it good news or bad news?" questioned Jerry.

"That depends on what it is you're looking for. Your pleasant weather will soon come to an end. The boundary of the incoming storm is about ten miles west of Clear Lake. There are several heavy rain squalls over there. Sustained southerly winds are in the twenty-five to thirty miles per hour range with gusts up to forty. If you want some exciting sailing, you're probably going to get all the excitement you're looking for, and more. The storm is moving in your direction at about ten miles per hour, so it should reach Pioneer Island in about two hours. You should experience a gradual increase in wind strength as the storm approaches. Enjoy your sailing."

"Thanks Mike," replied Jerry.

Sounding concerned, Connie asked, "Can this boat handle that much wind?"

"With this boat, we have lots of flexibility," replied Jerry. "If the wind starts getting too strong, we'll partially retract the telescoping mast and roll up the bottom of the sail. The stronger the wind gets, the less sail we need to deploy."

"But this is a big lake," protested Connie, "and winds up to forty miles per hour can generate some big waves."

"If the situation gets too rough, we'll completely retract the mast and sail," Jerry replied. "Then, we'll retract, deflate, and stow the outriggers. When this has been done, our boat will again be a submarine, and we can dive to a depth that isn't affected by the surface storm. No matter how stormy things are on the surface, the depths are always peaceful and quiet."

"In other words, I have nothing to worry about?"

"Not a thing," assured Jerry. "Just relax and enjoy the experience."

"The only thing we need to be concerned with is losing the things that are on deck," commented Moose. "Strong winds could blow some of this stuff away. I think it's time to put away everything that isn't tied down."

After helping his companions clear the deck, Jerry said, "I'm going below to check the sonar data. I'm curious about whether this side of the lake has a deep underwater canyon."

"I'll join you," stated Connie.

When they were below deck, Jerry asked, "How are you feeling?"

"I'm starting to feel pretty good. The pain killer that I took has taken effect."

"I am glad you feel well enough to enjoy our sailing excursion."

Jerry put his arms around his wife, "Seeing that saber-tooth on top of you put a real scare in me. It makes me shudder to think what a close call you had."

In response to Jerry's embrace, Connie snuggled up against him and enjoyed the love and security that she felt with his strong arms around her. She closed her eyes and mentally blocked out everything except Jerry's love, which seemed to flow into her very being. After relishing in the feeling for several moments, she said, "My brush with death really makes me appreciate the special relationship that we've enjoyed for so many years. This is a very dangerous planet, and each day that we have is precious, so let's enjoy them to the fullest."

"By their very nature, some of our most exciting and enjoyable adventures will be fraught with danger."

Backing away from her husband, Connie looked at him and said, "I hope I didn't sound like I was implying that we should avoid adventure because it might be dangerous. I only meant that we should appreciate the time that we have and make sure that we enjoy everything we do."

"A close call with death does tend to enhance one's appreciation for just being alive."

"I also have a new appreciation for Pioneer Island. Can you imagine trying to build a home in the countryside among the fierce creatures that live there?"

"That would be challenging, but I prefer the lesser challenge of making a safe home on Pioneer Island."

"I wonder if there are any life-threatening hazards hidden in its dense forest."

"A few days of exploration should help answer that question," replied Jerry.

"As isolated as the island is from the countryside, I wonder if any dangerous animals besides bears ever swim to it."

"I don't know, but our lives depend on being alert for and prepared for any possibility."

"In view of my perilous experience, I think it'll be a long time before anyone gets careless about being alert for danger."

Jerry smiled and nodded in agreement. "Let's take a look at our sonar data."

A few moments later, Jerry said, "It looks like we might have a deep underwater canyon. We're about two miles north of where we were when we first detected deep water and it's also deep here, about eighteen hundred feet. The drop-off occurred about where I thought it might. And again, it was very abrupt, indicating a nearly vertical underwater cliff."

While Jerry studied the sonar data, Connie observed whatever fish came within viewing range. After about ten minutes had gone by, Jerry said, "We've reached the west side of the deep water, and once again, it abruptly ends with a nearly vertical underwater cliff. Present depth is about 280 feet."

"If it is a canyon, I wonder if it extends the length of the lake?"

"I think that it probably does. I've sent sonar pulses to the north and to the south, and I was unable to find the underwater cliffs that would be there if this were just a deep crater-like hole. This canyon is something we'll have to investigate. I would like to take this boat down and see what lives down there, but right now, let's go topside and enjoy some sailing."

A few moments later, Connie and Jerry joined Moose and Dianne, "It's beginning to look like Mike's forecast might be right. The wind is getting stronger, and that heavy cloud bank in the west is now much closer," Moose said.

"He did predict rain," remarked Connie, "and it sure looks like we're going to get drenched before we get home."

"I haven't been rained on in so many years that I think I am going to enjoy it," commented Moose.

Jerry scanned the huge lake and noticed how rough the water was starting to get. Then, he looked at the approaching storm west of Pioneer Island. His gaze shifted to the large sail stretched tight by the force of the wind. "It's us and one small boat against the elements, and I welcome the challenge," Jerry said, looking at his companions.

"And what a contrast those elements are to the controlled environment onboard the Challenger," remarked Connie.

"After living in that pleasant but never-changing climate for such a long time, some blustery, rainy weather might be exciting," stated Dianne.

Turning to Moose, Jerry said, "Let's deploy our jib and increase our speed a bit."

"Good idea," agreed Moose.

A short time later, with both the main sail and jib fully deployed, and with the wind steadily gaining in strength, Moose said, "This boat is a marvelous piece of equipment. After using solar power all afternoon, we're now zipping along at a pretty good clip with nothing but the wind for power, and if Mike's right, the wind's going to get much stronger, further increasing our speed."

"If it gets strong enough, we'll have an opportunity to test this boat's capabilities," stated Jerry.

"And an opportunity to test some sailing skills that you haven't used since leaving Earth," commented Connie.

"I might be a little rusty, but I haven't forgotten. I did have extensive training on this boat and one of its sister ships."

"Maybe, you could teach us the fundamentals of sailing," suggested Connie.

"Be more than happy to."

During the next hour, Jerry explained the basics of sailing and the particulars of operating the boat they were on. Having had a great deal of sailing experience on a variety of boats, Moose easily grasped the details Jerry presented. Even though Dianne and Connie had never been sailing, they were eager students and learned quickly. With a little experience, they too would become skilled sailors.

Noting their location, Jerry said, "We're now only about two miles from Pioneer Island, and it looks like the storm has already arrived on its west coast."

The dark storm clouds were brilliantly lit by a powerful lightning bolt that appeared to strike Pioneer Island. "I think it's time to convert this boat into a submarine. I don't want to be caught on the surface in a sailboat during an electrical storm," Jerry commented.

"Mike didn't tell us that this system contained thunder and lightning," commented Moose.

"Weather forecasting still isn't a perfect science," remarked Jerry.

The interstellar pioneers quickly rolled up and stowed their sails. They retracted the tall telescoping mast. Last, they retracted, deflated, and stowed their outriggers.

With the lake now very rough and the little boat pitching and rolling with the waves, the pioneers paused to take a final look at the rapidly approaching electrical storm. They watched a powerful lightning bolt strike a tree on Eastern Island, instantly exploding it into a flaming torch. Three seconds after the explosive flash, they were jolted by the sudden crack of thunder so loud that it sounded like the entire sky had been split open.

"I am glad that one didn't hit us!" shouted Jerry. "Let's dive!"

Jerry immediately dropped through the hatch into the sub's interior and headed for the controls. With the image of the exploding tree vividly in their minds, Dianne and Connie needed no urging to immediately follow Jerry. Being the last one through the hatch, Moose closed it tightly while Jerry initiated the diving sequence. Within seconds, the little submarine disappeared from the surface of Clear Lake and headed for a depth of sixty feet.

"That was an awesome display of the raw power of nature," remarked Connie. "What would be left of us had one of those lightning bolts struck our boat?"

"That is something that I would rather not find out," responded Jerry.

"I can't believe how quiet and peaceful it is down here even though there's a powerful storm raging on the surface," commented Connie.

"It's also quite dark," noted Dianne. "Everything has a sense of unreality about it, but even though there isn't much light, the water's so clear that I can still see for quite some distance. In its own way, the low light level adds a special kind of beauty to the depths, kind of like the countryside on a moonlit night."

"It does have a romantic appeal to it," commented Connie.

"Especially, when you consider that there is a violent storm raging only twenty yards above us," added Dianne.

While they relaxed and enjoyed the quiet peacefulness of the depths, Jerry navigated the little submarine around Eastern Island and into the wind protected water of East Bay. "Judging from the increased lighting, I would guess that the thunder shower has passed. Let's surface and use this opportunity to go home before the next shower arrives," Jerry said.

A few minutes later, they were standing on deck appreciating a break in the storm system. "I love fresh smells after a heavy shower," commented Connie.

"And look at that beautiful rainbow in the east," said Dianne.

Connie turned and gazed at the rainbow for a few moments. "Its elegant beauty makes it easy to understand why it became the Biblical symbol of hope after the great flood. Even though it has a simple scientific explanation, its does make me feel elated and hopeful."

"A display of nature's awesome firepower, immediately followed by a display of soft beauty that is so colorful and peaceful. What a contrast," Dianne commented.

"Based on what I see in the West, the next display of firepower isn't very far away," added Jerry.

"I think he's suggesting we get into the boat and head for home," said Connie.

A few minutes later, they stood on the beach and watched the little submarine slip below the surface. Jerry had decided to anchor it a few yards off the bottom, so it would be protected from lightning strikes and whatever else the storm might throw at it. A small orange buoy marked the sub's location.

After a short hike through dripping rain-drenched forest and a climb up a wet, slippery rock-slide, the weary pioneers hiked to their habitation capsule, arriving only moments before the next thunderstorm hit. When all were inside with the door tightly closed, Dianne said, "I am glad this capsule is rugged and well-built."

After watching the electrical storm through one of the large windows for a few moments, Moose remarked, "I am glad that it is equipped with a well grounded lightning rod."

"All things considered, this is a safe comfortable home," commented Dianne.

"I feel tired enough to sleep until noon tomorrow," said Connie.

"You should be tired," commented Jerry. "This has been an extremely active day, and there was your harrowing encounter with those saber-tooth cats. That, all by itself, could leave you physically and emotionally drained."

"I could use a few days off, during which we just relax and do a few easy things close to home," remarked Connie.

"I think that's a good idea," agreed Dianne.

"I think we can find enough interesting things to do around here to entertain ourselves for a few days," Moose said to Jerry.

"We could probably do that without even leaving Stellar Plateau," commented Jerry. "Depending on how long this storm hangs around and how long the breaks are between showers, we may not have any good opportunities to travel very far. So, let's rest for a few days."

ELEVEN

Life Starts to Become Routine

TIME: Day Six, Late Morning.

The interstellar pioneers were still sound asleep, even though Alpha Centauri A had long since arisen. Five nights with not quite enough sleep and five long days filled with productive activity had brought them to the point of needing some well-deserved extra rest. Nature had obligingly accommodated their need for extra rest by concealing Alpha Centauri A with heavily overcast skies, making it quite dark inside the capsule. However, heavily overcast skies sometimes have another side to them, and the quiet peacefulness inside the capsule was suddenly shattered by a loud, sky-splitting boom of thunder. The sharp deafening boom from a nearby lightning strike instantly jarred everyone awake.

Connie and Jerry both sat up, "Nature's alarm clock calls," Jerry said.

While looking out the large plastic window near their bed, Connie said, "What a cloud burst!"

"The driving wind magnifies the force of the rain and makes it seem heavier than it actually is," commented Jerry.

"That may be, but wind or no wind, this is a deluge."

The noise generated by the storm dramatically increased. Walking across the capsule to a down-wind window, Jerry said, "Look at this. There are hail stones bouncing all over the place."

"Wow! That's awesome! I wonder how often hail storms like this one come through here."

"I hope they're not very frequent. Growing fruit trees and vegetable gardens will be impossible if intense hail storms are a frequent occurrence."

"The plant life is definitely taking a beating. The ground is already white with ice, and it's still coming down."

For the next two minutes, Jerry and Connie gazed in fascination at the bouncing hail stones. Then, just as suddenly as it started, it abruptly stopped, and within minutes, Alpha Centauri A and B flooded the plateau with the brilliant light of day. And the light of day had a special eerie brilliance to it as it reflected off a landscape covered with bright white hail stones.

"What a weird scene," remarked Connie.

"Once again, the potentially destructive power of Nature has been demonstrated to us," commented Jerry.

"It certainly is a dramatic contrast to the tame environment we took for granted onboard the Challenger. Nature is certainly letting us know that violent weather is a force that we'll have to contend with, at least occasionally."

A worried look of concern spread across Connie's face. "What are you thinking about?" Jerry asked.

"I am wondering if the infant pterodactyl on Western Island survived all of this."

"We can easily find out. Using an RPV, Mike installed a camera inside the infant's shelter. Let's take a look."

First, Jerry tuned in to the signal from a camera on the Western Island cliff top. Panning the area, Jerry and Connie saw that the shelter had survived the storm and that the cliff top was covered with hail stones.

On another screen, Jerry tuned in to the camera inside the shelter. At first, the shelter looked deserted. Then, they noticed movement in a pile of leaves and grass, followed by the emergence of the baby pterodactyl's head.

"Thanks to a sturdy shelter and a pile of bedding, that chick looks quite comfortable," commented Connie.

"That shelter definitely is well built. It has withstood the full force of this storm without apparent damage, and I am amazed by how little rain has leaked into it."

"The male did a good job with those pine boughs you cut yesterday. He has woven them and tough vines into the driftwood to tie the whole thing together."

"It is good for the infant that I cut them. If the male had to scavenge for material, he would never have completed the shelter before the storm arrived."

"I wonder where the adults went during the hail storm."

"They probably took shelter in the forest on the downwind side of that cliff."

After a brief pause, Jerry asked, "How do you feel this morning?"

"Except for some aching bruises and a sore shoulder, I feel great."

"Any indication that the puncture wound might be infected?"

"No, I feel fine, but after breakfast, I'll have Dianne draw a blood sample, which we'll analyze to see if there are any alien microbes circulating in my system. If we find any, we'll check to see if my immune system is producing the appropriate antibodies."

"You've really gotten personally involved in our medical research."

"Believe me, I didn't plan this injury. But if my body is able to effectively deal with whatever nasty microbes were present in that carnivore's mouth, it will sure help build confidence that our immune systems can protect us here on Alcent."

"I wouldn't expect the mouth of a meat eater who never uses dental floss to be a very sterile place, so I can't argue with you on that point."

"Dianne took the fluid she suctioned out of my shoulder wound and put it into the robot lab last night to have it analyzed. That analysis should have been completed hours ago, so we should have a good reading on what kinds of microorganisms lived in that cat's mouth and how much risk I might be facing. Likewise for the fluid I suctioned out of Moose's sty-tick wound."

Jerry affectionately embraced his wife, "I admire the courageous way that you are facing a situation filled with the potential for such danger."

Connie beamed a happy smile at Jerry, "I have confidence in my immune system and in our medical technology."

After a few moments of silence, Jerry said, "I am going outside to look around. I want to see how much damage this hail storm caused."

"I'm coming with you."

"Let's collect some hail stones and put them in the freezer for later analysis. As violent as this storm has been, these hail stones may have been formed high in the stratosphere and contain bits of dust from some other part of this planet."

"What do you expect to learn from them?" asked Connie.

"I don't know. I just think we should do the analysis."

Jerry and Connie collected several dozen hail stones ranging in size from 1/4 to 1/2-inch in diameter and put them in the freezer. Then, they went back outside to explore the eerie scene.

Shortly thereafter, Moose and Dianne joined them. "This is unreal," remarked Moose.

"Even though the air feels warm, all this ice laying around makes me feel chilly," remarked Dianne.

"You've just gotten soft from all those years of continuous comfort on the Challenger," teased Connie.

"There might be some truth to that," admitted Dianne.

"Let's walk to the south end of the plateau and back, and then, let's have breakfast," Connie suggested.

Everyone agreed, and then, with the crunching sound of ice pellets crushing under their feet, they set out to soak up the sights and sounds of their ice covered plateau and inspect damaged plant life. In about an hour, with most of the hail stones already melted, they returned to the capsule hungry for a hearty breakfast.

After breakfast, Dianne and Connie anxiously plunged into their medical research hoping for a good outcome.

Meanwhile, Moose said to Jerry, "I think we should go down to the submarine and retrieve Charlie. I want to inspect him and see how difficult it will be to repair the damage inflicted by the saber-tooth."

Agreeing to Moose's suggestion, Jerry accompanied him to East Bay. After bringing the submarine to the surface, they entered it and examined Charlie.

In less than an hour, Moose found and repaired a severed control line between Charlie's right leg and his inertial guidance system. With the line repaired, Charlie was able to stand up and walk around without losing his balance.

"It appears that most of the remaining damage is just bent structure and ripped skin. But now that he can walk, let's take him home and do a more thorough checkout of his circuitry," Moose said.

"I am amazed that Charlie suffered so little critical damage during the attack by the saber-tooth."

"Making him durable was one of my objectives when I designed him."

After returning to the capsule, Moose and Jerry spent the rest of the day working on Charlie while Dianne and Connie diligently pursued their medical research.

Late that evening, after they were in bed, Jerry said, "I am very thankful that your shoulder wound hasn't developed any complications."

"I am too," replied Connie, "but it's too soon to say that there won't be any. Once they've entered the human body, some germs can lie dormant for long periods of time before they attack. As deep as my puncture wound is, there may be germs in it that weren't present in the fluid Dianne removed from it. However, I am encouraged by the way my immune system is reacting to the ones that we did isolate."

"Hopefully, the wound will heal properly, and you'll be left with nothing but a small scar that will serve as a conversation piece in the distant future, when you'll be telling stories about the early days to our grandchildren."

"I like that scenario, and I promise that I will do everything I can to bring it about."

"Some restful, low-risk days like today was might help you keep that promise."

"Today was rather uneventful. Except for that hail storm this morning and an occasional passing thunder shower, not much happened. What a contrast to yesterday."

"A few more days like today and life here might start to feel just as routine as living back on Earth," joked Jerry.

Connie chuckled and said, "We might be able to establish a routine here on the plateau, but we'll never have to go very far for some wild adventure, and you and I are both anticipating more days like yesterday, despite the hazards."

TIME: Day Seven.

At the breakfast table, Jerry said to Moose, "Let's build a trail up the rock slide. Even working between showers, it shouldn't take us more than two or three days to get it roughed out."

"Good idea," Connie said, before Moose could respond, "Using a rope to scramble up and down that steep slope is a bit cumbersome."

"I like the idea too," agreed Dianne.

"I guess it's unanimous," stated Moose. "But I think you're being too optimistic on how long it will take."

"How much time it will take depends on how fancy we get and how steep we make the grade. I think we should be able to rough out a functional trail in just a few days, if we follow the path of least resistance. It won't be perfect, but we can improve it later."

"A trail with a grade as steep as fifteen to twenty percent would be a big improvement over what we have now," commented Moose.

"With that kind of grade, we'll have about 800 to 1000 feet of trail to build," said Jerry. "If we follow the route I've been considering, the trail will have six switchbacks. We can make most of the trail by simply removing selected rocks and rolling them down the rock slide. Starting an avalanche is the biggest risk we'll face, so we'll have to be careful not to remove rocks that are supporting rocks that are above us."

"If we have to, we can always shore up some areas with small logs. There are plenty of trees between the bottom of the cliff and East Bay that we need to cut down anyway to thin out the forest along our path to the water. That will give us better distance vision to spot bears and other predators that might decide to visit this island."

"Thinning out that stretch of forest is an important job," acknowledged Jerry.

"Cutting down the trees we need for the trail from that area is a practical way to begin that project while building the trail," commented Moose.

"When you're finished eating, we can start moving rocks."

"I've had some experience working with rocks, and it's hard work. I think I should eat a little more; I will need the energy."

Several minutes later, Moose and Jerry picked up their tools and weapons and headed for the rock slide.

Meanwhile, Dianne and Connie decided to do biological research on some of the plants and other organisms living on the plateau, along with continuing their medical research.

TIME: Day Nine, Mid-Afternoon.

Moose and Jerry were standing at the bottom of the rock slide looking up at the trail they had just completed. After admiring it for a few moments, Jerry said, "I think it looks pretty good, considering that we did it in less than three days. As I recall, you didn't think we could do it that fast."

"Well, we did work hard, and we put in some long days. Also, we did get some help from the weather. We didn't get any rain all day yesterday or today. That storm system moved through faster than predicted."

"But, more important than any of that, we used our intelligence," commented Jerry. "We routed the trail in a way that required minimal movement of rocks, and we made some key stretches of the trail by muscling in some logs and anchoring them in place."

"We did lay it out for the easiest possible construction, but we still worked hard, and I'm ready for some fun. Let's go swimming, and then, let's see if we can catch another one of those rainbow pike. We're out of seafood, and I'm hungry for a big dinner."

"That sounds good to me. Let's give our wives a call and see if they would like to join us."

"I think they will, and they might also like to try out our new trail," commented Moose.

Jerry reached for his communicator and beeped Connie. After telling her what he and Moose had in mind, she said, "We'll be right there."

While waiting for Dianne and Connie, Moose said, "I'm hungry for some good smoked fish."

"That does sound good, but there aren't any seafood markets around here, so I guess we'll have to make our own."

"Smoking fish was one of my hobbies back on Earth. I developed some special flavors."

"I remember that. You were even somewhat of a gourmet cook in that specialty. Are you going to resume the hobby here?"

"It would be easy to do," Moose answered. "We have an unlimited supply of fish, and it wouldn't be very difficult to build a small smokehouse. We also have quite a variety of trees and shrubs growing here on the island. Burning green wood with not quite enough oxygen will produce lots of smoke. The question is, which tree or shrub will produce the most flavorful smoke?"

"Also, there's another important question: do any of the trees or shrubs produce smoke that will make the smoked fish poisonous?"

"Maybe tomorrow we should cut samples from different trees and shrubs and test the smoke for toxins and fragrance," suggested Moose.

"Besides building a small smokehouse, that could keep us busy all day."

"But it would be fun, and as hard as we've worked building this trail, I think we deserve a day of recreation."

A few minutes later, Dianne and Connie appeared at the edge of the plateau and proudly marched down the new trail carrying Moose's fishing tackle and a snack for their husbands. "I like it," Dianne said. "It's sure beats climbing the rock slide while hanging onto a rope."

"In time, we'll make it wider and add some guard rails, but this is functional, and by being careful, it's also quite safe," Jerry said.

"Let's head for the beach," said Moose. "I'm hot and sweaty, and need a good swim."

"Me too," said Connie. "I've been doing research all day, and I'm ready to kick back."

"Aren't you worried about infecting your shoulder?" asked Jerry. "It's not completely healed yet."

"I covered the wound with a waterproof bandage. It should be okay."

When they reached the beach, Jerry said, "Let's use the submarine as a diving platform."

Jerry used his communicator to command the submarine, which was still anchored underwater, to rise to the surface. While the sub rose to the surface, the pioneers placed their fishing tackle and snack food in the inflated boat and rowed out to it.

When all had their fill of diving and swimming, Moose and Jerry entered the inflated boat and headed for the same spot where Moose had previously caught a large rainbow pike. Dianne and Connie sprawled out on the sub's deck.

With Moose manning the oars, Jerry selected the same lure from Moose's tackle box that had been successful for Moose. As they approached their destination, Moose stopped rowing and let the boat drift.

After a few minutes of drifting, Jerry cast out the lure. He waited a few seconds to give the lure a chance to sink a few feet, then, began reeling it in with an erratic stop-start jerking motion to simulate an injured fish.

In a matter of seconds, Jerry received a massive strike, sharply bending his fishing rod and quickly removing line from the reel. Worried that all the line would be removed and broken, Jerry tightened the drag causing the fish to change direction. Jerry quickly reeled in the slack line. When the line became tight, the fish leapt out of the water, briefly standing on its flapping tail.

"That's a beauty!" exclaimed Moose.

The fish headed for the bottom, rapidly stripping line off the reel. Upon reaching the bottom, it headed away from Jerry. However, the tightened drag again forced the fish to change directions, and Jerry quickly reeled in the slack line.

A few minutes later, Jerry managed to reel the now exhausted fish up to the boat where Moose netted it and hauled it in. "It's a beauty!" exclaimed Moose. "But it doesn't look quite as big as the one I caught."

"But I didn't have to make a whole bunch of casts to catch it. With just the right touch, it's possible to catch dinner on the first cast. With a little practice you might be able to do that too."

Moose stared at the fish, "I don't think there's any doubt that the one I caught was bigger, but that doesn't surprise me, catching the big ones does require a special kind of talent."

"This one's big enough to give us a few meals. I am guessing that it weighs at least fifteen pounds, maybe even twenty."

"The one I caught was over twenty."

"You'd best enjoy that record while you can: I don't think it's going to hold up."

"Now, that's a statement I can agree with, because I plan to break that record myself."

TIME: Day Ten, Late Afternoon.

Moose and Jerry had collected and tested samples of seventeen kinds of young, tender, sap-rich wood. Testing consisted of burning them individually and channeling the smoke into the robot lab's spectrographic gas analyzer. Computer analysis of the data provided Moose and Jerry with a list of the chemicals contained in the smoke. Also, unburned samples of wood, sap, and bark were analyzed by the lab, and their component chemical compounds were identified.

They were busy discussing test results when Dianne and Connie joined them. Connie leaned over Jerry's right shoulder in a way that was intended to get his attention. "Does any of that wood contain anything toxic enough to cause medical problems?" she asked.

Jerry briefly entertained the promise implied in the unexpected physical distraction and decided to pursue it later. "Only one contains toxins," he answered. "In their natural state, they don't appear to be strong enough to be fatal, but I think you should look at the data. Some additional testing might be needed."

Jerry showed Connie and Dianne the video of Moose cutting the sample from the shrub in question. Then, he showed them the results of the chemical analysis of its sap and smoke.

Dianne and Connie briefly reviewed the data. "I agree with your analysis and your suggestion that we do more testing," Connie said.

"That would be the prudent thing to do," agreed Dianne.

Moving on, Jerry presented video of a tree and said, "The sap from this tree has a very high sugar content and a good flavor. It's definitely as good as maple syrup. I am going to tap the tree and attempt to collect a quart of it. If I am successful, let's plan on having pancakes for breakfast tomorrow."

"When I was a kid, pancakes soaked with butter and drowned with maple syrup was a favorite breakfast of mine," Connie said, with her mouth watering.

Then, while showing video of them, Moose said, "We found two trees and three shrubs that produce fragrant, flavorful smoke that should allow us to produce some delicious smoked fish. And I believe there's enough difference in the smoke to produce smoked fish with five distinctly different flavors. Along with marinating the fish in special spice solutions, I guarantee that we'll have some tasty eating."

"As enthusiastic as you are, it looks like you're ready to back up your words with action," Dianne said.

"First, we need to build a smokehouse. And there's a tree over there that was knocked down by the storm. I'll cut some small logs out of it with a chain saw and cut them into boards with our sawmill. Then, I'll nail them together. It shouldn't take me more than a few hours to build a crude, but functional, smokehouse. Then, we'll need to catch more fish."

"I can help you with both of those tasks," offered Dianne.

"I'll go with you and help you tap this planet's version of Earth's maple tree," Connie said to Jerry.

Remembering the way that Connie had distracted him only a few minutes earlier, Jerry smiled at her, "This could turn out to be an enjoyable outing."

Trying to act like she didn't know what he was talking about, Connie replied, "I've never tapped a maple tree. I don't know how enjoyable it will be."

"Tapping a maple tree is an art, but with enough forethought, I'm sure we'll use the right technique for the best results."

"Perhaps, you will take a little extra time to demonstrate this technique for me, so that I will be able to fully appreciate the art work involved."

"I'll be more than happy to do that for you."

"I think we should get started. Where is this maple tree?" Connie asked, with a subtle, but noticeable, degree of eagerness in her voice.

While pointing at the nearest grove, Jerry said, "There are several of them in that grove."

"I'm glad they're right here on the plateau. That makes them conveniently close. If your technique fulfills expectations, we could do another one tomorrow."

"That favorite breakfast of yours that you were talking about earlier is starting to sound like a special dessert."

"I've sometimes thought of it that way."

Jerry and Connie looked at each other and silently decided that there had been enough conversation. So, they picked up the things they thought they would need and started walking toward the nearby grove.

TIME: Day Eleven, Early Dawn.

Dianne awoke early and quietly slipped out of bed. Looking out the window to the East, she gazed at the soft red bottoms of distant clouds and listened to the chirping of birds anticipating the new day. She noticed the red color of the sky reflecting off the lake giving it the appearance of a sea of subdued fire.

Consumed by the beauty of the scene, she failed to notice that Moose had gotten up and was standing behind her. She was startled when he said, "We are very fortunate to have the opportunity to build a home in the presence of such natural beauty."

"How long have you been standing behind me?"

"Just a couple minutes."

"I really must have been mesmerized to have not noticed you."

"You were definitely preoccupied with it."

"This kind of beauty can easily put me in a trance."

Dianne and Moose silently enjoyed the magnificent beauty before them. "Would you like to go down to the bay with me? I want to try my hand at fishing," Dianne said.

"Not much doubt about my response to that question. We did finish the smokehouse last night, and I would like to fire it up."

About an hour later, when Connie and Jerry were finishing their breakfast, they looked outside and saw Dianne and Moose returning with a large rainbow pike. Stepping outside to greet them, Jerry said, "That looks like the largest fish we've caught so far."

Bubbling over with excitement, Dianne said, "It took me a full ten minutes to tire him out enough so Moose could net him and lift him into the boat."

"Are you saying that you caught this giant?" asked Jerry.

"Yes! And it was such a vigorous battle that my arms are still aching."

"That really surprises me," remarked Jerry.

"You're surprised that my arms ache?"

"No, I'm surprised that you caught that fish."

"Why is that?"

"Just two days ago, your husband told me that catching the big ones requires a special kind of talent. There was no doubt in my mind that he was implying that only he has this talent. And now, you show up with a fish much bigger than the one he caught."

Jerry's remark caused everyone to stare at Moose, who immediately blurted out, "Well, she did have a good coach."

Everyone continued to stare at Moose for a few moments longer, then Dianne decided to rescue him by saying, "I must admit that Moose did give me some helpful tips."

"Thank you," stated Moose.

"It really was a team effort," Dianne continued. "I would've had a difficult time landing this monster by myself. Let's weigh him and see just how heavy he is."

A few moments later, she proudly exclaimed, "Thirty-three and one-half pounds!" She looked at Moose, "That should be enough fish to test your smokehouse."

"It sure is," agreed Moose enthusiastically.

"Are you going to marinate the fillets first?" Jerry asked.

"I would like to start out by trying the natural flavor of the fish combined with the natural flavor of the smoke."

"Which smoke?" asked Jerry.

"One of the shrubs we tested yesterday produced a smoke with a really spicy aroma. For lack of a better name, let's call it the spice bush. Anyway, I want to try it first. I think smoke from it will give the fish a spicy flavor not too different from Cajun spices, but perhaps milder."

"That sounds so good that my mouth is starting to water," commented Jerry.

"Mine too, but I haven't had breakfast yet. I should eat before I start smoking fish."

"There's a half bowl of pancake batter and a pitcher of syrup on the counter," said Connie. "The syrup is what is left from the maple syrup we collected. It is excellent, every bit as sweet as Earth's maple syrup, but the flavor is stronger. To me, it tastes like maple syrup accented with a bit of butterscotch flavor."

"Sounds delicious," Dianne said.

"I can't wait to try it," Moose said quickly.

"I'll fix the pancakes," volunteered Connie.

"While you're eating breakfast, I'll cut some spice bush for the smokehouse fire," Jerry said to Moose.

"We are going to have a delicious smoked fish dinner tonight!" declared Moose.

After breakfast, Moose cut the fish into fillets, placed them on racks in the smokehouse, and got the fire going. As the day wore on, Moose and Jerry busied themselves tending the smoky fire, exercising special care to avoid making it too hot inside the smokehouse.

While doing this, they made detailed plans to build an elevator for the cliff at the south end of the plateau. They decided to have the pulleys and axles made on the Challenger and to make the car and support structure out of wood. The elevator would be powered by an electric motor sent down by Mike with the pulleys, axles, brackets, bolts, and cable.

Dianne and Connie spent the day doing medical and biological research. They also started meticulously exploring South Bay with the marine explorer. With the water in South Bay being about five degrees warmer than East Bay, it would become the choice swimming area.

By mid-afternoon, Moose could no longer resist the temptation and announced, "I think it's time to do a taste test."

He removed a fillet and put it on a plate to cool off for a few minutes. "It certainly looks good," he said, "and it smells pretty good too. In fact, it's making my mouth water."

Moose began picking the fillet apart to see if it was completely baked. "It looks done as far as the cooking is concerned, but if we lower the heat a bit, we can leave the fillets in a while longer to dry them out some. I like smoked fish on the dry side."

"I do too," agreed Jerry.

Moose tasted it, "This is delicious, but another hour in the smoke would make the flavor a bit stronger."

Moose handed Jerry a piece of fish. Jerry tasted it and said, "This is good."

"But I think another hour in the smoke will make it even better," argued Moose.

Jerry savored another mouthful of the freshly smoked fish. "This is already so delicious that I'm not sure that it can be made better.

"I think it can, but to give your opinion some weight, I'll take half the fish out and smoke the other half for another hour."

"While you're doing that, I am going to talk to Mike about this elevator design, so he can make the things we need and send them down."

Jerry called Mike and after discussing the details of the design, Mike said, "I'll make sure that you have the things you need by noon tomorrow."

Mike continued after a bit of silence, "On another subject, I've been tracking your favorite bear; and early this morning, he left your island and headed south. He is now taking a nap on the next big island."

"I don't know why he left, but I'm not going to miss his presence," replied Jerry.

"Maybe, we frustrated his ambitions too many times, or he may simply be a nomadic bear."

"Somewhere on this island, we still have the mystery bear. I am surprised that one of our surveillance cameras hasn't spotted her on the beach by now. But with all the rain we just had, there are probably lots of small pools and streams all over this island to drink out of."

"You're assuming it's a female."

"I think it's a female with cubs in a well-hidden den. You've done a fairly extensive search of the forest with RPVs and haven't found her, so that's the best explanation I can come up with. But, I suppose it's also possible that she left before we had all of our surveillance cameras in place."

"A female with cubs can be very dangerous, and as time goes on, the situation might become even more dangerous for you guys."

"What do you mean by that?"

"I've noticed that you guys are having a difficult time at the dinner table, that is to say, a difficult time getting away from the table. With all that good alien food you're discovering, you're bound to get fat, and you know how that can slow you down."

"As physically active as we are, you don't need to worry about us getting fat."

Having overheard the last few remarks, Connie said, "Speaking of physical activity and food, Dianne and I have located a couple areas where we would like to start experimental gardens. We would appreciate it if you and Moose would work the soil for us."

"It's a little over two hours until dinner time," responded Jerry. "Spading that soil over will give us an opportunity to work up an appetite, so we can feast on some delicious smoked fish."

"Why do I feel like that comment was made for my benefit?" questioned Mike.

"I was merely taking advantage of an opportunity to assure you that we're working hard and won't get fat and slow."

"I think you made that statement to make me hungry for smoked fish," retorted Mike.

"That possibility might have been a little side thought back in some recessed corner of my mind."

"Baloney! Making me hungry was your main objective."

"Well, I just want to make sure that you're ready for a seafood feast when you come down in a few weeks. We plan to prepare a banquet for the next group that comes down, and I'm assuming that you will be part of that group."

"That's an assumption I can live with."

Dianne got Jerry's attention and said, "Let me know when you and Moose are ready to start working the soil for our experimental gardens. I want to be there. I need to watch for bugs and worms living in the soil and to collect some of them to study in the lab."

"I am ready to start right now. Moose can join us when he's done smoking fish."

"I'll pick up some specimen containers," replied Dianne.

"This is going to be slow, difficult work," commented Jerry. "Soil that has never been tilled is usually root-bound and difficult to break up."

"Fortunately, these are small experimental gardens. If you and Moose will do the hard work, Connie and I can do some additional soil preparation tomorrow when we plant the gardens."

"That's a good plan. I'll get some tools."

Jerry picked up a shovel, a spading fork, and a grub hoe. "I'm ready to start digging," he said to Dianne.

Dianne showed Jerry the selected garden areas. He vigorously began the backbreaking project of hand tilling the soil while Dianne alertly watched for and collected some of the little critters living in the soil.

A half hour later, Moose applied his muscle power to the project. After a few minutes, he said, "This is hard work."

"I am not going to disagree with you," Jerry said, drenched in perspiration. "Using muscle power is fine for these small gardens, but before we do any large gardens, we need to bring down some power equipment."

"I can't disagree with that, but I am enjoying this, even though it is tough." After a few moments of thought, Moose said, "Maybe, I misstated that. Maybe, I am enjoying this because it is hard work. Strenuous physical activity always gives me a kind of healthy feeling that I don't seem to be able to get any other way."

"Hard work always makes me feel good too," agreed Jerry.

"If I had known you guys were going to enjoy this so much, I would have selected much larger areas," Dianne said quickly.

"These areas are big enough," Moose instantly responded. "By the time we are done, I will be ready for a hot shower, a big dinner, and a good night's sleep."

Dianne smiled at Moose, "I really appreciate the help you're giving me, and I believe you will sleep good tonight."

Two hours later, both experimental gardens were ready for planting, and the three tired, hungry gardeners headed for the shower. They had sore aching muscles and felt like basking in the hot shower. However, they took quick showers. They knew that Connie was putting the finishing touches on a large feast featuring freshly smoked fish.

TIME: Day Twelve, Late Morning.

Dianne and Connie were busy planting their experimental gardens. They put seeds directly into the ground and transplanted an assortment of plants brought down from the Challenger.

"It'll be interesting to see how these plants do in this environment," commented Connie.

"I wonder how they're going to react to the insects and diseases that they encounter here."

"If they encounter problems they're unable to cope with, our resident plant doctor will have to make some house calls."

"This is the first time I've ever been called a plant doctor," stated Dianne, "but I might very well become one. The defenses these plants developed back on Earth might not be adequate here."

"In that event, your skills will be tested."

"I should be able to develop a treatment for any problem that this environment subjects our plants to. If I succeed at keeping them healthy, we should have a nice variety of salad greens to eat in as little as a month or two."

"Maybe some ripe tomatoes too," remarked Connie. "These plants are loaded with green ones."

"Throw in a few pea pods and some grated sweet onion, and we'll have some good salads."

"And not too long after that, we should have string beans, carrots, potatoes and sweet corn," added Connie.

"I am really looking forward to some natural home grown foods."

"Me too! Our food synthesizers have served us well over the years, but after a while, that subtle psychological feeling that the foods are somehow artificial just seems to grow, even though they aren't."

Meanwhile, on the south end of the plateau, Moose and Jerry were busy cutting and shaping wood for the elevator car and its support structure. Suddenly, their activities were interrupted by a beeping communicator. It was a call from Mike who said, "If you guys will move away from where you're standing, I think I can land the items you requested very close to where you're working."

Looking up and searching the sky, Moose and Jerry saw a circling, descending para-wing. Then, they noticed that a pair of pterodactyls were flying close to it. When the para-wing turned into its final approach glide, the pterodactyls took up positions a little behind it and to either side.

"I wonder if those are the birds from Western Island?" questioned Jerry.

"When they get closer, we'll be able to tell, but right now, I think we should move out of the way. That thing is headed directly at us."

The capsule full of supplies landed within fifty feet of where Moose and Jerry had been standing. The pterodactyls did not land, but circled and watched with interest as the para-wing collapsed on the ground.

Jerry warily observed the circling pterodactyls, "They sure look like the birds from Western Island."

"I think you're right, and they're very interested in that para-wing."

"Pterodactyls are the largest fliers on this planet. Since we arrived, they've seen things in flight that are larger than they are. If they're as intelligent as we think they are, I would expect them to be curious about these large flying objects."

"If we fold up the para-wing and put it away while they're watching, I wonder if they will figure out that it's an inanimate object and not some new flying creature that they need to be concerned about."

"They do have an infant on Western Island," stated Jerry. "Maybe, they're trying to figure out if this is a flying creature that could be a threat. Perhaps, folding it up and putting it away will put their minds at ease."

"That's possible, but I don't think we've been around them long enough to know if we can trust them to not attack while we're folding up something that they might see as a threat."

"Let's stay alert and be prepared."

"I agree," stated Jerry.

Moose and Jerry both checked their 10.5-millimeter pistols to make sure that they were loaded and ready for use. Then, while watching the circling pterodactyls, they walked over to the para-wing, unhooked it from the capsule, folded it up, and packed it into its storage compartment in the upper part of the capsule.

When this task was finished, the pterodactyls headed toward Western Island and Moose and Jerry went back to elevator construction.

TIME: Day Fifteen, Lunch Time.

The interstellar pioneers were at the south end of Stellar Plateau admiring their new elevator. "It certainly looks rugged," declared Dianne, "but is it safe to ride?"

"We loaded 2,500 pounds of rocks onto it and hauled them up and down several times," responded Moose.

"Then, it should certainly be safe for the four of us," commented Connie. "Let's go down to the beach and enjoy a picnic lunch."

A few moments later, all were in the elevator and slowly descending along the south face of Stellar Plateau. "This isn't very fast," remarked Connie.

"That's true," agreed Jerry, "but it is convenient. As slow as it is, it still only takes about a minute, and that's much faster than hiking down the trail we built on the rock slide. Not to mention that you'd still have to walk the beach to get to South Bay."

"What would happen to us if the support cable were to break?" asked Dianne.

In response, Moose showed Dianne and Connie the guide cable located at each corner of the car and said, "Each of these cables passes through a friction brake that will automatically engage if the main support cable breaks."

"Then, we'd be stranded at whatever height the support cable broke," commented Connie.

"No, the friction brakes can be used to maintain a controlled descent," responded Moose.

A few seconds later, the elevator came to a stop at the base of the cliff, and Connie said, "I like it. You guys did a good job."

Shortly, all were seated at a picnic table located on the sandy beach, only a few feet from the water. Dianne briefly considered the table's location, "A picnic table on the beach, and an elevator to get to it, what a convenient setup."

"And it's a rugged outdoor table," added Connie.

"We didn't spend much time on it," stated Jerry. "It's just a few slabs of wood bolted to some legs."

"It definitely has a crude backwoods appearance," remarked Moose, "but it's perfect for our needs, and it makes me feel like I'm on a camping trip."

"If you guys keep building things, this island will soon feel like home rather than a camp-out," said Dianne.

"I'm not sure if that's a complaint or a compliment," Moose said to Jerry.

"I'm not sure either," replied Jerry, "but they've been busy planting and tending gardens, and a garden filled with fresh vegetables can sure make a campsite look and feel like home."

"My remark was intended to be a compliment," declared Dianne. "But even after we've been here for a few years, and have all the conveniences of home, I think I will still feel like we're camping out, because we'll still be a lone human outpost on a hostile planet."

"As if we need a reminder that we are on a hostile planet, there's a pair of pterodactyls circling, and they seem to be investigating us," Connie said.

Jerry looked up, "They aren't the pair from Western Island, and they're closer to us than I feel comfortable with."

Jerry got up from the table, picked up his rifle, and prepared for defensive action. Moose, Dianne, and Connie followed his example.

"Even though they're uncomfortably close, they aren't doing anything of a threatening nature," commented Connie.

"No, they aren't," agreed Jerry. "They may be doing nothing more than wondering if we would be a good alternative to eating seafood all the time."

"That's a comforting thought," responded Connie.

At that moment, the male pterodactyl from Western Island arrived on the scene and made some loud squawking sounds that got the immediate attention of the circling pterodactyls. They turned to meet him and made some squawking sounds in return.

271

With giant predators apparently carrying on a conversation directly above them, the humans watched in spellbound amazement. After a couple minutes of back and forth squawking, the new arrivals left, flying off toward the northeast. Then, the male from Western Island circled once, let out a squawking sound that seemed to have a reassuring tone to it, and then left.

Jerry looked at his fellow pioneers and asked, "What do you think of that?"

"I think the new arrivals were told to leave us alone," replied Connie.

"But was it a warning, or was he simply telling them that we are friends?" questioned Jerry.

"Either way, it looks like removing that tree from his cliff top home has made him feel indebted to us," responded Connie.

"That's probably true," agreed Jerry, "but there are some other possibilities that we need to consider. Is it possible that the pair on Western Island has observed us long enough to have concluded that we are far superior to them and that we are capable of defending ourselves with lethal force? Is it possible that the new arrivals are friends of the Western Island pterodactyls and that the big male simply informed them of our capabilities?"

"If we say yes to those questions, then we are saying that pterodactyls are smart enough to do deductive reasoning," Dianne commented.

"And we're also saying that they're capable of communicating on a fairly advanced level," declared Moose.

While continuing to speculate on how intelligent the pterodactyls might be, the pioneers enjoyed their picnic lunch. When Jerry finished eating, he changed into his swimming trunks and stretched out on the sand next to the water's edge. Shortly, Connie joined him.

"You removed your bandage and stitches this morning, and it looks like your puncture wound is completely healed," Jerry said.

"It is, and my shoulder feels good too. So, except for this small scar, I seem to be fully recovered from my brush with death."

"Does that mean that you're ready to return to the countryside for some additional adventure?"

"I think I will be content to put on a video headset and explore the countryside with an RPV."

"When we sail around the lake, we should see some interesting sights and learn a lot using that approach."

"And we can enjoy the adventure from the safety of our submarine. The next time I am attacked by a carnivore, I might not be so lucky."

"I hope that there won't be a next time," said Jerry softly.

"Considering where we are, that might be somewhat unrealistic."

"Unfortunately, I think you're right."

"I am really looking forward to our exploratory voyage around the lake," Jerry said. "It'll not only be fun, but we'll also discover lots of plants and animals, greatly adding to our basic knowledge about our new home."

"We'll also gain a great deal of knowledge about the underwater world," remarked Moose. "Just think, there may be many different kinds of fish living in other parts of the lake."

"My husband's mind never seems to be very far away from food," remarked Dianne.

Moose looked at his wife and said, "Don't tell me you've already forgotten how excited you were when you caught that big rainbow pike a few days ago?"

"That was pretty exciting."

"And haven't you been enjoying the smoked fillets?"

"I must admit, they are delicious," agreed Dianne while nibbling on one.

"I have nothing more to say in my defense," stated Moose.

Watching Dianne munch on the smoked fish fillet, Connie conceded, "As a member of the jury, I must say that I think the defense won this one."

Dianne made fleeting eye contact with Connie. She continued to enjoy her smoked rainbow pike. Moose smiled in smug satisfaction.

"When do you think we can go on our voyage of discovery?" Connie asked Jerry.

Jerry briefly considered the question, "There are some things we should do here on the island before we take off on a week-long sailing trip. We've been here more than two weeks, and we still haven't explored this island's forest. I would like to spend a few days poking around in the bushes before we leave for a week."

"While you're doing that, Dianne and I can continue our research on the things we found living in the soil in our gardens."

"We also need to observe the insects that visit our gardens and determine if they're beneficial or detrimental," Dianne said.

"Since we're talking about food, we need to find out if some of the other species of fish that live around this island are edible," stated Jerry.

"Now that's a project I wouldn't mind devoting some time and energy to," commented Moose. "Being the devoted husband that I am, I've noticed that my wife seems to have developed a real taste for smoked seafood."

They all stared at Dianne waiting for a response. "I admit it. It is delicious," she said, shrugging her shoulders.

Moose gave Dianne a loving smile.

"I like the idea of going sailing for a few days," Dianne said to Jerry. "What a fun way to get acquainted with our little corner of this planet. I think I could be ready to go in about three days."

"Unless something unforeseen develops in the next few days, let's plan on going," stated Jerry.

"I'll be ready," declared Connie, "but right now I'm ready to go swimming. It's time we check out the water of South Bay."

"I'll go with you," stated Jerry.

"I'll stand guard," declared Moose.

"I'll help you," offered Dianne, "and when they return, maybe we can go swimming together."

"That sounds good to me."

TWELVE

A Shocking Discovery
Makes Life More Complicated

TIME: Day Sixteen.

The interstellar pioneers were enjoying their breakfast when they received a call from Mike. After the usual greetings, Mike said, "I have some video that I think you'll find interesting."

Before anyone could respond, Mike's image disappeared from the screen and was replaced by an image of the Rocky Point Bay waterfront. A large bear stepped out of the forest onto the beach followed immediately by two small cubs that looked like playful fur balls. The bear family walked along the waterfront for about a hundred yards until they came to a tree that the mother liked. After sending her cubs up the tree, she entered the water of the bay and swam out a short distance. Then, she submerged her head and body. With only her hind legs sticking out of the water, she reached down and grabbed a large abalone.

Once back on shore, she called her cubs. They scrambled down the tree and bounded up to her. When she presented them with the abalone, they smelled it and pawed it. Then, they circled it seemly at a loss as to what to do with it. Having aroused their curiosity, she opened the shell while they attentively watched. Then, she gave each cub a piece of abalone to chew on.

"Looks like our mystery creature has finally appeared," commented Jerry.

"If you would like to collect a hair sample for analysis, she and her cubs are still on the beach," said Mike as he turned off the video and switched to live coverage from the surveillance camera on Cliff Point.

"While we're doing that, let's attach a transmitter to her, so we can track her movements," said Jerry.

"It'll be interesting to see how the hair analysis turns out," commented Moose.

"There's no doubt in my mind that her hair will match the hair we found in the thorn bush at the north end of the island on our second day here," declared Jerry.

"Those little cubs sure are cute," stated Connie.

"I'm amazed by how small they are," commented Dianne.

"They're such playful little fuzz balls that it seems like they would be cuddly little pets to have," remarked Connie.

"Your cuddly little pets would have the potential to turn into 1500-pound pets in a few years. Anyway, I think their mother might take exception to your idea," Jerry commented.

"If she's anything like the bears back on Earth, she would probably fight to the death in defense of her cubs," agreed Connie.

"It'll be good to have a radio on her, so we can keep our distance while we explore the forest," remarked Moose.

"If she's using this island as a safe haven on which to raise her cubs, she's probably going to be here for a few years," said Dianne.

"That shouldn't be a problem if we always know where she is," stated Jerry.

While the group continued to observe the bear family, Mike said, "On another subject, the pterodactyls that arrived yesterday are busy making repairs to the shelter on Rock Island, so it looks like you have some new neighbors."

"Some new neighbors who are apparently expecting to give birth," added Connie.

"It's a good thing they don't know that you're a doctor, or they might expect you to make a house call," remarked Dianne.

"You're letting your imagination run away with you," responded Connie.

"Am I? Let's suppose that they're intelligent enough to recognize us as vastly superior beings based on what they see us do. Think about it! When they see us do things that are incomprehensible to them, isn't it possible that they might think us capable of doing just about anything?"

"Are you suggesting that at some point, they might look upon us as gods who can treat any medical problem they might have, or any problem of any nature for that matter?"

"That is a possibility," declared Dianne. "Throughout most of history, humans have had a tendency to make gods out of forces they were unable to understand. Suppose these pterodactyls have the intelligence level of prehistoric humans, isn't it possible that they could see us as gods? After all, we did descend out of the heavens, and we routinely bring down supplies."

Connie considered Dianne's comments, "If they eventually conclude that we are benevolent, all-powerful creatures, they might look for ways to pay us homage or even worship us. I don't think I would be comfortable in that position. What would happen the first time that we disappoint them?"

"And what would happen among them if they were to start competing for our favors?" questioned Dianne.

"I don't think that I want to be worshipped either," stated Jerry, "and I certainly don't want to be in the position where they frequently and aggressively seek favors from us. The ideal situation would be for them to just respect our capabilities, be our friends, and otherwise leave us alone."

"That seems to be exactly what the pterodactyls on Western Island are doing," remarked Moose.

"Hopefully, the new arrivals will do the same," stated Jerry as he got up from the table. "I am going to outfit an RPV, tag that bear, and collect some hair before she disappears into the forest."

"I'll do the hair analysis," volunteered Dianne.

"Thank you," responded Jerry. Then, turning to Moose he said, "After I tag her, let's start exploring our forest."

"What part of the forest do you want to look at today?" Moose asked, following Jerry out the door.

"Let's hike north from the bottom of the rock slide and follow the island's crest to Rocky Point."

"What do you expect to discover? This island has been rather thoroughly explored with RPVs."

"We may not discover anything of consequence, but I need to gain the familiarity that comes from setting foot on the soil, scrambling over logs, and poking around in the bushes. I can study RPV video all day, but until I set foot on the soil, I won't have the feeling that this land is ours."

TIME: Day Sixteen, Late Afternoon.

Moose and Jerry arrived at Rocky Point after a strenuous hike through dense forest. It took them most of the day to reach this destination, even though the straight-line distance from Stellar Plateau is only about three-and-one-half miles. Progress was slow, because they proceeded with extreme caution, and at times, they had to work their way through or detour around dense undergrowth. Also, they stopped numerous times to investigate things of interest.

The difficult, time-consuming hike made Moose and Jerry tired and hungry. They sat on a large boulder eating a snack, enjoying the scenic beauty of Clear Lake.

Shortly before arriving at Rocky Point, Moose and Jerry decided that they had done enough hiking for one day and called their wives to ask them for a ride home. Connie and Dianne were on their way with the submarine.

"On the way home, why don't we sail into Red Fish Lagoon and catch a couple redfish," suggested Moose. "I would like to find out if they're edible and taste good."

"Good idea, but I'd like some abalone steak."

"Me too! Why don't we pick up a couple large ones? I could smoke some of it and find out how it will taste."

"Do you have any doubt about how it will taste?" questioned Jerry.

"No! It will be good! However, it sometimes takes a little experimenting to create the perfect smoking technique. That's a good project for tomorrow, unless you're planning for us to do more forest exploration."

"We do have more exploration to do, and it's such slow going that it will probably take a few days to finish the job."

"It seems like we should be able to safely delay completion of that project," commented Moose. "We didn't discover anything of consequence today, and if tomorrow's going to be more of the same; then, I think I would rather spend it experimenting with smoking abalone."

"I can count on you to always be thinking about food."

"I have a feeling that when you taste my smoked abalone, you're going to appreciate my talent with smoked delicacies."

"I already appreciate your talent in that area, especially after hiking through the forest all day," Jerry said, enjoying a piece of smoked fish.

"What does that have to do with how good my smoked fish tastes?"

"To start with, I've worked up quite an appetite. Besides that, this fish has a flavor that just seems to make it a natural part of outdoor activity, especially hiking and camping."

"I agree," said Moose, reaching for another piece of smoked fish.

"I am surprised by your assertion that we didn't discover anything of consequence today," Jerry said.

"What do you mean? All we saw were lots of birds and small mammals, and they didn't look much different than similar creatures back on Earth."

"But, that is significant! We hiked the entire length of the island without encountering any dangerous creatures. Except for the bears, Pioneer Island might be a very safe place to live," Jerry said. "All the same, I think I will explore a little more around the base."

"Alone?"

"Why not?"

"There is safety in numbers, and we don't know for sure that this island is safe for us."

"But just a few minutes ago, you said that you didn't want to do any forest exploration tomorrow," Jerry said. "You said that we would probably just see more of what we saw today and that we wouldn't discover anything of consequence."

"Just because I said that doesn't mean that I think it's a wise idea for you to wander around in the forest by yourself," Moose countered. "We are on an alien planet, and we just don't know what dangers might exist."

"It sounds to me like you're having a flashback to our football days when protecting me was one of your responsibilities."

"That's possible" agreed Moose.

For a few moments, Moose thought about his college football days and all the times he had saved Jerry from being sacked. "I did take that responsibility quite seriously, and I did a good job at it too, I might add."

"I can't dispute that, and to put your mind at ease, I have no intention of exploring the forest alone. I think my wife might like to accompany me."

"She would be excellent backup in case of unexpected trouble. She has proven to be very quick with her rifle. You might say that she has met the test of combat. Also, she can provide medical assistance if the need arises."

"You've convinced me. You can stay home and smoke your abalone. We will expect a sumptuous feast tomorrow night when we return."

"No problem."

"Getting back to today's exploration, I'm surprised that we didn't see any predators," commented Jerry. "With the abundance of small mammals and game birds living on this island, it seems like a feline predator about the size of a house cat should be able to thrive here."

"Before we landed, we had Charlie walk through the forest leaving a trail of blood droplets, and he was tracked by a small animal that looked like a cross between a large weasel and a small mink. So, we know for a fact that there are small predators here."

"Perhaps, we didn't see any of them because they did not want to be seen."

"That might be the case," agreed Moose. "Out of necessity, hunters of this type are masters of stealth, and they could've easily hidden from us."

"That's true, but even though we didn't see any of them, they must be a fairly numerous."

"Why?"

"Because we saw numerous species of small mammals, and if they're anything like their earth counterparts, they're capable of rapid reproduction. To keep their populations in check, hunters must also be fairly numerous."

"As far as keeping the mammal population in check is concerned, the land hunters are undoubtedly getting help from predatory birds. We saw several of them today, and there's an owl nest right on Stellar Plateau."

"And those owls are large enough to prey on the kind of small predator that tracked Charlie," commented Jerry.

"We need a name for the hunter that tracked Charlie. Since it looked like a cross between a weasel and a mink, why don't why call it a weamink?"

"I suppose that name is as good as any."

For the next several minutes, Moose and Jerry gazed at the panoramic scenery, each silently lost in thought. Shifting his gaze, Jerry said, "Some of those rocks have highly reflective crystals in them. They sparkle like gem stones."

Moose turned toward Alpha Centauri A to view the glittering rocks. After a few moments, he said, "There's a reflection over there that's especially bright, almost what you'd expect from a small mirror."

"That is brilliant. Let's take a look at it. Who knows, we may be living on a treasure island loaded with large gem stones."

"Who would we sell them to? There's no market here, and we can't ship them back to Earth."

"It would be frustrating to discover a vast supply of gems and not have a market for them," remarked Jerry.

Moose and Jerry walked over to the source of the reflection, and right there in front of their feet, they saw a small piece of shiny metal wedged between two rocks. Astounded by the implications of what they were looking at, Moose and Jerry were speechless for a few moments, while their minds raced through possible explanations for the origin of the metal.

"Is this discovery consequential enough to make your day of exploration worthwhile?" Jerry asked Moose.

"Consequential? I am shocked by the implications of what we're looking at! We might not be alone!"

"That is a definite possibility," agreed Jerry.

"It sure is! Where did that piece of metal come from? How did it get here?"

"There is a remote possibility that it broke loose from one of the vehicles that we've landed here."

"I doubt that," commented Moose. "Our equipment is very well built."

"Then, it either came from another planet, or there are intelligent creatures living somewhere on this planet with the technology to work with metals. But it seems like our reconnaissance would have spotted some indication of their presence."

"If it came from another planet, the most likely candidate is B-2," declared Moose.

"If it came from there, I wonder which of the two sides in the great war sent a spacecraft here, how long ago, and was it manned or unmanned?"

"If the spacecraft was manned, it may have been heading for one of the islands in this lake for the same reasons that brought us here."

"This is a choice area, so that is possible."

"I wonder if there are any survivors."

"Why wouldn't there be survivors?" questioned Jerry.

"A piece of metal that small indicates that the spacecraft might have disintegrated. Maybe, no one survived."

"If the metal came from a spacecraft."

"What else could it have come from?" asked Moose.

"What if intelligent beings safely landed here, explored for a few weeks, and then left. Isn't it possible that piece of metal could be the remains of a food container or beverage can?"

"That's possible, but what if they safely landed and were unable to leave. There could be intelligent beings living on one of the other islands in this lake, or on one of the islands in the big lake up the river to the north. If they're somewhere in this area, they've certainly seen our shuttle flights, and consequently, they know that we're here. In fact, they would know exactly where we are! But we don't know where they are or if they even exist."

"It seems that our lives are a bit more complicated now than they were a few minutes ago," Jerry said, calmly.

"That may be the understatement of the century!"

Jerry crouched down and carefully removed the rocks from around the piece of metal and picked it up. "The first thing we need to do is analyze this alloy to see what elements it contains. That information, along with its physical properties, should give us a pretty good idea what it may have been used for."

"We also need to search for more pieces of metal and items that may have been brought here by intelligent beings."

"Unfortunately, they're going to be difficult to find," stated Jerry. "If this is part of a spacecraft that broke up and if this happened several years ago, any pieces that came down in the forest will have been buried by falling leaves long ago. Our best bet might be to search the lake bottom with the submarine."

"Pieces on the lake bottom would eventually be buried by sediment."

"While that's true, it wouldn't happen as quickly as in the forest. Falling leaves from just one season could easily bury a small piece of metal, and searching with metal detectors would be a very time consuming process."

"Much of Stellar Plateau is open. I could search it tomorrow while I'm tending my smokehouse. Also, the rock slide might be a good place to search."

"After what we've just discovered, you're still planning to smoke abalone tomorrow?"

"Of course. I don't think we should discontinue living our lives just because we might not be alone. We should live the way we want to, while being alert to the possibility of attack by technologically advanced beings. Your question implies that you feel otherwise."

"No! I don't. I agree with your thinking, but we do need to find out as quickly as possible where this piece of metal came from. If there are technologically advanced beings living here, we need to find them and determine if they pose any danger to us."

"If there are advanced beings living on this planet, there numbers must be small. It seems like our orbital reconnaissance would've easily found a large society."

"That sounds reasonable," commented Jerry, "but since we don't know what kind of beings we're looking for, I don't think we should make that assumption. We need to use the Challenger's instruments to make a determined search of this planet for anything that cannot be explained as a natural occurrence."

Jerry reached for his communicator and punched in Mike's number. After reporting the situation and discussing it with him, Jerry asked, "How much progress have Michelle and Shannon made at understanding each other's language?"

"They're fluent enough to have regular gossip sessions."

"I heard that remark," declared Michelle, "and I would like to point out that all of our conversations have been very informative."

"Does that answer your question?" asked Mike.

Jerry chuckled a bit, "I would say they're fluent."

"We're fluent enough so that I can find out if Rex and Shannon know if any spacecraft were ever sent here," stated Michelle.

"I would also like to know which side sent them, how long ago, and were they manned or unmanned?"

"I will send the information request right away, but because of the distance involved it will be a few hours before I receive the response."

"That time delay must make conversation a bit cumbersome," commented Jerry.

"It does, but we've adjusted to it quite well."

"I concluded that from Mike's comment."

"Just because Shannon is deeply interested in social customs back on Earth, Mike likes to tease us that we just spend a lot of time gossiping; when in reality, we're learning about each other's culture, and I find that very interesting."

"Maybe, Mike needs more projects to occupy his mind."

"Life has been getting a bit routine," said Mike, "but now, I can help you solve the mystery of that piece of metal."

"I would like you to start by doing a meticulous reconnaissance of all the islands within a couple hundred miles of Pioneer Island. Search for any evidence that technologically advanced beings might be living here," said Jerry.

"How about the countryside around Clear Lake?"

"Do the islands first. From what I've seen of the countryside, aliens would have a difficult time surviving there. Even if they came here well armed, they would've had to face the prospect of eventually running out of ammunition, and they would've found a way to move to an island before that happened."

"We'll start the search right away."

"I am going to analyze this alloy. When I find out exactly what it is, we can compare it to the alloys used in the construction of the spacecraft we captured."

"That might tell us if that piece of metal came from B-2," said Mike.

Before Jerry could make another comment, Moose tapped him on the shoulder and said, "There's a submarine surfacing over there, and it looks like ours."

"Until a few minutes ago, I would've made that assumption without so much as a second glance," Jerry chuckled.

"But, as you said a few minutes ago, our lives are now a bit more complicated."

TIME: Day Seventeen, Early Morning.

Over breakfast, the pioneers discussed the implications of the previous day's discovery. Mike and Michelle joined the discussion via the communications system.

Holding it up for all to see, Jerry said, "I am convinced that this piece of metal originated on B-2. It is identical to the alloy used in some parts of the derelict satellite that we captured. The question is: which side in the great war sent a spacecraft here?"

"We sent Rex pictures of the inscriptions on some of the parts in that satellite," remarked Michelle. "He said that they are in the language of their enemies in the great war."

"Since we destroyed their biological warfare complexes, I think we should assume that they're also our enemies," added Mike.

"I'm glad that they're too far away to bother us," stated Moose.

"Are you sure about that?" asked Jerry. "Keep in mind that they may have already demonstrated their ability to come here."

"But the great war has left their country in a shambles, and I can't imagine that they could come here now," argued Moose.

"Earth's history is filled with examples of very determined nations recovering from the devastation of war in just a few years," declared Jerry.

"That's true," agreed Moose, "but would this nation's recovery effort be directed toward rebuilding their society or toward seeking revenge against us?"

"That would depend on the ambitions of the political system that's in place," commented Jerry.

"According to Shannon, that country was run by a brutal dictator during the great war," remarked Michelle. "As the war dragged on for decades and turned into a stalemate, she thinks the military killed the dictator and took over."

"If they're in charge, they may be more interested in revenge against us than in rebuilding their country," Jerry commented.

Then, turning to Connie, Jerry asked, "Would you care to speculate on how their minds work?"

"Based on what we've seen, it is difficult to find adequate words to describe their psyche. Such terms as cruel, sadistic, and malicious don't begin to describe their lust for inflicting death and destruction. After all, they were conducting a campaign of genocide against half of their planet when we shut them down."

"During one of our early orbits over their territory, I sensed intense hatred, a foreboding feeling of evil. I felt in grave danger. I sensed that they would've killed me if they could have," Dianne added.

"Are you and Connie suggesting that they will use whatever manufacturing capability they have left to make armed spacecraft to attack us; rather than, make products to improve the lives of their people?" Mike asked.

"They are extremely evil and vengeful," Dianne replied, "They were attempting to kill all warm-blooded life on half of their planet; rather than, let the war be over and devote their energy to rebuilding their country. We stopped them, and I think we should assume that they will seek revenge against us. Their attacks on us might even be carried out by suicidal fanatics."

"But can they get here?" questioned Moose.

"We don't know, but apparently, they've come here before," replied Jerry.

"According to Rex, both sides moved critical manufacturing facilities underground during the course of the great war," Michelle said. "Much of this was attacked with nuclear weapons, but some facilities on both sides did survive."

"Even though their resources are limited, if they have a fanatical determination to get revenge, they will find a way to attack us," stated Jerry.

After a few moments of silence, Moose reluctantly agreed, "And there's little doubt that they know where we are. All they had to do was track us when we left and monitor our daily communication with Rex and Shannon."

"I think we're in agreement that they could get a spacecraft here and that they may be possessed with a fanatical determination to get revenge; however, even fanatics respect overwhelming military power," Mike said. "They've seen firsthand what we can do with our antimatter particle beam gun. I'm not sure that they would want to have another encounter with its destructive capability. They may decide to just rebuild their military and not do anything to risk bringing us back to attack them again."

"Or they might try to figure out a way to destroy the Challenger," remarked Jerry, "and if that's successful, then attack us."

"If they have the intelligence to get here, they should also be able to figure out that in the vacuum of space our antimatter particle beam gun could destroy them at a range of several million miles," argued Mike. "They should realize that an attempt to attack us would be an exercise in futility."

"We can only destroy them if we're able to detect their presence," countered Jerry. "What if stealth technology is incorporated into the design and construction of their spacecraft?"

"We do have reconnaissance satellites orbiting B-2," commented Mike, "so we will get adequate warning of an impending attack. Since their rockets still rely on chemical propulsion, a vehicle capable of reaching us with a meaningful payload would be quite large and easy to detect when it is launched. Its speed would be low enough, so that it would take a few years to get here, giving us plenty of time to find it and destroy it."

"You sound very confident," commented Jerry.

"With their level of technology, I don't think it's possible for them to build a spacecraft that I can't find when I have a few years to work the problem."

"We haven't yet presented you with a problem that you weren't able to solve," remarked Jerry.

Mike smiled in satisfaction, "Thanks for the compliment."

After a few moments of silence, Jerry said, "Our original mission plan calls for stripping the Challenger of everything useful and bringing it down here, but now that we have a potential external threat, that plan is no longer viable."

Before Jerry could continue, Moose interrupted him, "Our lives are now a bit more complicated than what was envisioned by our mission planners back on Earth."

"That's true," agreed Jerry, "but with proper planning we can deal with this new complication. Specifically, we must develop plans to keep our shuttles and the Challenger functional for as far into the future as we possibly can."

"It is good that we made our long journey at .73c rather than .77c," remarked Mike. "Because of that key decision, we still have an ample supply of antimatter. We can even return to B-2 and cripple the war making ability of an enemy, if we have to."

"Let's hope that it doesn't come to that," stated Jerry. "But, in case it does, let's be prepared."

"I will get some people working on the development of operational procedures and maintenance plans to keep our shuttles and the Challenger operational far beyond their design life spans," stated Mike.

"Good!" replied Jerry. "Now, let's get back to the more immediate problem: are there humanoids from B-2 living here on Alcent?"

"Rex doesn't know for sure, but he thinks their opponents in the great war did send a manned spacecraft to Alcent about thirty years ago, shortly before the war started," Michelle said. "He does not know what the mission's objectives were, but he said that the brutal dictator in charge at that time had a fanatical desire to expand his empire. He used a form of religion to control his subjects. He even had religious police who would persecute and sometimes kill individuals who refused to bow to his religious dictates. He maintained that he was God's representative and that he had divine powers. Rex speculates that the evil dictator may have been trying to expand his empire to other planets to satisfy his ego and bolster his claim to divine powers."

"If Rex's speculation is correct, we may have some evil fanatics living here on Alcent," suggested Jerry.

"If they arrived here twenty-five to thirty years ago, there may not be any of them alive anymore," commented Connie. "I was almost killed less than a week after our arrival."

"And on that day, I could easily have been killed," added Moose.

Jerry said, "While it's possible that none of them are alive anymore, we must assume that they came here prepared to survive and multiply, and that means they were well-armed and the crew included both males and females."

"But Rex does not know for sure that a manned mission was sent here," argued Moose. "All we have to go on is a small piece of metal, which could just as easily have come from an unmanned spacecraft that broke apart in the right place for a piece to fall on Pioneer Island."

"That's true enough," agreed Jerry, "but until we can prove otherwise, our security requires that we assume that a manned mission came here and that there are survivors. Even though they might be living thousands of miles from here, we need to be alert to the possibility that they could be living in our immediate vicinity."

"Wherever they are, they may be preoccupied with surviving and building their own society," Connie offered. "The demands of accomplishing those objectives may have caused them to drop their fanatical religion and extremist political system. They may not be a threat to us."

"That's a possibility," acknowledged Jerry, "but I will need to see proof of that before I can accept it."

"Me too!" exclaimed Dianne.

"If there are intelligent humanoids living on Alcent, it shouldn't be all that difficult to find indications of their presence," said Mike.

"Let's start with what we know, namely that their best chance to survive and prosper would be to live on an isolated island like we are. Also, we've explored Pioneer Island thoroughly enough to know that they aren't living here," Jerry said. "All of our beaches are constantly being scanned by surveillance cameras, so they cannot come here without us knowing about it. But for our own peace of mind, we need to take a look at the other islands in this lake. The best way to do that is with RPVs."

"There are people up here who would like to fly those RPVs and help you with the search," remarked Mike. "But there is one small problem: the RPVs don't have the endurance to do an extensive search after flying to the islands and still have enough juice to return."

"We'll either have to park them in the sunshine to recharge their batteries for the return flight, or we can land them on the deck of the submarine and use it to ferry them to the islands," said Jerry.

"Sounds like our multipurpose boat is about to become an aircraft carrier," commented Moose.

Being a student of naval history, Jerry formed some mental images of some of the giant flattops that the U.S. Navy had operated in the past. "It requires a real stretch of the imagination to call our boat an aircraft carrier," he said to Moose.

"But, if we discover hostile aliens living in our immediate vicinity, we could spy on them as well as attack them with RPVs launched from our boat, so in effect, it could function much like an aircraft carrier."

"In a limited sense, that's true," agreed Jerry, "but today it's going to function like a special purpose search vessel to complement reconnaissance done by the Challenger. If intelligent humanoids came here twenty-five to thirty years ago, we will either find them or evidence that they've been here."

"Sounds like a perfect job for a little aircraft carrier loaded with reconnaissance aircraft," stated Moose.

Convinced that Moose was determined to win the semantics argument, Jerry simply nodded in agreement. Then, he gave his attention to Connie, who asked, "Which island are we going to search first?"

"We'll start with the next island to the north. It's the second biggest in this lake and is just as isolated from the countryside as Pioneer Island."

"I would like to go with you," said Connie.

"I would enjoy having you come with me," replied Jerry.

"Sounds like you're trying to turn our little aircraft carrier into a love boat," commented Moose with a grin.

"I guess I inadvertently phrased my response with a double meaning, but I think you know what I meant."

"Just the same, I wouldn't want to get in the way, so I think I will stay here and search the rock slide and this plateau for spacecraft parts and any other indication that we aren't the first aliens to visit here. Also, I can tend my smokehouse while I search."

"I have some research projects I need to continue working on, so I will stay here with Moose," Dianne said quickly.

Jerry turned to Moose, "Before you fire up your smokehouse, I need you to help me check out the RPVs and get them onto the deck of our boat."

Moose nodded in acknowledgment of Jerry's request. Then, Jerry turned to Connie and said, "I should be ready to leave in about an hour."

"I'll pack our supplies for the day."

"Pack enough for a long day, because it's possible we might look at all four of the northern islands."

"Okay."

"Don't eat too much while you're gone," Moose said, "because I will have some delicious, freshly smoked abalone fillets waiting for you when you return."

Connie looked at Moose and did her best to show him a naughty grin. "Don't worry, we'll be hungry. After all, we do have all day to work up an appetite."

Moose grinned and said to Jerry, "Your day might be a bit more involved than just looking for aliens."

"I am capable of dealing with any opportunities that come up," responded Jerry.

"So am I," remarked Connie.

"You people are sure having a tough life down there," Mike stated quickly. "Every day just seems to be filled with fun and excitement, and you have an abundance of delicious real food to enjoy."

Jerry smiled, "Making sure that it's safe down here for the rest of you has put quite a strain on us, but we're shouldering the burden as best we can."

"Yeah, and it looks like a real struggle too," Mike chuckled. "I sure hope that creating an abalone delicacy doesn't burden Moose with an overwhelming amount of stress today."

Determined not to have his project belittled even in a joking way, Moose asserted, "Discovering and developing local food sources is essential to our future health and prosperity."

Mike laughed, "Yeah, that's true. I just hope meeting that important responsibility isn't so stressful that you end up with high blood pressure."

"You don't need to worry, because I have so much natural talent in this field of human endeavor that it's actually a recreational activity for me."

"I think those last four words do a pretty good job of describing your life down there to date," bantered Mike.

"There might be some truth to that, but remember our lives have gotten a bit more complicated recently."

TIME: Day Seventeen, Late Morning

Jerry and Connie approached the first island to the north of Pioneer Island. While scanning the south end of the island with binoculars, Connie said, "It sure doesn't look inhabited."

"I doubt that it is," commented Jerry. "If it were, it seems like our orbital reconnaissance would've spotted boats of some sort in the water around the island."

"That should apply to all the islands. I can't imagine humanoids living on an island in a big lake and not having boats for fishing and transportation."

"But what seems reasonable to us might not be to them. The only way that we can be absolutely certain that we are alone in this area is to take a good look at all the places where they might be expected to live."

Connie agreed with Jerry. Then, after thinking about the situation for a few moments, she said, "I hope we don't find any aliens here, because if we do, and they're hostile, we'll have to kill them before they kill us. The idea of genocide against a species of humanoids is repugnant to me."

"Killing them wouldn't be our only option. We could leave Pioneer Island and live somewhere else."

"But, that is the problem. I am starting to think of Pioneer Island as home, and I really do not want to leave."

After a continued search of the island with binoculars, Connie said, "During our long voyage from Earth, I had assumed that this planet would be kind of like the way Earth was during its dinosaur age. It never occurred to me that we might also find humanoids here."

"You may be jumping to conclusions too quickly. All we've found, so far, is one small piece of metal."

"That's true, but that small piece of metal has enormous implications. The need to be constantly on guard for potentially hostile aliens adds a dangerous complication to our lives, kind of like a lurking storm cloud casting a shadow over what could otherwise be a simple peaceful life."

"But if they're here and living thousands of miles away from us, we'll still have the kind of life that you want. This is a large planet, and the probability that they came to the same place we came to is very small."

"That's true," agreed Connie.

"And it's possible that the piece of metal we found came from an unmanned probe and that there never was a manned mission. Even if there was, there might not be any survivors."

"I would be content with any of those possibilities."

"In a few days, we'll know if we're alone as far as the islands in this lake are concerned," stated Jerry as he picked up his communicator and punched in Mike's number. "Your eager pilots can start launching their RPVs," Jerry said.

Mike acknowledged, and almost immediately, the first RPV took off and headed for the island. As the small makeshift aircraft carrier slowly cruised northward along the island's east coast, the remaining RPVs took off at regular intervals until all eight were airborne. When each RPV completed the search of its area of responsibility, it returned to the boat for a recharge. When the eighth RPV was recovered, the carrier headed northwest to the second island in the chain.

"We've taken a good look at the eastern half of the island, and there's no indication that humanoids have ever lived there," Mike remarked.

"The search went so smoothly, that I think we might be able to look at the rest of the northern islands yet today," remarked Jerry. "That will leave the two southern islands for tomorrow."

Stifling a chuckle, Mike said, "But if we do all four of the northern islands today, you might get home too late for Moose's smoked abalone dinner."

"If it's as good as his smoked fish, we'll be able to feast on it no matter what time we get home," said Connie.

"I wouldn't mind showing up for that feast," said Mike.

"Hang on for two more weeks, and I think you'll be free to come down," remarked Jerry.

"I hope so. I am definitely ready to bask in the outdoor living that you've been enjoying."

About twenty minutes later, the little aircraft carrier arrived at the second island. RPVs were launched at regular intervals while the carrier sailed slowly northward along the island's eastern shore. After about forty-five minutes, the carrier reached the north end of the island. Satisfied that there weren't any aliens living on the eastern half of the island, Jerry decided to go to the third island.

Connie looked at her watch, "It's 12:30 and I'm hungry. Let's eat lunch."

"Good idea, I'm hungry too."

"We couldn't ask for a more pristine setting in which to enjoy our lunch," commented Connie.

Jerry smelled the fresh air and gazed across the clear, pollution-free water to the distant, snow-capped mountains. For a few moments, he relished in the quiet peacefulness that surrounded them. "One of the things that adds a special air to this setting is that we're alone; at least, I think we are," he said.

"I like being alone. For me, the presence of aliens would detract from the pristine nature of this area, spoiling it to some degree."

"In what way?"

"It's a matter of attitude. We came here with the idea of living in harmony with our environment, doing what we can to preserve its pristine nature. The aliens we're looking for came from a society so barbaric that it was conducting genocide against half a planet until we stopped them."

"But that was in the context of a 30-year war. The ones that came here might not be barbarians. If they're still alive, they may have developed a benign life style, killing only what they need for food or in self-defense."

"That's possible, but based on what we saw on B-2, I am inclined to think they're more likely to be plunderers. Anyway, after traveling across more than four light-years of interstellar space, I'd hoped we'd have a pristine planet all to ourselves, and that we could build a society that would take good care of the environment. Aliens from B-2 might not be as conscientious as we are."

"That is a legitimate concern, especially if they're living close enough to have an effect on us."

"Their possible presence is already having an effect on us. Instead of enjoying the romantic aspects of this beautiful setting, we're discussing aliens."

"That's a good point," conceded Jerry.

Jerry and Connie continued their discussion and arrived at the third island at about the time they finished their lunch. After searching its eastern half and finding no evidence of aliens, they continued on to the fourth island. Much to Connie's liking, the search of it also proved fruitless.

As they rounded the north end of the northernmost island, Connie said, "It's only 3:30. If our return trip takes the same time as it took to get here, we'll be home at about 10:00."

"I think we can be back by 9:00," stated Jerry. "We only have two more RPVs to recover, and we'll be done searching this island. We should be able to make pretty good speed on the way back. Our batteries are fully charged, and we have a favorable wind, so let's deploy our sails. I would like to be back well before second sunset, so we don't have to hike through the forest in the dark."

"Are you worried about safety in the forest, or is it possible that you're able to smell smoked abalone, even though you're twenty miles from home?" Mike asked.

"My nose isn't quite that good, but I did talk to Moose a few minutes ago, and he said the smoked abalone is delicious."

"With a dinner like that waiting for me, I think I could get enough speed out of that boat to get home well before 9:00," declared Mike.

284

"It isn't just a matter of speed, we still have a lot more reconnaissance to do, and we need to be reasonably thorough," responded Jerry.

"Our RPV pilots are getting quite efficient, and I believe we'll finish the recon sooner than you think."

"Okay, show me how good they are. Then, when we've finished that project, I'll push this boat to the limit and find out how much speed I can get out of it."

"It's about six miles from the first island to East Bay, so you will have a pretty good run on which to play with the speed."

"Keep in mind that this boat wasn't designed to win any races. It's able to do a lot of different things, but going fast isn't one of them."

"True enough, but it's not an old barge either."

"I have enough charge on the batteries to run the motors at full power. The only question is whether there will be enough wind to use the sails effectively."

Mike displayed the latest weather information on his computer screen, studied it, and said, "It looks like you'll have westerly winds of twelve to twenty mph."

"The high end of that range would sure make playing around with the sails worthwhile. With that much wind power added to the battery power, I should be able to get at least twenty mph out of this boat."

"So it will take you less than twenty minutes to get home after we've finished the recon."

"If the wind's in the high end of your predicted range."

"Discussing sailing makes me wish I could be there. I've been in this starship for so many years that I'm really ready for exposure to the elements."

"Be patient for two more weeks. If all goes well, you'll be free to come down."

"I think I'll make the time go faster by occupying my leisure time with a challenging project."

"What are you thinking about doing?"

"I would enjoy designing and building a water glider."

"That kind of boat could take many different shapes. Do you have a basic concept in mind?"

"A modified two-person kayak equipped with a large sail, outriggers, and hydrofoils might be a good starting point. Speed will be my main objective. I want to be able to easily ride the hydrofoils even when the wind isn't real strong, so minimizing weight will be a key consideration."

"To easily achieve stability and control, you might consider adding some motion sensing vanes with a direct link to control vanes. That would leave the pilot free to play with the sail to achieve maximum speed without having to worry about flipping the boat over."

"That's a good idea, but I might go high-tech and use a modified inertial guidance system to assist with the stability and control, or I might use a combination of the two approaches. The goal will be to make this water glider as safe and as easy to operate as possible while making it as fast as possible. On a windy day, I want it to be fast enough to make your adrenaline flow."

"Streaking around on this lake with that kind of toy would get me high. Of course, when you bring it down, it will have to be tested for safety, and you'll probably need a test pilot for that."

"That job just might be reserved for the project's chief engineer. However, the boat will seat two people, and the chief engineer might need an assistant in case unforeseen problems come up."

"That's good sound reasoning. Sign me up for the copilot position."

"Consider it done."

"How long do you think it will take to complete the project?"

"This toy will be so much fun to play with that I have a feeling that most off duty personnel are going to volunteer to work on it. I see no reason why we can't have it ready to bring down with us in two weeks."

"That sounds a bit ambitious, but proper motivation will always get a job done quickly."

TIME: Day Seventeen, 8:20 P.M.

Jerry and Connie arrived in East Bay, tired but happy. They were tired from a long day of sailing and searching for aliens, but they were happy that they found no evidence to indicate their presence.

While Jerry and Connie put their weapons and gear into the inflated boat for the short trip to shore, Mike's RPV pilots launched their aircraft and flew them into the forest.

When the last RPV disappeared into the forest, Connie said, "I've been looking at this lake all day and haven't had an opportunity to go swimming, and I think a good swim would really be refreshing."

Jerry checked the position of Alpha Centauri B and said, "We're certainly back early enough so that we can squeeze in a quick dip before it gets dark."

While Connie was undressing, she stole a quick glance at Jerry to see if he was watching her. Noting with satisfaction that he was, she completed the removal of her clothing and dove into the cool water followed immediately by Jerry.

They swam under and around their multipurpose boat enjoying the pleasant evening and the peaceful solitude of East Bay. As the minutes ticked away, their swimming evolved into a playful game with the rules being invented as the game progressed. Eventually, the game came to a satisfying conclusion that left both contestants feeling like winners. They climbed out of the water onto the deck, toweled off, and dressed.

"You were right, that was refreshing," Jerry said, glowing with contentment.

Looking around at the scene lit by the soft orange glow from Alpha Centauri B, now low on the western horizon, Connie said, "That orange light no longer seems eerie to me; it now seems to have a warm romantic tone to it."

Jerry gazed across the water of East Bay to Eastern Island and noted the warming effect of the soft orange hue on its pristine beauty. He turned his gaze in the opposite direction and noted that much of East Bay's shoreline was deeply shadowed. "I think we should head for home before it's completely dark in the forest," he said.

"We shouldn't have any problems. By now, our RPV pilots have had plenty of time to thoroughly scout our trail."

"That's true, but we're going to use extreme caution anyway."

Jerry and Connie rowed ashore. Then, they followed Charlie through the forest without incident. A short time later, they arrived in the capsule to the aroma of freshly baked bread and smoked abalone.

"Dinner smells so good that it's making my mouth water," stated Jerry.

"After being out all day, it's a real pleasure to find a good dinner waiting for us," remarked Connie.

Pleased by their comments, Dianne said, "I'm glad both of you are hungry. We've already eaten, so we'll play the roles of cook and waitress. You can pretend you're dining out at your favorite restaurant."

"We don't have any money," declared Connie.

"Then, I guess you'll have to wash the dishes," suggested Dianne.

"That's certainly a bargain price for a good dinner," responded Connie.

"Now that the negotiations are out of the way, it's time for you to sit down, relax, and enjoy some exquisite dining pleasure," Moose commented.

"That's an invitation I can't refuse," stated Jerry.

Jerry and Connie sat down and as soon as they were comfortable, Dianne placed a salad in front of each of them. "This salad is a first. It is made entirely from native greens, tubers, and herbs," she said.

"Is it safe to eat?" questioned Jerry.

"I've thoroughly checked out each ingredient in the lab, and I've also eaten them," replied Dianne.

"You look healthy to me. How long ago did you eat them?"

"I ate all of them yesterday, but that wasn't the first time. With Connie's help, I've been medically monitoring myself, and I haven't suffered any ill-effects."

Noting that the salad looked good, Jerry tasted it, then said, "It does taste good, in fact, it's very good. Where did you find all the ingredients?"

"The vines we see climbing some of the trees here on the island are fed by a clump of tuberous roots. These tubers not only have a delicious mild flavor, but they're also highly nutritious. The brownish-orange ingredient in your salad is from shredding some of these tubers. This starchy root also tastes good cooked. I diced and steamed some of it to serve as a vegetable dish."

"What about these crisp dark green leaves?"

"They're from an aquatic plant that grows about six feet tall in shallow water. The leaves are from the part of the plant that is above the water. The greens in your salad are from plants growing in shallow water near the mouth of South Bay."

"I love the flavor of the dressing," commented Connie.

"That flavor comes from two plants that I've classified as herbs. Each has a flavor that seems to complement the other. The dressing was easy to make. I just put some stems and leaves in a blender with some water and a little starch. Next, I cooked it for a few minutes, and then, I chilled it."

"For being that simple to make, it sure tastes great," stated Connie.

"Thank you," replied Dianne.

When Connie and Jerry finished their salads, Dianne served them smoked abalone, smoked fish, a special imitation rice dish, the diced root vegetable dish, and freshly baked bread. After he had tasted everything, Jerry exclaimed, "This is excellent! If I am going to get this kind of dinner when I go out searching for aliens, I think I'll have to do that more often."

"It's a great way to celebrate that you didn't find any," commented Dianne.

"It might be too early to celebrate," commented Jerry. "We still have lots of searching to do."

"That's true, but each day we don't find any aliens is worth celebrating," stated Dianne.

THIRTEEN

Condition Critical
A Grave Medical Challenge

TIME: Day Eighteen, Mid-Morning.

The pioneers finished their reconnaissance of the small island two miles south of Pioneer Island and found no evidence to indicate that it had ever been visited by aliens.

Twenty minutes later, they arrived at the southernmost island. "It sure looks peaceful," Connie said.

"And mysterious," added Dianne.

"That's what you said about the last one," stated Connie.

"It did look mysterious," asserted Dianne. "These islands are covered with pristine forests never before looked into by humans. Why shouldn't they look mysterious to me?"

"That's a good point, but in my case, this is the sixth island that I've looked at since yesterday morning, and we haven't found anything on any of them that is much different than Pioneer Island. But more than anything else, I am especially pleased that we haven't found any aliens."

"I'm happy about that too," replied Dianne.

"As quiet as this island looks, I doubt that there are any living here either," commented Connie.

"It looks like you're probably right, but this island does have a sense of mysteriousness about it."

Connie picked up her binoculars and closely surveyed the part of the island in their vicinity. Then, she said, "I don't see anything unusual compared to the other islands." Then, she handed the binoculars to Dianne.

Dianne closely scrutinized the island while they cruised slowly southward. She watched one of the RPVs sail into and out of the forest repeatedly as its pilot searched the island's waterfront from the safety of the Challenger. After a few minutes had gone by, Dianne handed the binoculars back to Connie and said, "I don't see anything that looks suspicious, but there's something mysterious about that island. I can feel it."

"Perhaps that's because you're a biologist, and you have a strong desire to study the plants and creatures that live there. Once you become familiar with them, the island won't seem so mysterious."

Dianne thought about Connie's comment for a few moments. Then, she said, "I've had a desire to do research on the plants and creatures that live here since our arrival, but I haven't felt a sense of mysteriousness about it."

"From the sound of your voice, I sense that you feel some uneasiness about this. Do you think we might be in danger from something on this island?"

"I don't know, but I do feel some anxiety."

"Are your feelings anything like what you felt when we were orbiting B-2?"

Dianne considered the question for a few moments, "The sensation that I have now isn't as strong, but I think it's real. I feel like something or someone is trying to probe my thoughts, but isn't quite able to make contact."

"Does it feel like a hostile probe or a friendly probe?"

"I can't tell; it's just too feeble."

"The last time your thoughts were probed, we ended up getting involved in the final phase of a thirty-year war."

288

"But the mental probe from the beings that we ended up attacking was very intense and filled with hatred. Even though this probe isn't like that, it could still be from the aliens that we're looking for; and even though this island looks deserted, they could be living here."

"I think we should tell Jerry and Moose about what you're sensing."

"Moose is flying one of the RPVs, and I don't think we should disturb him or he might crash it into a tree."

Connie laughed, "I think Jerry's talking to Mike about the exploration of this island, so let's talk to them."

Dianne and Connie approached Jerry, but before they could say anything, they heard Mike exclaim, "We've just found something that you need to see!"

"Show me!" Jerry said, putting on a video headset.

When the image appeared, Jerry's attention immediately focused on an old rotted stump that was almost completely concealed by vines, but the vines did not conceal the shape of the stump's top. Surprised by its appearance, Jerry stared at it for a few moments before he remarked, "A stump with a flat top is a curious thing to find on a planet where dinosaurs are the dominant species."

"Are you saying that you haven't seen any dinosaurs running around with saws?" Mike laughed.

"Some of the dinosaurs we've seen don't need chain saws to knock trees down," replied Jerry. "The obvious implication here is that this tree was cut down by the aliens that we're looking for, but let's not rule out other possibilities, however remote they may be."

"It appears that there's a factual basis for what you've been sensing," Connie said to Dianne.

Having overheard the remark, Jerry asked, "Would you mind explaining that comment to me?"

While Dianne and Connie reported to Jerry, the search continued, and more old stumps with flat tops were found, all in the same small area. Mike said, "What's puzzling about this is that we aren't finding an old log cabin. With so many trees cut down in such a small area, it seems like there should be a log structure of some sort within the area."

"The logs could have been used for some other purpose, such as building a boat or raft," commented Jerry.

"Are you suggesting that the aliens were here, built a boat, and left?" questioned Connie.

"That's a possibility."

"But why would they leave a location that has so many pluses and so few minuses?"

"What's attractive to us might not have been to them, but we don't know that they've left; it's only a possibility."

"Maybe, they did build a log cabin, and it was destroyed by fire," suggested Moose. "As prolific as the vegetation is here, the site would've been quickly overgrown."

"But why wouldn't they have built a new one?" asked Dianne.

"One of our big concerns is whether or not our immune systems can handle the microbes on this planet. Perhaps theirs didn't, and they were killed by disease," Moose replied. "Then, maybe their cabin was struck by lightning and set on fire. Within a few years, the site would've been overgrown making it look to us like they moved on."

"That scenario is certainly possible," acknowledged Jerry, "but how likely is it that a lightning strike would've occurred at precisely the right place to destroy the evidence that aliens had once lived here?"

"I don't know, but it is possible," replied Moose.

"I think we're going to have to go ashore and poke around in the bushes and see what we can find," stated Jerry.

"Before you do that, there is another possibility you should consider," remarked Mike, "and that is that they may have tunneled into the hillside and used the logs for internal support. They may still be living on the island, although I must admit that it does look deserted."

"I'm counting on you and your RPV pilots to make sure that it is before we go ashore."

"We'll do an exhaustive search."

"While you're doing that, we'll circle the island and inspect the waterfront."

"I have a theory for you to consider," Connie offered. "Let's assume that their immune systems weren't able to handle the microorganisms here and that they were killed by them. If they went to bed when they got sick, they could've died in their homes. If they lived in underground homes and those homes had small entrances, they could now be overgrown with brush and be difficult to find. To us, the island would look like it had been deserted by the aliens; when in fact, they lived here and died here."

"While that scenario is possible, it seems to me that it would take quite some time to build an underground home," commented Jerry. "If they were killed by microbes, wouldn't they have died before completing such a home, and wouldn't we see some unused logs laying around?"

"Not necessarily, while some diseases kill quickly, others take a long time to develop."

During the next two hours, the interstellar pioneers slowly circled the island and intensively searched its waterfront, while the RPV pilots searched its interior. Mike summed up the results by saying, "It looks to me like no one has lived on this island for quite a long time. So the question remains: what happened to the trees that were cut down?"

"I am convinced that they were used to build a raft or boat of some sort," stated Jerry.

"Why do you think that rather than the scenario that Connie proposed?" asked Mike.

"Something that I noticed about the stumps. All of the big ones are close to the water, and you can tell from the saw-cuts that these trees were dropped into the water. The logs from these trees would've been too heavy for use in building a log cabin or to shore up an underground home, but they could've been used to make a raft. I think the logs from the smaller trees were used as cross members to secure the big ones together, to build a shelter on the raft, and perhaps to make masts for sails."

"But where did they go?" asked Connie.

"I don't know, but we're going to try to find out," replied Jerry.

Jerry noticed that Dianne was staring at the island so intently that she seemed to be in a trance. All turned their attention to her, but no one did anything to disturb her. After about a minute had gone by, Dianne came out of her state of intense concentration and said, "I just experienced what I think was another attempt to establish mental contact with me."

"Are you sure?" asked Connie. "We've taken a pretty good look at this island, and it does look deserted."

"I agree that it looks deserted, but I have a strong feeling that it isn't, at least not completely."

"Are you suggesting that all the aliens are gone except for one or two?" questioned Jerry.

"I have a feeling that there's only one on the island."

"Is there a basis for that feeling?" asked Jerry.

"During the attempted contact that I just experienced, I felt like there was an aura of intense loneliness hovering around my mind."

Connie asked, "Was that aura of loneliness continuous, or was it interrupted by moments of excitement or hope?"

Dianne closed her eyes and tuned out her surroundings while she focused her mind on the recent experience. After a few moments she said, "I think there were some fleeting moments of hope and excitement."

"An intelligent humanoid living in isolation on an alien planet for a long period of time could exhibit that kind of aura," commented Connie. "Suppose this individual has been alone for twenty to thirty years, he might be so hungry for companionship that he would even attempt contact with an alien species that could turn out to be hostile to him. Particularly, if he is old or ill and doesn't think he has much time left anyway."

Dianne shuddered, "I would become horribly lonely if I had to live alone on one of these islands for the rest of my life."

"If there is an alien living alone on this island, is he alone because the others have died, or is he alone because he was deserted by his colleagues?" Connie asked.

"The evidence we have indicates that a large raft was built, and that they left," replied Jerry.

"But why would his colleagues have left without him?" questioned Connie. "It doesn't seem likely that there would've been enough of them, so that they could afford to discard one of their members."

"It sounds like you're arguing in favor of the premise that they never left this area," responded Jerry.

"This is a huge lake, and a large raft could've been built simply to navigate it. If we can prove that they never left this area, and that they're all dead except for the one attempting to contact Dianne, then we can stop searching the planet for them."

"It's important to keep in mind that we have no evidence that they lived here, only that they were here long enough to cut down trees that appear to have been used to build a raft," Jerry said.

"If we could find the being that's attempting to contact Dianne," said Moose, "maybe we could get some answers to some of our questions. Right now, we don't even know for sure if this being is one of the humanoids from B-2, it could be some other kind of entity that's native to this planet."

"That's possible," conceded Dianne, "but I sense that it's one of the aliens we're looking for."

"Do you have any idea where on the island this alien might be?" Jerry asked Dianne.

Dianne considered Jerry's question for a few moments. "I sensed the attempted mind probe most strongly after we passed around the island's south end and started heading north," she said.

"Let's go there and carefully search that part of the island."

When they arrived at the island's south end, they surveyed the overall lay of the land and noted that the rocky beach was quite similar to that at the north end of Pioneer Island. But set back about fifty yards from the water was a steep cliff that rose about two hundred feet. The top of the cliff sloped gently downward toward the north so that there was no inaccessible plateau on the cliff's top. This feature led Jerry to comment, "An alien living here would not find safety from large animals by living up there."

"If you were living here and were out of ammunition, where would you want to live?" Jerry asked, looking at his colleagues.

Moose was first to respond, "I would try to find a cavern with an entrance barely big enough for me to squeeze through."

"Such a cavern would be convenient, but where would you live if one didn't exist?" asked Jerry.

For a few moments, Moose thought about the problem of surviving. "The bears that visit these islands are huge, up in the 1,500-pound range. They are strong, ferocious animals. I doubt that a lone 250-pound humanoid lacking construction equipment could build a structure that would withstand assault by one of these bears. Without weapons, I don't think that I could survive here for a long period of time without a secure refuge, such as a cavern with a small entrance."

"If we assume that such a cavern exists, we must also assume that its entrance is well concealed, or we would've found it," commented Jerry.

"There are lots of trees and bushes growing against the base of that cliff," observed Connie. "I would like to fly one of the RPVs and look behind some of them."

Before Connie could begin searching, Dianne said, "I don't think an extensive search will be necessary. I think this alien has decided that he definitely wants to be found. An image of a large tree has just appeared in my mind, and it looks just like that one over there. I now see an image of a cave entrance at the end of a large branch about twenty-five to thirty feet up the tree."

"I wonder why he's decided to show us where he is," questioned Jerry.

"He might be looking for companionship," suggested Connie.

"I don't think that would be enough of a reason for him to assume the risk that we might be hostile," argued Jerry.

"I don't know what this alien's normal life span would be," Dianne commented, "but if he were middle age when he came here, he would now be quite old. Perhaps, he is ill and is hoping that we are friendly and able to help him."

"We don't know that this is an alien from B-2," Moose remarked. "It could be an entity that is native to this planet that is trying to play upon our sympathies and lead us into an ambush."

"That's possible," acknowledged Jerry. "I think it's time to investigate and find out. I am going to fly one of our small RPVs inside of that tree's foliage. If I find a cave entrance, I will inspect it and investigate the cavern."

Turning to Dianne, Jerry said, "I want you to put on a headset and clearly hold the images from the RPV in your mind while staying open to communication from the alien."

Then, to Connie and Moose, Jerry said, "In case this is a trap of some sort, I want you two to be alert to everything going on around us."

Jerry looked briefly at the tree and noted that it stretched nearly to the cliff top, making it almost 200 feet tall. While all tingled with excitement, Jerry put on a headset, launched an RPV, and headed it toward the large tree. Flying in under the tree's foliage, Jerry circled and inspected the tree's trunk noting that it was at least ten feet in diameter and that its bark was rough enough to provide hand and foot holds for a humanoid wanting to climb it. Jerry quickly found a well-worn path up the tree where deeper cavities had been carved into the bark. Jerry judged the spacing to be about right for easy climbing for a humanoid about six feet tall.

Jerry flew the RPV upward following the improvised ladder. At a height of about thirty feet, the carved out ladder came to a branch that looked to be nearly three feet in diameter at its base. Jerry noted that the top of the branch showed some wear as though it had been walked on repeatedly for many years.

He flew the RPV along the top of the branch following it for about thirty-five feet before coming to the solid rock wall of the cliff. Here, unable to grow outward any farther, the branch split and grew to both the left and the right hugging the rock wall. Noting that the wear pattern turned to the right, Jerry followed this fork of the branch for about twenty feet before finding a cave entrance a few feet above the branch.

For the benefit of Moose and Connie, Jerry said, "I've found an opening in the cliff, and as we suspected, it's big enough for one of us to crawl through, but much too small for the big bears."

"I would sure like to see what's inside," stated Connie.

"I would too," declared Jerry as he flew the small RPV slowly into the cave. In just a few feet, the tunnel started to broaden. Then, in a few yards, it turned gently to the left and sloped upward. About fifty feet from the entrance, Jerry found a fairly large cavern.

Immediately catching Jerry's attention was a bright patch of sunlight on the cavern floor. Looking upward, he noted that the cavern extended all the way to the cliff top. Even though it narrowed considerably, there was still a fairly large hole at the top letting in an ample amount of sunlight.

Jerry surveyed the cavern and noted that it was about thirty feet wide and perhaps fifty feet long. Near one end, Jerry found a pile of firewood and a fire pit made out of stones. Next to the fire pit were some scorched abalone shells that had apparently been used as cooking pots.

A short distance from the fire pit, Jerry found a table and chair made from artistically carved wood and tied together with fiber that appeared to be from vines. On a rock ledge a few feet behind and above the table, Jerry saw water seeping out of a small crack in the rock wall. An abalone shell placed tightly against the wall to catch the water was full and overflowing with the overflow disappearing into a crack in the ledge.

Next, Jerry slowly rotated the RPV to view the rest of the cavern. At the end of the cavern opposite the fire pit, Jerry found the cavern's occupant and exclaimed, "I've found him, and he looks very much like the humanoids that inhabit B-2!"

"What is he doing?" asked Connie.

"He's in bed, either asleep or in a trance."

"It's probably the state he needs to be in to achieve telepathic communication," suggested Dianne.

"Are there any weapons next to the bed?" asked Moose.

"I see a spear with a neatly crafted rock point and a bow with a quiver full of arrows. I also see a hunting knife with a metal blade that looks like it is twelve to fifteen inches long."

"Unless we provoke him, I don't think we need to worry about those weapons," stated Dianne.

"Those might be primitive weapons, but when skillfully used, they are deadly," asserted Jerry. "The fact that he is alive proves that he is skillful in their use."

"He looks old, and I don't think he is as capable as he once was," commented Dianne.

"He may be old, but he looks lean and muscular to me," remarked Jerry.

"But I think he has a serious injury and needs our help," countered Dianne.

"Why do you think that?" asked Connie.

"He is suffering great pain. I can feel it."

"Any idea what's causing the pain?" questioned Connie.

Jerry focused the RPV's cameras on the alien's head, then slowly moved down his body.

"His head and upper body look healthy, but his lower body is covered with what looks like a hand woven blanket. It's impossible to tell where the pain is coming from," Dianne said.

"If he has a medical problem, his situation must be desperate, or he wouldn't have led us to his home," commented Jerry.

"But if he brought us here because of a life-threatening medical problem, it seems like he would find a way to indicate to us what it is," remarked Dianne.

"It's possible that his situation has deteriorated to the point that he has used his last ounce of energy just to bring us here," suggested Connie.

"You may be right, because I am no longer sensing anything," stated Dianne. "I think he has passed out."

"Has he passed out, or has he died?" questioned Connie.

Hoping to answer Connie's question, Jerry flew the RPV close to the alien and focused on his chest. "He is breathing, but not very strongly," he said, after a few moments.

"He is trembling weakly," Dianne noted.

Checking data from the RPV's infrared detector, Jerry said, "His body temperature is 104.7 degrees."

"If we're going to save him, we need to get to him soon," Connie said quickly.

Deciding to tease his wife a bit, Jerry commented, "Yesterday, you said you hoped we wouldn't find any aliens, because their presence would add an unnecessary complication to our lives. Now, you want to save one's life."

"But he's sick and suffering. He needs our help."

Jerry smiled at getting exactly the reaction he expected. "I'm glad you feel that way. If we can save him and learn to communicate with him, there is much we can learn from him. After all, he has lived here for a long time."

"You're assuming that he'll be friendly and willing to give us information," remarked Moose. "If we allow him to die, we won't have to live with the risk of having an alien with unknown intentions in our midst."

"I think the potential for gaining useful, perhaps even critical, information is worth the risk," replied Jerry. "If he turns out to be a nasty individual, we can always deal with him."

"That's true, but if we save him and he turns out to be a nasty individual who is very cunning in his ways, he might do us great harm before we discover his true nature."

"That's possible," admitted Jerry. "We'll have to always be on guard until we get to know him very well."

"These alien humanoids are similar to us," Connie said. "I think it's important to keep this one alive and study his physiological processes, especially his immune system. If he's different from us in some crucial way that has allowed him to survive here, I would like to discover that. Also, I would like to find out if he's had any illnesses of consequence."

"You make him sound like a humanoid lab animal," commented Moose.

"The medical tests I will do on him won't be any different than the ones I do on us, just more intensive."

"All things considered, I am convinced that the potential benefits of keeping him alive far outweigh the risks, if we never let our guard down," Jerry asserted.

Jerry took several minutes to inspect the cavern looking for possible hazards, such as traps rigged to kill an intruding carnivore. When he satisfied himself that there weren't any, he handed the RPV control unit to Dianne and said, "Keep an eye on that alien. Connie and I are going in."

Jerry and Connie checked their pistols and strapped them on. Then, they checked their rifles and shouldered them. Connie handed her medical cases to Jerry who placed them in the inflated boat. With Moose alertly on guard and Mike's RPV pilots surveying the vicinity, Connie and Jerry headed for shore.

Once there, Jerry climbed the tree to the large branch and stepped onto it. With a piece of rope he hauled up Connie's medical cases. Then, she climbed the tree and followed him to the cave entrance.

Jerry beamed a bright light into the cave and carefully inspected it to where it curved out of sight. Not seeing anything suspicious, he strapped the light to his head and cautiously entered. Very slowly, Jerry crawled down the tunnel as it curved to the left and upward. Pushing her medical bags in front of her, Connie followed him.

Noticing how smooth the tunnel floor was, Jerry wondered how many times the alien had pushed or dragged objects into and out of his refuge. He must have countless stories to tell, thought Jerry, and after living in isolation for all these years, he might be eager to tell them, if he's been able to maintain his sanity and memory.

When Jerry and Connie reached the cavern, they stopped and looked around. After a few moments, Jerry said, "It looks safe, let's go in."

While warily approaching the alien, Connie inspected the cavern and said, "It looks like he was able to make himself reasonably comfortable considering his situation."

"If he's lived here for thirty years, he's had plenty of time to fashion some comforts."

"He's also kept his home quite clean and orderly. If he has taken care of himself as well as he has maintained his home, that might help explain how he has survived for so many years without medical help."

"Let's see if we can keep him alive for a few more years."

"I'll do my best, but first, I'll have to find out what's wrong with him."

Not seeing any problem on the alien's upper body, Connie removed the blanket covering his lower body. The appearance of his right leg made two problems immediately obvious. The calf had a deep four-inch long gash in it and was swollen and horribly discolored. Also, the ankle was swollen and the foot was turned out at very unnatural angle.

"There's little doubt that he has multiple fractures in that ankle. However, the injury to his calf is the one that might be life-threatening," Connie said. "Apparently, it has become infected by a microbe that his immune system is having difficulty coping with."

Next, Connie checked the alien's vital signs. "His condition is critical. To save him, I'll have to kill the invading microbe, and I don't even know what it is. There may even be more than one kind. All I can do is inject him with each antibiotic that I have and hope that at least one of them will be effective and that none of them kill him. His system may be different than ours in some way that will make our antibiotics toxic to him. But by the time I did the lab work to find out which antibiotic would be effective and whether it would be toxic to him, he would probably be dead. So I have no choice but to use the shotgun approach."

Connie had six distinctly different broad spectrum antibiotics in her medical bags. First she drew a blood specimen for lab analysis, then she injected the alien with what she judged to be the maximum safe dose of each of five of the antibiotics.

Turning to Jerry, she said, "I have one more antibiotic to give him, but it's most effective when administered intravenously. Also, he looks like he is suffering from dehydration. It's possible that he hasn't had anything to eat or drink for several days, so I need to get some water and nutrients into him. If you would tie down his right arm and rig a support for the I.V., I would appreciate it."

Jerry cut a short piece of rope and gently secured the alien's forearm to the bed structure. Then, Jerry tied the alien's spear to the small bedside table and attached the I.V. bottle to it with a short piece of cord.

Connie looked at the setup in an admiring way and said, "What a unique way to use a man's spear to save his life."

Jerry grinned, "This just might be the first time that a spear has ever been used in this way."

Then, Jerry looked down at the unconscious alien and asked, "What do we do next?"

"We have to wait for the antibiotics to work and hope that they do. While we wait, we'll monitor his vital signs and do what we can to keep him alive if they start deteriorating."

"How long do you think we'll be here?"

"It may take a day or two before he recovers to the point where we can move him."

"Move him?"

"If we're successful in curing this infection, then I'll repair that ankle. If it's a multiple fracture that's as serious as it looks, I'll have to open it up to fix it. There might be some delicate microsurgery involved, and that would be a lot easier to do at home than here in this cave."

Not wanting to miss an opportunity to tease his wife, Jerry said, "Yesterday, you hoped we wouldn't find any aliens; now, you want to bring one into our home."

"Finding a lone individual desperately in need of help is different than finding a large powerful group living nearby," Connie replied, quickly.

"But if we take him home with us, and you're able to cure him, he might not want to leave."

"If he turns out to be a warmhearted individual, he could be a real benefit to us."

"And what if he turns out to be cold-hearted to the point of being evil?"

"Then, I would consider him to be no different than a malignant tumor that needs to be either removed or neutralized."

"Judging from the appearance of that leg and ankle, he's not going to be much of a threat to us for quite some time. We should use that time to learn how to communicate with him and try to gain some insight into how he might behave when he's back to normal."

"Michelle has made marvelous progress learning Rex's language," stated Connie. "Perhaps, she could do the same with this alien."

"There's a possibility that this guy might understand Rex's language; even though, he apparently is from the other side in the great war."

"That might be true, but I'm not sure that it would be wise to speak to him in Rex's language."

"What bothers you about that?" asked Jerry.

"What if the great war was the final war between ethnic groups who have hated each other for centuries. This alien could see Rex's language as the language of a hated enemy and associate us with that enemy simply because we used the language."

"Perhaps, it would be best to just teach him English," stated Jerry. "If he decides he wants to join our society and become an effective part of it, he will have to learn English anyway."

"That's true, but first, he has to survive the battle that's raging inside him, and I think we'll know the outcome of that in the next few days."

"If we're staying here for a few days, we're going to need some camping supplies, including some pretty good lights. Unless this cavern has luminescent walls, it's going to be very dark in here tonight. If our patient regains consciousness, I think it's important that we have enough light so he can see the medical set up and realize that he's being helped."

Having watched and listened to everything that was going on via the RPV, Dianne decided that it was time to join in and said, "Moose and I can go home and get everything that we need to be comfortable for a couple days."

"I need some lab work done on the blood specimen I took from this alien," Connie said.

"If you'll attach it to this RPV, I'll take it home and do the lab work while Moose puts our supplies on the boat."

"It would sure be helpful if you could identify the microbes that I'm trying to defeat. Then, I would have some guidance on what to attack them with."

"If they're present in your specimen, I'll find them and get you some pictures."

"To make sure that we find them, I'll give you an additional specimen to examine," Connie replied.

While Jerry directed a beam of light on the gash in the alien's leg, Connie collected a sample of the fluid oozing out of it. Then, she attached it to the RPV along with the blood specimen.

After completing this, Connie said, "You might bring along an extra air mattress and some extra blankets. We need to give this alien something clean to sleep on, after we give him a bath."

"Anything else we need?"

"No, but I'll call you if I think of something."

Four hours later, Connie received a call from Dianne, who said, "I've identified the microbe that's causing our patient's problems, and the antibiotic that you are administering with the I.V. is effective against it. However, there is a possible complication, in that this appears to be a very nasty little bug that is capable of severely damaging any fleshy tissue that it chooses to invade. I think it could easily be fatal if it were to establish a colony in a vital organ."

"So even though we're killing the bug, we might lose our patient anyway, because he may have already sustained life-threatening damage to a vital organ."

"That's the way I see it. Has he gotten any better since you started treatment?"

"His vital signs are stable; in fact, I'm even seeing some modest improvements."

"Maybe, you got to him soon enough to prevent critical damage. Perhaps, he's lucky that we found him when we did."

"It wasn't just luck; he revealed his location to you. Apparently, he had reached the conclusion that he was dying and that we were his only chance for survival."

After a brief pause, Connie asked, "When are you coming back? All of our food is on the boat, and I'm starving."

Moose has our supplies loaded, so we'll be there in about forty-five minutes. Have you thought of anything else you want us to bring?"

"Bring extra food, including some that's ready to eat."

"Knowing my husband, that's probably the first thing that he put on the boat."

When Dianne and Connie concluded their conversation, Jerry said, "It's starting to get dark in here, I think it's time to build a campfire."

"That would add a warm, cozy atmosphere to this place."

Checking the alien's firewood supply, Jerry found some dried grasses and kindling wood as well as a large supply of firewood. After placing some of each in the fire pit, he lit it and soon had a brightly burning campfire.

When Moose and Dianne returned, Jerry went out to help bring in the supplies, while Connie stayed with the alien. The first items brought in were the lights and the evening meal. Dianne and Connie set up the lights, put the finishing touches on dinner, and laid out the meal on the alien's table. While they were doing these tasks, Jerry and Moose completed the laborious job of hauling the rest of the camping supplies up the tree and dragging them through the tunnel into the cavern.

Then, the interstellar pioneers filled their plates and sat on the cavern floor next to the blazing campfire to enjoy a hearty dinner. Being famished, they ate in silence for a few minutes; then, while gazing around the cavern, Connie said, "Camping in here makes me feel like I'm visiting the home of one of Earth's prehistoric cave dwellers."

"From the appearance of this cavern, I think this guy has been living more comfortably than Earth's cave dwellers ever lived," stated Jerry.

"That might be because he has enjoyed one big advantage over Earth's cave dwellers, and that's knowledge," Moose commented. "To me, it's inconceivable that he would've been allowed on an interstellar mission unless he was very intelligent and excelled in the training for the mission."

Dianne looked at Moose, "But you became a part of this mission without any training for it."

"That's because my best friend was in a position of authority and was fully aware of my knowledge and capabilities."

As he finished speaking, Moose shifted his gaze from Dianne to Jerry, who looked at Dianne and asked, "Are you implying that I made a mistake by sneaking Moose onto this mission?"

Now feeling the combined stares of Moose and Jerry, Dianne quickly replied, "No! I'm not implying that at all. I am very happy that you thought highly enough of Moose to give him the opportunity to be with us. I was only pointing out that this alien didn't necessarily have to excel in a training program to be part of an interstellar mission."

"Are you implying that I'm only here because of friendship and that I didn't excel in my profession?" Moose teased her.

Shifting her gaze back and forth between Moose and Jerry, Dianne said, "This seems to be pick-on-Dianne night. I think my easiest way out is to just simply admit that this alien wouldn't be here unless he was very intelligent and extremely capable at the time the mission departed."

Moose and Jerry exchanged smiles of satisfaction. "It's also quite likely that this alien was rigorously trained in survival techniques, including the manufacture of lethal weapons from available materials. I am impressed with the quality of those stone tipped weapons," Jerry said.

"But even as well-made as they are, they seem inadequate as a defense against the big bears that visit these islands," commented Moose.

"Apparently, he has been quite adept at avoiding the bears, and these weapons were only a last resort," speculated Jerry.

"I suspect they were used primarily to hunt small game for food," remarked Moose. "Some of the waterfowl we've seen look like they might be a good source of food and an easy target for someone skilled in the use of a bow and arrow."

"As interested as you always are in good food, I'm surprised you haven't yet treated us to some barbecued waterfowl," commented Jerry.

"I've been preoccupied with seafood, but the birds are next on my list. Also, I'd like to bag one of those ostrich-like dinosaurs that we've seen in large numbers. However, that would require a trip to the countryside, and that's not a very friendly place, so I'm not eager to shoot one of them. Once I dropped one, the smell of fresh blood would probably attract every nearby predator."

"Aw you're just a chicken," teased Jerry.

"Not too long ago, I rode a ten-ton styracosaurus into a face-off with a pack of ten-ton T-Rexes. I haven't seen you do that yet."

"No, but I did walk under a 100-ton sauropod, reach up and touch him."

"I think you both have enough courage to get yourselves killed," stated Dianne.

"I came close to being killed by a saber-tooth during that little adventure," remarked Connie. "For the time being, I think I will be content to explore the countryside with an RPV from the safety of our boat."

"I wonder if this alien ever made any trips to the countryside?" questioned Jerry.

"He would've needed a boat to do that, and we haven't seen one," responded Moose. "Besides that, armed with only stone-age weapons, I doubt that he would've survived such a trip."

"There are lots of bushes on the waterfront, and he could easily have a small boat hidden away," remarked Jerry.

"But if he's all alone here, why would he bother hiding his boat?" questioned Dianne.

"If he saw one of our robot labs land, he may have been hiding from us," replied Jerry. "Those para-wings are big and would've been easy to spot. If he missed all the robot labs, he would certainly have heard and seen our personnel shuttle take off on the day that we arrived."

"That was an awesome sight," stated Connie. "He could easily have reacted to it with a mixture of joy and fear."

"Whatever his feelings were, he did choose caution as the wisest course of action, and he kept himself hidden from us," declared Jerry.

"Speaking of feelings," Jerry said, after a few moments. "I wonder how he would react to seeing us sitting around this campfire if he were to regain consciousness right now."

"If he's as intelligent as we're giving him credit for, he should recognize from the medical setup that he's being helped," Connie commented. "Unless he's totally cold-blooded, he should be appreciative of our presence and think of us as friends."

"Or he could be suspicious of our motives," commented Jerry.

"What do you mean?" asked Connie.

"He might think that we are cold-blooded and that we're only keeping him alive because we're hoping to pump some information out of him, and once we have that, we'll dispose of him."

"That possibility is a good reason to never speak to him in Rex's language," remarked Connie.

"Let's keep in mind that we are here by invitation," stated Dianne.

"How do you figure that?" inquired Moose.

"By revealing his location to me, he in effect invited us into his home."

"But let's not forget that that invitation was an act of desperation," asserted Moose. "It doesn't mean that he'll be sympathetic toward our goals once he has regained health."

"Even if he isn't sympathetic toward our goals, he has already helped us a great deal," Jerry said. "The fact that he has survived here for many years with nothing more than stone age weapons at his disposal bodes well for our future."

"Whether he wants to or not, he can help us a lot more than that," declared Dianne.

"In what way?" asked Jerry.

"We can take a tissue sample from him and send it up to the Challenger for DNA analysis. Once we have a complete DNA profile on him, we can compare the genetic blueprint for his immune system to the genetic blueprint for the human immune system. If we can establish that the design and function of his immune system is essentially the same as ours, then we can confidently bring down all of our people."

Jerry looked at his wife and asked, "Would the doctor care to comment on that?"

"All the evidence we have indicates that he has lived here for a long time, perhaps as long as thirty years. It also looks like he has lived here alone, which means he has not had any medical help, which means that his immune system has served him well. If his immune system is fundamentally the same as ours, then I will vote in favor of bringing everyone down."

"Would your level of confidence be high enough so that you would have no problem bringing down our daughter?"

Connie considered the question for a few moments, then said, "As far as diseases and infections are concerned, I would have no problem bringing her down."

"What about the bug currently infecting this alien? Why is his immune system having trouble with it, and is it a threat to us?" Jerry asked.

"It might be that his immune system is starting to break down because of his age, or the bug may have gained entry to his body at a time when he was in a weakened condition because of some other factor. As far as the threat to us is concerned, I believe that our immune systems can handle this bug; if not, we have an antibiotic that is effective against it."

"How long will it take to do a DNA profile on this alien and a genetic code comparison of immune systems?" Jerry asked Dianne.

"My assistants are tired of being confined to a spaceship, and they're eager to come down. With that kind of motivation, they'll probably work day and night on the project. My guess is that it won't take them more than a few days, certainly less than a week."

"This DNA project does pose some risk for the people on the Challenger," stated Connie. "Sending up a specimen for analysis creates the possibility of accidentally putting some of Alcent's microbes into the Challenger's environment. Some of these might be lethal to humans, and we might not be able to develop a cure quickly enough to save the lives of those infected. This DNA project could take away from the people on the Challenger the option of living out their lives in space, should it prove to be impossible to live here."

"Both of our shuttles have been down here and have returned to orbit," commented Moose.

"But they haven't entered the Challenger," argued Connie. "They're orbiting in formation with the Challenger, and no one has entered either of them."

"That's true," acknowledged Moose.

"It appears that we have a dilemma here," commented Jerry. "We now have a possible way to prove that the human immune system can deal with the microbes that exist here, but an accident could doom the people on the Challenger if it turns out that our immune systems aren't up to the job."

"I think we need to do this DNA project," asserted Dianne, "and I think we should be able to set up a procedure that reduces the risk to almost zero."

"But we cannot reduce it to zero," stated Connie.

"No, but we can get very close," argued Dianne.

"We've been here for nearly three weeks and none of us have gotten sick," remarked Moose.

"There are diseases that take much longer than three weeks to develop," stated Connie.

"And that's the reason we need to do this DNA project," declared Jerry. "If it turns out that our immune systems are essentially the same as this alien's, then we won't have to be anymore concerned about illnesses here than we were back on Earth. We could freely travel back and forth between Pioneer Island and the Challenger. We could bring down materials and equipment and start building our homes. We could have children and start building the new civilization that we came here to create."

Dianne turned to Connie, "I think it's time to work out a fail-safe procedure for doing the project."

"We can bring the personnel shuttle down tomorrow to pick up your specimens," stated Jerry.

"We'll have the procedure worked out by then," declared Dianne.

Connie reluctantly nodded in agreement.

Noticing this Jerry commented, "You seem to be troubled by the need to do this project."

"I realize how important the project is, but finding this alien on the verge of death because of a horrible infection clearly illustrates that microorganisms might be the greatest danger that we face here. I'd hoped that we could define that danger quite well before exposing our daughter to possible risk. No matter how good a procedure we set up and how strictly we follow it, the possibility of human error or having an accident will still exist."

"But if our immune systems are essentially the same as this alien's, then we should be able to assume that the risk from microbes is no greater here than on Earth."

"That's true, but I wish we could prove that without exposing our daughter to possible risk."

"Like us, our daughter is a pioneer. Being a pioneer often involves risk taking. We must do everything we can to minimize the risk, but then, we must go forward. In this case, it is necessary to take a risk in order to minimize a risk."

Connie again nodded in agreement, then she looked at her wrist monitor, "This alien just might pull through; his vital signs are continuing to slowly improve."

"Any guess when he might regain consciousness?" queried Dianne.

"I don't know, but I would like him to be clean and comfortable when he does. So as soon as we've finished dinner, let's give him a bath and some clean bedding. Also, let's put an air mattress under him."

"OK," said Dianne. "Being clean and comfortable when he wakes up should help convince him that we care about him and that we're not just trying to keep him alive for our needs."

An hour later, while bathing the alien, Dianne asked, "How long ago do you think this guy injured himself?"

"Judging from his condition, he had the accident at least a week ago, maybe two," Connie replied. "Considering the mess that he's made, I don't think he's been out of this bed for several days."

"He definitely needs a bath and clean bedding."

"Being clean and having an air mattress under him should make him feel a lot better when he regains consciousness."

"But that leg infection and fractured ankle are going to be agonizingly painful for him. Have you added any analgesic to the I.V.?"

"I haven't because of the possibility of an allergic reaction."

"He could've reacted to one of the antibiotics that you gave him."

"That's true, but I had no choice except to hit him with everything. Now that he seems to be recovering, I will add a small amount of analgesic to the I.V. If he doesn't react, I'll increase the dose. If there's no adverse effect from that, I'll add a drug to reduce the swelling and see if he tolerates it. If he does, I'll increase the dose."

"If this guy's lucky, he won't regain consciousness until sometime tomorrow. By then, all of our drugs will have had a chance to work, and he should wake up feeling fairly good."

"If he hasn't already suffered critical damage to one or more vital organs," remarked Connie. "When we get back to our camp, we can give him a more thorough exam."

"I wonder if we'll be able to move him by tomorrow afternoon."

"If he continues the slow steady improvement, I think we should take him home tomorrow even if he hasn't regained consciousness. The immediate danger of death will have passed, and I need to give him the kind of exam that is possible with the equipment we have at home."

"It's going to be a difficult job taking him out that narrow tunnel and lowering him thirty feet down the tree without aggravating his condition."

"I think we should dump that problem on our husbands and let them apply their engineering talents to it," stated Connie.

"They'll probably figure out an easy way to do the job."

A short time later, Connie and Dianne finished making the alien comfortable and joined Jerry and Moose who had just finished exploring the cavern and were again seated next to the campfire.

"How is your patient doing?" Jerry asked Connie.

"I think he's going to make it."

"I don't think there's any doubt that he is very strong willed in his determination to live," noted Jerry.

"That's an important factor in surviving any serious illness," commented Connie.

"I am amazed at how well this man has lived without any guns or modern equipment," Jerry noted. "The only thing in this cavern to connect him with an advanced society is a hunting knife with a high quality stainless steel blade."

"He is definitely very well-equipped with ingenuity and survival skills," commented Moose.

"I think the fact that he has nothing modern except for his knife indicates that he was deserted by his colleagues," Jerry said. "If they'd died here of disease, then he would have the tools, weapons, and equipment that they brought with them."

"But why did they desert him with nothing but a knife for defense?" questioned Dianne.

"Apparently, he was left here to die," replied Jerry. "Perhaps, their intention was to take all of his weapons, and the knife was just overlooked."

"So what crime did he commit that was deserving of the death penalty?" asked Connie. "Is it possible that I am trying to save the life of a psychopathic killer?"

"If that's why he was deserted, we certainly don't need him to get well and live with us," stated Moose.

"There is another possibility to consider," Jerry suggested, "and that is that he may have been staunchly opposed to something the group was doing or was planning to do, and they deserted him simply to get him out of the way."

"If that's the case, it would be helpful to know what sort of evil activity this man was trying to prevent," remarked Dianne. "If the group has survived and prospered, we might have a tribe of evil humanoids living somewhere in this vicinity that we'll have to deal with sometime."

Moose frowned, "It looks to me like we have a potential problem either way. Either we're trying to save the life of a dangerous man, or we're going to have a group of ruthless, evil beings to contend with."

Jerry grinned at Moose, "It seems like our lives are a bit more complicated than they were a few days ago."

"How can you joke about something as potentially dangerous as this?" retorted Moose.

"I'm not trying to belittle the problem, but we do have the tools to deal with it, so long as we stay alert to all possibilities."

"And there's something else to consider," commented Connie. "Let's suppose this alien was abandoned thirty years ago because of a criminal act. Thirty years is a long time, and people sometimes change drastically with time. After living in isolation with nature for thirty years, he could easily have undergone some drastic changes in his thinking."

"But those changes could just as easily be for the worse as for the better," commented Moose.

"That's true," admitted Connie. "We'll just have to watch him until we know him very well. For that reason and to monitor his medical condition, we'll have to sleep in shifts tonight. I can watch him until around 3:00 to 4:00 A.M., and then, I'll need to be relieved."

"I'll stay up with you and help you stay alert," Jerry said. "Even though the alien has found security in here for a long time, I think we need to be on guard anyway."

"Wake me up when you need to be relieved. Moose and I will take over," Dianne said to Connie.

FOURTEEN

Saved By a Savage Attack

TIME: Day Nineteen, Late Morning.

The interstellar pioneers sat around their campfire eating breakfast. They chatted about their first night away from the security of Stellar Plateau and the novelty of being the first humans to have spent the night in the home of an alien.

When they were almost finished with breakfast, their conversation was interrupted by the alien, who had just regained consciousness. They all turned to face him as he raised and turned his head in their direction.

The alien gazed at the humans for a few seconds; then, he shifted his gaze to the medical setup. After scrutinizing the I.V. for a few moments, he looked at his clean comfortable bedding. Noticeably satisfied with his greatly improved situation, he shifted his gaze back to the pioneers. An expression of gratitude seemed to pervade his facial features. Then, weakness overcame him, and his head slumped down on the pillow provided by the pioneers.

"He certainly doesn't seem to be alarmed by our presence," commented Jerry. "In fact, he seems to be quite comfortable with the idea of having us here."

"And it looks to me like he is grateful to us for what we've done for him," noted Connie.

"He should be; after all, we've saved his life," Moose said.

"It'll be a few days before we'll know for sure that we've saved his life," remarked Connie.

"But if he thinks that we've saved his life, he should trust us and be happy that we're here," argued Moose.

"There might be more to it than that," remarked Dianne.

"What do you mean?" asked Jerry.

"He may have concluded that we would help him before he revealed his presence to us."

"How could he have known that?" questioned Jerry.

"Don't forget that he contacted us using his telepathic powers. It's possible that he may have first used those powers to probe our minds. Even though there is a language barrier, he may have been able to detect whether we are kindhearted or cold-blooded."

An expression of concern appeared on Jerry's face as he considered the implications of what Dianne had just said. "If he can probe our minds, is it possible that he might also be able to get into our minds and control us?" he asked.

"The ability to mentally transmit information directly into our minds is nothing more than a form of communication. Having the ability to communicate is not the same as having the ability to control," Connie commented.

"But he is a member of an intelligent alien species that we know very little about," argued Jerry. "I don't think that it would be wise to assume that his telepathic powers are limited to communication."

"I'm not advocating that we make that assumption, but if he is capable of telepathically controlling the activities of those around him, then his colleagues could not have deserted him thirty years ago unless he allowed them to do so."

"What if his colleagues had telepathic powers greater than his?" questioned Jerry.

301

"Then he would not have been able to prevent them from deserting him," replied Connie.

"You're saying that there might be a colony of humanoids somewhere on this planet that might have a telepathic ability to control us," Moose blurted. "If we ever have to fight them, our superior weapons won't give us any advantage if they can prevent us from using them."

"That is a sobering thought," commented Jerry, "but let's not forget that they were unable to keep us from destroying their genocide machines."

"I think it would be extremely difficult to control another person with telepathic powers unless the targeted person allows it to happen," Connie said.

"That might be true," agreed Dianne, "but telepathically planted suggestions could certainly influence the activities of a person who is unaware that the suggestions are being planted. Hypnotists do quite well with verbally planted suggestions."

"But hypnotists can only hypnotize those who are willing to surrender control," countered Connie.

"If both of you are correct," Jerry said, "I think our best defenses are to be aware that suggestions might be planted and to be stubbornly determined to remain in control of our own actions."

"I think that is a good policy for each of us to follow," stated Connie, "especially now that it appears likely that there might actually be a colony of telepathically capable aliens living somewhere on this planet."

"And there's also this alien whose life we are trying to save," remarked Moose. "Even if it turns out that he cannot telepathically control us, I don't know if I like the idea of having an individual around who can read my mind."

Displaying a mischievous grin, Dianne asked, "Is there something that you're trying to hide?"

Moose squirmed and said, "Of course not, it just seems rather spooky to have to constantly guard my thoughts."

"This alien might turn out to be a considerate individual who would always respect the privacy of our thoughts," commented Connie.

"I still don't like the idea that my thoughts might be open to him any time he decides to look at them," countered Moose.

"I think we should be alert to that possibility without jumping to conclusions until we get to know him and the extent of his powers," commented Connie.

"There is another possibility to consider," remarked Jerry, "and that is that this alien could turn out to be a vital ally if there is a colony of aliens nearby that have telepathic powers. If he is grateful to us for saving his life and upset about having been deserted thirty years ago, he might choose to assist us. He might be able to sense when the others are attempting to use their telepathic powers against us."

Moose reluctantly acknowledged, "I understand the importance of saving his life and caring for him while he recovers, but I don't like the idea that my thoughts might be open to him any time he cares to look at them."

"I don't think that will be a problem until he understands our language," commented Dianne. "If your thoughts are in English, and he tunes in to them; what good will it do him? I think that until he understands English, he will only be able to pick up your mood, or see images that are in your mind, or transmit images into your mind."

"That means that he cannot plant suggestions in our minds until he understands our language," stated Jerry. "If he attempts to plant suggestions using images, it should be obvious that something unusual is happening."

"Are you suggesting that we delay teaching him our language until we learn more about him?" asked Connie.

"I think that would be the prudent thing to do."

"We communicated very well with Rex using images," remarked Dianne.

"Let's learn as much as we can about this alien and those that came with him by communicating with images," Jerry stated. "If we eventually decide that we can trust him, then let's teach him our language."

"I like that approach," declared Moose.

"I think it's time to remove the I.V. I've pumped enough drugs and nutrients into him to last for a while," Connie said. "He is no longer dehydrated, and it appears that we've killed the microbes that were ravaging his body."

"How long before we can move him to Stellar Plateau?" Jerry asked Connie.

"I think he has recovered to the point where we can safely move him, if you and Moose can devise a way to do that without aggravating his condition."

"All we have to do is immobilize his injured leg and strap him to a sturdy stretcher. We can easily carry him. I doubt that he weighs more than about 180 pounds. We can use ropes to lower him down the tree."

"It might be beneficial to show him what we're planning to do before we start moving him," Connie commented. "If he knows what the plan is and approves, then he won't do anything to resist. In his weakened state, I don't want him to get alarmed and do something foolish."

"If he's still awake, let's introduce him to one of our video headsets," Jerry said. "With it, we can show him our boat, a map of this lake, and which island we're taking him to. We can show him some video of our camp. Then, we can show him the stretcher and indicate to him that we're going to put him on it."

"After all of that, he should be smart enough to figure out what our intentions are," commented Connie.

"And by using his telepathic powers he should be able to tell us if he has any objections," remarked Dianne.

"So far, all telepathic communication has been with you," Jerry said to Dianne. " I don't know what the reason for this is, but I am going to assume that if he wants to communicate with us, it will be through you. So while I show him what we're planning to do, I want you to relax and keep your mind open."

After Dianne acknowledged the request, Jerry picked up two video headsets and calmly approached the alien followed by his fellow pioneers. The alien was not alarmed by their approach, because he had already decided that these strangers had come into his home to help him.

When he had the alien's attention, Jerry showed him the headsets. Then, he handed one of them to Moose who put it on. Using gestures, Jerry indicated to the alien that he wanted him to wear the other headset.

After a few moments, Dianne said, "An image of the alien wearing a headset has just appeared in my mind."

"That was quick," remarked Jerry.

As Jerry leaned over the alien to put the headset on him, the alien lifted his head to make the task easier. When the headset was comfortably in place, Moose launched the little RPV that the pioneers had brought into the cavern and flew it down the tunnel and out of the cave. Then, Moose flew the RPV out to the boat and slowly circled it to give the alien a good view. Next, Moose landed the RPV on the boat.

While Moose was doing this, Connie removed the I.V., and Jerry accessed the Challenger's computer library to call up specific images to show the alien.

After landing the RPV, Moose took off his headset and gave it to Jerry who put it on, so he could view the images he planned to show the alien. First, Jerry used the computer to create an image of the boat with the pioneers and the alien on it. Then, he showed the alien an image of Clear Lake. Next, he slowly zoomed in on an area that included Pioneer Island and the alien's home Island. Then, he used computer graphics to show the boat moving from the alien's home island to Pioneer Island. Next, Jerry used the video cameras on Stellar Plateau to present images of their camp. Finally, he used the computer to create an image of the alien lying on a table with Connie working on his broken ankle.

A few moments after Jerry turned off the video, Dianne said, "I have an image in my mind of us and the alien on our boat."

"I now have an image of the alien standing on one leg while being supported between Moose and Jerry. Apparently, he thinks he can make it to our boat without being carried on a stretcher," Dianne said.

A few moments later, Dianne said, "I now have an image of the alien with a glass of water in one hand and some food in the other."

"It appears that our therapy has knocked out the alien's infection and made him feel much better," remarked Connie. "He's not only hungry, but he thinks he's strong enough to hobble his way to our boat with a little assistance."

"I'll get him some water and some breakfast," announced Dianne.

"While you're doing that, I'll bandage his leg and immobilize his broken ankle," stated Connie.

Turning to Moose, Jerry said, "Let's break camp and put our equipment on the boat."

About an hour and a half later, all were onboard the boat and sailing toward Pioneer Island. Deeply interested in the boat, the alien looked intently at the solar sails. Then, he noted that Alpha Centauri A was almost directly overhead in the midday sky. Having determined that the boat must be electrically powered, the alien looked at the stern and listened intently for the sound of an electric motor, but was unable to hear even a faint hum. The alien was deeply impressed that these strangers had seen fit to use their advanced technology to create a propulsion system that would power this boat in absolute silence, and a pleasant smile of approval appeared on his face.

Comfortably seated in a portable lounge chair, the alien relaxed in the warm sunshine with a gentle breeze caressing his body. Hearing only the sound of small waves lapping against the sides of the boat and pleasant conversation among his new-found friends, the alien soon became drowsy and fell sound asleep.

About a half hour later, he felt a gentle prod on his right shoulder and awoke to find Dianne next to him and pointing up at something in the western sky. He looked upward and saw the personnel shuttle heading north. Dianne handed him a pair of binoculars, which he eagerly accepted and immediately focused on the shuttle. He watched it turn to the east and then to the south as it glided into the last leg of its landing approach. After landing, it turned and headed toward South Bay.

Arriving at the south end of Pioneer Island at about the same time as the shuttle, Jerry decided to follow it into South Bay. The shuttle dropped anchor about thirty yards offshore. Jerry dropped anchor a short distance away from the shuttle. He turned to Moose, "Let's unload it and send it back up."

"We have about four thousand pounds to unload," commented Moose. "It's going to take a couple hours to haul all that to shore."

Stepping into the inflated boat, Jerry said, "The sooner we get started; the sooner we'll get done. Anyway, I think we can get the job done in much less than two hours. If we swim rather than ride in the boat, we can put more in it. When we're ashore, we can haul the boat in with a piece of rope."

An hour and twenty minutes later, Moose and Jerry moved the last boatload of cargo ashore. Dianne and Connie had already carried the items that they could lift to the elevator and hauled them up to Stellar Plateau. With two additional trips on the elevator, Moose and Jerry lifted the remaining cargo up onto Stellar Plateau. Then, they returned to the solar sail boat to pick up the alien.

When they were all were on the plateau, Jerry said, "Let's launch the shuttle, so our colleagues on the Challenger can get the DNA project started."

Dianne glanced at the alien. "I wonder how this alien would react if he knew that his DNA might turn out to be the final piece of evidence that we need to prove that it is safe for humans to live here," she said to Connie.

"I don't see how he could possibly object to helping us in that way," commented Connie. "After all, we've saved his life. In my opinion, he was no more than a day or two away from death when we found him."

"You would never know that by looking at him now," remarked Dianne. "He seems to be making an amazing recovery."

Connie considered Dianne's remarks, looking at the alien. "We did give him some very effective medical help, but even so, I am surprised by his speedy recovery," she said.

"Me too!" exclaimed Dianne. "It's only been about 24 hours, and he not only seems to be feeling pretty good, but he also seems to be mentally sharp and keenly alert. He has been very interested in everything that we've done."

"That's perfectly understandable," noted Connie. "He's been alone for a very long time. Now, he finally has some visitors, and the visitors are from another planet. To him, we are the aliens. He should be interested in us and our technology."

"Since he's so eager to learn about us, let's give him a good vantage point to watch our shuttle takeoff," Jerry said. "It's not only an impressive display of advanced technology; it's also a spectacular sight, a sight that I also enjoy watching."

A few minutes later, they were at the southeast corner of Stellar Plateau observing the shuttle taxi out of South Bay. Once out of the bay, the shuttle immediately accelerated to hydrofoil speed. Then, its powerful NTR burst into action with a thundering roar. In just a few seconds, the shuttle seemed to leap off the lake into a steep climb as if having a mind of its own that yearned for a speedy return to orbit.

Jerry stole some brief glances at the alien to observe his reaction at the shuttle's departure. "If I am correctly interpreting his facial expressions, I must conclude that our guest is deeply impressed with our technology. I also sense a yearning on his part to ride our shuttle into orbit," Jerry said.

"That seems like a reasonable reaction; after all, he is an interstellar astronaut," Moose commented.

"But the gleam that I detected in his eyes is a gleam that I've seen only in the eyes of test pilots about to go up in a hot new aircraft," remarked Jerry. "I think it's quite likely that he was the mission pilot, and once they arrived here, that skill was no longer essential, making it easy for his colleagues to desert him in response to whatever conflict they had."

"That concerns me," stated Moose.

"What concerns you?" asked Jerry.

"The strong possibility that he was the mission pilot concerns me. Think about it! We don't know why he was abandoned by his colleagues. It may have been because of ruthless criminal behavior on his part. If he was an excellent pilot, it won't take him long to figure out how to fly our shuttles once he learns our language. Then, he could steal one if given the opportunity to do so."

"And what would he use it for?" asked Jerry.

"He might use it to punish those who deserted him thirty years ago, if he knows where they are."

"I think you're letting your imagination get the best of you," responded Jerry.

"That may be, but what I'm suggesting is possible."

"While that's true, you have to consider the fact that this alien isn't exactly a young man anymore. He might just want to live out the rest of his life in a peaceful relaxing way. He might even want to become a member of our society for social reasons and to enjoy the benefits of our technology."

"Well, I don't think we should trust him until we know a lot more about him. Right now, it's possible that he's being very friendly only because he needs us."

"Because of his needs, he's not going to be in any kind of physical condition to steal a shuttle for at least six weeks," stated Connie. "It's going to take at least that long for his ankle to heal, after I do the surgery."

"During that time, I think we should assume the best and treat him as an honored guest while we learn about him and his past," Jerry said. "If we determine that he will be a threat to our well-being, we can always take appropriate action."

"That self-propelled wheelchair that he's sitting in seems to be making him feel like an honored guest all by itself," commented Dianne.

"He's definitely pleased that we've provided him with an easy way to move around," observed Connie.

"It was thoughtful of you to have it sent down," commented Jerry.

"Just taking care of my patient."

"It's actually more than that," commented Jerry.

"What do you mean?" asked Connie.

"Giving him the means to easily move around should indicate a degree of trust on our part. Now, the burden is on him to show that our trust is justified. Also, if he thinks that he's being treated the same as we would treat one of our own, he might conclude that we're trying to tell him that he's welcome to join our society. Again, the burden is on him to avoid doing anything that would cause us to revoke the invitation."

"I really didn't have all of that in mind when I requested that the wheelchair be sent down. I was just trying to be a good doctor. However, I agree with your thinking."

Jerry looked at Moose, who thought about the situation for a few moments. "Giving him as much freedom as possible is sort-of-like giving him enough rope to hang himself," Moose said.

"You're sure in a distrustful state of mind today," stated Jerry. "But you are right. If he abuses his freedom, he will face undesirable consequences."

"That's a rather mild way of stating what I just said."

"Whether or not we trust him, there can be little doubt that we will learn more about him by giving him as much freedom as possible than what we would learn by restricting him and directing his every activity," Connie said to Moose. "The implications behind the free choices that he makes in day-to-day life should reveal much about him."

"That's probably true, but if he's clever, he can conduct himself in ways that are designed to deceive us," argued Moose.

"If he does, I think you'll see right through his deceptive activity as suspicious as you are," responded Connie.

"I don't think I'm being overly suspicious just by considering possibilities. After all, our shuttles are essential pieces of equipment."

"Until this alien learns our language, he will have a very difficult time learning how to operate our shuttles," commented Jerry. "While the flight control computers make shuttle operation quite easy, it's impossible for him to learn how to operate those computers until he learns English. Also, if he was deserted thirty years ago and wants revenge against those who deserted him, wouldn't it be simpler for him to make friends with us and attempt to enlist our help?"

"If he does, and we refuse to help; then, I think theft of a shuttle becomes a real possibility," stated Moose.

"For that scenario to have any credibility, those who deserted him have to still be alive, he has to know where they are, and he has to have a desire for revenge," Connie said.

"If they're still alive, his telepathic ability might enable him to know where they are," remarked Dianne. "If he considers us to be his friends, he might be willing to tell us where they are, saving us the job of searching for them."

"By the time his ankle heals, we should attempt to have answers to all pertinent questions about him and those who came here with him," Jerry said.

"Dianne and I are planning to do the ankle surgery tomorrow morning," stated Connie.

"After he has had a little time to recover from the stress of surgery, I'll begin the process of getting information from him," Dianne said. "Hopefully, it won't take very long to get enough answers to put my husband's mind at ease. I don't want him to get high blood pressure from worrying about this alien's intentions toward us."

Connie quickly assured Dianne, "Don't worry, if he gets high blood pressure, I can treat him for that."

"Would you use drugs, or would use psychological counseling to help him deal with the stress caused by excessive worrying?"

"I would have to do a careful diagnosis to determine which therapy would be most effective."

Moose looked at Jerry and said, "I think I'm being picked on for doing nothing more than expressing legitimate concern about a potential problem."

Jerry chuckled, "Why do I get the feeling that you're enjoying the attention?"

"That question should be easy for him to answer," Dianne said quickly.

"Our guest seems to have picked up the present mood of our conversation, for he seems to be softly laughing too," commented Connie.

"So, even the alien that I am concerned about gets a good laugh at my expense," remarked Moose.

"I still get the feeling that you're enjoying the attention," commented Jerry.

In response, Moose grinned at Jerry.

"I think we should forget about the alien for a while and take care of the cargo that we just unloaded. Let's start by putting together the ATV (all-terrain-vehicle). Then, we can use it to haul the rest of the items home," Jerry said.

"It shouldn't take us more than an hour or two to put it together," declared Moose.

"I think you're probably right," agreed Jerry. "All the small parts have already been assembled into major components. All we have to do is put them together, so let's get started."

As Moose and Jerry went to work on the task at hand, Dianne asked, "Do you guys need any help?"

"Thanks for asking, but this ATV was designed for quick easy assembly. We should be fine," Jerry replied.

"Maybe, you could fix us some dinner," suggested Moose. "By the time we've finished here, I am going to be starving."

"That doesn't surprise me," commented Dianne in a playful tone. "Do you have any particular kind of dinner in mind?"

Moose ignored Dianne's teasing remark, smiled at her, and said, "I wouldn't mind sitting down to a large spicy pizza with a salad on the side."

"You just might be in luck," replied Dianne. "Some of these boxes contain a new supply of groceries. I believe pizza-making ingredients are included."

Dianne looked through the supplies, found the box she was looking for, picked it up, and handed it to Charlie.

While she was doing this, Connie asked Jerry, "Would you like us to take the alien with us or leave him here?"

"He has the controls to his wheelchair. Let's let him make that choice."

"What do you hope to learn by presenting him with that choice."

Jerry looked into his wife's eyes, displayed a sly grin, and said, "We might find out whether he prefers to be with men or with women."

"I don't know if I like giving him that choice. I might feel rejected if he chooses to stay here with you guys, especially when you consider that he probably hasn't seen a woman in thirty years."

Making some subtly suggestive movements, Dianne added, "We could end up feeling unattractive."

Moose noticed Dianne's body language. Then, his face lit up with a broad smile as he recognized the opportunity that the women had just presented him. In a compassionate tone, Moose said, "If the alien decides to stay here with us, I could arrange for counseling to help you deal with your bruised egos, but this would occur only after a careful diagnosis of your traumatized emotions."

Caught off-guard by Moose's remark, Dianne and Connie looked at each other with wide-eyed expressions of surprise. "I think my husband's been studying elementary psychology," Dianne said.

"That may be, but I don't think we're going to have damaged egos for him to repair, because it looks like the alien has taken quite an interest in the parts to the ATV," Connie said. "Evidently, he's mechanically minded and has already started mentally assembling it. I think that he will stay here and watch our husbands put it together."

Connie proved to be correct. When she, Dianne, and Charlie started walking toward home, the alien glanced at them briefly, then returned to watching Moose and Jerry.

Two hours later, with a large bowl of salad on the table and a large pizza in the oven, Dianne and Connie stepped out onto the front porch to watch Moose, Jerry, and the alien drive up in the new ATV. Apparently, Jerry had claimed captain's privileges, for he was seated in the driver's seat.

The ATV had two front seats and a truck bed able to accommodate 1000 pounds of cargo, or a seat for two people could be installed in the bed leaving room for 500 to 600 pounds of cargo. The vehicle was four-wheel drive with each wheel having its own electric motor. Its fairly large low-pressure tires were equipped with large lugs, giving them excellent traction. This feature made it possible for the ATV to be used as a light tractor to pull soil-working equipment.

All admired the ATV, acting very much like children with a new toy. "I think Dianne and I should take it for a test-drive after dinner," declared Connie.

"Good," said Dianne, "and we can pick up some of the supplies that came down today."

"I smell something good," remarked Moose, "and it's making my mouth water."

"Dinner does smell good," agreed Jerry, "and it's such a pleasant evening that I think we should eat outdoors."

A few minutes later, all were seated at the picnic table. Before they started eating, Jerry said, "I think it's time to introduce ourselves to our guest."

One by one, the pioneers pointed to themselves and announced their names. The alien repeated each name. Then, he pointed at himself and said, "Zebronyrick."

Each pioneer struggled with the name attempting to correctly pronounce it, so the alien slowly said, "Zeb-ron-y-rick."

After each pioneer correctly pronounced his name, the alien smiled in satisfaction. Then, he pointed at himself and said, "Zeb."

"Why didn't he just say *Zeb* in the first place?" Moose mumbled.

"I think our guest found some amusement with our struggle to pronounce his full name," commented Jerry. "Perhaps, he has a sense of humor."

Zeb was the last to begin eating. He watched each pioneer for a few moments; then, he imitated their manners. First, he tasted the salad. After a few moments, he looked at Dianne and Connie and smiled in approval. Then, he tasted the pizza; again, he smiled in approval.

"Apparently, our dinner is a big hit with our guest," Dianne said to Connie.

"This might be the first time that he's been out to eat in thirty years," commented Connie.

"That would make this a special occasion for him," noted Dianne. "Especially, when you consider that he's eating a meal prepared by beings from another planet."

"He's definitely enjoying the occasion," stated Connie.

A half hour later, Connie asked Dianne, "Are you ready to go for a ride?"

"Yeah, let's go. We can do these dishes later."

"Why don't you just enjoy yourselves," suggested Moose. "I'll take care of the cleanup duties."

Dianne smiled at Moose and said, "Thank you." She turned to Connie and said, "I love it when my husband is well-fed. It always puts him in such a good mood."

"What do you mean? I'm always in a good mood," Moose said quickly.

Dianne looked affectionately at Moose for a few moments. "Well, I suppose that's true."

A couple minutes later, Dianne and Connie were in the ATV heading south. "This is great!" exclaimed Connie. "We'll no longer have to walk everywhere we go."

"And we won't have to carry everything that we want to move around," added Dianne.

"Life here on the plateau will be easier. I wish we had one of these down on the rest of the island."

"Maybe, you could talk your husband into having another one sent down."

"That shouldn't be too difficult," responded Connie.

While watching Dianne and Connie drive off in the new ATV, Moose said, "They're acting like they just took delivery on a new car."

"In other words, they're as excited as we are," commented Jerry.

Zeb picked up the mood of the occasion and seemed pleased that everyone was enjoying the new vehicle. Noticing this, Jerry said, "I think our guest is starting to realize that it would be very beneficial to him to join our society."

"That may be, but he still has to prove himself trustworthy."

"If I were a gambler, I would bet that he will."

"Time will tell," stated Moose. "But your comment did have a word in it that I like."

"What word is that?"

"Beneficial," replied Moose. "I think it would be very beneficial to us to bring down another ATV. We could use it for getting around on this island. Most of the waterfront is passable to an ATV. The few places that aren't could easily be made passable by moving a few rocks or clearing some brush or cutting down some trees."

"In other words, you want to build a road around the island."

"A rough trail that's passable to an ATV could hardly be thought of as a road."

"That's true, but whether we call it a trail or a road, once we start driving around instead of walking around, we will have taken a significant step in the creation of a modern society."

"I'm ready for that step," declared Moose.

"Are you trying to say that your legs aren't as young as they used to be?"

"I believe that I could still keep up with you in a foot-race, but I am ready for the convenience of having some wheels to get around with."

"I'm not sure that's a good idea."

"What do you mean?"

"As much as you eat all the time, you're probably going to get fat if you start driving instead of walking."

"With all the work that we have to do to turn this island into a comfortable home, I think I'll get more than enough exercise to burn off the excess calories. Besides that, I don't eat much more than you eat."

"I don't know about that; it seems like you're always hungry."

"Why shouldn't I be; look at the active outdoor life that we live. Good clean living is supposed to make me hungry."

"Are you sensitive about your voracious appetite?" Jerry joked.

"I'm not sensitive about it, but you seem to be implying that there's something wrong with me because I've been blessed with a highly developed sense of taste that enables me to enjoy the delicate flavors of choice foods. In addition to my highly refined sense of taste, I live an energetic life style that stimulates my appetite. Also, I am constantly being tempted by an abundant supply of delicious delicacies."

"You sure use a lot of big words to explain something that you're not sensitive about."

"Being able to fluently express myself is one of the benefits of my extensive education. And I might add that I've found that this is a valuable ability. On more than one occasion, my expert ability to communicate has allowed me to present my point of view in a way that allowed me to prevail over others with differing points of view."

"Are you telling me that you rarely lose an argument?"

"I am exceedingly articulate, and I can't remember the last time that I failed to persuade others to accept it."

"Aren't you too young for that?"

Completely puzzled by Jerry's question, Moose asked, "Too young for what?"

"It seems to me that you're too young for your memory to be going bad."

"There's nothing wrong with my memory! In fact, it has just occurred to me that I promised our wives I'd do the dishes, so before I do anything else, I suppose I should do that, or they might be looking for an explanation as to why I didn't keep my promise."

"That shouldn't be difficult for one who has an expert ability to prevail over others with a differing point of view."

"But wives can sometimes be quite emotional and unwilling to consider a well thought out explanation."

"So your enhanced ability to express yourself does have some limitations."

Moose considered Jerry's remark for a few moments. "I think I will start by putting away the leftover food."

Jerry chuckled, "I'm surprised that there is any leftover food."

"Zeb and I did justice to the meal, but we could've used a bit more help from you."

"I ate my share, but I never could keep up with you. I think Zeb kept up with you only because he hasn't eaten much during the past week, and now, he has some catching up to do."

Jerry noticed that Zeb became quite attentive when he heard his name mentioned, but he did not seem alarmed. Apparently, the mood of the conversation put Zeb's mind at ease thought Jerry as he turned to Moose and said, "I'm going to take Zeb inside and use the video screen to give him some general information about us, like where we're from, how we got here, and some scenes from Earth.

"Well, don't give him anything that he might use against us. He is an alien, and we don't know if we can —"

Moose's comment was interrupted by a loud cry of alarm from Zeb who was urgently pointing skyward. Moose and Jerry quickly turned to see what Zeb was alarmed by. What they saw filled them with terror, for there was a large pterodactyl in the midst of an attack dive with their wives as the target. Instantly, Moose and Jerry leapt from their chairs and grabbed their rifles, but before they could aim and shoot, the calm, quiet air of the evening was shattered by a savage blood-curdling scream. The diving pterodactyl broke off its attack to answer the challenge, but it was too late. As he spread his wings to pull out of his dive, the big male pterodactyl from Western Island struck him, quickly burying his talons into his back. He finished the job by grabbing his victim's neck with his powerful beak and clamping tight with a bone-crushing crunch. The big male released his mortally wounded victim, which fell from the sky crashing into the plateau with a dull thud a mere three yards away from Connie and Dianne.

Sitting in the driver's seat, Connie quickly sped away from the fallen pterodactyl, because she didn't know if it was dead or just wounded. In the passenger's seat, Dianne drew her 10.5 millimeter pistol and turned to face the fallen creature. She also made quick wary glances skyward looking for other attackers, but she saw only the big male from Western Island circling the scene looking very much like an alert sentry.

Meanwhile, Moose and Jerry were running toward them with rifles ready to fire followed by Zeb in his self-propelled wheel chair making a valiant effort to keep up. When they reached their wives, a noticeably shaken Dianne stepped out of the ATV and turned to her husband for support. After receiving a reassuring hug, she silently gazed at the fallen pterodactyl for a few moments. She turned to Connie and shuddered as she said, "One of us was only a few seconds away from becoming a meal for that creature."

"We haven't even been here three weeks, and this is my second brush with death," Connie commented, soberly. "In both cases, I would've been torn apart and eaten by a predator."

"That's a chilling thought," stated Jerry as he wrapped an arm around his wife to comfort her.

Dianne pointed skyward and said, "We are fortunate that the big guy circling up there came to our rescue."

"I wonder why he did that," questioned Connie. "Was it out of loyalty to us for having helped him, or was he just killing an enemy?"

"I don't know if we'll ever know the answer," Jerry replied, "but whatever the reason, I am glad that the big guy was in position to protect you and that he did the job so effectively. Zeb yelled out a warning, but it all happened so quickly, that I don't know if we could've shot the attacker in time to save you."

Pointing at the fallen pterodactyl, Moose said, "I think we should take a closer look to make sure that it is dead; if it isn't, we need to finish the job."

The pioneers cautiously approached the fallen pterodactyl with their guns ready for action. However, when they got close to it, it became quite obvious that the creature was dead.

Having recovered from the shock of their unexpected brush with death, Dianne and Connie proceeded to inspect the wounds inflicted by the big male from Western Island. The severity of the neck injuries caught their attention immediately. "I am amazed at how much force these pterodactyls can exert when they close their beaks," Connie said. "This one's neck isn't just broken in two spots; the bone is completely crushed."

"The bones of a flying creature are usually hollow and very light, making them easier to crush than those of a land animal," remarked Dianne. "But even so, I am surprised at the amount strength that has been shown, and I wouldn't want that beak clamped onto any part of me."

Next, Connie examined the talon-inflicted wounds. "Judging from the amount of blood on this creature's back, I would guess that one of the big guy's talons ripped a large hole in a main artery," she commented.

Dianne gazed at the dead pterodactyl's talons, "Those are awesome weapons. They look like curved daggers."

"We were only seconds away from an agonizing death inflicted by those daggers," Dianne trembled.

"We're lucky that the big guy used his deadly weapons to save us," responded Connie. "I wish I knew if he was killing an enemy, or if we actually do have a loyal 400-pound flying guard dog."

"It's difficult to believe that a fierce, wild creature who doesn't need us for anything would voluntarily decide to be our protector, but it's starting to look like that might be the case," Dianne said.

"But why would he do that?" questioned Connie.

"We can only speculate," replied Dianne, "but it's possible that pterodactyls are intelligent enough to think about the future. Considering what the big guy has seen us do, he may have concluded that we would be valuable friends to have in case he ever needs our help."

"This dead pterodactyl gives us an opportunity to gain some direct information about their intelligence," stated Connie. "We could open the skull, remove the brain, and study it in the lab. While we won't be able to determine how intelligent these creatures actually are, we should be able to determine what they're potential is."

"It's an opportunity that we need to take advantage of," declared Dianne. "In fact, we should study all of its organs."

"If we're going to do that, we need to get started soon," stated Connie. "Once the postmortem processes have had a chance to do their damage, it'll be more difficult to get the information that we want."

"And there's also the possibility that nocturnal scavengers could eat most of this carcass by morning," commented Dianne. "There are lots of birds here, and I suspect that even those that aren't scavengers will have a difficult time passing up an easy meal."

"That's a good point," agreed Connie. "I am tired, but if we get started right away, we should still get a good night's sleep. It shouldn't take more than a few hours to remove and preserve tissue samples and organs for future study."

"I think we should also open up its digestive tract and attempt to determine what kinds of creatures it has preyed upon in recent days," suggested Dianne.

A rather squeamish looking Moose said, "You're going to open up this creature's guts after the meal we just ate?"

Surprised at Moose's comment, Dianne said, "Why not? We are scientists, and one of the reasons we're here is to study extraterrestrial life."

"But the sight and smell of partially digested prey might be enough to cause me to lose my dinner."

"You don't have to watch us, but it would be nice if you would help us get set up," Dianne responded. "We are going to need some lights, because it's going to be dark before we finish. Also, you could stand guard in case some overly aggressive scavengers show up."

Before Moose could respond, Jerry said, "I think we can do that."

"We don't have much of a breeze, but we can take advantage of what little there is by doing guard duty upwind from the carcass," Jerry said to Moose. "Then, your highly refined sense of taste won't overreact to the odors and cause you to lose your dinner."

Moose grinned, "This is one of those rare occasions when my ability to appreciate delicate flavors is a burden that I have to endure."

"The next couple hours will put you to the test," Jerry chuckled.

"What test is that?"

"I am going to find out if you will make a good hunting partner for me?"

"What does being a connoisseur of fine foods have to do with being a good hunting partner?"

"Nothing, but being easily nauseated could be a problem. When we make a kill, we will most likely have to quickly butcher it and make a hasty retreat with whatever we can carry. There won't be time to nurse nausea problems caused by the odors involved in the butchering process."

Jerry noticed that a blank expression appeared on Moose's face while his eyes were staring off in the distance as if he was trying to see the distant countryside. After a few moments, Jerry said, "It looks to me like you're trying to visualize a successful hunt."

"I was, and you're right; there won't be time to contend with nausea problems. So, I am going to find out just how serious this problem might be for me."

"How do you plan to do that?"

"If you'll do the guard duty, I will assist our wives with the dissection of this dead pterodactyl."

"That will be a realistic test."

Looking skyward, Jerry said, "I think I should stay here and guard the carcass while you help our wives get the equipment they need. All these birds that are beginning to show up look hungry. You need to bring me a shotgun."

Moose looked at the birds and commented, "They remind me of sea gulls, and if they're like sea gulls, they'll eat just about anything that's edible."

A short time later, Connie, Dianne, and Moose started dissecting the dead pterodactyl. At first, Moose had a difficult time controlling his queasy stomach. However, as time progressed, his dogged determination to maintain control allowed his mind to make steady progress in gaining dominance over the nausea, which was a deep-seated reaction to blood and guts that dated back to a bad childhood experience.

By the time three hours had gone by, Moose gained complete control over his nausea problem, and the trio finished removing and preserving organs and specimens of interest.

From the beginning, one of Dianne's assistants onboard the Challenger used Charlie's video capabilities to record every aspect of the procedure. But now that the operation was finished, Charlie was marched a short distance away from the carcass, so that his video capability could be used to observe and record the expected feeding frenzy of all the flying scavengers that were getting increasingly more bold and impatient.

Leaving the scene, Connie said to Dianne, "I am exhausted, and I feel like collapsing into bed for about ten hours. If I had a coin, I would flip it with you for the first shower."

"Why don't you go first; I want to check our specimens to make sure they're properly preserved."

By the time the pioneers traveled twenty-five yards, the scavengers had already begun fighting over the choice parts of what remained of the dead pterodactyl. An almost deafening noise was created by the loud squawking of challenges and counter challenges, occasional shrieks of pain issued by fighting competitors, and the sound of hundreds of flapping wings.

The pioneers stopped to look back at the tumultuous scene, but were unable to see anything because neither Aphrodite or Nocturne were in the night sky and they had only starlight to see with. Noting the sounds of combat, Moose said, "Those birds must have excellent night vision if they can see well enough to fight."

"Nocturnal hunters and scavengers do have excellent night vision," stated Dianne.

"I know, but I'm still amazed by it," remarked Moose. "They're carrying on like it's daylight out here, and I can't see a thing."

Besides its headlights, the ATV was equipped with a brilliant searchlight. Currently seated in the driver's seat, Jerry said, "I would like to see what's going on back there."

Jerry turned the ATV around and pointed the headlights at the scene. He used the searchlight to pan the area above the remains of the pterodactyl. Moose said immediately, "They remind me of a school of piranhas in the midst of a feeding frenzy. There must be hundreds of them. Where did they all come from?"

"They've been arriving one and two at a time while you were working on the pterodactyl," replied Jerry.

"That's a terrifying scene!" exclaimed Connie as a cold chill ran up and down her spine. "If we had been caught in the middle of that, we could easily have been overwhelmed, and then, we might have become part of the meal."

"We would've been very busy with our pistols," remarked Moose, "but there are hundreds of them."

"The barrel of my shotgun would've gotten very hot," stated Jerry, "but I would not have been able to kill those that were very close to you."

"The loud banging sound of rapidly firing guns is unfamiliar to them and may have scared away those that we didn't kill," Moose commented.

"That's a comforting theory," stated Connie, "but I'm sure glad that we didn't have to test it."

"I wonder if these birds ever make a massive group attack on a large living creature in an attempt to overwhelm it with the force of numbers," Jerry said. "If they do, they could pose a serious danger to us, especially to our children."

"I haven't seen them prey on anything except marine life along the waterfront and small creatures of opportunity," responded Dianne. "I can only speculate, but I don't think that they have the intelligence to form a large group for the purpose of bringing down a large animal. I believe that this group formed in response to the scent of blood and the possibility of an easy meal. Rather than work together to attack a large animal, I think they're more likely to fight each other for a share of an already dead animal."

"But what if a small child became injured in a way that caused bleeding, and the scent of blood attracted a large number of these birds," Jerry said. "Would the child look vulnerable enough so that they would attack it? I am concerned that the more aggressive members of the flock might attack the child while he is still alive in order to gain advantage over their competitors. Then, the rest would join in, and the child would quickly be overwhelmed and devoured."

"That's a question that I can't answer," responded Dianne.

"I think I have a way that we can find out," stated Moose.

"What do you have in mind?" asked Jerry.

"Charlie has been invaluable to us," stated Moose. "Why don't we make a child-sized version of him. March him into an area frequented by these birds, have him fall in a fake accident, then have him stumble along with blood oozing from a fake injury. Then, we simply watch the birds to see how they respond."

"I like the idea," stated Jerry. "How soon can you get the project started?"

"I'll put in a call to the Challenger yet tonight. Some of the people who helped me make Charlie will still be up. They can start the project in the morning."

"How long do you think it will take them to finish it?"

"By working in shifts around the clock, they should be able to do it in less than a week."

"Good! When they're done, we'll bring it down and run the experiment. And whatever response we get from these birds, we will verify by repeating the experiment several times with variations to see if we always get the same reaction."

The pioneers watched the feeding frenzy for a few minutes, then headed home looking forward to a night of peaceful sleep inside their rugged habitation capsule.

FIFTEEN

An Unexpected Erotic Response

TIME: Day Twenty, Early Evening.

The interstellar pioneers relaxed at their outdoor table enjoying a pleasant evening and another delicious seafood dinner.

Connie said, looking to the south, "It's amazing how quiet and peaceful this plateau is compared to the wild savagery that went on here last night."

"Last night's dinner was equally peaceful," noted Jerry.

"Maybe that's why I was almost killed," stated Connie. "For the most part, our life here on the plateau has been peaceful, so peaceful that we've become complacent."

After making the comment, Connie stood up and searched the sky and landscape in all directions. Then, she sat down and said, "There doesn't appear to be anything of a threatening nature in our little corner of this planet. The only big creatures around are the two pterodactyls from Western Island, and they appear to be soaring around purely for the pleasure of flying."

"Maybe, they're also looking for anything that might be a threat to us," commented Dianne.

"After the way the big guy came to our rescue last night, I am inclined to agree with you," Connie remarked. "In fact, I am starting to think that we just might have a pair of flying guard dogs."

"Time will tell, but in any case, it does look like they will play a part in our daily life, so I think we should give them names," Dianne responded.

"Speaking of names, I think we've been using the name *pterodactyl* rather loosely," commented Connie. "For lack of a better name, we've been calling these creatures pterodactyls ever since we arrived here, but in many respects, they look more like giant golden eagles."

"And their talons protrude from webbed feet that look like they belong on a giant goose," remarked Moose.

"I've never seen a goose with long, sharp talons," remarked Dianne, innocently.

"You know what I mean," responded Moose. "If you cut off the talons, the feet that you have left look like they belong on a giant goose."

Noticing a broad grin of satisfaction on Dianne's face, Moose said, "You're developing quite a talent for teasing me while sounding serious, and I fell for it again."

"Somehow, I get the feeling that you enjoy the attention," replied Dianne.

Moose didn't say anything, but simply looked at his wife affectionately and warmly smiled at her.

Dianne relished Moose's silent expression of affection for a few moments, then turned to Connie and said, "You're right. These creatures are significantly different and far more advanced than Earth's extinct pterodactyls, but we have good reason to believe that these creatures have had an additional 500 million years to evolve."

"Evolution is a slow process, but that is a tremendous amount of time," commented Connie. "With that much time, even a slow process can produce marvelous results."

"In the case of these pterodactyls, evolution has developed a magnificent species that not only dominates the sky, but is also able to dive deep and catch fish. As if that's not enough, they're also able to prey on land animals," Jerry said.

"Apparently, the one that we dissected last night preferred to eat land animals," stated Dianne. "I wasn't able to find any fish parts in its digestive system."

"And it had every intention of putting one of us into its digestive system," added Connie.

"But the local king of the sky quickly put a stop to that," remarked Moose.

"That's the name we're looking for," asserted Connie.

"What is?" asked Moose.

"King," responded Connie.

Moose thought about it for a few moments. "I was just making an off-the-cuff comment, but I think the big guy just might be the boss in this area as far as pterodactyls are concerned. As near as I can tell, he is the biggest pterodactyl that I've seen so far. His wing span exceeds fifty-two feet, and the computer estimates his weight to be about four hundred pounds."

"When I was a kid, we had a dog named King," Dianne said. "He was a big German shepherd, and he was intelligent, loyal, and protective. I like the idea of giving the big guy the name *King*."

"If we give him the name *King*, then *Queen* is the obvious name for his mate," suggested Connie.

The pioneers thought about it, looked at each other, and nodded in agreement. "Okay, it's official: their names are *King* and *Queen*," Jerry said.

"How did the ankle surgery go?" he asked Connie, after a few moments of silence.

"I don't know how Zeb injured that ankle, but it was a nasty multiple fracture with torn ligaments. It took us more than three hours to repair everything."

"How long do you think it will take for it to heal?"

"He is an alien, and I don't know how quickly his body can heal an injury as serious as this one. However, if I had a similar injury, it would probably take two months before I could begin to gingerly walk on it and an additional two months to fully recover."

"So, it's quite likely that he will be dependent on us for at least two months."

"I think that's a reasonable guess."

"So, if he has any common sense at all, he'll avoid doing anything to alienate us for at least two months."

"That's what I would expect of him," agreed Connie. "In fact, he might even look for ways to be helpful in an attempt to convince us that it is to our advantage to continue to care for him."

"Even to the extent of being cooperative with our objectives?"

"I think so. Why? What do you have in mind?"

"Zeb has lived here for a long time, and there is a great deal of information that he could give us. We don't know what kind of individual he is and what he will do when he no longer needs us, but while he is dependent on us, he is likely to be cooperative. So, I think we should begin teaching him English. If he's willing to work with us, I think we can teach him enough in just a few weeks so that he could carry on a conversation with us. By the time he is back to normal, I would like to know what happened to his colleagues and where they are, if they're still alive. Also, I want to know why he became separated from them. On a more casual note, but also important, I would like to sit down next to a campfire and listen to him tell stories about his experiences on this planet."

"My only concern with your plan is that if he becomes fluent in our language, he might be able to learn how to get into our computers and operate some of our key pieces of equipment," Moose said. "If that were to happen, and if he turns out to be a bad individual; then, when he no longer needs us, he could do serious damage to us."

"But that possibility is probably two to four months away. If everything goes according to plan, everyone will be down here by then, and there will be enough of us to keep an eye on him. If we have any reason to be suspicious of him, we can always take appropriate action."

"But teaching him English before we know him does expose us to additional risk," argued Moose.

"That's true," admitted Jerry, "but teaching him English will help us get to know him sooner. Besides that, it's not just him that we need to worry about. We must find out what happened to his colleagues. If they're still alive, have they multiplied and prospered? Where are they? How strong are they? Are they a threat to us?"

Moose thought about it for a few moments. "Despite my concern, it looks like we have to increase our present risk to gain knowledge that might reduce our future risk," he said.

"That's the way I see it," stated Jerry. "However, I don't think the risks involved in teaching him English will be all that great, if we're careful to teach him nothing more than simple conversational English. To get into our computers and steal a key piece of equipment, he would need a good understanding of the sophisticated technical language involved. And, we are not going to teach him that."

"Let's not forget his telepathic abilities," cautioned Dianne. "Once he understands even simple conversational English, he may be able to read our thoughts and probe our memories, and that could lead to all sorts of problems."

"But could he do that to an individual without the individual being aware of what's happening?" asked Jerry.

"That question is impossible to answer," replied Dianne. "We simply don't know enough about telepathic powers."

"It seems to me that when we were in orbit around B-2, you were convinced of the presence of life on the planet before Rex revealed his presence," Moose said to Dianne. "We were on the observation deck together, and you told me that you could feel the presence of life. Could it be that your feeling was a response to Rex using his telepathic power to probe your mind?"

"That's possible, but did Rex make any attempt to conceal his probing effort, or did he want me to know that he existed to find out if we would make some attempt to contact him in response?"

"I think Dianne is right," remarked Connie. "We don't know enough about telepathic powers to know if it's possible for Zeb to probe our thoughts and memories without us being aware of it."

"I wonder if Rex could answer that question?" asked Jerry.

"I'm sure he knows as far as his species is concerned, but his knowledge of the human mind is limited," responded Dianne.

"But there was an extensive exchange of information between your mind and his mind through the use of telepathic images," remarked Jerry. "He may have learned enough about your mind to at least have an opinion."

"Michelle is in contact with Rex and Shannon every day. She could explain our situation to them and see what the response is. However, what they say might only apply to my mind. For whatever reason, both Rex and Zeb communicated telepathically only with me."

"Are you implying that there might be something unique about your mind that allows telepathic communication?" asked Connie.

"That is a possibility."

"If that's the case, then it's possible that only your mind would be open to covert telepathic probing by Zeb once he understands our language," commented Connie.

"That's possible, but again, we simply don't know."

"We seem to have more questions than answers," commented Jerry.

"Unfortunately, that is true," stated Dianne. "But humans have never before had to face the possibility of having their minds covertly probed by a being with telepathic powers. We don't know much about this, but eventually, we will find answers to our questions. Until then, we need to do what we can to protect ourselves."

After a few moments of thoughtful silence, Jerry said, "The possibility of having our minds covertly probed is another reason to teach him only basic conversational English until we know him better. We have very extensive vocabularies, and much of what's in our minds is in the form of technical terms that Zeb just simply won't be able to understand, even if he is able to probe our minds covertly. So let's begin teaching him English, but let's keep it simple."

"That should protect the technical knowledge in our minds," said Dianne. "However, thoughts and memories of life's everyday experiences will not be protected."

"I think that's a risk that we'll have to take," stated Jerry. "He has lived here for a long time and has knowledge that we need."

"Simple English combined with the images that he's able to project into my mind would enable me to gain a wealth of information from him, if he's willing to cooperate," Dianne said.

"If he wants us to nurse him back to health, he'd better be cooperative," declared Connie.

At that moment, everyone noticed that Moose was smiling broadly. Then, the smile turned into a bout of soft laughter that seemed to say that Moose was deeply amused about something. Everyone silently stared at him patiently waiting for an explanation. When none was given, Dianne said, "All right! I give up! What is so funny?"

"I was just thinking about all the fun Zeb is going to have if he's able to get into my mind and tune in to the memories that I have from the years when I was young and carefree."

Dianne gazed at Moose for a few moments. She decided to put her husband on the hot seat, "Why have you mentioned memories from those years rather than memories of the experiences we've had together? Are you implying that the girlfriends you had during your playboy years were more exciting than I am?" she asked.

"Whoops! I think I just said the wrong thing," Moose said to Jerry.

"I believe your thinking is correct," Jerry responded, after catching Dianne's expression.

"Well, how do I get out of this one?"

"You're on your own old buddy."

Moose turned to his wife and racked his brain for the right thing to say. After a half-minute of steadily building tension, he said, "I wasn't implying that our life together hasn't been exciting and fulfilling, but when I was single, I lived a recklessly wild life style at times."

Now, it was Dianne's turn. "We had our honeymoon on a starship in interstellar space. We're now living on a wild alien planet inhabited by dinosaurs. And, you recently rode a ten-ton styracosaurus into a face-off with a pack of ten-ton T-Rexes. Have you ever had a life style more recklessly wild than ours?"

Moose smiled broadly, gave Dianne a big hug, "You win this one."

While displaying a contented smile of satisfaction, Dianne turned to Jerry, "I think we need to teach Zeb simple English, so he can entertain himself by telepathically exploring my husband's memories."

"Having an alien being poking around in my subconscious mind seems rather spooky," commented Moose. "However, I have nothing to hide."

"We don't know if he has the ability to do that," stated Dianne, "but teaching him our language might be the best first step in the process of finding an answer to that question. We'll just have to stay alert to the possibility that a covert mental probe might be happening."

Facing Dianne, Jerry said, "I agree, and since Zeb has communicated only with you via telepathic images, I think you're in the best position to take the lead in teaching him English."

"I will enjoy doing that," replied Dianne, "but I will need some help, or I won't have much time for research."

"We'll all be available to assist you," stated Jerry.

Connie nodded in agreement and said, "That still leaves the question of whether or not we should talk to Rex about the possibility that Zeb will be able to covertly probe our minds once he understands English."

"The answer to that question boils down to whether or not we want the humanoids on B-2 to know that one of their kind is living here?" Jerry replied.

"What concerns you about that?" asked Connie.

"In view of the attack that we carried out, we undoubtedly have a hate-filled enemy on B-2 with a burning desire for revenge. If that enemy were to find out that one or more of their kind are living here, they might find a way to make contact. At the very least, they could then gain some knowledge that would help them plan an attack."

"But Rex would never tell anyone that one of their kind is living here, if he thought that doing so would put us at risk."

"I think that's true," commented Jerry, "but Rex has friends and colleagues who know about us. Some of them might have access to the messages we transmit and see them before Rex has had an opportunity to keep them confidential."

"Not only that," remarked Dianne, "but the very question that we need an answer to might come into play; and that is, if these humanoids have the ability to covertly probe each other's minds, then it would be impossible for Rex to keep the information confidential."

"That's exactly what concerns me," stated Jerry. "In a war that has gone on for thirty years, we have to assume that each side managed to plant numerous spies. Some of them might be so deeply entrenched that they're still around. Eventually, one of them would find out that one or more of their kind are living here, and that could lead to trouble for us."

"So you're saying that we must not tell Rex about Zeb," questioned Connie.

"Not until we know for sure that Zeb is trustworthy."

"So, that means that we need to find out ourselves whether or not Zeb can covertly probe our minds," commented Connie.

"I don't see any alternative," stated Jerry. "Eventually, we'll have the answer to that question. But until then, we must stay alert for any clues that indicate that our minds are being probed."

Everyone quietly thought about the situation for a short time; then, Moose nonchalantly commented, "It seems like our lives have become a bit more complicated ever since we found that shiny piece of metal among the rocks at the north end of this island."

Jerry laughed at the innocent way that Moose intentionally understated the current problem. Then, he said, "That was a rather shocking surprise, but something unexpected can happen at any time, and that's what makes our life such an exciting adventure."

"We haven't had very many dull moments," responded Moose.

"Years ago, when I invited you along on this mission, I did promise you an adventure beyond your wildest dreams."

"You've certainly fulfilled that promise!"

"I have an adventure in mind for tomorrow that I think will continue the fulfillment of that promise," Jerry said calmly.

Before Moose could comment, Connie said, "It's probably something dangerous that has the potential to get someone killed."

Jerry made eye contact with his wife. He nodded in agreement, but his body language seemed to say that he respected the dangers and would be triumphant over them. When he saw that Connie would say nothing more for the time being, he turned to Moose.

"What adventure do you have in mind?" asked Moose in a way that implied that he wasn't sure that he really wanted to know.

"First, I want to say that the seafood that we've been eating has been excellent, but we've been eating seafood almost every day, and I'm ready for a change in the menu."

"Sounds like we're going hunting," commented Moose.

"I am really hungry for barbecued steak, and I don't mean steak from our food synthesizers. I haven't had a real steak since we left Earth."

"Real steak comes from beef, and there aren't any cattle running around here," remarked Moose.

"But there is an abundant supply of dinosaurs ranging in size from very small to the 100-ton sauropods. The species that I think might be a good source of steaks reminds me of the ostrich in some respects. In fact, I think ostri-dino would be a good name for them."

"I think they're bigger than ostriches," noted Dianne. "However, if their dinosaur hides were covered with feathers, they would resemble ostriches."

"There are plenty of them roaming the countryside," stated Moose. "In fact, ostri-dinos just might be the most numerous of all the dinosaurs."

"That will make them easy to hunt, and if they turn out to be good to eat, killing one occasionally certainly won't hurt the species any. They're so numerous that they're probably a prime source of food for many of the predators."

"So, what's your plan?" asked Moose.

"There are hundreds of them living in Sauropod Meadow. Some of them drink water out of the lake. If we cruise slowly along the waterfront, it shouldn't take long to find a choice specimen. We simply shoot it, go ashore and quickly carve out some chunks of flesh to make into steaks. Then, we leave before dangerous predators show up. I would like to avoid killing other animals in defense of our kill."

"The one time I went ashore over there, I came within a fraction of a second of being killed," stated Connie.

Dianne looked at Moose, "The only time that you went ashore over there, you could easily have been killed in a fight between T-Rexes and styracosauruses."

Moose turned to Jerry, "I'm not sure that our wives approve of your plan."

"Well, it will be dangerous," argued Connie.

All eyes were upon Jerry as he thought about how to sell the plan to his wife. After a few moments, he said, "It will be dangerous, but I think I have an idea how to take some of the danger out of the hunt."

Jerry looked into the eyes of each of his colleagues. "Do you remember the day that we landed our first robot lab on top the big boulder in Sauropod Meadow?"

All nodded, then Jerry continued, "We were watching and listening to herds of dinosaurs peacefully grazing in the meadow when all of a sudden a spin-chilling roar reverberated throughout the Challenger. It was the defiant challenge issued by the leader of a group of T-Rexes that boldly marched into the meadow. All creatures except for the giant sauropods ran in response to the challenge."

Dianne shuddered, "Those T-Rexes are part of the danger that you will face over there."

"That's true," agreed Jerry, "but indirectly, those T-Rexes can protect us."

Sounding incredulous, Connie asked, "How are you going to get them to do that?"

"That defiant challenge is stored in the Challenger's data banks. If we take a powerful amplifier and a couple large speakers with us, we can sound out that challenge just before we go ashore to butcher our kill. I would guess that we will then be all alone with our kill for several minutes, and that's all the time we'll need."

Moose grinned broadly and said, "I think that idea will work, but there's only one problem: we don't have a powerful amplifier or large speakers down here."

"No! We don't, but our personnel shuttle could deliver them to us early tomorrow morning. I want to bring down another ATV anyway. I'm sure that each of you has something you'd like brought down. It shouldn't be that hard to fill up the personnel shuttle."

"In view of what happened last night, I think we should bring down a radar unit to monitor pterodactyl activity in this area," Connie suggested.

"I agree," Dianne said.

Jerry thought about the request. "The radar could be monitored by a computer that would send out a warning signal whenever a pterodactyl gets too close. Our communicators could be programmed to receive the signal and sound an alarm."

"I really like that idea," declared Connie.

"Me too," echoed Dianne.

"We could also program our communicators to keep the computer informed where each of us is located," Moose suggested. "Then, as long as we are within the radar's range, the computer could monitor pterodactyl activity in each person's vicinity and send out individual warnings."

"I like the idea of setting it up that way," commented Dianne. "The next time some pterodactyl decides to attack, King and Queen might not be around to defend us."

"Not only that, but when all of us are down here, there will be too many of us for them to defend," stated Connie.

"Also, we don't know if King was defending us, or if he was just killing an enemy," noted Dianne.

Jerry picked up his communicator, called Mike, and relayed his shopping list. Then, each of the pioneers talked to Mike in turn with their shopping lists.

When they were finished, Dianne and Jerry took Zeb into the habitation capsule to begin teaching him English and to give him some information. Jerry used the largest video screen and the computer library to present a star map and show Zeb where they were from. Next, Jerry showed Zeb the Solar System. After showing Zeb Earth as seen from space, Jerry took him on a brief scenic tour of the planet. Obviously deeply interested, Zeb watched in spellbound fascination. When Jerry decided that he had shown Zeb enough, he turned off the video and turned to face Zeb and did his best to present Zeb with an expectant expression that seemed to say, "Okay, now it's your turn."

Zeb responded by heading his wheel chair toward the door. Once outside, Zeb pointed at Alpha Centauri B located just above the horizon in the western sky. Alpha Centauri A had already set.

Jerry turned to Dianne and said, "I think he just told us where he is from. Let's take him back inside and show him B-2 from space and see if he'll show us which continent he's from."

When they were back inside, Moose and Connie joined them, and Jerry displayed a slowly rotating image of B-2 on the large video screen. Zeb perked up immediately and watched with deep interest. Then, a very distant expression appeared on his face that slowly changed to sadness causing Dianne to say, "I think he's homesick."

After about a minute had passed, Zeb moved close to the video screen, pointed at himself, and then at the continent currently visible on the screen. This caused Dianne and Jerry to look at each other with puzzled expressions. "He just pointed at Rex's home continent, but Rex said the manned mission to here came from the other side in the great war."

"It would appear that someone's not telling the truth," noted Dianne.

"Or Zeb might be one of those deeply entrenched spies I mentioned earlier," returned Jerry.

"That's incredible!" exclaimed Dianne.

"What do you mean?" asked Jerry.

"I think that it's incredible to the point of being unbelievable that a spy could rise high enough in the enemy's air force to be selected to be part of the first manned mission to another star."

"If he actually pulled off something like that, he is an extremely capable individual," stated Jerry.

"This would be a possible explanation for why he was deserted by his colleagues," speculated Moose. "Imagine their reaction if they found out after arriving here that Zeb was a spy."

"We could have Michelle speak to him in Rex's language and see how he reacts," Connie said.

While Zeb continued viewing the slowly rotating image of B-2 with a distant, forlorn expression on his face, Jerry thought about Connie's suggestion. After a few moments, he said, "If we do that and find that Zeb is fluent in Rex's language; then, we can delay teaching him English until we find out if we can trust him. Using this approach, only Michelle will be at risk of having her mind covertly probed in a telepathic way. And, she does not know how to operate either of our shuttles, or the Challenger, or any of the Challenger's essential systems."

"That would limit the amount of damage Zeb could do to us if he turns out to be an enemy," Moose commented.

"But do we want to expose Michelle to the risk?" asked Connie.

"I will discuss the situation with her and Mike and let them decide," stated Jerry.

"I don't think that there's much risk to her as long as she's onboard the Challenger and stays off the observation deck," Dianne said. "Rex was only able to communicate with me telepathically when I was on the observation deck. It seems that the energy field generated by Rex's mind to communicate with me was blocked by the metal in the Challenger's hull, but the transparent plastic hull on the observation deck allowed it to pass through."

"If Zeb is fluent in Rex's language, Michelle might not be able to come down here when everyone else does," remarked Jerry. "She might have to stay on the Challenger until she feels that she can trust Zeb to stay out of her mind."

"How do you ever trust a professional spy?" Moose asked.

"We don't know if he was a spy," replied Jerry. "We're only speculating."

"But if he was a spy and rose high enough in the enemy's air force to become part of an interstellar mission, then, he is an absolute master of deceit," Moose argued.

"If he was a spy, he may have been chosen for that career because of his telepathic ability," Dianne added. "What I am trying to say is that his telepathic ability might be far greater than that of others in the society he came from. He may even have received special training in how to use his telepathic ability in covert ways."

"We may be nursing an extremely dangerous individual back to health," stated Moose.

"Because of that possibility, it is imperative that we get answers to all of our questions before he has fully recovered," stated Jerry. "Also, it is imperative that we change our earlier decision and avoid teaching him English until we have good reason to trust him. If Zeb is from the continent he claims to be from, he should understand Rex's language, and it won't be necessary to teach him English if Michelle will agree to talk with him. When I explain the situation to her and Mike, I am confident that she will agree to accept the risk, which should be minimal as long as she stays on the Challenger and off the observation deck."

Speaking to Dianne, Jerry said, "Also, we can supplement Michelle's dialog with Zeb if you'll keep your mind open to telepathically transmitted images from him, and we'll use video to present him with images."

"I don't have any problem with that," responded Dianne, "and if Michelle agrees to talk to Zeb, he'll have ample opportunity to answer our questions and convince us that he is trustworthy."

"One thing I don't understand is that with a full scale war impending, why would a nation want one of its spies on an interstellar mission? Wouldn't he have been more valuable in the enemy's air force?" Connie asked.

"Are you trying to say that for that reason he wasn't a spy and that he might be lying about where he's from?" asked Jerry.

"That's possible."

"To answer that question, I think we have to ask why a nation would launch an interstellar mission when they were planning a full-scale war," Jerry responded. "Maybe, they were hoping to find a technologically advanced society on this planet and that there would be technology here that would give them a decisive advantage in the impending war. If Rex's country had no interstellar mission in the works, the only way that they could've protected themselves from such a technological bonanza would've been to place a spy on the mission."

"That sounds reasonable," remarked Connie. "If you're correct, and Zeb's true role was discovered after arriving here, he's lucky that he was only deserted, he could've been shot."

"Perhaps, his colleagues planned to shoot him, but he stopped them," commented Dianne.

"How?" asked Connie.

"Maybe, in a covert way, he telepathically planted suggestions in their minds that deserting him without weapons would be a worse fate than shooting him."

"That would be a unique method of self-defense," stated Jerry. "The possibility that he may be able to do that supports our decision to avoid teaching him English until we've determined that we can trust him to stay out of our minds."

"How soon we can trust him might depend on how soon he feels he can completely trust us," stated Connie. "Right now, he could think that we're only keeping him alive because we want information from him. Likewise, we have to consider the possibility that he's trying to be helpful because he needs us. However, if it turns out that he is from Rex's country, we might be able to completely win his trust by telling him about the horrible war that took place and our part in putting a stop to the final phase of it. If he still has patriotic feelings toward his homeland, he might be motivated to ally himself with us."

"It seems like that would be a normal reaction to what we've done," agreed Jerry. "If our speculations are correct, his knowledge and capabilities will make him a valuable asset to our society, especially when you consider that he may have lived here for thirty years."

"The key test will occur when Michelle appears on the video screen and addresses him in Rex's language," Connie said. "How he reacts might be more important than what he says."

"We might try that tomorrow after breakfast," stated Jerry. "I will discuss it with Mike and Michelle shortly, and if they agree, we'll do it then. In the meantime, you might show him additional scenes from Earth."

Turning to Dianne, Jerry said, "Keep your mind open for telepathic images in case he wants to tell us anything."

Dianne and Connie nodded in acknowledgment of Jerry's request. Then, Jerry contacted Mike and Michelle.

TIME: Day Twenty-One, Shortly After Breakfast.

The pioneers and Zeb were seated in the habitation capsule facing the main video screen. Zeb expectantly awaited the presentation of more video about Earth, but instead, Michelle appeared on the screen wearing a broad friendly smile. She paused briefly; then, she said, "Hello Zeb! My name is Michelle. Do you understand this language?"

When Michelle spoke, the effect on Zeb was electrifying. He became so excited that he forgot his broken ankle and started to jump up out of his wheelchair, but a jolt of pain from the ankle caused him to immediately sit back down. "Yes, I understand! But how do you know my language?" he exclaimed.

"Before we came here, we visited your home planet. We have friends there who are teaching me their language," Michelle replied.

"I am glad they are. I haven't had anyone to visit with in a very long time."

"How long have you been alone?"

A distant expression appeared on Zeb's face as he appeared deeply lost in thought. "It's been so long that I've lost track of time, but I think it might be close to thirty years."

"I am amazed that you were able to survive alone on such a hostile planet."

"I have had many close calls, but I have been lucky."

"I suspect that you've had more than luck on your side."

"I had survival training before coming here, but I'm lucky that I never had any injuries like the one I have now. If you people hadn't treated me, I would be dead by now. Please say thank you to your friends for helping me, and tell them that I will find ways to repay them."

Michelle interrupted her dialog with Zeb, and told her colleagues what he had just said.

Connie had diligently applied her medical skills to save Zeb's life and repair his injuries. Hearing his heartfelt expression of thanks made her feel warmly appreciated. She smiled at Zeb in a way that told him that she was happy to hear his expression of appreciation.

Zeb nodded and smiled warmly to indicate that he understood. Then, he noticed that Moose was eager to say something, so he turned his full attention to him.

Moose turned away from Zeb and faced Michelle on the video screen. "Tell Zeb that I would like to know what he has found that is good to eat."

"It doesn't surprise me that that would be the first thing my husband would want to know," remarked Dianne.

After a bit of laughter at Dianne's remark, Moose exclaimed, "Well, it is an important question!"

Wondering what the laughter was about, Zeb asked Michelle for an explanation. After receiving one, Zeb said, "When I was a young man, my friends used to tease me that I had an insatiable appetite for fine foods. Tell Moose that I understand his keen sense of taste."

While Michelle did this, Zeb faced Moose waiting for a reaction. Pleased with Zeb's comment, Moose smiled and said, "Maybe, Zeb and I have a mutual interest to pursue."

After hearing the translation of Moose's comment, Zeb said, "Tell Moose that if he will take me on a tour of this island, I will show him which plants produce edible parts and which are especially delicious. The warm moist climate here has produced an abundance of plant life. There are quite a variety of trees and bushes that produce fruit, berries, and nuts. Other plants produce edible seeds. Some plants have stems and leaves that are quite tasty. Some have edible roots."

After Michelle told Moose what Zeb had said, Moose had a difficult time containing his excitement. He turned to Jerry and said, "I think we should skip today's dinosaur hunt. I'd like to take Zeb on a tour of the island."

"I understand your excitement, but I am hungry for some charbroiled steak. You can tour the island tomorrow."

Reluctantly, Moose said, "Okay, I guess you did have the hunt planned first, but let's not make any other plans for tomorrow. We now have an opportunity to gain a tremendous amount of information in just a few hours that would have taken us months, if not years, to learn."

"The ATV that's coming down today will make it easier to take Zeb on a tour of the island," remarked Jerry.

"I can't argue with that. We can assemble it tomorrow morning. In the interest of safety, I think we should set up our radar today."

"I can live with that plan," responded Jerry.

Speaking to Michelle, Connie said, "Tell Zeb that I would like to know about any illnesses, injuries, and infections that he has had while living here."

Michelle relayed the request to Zeb, who responded, "I will discuss my medical history with Connie whenever she wants to. I don't think I will have a very demanding schedule during the next few weeks," Zeb chuckled.

After Michelle relayed the response to Connie, Jerry said, "I am going to display a slowly rotating image of B-2 on another screen. Ask him to show us the launch site of his interstellar mission."

When Zeb heard the question, he put his finger on a point that Jerry judged to be no more than fifty miles from one of the mountain fortresses that he had attacked. Knowing that Mike was watching, Jerry said, "Mike, please check our recon data to see if the ruins of a space center are at that location."

When Mike acknowledged the request, Jerry said to Michelle, "I think we may as well be candid and ask him the direct question: How did you become part of an interstellar mission launched by a country with hostile intentions toward your homeland?"

Michelle relayed the question to Zeb, and then, continued the conversation with Zeb while translating his responses to her colleagues.

"An uneasy peace existed between our nations during the many years that it took to design and build the hardware used to carry out the interstellar mission," Zeb responded. "Politicians felt that a joint historic space mission would promote peace, but war broke out a few days before we arrived here. I was accused of being a spy, and I was deserted by my colleagues."

"Were you a spy?"

"With a war in progress, I would have been alert for anything that would help my country."

"How many were on your mission?"

"There were eight of us, four from each nation."

"What happened to the other three from your country?"

"Two of them turned out to be spies for the other side. The third was to become my wife, but they forced her to go with them for reproductive reasons. Her name was Zonya."

"Do you know where they went?"

"They built a large raft and incorporated our landing capsule into its structure. I believe they followed the river to the ocean and then used the prevailing winds to sail far to the south."

"Do you know if they're still alive?"

"With my telepathic powers, I stayed in contact with Zonya for as long as I could. However, they sailed beyond the range of my telepathic ability, and I don't know if any of them are still alive."

"Your life must have been filled with terrible emotional pain having to live alone with the knowledge that your loved one was being held captive."

"My life was filled with great sadness for a long time. I felt helpless, because there was nothing I could do. In effect, my island was my prison. I could not follow them by land, because I did not have adequate weapons. I could not follow them by sea, because I did not have tools to build an ocean going vessel by myself."

"If Zonya is still alive, would you like to see her?"

"Yes!"

"Do you want us to help you find them?"

"I would like that, but you've done so much for me already that I really cannot ask more of you."

"We need to find them for reasons of our own. Perhaps, you can help us."

"If I were onboard your starship, I could search for them with my telepathic ability. Putting your starship in the lowest possible orbit would make my search easier."

"If we haven't located them by the time our quarantine is over, we may enlist your help. We will discuss it, and Captain Jerontis will make that decision."

Mike interrupted the discussion with Zeb with the announcement: "The personnel shuttle is on its way down and should arrive in South Bay in about fifteen minutes."

"Let's go out and watch the shuttle come in. I want to unload it right away, so we can head for the countryside for our dinosaur hunt," Jerry said.

"What about our ongoing discussion with Zeb?" Michelle asked Jerry.

"I am going to give him a communicator and take him with us. As much as possible, I want to include him in our everyday life. If he has a communicator, he can stay in contact with you. The kinds of questions he asks and the comments he makes relative to our everyday activities should give us an insight into his personality and character much more quickly than if we don't include him. Besides that, I want him to feel like he is part of our society. That will give him an incentive to be loyal to us if a situation ever comes up where he'll have to make a choice between us and those who deserted him. I don't want there to be any doubt in his mind that he should ally himself with us."

"I agree with your reasoning," stated Connie.

A few minutes later, all were in the ATV headed for South Bay. Suddenly, they were jolted by a sonic boom. They stopped, looked up in the northwestern sky, and saw the shuttle begin a 180-degree right turn that would put into the final leg of its landing approach.

"I love to watch our shuttles land and takeoff," said Jerry. "Even though they're rugged and powerful, they always look graceful because their control systems are so finely tuned."

"I also enjoy the smooth graceful way they operate," commented Connie, "but I especially appreciate how rugged and dependable they are."

"Are you talking about me or about our shuttles?" Jerry asked.

Connie snuggled up to her husband and said, "I've never really compared you to our shuttles, but I guess you do have some things in common with them."

Jerry responded by affectionately putting his right arm around his wife as they observed the incoming shuttle.

After the shuttle landed and began taxiing toward South Bay, the pioneers drove to the south end of the plateau and rode their elevator down to the sandy beach. While awaiting the shuttle's arrival, they gazed out over the pristine water and enjoyed the scent of clean air lightly perfumed by flowering plants.

After unloading the shuttle, the pioneers returned to the plateau. They watched the shuttle taxi out of South Bay and begin its takeoff run. When the shuttle reached hydrofoil speed, its powerful NTR roared to life and in just a few seconds it leapt off the water and pitched into a steep climb. Deeply impressed by the performance of the sleek powerful vehicle as it rapidly climbed out of sight, Zeb said to Michelle, "That is a marvelous piece of equipment. What is it powered by?"

"It has a nuclear reactor."

"I suspected that might be the case," commented Zeb. "We had to use chemical rockets on our interstellar voyage, and that greatly limited the scope of our mission. Nuclear rockets were still in an experimental stage when our mission was launched."

"Because of the distance involved, our voyage would have been impossible with chemical rockets or even nuclear rockets. We used an antimatter propulsion system."

"On my planet the thought of using antimatter was only a wild theory."

"Well, it does work," declared Michelle.

"I was the pilot on our mission," stated Zeb. "I enjoy flying, but I haven't been flying in a long time, and I would like a ride on your shuttle."

"You may have an opportunity after our quarantine is over, but that will be Captain J.J.'s decision."

TIME: Day Twenty-One, Early Afternoon.

The pioneers, including Zeb, sailed toward the eastern shore of Clear Lake. With a mostly clear sky and very little breeze to take advantage of, they deployed their solar sails and cruised at about twelve mph.

Pointing skyward toward the northwest, Connie said, "It looks like we may soon have an operational test of our new radar warning system."

Suspecting that Connie was pointing at approaching pterodactyls, everyone looked up to see them. "I think they're about a half mile away," Jerry said. "If they keep coming toward us, we'll get our first warning at 500 yards. At 300 yards, we'll get a second warning. At 100 yards, our communicators will sound off with loud, urgent sounding screeches that will be impossible to ignore."

The pterodactyls kept coming, and as programmed everyone's communicator sounded an alarm at 500 yards and a second alert at 300 yards. The pterodactyls passed directly over the pioneers, but the urgent 100-yard alarm did not occur because they were flying at an altitude of about 400 feet.

"I like this system. It just might save one of our lives someday," Connie said.

"I'm glad we have it. We should have installed it sooner," Jerry remarked.

"Fortunately, we haven't suffered because of not having it in place," commented Connie.

"We've been lucky," stated Dianne.

"What does the third warning sound like?" asked Connie.

In answer to the question, Jerry contacted the radar control computer and requested that it send out the 100-yard alarm. Almost immediately, everyone's communicator began shrilly shrieking. Even though she expected it, Connie was so startled by the sudden sharp sounds that she flinched and exclaimed, "You're right! That sound is impossible to ignore!"

About a mile beyond the boat, the pterodactyls started circling. Noticing this, Moose said, "It looks like it's time for a seafood lunch."

Moose hardly finished speaking when one of the creatures dove into the lake. Moose picked up a pair of binoculars for a better view of the action. Less than twenty seconds after the pterodactyl dove in, large fish were frantically leaping out of the water. The airborne pterodactyl quickly grabbed one of these with its talons. Within seconds, the other pterodactyl emerged from the lake with a fish securely clamped in its beak.

"I've seen them do this several times, but I am still amazed at how deadly efficient they are," Moose said.

Shortly, the pterodactyls again flew over the pioneers on their way home. Watching them closely, Moose commented, "The fish captured by the one that was in flight is really huge. I'll bet it weighs a hundred pounds. I'd like to catch one of those."

"This isn't a fishing trip," responded Jerry. "It's a hunting trip."

"I know, but if we changed course a little bit, we could sail right through the area where those fish are. And if we slowed down, I could put a lure in the water and troll on our way through. It wouldn't delay us that much, and I might catch one of the big ones."

Intervening on Moose's behalf, Connie said, "From a medical perspective, I think Moose has caught a severe case of fishing fever. I recommend that you honor his request, so that we don't have to watch him suffer for the rest of the day."

"That's the best medical advice I've heard in a long time," declared Moose, grinning broadly.

Jerry looked at Moose, then at his wife, then at Dianne, who said, "I don't want to listen to him snivel about the big one that he might've caught. So, I think we should do some fishing while we're here. Besides, if we catch one, it'll give us an opportunity to check out one more species of fish."

"I think I've been out-voted," remarked Jerry. "Get your gear ready," he said to Moose. "I'm going below to use the sonar to locate those fish. I'll take you through the thickest part of the school."

"That's the kind of talk I like to hear," declared Moose.

A short time later, as they approached the large school of fish, Moose said, "I think we should pull in our solar sails and outriggers. If I manage to hook a big one, he's going to be all over the place before I tire him out and land him. I don't want to risk tangling the line on the outriggers or damaging the solar sails."

"Good idea," agreed Jerry.

A few minutes later, with the boat in a clean configuration and running on battery power, they headed into the school of fish towing a large triple-jointed lure designed to act like a crippled fish. In just a few minutes, Moose's fishing pole bent almost in half when the lure was savagely struck by a hungry fish.

Moose fought the wildly active fish until his arms and shoulders ached with pain and cried out for rest, but the battle continued. In its struggle for freedom, the fish swam with speed and power, abruptly reversing direction numerous times. It alternated between heading for the bottom and leaping out of the water, but all to no avail, for it was securely hooked. After a full half hour had gone by, Moose and Jerry landed the fish.

Moose immediately exclaimed, "That's the biggest fish I've ever caught in a lake. I'll bet it weighs over a hundred pounds."

"Easily over a hundred," agreed Jerry.

"Aren't you glad we talked you into this?" asked Moose.

"Yes, but I still want charbroiled steak."

"Let's go get some," said Moose. "If this fish is good to eat, I'll freeze part of it and smoke part of it. It will be part of the feast that we're planning for our colleagues when they come down here in about ten days."

"If everything goes as planned, we'll start bringing them down sooner than that," commented Jerry.

"At this time, I have no medical reason to prevent that," stated Connie.

"In four to six days, we'll have the genetic blueprint for Zeb's immune system, and we'll know how closely it compares to our immune systems," Dianne said.

"I am betting that the comparison will be favorable," commented Jerry. "If it is, and the four of us pass thorough medical exams; then, everyone will be free to come down. And I think charbroiled steak would be a delicious addition to the welcoming feast."

The pioneers deployed their solar sails and resumed their voyage to the countryside. A half hour later, they arrived at the location of Moose's styracosaurus/T-Rex encounter. Here, they launched two RPVs. Jerry flew one to the north and Moose flew one to the south in search of an ostri-dino or some other small dinosaur that looked like it might be a good source of meat.

A few minutes later, Jerry announced, "I've found a herd of ostri-dinos grazing in Sauropod Meadow, and some of them are only about a hundred yards from the lake."

Jerry returned the RPV and put the boat on a course toward the herd. Fifteen minutes later, they arrived and dropped anchor about 100 yards offshore.

After inspecting the herd, Jerry said, "They don't seem to be thirsty; they're just peacefully grazing."

"How far inland are you prepared to go for a steak dinner?" asked Moose.

"I'd like to stay close to the water."

"I like that plan," remarked Connie.

"I do too," stated Jerry, "but the fact that they're peacefully grazing indicates that they're not concerned about predators, so there probably aren't any around at the moment."

"The saber-toothed cats that almost killed me were so well hidden that we didn't know they were there," Connie argued. "These ostri-dinos are about the right size to be good prey for those cats. If some of them are downwind and concealed, the herd won't be aware of them."

"That's a good point," agreed Jerry. "Let's wait for a while. Maybe, one of the ostri-dinos will get thirsty, but if not, I am prepared to go inland a short distance, if it looks safe. I want some charbroiled steak. Even the water's edge isn't free of danger. It's just closer to our boat, and escape is easier. While we're waiting, I want you and Dianne to launch two RPVs and search this area for predators."

Turning to Moose, Jerry said, "Check the amplifier and speakers. Make sure they're ready to blast out the T-Rex challenge."

After a half hour passed by, none of the ostri-dinos came to the lake to drink. "I don't think they're thirsty, and the herd seems to be slowly drifting away from the lake," Jerry commented.

"Have you found any predators?" Jerry asked Dianne and Connie.

Almost in unison, they said, "No!"

Jerry said, "Let's move closer to shore."

After moving in to about twenty-five yards offshore and dropping anchor, Jerry turned to Moose and said, "Grab your rifle. Let's go hunting."

Jerry turned to Dianne and Connie, "Have your rifles ready in case we need help, and be ready to blast out the T-Rex challenge."

Moose and Jerry stepped into the small boat and rowed to shore. After beaching the boat, they looked around warily. Unable to discover anything of a threatening nature, they began stealthily moving closer to the herd.

At about fifty yards, Jerry selected an animal on the edge of the herd that he thought might be a source of some choice cuts. Jerry raised his rifle and took aim, but the animal moved a few steps with its head bobbing around. Jerry waited patiently, because he wanted a good clean head shot. When the animal stopped moving and returned to grazing, its head was fairly stable for a few seconds, which was all the time that Jerry needed.

His rifle boomed, and the animal dropped right where it stood, never knowing what hit it. The sound of the rifle shot was followed immediately by the loud T-Rex roar from the speakers on the boat. Instantly, the ostri-dino herd stampeded inland, and the entire area became quiet in response to the deafening roar.

Jerry and Moose ran up to the fallen ostri-dino, which was still kicking even though its brain was fatally injured. Jerry circled the animal and approached from its back. Then, he drew his long sharp hunting knife and cut into the animal's neck searching for a major artery. Almost instantly, his knife found a main artery, and the fallen animal's still beating heart sent hot blood gushing out, which formed a small pool.

"You're really a bloodthirsty cutthroat!" Moose exclaimed.

"It might look that way, but this is an essential part of the job. By bleeding the animal, we'll get much better steaks, and this will quickly complete the dying process."

Moose accepted Jerry's response without comment while warily searching the surrounding area for indication of danger. He looked at the still bleeding ostri-dino and said, "What a strange looking creature. Why would an animal have wings if it can't fly?"

Jerry commented, "The wings aren't large enough to allow flight, but they're large enough to help the animal make abrupt turns when running at high speeds. A closely pursuing predator without wings might have a larger turning radius allowing the ostri-dino to gain distance on the predator."

Moose considered Jerry's comment and said, "That sounds reasonable."

Moose studied the ostri-dino for a few moments, "Apparently, they use their wings a lot, because they have very well developed breast muscles, much like birds that fly."

Jerry nodded in agreement; then, noting that the bleeding had slowed to a small trickle, he said, "It's time to get our meat and leave."

Jerry knelt down next to the animal and expertly peeled back a section of hide to reveal breast muscle. Then, he cut away several pieces of flesh and put them into tough plastic bags that he zip-locked shut.

Then, Jerry contacted Connie and said, "Blast out the T-Rex challenge again."

Almost immediately, Moose and Jerry were hit by the deafening T-Rex roar. Moose trembled and said, "That roar sends shivers up and down my spine, even though I know that it's only coming from the speakers on our boat."

"I have more butchering to do, and if there are any predators in the area, I want to keep them away from us," Jerry said.

Jerry moved to the upper part of the legs peeled back the skin, and cut several pieces of thigh meat, which he stuffed into plastic bags. He stood up, looked at all the meat bags and said, "Not a bad hunt. I think we have about 150 pounds of fresh meat."

"I hope that it's edible and tastes good."

Looking skyward, Jerry said, "I think we should get out of here. The sea birds that showed up in large numbers on the plateau the other night are arriving. Other scavengers can't be too far behind."

Jerry asked for the T-Rex roar. Then, he loaded the bags of meat into two backpack frames. Jerry shouldered his pack while Moose stood guard. Then, Moose strapped on his pack while Jerry stood guard.

They took one last look around, before beginning the 150-yard hike back to the lake. They had taken only a few steps when a medium sized T-Rex stepped out of the forest to the south and rapidly marched northward on the beach.

"We got trouble!" exclaimed Moose as he moved his rifle into a position from which he could quickly fire. Jerry did the same, but neither man fired, they just closely observed the T-Rex.

After a few moments, Jerry said, "I don't think that it has seen us. I would like to avoid killing it, if possible."

A few moments later, Moose said, "It doesn't seem interested in us or the scent of blood coming from our kill, and what little breeze we have is carrying the scent in that direction. Apparently, it isn't hungry."

"It's not as big as some of the T-Rexes we've seen."

"It looks huge to me!" exclaimed Moose.

"But, it's not as big as they get. Perhaps, we can scare it away with the T-Rex challenge if we turn up the volume to the maximum. If that doesn't work, we can wait a few minutes for it to move on. And if it doesn't, we'll have to kill it. We can't hang around here too long. I don't want to get caught in the middle of a scavenger feeding frenzy."

Jerry contacted Connie who did as requested. When the now even louder T-Rex roar blasted out, the T-Rex on the beach stopped, listened, and headed directly toward the boat at increased speed.

Puzzled by the reaction, but quick to take advantage of it, Jerry said to Connie, "Move farther off shore and head north. Keep blasting out the T-Rex roar. Perhaps, you can lead this one away from us, so we can get to our boat and out onto the lake."

Dianne and Connie did as directed, and the T-Rex followed even to the point of entering the water. However, it could not swim and stayed close to shore.

Seeing that the T-Rex was preoccupied with the boat, Jerry said, "Let's run for it, but let's watch our backs. I don't want to be killed by something else while being distracted by a T-Rex."

With haste tempered by caution, Jerry and Moose made their way to the small boat without incident. They pushed off, got in, and rowed straight out into the lake. When they were a safe distance from shore, Dianne and Connie changed course to pick them up.

When they were safely on the sailboat, Moose and Jerry stared at the T-Rex pacing the beach. Its size and obvious killing capability made their spines tingle when they thought about the fact that they had been close enough for it to have charged them.

"That's an awesome killing machine," declared Moose.

"I get the feeling that flirting with danger really gets you high," commented Dianne.

Acting very cool, Moose calmly said, "Well, I'll have to admit that being close to a T-Rex does cause a bit of an adrenaline rush."

"That sounds to me like *a bit of an* understatement," responded Dianne.

Moose smiled at his wife in a way that acknowledged the validity of her comment.

"I wonder why that brute ignored the smell of fresh blood and responded to the roar from our speakers with such determination," Jerry said.

"I don't know," replied Moose, "but I'm glad that it did. If it had charged us, we would've had to kill it. Even lethal hits with explosive bullets might not have prevented it from killing us in its death throes."

Since Zeb was confined to his wheelchair, he wasn't able to participate in the action, but he was a wildly excited spectator and obviously pleased with the outcome of the whole episode. Noticing that his newfound friends seemed to be puzzled by the T-Rex's behavior, Zeb contacted Michelle and said, "Could you please ask Jerry why he called the female T-Rex."

Michelle was puzzled by the inquiry, because she wasn't aware that Jerry had called a female T-Rex. Curious about why the question was asked, she eagerly relayed it to Jerry.

Jerry was also puzzled by the question, but his face lit up with amusement as it began to dawn upon him what he might have unintentionally done. Then, he said, "Tell Zeb that I used the T-Rex challenge to scare away predators. Ask him why he thinks I was calling female T-Rexes."

Michelle relayed the message and question. Then, she translated Zeb's reply, "That wasn't a T-Rex challenge; that was the male T-Rex's mating call. They try to sound as loud and ferocious as possible in an attempt to impress females that are in heat."

Realizing what they had done, the pioneers laughed about it. "Whose idea was that anyway?" Dianne asked.

"It was Jerry's," replied Connie.

Dianne's face lit up with a broad, naughty grin. "Your husband must have some pretty big balls if he feels the need to proposition female T-Rexes. How do you satisfy such a man?" she asked Connie.

Connie flashed Dianne a smile of smug satisfaction and said, "He usually sleeps pretty good by the time I get done with him; and I might add, I do too."

After making the remark, Connie turned to Jerry and gazed at him affectionately. Jerry responded by saying, "I have no complaints."

Jerry noticed that Moose was chuckling and asked, "What's on your mind that's so funny?"

"I was just thinking about how I'd thought that your idea was a very clever way to scare away predators. Had I realized that we were trying to impress female T-Rexes, I might have been a lot less comfortable when we went ashore."

"I still think it was a clever idea. What creature would want to get caught between a couple of ten-ton T-Rexes with the mating urge?"

"Not me!" exclaimed Moose.

"I wonder how long that T-Rex is going to pace the beach," Connie said.

"She looks very frustrated," commented Dianne.

"She'll get over it," stated Jerry.

"That's my buddy. First, raise their hopes; then, leave 'em frustrated. Really insensitive," Moose commented.

"But it worked," said Jerry. "We went ashore and had a successful hunt without killing anything except the animal that we took for food. If the meat is good, we can eat steak every day and still have more than enough for our welcoming feast."

Proud of the results of the hunt and wanting to retain the freshness, Jerry put the bags of meat into several ice chests and covered them with ice. While he was doing this, his colleagues set sail for home.

Even though it was late afternoon, Alpha Centauri A was still high enough in the sky to provide considerable energy to the solar sails. In addition, there was now a steady breeze blowing out of the north, so the wind sails were also deployed. The combination of solar energy and wind power enabled them to make the return voyage in less than an hour without using any battery power.

After arriving home, the first thing Jerry did was enter two samples of thigh meat and two samples of breast meat into the robot lab for analysis. All four tested negative for toxins, so Jerry fired up the barbecue pit.

About twenty minutes later, the aroma of sizzling steaks pervaded the air of the campsite. Moose commented, "I don't know what they're going to taste like, but they smell so good that my stomach is starting to rumble."

"Mine is too," echoed Jerry.

"I think the aroma is getting to our wives. They're preparing the rest of the dinner more quickly than usual."

"Well, the steaks do smell pretty good, and we've had a long day. They're probably as hungry as we are."

Soon, all were seated around the outdoor table. Jerry was first to sample the steak. Everyone watched him and waited for his reaction. In just a few moments, Jerry said, "It's tender and juicy, and it tastes every bit as delicious as any steak I ever ate back home."

Now, everyone cut a small piece from their steaks and critically tasted it. "This is good," stated Moose. "I think I'll experiment with smoking some of this in various ways to see what I can come up with."

"When it comes to food, my husband's imagination can be quite creative," remarked Dianne. "I'll bet it won't be long and we'll have ham, sausage, and jerky."

Moose took the comment as a compliment, smiled at his wife, and nodded in agreement.

"If we grind up some of it, I'll bet I could make a delicious meat loaf," Connie said.

"The challenge would be to do that using nothing but local ingredients," Dianne responded.

"Zeb wants to take us on a tour of the island to show us what's good to eat," said Connie. "Maybe, after we've done that, I will be able to meet that challenge."

"Let's do that tour tomorrow," suggested Jerry.

SIXTEEN

Grocery Shopping in the Wilderness

TIME: Day Twenty-Two, Mid-Morning.

Jerry and Moose were on the beach of South Bay. They finished assembling the second ATV and stepped back a few paces to admire it.

"It's not a race car, but it's going to make getting around the island a lot quicker and easier," noted Jerry.

"And we'll be able to haul things instead of carrying them," added Moose.

"I am definitely ready for the convenience."

"Let's take it for a test drive."

After they checked out the ATV's capabilities, Jerry said, "Everything works; we're ready to go."

"It's going to be fun blazing a trail around the island with this rig."

"Why is that?" asked Jerry.

"This is a rugged, well-designed ATV that's able to handle rough terrain. I'm eager to find out just how good it is."

"But for the most part, our trip is just going to be an easy drive on the beach."

"But there are places where the forest extends right to the water's edge. In some of those places, the land is rough, rocky, and littered with fallen trees. Getting through those areas will challenge us and this ATV."

"But we can meet that challenge," stated Jerry. "We can cut a path through the fallen trees with our chain saws, and we have a winch to pull the pieces out of the way. And if they aren't too big, we can even pull some rocks out of the way if we need to."

"You make it sound more like hard work than like fun."

"It will be work, but finding a way through difficult terrain will be fun work."

"I don't know which I'm more excited about: the challenge of driving this ATV around the island, or learning about the plants that kept Zeb alive and healthy."

"It will be an interesting day. I'd like to get started."

"They must have heard you," said Moose as he pointed to the top of the cliff where Zeb, Connie, and Dianne were getting on the elevator.

A few minutes later, all were in the ATV. With an ice chest full of food and beverages and two large thermos bottles full of hot beverages, the pioneers set out on an all-day exploratory tour of the island. They planned to drive north along the west shore and then return home along the east shore.

However, before they had even left South Bay, Zeb stopped them to show them several small patches of cane-like plants growing along the edge of the forest. He pointed out that the pulpy core of the canes could be eaten raw and that it had a sweet, mild flavor. He said that the canes grew all year and were a mainstay of his diet. He noted that harvesting the canes seemed to stimulate the plant's root system to send up new shoots.

Under Zeb's direction, Moose cut a choice cane and handed it to Zeb who immediately opened it and started eating the white core. He offered a sample to Moose who was tempted to try it, but Dianne stopped him and said, "Even though Zeb is a humanoid and has eaten this for a long time, we won't know for sure that it's safe for us to eat until we test it. There may be some fundamental differences between Zeb's digestive system and ours. In a few days, we'll have his complete genetic blueprint, and we'll be able to compare his system to ours."

Moose nodded.

Dianne noted that the most mature plants were about nine feet tall with canes about two inches in diameter at the base. Then, she collected a choice sample of the cane, and they moved on.

The pioneers stopped numerous times to examine plants at Zeb's direction. He showed them vines and shrubs that produced edible berries; as well as, other shrubs that produced edible nuts. He also showed them fruit and nut trees. Zeb also identified plants whose berries had made him sick.

In order to gain as much knowledge from Zeb as possible, Jerry showed him how to fly an RPV. The ease with which he learned how to do this made it obvious that he had been a pilot at one time.

Zeb flew the RPV on short trips into the forest. In some parts of the forest, there were small areas where the large trees were almost nonexistent for various reasons. It was in these small open areas that enough sunlight reached the ground for the low-lying berry and nut producing vines and shrubs to flourish.

In one of these areas, Zeb pointed out a plant with foliage much like a horseradish. The leaves were crisp and had a mildly tart flavor. Unlike the horseradish, the tan carrot-shaped roots had a mildly sweet flavor. These plants flourished year around, and mature plants to harvest could always be found.

"I've seen some of these plants on Stellar Plateau. From the way Zeb has described the flavor, shredded roots and leaves might work very well in a meat loaf," Connie commented.

"Steamed roots might make a good side dish," added Moose.

Even in the dense parts of the forest, Zeb identified food sources. In some locations, conditions were right for mushrooms to flourish. Zeb pointed out three species that he had eaten frequently. He also identified numerous poisonous varieties.

"Sliced mushrooms can work wonders in a meat loaf," stated Connie.

So many stops were made to collect samples, that the pioneers did not reach Redfish Lagoon until mid-afternoon. Here, Zeb showed them a rice-like plant growing abundantly in the shallow marshy water along the shoreline. He explained that the island he lived on had several marshy areas along its shoreline where this plant grew abundantly. Its seeds were ripe by late spring with a second crop available in early fall. Cooking a mixture of this grain and the pulp from the canes made a sweet hot cereal with a mild flavor.

It was at Redfish Lagoon that they met their first serious trail blazing challenge. The lagoon had very little sandy or rocky beach. For the most part, swampy marshland separated the lagoon's open water from the solid land of the forest.

To get around the lagoon, the pioneers had to rough out about a half mile of trail through the forest. It took several hours to cut through enough fallen trees to make a trail for the ATV. When they finally arrived on the north side of the entrance to the lagoon, it was early evening and Jerry said, "I think we should go home and finish our tour tomorrow."

Dianne thought about all the specimens already collected and said, "I have a great deal of research to do tomorrow. I want to find out if all the things Zeb showed us are safe to eat."

"I would like to help with that," stated Connie. "Plus, I would like to make a meat loaf for tomorrow night's dinner."

Moose looked at Jerry and said, "I guess that leaves it up to us and Zeb."

"And Michelle," stated Jerry. "We can't do this without her until Zeb learns English."

"Maybe, we should start teaching him," suggested Moose. "I'm starting to get a feeling that we can trust him. His helpfulness seems to be coming from the heart. It's just too real to be faked."

"I am inclined to agree with you," stated Jerry. "But before we teach him English, I would sure like to know if he can telepathically probe our minds in a covert way. If he can, then, not teaching him English is the best way that we have to prevent him from tuning in to our thoughts and memories."

Moose nodded in agreement and said, "I guess the language barrier isn't that much of an inconvenience as long as Michelle is available to be a translator."

"I think she's enjoying the job," commented Connie. "It keeps her involved in our daily adventures."

"Speaking of adventure, I think we should drive up to Rocky Point before we go home," suggested Dianne. "It's less than two miles, and I believe we can make the drive without cutting our way through any fallen trees."

"Do you have any particular objective in mind for wanting to make this drive?" asked Jerry.

"No, I just think it would be fun. We've worked hard all day, and we've learned a lot. Now, I think it's time to enjoy ourselves. It's a pleasant evening, and I think a pleasure drive along the waterfront just might be fun."

"You've twisted my arm just enough to convince me," replied Jerry. "But I am hot, sweaty, and covered with sawdust and grime. Before we make the drive, I'm going for a quick swim as soon as we find some choice beach."

"That shouldn't be difficult," remarked Dianne.

In only about two hundred yards, Jerry stopped the ATV and said, "This is some good looking sand, and the water looks very inviting. I'm going in."

"I'm coming with," declared Connie. "I thought we might go swimming at the end of the day, so I brought along some clean clothes for us on the return trip."

Connie opened her travel bag and removed the clean clothes and two towels. "It looks like I forgot our swim suits," she said.

Jerry looked up and down the beach, "This seems to be a rather deserted section of beach. I think we can get along without the swim suits. I'll race you into the water."

Jerry was quick, but not quick enough to win the race. Connie beat him by one full step.

Both charged into the water until it was too deep to run. Then, they swam with power and speed. By the time they were 150 yards offshore, Connie was three yards ahead of Jerry. She stopped and said, "It looks like I'm still faster than you in the water."

"That's okay; as long as you stop and let me catch you."

"I've never minded being caught by you."

After an affectionate embrace, Jerry and Connie took several deep breaths and dove into the underwater world to check it out. The water was so clear that distance vision was great. Even though they only went down about fifteen feet, they were easily able to see the bottom, which was thirty-five feet below them.

After looking around for about a minute, they surfaced for air and playfully splashed around on the surface for several minutes. "I rather enjoy swimming in the nude. It gives me a certain sense of unrestricted freedom," Connie remarked.

"It does have some advantages," commented Jerry.

"It makes me feel rather sensual."

"I know what you mean."

Jerry and Connie took several deep breaths, then disappeared beneath the surface.

Meanwhile, back on shore, Moose said, "I hope they come in pretty soon. I need a good swim too."

"Be patient; we'll get our turn."

"They've sure been underwater for a long time. I hope nothing has happened to them."

"You don't need to worry. They're both excellent swimmers with good breath endurance."

"I know, I just hope nothing has happened to them."

"I think they're just enjoying the underwater world."

At that moment, Jerry and Connie broke the surface and headed for shore. When they arrived, Connie beamed a glowing smile at Dianne, "That was refreshing. I feel great."

Dianne turned to Moose, "It's our turn, and it seems as though I also forgot to bring our swim suits. It never occurred to me that we might go swimming today."

Noticing that Dianne had packed some towels and clean clothes, Moose wondered if she really did forget the swim suits. But Moose didn't bother to search the travel bag because he saw that Dianne was already strolling toward the water, discarding her clothing item by item along the way. Moose quickly removed his work boots; then, he added the rest of his clothing to the trail left by Dianne.

A few minutes later, Moose and Dianne were a hundred yards offshore playfully engaging in delightful carefree activity that seemed to them to be a well-deserved reward for a very productive day of hard work.

As the minutes ticked by, their improvised game gradually worked its way to a thrilling conclusion. "That was a pleasurable way to add a pleasing touch to a fruitful day," Dianne said in Moose's embrace.

"You might call it the best part of the day, maybe even the climax of the day."

"Whatever caused you to make a comment like that?" Dianne asked, glowing with satisfaction.

"I thought it was appropriate."

"In a few days, we're going to have a decision to make," Dianne said.

"What's that?"

"I will be capable of getting pregnant. I think it would be nice if our first child could be the first baby conceived here on Alcent. Matthew is the only child conceived on Earth and born in space. Denise is the only child conceived in space and born in space. I would like our first child to be the first conceived here, and hopefully, the first born here."

"I like the idea. It will definitely be an historic event when the first child is born here."

"In a few days, we'll have Zeb's genetic blueprint. If his body is nearly identical to the human body in its biological processes, and if we can pass a thorough medical exam, then there will be no reason why we can't get pregnant."

"We've waited a long time to start a family. I am ready."

A few minutes later, Dianne and Moose were back on shore. Dianne beamed a smile at Connie, "You're right, that was particularly refreshing!"

"Now that everyone's feeling refreshed, I think it's time for an evening pleasure drive," Moose said.

"Let's go," said Jerry. "We still have a full hour before first sunset. That should give us plenty of time to drive to Rocky Point and then back home before dark."

Five minutes later, the pioneers rounded Cliff Point and headed toward the foot of Rocky Point Bay. When they rounded the foot of the bay and started heading north, everyone's communicator started beeping. Then, the early warning computer on Stellar Plateau announced: "You are now within two hundred yards of the bear with cubs."

Jerry immediately stopped the ATV and said, "The radio tag we put on her is working well."

He turned on the ATV's video screen and called up a map of the island's north end. A blinking red dot on the map indicated the bear's position.

"If we continue up the coast, we'll pass within about a hundred yards of her," Jerry said. "With the breeze coming out of the northwest, she won't smell us until we are fifty to one hundred yards past our closest approach."

"Are we going to continue on our way?" Connie asked.

"I think we should. We need to find out how she reacts to the scent of humans."

Jerry turned to Moose and said, "Launch an RPV and find them, so we can watch them."

"That won't be difficult. I'll just home in on the radio signal."

A few minutes later, Moose located the mother bear and her cubs. He approached them from downwind, found a suitable rock, and landed the RPV on it. He aimed the RPV's cameras at the bears, and they appeared on the ATV's video screen. The RPV's microphones picked up and relayed the sounds of the forest, which seemed calm and peaceful.

"They appear to be on a pleasure stroll," noted Connie.

"But they are heading toward the beach," stated Jerry.

"Maybe an abalone dinner is on her menu," remarked Dianne.

As Jerry resumed driving northward, he said, "It'll be interesting to see if she changes her mind when she picks up our scent."

About a minute later, Jerry judged that they were directly upwind from the bears. He stopped and said, "It'll take a minute or two for this breeze to carry our scent to them."

The pioneers anxiously watched the bears on the video screen. When their scent reached the mother bear, she stopped and sniffed the air repeatedly.

"She's making quite an effort to identify our scent," remarked Dianne.

"Has she ever seen any of us?" asked Connie.

"I don't think so," replied Jerry.

Next, the pioneers heard a low, menacing growl emanate from the ATV's speakers. At the sound of the growl, the cubs immediately scrambled up the nearest trees, and the forest in the vicinity of the bears became ominously silent. The mother checked her cubs' positions and seemed satisfied that they were safe. After issuing another low growl, which was apparently a command for the cubs to stay in the trees, she cautiously moved forward.

"It looks like she's going to investigate us," stated Jerry.

"What do we do now?" asked Connie.

"I think we should stay put and give her a chance to see us. I would like to find out how she reacts to the sight of us."

Turning to Moose, Jerry said, "Follow her with that RPV, so we can watch her every move."

"What if she decides to attack when she sees us?" asked Connie.

"I don't think that she will. Right now, she has her cubs high up in the trees a hundred and fifty yards away from us. She shouldn't see us as an immediate threat to them. If she attacks anyway, then we have another problem bear on our hands, and the assumption that we can peacefully coexist with these animals might not be valid. If she attacks, it might be because she sees us as prey. We need to know."

"But what do we do if she does attack?" questioned Connie. "Are we going to kill her in self-defense? If we do, what happens to those cute little cubs? They're such innocent looking little fur balls."

"We're about thirty yards from the forest, and we have a half mile of open beach in front of us. Moose will keep her in sight with the RPV. If it looks like she's going to charge, we can quickly accelerate to fifty mph. It won't be a smooth ride, but I believe we can do it. I doubt the bear can run that fast; she's just too bulky. If she can get close to that speed, she certainly won't be able to maintain it for a half mile. As a last resort, we do have our guns."

"I would hate to have to kill a mother with cubs," said Connie.

"I don't want to either," responded Jerry, "but we have an opportunity to learn more about the risk these animals pose, and we have to take advantage of that opportunity."

Realizing that Jerry was right, Connie checked her rifle and pistol to make sure that they were ready for action.

Everyone stared at the video screen as the mother bear cautiously moved toward them. When she approached the edge of the forest, she slunk down and slowly crawled forward. She stopped behind a couple bushes. Then, as flat to the ground as she could make herself, she silently wiggled into position between the bushes. There, she intently stared at the ATV and its occupants.

Connie looked at the forest, located the two bushes, and said, "She's extremely good at stealth. Even though I know exactly where she is, I cannot see her. She blends right into the shadows. If it weren't for our technology, we wouldn't even know that she's there."

"Something to think about next time we go for a walk on the beach," commented Dianne.

Connie's inner being responded to Dianne's suggestion, and an involuntary chill ran up and down her spine. Within moments, the chill passed and she said, "A walk on the beach definitely has more potential for adventure here than it did back on Earth."

"No question about that," agreed Dianne, "and that's one of the reasons why I'm glad we're here."

"It looks to me like she has no intention of attacking at the moment," noted Moose. "In fact, I think she's wary of us."

"She has cubs to care for and protect, and she can't do that unless she stays alive," stated Dianne. "It seems reasonable that she would try to determine what dangers we pose to her and her cubs without placing herself at risk."

"But this is quite a contrast to the bear we encountered shortly after we arrived here," commented Moose. "That bear doggedly stalked us. I believe it wanted to eat us."

"But that was a male," argued Dianne. "It didn't have cubs to worry about."

"Or it may have just been a mean-tempered animal," remarked Connie. "Perhaps, most animals in this species aren't that way."

"There might be another factor involved," remarked Jerry.

"What?" asked Dianne.

"The male saw Moose and me as individuals much smaller than itself. This bear sees an ATV with five occupants. To it, we might look like one large, strange creature. Since it has never seen any kind of vehicle, it can't possibly know that this ATV is a machine containing individuals."

"That means that we aren't going to get an answer to your question as to how this bear will react to us as individuals unless we get out of this ATV," Dianne said.

"I could get out and walk around," offered Connie.

"I don't like that idea," objected Jerry. "That could put you in serious danger. I would prefer to do that myself."

"I am just as fast on my feet as you are," argued Connie. "Besides that, you're behind the wheel, and you are more of a daredevil driver than I am, in case we need to leave in a hurry."

"And Moose is flying the RPV, so that leaves it up to me and Connie," added Dianne.

"Too bad we didn't bring Charlie along," commented Jerry. "We could've used him for this."

"We couldn't," stated Moose. "There's a malfunction in the temporary repairs we did on him after the incident with the saber-toothed cats."

Jerry looked at the video screen and said, "That bear sure is staring at us intently, and she's still doing her best to stay hidden. I don't get the feeling that she's going to attack any time soon."

Jerry thought about it for a few moments and decided that he would like to be the driver if the bear charged. He turned to Connie and said, "I'll agree with your plan, but I want you to stay in front of the ATV and be prepared to jump back in on the run."

"I'll leave my rifle behind. I can jump in more quickly without it."

Connie checked her 10.5-millimeter pistol to make sure it was loaded with explosive bullets. Then, she said, "This ought to be lethal enough to stop a bear, if I have to shoot."

Connie set the gun to automatically fire three rounds with each pull of the trigger. Then, she stepped out of the ATV and walked away from it at a leisurely pace. The bear instantly lifted its head a little bit and stared at Connie, apparently, puzzled by what had just happened.

When Connie was about fifty feet in front of the ATV, she stopped. Now, Dianne stepped out of the ATV and leisurely strolled toward Connie.

The bear raised her head a little bit more and inquisitively stared at the puzzling scene. "Our wives have really gotten her attention, but she still doesn't appear to be interested in attacking," Moose said.

"She might be too confused to attack," Jerry said. "When she first saw us, she might have concluded that a strange new creature now inhabits this island. Then, she saw the new creature break up into individual creatures. She might have enough intelligence to be aware that something peculiar is happening, but not enough to figure out what."

"In other words, we aren't going to find out how she'll react to us as individuals until one of us encounters her alone," commented Moose.

"I think you're right, so let's really confuse her by putting the strange new creature back together."

Speaking to Dianne and Connie, Jerry said, "She's watching you closely, but I don't think she's going to attack. Come on back, and let's move on. I want to find out what she does at the sight of us leaving."

Dianne and Connie returned to the ATV, and the pioneers resumed their drive to Rocky Point.

The bear watched attentively, but remained concealed. She waited until they were well on their way; then ambled onto the beach. After sniffing the tire tracks and the footprints, she stood up on her back legs, stretched to her full height, and looked northward. Assuring herself that the strange new creatures had left, she returned to the forest and headed in the direction of her cubs.

The pioneers drove northward, but the sandy, gravely beach gave way to an impassable, rocky beach when they reached the vicinity of Rocky Point. After stopping the ATV, Jerry grabbed the roll bar above him, stood up, surveyed the area, and said, "Making a trail through this rock pile is going to be a challenge."

"But it's a challenge that we can handle," declared Moose.

"Let's take a look at it and map out the path of least resistance. Then, we'll know just how big of a job it's going to be."

"After that, I think we should experiment with our winch and find out how good it is at moving rocks."

"Haven't you two done enough for one day?" asked Dianne.

"Seems like you guys should be able to just relax," commented Connie.

"This ATV is still a new toy," responded Jerry, "and it's still fun to check out its capabilities. It was designed to handle rough terrain. It's possible that by pulling a few key rocks out of the way, we might be able to drive across this rock pile yet tonight."

"It's also possible that the job might be too big for the winch," commented Moose. "We may have to bring along some explosives when we come back tomorrow."

"This ATV might be a new toy, but your plan sounds like work to me. I'm glad I'm not included, because I'd like to be lazy for the rest of the evening," Connie remarked.

While Jerry and Moose scrambled over the rocks looking for the easiest way through; Zeb, Connie, and Dianne found a spot from which to enjoy the scenic views. Once settled, they helped themselves to food and beverage, and engaged in casual conversation.

"If all of the things that Zeb showed us today pass our lab tests, we're going to have quite a menu of local foods to select from," Dianne said, enjoying a sandwich. "You shouldn't have any problem making a delicious meat loaf for tomorrow night's dinner using only local ingredients."

"Spices and fillers shouldn't be a problem, but I wish I had some eggs to put in it."

"There are lots of waterfowl around here. Maybe, Zeb knows which ones produce edible eggs."

Connie picked up her communicator, called Michelle, and explained the question to her.

After Michelle discussed it with Zeb, she reported: "Zeb said that eggs have been a regular part of his diet. He has eaten the eggs of several species, but he prefers the eggs from the large waterfowl that resemble Canadian geese. These birds weigh about fifteen pounds and their eggs are fairly large. He only needed one egg along with side dishes to make a good meal. Winters here are very mild allowing these birds to nest year around. Different birds nest at various times on a random basis making the eggs constantly available. When they nest, they usually lay about a dozen eggs over a ten-day period before starting the incubation of them. They nest in the forest near the water and protect their eggs by finding very well concealed nest sites. Until incubation starts, the nests are unattended for several hours each day. Taking a couple eggs while being careful not to disturb the nest site never attracted the birds' attention, and they never missed the eggs. He also said that these birds are quite tasty."

"Ask him if he can find me some eggs tomorrow morning."

A few moments later, Michelle replied, "Zeb said the nests are so well concealed that they're difficult to find, but if you'll let him use an RPV, he'll try to locate one. Back on his island it would be easier because these birds usually reuse their nest sites until disturbed by some predator, then they relocate."

"How serious are you about putting eggs in your meat loaf?" Dianne asked.

"They're not essential, but they would give it a better texture. Why did you ask that question?"

"I was just wondering if the eggs are important enough to make them worth a boat trip to Zeb's island. It would be kind of like going shopping."

"I like the texture that eggs give a meat loaf, but I don't know that it's worth a special trip to Zeb's island."

"The whole trip wouldn't take more than a couple hours. That allows for a half hour of travel time in each direction, and with an RPV, Zeb could quickly check all known nesting sites."

"The most dangerous part of the trip would be going ashore to get the eggs," noted Connie.

"Zeb should be able to warn us of any dangers; after all, he has lived there for thirty years."

"But we don't know if we can trust him to do that," argued Connie.

"I think we can. He still needs our medical help, and that gives him a personal interest in keeping us alive."

"I don't think our husbands will like the idea of us doing this."

"Tomorrow, they'll be busy completing the trail around the island and won't have time for a trip like this. Besides that, I don't think that we need their permission to go shopping."

"I don't think so either," agreed Connie, "but this isn't exactly a trip to the grocery store. We should at least talk to them about it. I'm sure that they will be concerned about our safety."

"Safety is a legitimate concern, but if they can be out all day without us, we should be able to go on a two-hour trip without them. After all, you and I did extremely well in survival training. We were near the top of the class, and we are experts with our weapons."

"That's all true, but a short time ago, I was unable to see a bear, even though I knew exactly where she was. Bears do frequent these islands. Also, I was nearly killed by a pair of saber-tooth cats that we were unaware of. It looks to me like the predators on this planet are very good at what they do. It's possible that our survival training didn't fully prepare us for the dangers that we face here."

"You're starting to make me think that eggs aren't that important to your meat loaf."

"You're starting to make me think that you would like to go on an exciting adventure without our husbands."

"There might be some truth to that." Dianne chuckled, "Not to mention the fact that we would be in the company of a strange man."

"Who happens to be crippled at the moment and uses either a wheelchair or crutches to get around."

"But he did see both of us nude not long ago, and I noticed that he did look."

"Can you blame him? He hasn't seen a woman in thirty years. Besides that, to him, we are the aliens, and he should be curious about us."

While conversing and eating, Dianne and Connie gazed out over the lake in various directions, appreciating its serene beauty. The most dominant sounds, in their otherwise quiet evening, were the occasional drone of the electrically powered winch and the crashing noise of the rock that it was moving. After a while, these sounds were replaced by the hum of the ATV's electric motors as it made its way over the rocks working its way toward them.

Soon, the ATV stopped near them, and Jerry announced, "The challenge wasn't as great as we thought it might be. Thanks to this rig's ability to handle rocky terrain, we only had to move five rocks. It's a slow bumpy ride, but we can now drive across the point."

When Moose stepped out of the ATV, Jerry asked Connie, "Would you like to enjoy the thrill of a rough ride over a rock pile?"

"Sounds like fun," replied Connie as she eagerly stepped into the ATV.

A few minutes later, when they returned, Connie was driving and Jerry was sitting in the passenger seat. Connie exclaimed to Dianne, "That was fun! Now, it's your turn!"

Moose got into the driver's seat to demonstrate the trail that he and Jerry had made. But, a few minutes later, when they returned, it was Dianne who was driving. "Climbing around on a rocky slope with this machine could easily be made into a real sport," she said, looking excited.

After briefly gazing at the western sky, Jerry said, "I don't want to bring this party to an end, but first sunset is only minutes away, and I think we should head for home."

To Dianne, who was still in the driver's seat, Jerry said, "Turn on the video and check the location of the bear family."

Dianne did as requested. "They're on the beach about a half mile south of us," she said.

"Looks like we have a problem," commented Connie.

"I think it's an opportunity," stated Jerry. "We can drive south at a leisurely pace, occasionally honking the horn to let her know we're approaching. I expect that an early alert to our approach will cause her to take her cubs into the forest, but she could defiantly stand her ground. I want to find out which alternative she chooses."

The pioneers headed south. When they were about three hundred yards from the bear family, they started honking the ATV's horn and flashing its headlights. This instantly got the mother bear's attention. She stood up on her back legs for a better view. For a few seconds, she observed the steady approach of the strange new creature that had entered her life. Then, she uttered a low pitched growl that sent her cubs scurrying into the forest. She watched for a few more seconds; then, she dropped down to all four feet, picked up the remains of an abalone, and followed her cubs.

By watching the blinking red dot on the ATV's video screen, the pioneers monitored the bear's retreat. "Apparently, there's no panic on her part. She's just leisurely moving out of our way," Jerry noted.

"She seems to have no desire to subject her cubs to unknown danger," commented Connie.

"This might be a bear that we can coexist with," stated Jerry, "but we need to find out how she will react to the approach of one of us on foot, and we need Charlie for that job."

Moose thought about Charlie's malfunction and said, "I can repair him the day after tomorrow."

"But if she looks upon Charlie as prey, she could destroy him," protested Connie.

"Not if we rig Charlie with the right equipment," declared Jerry.

"What do you mean?" asked Connie.

"We don't want this bear to think of us as prey, so if she attacks Charlie, we need to teach her a lesson that she'll remember for a long time."

"How?" questioned Connie.

"We need to rig Charlie with some electrical equipment that will put out a strong shock every second or two while he is under attack."

"I like the idea," stated Connie. "Any large dangerous animals that come to this island should be introduced to the human race by an electrified Charlie."

Dianne nodded in agreement, "That would be a good way to teach dangerous animals to respect us."

"As long as they aren't smart enough to tell the difference between Charlie and real people, it should work," commented Jerry.

"Charlie looks like a real human," declared Moose. "He walks, runs, and talks like a real human. And we can certainly make sure that he carries the human scent."

"Scent is another good way to teach dangerous animals to leave us alone," suggested Dianne. "Many predators have an extremely sensitive sense of smell, so why don't we equip Charlie with a number of small canisters of highly irritating aerosols."

"Good idea," commented Jerry. "Back on Earth, the lowly skunk does a pretty good job protecting itself with a noxious chemical spray. Many predators simply leave it alone."

Speaking to Moose, Jerry said, "Contact Mike and ask him to work out the details for electrifying Charlie and equipping him with irritating chemicals."

Moose picked up his communicator, called Mike, and discussed the project with him. Mike concluded the conversation by saying, "I'll send down the things you need either tomorrow evening or the morning of the next day."

The pioneers leisurely completed their drive home arriving after first sunset but before second sunset. After discussing their discoveries and achievements of the day, they retired to bed feeling good about their accomplishments and quickly dropped off into a deep well-deserved night of sleep.

TIME: Day Twenty-Three, After Breakfast.

Jerry and Moose prepared to leave the capsule to continue working on the ATV trail around the island.

"I don't think we'll have any problem completing the trail today," commented Jerry. "In fact, we might even be done by mid-afternoon."

"I don't know about that," responded Moose. "It's going to take a while just to get from South Bay to East Bay. There are lots of trees growing right to the water's edge on more than half of that stretch of coastline."

"But if we can make it to East Bay by lunch time, it should be easy to get to Rocky Point by mid-afternoon."

"I can't argue with that. Most of the east coast is sandy beach. There are only two small stretches of waterfront where the forest extends to the water, and there aren't any rock piles before Rocky Point."

"I'd like to finish at least by late afternoon, so let's get started."

"Aren't we taking some food along?" questioned Moose.

"If we don't get past East Bay by noon, we'll be close enough to home, so that we can eat lunch right here."

"I think I'll take something along anyway. We'll be working hard, and I'll probably need a mid-morning snack."

"That doesn't surprise me," teased Dianne.

Jerry and Connie chuckled softly at Dianne's comment while Moose ignored it and packed some food.

A few minutes later, as they were leaving, Jerry turned and said to Connie and Dianne, "We'll see you later. Don't work too hard."

Connie responded, "We won't. We're just going to check out the specimens we collected yesterday and make dinner."

"Well, don't push it too hard. Just relax and enjoy the day."

"Is that the captain's direct order?" asked Dianne.

Jerry grinned, "No, it's just a suggestion."

"It's a good suggestion," replied Dianne. "Maybe, we'll take the boat out for a couple hours sometime today."

"That's one way to relax and have fun," commented Jerry as he turned and left.

"See how difficult it was to get the Captain's approval for our shopping trip," Dianne said to Connie, smugly.

"You didn't exactly tell him the whole story, like the fact that we might be sneaking around in the forest on Zeb's island."

"He didn't ask where we're going."

"And you didn't volunteer any information either."

"Neither did you."

Connie thought about the truth of Dianne's remark, "Maybe I have a subconscious desire to make this trip even while my conscious mind is telling me not to."

"You are a competent psychiatrist. You should be able to figure out what's going on in your head that would cause that kind of mental conflict."

Connie thought about it and said, "Maybe, I need to prove to myself that we can successfully face possible danger without the support of our husbands. Maybe, I need to do that to feel truly at home here."

"Having the freedom to move about on one's own is part of feeling at home."

"Back on Earth, I took that freedom of movement for granted, but here, every little trip, no matter how short, can bring one face-to-face with death."

Connie paused briefly, "Perhaps, there is another factor coming to the surface," she said.

"Want to tell me about it?"

After a short pause to organize her thoughts, Connie asked, "Do you remember how at the end of our survival training each of us had to live alone for two weeks in a remote tropical jungle?"

"I will never forget that experience! Why are you bringing that up?"

"During those two weeks, I had a vivid dream every night that I would be killed by an animal on this planet."

"That must have been scary when you were alone in the jungle."

"It was a real nightmare."

"But you didn't put out a call to be picked up, like some people did."

"I didn't want to be washed out."

"Did you talk to anyone about those dreams?"

"No! And it was for the same reason. I was afraid that I'd be labeled as someone with a deep-seated abnormal fear and be washed out."

"I think you should be proud of yourself. By maintaining a tough mental attitude, you passed the final test of survival training despite having to endure terrifying dreams every night. But now that you're here, I hope that you don't subconsciously seek out dangerous situations to be triumphant over just to prove that those bad dreams were meaningless."

"That is something that I'll have to think about and guard against."

"If I were your patient and told you what you just told me, what would you do?"

"I would try to discover the origin of those horrifying dreams and help you to understand them. While doing that, I would caution you to avoid looking for dangerous situations to overcome, so that you wouldn't end up turning those dreams into a self-fulfilling prophecy."

"That sounds like a good approach. Want me to repeat those words of caution to you?"

"That won't be necessary. I think I can follow my own advice. However, if we go to Zeb's island to get some eggs, I want to be the one who goes ashore to get them."

"I think we should both go ashore. Two people looking for danger should be safer than one."

"We may not be going to Zeb's island. He might find some eggs here. Let's give him an RPV, so he can start the search."

During the next two hours, Zeb searched for eggs. Although he located several nests, they were all deserted except for one, and this one was occupied by a hen who was already incubating her eggs.

Speaking through Michelle, Zeb said, "On my island, I know the locations of nineteen nests. Do you want me to keep searching here, or do you want to take me there, so I can check those nests?"

"Do you have any idea what the probability is of finding eggs that aren't yet being incubated?" Dianne asked.

Zeb considered the question for a few moments, then replied, "I think the odds are better than even. Over the years, I've gained some familiarity with the nesting habits of the birds that use those nests. There are three pairs that seem to prefer nesting at about this time of the year. There's a pretty good chance that one of those nests will have eggs that we can take."

Turning to Connie, Dianne said, "I think we should go check them out. If one of those nests has eggs, this could end up being a quick easy trip, a joy ride on a pleasant day."

Connie nodded, and a short time later, they were sailing out of South Bay on their way to Zeb's island. Since it was a mostly clear day with very little wind, they deployed the boat's solar sails.

The little boat with its interstellar occupants moved silently at about ten mph. Zeb was below deck taking advantage of the boat's transparent hull and Clear Lake's amazingly clear water. Dianne and Connie were on deck enjoying the pleasant, late morning air. With the boat under the control of its navigation computer, they were free to be lazy and just enjoy the cruise.

Connie surveyed the deep blue sky with its widely scattered cumulus clouds and soaring sea birds. Then, she slowly scanned the lake in all directions. Her gaze eventually settled on the south end of the receding Pioneer Island. She thought about all the things they had already done to turn it into a secure home on a hostile planet. So far, everything had gone very well: no deaths, no crippling injuries, no serious illnesses. Also, an abundant supply of nutritious food from a big variety of sources had been discovered. If all continued to go so well, all of the Challenger's personnel could come down in about a week. They would live in temporary shelters while permanent homes were built.

Cruising on this lake sure is quiet and peaceful, thought Connie. Wondering why Dianne hadn't said anything to interrupt her thoughts, Connie turned to see what she was doing and found her stretched out on an air mattress sound asleep. Wearing only short shorts and a halter top, Connie became aware of the radiant heat of Alpha Centauri A and the gentle caress of the pleasant late morning air and thought, I guess if I were sun bathing, I would probably fall asleep too.

Connie wondered if the present peacefulness was lulling them into a false sense of security. She considered the possibilities: our radar will warn us of pterodactyls; our sonar will warn us if a large marine creature approaches. What other dangers are there? Connie scanned the lake and the sky and saw only sea birds. Then, she recalled the savage feeding frenzy of the sea birds on the dead pterodactyl. Connie wondered; what provokes these birds into a feeding frenzy like that one? What if Dianne and I were both sound asleep? Do we need to be dead or just look defenseless? Maybe, it's the sight and smell of blood that attracts them. Maybe, they respond to the pterodactyl battle cry knowing that death might occur.

With more questions than answers, Connie decided to stay alert for as yet undiscovered dangers, but to stay relaxed and enjoy the peaceful cruise too. When Zeb's island was only a few hundred yards away, Connie woke Dianne and summoned Zeb from below deck. Using gestures and telepathic images, Zeb informed Dianne where he wanted to begin the search for eggs. While Dianne piloted the boat, Connie and Zeb put on headsets. Connie wanted to see how well the nests were hidden and what difficulties she would encounter while robbing one of a couple eggs.

A few minutes later, Zeb launched a small RPV and flew it toward the first of the three nests that he thought most likely to contain eggs. About a minute later, Zeb reported that the nest was occupied by a hen and that he didn't know if she was already incubating her eggs or if she was there to lay an egg.

Zeb proceeded to another nearby nest, checked it, and announced that it was empty. After checking three more nests and finding them empty, Zeb returned the RPV to the boat.

Under Zeb's direction, Dianne piloted the boat to the next nesting area. When they arrived, Zeb spoke through Michelle and explained, "There are five nests here. Two of the three that I think might be in use are here."

Wanting to see what the nests looked like and how well hidden they were, Dianne asked Connie to stand guard while she wore the second headset. Dianne then directed Zeb to show her all five nest sites. Even though nine eggs were discovered at the second nest, Dianne insisted on seeing the remaining three for reasons of her own.

While Zeb returned the RPV, Dianne handed the headset to Connie, so she could replay the video of the egg containing nest. After looking at it, Connie said, "That nest is in the middle of a patch of thorn bushes. How does that bird get to it without being scratched up?"

"Replay the video and look at the small opening that Zeb flew the RPV through," suggested Dianne.

Connie did as directed and said, "I don't know if I can fit through that opening. I would have to stretch out on my stomach and literally inch my way along. If that bush has dropped any twigs, I could end up with thorns stuck in me. "

"I thought you wanted some eggs for your meat loaf."

"I do, but I don't want to get seriously injured while getting them."

"Getting poked by a thorn isn't exactly a serious injury," teased Dianne. "It really wouldn't be much different than getting a shot at the doctor's office. And don't you doctors usually tell your patients that it won't hurt all that much."

Connie stared at Dianne, "I think you're punching below the belt, but you do make a good point."

"I think there's something more serious than being scratched by thorns that we need to think about," Connie said, after a moment's thought.

"What?"

"While I am slowly inching my way through a small opening among thorn bushes, I will be vulnerable to attack. With my upper body encased by thorn bushes, I will not be able to quickly respond to an animal that attacks my lower body."

"I will be there to protect you."

"We could just cut a larger opening through the thorn bushes," commented Connie.

"The hen might notice that and desert the nest," objected Dianne.

"That would probably be the case."

"If Zeb could successfully steal eggs over the years without disturbing the nests, then we should be able to too," commented Dianne.

Connie looked at Zeb, then at herself and said, "I think I can slip through a smaller hole than he can. Let's go ashore and try it. After coming this far, I don't want to admit defeat."

Speaking through Michelle, Connie explained the plan to Zeb.

"I have taken eggs from that nest a number of times over the years," Zeb replied.

Michelle said to Connie, "You sure are determined to have some eggs to put in your meat loaf. Why don't you just play it safe and make the meat loaf without eggs?"

"It's a matter of principle," replied Connie. "When I set out to do something, I like to be successful, no matter what the task is. I like to overcome any obstacles that show up."

Dianne and Connie checked their pistols to make sure that they were loaded with explosive bullets. Then, they checked their rifles and were about to step into the small boat to go ashore when they noticed that Zeb appeared to be in a trance. They looked closely at him wondering what was happening, but they did not disturb him because he appeared to be breathing normally and not in any medical trouble.

When Zeb came out of the trance, he spoke through Michelle and said, "There is a bear downwind from the nest, and I sense that he's in a belligerent mood."

With a bit of a chuckle in her voice, Dianne said, "Speaking about obstacles that just happen to show up. How do you plan to overcome this one?"

"Forget the bear and the eggs for a moment. We just learned something about Zeb: his telepathic ability is able to detect the presence of bears and what mood they're in."

"That explains how he was able to avoid being killed by a bear during the thirty years that he lived on this island."

"If he can detect the energy field generated by a bear's brain, maybe he can detect the presence of any large animal and the mood that it's in," Connie commented.

"He didn't give us an early warning when a pterodactyl had one of us in mind for its dinner."

"Maybe his telepathic ability only works when he shuts out all distractions and totally focuses his mental energy."

"Either that's the case or his telepathic ability doesn't work with pterodactyls," remarked Dianne.

"You're ignoring a third possibility."

"Not really. I just don't believe that he would've avoided warning us if he had known we were about to be attacked. After all, he just warned us about the bear."

"I don't think so either," responded Connie, "but I would sure like to find out just how extensive his telepathic abilities are. In regard to our bear problem: Can he pinpoint the bear's location or does he just know approximately where it is? Can he see what the bear sees? Can he influence the bear's behavior by transmitting images into its mind?"

"I would like to know what it is about his brain that gives him a telepathic ability."

"Your assistants are doing a DNA profile on him. When you have his genetic blueprint, you should be able to discover the differences between his brain and our brains."

"I think we can," stated Dianne. "After we've compared his immune system to ours, we'll tackle that problem."

"I am interested in helping you with that, but right now, I think we should get back to our bear problem."

Speaking through Michelle, Connie asked Zeb if he knew the bear's location well enough to approach him with an RPV from downwind. Zeb said that he did, and Connie directed him to do so.

When the RPV was in place and had its cameras trained on the bear, Connie said, "Let's find out if this bear has any interest in the human sent."

Connie picked up a small RPV and smeared some of her skin oil and perspiration on it. Then, as an after thought, she added her female scent to it. Next, she handed the RPV to Dianne, who added her scent to it.

Connie put on a headset and slowly flew the RPV toward the bear approaching him from upwind while Dianne watched video of the bear. The bear picked up the scent when the RPV was still more than two hundred yards away.

The bear flared his nostrils and sniffed the air several times. Then, as if annoyed by the scent, he growled and set off to investigate it.

"It looks to me like Zeb was right," stated Dianne. "This bear is in a belligerent mood. He's making no attempt at stealth in his effort to find the source of our scent. There's no doubt in my mind that he would attack us if we were there, and we would have to kill him."

"I will keep the RPV out of sight, so that he will not know where the scent is coming from. If he continues to follow it, maybe I can lead him at least a half mile upwind from the eggs we want."

"That sounds like a good plan."

Determined to find and attack the source of the scent, the agitated bear aggressively pursued it, occasionally letting out a menacing growl.

"I wonder why this bear is in such a bad mood," questioned Dianne.

"I don't know, but I wouldn't want to be on that island with nothing more than the weapons that Zeb had at his disposal for the last thirty years."

A few minutes later, Connie found a large boulder at the north end of the island and landed the RPV on top of it. "I think this rock is big enough so that the RPV will be out of reach, and it's in an open area," she said. "With the radiant energy of Alpha Centauri beating down on it, the scent we put on it should evaporate off quite rapidly making it quite strong around the rock. I think the bear will circle the rock a number of times trying to figure out how to get to the source of the scent. By the time he loses interest, we should have our eggs and be on our way home."

"That's a good theory, but I think I would like Zeb to keep an eye on him and let us know if he starts coming back."

With the mean-tempered bear temporarily preoccupied, Connie and Dianne stepped into the small inflated boat and began rowing ashore. When they reached shore, they beached the boat and cautiously entered the forest. Slowly and quietly, they made their way toward the nest. Frequently, they stopped and listened to the sounds of the forest while intently scanning their surroundings for signs of danger. Even though the nest was only about a hundred and fifty yards from the edge of the forest, it took Dianne and Connie nearly seven minutes to get to it.

When they arrived at the small clump of thorn bushes, they slowly circled it looking for danger. Not finding any, Connie said, "I'm going in."

She put down her rifle, stretched out flat on her stomach, and slowly inched her way through the small opening into the clump of thorn bushes. When she reached the nest, she selected three eggs and put them in a small bag. Then, she began inching her way backwards out of the thorn bushes.

When Connie was free of the bushes, she stood up, brushed the dirt off herself and said, "I could use a quick swim."

"You do look like you've been rolling around in the dirt."

"A little swimming will clean me up. Then, I'm going to do some sun bathing on the way home, while you stand guard."

"I guess it is my turn," agreed Dianne.

At that moment, an image appeared in Dianne's mind with a mood of urgency attached to it. The image clearly depicted a bear heading south along the waterfront. "I think we should get out of here," stated Dianne. "The bear that we decoyed away from this area is returning."

Not wanting to kill the bear, Dianne and Connie hastily made their way to the beach. But even though they were in a hurry, they did not throw away caution. They moved as fast they could while staying alert to their surroundings.

In less than two minutes, they were on the beach. As they began pushing their little boat into the lake, the bear rounded a bend about two hundred yards away and immediately broke into a charge. However, less than a hundred yards into the charge, he skidded to a dead stop and flattened out on the sandy beach as if trying to make himself invisible. Several seconds later, as Dianne and Connie reached the submarine, the bear got up and resumed his charge quickly covering the remaining distance. He then charged into the lake and swam in pursuit of his quarry. But it was too late, his quarry had escaped. By the time the bear was even half way to the submarine, Dianne and Connie had it on the move and heading toward Pioneer Island. As the submarine steadily pulled away, the bear decided that he could not catch it and returned to Zeb's island.

"I wonder what caused that bear to skid to a dead stop right after breaking into a ful! charge," Connie said.

"I suspect Zeb had something to do with that," remarked Dianne with a bit of a chuckle.

"You're suggesting that he is able to project images into the mind of a bear."

"At the moment, that's the best explanation we have for what the bear did. Imagine a bear charging what looks like an easy meal, and then, the image of us fades from his brain and is replaced by the image of a ferocious T-Rex. Wouldn't that cause him to do what he did?"

"If I were that bear, I certainly would've skidded to a halt and tried to look invisible, but I don't think I would've resumed the charge in ten to fifteen seconds like he did. Unless, the T-Rex image faded out and the image of us reappeared."

"That might be what happened," suggested Dianne, "and I have a possible explanation. When the bear began its charge, it seems reasonable to assume that his brain was intently focused on making a kill. That intense concentration may have made the bear's brain resistant to a telepathically projected image. Placing the image of a T-Rex in the bear's brain may have required so much mental energy that Zeb was simply unable to maintain the image for more than ten to fifteen seconds."

"That ten to fifteen seconds was the margin of safety that we needed to avoid killing the bear."

"Maybe Zeb realized that and broke contact when he saw that we were safe."

"That's possible," agreed Connie, "and he does look tired. He can hardly keep his eyes open. I think he's about to doze off, and that supports your theory about the mental energy required to place a T-Rex image in the bear's brain."

"We don't know if that's what he did. We're only speculating."

"When he wakes up, let's discuss it with him. Right now, I'd like to take a look at our eggs."

Connie reached into the small bag, took out the eggs, and handed one to Dianne. "These are a lot bigger than the eggs I used to buy at the grocery store back on Earth," she said.

"I would guess that one of these is equal to three large chicken eggs."

"I won't need more than one in my meat loaf."

"I'll use the other two to make an omelet tomorrow morning," stated Dianne.

"I don't think there's a problem, but we should do the lab tests anyway just to make sure that they're safe to eat."

Dianne nodded in agreement.

"I need to get cleaned up," stated Connie while bringing the boat to a stop. "Perhaps, you could stand guard while I go swimming."

"Okay, and when you're done, I want to go for a quick swim too."

After about fifteen minutes of playful, slow-paced swimming, both underwater and on the surface, Connie climbed out of the water. She looked at Dianne and asked, "Do I still look like I've been rolling around in the dirt?"

"You look like you just stepped out of the tub, and now, it's my turn," stated Dianne as she stepped to the edge of the deck and dove in.

About ten minutes later, Dianne climbed out of the water and said, "That was great! I feel rejuvenated and filled with energy."

"Good, because I feel like taking a nap."

"I can't believe that a little grocery shopping trip would tire you out so much that you need a nap. Maybe, you and Jerry should have spent more time sleeping last night."

"It doesn't take us all night. Anyway, I always sleep well afterwards."

"Since you're tired now, that means you didn't sleep well last night, and that means you didn't."

"I slept very well last night. I am only sleepy now because it's such a warm, pleasant day, and I feel like being lazy for a while."

Dianne smiled in satisfaction at Connie's reaction. Then, she got the boat underway while Connie stretched out on an air mattress. With the radiant heat of Alpha Centauri A pouring down on her, Connie felt pleasantly warm and relaxed. She listened to the soft peaceful sound of small waves splashing against the boat's hull. She felt the sensual caress of the gentle breeze flowing over her almost nude body. I thank God that we can have such peaceful relaxation on this planet that is so filled with danger, she thought. She became very drowsy and was soon sound asleep.

Meanwhile, Dianne noted that Zeb had recovered from his earlier drowsiness, so speaking through Michelle, she questioned him about his telepathic ability with animals, bears in particular. Dianne found Zeb in a talkative mood, and their conversation lasted all the way home.

TIME: Day 23, Dinner time.

Since it was a warm pleasant evening, the pioneers decided to eat dinner at their outdoor table. Before sitting down, Moose said, "This looks like a real feast, and it smells so good, it's making my mouth water."

Jerry briefly surveyed the various dishes. "You've prepared a bigger variety foods than at any meal we've had here so far," he said to Dianne and Connie.

Obviously pleased Dianne proudly proclaimed, "Everything that went into these dishes was obtained locally."

"Even the spices are from local plants," Connie declared with satisfaction.

"It looks to me like we don't need our food synthesizers anymore," commented Jerry.

"That's true," agreed Moose, "but I don't think that we should throw them away just yet. After all, it is possible to create some rather unique delicacies with that technology."

"I wasn't implying that we should throw them away. What I am suggesting is that as far as food is concerned, we could bring everyone down right now and show them a broad variety of tasty foods to eat. In other words, we've accomplished one of our major objectives."

Jerry established eye contact with his wife. She immediately sensed the question in his mind and said, "From a medical perspective, I haven't discovered anything that would prevent us from bringing everyone down."

Jerry turned to Dianne, who said, "The DNA analysis on Zeb is proceeding smoothly. In two or three days, we should have his genetic blueprint and be able to compare his immune system to our immune systems."

"If the comparison is favorable, we'll be able to bring everyone down with a lot more confidence than would have been possible without Zeb," Connie added. "In many ways, he has turned out to be a big help."

"All the samples we collected yesterday under his direction turned out to be safe to eat," stated Dianne.

"He has provided us with a wealth of information," commented Jerry.

"That's true," agreed Moose, "but I don't think we should completely trust him just yet."

Dianne made eye contact with Connie, and even though no words were spoken, they seemed to understand each other's thinking. Then, Dianne turned to Moose and said, "You might not be ready to completely trust him, but he did help keep us out of trouble today by twice warning us of the presence of a bear when we were on his island."

Jerry immediately stared at Dianne and Connie and exclaimed, "You were on Zeb's Island today! What were you doing there?"

"We needed some eggs for our meat loaf, and Zeb said he knew where we could find some," Connie responded.

"Seems like you subjected yourselves to considerable risk just for a few eggs."

"We didn't take any more risk getting the eggs than you and Moose took getting the meat." Connie chuckled, "And we didn't add to our risk by calling a female T-Rex to the scene."

Jerry couldn't help feeling pride at his wife's quick wit. He smiled at her affectionately, "I get the feeling that it's going to be a while before I stop hearing about that incident, but even though I didn't know that's what I was doing, it did work. All other animals did leave the scene."

"We only had one animal to contend with, and we managed to lure him away from the scene," Connie said.

"How did you do that?" asked Jerry.

While Jerry and Moose listened attentively, Connie gave them a detailed account of the egg gathering expedition.

When she finished, Dianne commented, "If we're going to make eggs a regular part of our diet, I think we need to domesticate some birds to provide us with them. It would be a bit inconvenient to have to go tramping through the bushes every time we need a few eggs."

"But that would take away the adventure," teased Connie.

"Living here is all the adventure I need," declared Dianne.

"I agree with your idea," stated Jerry. "The trick will be to get birds that are accustomed to nesting two or three times a year to produce eggs all the time."

"That won't be difficult," stated Dianne. "I can stimulate egg production with hormones, or I can alter the birds genetically."

"I think we should start the poultry project as soon as we have the time to do it," Jerry commented.

"This is the first time in my life that I've eaten meat loaf made entirely from things grown in the wild," he said, "and it is excellent. Thinking about the effort that went into obtaining each of its ingredients really makes me appreciate how good it is."

Jerry turned to Dianne, "Were you able to find out from Zeb how effective his telepathic ability is with animals?"

"He said that he cannot contact any of the dinosaurs or pterodactyls, but that he is able to get into the minds of some of the mammals, especially those that are large predators."

"That's convenient," commented Jerry.

"He told me some stories about how he has used this ability to avoid being killed by bears. His favorite trick is to place an image of an angry T-Rex in the bear's mind."

"I see some humor in that," Jerry laughed.

"In what way?" asked Connie.

"I can picture a bear aggressively pursuing Zeb, fully intent on making a meal out of him; when all of a sudden, Zeb's image disappears from the bear's mind and is replaced by the image of a T-Rex. Instead of seeking a meal, the bear would have to instantly figure out how to avoid becoming a meal. Seeing a large predator make that kind of an abrupt change in plans purely because of an illusion would get a laugh out of me."

"Setting the humor aside, I am impressed with the concept. It's definitely a unique way to deal with an enemy," Jerry continued. "I wonder how effective Zeb is with that technique."

"He's very effective," declared Dianne. "Earlier today, we watched him bring a charging bear to an immediate screeching halt."

Dianne recalled the scene and visualized what had happen. "Now that I think about it, it was very amusing that Zeb could so completely fool such a large animal using nothing more than a special mental power."

"I wish I could do that," Moose said.

"That would be a useful skill," commented Jerry, "especially, if we could get into the minds of all predators."

"When we have Zeb's complete DNA profile, we might be able to determine what it is that's different about his brain that gives him this ability," Dianne commented.

"That could be a dangerous knowledge to have," remarked Connie.

"Why?" questioned Dianne.

"You are a very competent genetic engineer. You might be tempted to genetically alter the human species so that some of our offspring will have the same telepathic ability that Zeb has. Can you imagine raising children who could read your mind, but you could not read theirs?"

"That could make a rebellious teen-ager extremely difficult to deal with," admitted Dianne.

"But it would be a useful survival skill," stated Jerry.

"I was a rebellious teenager" stated Moose. "My parents and those in authority had enough trouble with me as it was. Had I been able to read their minds, I might have been impossible to deal with."

"For having been a juvenile delinquent, I think you turned out pretty well," commented Dianne.

"Thanks to my high school science teacher, I managed to get my life turned around."

"I'm glad that he straightened you out. If he hadn't, you wouldn't be here, and I wouldn't have such a wonderful husband. But what really impresses me is the simple way that he influenced you to mend your ways."

"I agree," commented Moose. "The profound changes that he effected in my life clearly show that constant exposure to a simple message can be very persuasive. As I've told you many times, he had a sign on his desk that said, MY FUTURE DEPENDS ON THE CHOICES THAT I MAKE TODAY. That message didn't mean much to me at first, but it was so prominently displayed that I couldn't help seeing it everyday. Over a period of time, it got me thinking about my future. I decided what things I wanted to do and started making choices that supported my goals."

"If you'd had the ability to read people's minds, do you think that message would've still gotten through to you?" Connie asked.

"I think it would have, but I would've been very difficult to deal with during my rebellious years," Moose said.

After a few moments of silence, he continued, "I don't know that I would enjoy raising a child that could read my mind. Even if he were a perfect child, I still would be put in a position of having to constantly guard my thoughts. Raising children is difficult enough without having that added burden."

"But there would be benefits to shouldering that burden," argued Jerry. "For example, when your children become teenagers, they might decide to explore the wilderness with or without your permission. It seems to me that you would be far less worried about them if you knew that they could mentally sense the presence of predators."

"That's true," admitted Moose. "But with our technology and weapons, I'm not sure that we need additional survival skills, especially one that could cause problems for parents. Besides that, Zeb's telepathic ability only works with mammals, and most of the predators are dinosaurs."

"I suspect that when Dianne figures out how Zeb's telepathic ability works that she will also figure out why it doesn't work with dinosaurs," Jerry said. "Then, with her genetic engineering skills, she will figure out how to alter the human species so that our offspring could telepathically communicate with dinosaurs and mammals."

"You're giving me tremendous credit that I haven't yet earned," stated Dianne. "You may be expecting me to do the impossible. Dinosaur brains may be so incompatible with the brains of mammals that it will be impossible to achieve telepathic communication with them."

"I guess I am getting out in front of the research results," admitted Jerry. "However, if it becomes possible to give our offspring the ability to mentally detect predators and influence their behavior, we will have a very big decision to make. The problems that this ability would cause in our everyday lives will have to be weighed against the increased probability that our new civilization will survive and prosper. We are few in number, and this is a hostile planet. As I see it, an effective survival skill should not be lightly discarded."

"What you're saying makes sense," agreed Moose, "but I am not comfortable with the idea of raising children who would always know what I am thinking. It seems like that would put me at a severe disadvantage. It might even put my sanity in jeopardy."

Dianne turned to Connie, "I agree with what you said earlier: understanding how Zeb's telepathic ability works might be dangerous knowledge to have."

"It sure took a lot of discussion for you to reach that conclusion," replied Connie.

"It wasn't the discussion as a whole; rather, it was my husband's concluding remark. I certainly don't want to be the one responsible for jeopardizing his sanity."

Connie laughed at Dianne's comment; then, she looked at Moose who said, "I'm serious! Kids who could read my mind would drive me crazy."

Amused by Moose's excited emotional state, Jerry laughed softly, "You're taking this all rather seriously in view of the fact that a possible threat to your sanity is still years away, if it ever happens at all."

"Just thinking about it seems to be threatening his sanity," commented Dianne.

Connie turned to Dianne and said, "What's really puzzling about this is that this whole conversation started when Moose said that he wished he had the ability to do what Zeb does. Now, he seems to be deeply troubled by the possibility."

"You people are twisting things around. I stand by my earlier statement. I do wish I had Zeb's ability. It would be a real advantage here on this hostile planet, and it would be a real advantage for parents to be able to read the minds of their children. But children having that advantage over their parents could lead to disaster. Anyway, I don't see how you can make fun of me over something so serious. Think about it; you're talking about genetically altering the human race."

"Only the small part of it that lives on this planet," stated Jerry. "But you're right, it is a serious matter, and when the time comes, we'll have a big decision to make."

"Actually, we'll have two decisions to make," commented Dianne.

"What do you mean?" asked Jerry.

"If we learn how to genetically alter the human species to give it a telepathic ability, do we transmit that information to Earth, or do we keep it to ourselves?"

"I think we should keep it to ourselves," declared Jerry. "I believe that the trouble that knowledge would cause back on Earth would outweigh any possible benefits."

"I agree," stated Moose. "But now that I've said that, I will have to admit that back when we were playing football, it would've been very helpful to have always known what the defense was planning to do."

"That really would've made us look good, but during our last two years, we won all of our games anyway."

"But it would have been fun to have always had the best offensive scheme to take advantage of the defense."

"If we learn how to give the human species a mind reading ability, we must never transmit that knowledge to Earth," Jerry said to Dianne. "Application of that knowledge could be very disruptive to their society. For example, competitive sports would be forever changed in that deceptive plays would no longer be possible."

Connie giggled, "What would happen to slick politicians if deception were no longer possible?"

"What would happen to the legal profession if members of the jury could see right through the deceptive maneuvers of some trial lawyers?" Dianne asked.

Moose and Jerry grinned from ear to ear considering the possibilities suggested by the two questions. "Maybe, you should reconsider your decision. Maybe, we could shake up Earth's society in some very beneficial ways," Moose said to Jerry.

"Perhaps the benefits would outweigh the problems," responded Jerry.

Dianne and Connie looked at each other. "Isn't it amazing how asking the right questions can cause someone to immediately reconsider a decision that only moments before seemed irrevocable?" Dianne said.

Connie nodded in agreement. She and Dianne watched Jerry for a reaction.

"I haven't yet made the decision. I was merely stating what was in my mind at the moment."

"It sure sounded like a decision," commented Connie.

"When I think out loud, I sometimes do it in an assertive way. But as all of you know, I am flexible in my thinking, and I am always open to ideas."

"I can't deny that," replied Connie, "and that is one of the things I like about you."

"It will definitely be a monumental discovery if I am able to figure how Zeb's telepathic ability works and what genetic alterations I need to make in order to give our offspring that ability," Dianne said. "We are a scientific expedition, and discovering new knowledge is one of the big objectives of our mission. However, I never in my most imaginative dreams ever thought that I would learn how to give the human species a telepathic ability. But now, it looks like that will happen. It will be a revolutionary discovery. We will have the ability to advance the human species to a new level. But will we want to do that? Will we transmit the knowledge to Earth?"

"Our situation is far different from what exists on Earth," said Connie. "Society on Earth has been evolving for tens of thousands of years and application of this knowledge could be very disruptive. But here on Alcent, we are a tiny group of people. We are the beginning of a new society. It's possible that we could have a telepathic ability and agree to laws governing its use. It's possible that our society could evolve in ways that incorporate this ability to full advantage."

"When the time comes, we will have some big decisions to make," stated Jerry, "but all of us are here because we made the right choices throughout our lives, and we will make the right choice this time too."

Jerry turned to Dianne, "I would like to learn more about how Zeb has used this special ability over the years. Perhaps, you could tell us the stories that he told you about his bear encounters."

Dianne narrated the stories that Zeb had told her. By the time she finished, Moose and Jerry gained a new respect for Zeb and his survival skills.

Moose shifted his gaze back and forth between Dianne and Connie and said, "Your day was far more exciting than ours. All we did was work."

"Our day might not have been very exciting," said Jerry, "but we did finish another project."

"Are you saying that we can now drive completely around the island?" asked Connie.

"That's right."

"Did you run into any unexpected difficulties?"

"Cutting a trail through the forest from South Bay to East Bay took more time than I expected. The forest is so dense and tangled with lush undergrowth that it was mid-afternoon before we finished that stretch. It took no time at all to get to Rocky Point. When we arrived at the point, we moved a few rocks to make the drive across it easier."

"It sounds like you worked very hard today. You must be tired."

Moose cut in, "We worked our butts off. I think we should take a couple days off and save some of the hard work for the people coming down in a few days."

"You must be getting old," commented Jerry. "I remember a time when hard work didn't seem to bother you all that much."

"I can still do more than my share," retorted Moose. "I just think that we should take a few days off and enjoy the solitude that we have. In a few days, everyone will probably be free to come down. Then, it will be a lot more crowded here, and our peace and quiet will be gone."

"You make it sound like we're about to be hit with a population explosion," commented Jerry. "There will only be twenty-nine of us, and we have an entire planet at our disposal."

"That's true, but we'll all be living right here on the plateau, and it won't be as quiet and peaceful as it is now."

"I sense that the prospect of everyone coming down is a bit upsetting to you," Connie said.

Moose thought about it for a few moments and said, "Not really. I've just enjoyed having the whole place to ourselves. I feel like we've been camping in some remote wilderness area, and now, it is time to return to civilization. Only, in this case, it's coming to us."

"I've also enjoyed our solitude," stated Jerry. "Perhaps, we should take the next couple days off. After we bring everyone down, we're going to be busy building homes and getting everyone settled in. It's going to be a very different life. A few days vacation would be good for us."

"I could use the time to play around with my smokehouse."

"Do you think you could come up with something comparable to ham?" asked Jerry.

"I am going to try. I am also going to try to create something similar to beef jerky, and I'm going to experiment with making sausage."

"I thought you were going to take some time off," remarked Connie. "It sounds to me like you're going to be quite busy."

"My husband never gets tired when he's busy creating good things to eat. In fact, that seems to be his favorite leisure time activity."

Moose looked at Dianne suggestively, "Let's just say that creating tasty food is my second most favorite leisure time activity."

"I am happy to hear than I'm still ranked above smoked sausage on your priority list," Dianne smiled.

Connie gained Jerry's attention, "Why don't you and I take the boat out tomorrow. Perhaps, we could explore part of the western shore of this lake. We haven't been over there yet."

"That would be fun, but the weather might not cooperate. I talked to Mike while driving home from Rocky Point, and he said a small storm system is coming our way. He's predicting that we'll have rainy weather tomorrow."

"If it's a small system and moves through here in just one day, we can sail over there the day after tomorrow."

"Maybe on the day after that, Moose and I can take the boat out," suggested Dianne.

"Good idea," agreed Moose. "After everyone comes down, we'll have to get on a waiting list to use the boat."

"It will definitely be a popular piece of equipment for a while," agreed Dianne.

"After we get our homes built, we'll make some boats, so that our submarine can be used primarily for research," Jerry said. "I want to thoroughly explore the depths of this lake. If there are any dangerous creatures living in it, I want to find them. Also, I want a full knowledge of what resources it contains. In other words, I want to know everything that there is to know about it."

His colleagues nodded in agreement, "If tomorrow's weather isn't good for sailing, I'll get together with Michelle and spend a major part of the day talking with Zeb. I really haven't yet had time to sit down and have a lengthy conversation with him, and it's time I do that," he continued.

"That should be interesting," commented Connie. "I might join you for part of that, but first, I should do a medical evaluation of each of us."

"I thought we were going to take a few days off to relax," remarked Dianne.

"Can you think of a better way for me to relax than to leisurely do something that I enjoy?" asked Connie.

"I've never thought of a medical exam as a recreational activity," replied Dianne.

"I don't know about that," commented Jerry. "I still remember that medical exam she gave me right after we left Earth. I can honestly say that it put a smile on my face."

Connie grinned and turned to Dianne, "As far as I can tell, he's been a well satisfied patient ever since."

"After those comments, you expect me to trust you to give my husband a physical tomorrow morning. Maybe, I'd better assist you."

"I knew I could count on you," stated Connie. "With your help we'll get the medical work done early, and then, we can take the rest of the day off."

"Somehow, I get the feeling that I've been finagled into helping you with your work on my first day off in quite some time."

Connie smiled, "Even with the lab work, it won't take us more than an hour or two. Then, we'll have the rest of the day to do whatever we want."

"That sounds good to me," responded Dianne.

"What do you think you might want to do tomorrow?" Connie asked Dianne.

"I'd like to wander around here on the plateau looking for interesting plants and creatures to study."

"That sounds like work. You just told me that tomorrow's your first day off in a long time."

"But I enjoy my profession. Especially, when I can work at a leisurely pace. Learning about the things that live here is fun for me, but it is a big job. It's going to take a long time to catalog all of the life that exists just here on the plateau; then, there's the rest of the island, the marine life in the lake, and the life in the countryside surrounding the lake."

"How can you talk about leisure time in the same breath that you outline a lifelong project?" asked Connie.

"I'm not going to do the whole project tomorrow; I'm just going to wander around looking for things of interest, things that get my attention in some way."

"That might be interesting. Maybe, I'll join you when we're done with the medical work."

"I thought you were going to join your husband's conversation with Zeb."

"If it's raining, I'll do that; if we're between showers, I'll join you."

"You'd never make it as a biologist," commented Dianne.

"Why is that?" asked Connie in a surprised tone.

"We need to understand how various life forms behave in the rain as well as in the sunshine. And there are creatures that stay out of sight during sunny weather and come out only when it's raining. But, I guess you could always be a fair weather biologist."

"Okay! Rain or shine, I'll join you."

"That's a plan I can live with. Especially, after the way you finagled me into helping you."

TIME: Day Twenty-Four, Early Afternoon.

Dianne and Connie were exploring the plateau and enjoying the great outdoors.

"I love the way the air smells after it rains," remarked Connie.

"I do too. It just has such a fresh clean feel to it."

"We did need the rain. It was starting to get quite dry around here."

"As usual, Mike's forecast was right on," stated Dianne. "We've had several showers since midnight, but now it looks almost over, and this warm sunshine really feels good."

"We aren't necessarily done with the rain yet; there are still a few showers hanging around the area."

Dianne scanned the lake in all directions, "I see what you mean. That one in the northeast is really big. It could certainly take the fun out of a sailing trip."

"But it is producing a beautiful rainbow, one of the most colorful I've ever seen."

Suddenly, the heavy cloud formation was split from end to end by a powerful lightning bolt. Ten seconds later, a sharp booming crack of thunder reached the plateau, jolting Dianne and Connie with its sheer power.

"How spectacular can it get!" exclaimed Connie. "We're being treated to the beauty and violence of nature all at once."

For a few minutes, Dianne and Connie gazed in silence at the magnificent rainbow and occasional lightning bolt, then they resumed wandering the plateau.

"There sure are lots of wild flowers here," remarked Connie. "Have they always been so numerous?"

"Many of these plants have blossomed since our arrival."

"They're beautiful, and I really haven't paid that much attention to them. I think I need to take more breaks from work to enjoy the beauty that we have here."

"I need to study all the plants growing here. That's a big job, and you're welcome to help me with it. Then, you can learn about them while appreciating their beauty."

"That's a good idea," said Connie while pointing at a small shrub covered with pink blossoms. "That bush is exceptionally beautiful."

"And it smells good too," noted Dianne.

"It's little wonder that the air smells so good. It has not only been washed by rain, but it's also being perfumed by an abundance of wild flowers."

"This bush is buzzing with bees, and they look like the ones nesting in the dead tree we discovered a few weeks ago. Seeing them reminds me that we never did investigate that tree to find out if they're making honey."

"Why don't we do that now. We have the time."

"I don't know that I feel like being stung," replied Dianne.

"We should be able to figure out a way to investigate the inside of that tree without getting stung or even unduly disturbing the bees."

"If the bees don't agree with your plan, we could end up with numerous painful stings."

"I don't think these bees are overly aggressive," noted Connie. "When we used Charlie to check them out, they didn't bother him until he pounded on the tree. That would have to be seen as threatening and provoke a response."

"So, how do you plan to investigate their nest without provoking an attack on us?"

"I have cameras that are so small that I can snake them through a blood vein in search of trouble. It seems like we could use that instrument to investigate the bee nest. A couple hours of video should give us some pretty good insight into what their normal activity is. And if they're making honey, we can find out how much is in the tree. If they have a surplus, we can figure out how to get some of it without disturbing them in the process."

"And you guarantee that we're going to do all of this without being stung."

"I can't guarantee that, but why are you so concerned about being stung? It's no more painful than getting a shot at the doctor's office, and we know that that isn't very painful."

"That's what you doctors always say, but I know better. Besides that, we don't know for sure how toxic their venom is to the human body."

"Charlie was stung several times, and we analyzed the venom. Even though it is somewhat different than bee venom back on Earth, it is still in the same class of poisons. I believe the human body can handle the tiny amount that these bees are able to inject."

"What if we can't? What if one of us is stung and has an allergic reaction?"

"When we identified the chemicals in the venom, I had one of my assistants develop an antidote for it. I have an adequate amount of it in our medical supplies."

"I seem to have run out of objections, and you seem to be quite determined to investigate those bees."

"It is something that we need to do. If there is an abundance of honey in that tree, it would be nice to get some of it. But even more important than that, we need to find out how well the human body does handle their venom."

"It almost sounds like you're hoping to be stung."

"I don't particularly relish the idea of suffering one or more painful bee stings, but my daughter may be coming down in a few days. As active and curious as she is, sooner or later, she will suffer a bee sting. I need to know for sure if that's going to be a serious problem, and getting stung is one way to find out." "It looks to me like a mother's protective instinct is at work here."

"That's true, but setting aside concern for my daughter, if all goes according to plan, there will soon be twenty-nine of us living here. It's only a matter of time and someone will be stung. I need to know if that's going to be a medical emergency or just a painful annoyance."

"I am convinced. Let's investigate the nest."

"Let's take a look at our equipment options and work out a plan. The hole in that tree is higher than we can reach, and I don't think it would be a good idea to climb the tree."

"But I thought that you wanted to be stung."

"One or two stings is fine, but I don't want them to make a pin cushion out of me. One thing that might work is a thin rod to reach the nest entrance. I would think that the thinner it is, the less threatening it will look to the bees."

"My husband's fishing rod might work," Dianne suggested.

"That's an idea. If it had a ninety-degree bend near the end, we could reach the hole and enter it, and by simply feeding out line, we could lower our camera into the nest."

My husband is very possessive about that fishing pole. I'm not sure that he will be comfortable with us modifying it in any way."

"Let's talk to him. He's an engineer. Let's get him to modify it in a way that he is comfortable with that also meets our needs. Anyway, the possibility of adding honey to our menu will be a good incentive for him."

"That's true. His mind is never very far away from food."

A few minutes later, Dianne and Connie found Moose putting wood chips on the smoldering fire in his smoke house. Jerry was busy telling Moose some of the things he had learned from Zeb. Dianne and Connie listened with interest.

When Jerry finished his narration, Dianne and Connie explained their plan. Moose and Jerry listened attentively, their practical engineering minds were already at work.

When they finished, Jerry said, "Your plan should work and will be easy to implement."

"I can easily modify my fishing pole," Moose said. "All I need to do is take a piece of stiff wire, bend a small loop at one end for the line to pass through, put a ninety-degree bend in the middle, and then tape it on the end of the fishing rod."

"And I can make you a camera pack," stated Jerry. "I don't think you should use your medical cameras. The tiny cameras in our mechanical bugs will do a good job, and they are easy to remove from the bugs. Those cameras have a 120-degree field of view. By stacking three of them, I can make you a camera pack with a 360-degree field of view. That will eliminate the problem of trying to aim a camera hanging on the end of a fishing line."

"How long will it take?" asked Connie.

"Less than an hour," responded Jerry.

"It won't take me more than a few minutes," replied Moose.

"There is one possible problem," commented Jerry, "and that is that we don't know that the nest extends downward from the entrance. If the nest extends upward, your plan to lower the cameras into it won't work."

"If the dead tree is hollow because of decay and the action of bugs, insects, larvae, whatever; then, I would think that the nest probably extends up and down from the entrance," Moose said. "Why don't we attach an upward looking camera to the wire I'm adding to my fishing pole."

"Good idea," agreed Jerry, "and I will add a downward looking camera to the camera pack."

"I knew these guys could put it together for us," stated Connie.

"You did present us with a relatively simple problem," commented Jerry.

Moose chuckled, "This might be the first time in history that a fishing pole was used to look for honey. But if you find some, I will find a way to use it on some of the smoked meat delicacies that I'm creating."

Connie and Dianne looked at each other and smiled. "I guess we were right," Connie said.

"What was that all about?" questioned Moose.

"Just something Connie said earlier that I agreed with."

"That's an evasive answer."

"I know, but we can't tell you everything. We need to be a bit mysterious at times."

Realizing that he wasn't going to get a straight answer from his wife, Moose went back to nursing the smoldering fire in his smokehouse. When he was satisfied that it didn't need any attention for a while, he set out to modify his fishing pole.

Just over an hour later, Connie and Dianne arrived in the grove containing the bee nest. They stopped a few yards from the nest and observed a steady stream of bees entering and leaving.

"They're sure active," commented Connie.

"With all the rain we've just had, plants aren't hurting for water, so their blossoms should be producing an abundance of nectar. The bees are probably harvesting it as fast as they can."

"In other words, they're getting it while the getting is good."

"That's one way to put it. What I think is happening is they don't have to visit very many blossoms to pick up as much as they can carry, so it doesn't take them very long to fly out, fill up, and return."

"They don't seem to be paying any attention to us," noted Connie.

"Let's move a little closer and find out what happens."

Dianne and Connie moved closer to the tree, stopping about ten feet away. After about a minute, Connie said, "Still no reaction. I'm going in."

Walking slowly and trying to act non-threatening, Connie reached the tree without incident. Then, she slowly lifted the fishing pole up toward the nest entrance. When the end of the pole reached the level of the entrance, Dianne said, "Still no reaction. Apparently, the end of the pole doesn't look or smell like any of their enemies."

"Let's take a look inside," responded Connie.

"I'll put on a headset, monitor the images from the cameras, and give you direction."

A few seconds later, Dianne said, "Okay, I'm ready."

Connie slowly moved the modified end of the rod through the nest entrance and continued into the tree until Dianne said, "Stop."

Dianne looked at the imagery for a few moments and said, "This is a big nest. This tree is loaded. I see what look like honeycombs as far up and down as I can see. If these combs actually do contain honey, there is a huge supply here. Try lowering the camera pack."

Connie slowly reeled out line lowering the cameras into the lower part of the nest.

"What an amazing sight," commented Dianne. "These bees are hard at work. They aren't stopping what they're doing when approached by our camera pack. They're just totally ignoring it."

"Apparently, whatever enemies they have don't look or smell like our camera pack. Too bad we can't get a sample of what they're making to find out if it is similar to honey."

"I think we can. I can see the bottom of the nest. They're making honeycombs on the bottom. If you'll release the brake on the reel, the camera pack will crash into those honeycombs. The downward pointing camera should end up being coated with what they're making."

"Let me know when you've seen enough, and I'll do that."

"As long as we're here we should probably watch them for a few more minutes. Besides that, you haven't been stung yet, and that's something you wanted to investigate."

"Crashing our camera pack into the bottom of their nest might provoke them."

"But if they see it as an enemy and try to sting it, that still won't get you stung."

"Let me know when you're ready. I'll drop it, and we'll find out what they do."

"Before we do that, let's get some imagery of their nest activity. I want you to slowly raise the cameras back to the entrance, stopping when I tell you to."

For about fifteen minutes, Connie slowly moved the cameras around under Dianne's direction occasionally stopping to watch individual bees at work. Finally, Dianne said, "I think I have enough video to study, so that I can get a pretty good idea what goes on inside one of these nests. Let's drop the camera pack."

Connie released the reel's brake, and the small camera pack fell about six feet crashing into the honeycomb at the bottom of the nest. Then, she reeled it up to the nest entrance and removed it. Several bees followed the camera pack. Angered by the damage it had just caused, they were determined to chase it out of their nest.

Seeing a possible opportunity to get stung, Connie set the stock end of the pole on the ground and held the other end at arms length. With her other hand she reached out toward the camera pack. The dozen or so bees that had escorted the camera pack out of the nest continued to buzz around it and Connie's hand, but they did not sting her. After a few minutes the bees returned to their nest.

"I guess I'm just not going to get stung today," declared Connie.

"You don't have to sound so disappointed. After all, it is a painful experience."

"I don't need the pain, but I do need to find out how the human body reacts to their venom."

"As docile as these bees are, getting stung might be a rare occurrence, something that only happens with some very blatant provocation or in defense against known enemies."

Connie and Dianne looked closely at the thick sticky syrup coating the bottom of the camera pack. Dianne said, "It certainly looks like honey."

Connie sniffed it and said, "It smells like honey. Let's take it to the lab. I want to find out how sweet it is and if it contains any toxins."

"If it's sweet and safe, I know someone who will eagerly volunteer to taste it."

"If it tastes good, how long do you think it will take him to figure out how to get some of it out of that tree?" Connie chuckled.

"By the time he's finished smoking meat, he'll have a plan."

"Actually, harvesting some of that honey shouldn't be all that difficult."

"The trick will be to do it in a way that doesn't cause the bees to abandon their nest. The video that I watched shows that the back side of the tree is what's loaded with honey. All we should have to do is drill some holes into it and dig out some honey. When we're done, we plug the holes and use them again at some future time."

"Are you volunteering to drill the holes?" Connie asked.

"You're the one who wants to be stung, and drilling holes in the tree might provoke an attack."

"The problem is it might provoke a massive attack."

"That's possible, but if we quietly approach the back of the tree and drill the holes without a lot of noise or vibration, they might not bother us at all. If we carefully avoid breaking through the surface of the honeycomb, they might not be aware of what's going on beneath the surface."

"As docile as they seem to be, that's a good possibility. Let's analyze this stuff and then talk to our husbands about it."

A short time later, with the lab results in hand, Connie and Dianne met with Moose and Jerry. Connie declared, "It's very sweet, it's not toxic, and it tastes good."

"I'd like a taste," said Moose.

Connie handed him the small camera pack and a toothpick which Moose used to scrape off a bit of honey. After tasting it, he said, "This is delicious. How much is in that tree?"

"The tree is nearly three feet in diameter," Dianne said. "The hollow inside varies from about 1.5 to about 2 feet in diameter. It appears that about three fourths of the interior is filled with honey."

"Wow!" exclaimed Moose. "There could be fifty gallons or more in there. Why would they make so much?"

"It's food for them to eat during hard times," answered Dianne. "Evidently, they haven't had any hard times in recent years because it has probably taken them a few years to build up such a large supply."

"What would cause them to have a tough time?" asked Moose.

"An extended period of dry weather could cause many plants to not blossom very abundantly," replied Dianne. "In their struggle for survival, some plants might not flower at all. If the bees couldn't find enough nectar to live on, they would have to eat some of their stored honey."

"Evidently, the opposite has been the case," commented Connie. "Apparently, the flowering plants here on the island have seen ideal weather for the last few years, and the resulting abundance in flowers has resulted in the bees producing an abundance of honey."

"That does seem to be the case," agreed Dianne.

Moose tasted another bit of honey and said, "Whatever the reason for the abundance, we need to get some of it. This is really delicious. I wouldn't mind having some of this to put on some hot cinnamon rolls."

"You get the honey, and I'll make the cinnamon rolls," Dianne said.

"That's an offer I can't refuse. But, am I going to suffer multiple bee stings in the process?"

"I invaded their nest with a camera pack and didn't get stung," Connie said.

"But you didn't break into their supply of honey and attempt to steal a half gallon of it," commented Moose.

"You need to use stealth," suggested Connie. "Steal it without them knowing what you're doing."

"Do you have a plan in mind?" asked Moose.

Dianne answered, "Most of the honey is stored on the side of the tree opposite the entrance. If we could quietly drill a hole into the back side of the tree, we should be able to take some honey without them being aware of it."

"How large a hole do you have in mind?" asked Moose.

"I have medical instruments that allow me to do internal surgery through very small openings," Connie replied. "You drill me a one-half-inch diameter hole, and I will get some honey."

"Wouldn't it be easier if the hole were larger, like maybe three inches in diameter?" Jerry asked.

"Definitely. Then, we could just dig it out with a large spoon."

"In our tool chest, we have a drill bit with an adjustable head. I could drill a three-inch diameter hole, and I could do it fairly quietly, with very little vibration."

"If you're volunteering to do that, I'll stay here and finish smoking this meat," Moose said.

"Sounds like a convenient excuse to avoid the possibility of being stung," commented Jerry.

"It might sound that way, but I do have some real delicacies in my smoke oven. Being the master that I am, I just can't leave before they're done. There might be some definite loss in quality if someone else were to finish this job."

Looking at Connie and Jerry, Dianne said, "That's just one more demonstration of the ego that I have to contend with every day."

"You don't seem to mind," remarked Connie. "In fact, you seem to be quite content in your relationship."

"He does have a point," commented Jerry. "He is quite good at making delicious foods."

"Aw, the master finally gets some well deserved recognition," remarked Moose.

"I'll find out at dinner time if the praise was premature," stated Jerry.

"You won't be disappointed," declared Moose.

"Let's go get some honey," Jerry said to Connie. "Just to play it safe, I am going to wear some protective clothing. I wouldn't mind one or two stings, but there's always the possibility of a mass attack."

"I'll skip the protective clothing and watch you from a safe distance."

Jerry and Connie picked up the things they needed and headed for the bee tree. In less than an hour, they returned with two gallons of raw honey. Dianne asked, "How did it go?"

"It went smoothly," replied Connie. "Jerry drilled three holes. Then, he scooped out all the honey that he could reach. Before plugging each hole, he broke through the surface of the honey comb into the open space in the nest, so that the bees would be aware of the cavities we left. Hopefully, they will now fill those cavities. At some later date, we can pull the plugs and remove the fresh honey."

"It'll be interesting to find out how long it will take them to replace the honey that you and Jerry took."

"In a couple weeks, we'll drop the cameras in there and see how they're doing."

"You seem to have a fresh red welt on your forehead," Dianne said to Connie.

Connie held up her left arm, "I also have one right here on my wrist and another one on my hand."

"How painful are they?"

"About the same as a bee sting back on Earth."

"Three stings should be enough to find out how the human body responds to their venom."

"It'll tell us how my body reacts. I would like you to draw a blood specimen, so we can find out if this venom is affecting my blood chemistry in any significant way."

"I think we should treat you as a possible poison victim and check out all of your vital signs."

"Even though I feel just fine, I do agree with you."

"While we're checking me out, would you mind separating this honey from the wax?" Connie asked Jerry.

"I can do that," replied Jerry.

Speaking to Jerry, Moose said, "I'm done smoking meat for the day, so I'll join you, and you can give me the details of the honey collecting expedition."

About an hour and a half later, the pioneers sat down to enjoy their evening meal. The featured items were Moose's version of ham, sausage, and jerky along with hot fresh cinnamon rolls smothered with raw honey. Steamed mixed vegetables and a salad rounded out the meal. All items were locally obtained except for the ingredients used to make the cinnamon rolls. They spent a full hour leisurely enjoying their delicious dinner while making plans for the next day.

After dinner, Jerry noted that Alpha Centauri A had already slipped below the western horizon and that Alpha Centauri B would set in less than a half hour. Looking to the south and southeast, he noted that Aphrodite and Nocturne were high in the sky and that both would be in the full moon phase in two days. Two full moons will be a unique sight that we haven't yet seen thought Jerry.

He looked out over the plateau softly lit by the dim orange glow from Alpha Centauri B and the light of two moons approaching their full phase. The romantic aura of the scene gradually pervaded his mind, and he turned to Connie, "I feel like going for a moonlight swim in South Bay. Would you care to join me?"

"I'd be delighted," replied Connie. "Let's go."

SEVENTEEN

Vacation Sailing

TIME: Day Twenty-Five, Several Minutes Before First Sunrise.

Jerry and Connie were onboard the submarine cruising on the surface with battery power. They left South Bay and were rounding the southwestern tip of Pioneer Island in route to the west coast of Clear Lake. Jerry was at mid-deck piloting the boat while Connie was standing near the bow lazily enjoying the sensual caress of the mild early morning air. She took a deep breath while stretching straight and tall. She slowly exhaled and shook her arms and shoulders to rid herself of the last bit of early morning sleepiness. Feeling fully awake and relaxed, she gazed out across the vast open water of Clear Lake and anticipated a fun-filled carefree day. She turned and wandered from the boat's bow to its stern thinking, if Mike's forecast is correct, we are going to have perfect weather for a day on the lake.

When she reached the stern, Connie grasped the handrail and surveyed the sky. She noted a few widely scattered cloud formations, but it was the cloud bank in the eastern sky that caught her attention. As she gazed at this formation, its elegant, natural beauty seemed to fill her with a profound sense of peacefulness that grew into a joyful sense of warmth and well-being. As she continued to gaze at the soft billowing clouds, she became aware of their delicate curves and was struck by their sensual, almost erotic, appeal. She noted that the cloud bottoms were awash with a soft pink glow that added a buoyant warm aura to the scene. As Connie continued to feast her eyes on the delicate artistic beauty provided by nature, her sense of warmth and personal well-being became so strong that she was unable to contain it. She felt an overpowering desire to share her joyful mood with the man she loved, so she turned to Jerry and exclaimed, "It's wonderful to be living here! Please stop whatever you're doing and enjoy this beautiful sunrise with me!"

Surprised by the passion in Connie's voice, Jerry turned away from piloting the boat and gazed at her. He saw his wife silhouetted against the pre-sunrise glow of the eastern sky. Her golden blonde hair now being blown about by the gentle wind took on a reddish-blond tint. He noticed that her skin also reflected the warm glow. As he continued to gaze at Connie, he was struck by the way the pre-sunrise glow seemed to cause her to radiate a special angelic beauty. Jerry responded the only way that he could. He immediately slowed the boat to three mph and put it on auto-pilot. Then, he stepped into position behind Connie and put his arms around her in a warm loving way. While closely bound together by Jerry's embrace, Connie and Jerry enjoyed the special romantic effect of the warm pre-sunrise glow that filled the eastern sky and reflected off the lake.

A few minutes later, Alpha Centauri A peaked over the eastern horizon and its brilliant glare signaled the beginning a new day. Connie turned in her husband's embrace. She looked up into his eyes, kissed him warmly, and said, "Thanks for enjoying that with me. Our day is off to a great start. We're going to have more fun today than on any day since arriving here."

Jerry loosened his embrace of Connie, so he could back away from her one small step. With his hands warmly planted against her sides, he said, "You are really fired up this morning."

"I feel like a big load has been taken off our backs."

"What do you mean?"

"For the most part, I think we've accomplished our objectives for our first thirty days. Today, I want to forget about work. I want to celebrate our accomplishments. I want to relax and have fun."

"I like your objectives. You can expect full cooperation from me."

"As much as you enjoy sailing, I never had any doubt about that."

"Sailing has always been fun for me, and today promises to be an excellent day for it. We should have enough wind to use the sails effectively, but not enough to make the lake rough."

"And we have the lake entirely to ourselves."

"We're very fortunate in that regard. I've never enjoyed contending with large crowds."

"Privacy does have some advantages. As warm as it already is, I think that it will be hot enough this afternoon so that we can do some nude sunbathing."

"Now, you're getting me excited."

Connie smiled in satisfaction. She stepped forward and gave her husband a warm hug. They enjoyed the closeness of their embrace for a few moments. "I like the romantic mood that you're in."

"We're having a rather romantic morning so far," Jerry whispered.

Jerry nodded in agreement. He gazed into Connie's eyes as if expecting her to say more.

Connie sensed Jerry's thoughts, "Perhaps, my mood is partly the result of that romantic moonlight swim you took me on last night. I might still be basking in the afterglow."

"I don't think swimming has ever left me with an afterglow that I could get wrapped up in," Jerry teased.

"Do I need to be specific?"

Desiring to hear what she would say, Jerry gave her a naughty grin and nodded.

"It wasn't the moonlight swim," Connie responded. "It was that passionate episode on the beach that has left me with an afterglow."

For a few moments, Jerry pretended to be lost in thought. "Now that you've tweaked my memory, I vaguely recall that we did have some fun on the beach last night," he said.

"You might be a good actor, but you're not fooling me. You were a bundle of passion last night."

Jerry smiled warmly, "You're right; I was, and so were you."

Connie thoughtfully enjoyed the memory of the previous night for a few moments. "Last night was wonderful," she said. "I haven't yet gotten use to having two moons in the sky and that had a romantic effect on me. Plus, we are on a savage planet. The element of danger was present, and that added a degree of excitement. But most of all, I am happy with our new home and the great relationship that we have."

"Our marriage is special. I hope that it continues to be as warm and loving as it has always been."

"Our life together will be what we choose to make it. If we continue to be faithful to each other, treat each other with love and respect, and look for ways to make each other happy, then, we will not only continue to have a wonderful relationship, but it will get even better."

"That's a prescription I can live with."

"Did I sound like a doctor writing a prescription?"

"No, but you are a doctor, and I couldn't help saying that."

"Well, right now, the doctor is hungry and about ready to write a prescription for breakfast."

"I'm hungry too, but let's deploy the sails before we eat breakfast."

Twenty minutes later, with the sails and outriggers deployed, Jerry again put the boat on auto-pilot. "Okay, I'm ready for breakfast. In fact, I'm starving," he said to Connie.

Connie went below deck to prepare a hot breakfast while Jerry set up a portable table and chairs. In less than ten minutes, they were seated at the table, silently enjoying breakfast while surrounded by the pristine beauty of Clear Lake.

Connie broke the silence, "You seem to be deeply lost in thought. Would you mind sharing it with me?"

"I was thinking about some of the things that I did and some of the dreams that I had when I was a teenager back on Earth."

"Do you miss Earth?"

"Sometimes, I wish I could return to Earth for a few days to visit friends and family, but I would rather live here."

"What got you started thinking about Earth this morning?"

"The sunrise we just enjoyed reminded me of some that I enjoyed on backpack trips into wilderness areas. As you know, backpacking was one of my favorite activities. It was like entering a different world. It allowed me to temporarily escape the rat race of daily living. It was very relaxing and I deeply enjoyed the quiet peacefulness of the forest."

"That quiet peacefulness can be very beneficial. It can enable a person to get into a relaxed state of mind allowing one to think on a different level than what is possible during normal everyday living."

"It definitely did that for me. In fact, being in the wilderness seemed to stimulate my imagination in exciting ways. I would find a rapids in a mountain river and then scramble out to a rock in the midst of the rapids. While sitting on the rock, with the sounds of the rapids for a background, I would let my mind wander. Sometimes, I tried to imagine what it would be like to go back in time and visit Earth during the peak of the dinosaur age. Coming here isn't the same thing, but in a sense, it does fulfill that dream."

"Coming here is much more than a fulfillment of that dream. We're not just visiting a dinosaur dominated planet; we're also building a home among them."

"That's true, and living here is more wildly exciting than my daydreams ever were. I never once imagined that I would stand under a 100-ton sauropod, reach up, and touch his stomach."

"You also probably never imagined that we would befriend a pterodactyl who would then save my life by killing one of its kind."

"And I also never expected to see my best friend stranded on the back of a styracosaurus during a face-off with a pack of T-Rexes."

"Can you imagine what it would be like to put a pack on your back, hike into the wilderness, and do some overnight camping with those brutes lurking in the bushes?"

"I don't think that would be very relaxing. I would be too busy just trying to stay alive to ever find time to relax."

"But think about the advantages. To start with, you wouldn't have to make a daydream trip into fantasy land to wonder what it would be like to have dinosaurs around."

"You're not convincing me."

"But I thought you liked the sense of adventure that's always present on a backpack trip."

"There is such a thing as too much adventure. This isn't twenty-first century Earth; this is Alcent, a wild, primitive planet. Just living here is a full-time adventure."

"But spending a few days in the countryside would be a challenging test of your survival skills."

"Someday, we'll probably make such a trip, but we'll probably do it with ATVs, so that we can be well-supplied and well-armed. We'll use RPV's to scout our vicinity. During the night, we'll have two guards equipped with night vision goggles. It would be a dangerous adventure, but I think we could do it without suffering any casualties."

"There's no way to know that for sure. I was almost killed by a saber-tooth when we went ashore for just a few minutes."

"That's true, and with that in mind, I don't think we'll be making any extended trips into the countryside anytime soon, unless we have a very important reason to do so."

"I don't feel the need for such a trip. Living on Pioneer Island has been a lot like camping out and has given me all the adventure I need."

"In a few days, that's probably going to change, because I will most likely be giving the okay for everyone to come down and join us."

"Judging from the way you said that, I sense that you feel some reluctance about bringing everyone down."

Jerry thought about Connie's comment for a few moments. "There are only four of us here, five counting Zeb. We've had a vast wilderness area completely to ourselves, and I've enjoyed more adventure and solitude here than I ever had on any camping trip."

"I have too, but even after we bring everyone down, adventure and solitude will never be very far away."

"That's true, but Stellar Plateau has been a quiet, secluded place to live. I've enjoyed that quiet peaceful seclusion. After we bring everyone down, the plateau will be buzzing with activity, and building shelters will be the first thing on the list."

"How are we going to decide where to put them? Each couple will have their own idea about where they want to live."

"Probably the easiest way to avoid conflict will be to divide the plateau into public and private land. Then, we divide the private land into equally sized lots. The fairest way to decide which family gets which lot will be to simply draw numbers out of a hat."

"What about Zeb?"

"If he chooses to stay with us, he will also receive a lot, and we'll build him a shelter on it."

"For thirty years, his life has been the ultimate in quiet seclusion."

"I wouldn't like to have that much seclusion," declared Jerry.

"Does that mean that you now feel better about everyone coming down?"

"Let's just say that I have mixed emotions. I've like having the whole place to ourselves, but I am also looking forward to the challenge of building a new civilization."

"If Zeb chooses to live with us, then in return for building him a home, he could make his cave dwelling available for people to camp out in. Anyone who feels the need for some isolation could live on Zeb's island for a few days. They could explore the island during the day and have a secure place to sleep at night."

"Good idea," commented Jerry. "In fact, all the islands should be reasonably safe places to camp and explore, except for the bear problem. In time, we'll know just how much of a problem the bears are going to be. But that's okay, it's going to be a while before anyone is interested in going camping anyway. They've all been in space for so long that living on the plateau is going to feel like camping out, especially until we get permanent homes built."

"When all the homes are built, the plateau is going to look a lot like a village."

"But it won't be crowded. Even if we retain half of the land as public land, each family will still have a lot roughly three times bigger than a football field. And that should provide plenty of space to grow vegetables, fruits, berries, nuts, cereal grains, flowers, whatever."

"As readily available as food is in the wild, I don't think each family will face much of a challenge to grow enough additional things in order to eat very well," commented Connie.

"Speaking about food available in the wild, that honey we collected yesterday was delicious. I think it would be in everyone's best interest to make sure that those bees have a good year every year. One way to do that would be to beautify our homes with an abundance of flower gardens."

"Harvesting the honey would be much easier if we could get them out of that tree and into a bee hive. It would be even better if we could divide the colony and get several bee hives going."

"Our library should have all the information we need to care for bees."

"But that information applies to Earth's bees," stated Connie. "We don't know how these bees reproduce. We don't know what keeps them together in a colony. We don't know what would motivate them to leave a nesting site and search for a new one. And we don't know how to divide them into several colonies."

"That's all true, but while we're getting answers to those questions, it would be easy to make some boxes similar to what bee keepers on Earth make for their honey bees and locate them near the honey tree. Maybe, a few conveniently located nesting sites would cause them to move out of the tree or divide into colonies."

"It's worth a try," agreed Connie.

"I'll make the boxes tomorrow."

"I'm not planning to do much of anything tomorrow. It might be our last chance to be lazy in quite some time."

"I'll make the bee hives tomorrow morning, and then, I'll have the rest of the day to help you be lazy around home."

"Moose and Dianne are going sailing tomorrow, so except for Zeb, we'll be alone," commented Connie.

360

"I don't think Zeb will bother us much. He's been spending most of his time conversing with Michelle."

"He hasn't had anyone to talk to in thirty years, and ever since she decided to write his biography, he's been eagerly sharing his life with her at every opportunity."

"I'm glad she's doing that and that he's excited about it," said Jerry. "Depending on how good his memory is, we should learn a great deal about our home, and we might be able to find out what life was like on B-2 before the long war."

"When we left Earth, I never dreamed that we would discover an alien civilization or that we would have an alien living with us."

"It is an added but interesting complication to our lives. But setting that aside and looking at the big picture, all three of the earth-like planets that we know about are teeming with life."

"We actually know of four earth-like planets if you consider that Mars was earth-like early in its history, and when it was earth-like, life existed there too," Connie said.

"All the earth-like planets that we know about have spawned life. And that would seem to indicate that life must be fairly common throughout the universe, even if only one or two percent of sun-like stars have earth-like planets."

"Since the universe contains countless trillions of sun-like stars, I have to agree with you."

"That's fun to think about, but in our little corner of the universe, we will soon have a big decision to make."

"My intuition is telling me that you will make that decision tomorrow night and that you will decide to bring everyone down the next day."

"If I don't bring them down pretty soon, I just might have a mutiny on my hands. They might just decide to take the risk and come down anyway."

"I don't think they would do that. They're just too professional and too disciplined."

"While I believe that to be true, they've been in space for a long time. They're so excited about the possibility of coming down soon that they can hardly contain themselves. Mike told me last night that everyone is packed. They even have the cargo shuttle packed and ready to go."

"Besides all of that, Dianne tells me that her assistants are working around the clock to discover the details of Zeb's immune system."

"It's amazing to me that you can learn so much about Zeb just by studying his DNA."

"As soon as we have his genetic blueprint, all we have to do is feed that information into the computer, and it will create 3D imagery of any of his body parts that we choose to study. If we ask the computer to display his cardiovascular system, it will do that. If we want to study his skeleton, we can call up a display of it from any angle we care to view it from. We can call up an image of his brain. Hopefully, that will give us some clues as to where his telepathic ability comes from. But that will come later. The first thing we will do is display his immune system and make a detailed comparison to the human immune system."

"What's the current estimate on when this information will be available?"

Dianne talked to her assistants this morning, and they're promising sometime tomorrow night. If they find that Zeb's immune system is comparable to ours or inferior to ours, then the fact that he has survived here for thirty years would indicate that we can safely bring everyone down as far as the threat from microbes is concerned. If that's the case, tomorrow just might be our last opportunity to enjoy having the plateau to ourselves."

"What if Zeb's immune system turns out to be vastly superior to ours? Does that mean we don't yet bring everyone down? Or do we bring everyone down anyway?"

"I sense that you're thinking about bringing everyone down anyway."

"That is what I'm considering. Keep in mind that he has lived here for thirty years without medical attention. To have survived that long without medical help might require a superior immune system. Our situation is different; we have superior medical technology and a very competent doctor with very well trained assistants."

"I appreciate the compliment, but if we discover that Zeb's immune system has some unique capability that we don't have; then, I think we should try to understand that capability before we bring everyone

361

down. That way, I will be able to determine if our medical technology can do for us what his immune system does for him."

"How long would it take to determine that?"

"That depends on what we discover."

"That's a safe answer, but I guess it's the only answer you can give me."

"We could speculate on various possibilities, but that might take all day, and I would rather just kick back, relax, and enjoy a day of sailing with my favorite man."

"I can live with that. In fact, let's avoid serious conversation of any sort for a few hours and just enjoy sailing."

"The wind seems to be picking up a bit," commented Connie.

"Let's clear the deck," stated Jerry.

"I'll put away the dishes."

"And I'll put away the table and chairs."

Five minutes later, Connie emerged from below deck, and she and Jerry got down to the serious business of enjoying a day of recreational sailing on a pristine lake with seven hundred square miles of water, a huge lake by any standard of measurement. Best of all, in their minds, it was a huge lake with no one on it except them. There was the clear clean water teeming with fish that they could observe through the boat's transparent hull. There were sea birds soaring around. And there were soaring pterodactyls with their fifty-foot wing spans. The flying creatures were seen against the background of a beautiful blue sky sprinkled with a few fluffy cumulus clouds. All of this combined with warm temperatures would make it a very enjoyable day.

TIME: Day Twenty-Six, Mid-Afternoon.

Having spent the previous day enjoying the pleasures of sailing, Jerry and Connie were spending this day leisurely enjoying Pioneer Island. Expecting that everyone would soon be coming down, they were taking advantage of their opportunity to enjoy the peaceful solitude.

Meanwhile, Moose and Dianne were a little over twenty miles from Pioneer Island sailing eastward along the north shore of Clear Lake. While cruising along the edge of a small shallow bay, Moose noticed what was growing in the bay, "That sure looks a lot like the rice-like plant that is growing in some of the shallow areas around Zeb's island."

Because of the shallow water, they could not sail into the bay, so Dianne studied the plants with binoculars for a few moments. "I think you're right, and it's loaded with grain, but it's still green," she said.

"When do you think it will be ripe?"

"In two weeks, maybe three."

"I'd like to come back and harvest some of it. If it tastes good, it might become a key part of our diet."

"It's been a key part of Zeb's diet over the years," stated Dianne. "He said these plants produce a crop twice a year, one in late spring and one in early fall."

"Jerry and Connie found several patches of these plants growing in shallow areas along the west shore of the lake yesterday. As abundant as this grain seems to be, it could become a major part of our diet too. I wonder what it tastes like."

"I think that it must taste pretty good, or Zeb would've found something else to eat."

"That might be, but I would like to cook some of it and be my own judge on its flavor."

"Unless Zeb has some of the grain stored in his cave, you will have to wait a couple weeks."

"I'll be checking it often. As soon as any of it is ripe, I will harvest some."

"When you check on it, you will, of course, need to go sailing and spend a day on the lake."

"That would be a side benefit to my dedicated effort to make sure that our new civilization has enough to eat."

"Being a dedicated plant biologist, I will have to accompany you, so that I can study the ripening process of this potentially important plant, and before we eat any of the grain, I will have to check it out in the lab."

"If some of these plants were growing around Pioneer Island, we wouldn't be forced to spend a day on the lake."

"Darn the bad luck!" exclaimed Dianne.

"I wonder why there aren't any around Pioneer Island."

"I don't know, but my guess is that, in addition to shallow water, you have to have the right conditions on the lake bottom. Around Pioneer Island, the bottom is mostly sandy, gravely, and rocky. Maybe, this plant likes a silty bottom covered with decaying vegetation."

"It would be easy to find out if your theory is correct, but I don't feel like doing that today. In a couple weeks, when we harvest some of it, I will also get some bottom samples."

"Good plan," agreed Dianne, "I feel lazy today too."

"If we were to grind some of the grain into flour, I wonder if we could use it to make bread."

"That's going to depend on its flavor and on how much gluten it contains."

"What's gluten?"

"My husband who claims to be a master chef doesn't know what gluten is. I am surprised."

"I can't be expected to know everything. Anyway, baking bread has never been one of my specialties."

"Gluten is a tough elastic protein. It is abundant in wheat but is missing in most other grains. Because of gluten's tough elastic quality, it is able to hold the little bubbles of gas produced by growing yeast. This allows bread to rise."

"So gluten is essential to the bread baking process."

"Yes, it is."

"I'm excited about this grain," declared Moose. "If it contains gluten, is nutritious, tastes good, and is safe to eat; it could become the most common part of our diet."

"If it meets all those considerations, as abundant as it seems to be, we aren't going to have to grow much grain."

"I think we should experiment with growing different kinds of grain anyway. They will add variety to our diet."

"I've already started those experiments," replied Dianne. "I need to find out how well the grains we brought with us handle this planet's diseases and parasites."

"I know, but what I had in mind was to experiment with growing them in large enough quantities to be a meaningful addition to our diets."

"That will be next. First, we have to find out if grains from Earth do well here. If they don't, I will have to make some genetic alterations to them, so that they can deal with the problems they encounter here."

"So those that do well, we can grow in quantity next year. Those that have problems, we can't grow until you make the alterations and test them by growing them through a complete season. And if they still don't do well, you'll have to make more genetic alterations and grow them through another season. That means that it could take years before we can grow in quantity some of the grains we brought with us."

"That sums it up quite well," replied Dianne.

"I sure hope this wild rice checks out well."

"Zeb has been eating it for a long time, so there's a good chance that it will."

After looking at the wild rice for a few more moments, Dianne's gaze shifted to the meadows and trees. "I would like to explore the countryside for a while," she said.

"I don't think going ashore is a very good idea."

"I don't know about that; it looks quite safe to me. Anyway, I just want to look around for a while. I'm not planning to ride a dinosaur into combat."

"I didn't do that on purpose. It just happened unexpectedly."

"That's true, but you shouldn't be trying to sound so innocent."

"Why?"

"Because you're glad that it happened. You did something that no one else has ever done. It was the thrill of a lifetime, it was extremely dangerous, and you came through it with hardly a scratch."

"That sounds like a long-winded way of saying that it was a male macho thing."

"Well, you certainly did earn bragging rights."

"Yeah, I did, but whenever I think about that episode, there's one image that always appears in my mind, and it appears so vividly that it's almost as if I'm still there living it, and it's still terrifying."

"Want to tell me about it?"

"It was that moment in time when I looked into the eyes of a ten-ton T-Rex with a wide open mouth lined with foot-long daggers. Those teeth along with the streams of saliva flowing out of his mouth instantly sent a terrifying chill up and down my spine. At that instant, I knew what it would be like to be only seconds away from being eaten by a predator that could gulp me down in just a couple bone-crunching bites."

"That must have been terrifying."

"It made me appreciate the effective defense set up by the styracosaurus herd. They are large powerful animals and are very well equipped to defend themselves. Because of them, I am still alive and have a wildly exciting story to tell, one that I can tell our children someday."

"First, we have to have some."

"Sounds like fun. When would you like to get pregnant?"

"How about tonight under the light of a double full moon?"

"I like the idea, but shouldn't we wait until the decision has been made that we've passed our quarantine?"

"That decision will be based on recommendations made by me and Connie, and I already know what those recommendations are going to be."

"So if we attempt to get pregnant tonight, our actions will be based on insider information."

"That's one way to put it."

"You could share the recommendations with me. I won't tell anyone."

"Since I am suggesting that we get pregnant tonight, you already know what they're going to be, so I won't be telling you any secrets."

"I'm listening."

"Today is our 26th day here, and we haven't experienced any serious infections or illnesses. You could argue that 26 days isn't very long, but we've certainly exposed ourselves to the environment here. We've breathed the air, and we've all swallowed untreated lake water while swimming. We've all suffered scratches and abrasions. You were punctured by a sty-tick. Connie suffered a serious puncture wound at the hands of a saber-tooth. We've all suffered insect bites. Connie's bee stings healed without complication. Also, we've eaten raw food from here."

"I am convinced, let's get pregnant."

"I'm not done yet. In addition to everything I just said, my assistants are going to announce tonight that Zeb's immune system is basically similar to the human immune system but may be somewhat more capable."

"You already know that."

"I've known since early this morning."

"Why are they withholding this information until tonight?"

"Because I told them to."

"Why?"

"Because everyone may have decided to come down today, and I wanted to have this day alone with you. They've all been in space for nearly seven years, and one day more or less isn't going to matter that much."

"But they're so eager to come down. How could you get away with telling them to withhold the information until tonight?"

"I didn't directly tell them. I just questioned part of their work and gave them a short list of additional things to check for, just enough to keep them busy for today."

"That was a bit devious."

"Yes it was, but I have another motive in mind."

"What?"

"I want our first child to be the first child conceived here, and hopefully, the first child born here. I checked my calendar yesterday, and it indicated that I could probably get pregnant today."

"So you dreamed up some additional work to keep your assistants busy for another day."

"It was a challenge, but the work I've requested is worth doing, and they weren't able to voice any legitimate objections. But it is very likely that everyone will be coming down tomorrow."

"So that gives us today to get pregnant."

"I tested myself a few hours ago, and the test was positive. I should be ovulating today. So whether or not I get pregnant is up to you."

"I will certainly do my part," declared Moose with a broad smile.

"I was fairly certain I could count on you."

"I'm ready anytime you are."

"I think we should wait until this evening. We are going to have a double full moon, and that will be an exotic, romantic setting in which to conceive our first child."

"OK, so what would you like to do with the rest of the afternoon?"

"We've never been to this part of the lake before, so I would like to explore the countryside."

Moose looked worried. "Don't worry. I'm not planning to go ashore. I will use an RPV to take a good look around," Dianne quickly responded.

"That's the safest way to do it, and I think we should live our lives as safely as we can until we've had a chance to have a few children."

"I'll remind you of that remark the next time you ride a dinosaur into combat."

"There's not going to be a next time, once is enough."

"It sounds like you're losing your spirit of adventure."

"No! That's not it at all. I'm just ready to begin the adventure of raising a family, and to do that, I need to stay alive."

"I am glad you feel that way. We've waited a long time to have children, and I don't want to lose you now."

"We could store some of my sperm to guard against my untimely death."

"We need to do that for all of our men, but I sincerely hope that we don't lose anybody. I for one have no desire to try to raise children without a husband. I will if there's no other way, but please do me a big favor and stay alive."

Moose looked into his wife's eyes and said, "I assure you that I will do everything in my power to stay alive. It just simply isn't necessary to pull any daredevil stunts."

"You've already pulled off a unique daredevil stunt."

"But once is enough. I have a vivid memory to remind myself what it was like. Now I'm ready for a peaceful life involving activities like building a comfortable home to raise a family in."

"Having a happy, secure family life is very important to me. I'm glad that you feel the same way."

"It is a deep-seated feeling for me. I believe that how successful we are at building a new society is dependent on how successful we are at building stable secure families."

"True, but I would like to know why you think that way."

"The future of our society is dependent on our children. To properly develop, children need stability and security. A stable secure family life isn't the only way to provide that, but I believe that it is the best way."

"You speak with such conviction. I didn't know that you've studied child psychology."

"I haven't, but I once was a kid, and I remember what was sometimes missing in my life and in the lives of some of my friends."

Moose paused for a few moments, then asked, "What do you think is most important in raising children?"

Dianne considered the question for a few moments. "If we are to have a smoothly functioning society, all of our children need to have a good sense of values instilled into them," she said. "They need to have a good sense of what's right and what's wrong."

Speaking with conviction, Moose said, "When I was a kid, I was on the wrong path for a few years. If I hadn't changed my ways, I might have become a career criminal. Instead of being here with you, I might now be in jail, or maybe even dead."

For a few moments, Dianne thought about what might have been. She tried to imagine Moose sitting in a jail. Then, she tried to imagine her life without him, and she was overcome by sadness. "I can't imagine being here without you," she said tearfully. "I am so very thankful that you changed your ways and that you're here with me. Working together, we must make sure that our children never get on the wrong path."

Moose gave his wife a warm, reassuring hug, "Our children will receive plenty of love and guidance from me, but I just simply will not tolerate any of them getting into the kind of trouble I got into. I almost ruined my life, and I am not going to let that happen to our children."

"With me providing the gentle love and you providing the tough love, we should be successful."

"My tough love will be gentle most of the time. It will only be tough when necessary."

"We're going to be a good team. Maybe, we should start now instead of waiting for the double full moon."

"I'm as eager as you are," replied Moose, "but before we left Earth, Jerry promised me some exotic adventure."

"What does that have to do with getting me pregnant?"

"I think getting you pregnant on a sailboat on a huge, pristine lake under a double full moon fulfills part of that promise. A couple pterodactyls soaring around in the moonlit sky would make the setting even more exotic."

"But, I seem to be in the mood now."

Moose stared at his scantily clad wife and noted that she seemed to be on the verge of removing what little she was wearing. Her seductive manner immediately started to arouse him, but Moose made a halfhearted effort to resist and in an unconvincing way said, "I think we should wait until tonight."

"I don't feel like waiting. I really do want to get pregnant."

Dianne seductively removed her top. "Let's compromise. Let's do it now and again tonight."

"That's a great compromise."

"Only if you're still man enough to make it twice in the same day."

"Try me!"

"I intend to," said Dianne as she removed the rest of her clothing. She looked at Moose. "Well, what are you waiting for?"

Moose continued to gaze at his naked wife for a few moments. "I just want to admire your beauty in this setting for a few moments. Would you mind doing some suggestive poses for me?" he asked.

"Turn on some music and I will do an exotic dance for you."

"What kind of music do you want?"

"Punch *Music Erotic Dance* into the computer."

Moose did as instructed and some very enchanting music immediately began pouring out of the boat's sound system. For the next five minutes, Dianne performed a seductive dance routine that was so perfectly choreographed that her body movements and the music became one.

It was good that the boat was on auto-pilot because Moose was so captivated by the performance that he was oblivious to the course being followed by the little boat. It could easily have run aground in the shallow water along the shoreline, but the boat's auto-navigation system kept it in deep water at a safe distance from shore.

At the end of the performance, Moose said, "WOW! Where did you learn how to dance like that?"

"We were in space for a long time, and I had some free time on my hands. I worked up this routine in secret and saved it for a special occasion. Was my performance exotic enough for you?"

"It was out of this world. Something I would expect to see at the palace of an ancient Roman emperor prior to an orgy."

"Judging from that bulge in your trunks, you could've performed quite well at that orgy," Dianne teased. "So, do you still want to wait until tonight?"

"Are you kidding? That sexy performance of yours almost caused me to go off in my pants."

"How would that get me pregnant?"

"I guess that would've been wasteful on my part."

"It sure would have. Anyway, why are you still wearing your trunks? What are we waiting for?"

One second later, Moose said, "I'm not wearing any trunks, and we're not waiting any longer. Now, it's my turn to show you a little routine that I've worked out that I've been saving for this special occasion."

For several minutes, Moose teased and stimulated his wife with erotic caresses until she became so aroused that she cried out, "I can't wait any longer! I need you now!"

Moose immediately gave Dianne what she wanted. So thoroughly aroused were both of them that they quickly reached satisfaction.

Lying next to each other on an air mattress, they rested while soaking up the warm radiant energy pouring down on them from Alpha Centauri A and to a much lesser extent from Alpha Centauri B. If nature took the desired course, theirs would be the first child conceived on the new world. So complete was their satisfaction, and so comforting was the warm radiant energy striking them, that the hypnotic sound of small waves washing against the side of the boat quickly caused both Moose and Dianne to doze off into dreamland.

However, after just a few minutes of sleep, both were instantly awakened by the urgent chirping of their communicators. Recognizing the sound as the pterodactyl warning, Moose and Dianne immediately surveyed the sky and found a pair of pterodactyls approaching from the north. They grabbed their rifles and warily watched the big creatures approach. Then, their communicators chirped out a second warning. A few seconds later, the pterodactyls spotted the little boat and began circling it at an altitude of about five hundred feet.

After about a minute, Dianne said, "They seem to be keeping their distance."

"But with their diving speed, they could be on us in a matter of seconds."

"I want to take a closer look," she said.

Dianne put down her rifle and picked up the binoculars. She studied the huge creatures looking for the distinctive markings of King and Queen, but it was immediately obvious that these pterodactyls were strangers. "These birds aren't King and Queen," she said. "In fact, they are an entirely different species of pterodactyl. What concerns me the most is they don't have webbed feet, which means they can't swim, which means that they're not fish eaters unless they're able to grab them near the surface."

"Are you trying to say that this species preys on land animals and that they're wondering if we're good to eat?"

"I think that's the case. It looks to me like they aren't just circling aimlessly; rather, it looks like they're circling us, and that means they are investigating us."

"Then, we have a choice to make: Do we kill them now when they're easy targets, or do we wait until they attack? If they attack, they'll still be big targets, but we'll only have a few seconds to nail them?"

"I don't like the idea of killing these magnificent creatures unless we have to," replied Dianne. "I think we can safely wait. We're both crack shots, even against small moving targets, and these guys are big. Hitting them should be easy, and our rifles are armed with explosive bullets, so any hit should be lethal."

"I am comfortable with that, but I wanted to make sure that you are too."

"In a few seconds, we might have to shoot them or quickly go below deck. I get the feeling that they're about ready to attack."

"I don't want to retreat to below deck. These creatures could destroy our solar sails. I have another idea. Pick up your rifle and stand guard while I give them something to think about."

Dianne did as directed, and Moose quickly put his rifle down. Then, he opened the watertight hatch on a compartment containing emergency supplies. Very quickly, Moose located, removed, and loaded a flare gun. Next, he looked up and noted that the larger of the two pterodactyls was preparing to dive. Moose aimed and fired at the exact instant the large predator entered its dive. At a range of just over one hundred yards, the flare exploded creating a large smoke cloud directly in front of the diving pterodactyl. This smoke cloud combined with the loud boom from the explosion caused the diving pterodactyl to screech loudly in surprise and to immediately break off its dive and veer off to the side. Moose quickly reloaded the flare gun.

"Very good!" exclaimed Dianne.

"The other one is still circling us."

"But he's circling at a greater distance. He seems to be wary of us. I doubt that he's going to attack."

"His partner is heading for the hills, perhaps, in search of familiar prey."

"Maybe, this one will join him."

Dianne had barely finished speaking when the still circling pterodactyl turned and headed northward in pursuit of its partner.

367

"Either they aren't very hungry, or their usual prey is readily available, and they didn't want to make an issue out of attacking us," Moose commented.

"They've never seen humans before, and even though we are unknown to them, we must've looked like easy prey."

"But the flare I fired gave them some second thoughts."

"Are you saying that they're able to think?"

"I was using a figure of speech, but just the same, it should not have been difficult for the attacker to associate the exploding flare with us."

"Predatory birds have very keen eyesight," commented Dianne. "It's possible that the attacker actually saw the flare traveling from you toward him."

"If he didn't see the actual projectile, he certainly did see the smoke trail extend from me toward him. With even a minor amount of intelligence, he would have to have associated the exploding flare with the prey that he was attacking."

"That exploding flare must've been quite a shocking surprise considering that they've never before been shot at by their prey."

"They were surprised and scared away," commented Moose, "but they weren't injured in any way. So, will that shocking surprise deter these two from attacking humans again? If it doesn't, and they do attack humans again, will firing a flare at them cause them to break off the attack, or will they remember that they weren't hurt this time and continue their attack?"

"There's no way we can answer those questions. Firing the flare was a clever idea that worked well this time, but it might not work every time. The safest thing for us to do is to always respond with lethal force when our lives are threatened."

"That's true, but I wanted to find out if I could scare them away."

"I'm glad you did that. It was an exciting experiment, and I was ready with the lethal force just in case the flare didn't work. Now that I might be pregnant, I have to really be careful to stay alive."

"You can't possibly be pregnant yet. I realize that I have some very potent and ambitious sperm, but I don't think they could possibly have already done their job."

"Well, just in case they don't do their job by tonight, I am going to hold you to our plan to try again under the light of a double full moon."

Moose gave his still nude wife and admiring glance, "You don't seriously think that I would try to get out of that, do you?"

Dianne took a few moments to appreciate Moose's admiring gaze, "I think you'll do your part."

For a few moments, Dianne thought about how many years she had waited to finally become pregnant. She fervently hoped that their efforts would be successful. Noticing that she and Moose were still naked, she said, "Maybe we should put some clothes on."

"Why? There's no one here except us, and I rather enjoy being naked."

Dianne felt the warm gentle breeze caress her nude body and said, "I like it too."

Moose left the boat on auto-pilot but slowed it down to the point that its movement was barely perceptible. "I'm going swimming," he said as he dove in.

Dianne scanned the sky and saw nothing of a threatening nature, so she dove in too.

After leisurely swimming around for about ten minutes, they climbed back onto the boat. While drying off, Moose said, "I checked Mike's weather forecast earlier, and he's predicting a pleasant clear night with a gentle breeze and balmy temperatures."

"That's beautiful weather for what we're planning to do this evening."

"Maybe we shouldn't go home afterwards. With pleasant weather and a double full moon for light, I think it would be fun to camp out on the boat tonight."

"I don't know if that's a good idea," commented Dianne.

"Why?"

"After what we just experienced, how are you going to feel comfortable sleeping on the boat?"

"Our radar will warn us if pterodactyls approach. What else are you worried about?"

"We've only been here for twenty-six days. I don't think that's enough time to discover all the dangers that might be here. There might be some extremely dangerous nocturnal predators around that we're unaware of."

"That's a good reason to spend the night on the lake. Maybe, we can discover them, if they exist."

"I don't want to discover nocturnal predators when I'm sound asleep on the deck of this boat."

"Well, I think it would be fun to sail under the light of a double full moon. It would definitely be exotic and would include an element of danger. We can enjoy it until we're tired; then, we can go below deck and sleep for a while. After that, we can get up early and enjoy sailing in the pre-sunrise glow of early dawn. Shortly after sunrise, we can sail into South Bay and await the arrival of our friends from the Challenger."

"But, I didn't pack enough food for us to spend the night."

"I can't believe that you're worried about food. You usually accuse me of being overly concerned about food."

"Well, I didn't think we'd be out all night, and for some reason, we've both been eating more than I thought we would."

"I am beginning to think that you've lost your spirit of adventure. I've never heard so many objections to something as simple as sleeping out on a boat."

"Well, we are on a dangerous planet, and we are low on food."

"I can't eliminate the danger, but I can take care of the food problem," commented Moose as he pointed at his fishing pole.

"There's something else to consider; if everyone comes down in the morning, tomorrow is going to be an active day. If we stay out all night, we aren't going to get much sleep, and being tired will take some of the fun out of the day."

"That's true, but sailing in the moonlight with beautiful weather is just too good an opportunity to pass up. It'll be so much fun that it'll be well worth being tired tomorrow."

"I guess if I'm tired tomorrow, I'll just have to find a little time to take a short nap."

"It sounds like you've just agreed with me."

"Yeah, I guess I have, but tonight won't be very much fun if we're too hungry to enjoy it, so you'd better catch something for us to eat."

"That's a tough challenge," stated Moose as he reached for his fishing gear.

"I am going to try my rainbow pike lure. It has never failed. But before I start fishing, I should roll up the solar sails and pull in the outriggers. If I hook a big one, I want to be able to move around the boat without getting my line tangled up."

After putting the boat in a clean configuration, Moose said, "During all of our recent activity, I haven't paid much attention to our location. I am surprised at how far we've traveled."

"I haven't paid much attention either. Where are we?"

Moose had a portable video screen on deck. With this, he accessed the boat's navigation computer. A map of the lake immediately appeared on the screen. A small blinking red dot indicated their position.

In answer to Dianne's question, Moose said, "We're moving northeast along the northwest shore of the big bay in the northeast corner of the lake."

"Isn't there a big river flowing into this bay?"

"Yeah, there is, and about sixty miles up that river, there's another big lake. Someday, I would like to sail up that river and explore that lake. Wouldn't it be fun to take about a week to make a trip like that?"

"Now that's something I would like to do."

"I'm glad to hear that you aren't completely hopeless."

"You shouldn't interpret my concern about being out all night as an indication that I may have lost my adventurous spirit."

"Well you sure voiced lots of objections."

"I know I did, but I really do want to sail in the moonlight and camp out on the boat. It's just that I expect tomorrow to be an exciting festive day, and I just don't want to be too tired to enjoy it."

"I can understand that, so you sleep as much as you want. I'll stay awake and enjoy sailing until I am too tired to enjoy it, and then, I'll put the boat on auto-pilot and get some sleep."

"It sounds like you're not planning to sleep all that much."

"I've never needed much sleep when there's a party going on, and as far as I am concerned, the party has already started for us."

"Today has definitely been as much fun as I've ever had at any party, but partying always makes me hungry, so when are you going to catch us some food? I am starting to feel famished."

"It seems like we just had lunch a couple hours ago," teased Moose.

"I know, but we've had a lot of activity in the last couple hours. Plus, the thought of the spicy aroma from Cajun spices and the sizzling sound of fresh fish in the frying pan is making my mouth water."

"I think you really are hungry and aren't just teasing me about food," he said to her.

"Yes, I really am."

Moose picked up his fishing pole, offered it to Dianne, and asked, "Would you like the pleasure of catching our dinner?"

"I know how much you enjoy fishing, so you catch one, and I'll cook as much as we need for dinner."

Moose adjusted the boat's speed to what he thought would be a good trawling speed. Then, he dropped the lure into the water and observed its action for a few moments before feeding out about fifty yards of line.

In just a few minutes, Moose's fishing rod bent sharply, and he exclaimed, "I've hooked something big!"

As the minutes went by, Moose patiently played the fish until he was able to bring it near the boat. Then, Dianne reached into the water with a landing net and captured it.

When the fish was on deck, Moose looked at it and said, "This is the smallest rainbow pike we've caught so far. I doubt that it weighs more than about fifteen pounds."

"You're referring to this fish as small? How does it compare to what you caught back on Earth?"

"My favorite fresh water fish was the northern pike. Most of the ones I caught weighed between two pounds and seven pounds. The biggest one I caught weighed eleven pounds."

"It sounds to me like fishing is probably better here."

"Are you trying to tell me that I shouldn't refer to this fish as small?"

"In a round about way, I'm trying to say that, as far as fishing is concerned, you must feel like you are in a dream world."

"No doubt about that. Back on Earth I never once imagined that someday I would look at a fifteen-pound fish and say that it's the smallest I've caught so far, but then, I never imagined that I would move to another planet either."

"I am very happy that you are here with me, so let's celebrate with a fresh fish dinner."

"It doesn't get any fresher than this."

Within minutes, Moose had the fish cleaned and filleted. Dianne immediately selected some choice fillets for the frying pan. While she fixed dinner, Moose put the rest of the fish in the refrigerator and set the table.

After enjoying a delicious meal, Dianne put on a video headset and launched an RPV to explore the countryside. Moose stood guard and studied the slowly passing shoreline that was only about sixty yards away.

Finding interesting plants and creatures to study, Dianne continued her exploration of the country-side until Alpha Centauri A hung low on the western horizon. Then, she returned the RPV, took off the headset, and prepared to enjoy first sunset.

Moose turned the boat away from the waterfront and said, "I don't want to tempt any nocturnal predators to try to swim out to us."

Moose called up a map of the lake, did a position check, and said, "We've moved several miles into the bay, and we're not very far from the mouth of the river."

Moose looked at the map for a few additional moments and said, "We are a full thirty miles from South Bay, and I think it's time to start heading back."

Moose laid out the desired course on the video screen and instructed the boat's auto-pilot to follow it. Then, he programmed in the desired arrival time and said, "Well, there's nothing left for us to do now except enjoy the voyage. Since we're only going to be moving about 2.5 mph, it will be a silent, peaceful cruise on a beautiful, moonlit night."

"Let's enjoy first sunset and a double moonrise, and then second sunset."

"Is that exotic or what?"

"It is compared to what we were accustomed to back on Earth," replied Dianne.

Dianne looked to the east and said, "It looks like I got the order of events mixed up. Aphrodite has already risen, and Alpha Centauri A hasn't yet set."

Moose entered a question into the computer and received an immediate answer. "The double full moon will occur at 10:47 P.M., so both Aphrodite and Nocturne will rise shortly before first sunset," he said.

Gazing at Aphrodite, Dianne said, "It's just as large and beautiful as the full moon back on Earth."

"Even though it's much smaller than Earth's moon, it looks just as big because it's so much closer."

Dianne picked up the binoculars for a closer look at Aphrodite's surface detail.

A few minutes later, Nocturne began to appear on the eastern horizon slightly to the left of Aphrodite. With the binoculars, Dianne watched it slowly move above the horizon. "It appears slightly smaller than Aphrodite."

"Nocturne is actually much bigger than Aphrodite, but it is much farther away and consequently, looks smaller."

Dianne and Moose turned to the west and noted that Alpha Centauri A was laying on the horizon and beginning to slip below it. "This is really wild. We have two full moons and two suns in the sky," Dianne exclaimed.

Moose and Dianne enjoyed the exotic spectacle for a few minutes while Alpha Centauri A gradually disappeared below the western horizon.

Alpha Centauri B was now alone in the western sky. It lay low above the western horizon, and within a half hour, it would also slip below the horizon. Although not very bright when compared to Alpha Centauri A, it was many times brighter than the double full moon, and its dim orange glow colored the lake with a strange orange hue.

Moose and Dianne silently scanned the lake in various directions to soak up the effect of the peculiar lighting. "This is eerie," Dianne said.

"It's bizarre. It really drives home the feeling that we are not on Earth."

"How many times will we have to experience this before it feels normal?"

"I don't know if it will ever feel normal for me," commented Moose. "In just a few weeks, Alpha Centauri A and B will rise and set together. Six months after that, Alcent will be exactly between Alpha Centauri A and B. What will happen then will really seem bizarre. Alpha Centauri B will rise in the east at exactly the same time that Alpha Centauri A sets in the west. We simply won't have any darkness at night. This weird orange glow will light up our world all night long. How can something that eerie feel normal?"

"It'll really be bizarre if we happen to have a double full moon at about that time. Then, we'll have Aphrodite, Nocturne, and Alpha Centauri B moving through the nighttime sky together in a tightly knit little group."

"That will be a weird sight."

"With two moons and two suns, we might come to look upon a clear dark night with a sky full of stars as an unusual event."

"Since arriving here, we've only had one night that was clear and moonless," stated Dianne, "and the sky full of stars was spectacular."

"Clear dark nights aren't going to happen very often for us, but this is the time of the year when that can happen. Six months from now, we'll be well into a two to three month time period when dark nights will be impossible."

"That is going to take some getting use to."

Noting that Alpha Centauri B was about to slip below the western horizon, Moose and Dianne stopped conversing and watched their second sunset of the evening. In silence, they observed and appreciated the natural beauty of one of nature's wonders. Lost in peaceful thought, they continued to gaze across the open water at the western sky for a few minutes after Alpha Centauri B had set.

Suddenly, Dianne's communicator started chirping instantly pulling her out of her thoughtful mental state. Dianne answered the call and found that it was one of her assistants calling from the Challenger.

Dianne was informed that they had finished the additional work that she had requested. As expected, the additional work confirmed previous results, which showed that Zeb's immune system was basically the same as the human immune system, although more sophisticated in some respects.

Before discussing the results in detail with her assistants, Dianne called Connie and Jerry so that they could be included in the discussion. After nearly an hour of discussing Zeb's immune system relative to the human immune system, it was decided that shortcomings in the human immune system relative to Zeb's immune system could be easily compensated for with medical technology.

Consequently, Jerry accessed the Challenger's public address system and loudly announced: "WE HAVE JUST DECIDED THAT HUMANS CAN LIVE AND PROSPER ON ALCENT. ALL OF YOU ARE FREE TO COME DOWN. WE EXPECT TO SEE YOU SHORTLY AFTER SUNRISE TOMORROW."

Moose and Dianne listened to the Captain's announcement as picked up by a microphone onboard the Challenger. Jerry had barely finished speaking when loud cheering resounded throughout the starship.

Moose turned to Dianne and said, "You were worried about being tired tomorrow. How much sleep do you think our friends on the Challenger are going to get tonight?"

"Not much."

"Do you think they'll have any trouble staying awake and enjoying themselves tomorrow?"

"I believe they'll be pumped up from now until bedtime tomorrow night."

"I think they'll be so wildly excited tomorrow that some of their enthusiasm will rub off on you and keep you wide awake, so let's enjoy our moonlight cruise and not worry too much about sleep."

"That sounds like a good plan."

EIGHTEEN

The Beginning of the Future

TIME: Day Twenty-Seven, Early Morning.

With the last vestiges of nighttime darkness lingering overhead, the eastern sky was awash with the glow of early dawn, while the western sky was brightened by Nocturne and Aphrodite. Even though Alpha Centauri A was more than a half-hour away from rising, the air over Clear Lake was pleasantly warm. The region had been in the grip of unusually warm weather for more than two days.

Moose and Dianne sailed all night and approached the south end of Pioneer Island. They were on deck enjoying the mild early morning air.

"What a beautiful morning," remarked Dianne.

"Aren't you glad we spent the night on the lake?"

"It was fun," Dianne said, awash in contentment.

"Even though we didn't get much sleep, you don't seem to be very tired."

Dianne lazily stretched her sleep-deprived body, "I feel tired in a pleasant, laid-back sort of way."

"But you don't seem to be very sleepy."

"I'm not; there's too much excitement in the air."

Moose slowly took a deep breath. "I don't know what you mean; it seems to be ordinary air to me."

He had hardly finished speaking when the quiet early morning atmosphere was suddenly shattered by a sonic boom. "See what I mean; there's excitement in the air," Dianne said.

She looked high in the western sky. She spotted and pointed at what appeared to be a bright fast moving star. "That must be one of our shuttles."

"But its shock wave cannot have reached us yet," commented Moose as he turned to search the northern sky where he quickly spotted a second bright moving object. "That's the shuttle that jolted our senses."

"They sure didn't waste any time coming down. If they were any earlier, they would be landing in the dark."

"As it is, they're going to be on the water before sunrise," stated Moose.

"Maybe, they want to arrive early enough to enjoy their first sunrise in a long, long time and have lots of time to enjoy their first day here."

"I can't blame them for that. I wonder if I should try to catch a rainbow pike and welcome them with a fish feast for breakfast."

"They might really appreciate that, but we do have some fish left over from last night."

"That won't be enough."

"You're probably right, but I think we should get out of their way before you start fishing."

"They won't make their landing run this close to the island, so we're safe in that regard. And we're moving at about the right speed for trawling, so I am going to drop my favorite lure into the water and see what happens. At this speed, it'll be seven or eight minutes before we arrive in South Bay, and that should be enough time to snag a big pike."

"If we weren't trawling on the way in, we could go faster. I would like to be there to greet them when they arrive."

"I know we're going slow, but we should still be there at about the same time they are," said Moose as he dropped his favorite lure into the water.

Just then, Moose and Dianne were jolted by a second sonic boom, and Dianne picked up the binoculars for a better look at the shuttles. "It looks like the cargo shuttle will arrive first," she said.

"Half of them are on that shuttle."

"Splitting them up was a good idea. In case of a tragic accident, we would only lose half of our friends instead of all of them."

"Losing all of them would strike a hard blow at our prime objective. It would be difficult for us to start a new civilization with only four people."

"That's true. It would be difficult, but it wouldn't be impossible. However, I would have to resort to genetic engineering to expand our gene pool."

"I think it would be much better if most of us would survive long enough to have several children."

"I definitely agree, because I don't want to be put into a position where I would have to play God by deciding what our future population should look like and then start altering genes to make it happen."

"I wouldn't want that responsibility either," agreed Moose as he worked his fishing pole to put some erratic action on the lure.

Dianne followed the big shuttle with binoculars and watched it land on its hydrofoils. It ended its landing run about a mile from the south end of Pioneer Island. Dianne felt a growing excitement as she watched the cargo shuttle turn toward South Bay.

Then, Dianne trained her binoculars on the personnel shuttle and watched it make a perfect landing along a course considerably closer to Pioneer Island than that followed by the cargo shuttle. When it finished its landing run, it took up a position about one hundred yards behind the big shuttle.

After just a few minutes, the shuttles were less than two hundred yards from Moose and Dianne. On their present course, they would pass by at a distance of about fifty yards. Watching the shuttles approach enhanced their excitement.

It rose to an even higher level when Moose's communicator started chirping. When Moose answered the call, Mike Johnson responded, boisterously: "Good morning Moose and Dianne!"

"Good morning to you! And welcome to Alcent!" Moose exclaimed quickly.

"Very happy to be here! I have a million activities planned for today, most of which I haven't been able to do in years. You must have a busy day planned too; you're up awfully early."

"Actually, we've been up most of the night. We've been sailing since yesterday morning."

"That's something I haven't done in a few years. Maybe, I can go out for awhile later today. How is the fishing this morning?"

"Fishing's always good. Right now, I'm trying to catch breakfast for everyone."

"We'll be in South Bay in just a few minutes. If you haven't caught any by then, I'll be more than happy to show you how it's done."

Just then, Moose's pole bent sharply as he received a massive strike. "That won't be necessary; I have one on."

The fish swam rapidly away from Moose toward the cargo shuttle, which was now less than a hundred yards away. Moose tightened the drag to slow the fish down because of the risk of the line being cut by the shuttle's propeller. The fish responded by leaping completely out of the water less than ten yards from the shuttle and then swimming rapidly toward Moose who quickly reeled in the slack line.

"What a beauty!" exclaimed Mike. "Good luck landing him. I wasn't able to eat much this morning, but I'm starving now, and I haven't had fresh fish since leaving Earth."

"So far, I haven't lost any," stated Moose as he skillfully played the fish. After a few minutes, Moose had the fish next to the boat, and Dianne captured it with a landing net. While lifting it out of the water, she said, "This one is heavy."

Moose ran a knife through the fish's head, hung it on a scale, and proudly announced, "Thirty-seven pounds."

"More than enough for breakfast," commented Mike.

While Moose secured the fish and put away his fishing gear, Dianne piloted the boat toward South Bay. Wanting to arrive as soon as possible, she ran the boat at full power. Since Mike and the pilot of the personnel shuttle had slowed down considerably upon approaching South Bay, Dianne was able to catch up with them, and all three vehicles dropped anchor at about the same time.

Almost immediately, a large cargo loading door in the side of the cargo shuttle's fuselage was opened and a rolled up deflated pontoon barge was dropped into the water. The activation switch was remotely turned on, and the barge's pontoons immediately began to inflate. As the pontoons inflated, the barge unrolled and the deck planks automatically snapped into place. In less than a minute, the barge was ready for use. Measuring fourteen feet wide by twenty-eight feet long, the pontoon barge was easily able to haul eight thousand pounds and would find many uses besides hauling cargo ashore from the shuttle.

Jerry had parked one of the ATV's on the beach and was now swimming out to the barge towing the plastic cable from the ATV's winch. When Jerry reached the barge he attached the cable to it. Then, he looked up into the smiling eyes of his daughter who was very happy to see him.

"Hi daddy! Is this our new home?" Denise asked.

"Yes, it is."

"It sure has lots of water. Where did it all come from?"

"Rain clouds bring water in from the ocean."

"I watched you swim to this boat. Is swimming fun?"

"It sure is."

"Will you teach me how to swim?"

"Later today, I will give you your first lesson."

"I want to learn how to swim too," declared Matthew who was now standing next to Denise.

"If you need another instructor, I am available," volunteered Michelle.

Mike appeared next to Michelle wearing only a swim suit. "I need to find out if I still know how to swim," said Mike as he dove in. After swimming under water for about a half minute, Mike surfaced and yelled, "It sure feels good to be here."

Meanwhile, six people from the personnel shuttle were rowing ashore in a small inflated boat that they had just deployed. Upon seeing Mike and Jerry having fun in the water, the people still on the personnel shuttle quickly changed into swimwear and dove in to join them.

While all of this was going on, Moose and Dianne were standing on the deck of the submarine shouting greetings to all whose attention they were able to get. Then, Moose proudly held his catch high for all to see and yelled, "Fresh fried fish will be ready shortly for anyone interested in breakfast."

Several people shouted that they were hungry while Moose and Dianne stepped into their small inflated boat and rowed to shore. When Moose and Dianne stepped onto the sandy beach, they greeted the few new arrivals who were already there. Moose picked up his fish and headed for the elevator. Dianne accompanied him, "I'll drive you home; then, I'll return and pick up those who are hungry for an immediate breakfast. I have a feeling that I am going to be a busy taxi driver for a while."

"Judging from the way everyone hungrily stared at my fish, I think I'll be a busy cook for quite some time."

"You can't blame them for that. They haven't eaten real fish in years. But some of them are so wildly excited about finally being here that they're not going to be able to settle down enough to eat anything for a while. So, it'll probably be an hour or two before everyone wanders by for breakfast."

"And not too long after that, some of them will be looking for lunch. I could end up spending the whole day cooking."

"You'll have some help."

"I hope so. Maybe, the best way to handle lunch would be to prepare a picnic table banquet. I could lay out ample portions of all of the smoked delicacies I've made in recent days. Then, people could wander by and eat at their convenience."

"In a couple hours, I'll turn the taxi-driver job over to someone else and help you. I can make some salads and vegetable dishes to add to your lunch banquet."

"Starting at lunch time, I'll keep a bed of charcoal going in case anyone wants charbroiled steak or fish."

"Some fresh rolls would add a nice touch. Maybe, I can talk Connie into making some."

"Cinnamon rolls would be especially good," commented Moose.

"I'll suggest that to her."

"Maybe, we should get some help from the Challenger's chef. He served us very well during our long voyage."

"He is very talented," agreed Dianne, "but this feast will be made almost entirely from local foods that he's not familiar with. I think this has to be our show."

"Okay, but if he hangs around and asks questions about the foods we're serving, I will find a way to put him to work."

"I have no doubt about that."

"I like your idea to have a banquet table set up all day," Dianne said. "I suspect today will be an all day party, and people like to snack continuously at parties."

"Not only that, but I am proud of the smoked foods I've created, and serving them will be fun."

As Dianne brought the ATV to a stop at the campsite, Moose said, "Right now, I'm going to get set up to create the most delicious fish breakfast that any of these people have ever had. It will be second to none."

Driving away from the camp, Dianne called, "I'll have your first customers here shortly."

"I'll be ready."

When Dianne arrived back at the elevator, she looked down on a scene bustling with activity. South Bay was now far different from the quiet deserted place that she had become so accustomed to.

She felt the joy of the newcomers as she watched them find simple ways to celebrate their arrival on Alcent. She watched them experience great pleasure in doing ordinary everyday things that they weren't able to do during their long voyage through interstellar space. Some were swimming vigorously, while others were just playfully splashing around in the water. Some were running barefoot on the beach enjoying the open space and the feel of the sand beneath their feet, while others simply stood still and silently gazed across the water in appreciation of the vastness of Clear Lake. A few were wandering around looking at plants, birds, and insects.

Then, there were those who had chosen to celebrate later and busied themselves with unloading the cargo shuttle. Dianne noted that several boxes, bags, crates, and suitcases had been loaded onto the barge, and that Connie was slowly pulling it toward shore with the ATV's winch.

When the barge ran aground a few feet offshore, a wide plank was set in place, and the barge's passengers stepped ashore. Denise ran to her mother, closely followed by Matthew and Michelle. Connie dropped to her knees and gave her daughter and Matthew a big hug. Then, she stood up and warmly welcomed Michelle to Pioneer Island.

After visiting with Connie for a couple minutes, Michelle turned to Zeb and spoke to him in his language. Obviously excited by Michelle's presence, Zeb stood up and warmly greeted her.

Ready for breakfast and eager to see the view from the plateau, four individuals grabbed their luggage and stepped onto the elevator. Dianne awaited their arrival and greeted them when they reached the plateau. Then, the new arrivals slowly surveyed the surrounding area deeply enjoying the panoramic view. When they finished sightseeing, Dianne gave them a ride to the campsite where Moose served them breakfast while Dianne returned to the south end of the plateau to pick up another group.

Meanwhile, down on the beach, Connie and Michelle were walking barefoot with their children. When they approached a bush, they heard a bird chirping out a cheerful song. The song was immediately answered by another bird in a nearby bush.

Denise turned to her mother and asked, "Are songbirds making those pretty sounds?"

"Yes."

"I want to see them. Where are they?"

Connie pointed at the closest shrub and said, "One of them is in that bush. He's hiding behind some leaves near the top. If you look closely, you can see him. He's green with red stripes on his wings."

Both Matthew and Denise stared intently where Connie was pointing. Then, the bird fluttered into a new position and again chirped out its song.

"I see him!" they both exclaimed.

"He's really pretty!" Denise said.

She headed toward the bush for a closer look. Spooked by her rapid approach, the bird flew away, and Denise asked, "Did I scare him?"

"Yes, you did."

Then, a couple sea gulls flew over, and Denise asked, "Are those songbirds too?"

"They can make lots of noise, but they don't sing pretty songs."

"I like songbirds," Denise said. "They're fun to listen to."

Just then, King soared overhead and Denise exclaimed, "That's really a big bird! I'm afraid. Could he pick me up and carry me away?"

"Yes he could, but so far, he's been our friend. He saved my life one night when he killed another pterodactyl that was about to attack me."

"Were you afraid?"

"It happened so fast that it was over before I had a chance to be afraid."

"Will he protect me too?"

"I hope so, but if he doesn't, your father and I will."

Satisfied with Connie's answer, Denise continued to stare in awe at the big pterodactyl that was still circling South Bay and gazing down on all the new activity.

Noting her daughter's continuing interest, Connie said, "His name is King, and he lives on Western Island."

Then, a second pterodactyl arrived on the scene, and Denise asked, "Does that one live on Western Island too?"

"Her name is Queen, and she does live on Western Island. King and Queen are mates, and they have a baby that they are taking care of."

"They're sure taking a close look at everything going on here, but they don't seem to be alarmed by it," Michelle said.

"They've always been curious about us, but we've never given them any reason to think of us as enemies."

"How can we be sure that they aren't trying to decide which one of us would be a good breakfast?"

"We can't be certain, but these two are so skilled at catching fish that they don't need to view us as possible prey."

"Are you saying that we don't need to fear them as long as we don't threaten them in any way?"

"They've never acted threatening toward us, but they are wild creatures and are very capable killing machines."

"Fortunately, the most dramatic demonstration of that ability was when it was used to save your life."

"But we don't know if King intended to save my life or was simply killing an enemy."

"Whichever, the effect is the same; you and Dianne are both still alive."

"While the effect is the same, the implications are very different."

"I can't argue with that. If King was actually protecting you, we might have a pair of fierce flying guard dogs. But why would they want to be our protectors? They are wild creatures who are very skilled at taking care of themselves. What do they need us for?"

"A few days after our arrival, we solved a big problem for them."

"Are you suggesting that King was paying a debt?"

"Maybe, but they've also spent a lot of time observing us. If they have any intelligence at all and are capable of even elementary reasoning, they would have to conclude that we are vastly superior to them and that it might be to their advantage to be friends with us. They may even have decided that we could easily kill them if we wanted to."

"If they've concluded that we could kill them, why don't they just fly off to another part of the planet far away from here?"

"Maybe, they like us, or maybe, they think of us as benevolent gods. After all, they've seen our shuttles and para-wings descend out of the heavens, and they've seen our shuttles ascend back into the heavens. Maybe, they think it is to their advantage to try to win our appreciation whenever the opportunity arises, so that we will help them if they ever again need us."

"It seems like the answers to all of our questions about them begin with *if* or *maybe*."

"Unfortunately, that's true. We just don't have any concrete answers, and until we do, we have no choice but to respect the fact that they are wild creatures with awesome killing ability."

Michelle looked up at the huge flying creatures and was impressed by how graceful they looked. She watched them circle South Bay one last time before flying off toward the southeast. Then, she said, "I guess they've satisfied their curiosity."

"Either that or they're hungry and looking for a fish breakfast."

"I could go for that myself," responded Michelle. "It's been a few years since I've eaten real fish."

"I haven't had any since yesterday," stated Connie, smugly.

"You couldn't resist saying that could you?"

Connie simply smiled in response and Michelle said, "If you're not yet hungry for more fish, I'll eat your share."

"That won't be necessary; my appetite's been pretty good. In fact, it seems like I'm always hungry."

"Maybe, you're pregnant."

Connie smiled in response to the suggestion, "No, I think it's our active life style, plus the food here is really good. But Jerry and I have been thinking about getting pregnant soon."

"Mike and I have been talking about that too. And I've also heard others talking about it."

"It sounds like we might have a baby boom in nine to twelve months," commented Connie.

"They've all been waiting for several years to start their families. And we've been waiting for several years to expand ours."

"Hopefully, we'll have our homes built by then."

"The spaciousness of a large permanent home would be helpful in raising a large family," commented Michelle. "However, the prefabricated temporary shelters that we'll be living in while we're building our permanent homes will be quite comfortable. They'll have a bedroom, a bathroom, and a kitchen; and they will be equipped with electrical power and indoor plumbing. They will be small with a total floor space of only 16 X 32, but we'll be outside most of the time anyway."

"I think they will be adequate for two people, but for you and for us, there will be three people. For the sake of privacy, I would sure like to have a small second bedroom for Denise to sleep in."

"Mike and I've talked about that. We've considered several interior arrangements, and we've figured out a way to have a second bedroom. It'll be small but adequate for a child to sleep in."

"I'd like to see that floor plan."

"I'll sketch it out for you while we're eating breakfast."

"Okay," replied Connie.

Matthew interrupted the conversation between Connie and Michelle when he grasped one of Michelle's hands and asked, "May I play in the water?"

Michelle glanced at South Bay. Then, she gazed at the vastness of Clear Lake and wondered what dangers it might contain. After considering that four of her fellow pioneers had already been swimming in this lake for several weeks, Michelle looked into her son's eyes and noted how eager he was to have fun in the water, so she said, "Okay, but don't go out very far."

Denise immediately grabbed one of Connie's hands and enthusiastically said, "I want to play in the water too,"

Believing that it was safe for the children to play in the shallow water along the sandy beach, Connie said, "Okay, but let's head toward the elevator, so we can go eat breakfast."

Matthew and Denise repeatedly ran into and out of the lake, gleefully splashing water on each other. By the time they arrived at the elevator, they were completely soaked. Michelle opened her luggage and removed two towels and some dry clothing for them. After drying off and changing clothes, the children reluctantly stepped into the elevator cage at the urging of their mothers.

Denise stared at the open elevator car and its rugged rustic structure and said, "The Challenger has better elevators."

"Is this one safe?" Matthew asked, appearing worried.

"We use it every day," replied Connie in a reassuring way.

Connie was about to start the elevator's ascent but stopped when she heard "wait for us" and recognized Jerry's voice. A few moments later, Jerry and Mike boarded the elevator, and all six headed for the plateau.

As the elevator car steadily gained height, it wiggled and creaked renewing Denise's and Matthew's concern. Jerry assured them that it was perfectly safe, but the continued wiggling and creaking gave them the feeling of possible danger. As the open elevator car continued its ascent, Matthew and Denise looked down at the beach, now more than one hundred feet below them. The perception of great height added to the anxiety they felt. However, even though they were fearful for their safety, they couldn't help enjoying the thrill of ascending the face of a vertical cliff in an open-air elevator. But when the elevator car reached the plateau, Matthew and Denise were the first to step off.

Dianne greeted them and asked, "Did you enjoy the ride?"

Instantly, both children exclaimed in unison, "It was scary!"

After a moment of thought, Denise repeated her earlier comment, "The Challenger has better elevators."

"But was it fun?" asked Dianne in a persistent way.

"Yes, but it was scary," they repeated.

"Want to have some more fun?" asked Dianne.

Feeling a bit apprehensive, but not wanting to miss out on anything, Matthew hesitantly said, "Yes."

Denise followed his lead and also said, "Yes."

"Okay, I'll give you an ATV ride."

Both children looked at the ATV. "I've never had a ride in anything like that. Is it fun?" Denise asked.

Before Dianne could answer the question, Matthew declared, "I think it will be fun." Then, he eagerly ran toward the ATV. Afraid that she might miss out on some excitement, Denise immediately charged after him.

Michelle turned to Dianne and said, "If you could entertain your eager passengers for a few minutes, I would appreciate it. I want to take a brief look around before we head for camp."

"That should be easy. I'll just give them a ride and answer their questions."

"That could keep you busy all day."

"I don't mind. They're so eager to learn that teaching them is fun."

When Dianne started walking toward the ATV, Connie said, "I'll go with you and field some of their questions."

Mike turned to Jerry and suggested, "Why don't we walk to camp. That will give me more time to look at the plateau and give us a chance to discuss today's plans."

"Good idea," replied Jerry.

"Would you like to join us?" Mike asked Michelle.

"Thanks for the invite, but I think I will stay here and silently enjoy the scenery while I wait for an ATV ride."

"I'm not comfortable with leaving you alone," replied Mike.

"I should be safe here on the plateau. Anyway, I have my weapons, and I'll stay alert."

Mike considered Michelle's comments while looking around. Then, he gave her an affectionate hug and said, "I think you're right, but I will be looking back in this direction occasionally."

"Thank you for your concern."

Mike smiled at his wife reassuringly; then, he and Jerry headed toward camp.

For a few moments, Michelle watched Mike and Jerry walk away; then, she slowly turned and gazed in all directions. As she leisurely feasted her eyes on the natural scenic beauty surrounding her, a deep joyful happiness welled up inside her and filled her entire being.

She stepped to the edge of the plateau and looked down at the nuclear powered shuttles anchored in the bay. She focused her attention on the big cargo shuttle and recalled how she had become a part of this mission by hiding in it with Mike for a few days. She recalled the night on the Challenger's observation deck when Mike showed her the spectacular beauties of the universe. She remembered how he had patiently waited for her to become enthralled by the glittering beauty surrounding her. He then used his masculine charm to entice her into forever leaving the comfortable secure life that she had known on Earth in return for the uncertainties of being an interstellar pioneer. That night, long ago, Alpha Centauri A was nothing more than an unusually bright star that stood out prominently against the stellar background. It was so distant, while the comforts of Earth were so close. The hazardous journey to Alpha Centauri A would take nearly seven years, while the comforts of Earth were only a few hours away.

Michelle recalled that it was her emotions that made the decision to come here, for she was in love with Mike, was carrying his child, and did not want to pull him away from a lifelong dream. Mike had made it clear that he would not come here without her.

She fleetingly glanced at Alpha Centauri A and thought, now, it is no longer just a bright star; it is as brilliant as the Sun is back on Earth, and here on Alcent, it is my source of heat, light, and life itself. Now, it is the Sun that is nothing more than a bright star in the nighttime sky, and Earth is so far away that we cannot see it even with the Challenger's most powerful telescope. Earth is now so far away that two-way communication is even difficult, for it takes 4.35 years for a transmission to reach them and another 4.35 years for a response to reach us. Practically speaking, I have been cut off from my birthplace. This is now my home.

Her attention shifted to Zeb who was down on the beach sitting in his wheelchair watching the activities of the newcomers. Michelle thought, when I left Earth, I never imagined that we would discover a race of technologically advanced humanoids or that I would write a biography for one of them. Perhaps, I should also write biographies for Rex and Shannon. Three life stories taken together should give us pretty good insight into life on B-2 and here for that matter. We now know about three earth-like planets. I wonder why humanoid life evolved on Earth and B-2 but not on Alcent.

Michelle's gaze shifted to the now empty barge that was being moved back to the cargo shuttle for a second load. She noticed that Zeb was looking up at her, and she yelled, "Want to join us for breakfast?"

Zeb responded with an eager, "Yes," and headed toward the elevator, which Michelle immediately sent down.

While Zeb rode up on the elevator, Michelle took another look at the panoramic view and thought, what a wonderful place to live. I am glad I came here. By the time Zeb arrived, the ATV and its occupants had returned. Michelle gazed at the children and saw that they were wildly excited, "What did you do to them?" she asked Dianne.

Wearing a naughty grin, Dianne said, "Well, it's possible that I may have driven a little too fast, and maybe, I might have turned some corners with a little too much speed."

Dianne had hardly finished speaking, when Connie exclaimed, "That's a gross understatement! In reality, she came close to being a reckless driver. But now that I've said that, I do have to admit that it was thrilling."

"She is exaggerating with her reckless driving charge," countered Dianne. "We were never in any danger. I was just showing the children how much fun riding an ATV can be."

"She definitely accomplished that," stated Connie.

Michelle turned her attention to the children and again noted how delighted they were. But before she could question them, Denise said, "It was scary, but it was fun."

Michelle turned to Matthew, who said, "Living here is more fun than living on the Challenger."

Michelle beamed when she heard her son's comment. "I think we were unnecessarily concerned when we were worried about them adjusting to their new home," she said to Connie.

"They are definitely thrilled about being here," commented Connie.

The naughty grin returned to Dianne's face, and she said, "You can thank me for giving them their latest thrill."

"I think I should thank you for not killing us! That was a wild ride!" Connie exclaimed quickly.

Dianne looked at Connie, but before she could respond to her bantering remarks, Matthew said, "I'm hungry. When can we eat breakfast?"

"I'm hungry too," Michelle said. Then, she turned to Dianne and asked "Is it safe for me to ride the ATV or should I walk to camp?"

"It's fun, Mom. Hop in!" Matthew piped up.

"Does that answer your question?" Dianne asked Michelle.

"Well, I guess I could take a chance," commented Michelle as she joined Dianne, Connie, and the children in the ATV and headed for camp.

After about a minute had gone by, Michelle asked Dianne, "Why are you driving so slow?"

"I don't want you and Connie to feel like your lives are in danger. Besides that, I have to go slow so that Zeb can keep up with us in his wheelchair."

"Going fast is more fun," commented Matthew.

Meanwhile, Mike and Jerry were leisurely walking to camp and once again, Mike said, "This wide open space sure feels good. It seems like I've been cooped up inside a spaceship forever."

"Well, it was a rather long journey."

"That has to be the understatement of the year. I've been in space nearly seven years, and I've traveled a distance of 25 trillion miles at nearly 3/4 the speed of light, and you call it a rather long journey."

"Well, it was a rather long journey."

"It was an incredibly long journey, and I am glad that I am finally here."

"I still remember the time when you walked into my office and requested that you be replaced."

"I do too, and you don't know how happy I am that I didn't have to stay behind."

After a few moments of silence, Jerry said, "If you had been unable to persuade Michelle to leave Earth, do you think you actually would've stayed behind? Would you have actually passed up going on the greatest adventure in history?"

"I was prepared to do that, but I was confident that I wouldn't have to."

"But you weren't certain, because you did arrange for a replacement."

"I had to do that, because in order to make the stowaway plan work, I had to be free of the worries of keeping a starship ticking. But it all worked out, I have my wife and son here with me, and you were able to get your best friend on the ship."

"It's possible that my wonderful wife is alive only because of that replacement request you made years ago," Jerry said.

"What do you mean?"

"Remember the attack by the saber-tooth cats?"

"That was a close call."

"The first cat attacked Charlie and that attack was so sudden that that cat might have been able to kill Connie if Charlie hadn't been there."

"Now, I see what you're getting at. Building Charlie was Moose's idea, and if Moose weren't here, then Charlie might not have been built."

"It's possible someone else might have come up with the idea, but I prefer to give Moose the credit for saving Connie's life."

Mike chuckled softly. "What are you laughing at?" Jerry asked.

"I was just thinking about how upset some of the NASA bureaucrats were at you for putting Moose on the ship in my place."

Mike noticed that Jerry was now laughing in a seemingly self-satisfied way, so he said, "Why do I get the feeling that you enjoyed ignoring their multitudes of rules and procedures and acting on your own?"

"Cooperating with slow-moving bureaucracies has never been one of my strong points, and thumbing my nose at them was fun. Anyway, putting Moose on the ship was a spur of the moment idea that I wanted to implement, and it was impossible to do that working within the system. I had to bypass them."

"As it turns out, you made the right choice. It's possible that Connie is alive only because you bypassed the normal channels of authority and acted on your own."

After walking in silence and looking around for a few minutes, Mike said, "I'd sure like to take this entire day and do nothing except explore this place and maybe go sailing for a few hours, but that's going to have to wait until we get our projects done."

"There's only one big project that we should do today, and that's assembling our community bathroom. But that should be an easy one-day job. The building consists almost entirely of prefabricated panels that we just snap together. The floor panels have short adjustable legs for easy leveling, and the sinks, toilets, and showers were specially designed for quick easy installation."

"Besides sticking that stuff together, all we have to do is hook up the waste processing tanks, water supply, and electricity. I think we'll have the facility operational by early afternoon."

"I think you're being very optimistic."

"I don't think so. We have a highly motivated group of workers who want lots of time to explore the island today. During recent days, we've taken a detailed look at putting this thing together. We've formed crews to perform specific tasks. As much as possible, different parts of the project will be done at the same time. As we speak, the components for the facility are being unloaded from the shuttles. If you'll look back toward the elevator, you'll see that the trailer for hauling the components is already being assembled and some of the components for the building are being brought up."

Jerry stopped walking, looked back toward the elevator and said, "They are busy, and between hauling people and towing that trailer, our ATVs are going to be busy too."

"We thought about bringing another one down, but there wasn't room for it. In addition to the bathroom facility and trailer, we brought down tents, camp equipment, and personal items. Both shuttles were fully loaded."

"How much vacation time do you think we should have before we start building temporary homes?"

"We've been in space for so long that I think everyone will be content to live in tents for a few weeks in order to have ample time to enjoy outdoor recreational activities and do some exploring."

"That sounds reasonable. During that time, we can divide this plateau into plots of land and draw numbers out of a hat to decide who gets which plot."

"I like that idea. While we're vacationing, we can get acquainted with our property and start making plans as to what we want to do with it. It will be fun to look at a piece of land and think about where to build a home, where to plant a garden, where to plant fruit trees."

"That will be fun. Moose and Dianne, and Connie and I have been here for almost a month. We aren't really in need of a vacation. So, I think tomorrow we'll figure out an equitable division of the plateau. Tomorrow evening, we can draw numbers to see who gets what. Maybe, the next day, Moose and I will take the cargo shuttle up to the Challenger and start bringing down the materials we need to build our temporary homes. Then, we can start building them the next day."

"If you're going up to the Challenger, you might consider bringing down the other two ATVs. Also, there's another trailer up there that might be convenient to have down here. And don't forget the water glider that we built. It could add a lot of fun to our vacation. It will carry two people, and with any wind at all, it should zip around on this lake like a speed boat. It would provide a quick convenient way for people to take a look at the surrounding countryside."

"If I bring all that down, I'm not going to have much room for building materials."

"That's true, because everyone who came down today will probably have a list of appliances, equipment and personal items they'll want brought down too. We had the shuttles fully packed, and we just simply couldn't bring everything down that everyone wanted to bring down."

"I think Moose and I will make two trips up there, one the day after tomorrow, and another the day after that. And I think I'll ask for a couple volunteers to go with us to help load the shuttle."

"What if no one wants to interrupt their vacation to go with you?"

"Then, I'll have to offer them an incentive."

"What do you have in mind?"

"The two volunteers will be the first to use the water glider. It'll be theirs for four hours."

"It'll be theirs for four hours after you and I check it out to make sure that it's working properly."

"Of course. After all, we can't put our people at risk with an untried piece of equipment."

Mike and Jerry walked in silence for a few moments. "I smell fish frying, and it smells so good that it's making my stomach growl," Mike said.

"The seafood here is delicious. You're in for a gourmet treat."

After breakfast, Jerry and Mike selected a site for the community bathroom and construction started immediately. As Mike had predicted, the workers were eager to get the project done and worked with utmost speed and efficiency. The prefabricated pieces of the facility were quickly put together, and by early afternoon, the project was complete.

Everyone stepped back and admired the new building.

Matthew got Mike's attention and asked, "Does it work? I need to go to the bathroom."

"Go in and try it out," Mike replied. "Use this side. It is for boys, the other side is for girls."

While Matthew went into the building to put it to the test, Michelle asked, "How long will it be before we have hot water? I would like to try out one of the showers?"

"It won't be long," responded Mike. "We have lots of power right now. With a clear sky, we're getting peak solar power, and the breeze out of the south is strong enough for the wind turbine to generate a generous power output."

"This breeze is very warm, almost hot," commented Michelle.

"It is hot," stated Mike. "Current temperature is ninety-one degrees. Why don't you forget about taking a shower. Let's just go swimming."

"That's a good idea, but let's wait for Matthew."

A few minutes later, Matthew emerged from the new bathroom and said, "It works."

Then, he looked around and sounding concerned asked, "Where are we going to sleep tonight?"

"We're going to sleep in a tent," Mike answered.

"That's camping out, isn't it?"

"Yes, it is."

"I think that'll be fun," Matthew said eagerly.

An expression of concern gradually appeared on his face. "Will we be safe from dinosaurs in our tent?" he asked.

"There aren't any dinosaurs on this island," replied Mike reassuringly.

Matthew thought about the reply for a few moments. Seemingly satisfied, he went on to the next question, "How big will our tent be?"

"It will be large enough for us."

"I want to see it. Can I help you set it up?"

"Yes, you can."

Mike looked at Michelle and said, "Let's set up our tent and then go swimming."

Mike and Michelle selected a site about forty yards from the bathroom and, with Matthew helping, proceeded to set up their tent. Forty-five minutes later, the tent was set up, the air mattress beds were laid out, and personal items were stashed inside.

While Matthew was inside checking out his bed, Mike and Michelle were outside taking a look at their handiwork. Michelle said, "It looks pretty good as far as tents go."

"It's going to be our home for a while."

"I feel like I'm on a camping trip, except I've never had this large a tent on any of my camp outs."

"Ten by twenty is also larger than any tent I ever had on a camping trip, but all of my camp outs were backpack trips."

"The thing I like most about this tent is the panel floor supported three inches above ground by plastic rails. We don't have to worry about having a wet floor when it rains, and our beds will be flat and comfortable, no bumps under the air mattresses."

"I like the sturdy construction," stated Mike. "The material is tough, and the frame is strong. This tent will withstand some pretty stormy weather."

"Also, it looks like it won't be hot inside on a warm day like today. The material is very reflective, and the tent has large screened openings on all sides."

"I am happy with it," declared Mike. "Let's get Matthew and go swimming."

Michelle looked into the tent to see why Matthew hadn't yet come out. She turned to Mike and said, "It looks like Matthew is happy with it too. He's sound asleep in there."

"I don't think we should wake him. There are enough people here to keep an eye on him. Let's go swimming without him. We can take him later."

"Good idea. He got up as early as the rest of us, and he's been active. As fast as he passed out, he must be exhausted."

Michelle found Connie, who said, "Denise is taking a nap too. She ran out of energy a little while ago and stretched out on our bed. She fell asleep instantly."

"They've both been very active."

"And curious. I am pleased with how interested they are in everything they encounter."

"This is a big, new world for them," commented Michelle.

"I can't wait to take them for a submarine ride and show them the underwater world."

"Maybe, we should do that before we start teaching them how to swim. It'll give them some insight into the water world they'll be playing in."

"I am first on the list for the submarine," stated Mike. "We have a 4:00 P.M. reservation."

"How did you get the first reservation?" asked Michelle.

"We drew numbers, and I drew the third spot. Then, I managed to talk the first place people into trading with me."

"How did you do that?"

"They were in last place for use of the ATV that's down on the beach. I drew second place, so we did some trading."

"I like the trade. A trip into the underwater world and some sailing will be worth the delay in driving around the island."

"I think so too. Besides that, in a couple days, we'll probably have the other two ATVs down here anyway."

"I am hot and sweaty," stated Michelle. "I need a good refreshing swim."

"I do too," declared Mike.

"I'll wake the children in time for our 4:00 o'clock cruise," Connie said, "and we'll meet you on the beach. So, just relax and enjoy your swim."

"I will. I haven't been in years, and it's a good day for it."

An hour later, Jerry, Connie, Denise, and Matthew stepped into the ATV and headed for South Bay.

"Are we going swimming?" asked Denise.

"We're going for a submarine ride," replied Jerry. "I want to show you the underwater world."

"That's where fish live," stated Matthew.

"Will we see fish?" asked Denise.

"Yes, we will," replied Jerry.

"How deep is the water?" asked Matthew.

"In some places, it is as deep as this plateau is long," replied Jerry.

"That's really deep," stated Matthew.

"Is it scary that deep down?" asked Denise.

"Our submarine is very strong. It will protect us, and you will have fun."

A short time later, Jerry, Connie, Denise, Mike, Michelle, and Matthew were on the submarine and sailing out of South Bay. Even before leaving the bay, Jerry took the little submarine down to about ten feet off the bottom.

Denise and Matthew stared at the exotic underwater scenery in wide-eyed fascination. For them, this was like a journey into fantasy land, for they had never experienced anything like this underwater world teeming with life. They asked questions almost faster than the adults could answer them. It took a full hour of underwater cruising to satisfy their curiosity. Then, hunger took over, and they asked for dinner.

Honoring their request, Jerry said, "Let's surface. We have just enough breeze to do some pleasant sailing. While we're doing that, we can eat dinner."

"I am ready for some sailing," said Mike.

After surfacing, Jerry and Mike rigged the boat for sailing while Connie and Michelle served dinner to the children. Then, except for Mike, the adults ate dinner. Mike was too busy having fun sailing and said he would eat later.

A little later, when first sunset was only about a half hour away, Michelle said, "I think we should head for home. I would like to see my first double sunset from the plateau."

Mike agreed with his wife's suggestion and set course for South Bay.

Twenty-five minutes later, they stepped off the elevator onto the plateau, and Mike said, "We're here right on time. Alpha Centauri A is lying on the horizon."

A few minutes later, Alpha Centauri A disappeared below the horizon, and the orange light of Alpha Centauri B dominated the area.

For Matthew and Denise, this was truly amazing, for they had never before seen a sunset, let alone, a double sunset. As had been the case so many times on this day, they watched in spellbound fascination.

While looking concerned by what was happening, Denise asked, "Is the orange sun going to go away too?"

"Pretty soon, it will set too," responded Connie.

"But then it will be dark," commented Denise. "On our starship, it only got dark when we turned out the lights."

"Here it gets dark after both of our suns set."

"When will our suns come back?"

Connie pointed to the east and said, "Tomorrow morning both of our suns will rise over there, and a new day will begin."

Denise appeared puzzled by the fact that night and day would no longer be controlled by the flick of a switch. "Will we still have lights to see with at night?" she asked.

"Yes."

Matthew turned to Mike and asked, "Will we have lights in our tent?"

"Yes."

Matthew and Denise continued asking questions until Alpha Centauri B set. Then, the pioneers headed for camp, which now looked like a tent campground back on Earth, including a large blazing campfire.

When they arrived in camp, Michelle said, "This has been a long day, and I am tired and ready for about ten hours of sleep. But before I go to bed, I am going to take a shower, relax next to the campfire, and enjoy the nighttime scene for a while. If my energy holds up, I will stay up for first and second moonrise."

"I like that plan," stated Mike, "and since I haven't had dinner yet, I am going to try roasting some of Moose's smoked sausage over the campfire."

"Sounds like a good old-fashioned wiener roast to me," remarked Jerry.

"Kind of, except I won't be roasting wieners, I'll be roasting dinosaur sausage."

"I think you'll find that it tastes better than wieners," commented Jerry. "Moose did a good job making that sausage. The seasoning is excellent. The texture is good, and the smoke flavor has a pleasing taste."

"You're making me hungry. I think I'll take my shower later and eat dinner now."

"Save some for me," requested Michelle as she headed for the shower.

"I'll have one ready for you."

Twenty minutes later, feeling refreshed, Michelle joined Mike and Matthew by the campfire. Mike immediately handed her a roasted sausage in a bun and said, "Taste this."

Michelle did as directed and exclaimed, "This is very good! Can I have it?"

"It's yours. I'll make another."

"Can I have one more?" asked Matthew.

"You sure can," replied Mike.

Jerry turned to Connie, "It appears that the new arrivals like the food here."

Before Connie could comment, Moose said, "It seems like my culinary talents are once again being recognized."

"That almost sounds like bragging, but all of his creations have tasted so good that I cannot dispute his claim," Mike said to Jerry.

"I think it's his insatiable appetite that makes him a natural at food research and development."

"He does like to eat," agreed Mike. "It probably won't be long and he'll figure out how to make a good pizza using only local ingredients."

"That's a good idea," stated Moose. "I'll start working on that tomorrow, but it's going to be a couple weeks before the wild rice is ripe. At the moment, that's my only possible local source of flour. The tomato based sauce will also be a problem."

"It sounds like you've already thought about this," commented Jerry.

"Of course, pizza is one of my favorite foods."

While munching on a piece of sausage, Michelle said to Moose, "If your pizza turns out as good as this sausage, you're going to have lots of contented customers."

"I will experiment with it until it is," stated Moose in a matter of fact way.

Michelle thought about Moose's confident attitude for a few moments. "Your confidence is justified. I've eaten a big variety of excellent food today, and nearly all of it came from here."

"I cannot take credit for all of it," responded Moose. "Finding good food was a team effort. Each of us contributed to it in a significant way."

"I am amazed with what the four of you have accomplished," commented Michelle. "Think about it: you landed on an alien planet. Then, in less than thirty days, you not only explored this area and turned it into a home, but you've also identified and tested enough local foods to make us independent of our food synthesizers."

"We have accomplished a lot," agreed Connie, "but I am especially pleased that we've suffered no serious illnesses or infections."

"That is something to be thankful for," stated Michelle.

"While it is something to be thankful for, we must keep in mind that we've only been here four weeks," Connie said. "I think that it's too soon to disregard the dangers posed by microorganisms, but it is encouraging to note that our experience to date indicates that they won't be any more of a problem here than they were back on Earth."

"The fact that Zeb has survived here for a long time with an immune system similar to ours adds validity to that opinion," stated Dianne.

"But he was near death when we found him, and even though dangerous microorganisms are probably rare, they do exist. Finding them will continue to be one of my most important research projects."

"You will have help," declared Dianne.

"That's good, because it is a life-long project."

"I have a big project too," stated Mike, "but hopefully, it won't take the rest of my life to complete."

"What project are you talking about?" asked Connie.

"It's an important project. It will be hard work, but it will be fun."

"That really doesn't answer my question. What project are you talking about?"

"I am talking about designing and building a house."

Noticeably excited, Michelle quickly said, "I would like to help. When can we start?"

"First we need to build our temporary home, and I would like to get that done during the next few weeks. By then, we'll be tired of living in our tent."

"That's true," agreed Michelle, "but our tent is sturdy and quite spacious as far as camping tents go, and I think we should relocate it next to our temporary home and use it for dry storage. Since our temporary home will be small, we'll need the extra space."

"I agree, and the fact that our temporary home will be small leads into my concept for our permanent home. Basically, we need to gain living space quickly in the interest of being comfortable, and the quickest way to do that is to add a room to our temporary home. But, adding a room can be more than just adding a room. It can be the first step in building our permanent home."

Michelle thought about Mike's comments, "If I understand you correctly, you are planning to design a home that can be built in sections rather than one where the entire structure is built at the same time," she said.

"That's correct, but in addition, I plan to make our temporary home an integral part of the design for our permanent home. By doing it that way, we will actually be building the first section of our permanent home when we set up our prefabricated temporary home."

"I like the idea," commented Michelle. "Each section that we build will give us additional living space long before the entire structure is complete."

"That's the objective I want to achieve," stated Mike. "Considering the number of homes that we need to build, it will take years to complete all of them. However, building homes a section at a time will quickly provide additional space."

"That is a good idea," agreed Jerry. "Have you thought about what materials you're going to build your home with?"

"I am thinking about building the walls with rocks and the roof with some good solid timber."

"Are you building a house or a fortress?" asked Moose.

"I intend for my house to be my fortress. When I go to bed at night, I like to sleep peacefully."

"Does that mean sleeping in a tent will be difficult for you?" asked Connie.

"No, we'll have armed guards on duty besides all of our other security measures. But eventually, we'll all be living in permanent homes, and I think they should be rugged enough so that we can dispense with the guards."

"But there aren't any large animals on this plateau," stated Dianne.

"You haven't lived here long enough to know that that is always going to be the case. Besides, weren't you almost killed by a pterodactyl?"

"Both of your points are true," admitted Dianne.

"I like the idea of our home being a fortress," stated Michelle. "When we're in our home, we should be able to relax and not worry about danger."

"That's my objective," stated Mike.

"Can we build a rugged home that also looks good?" asked Michelle.

"Earlier today, I took a good look at the rock slide at the north end of this plateau. I was impressed by the colors and color patterns in some of the rocks. With some careful picking and choosing, we should be able to build a very attractive home."

"What kind of mortar are we going to set the rocks in?" asked Michelle.

"Our plastics technology is so good that we can easily manufacture resins with any characteristics we want, and we have plenty of sand on our beaches. We can make a mortar that is as strong as the rocks themselves. Also, we can add pigment to make the mortar whatever color we want, or we can go with the natural sand color."

"Talking about this is getting me excited," stated Michelle. "I'd like to start building tomorrow."

"First, we'll have to find out which piece of land is going to be ours, so that we'll have a place to build."

Michelle turned to Jerry who anticipated her question. "Tomorrow morning, we'll divide the plateau into public and private land," he said. "Then, we'll divide the private land into lots and have a drawing to decide who gets which lot. Anyone who isn't happy with the lot they get will be free to trade with whomever they are able to arrange a trade with."

"How could anyone be unhappy with any lot here on the plateau?" Michelle asked. "All lots will be choice view property. I feel almost like we are living in paradise."

"We did look at the entire planet before choosing this location," remarked Connie.

"Based on what I've seen today, I think we made the best possible choice," stated Michelle.

"As soon as we find out which part of this plateau is ours, I want to start turning it into our home," Michelle said to Mike. "We can start by deciding where on our land we want to build our house, plant a garden, and plant some fruit trees. We can even start gathering rocks for our house."

Mike grinned at Michelle and said, "You're awfully ambitious considering that just a little while ago, you told me that you were ready for a long night of sleep."

"Well, it is beautiful here, and the idea that this is going to be our home has really gotten to me. We're very fortunate to have such a picturesque place to live."

"When you think about how far we've traveled and all that we've been through, we really have a lot to be thankful for," Michelle said. "In fact, I think we should celebrate this day every year in thanksgiving for our safe arrival and our good fortune of finding such a wonderful place to build our homes."

"This day could also be viewed as the beginning of our civilization," commented Jerry. "When four of us arrived here a month ago, it wasn't certain that we could live here, but now, we are confident that our immune systems can defend us against this planet's microbes. Consequently, we've brought everyone down, and we are ready to build a new civilization, the first to be totally independent of Earth."

"We have a big job ahead of us," declared Connie, "but I am excited by the challenge."

"It will be a lifelong challenge," added Jerry.

"Looking at the big picture, it is much more than that," commented Connie. "Building a new civilization is a process that will continue for many generations. For each generation, it will be a lifelong challenge that must be successfully met."

"That's true," agreed Jerry, "but our challenge is to get our new civilization off to a good solid start. We must build a solid foundation for it, something that each succeeding generation can build on. We are the founding fathers."

"And the founding mothers," declared Connie.

With Michelle nodding in agreement, Dianne said to Connie, "Thank you for including us."

With Connie, Michelle, Dianne, Mike and Moose looking at him, Jerry felt like he was on the proverbial hot seat and quickly said, "I was using the term *founding fathers* in a gender-neutral way."

With Mike and Moose nodding in approval, Jerry said, "I had no intention of excluding the most important people in our lives."

Obviously pleased with Jerry's response, Connie smiled at him affectionately which seemed to say thank you for saying that. "With any luck at all, most of us should still be alive and healthy sixty to seventy years from now. That will give us plenty of time to do some foundation building," she said.

"I think making intelligent choices in our daily lives is far more important than relying on good luck," declared Jerry.

"I agree," stated Connie. "However, a little good luck now and then sure won't hurt anything."

"That's true," Jerry replied, "but I think lots of good luck is the natural outcome of making intelligent choices, and the more that we learn about Alcent in general and our local environment in particular, the better equipped we'll be to do that."

"I can't argue with that," responded Connie. "Knowledge is definitely the key to our success, both gaining new knowledge and preserving for future generations the knowledge and technology that we brought with us."

"That's all very important, but there's more to it than that," stated Moose. "When I was a kid, I made lots of bad choices that almost ruined my life. I had a bad attitude toward most of the people around me and toward society in general. Fortunately, I was able to pull myself out of it. If our society is going to be successful, I believe that we must instill in our children a sense of right and wrong and a sense of responsibility toward themselves and those around them, so that they will make responsible choices."

"That just might be essential," commented Jerry. "From what I've seen, the greatest nations on Earth are the ones that allow the most individual freedom. But individual freedom can only exist when individuals make responsible choices in their daily lives. When people abuse their freedom by making bad choices, laws are usually enacted to deal with them. As more and more laws get passed, personal freedom gradually disappears and personal initiative becomes stifled. Eventually, society becomes so bogged down with laws and regulations that little progress is made."

Connie listened attentively. She smiled at Jerry, "You sure use a lot of words to say that the success of our society depends on maximum individual freedom and that preserving individual freedom depends on individuals making responsible choices in daily living."

"I've always admired you for being able to get right to the point," stated Jerry.

"Is that why you married me?"

For a few moments, Jerry appeared deeply lost in thought. "I remember a morning in the medical lab when you needed very little time to get right to the point, and we did get married fairly soon after that," he said, grinning in a mischievous way.

Connie glowed as she recalled the memory of what happened in the medical lab shortly after leaving Earth, "I definitely got better results from that physical than any other I've ever given," she replied.

"I hope that you've never given another physical like that one," teased Jerry.

"I definitely haven't," responded Connie as she leaned toward Jerry who met her half way with a warm kiss.

Connie noticed Michelle smiling. "What are you so happy about?"

"While I wasn't in the medical lab with you that morning, I did help you prepare for that physical. Naturally, I am pleased that everything worked out so well for you. You ended up with a wonderful husband and a beautiful daughter who gets along very well with my son."

"Your son is a healthy child with a pleasant attitude toward life. He is easy to get along with."

"Since Denise is also that way, it is easy for our children to be good playmates."

"Can I say something?" asked Jerry.

Michelle and Connie turned to Jerry, and Connie asked, "What would you like to say?"

"There is a key word in your appraisal of Matthew."

"Which word got your attention?" asked Connie.

"Attitude."

"Why did that word attract your attention?"

"I believe that the success of our society is dependent on the kind of attitude that individuals in our society have. Specifically, as our children grow and develop into adults, I believe that it is very important to constantly nurture the development of a strong positive attitude in each of them. As our children become adults, it is important that each individual take responsibility for his or her own state of well-being. We must guard against them developing a frame of mind that allows them to readily blame others for personal short-comings."

Jerry had barely finished speaking, when Moose quickly said, "The last part of what you said hits me squarely in the head. When I was a rebellious teenager involved in illegal gang activity, I found it very easy to blame others and society in general for my lawless life style. It took a long time, and it was difficult, but eventually I figured out that my high-risk, unruly life style was no one's fault but my own. My dangerous life style was the direct result of me making bad choices in my day-to-day life. When I started taking responsibility for my activities and making wise choices, my life turned around fairly quickly."

Jerry grinned at Moose, "You sure use a lot of words to say that you agree with me."

"Would you prefer that I simply said that I know from painful personal experience that you are right."

"Actually, I didn't mind hearing your long-winded account of your lawless days."

As the pioneers continued their fireside conversation, Nocturne rose above the eastern horizon and flooded the plateau with moonlight. Matthew and Denise viewed their first moonrise ever in wide-eyed fascination and asked numerous questions about it.

Before Nocturne rose very high in the sky, both children were overcome by fatigue from their long active day and asked to be put to bed. After putting Matthew to bed, Mike and Michelle took a leisurely stroll around the plateau to enjoy their new home by moonlight. By the time they returned to their tent, Aphrodite was rising above the eastern horizon.

"What a novel sight to see a moonrise when we already have a moon hanging in the sky," Michelle said, looking at it.

"It looks rather bizarre, but I like it," said Mike.

"I think exotic is a better description than bizarre."

"I wonder how long we'll have to live here before the things that seem so peculiar now start to feel ordinary."

While gazing across the peaceful water of Clear Lake toward the two moons hanging in the eastern sky, Michelle said, "I don't know, but for right now, this alien scene is having a special romantic effect on me."

"Are you suggesting that we take advantage of the mood that you're in?"

"I would like that, and Matthew does need some brothers and sisters. Also, children are the building blocks in the foundation for our new civilization, and I think we should do our share in the building of that foundation."

Mike put his arms around Michelle in a warm, tender embrace and whispered, "You don't have to convince me. I am in the same mood that you're in, so let's find a secluded, moonlit area not too far away from the guards and celebrate the end of our first day here and the beginning of our future."

Pointing toward the east, Michelle said, "There's a grassy area on the other side of those bushes."

"That looks good. Let's take a blanket with us."

A few minutes later, Mike and Michelle arrived at the secluded area that they had selected. After spreading out the blanket and making herself comfortable on it, Michelle said, "This is some unusual grass. It's thick and not very tall. It feels like we have a well-padded carpet under our blanket."

Mike stretched out on the blanket beside Michelle, "This really is quite comfortable. I think I could quite easily sleep here tonight."

Michelle gracefully moved into a provocative pose, "Don't go to sleep just yet. I need your attention for a while."

Mike sat up and gazed at Michelle. As his eyes roamed over her body, his imagination became intensely fired up by the seductive way that she was presenting herself to him. In just a few moments, Mike's pulse quickened as his body prepared for action. "It seems like I don't feel sleepy anymore," Mike said huskily.

Greatly pleased with Mike's reaction to her alluring pose, Michelle smiled in satisfaction and reached out for him with open arms. Mike eagerly accepted her invitation, and for quite some time, they passionately enjoyed themselves in this exotic, romantic setting in their new home.

After they had fully satisfied their desire for each other's love, they sat up and gazed out across the water of Clear Lake. This peaceful, moonlit scene now seemed to have a very special romantic feel to it.

Feeling content and happy, Michelle said, "I think our love for each other is really something special. I hope we never lose these feelings."

"I will never forget that you left a life on Earth that you were very happy with because of your love for me."

"I didn't have any choice. I had to leave the security of that life for the uncertainties inherent in being on this mission."

"Why?"

"Because I am a hopeless romantic."

"What do you mean?"

"Don't you remember what happened on the observation deck long ago when we were still in orbit around Earth?"

"I do, but tell me about it anyway."

"The observation deck was really an exotic, romantic setting. With the spectacular beauty of the universe as a backdrop, you fired up my imagination and stimulated my desire to be a part of the greatest adventure in history. You also got me sexually aroused. Then, you took me to your apartment, and we made love with such fervent passion that it was more satisfying than any sexual experience I'd had in my life up to that time. That night I realized that I could not be truly happy without you and that neither one of us could be truly happy if I took you off this mission by insisting that we stay on Earth. I simply could not stand between you and your lifelong dream."

"If you had decided to stay on Earth, I would have stayed with you, and I would've done my best to make our lives happy."

"I know, but it would never have been the same as being here."

"I am happy that we are here," said Mike.

"I am too, and tomorrow, we can start building our future."

Mike stood up and gazed across the lake. Then, he looked around the moonlit plateau and down at Michelle. "I am very happy that we are here. Do you think we should sleep here on this blanket tonight?"

"That would be fun, and with the guards on duty, it would be reasonably safe, but if Matthew wakes up during the might, he will be worried if we aren't there."

"You're right. We need to make sure that he always feels safe and secure."

A few minutes later, Mike and Michelle entered their tent. They went to bed filled with joy and high expectations for the future, and they quickly dropped into a sound peaceful sleep.

BOOK REVIEW

Thank you for reading **THE ULTIMATE ADVENTURE**. I hope that you enjoyed it. This is my first book, and it is important to me to find out what you think of it. Please take a few minutes to answer the following questions:

Did you enjoy the story? _____ Why? _____

_____

_____

_____

What did you like the most about the story? _____

_____

_____

If you could change one or two things in the story, what would you change?

_____

_____

_____

I am currently writing a sequel. If you could have two or three things happen in the sequel, what would they be?

_____

_____

_____

_____

Would you like to be notified when the sequel is available for purchase? _____

If so, please print your name, address, and phone number: _____

_____

If you are interested in purchasing **THE ULTIMATE ADVENTURE** as a gift to a friend or family member, please fill out the order form on the next page.

Thank you for completing this book review. Please send it to:
Daniel L Pekarek
ALCENT ADVENTURES
P.O. Box 23781
Federal Way, WA 98093-0781

DLPekarek@aol.Com

ORDER BLANK

THE ULTIMATE ADVENTURE is an excellent gift to a friend or family member who enjoys reading quality science fiction/adventure. If you are unable to find it at your local bookstore, you can obtain copies by mail order.

Price $18.95 each
Include $3.50 for shipping and handling
Washington state residents add 8.6% sales tax

Your address:

Name:_____

Address:_____

City:_____ State:_____ Zip:_____

Telephone:_____

Payment: Check   Money Order   Credit Card: Visa   Master Card

　　　　　　　　Card Number_____

　　　　　　　　Name on card:_____ Exp. Date_____

Send your order to: ALCENT ADVENTURES
　　　　　　　　　　　　　P.O. Box 23781
　　　　　　　　　　　　　Federal Way, WA 98093-0781